THE RADLEY CURSE

THE
RADLEY CURSE

Aileen Armitage

PAN BOOKS

This edition published 1999 by Pan Books
an imprint of Macmillan Publishers Ltd
25 Eccleston Place, London SW1W 9NF
Basingstoke and Oxford
Associated companies throughout the world
www.macmillan.co.uk

This title first published in Great Britain 1998 by
SEVERN HOUSE PUBLISHERS LTD of
9-15 High Street, Sutton, Surrey SM1 1DF
Originally published in 1976 in Great Britain under
the title *The Brackenroyd Inheritence* and name of *Erica Lindley*.
This title first published in the U.S.A. 1999 by
SEVERN HOUSE PUBLISHERS INC of
595 Madison Avenue, New York, NY 10022.

British Library Cataloguing in Publication Data

Armitage, Aileen
  The Radley curse
  1. Love stories
  1. Title
  823.9'14 [F]

  ISBN 0 330 39657 9

Printed and bound in Great Britain by
Mackays of Chatham plc, Chatham, Kent

For my kinsfolk, the Armitages,
whose history reaches back through
the mists of Colne Valley antiquity.

I tell the things I know, the things I knew
Before I knew them, immemorially.

—VICTORIA SACKVILLE-WEST, *The Land*

Chapter 1

The master was coming downstairs. Fern Saxby, like all the other occupants of this imposing London villa in Elton Square, held her breath and hoped that the master's Monday morning humor, usually indicative of his mood for the whole week, would be sunny, for the weather decidedly was not. She ushered the two Hastings children hurriedly before her into the parlor to be ready to greet their papa and mamma.

"Now, remember, children, greet your papa first, and then your mamma. As soon as they enter, mind, don't wait until I have to nudge you," Fern advised them gently. A quick glance around the room reassured her that all was as it should be; though the grandfather clock in the vestibule was only now chiming eight, the parlor had hours ago been swept and dusted and the fire lit. No trace of skimped effort or sloth could be detected in the gleaming fire brasses by the fender to arouse Mr. Hastings' swiftly awakened disapproval.

Heavy footsteps approached the door. Fern ran her hands quickly over her smoothly coiled fair hair, then clasped them dutifully before her as the door swung open and Mr.

Hastings, his pallid wife on his arm, entered slowly and majestically. Lydia Hastings smiled timorously at her children and then glanced nervously at her husband. He, tall, graying, and imposing, stood glaring at his offspring expectantly.

"Good morning, Papa. Good morning, Mamma," two stifled voices breathed in unison.

Mr. Hastings nodded. "Good morning, children. Good morning, Miss Saxby."

He expected no reply from her, Fern knew, and from habit bred of the last two years' experience she walked across to the bell, anticipating the master's next command. Never on any one morning, except the week he had once been confined to bed with influenza, had the ritual of morning prayers in the Hastings household varied.

"Summon the staff to prayers," came the order as Mr. Hastings took his seat at the head of the chenille-covered table. Opening the great family Bible, he began to select the text for the day. Almost as soon as Fern released the bell rope the door opened and the servants shuffled in at the far end of the parlor. Under the vigilant eye of Bunting, the butler, they had all been awaiting the summons just beyond the green-baize door that marked the boundary between house and servants' domain.

Heads bowed now, they all stood respectfully before the master and mistress, the one inspecting their caps and uniforms critically before beginning to pray, the other surreptitiously smiling at her offspring while her husband's attention was diverted. Fern stood behind her little charges, midway between the seated Hastingses and the standing servants, as befitted her anomalous position as governess. A strange creature is a governess, she thought for the thousandth time, neither gentry nor common folk, but a curious hybrid, left to fend alone, vulnerable and friendless, in the no-man's-land that yawned between them. Mrs. Hastings, despite her undoubted warmth, dared not befriend a governess, however lonely she herself might feel. Nor dared Hetty and Rosa and Clara, the kitchen and parlor maids, for venturing to presume friendship with one above their own station would undoubtedly bring a

2

sharp reproof from the butler. Bunting knew well the boundaries of class, and firmly instilled the knowledge of these unalterable limits into the minds of his staff.

So I'm trapped, thought Fern as she stared directly ahead at the William Morris wallpaper and dimly heard Mr. Hastings' ponderous voice droning in prayer. Like the pimpernel entwined in the inexorable intricacy of the fronds on that wallpaper, I am trapped in this mesh of class boundary. If only Papa and Mamma were alive; if only we were all still comfortably wealthy and free.

Sighing, she turned her attention to Mr. Hastings' words. He was reading from Ecclesiastes, giving full emphasis to every word, conscious of his captive audience and of the resonance of his voice. From the corner of her eye Fern saw Hetty fidgeting restlessly.

"Vanity of vanities, saith the Preacher, all is vanity," intoned Mr. Hastings, pausing to lower his pince-nez a half-inch down his nose, the better to survey the effect of his words on his hearers. "What profit hath a man of all his labor which he taketh under the sun? One generation passeth away and another generation cometh."

Fern permitted herself a covert glimpse of the maids. Hetty, up before six to clear and relay the grates, was already trying to hide a yawn. Was she too speculating as to the uselessness of her labor? Fern wondered, for the grate would be dirty again tomorrow morning, and the next, and the next, and still even when the next generation came.

"All things are full of labor,". Mr. Hastings pontificated. "Man cannot utter it; the eye is not satisfied with seeing nor the ear filled with hearing. The thing that hath been, it is that which shall be, and that which is done is that which shall be done; and there is no new thing under the sun."

The staff shuffled to their knees for the Lord's Prayer while Mr. Hastings assisted his wife to kneel as gracefully as her rheumatically stricken joints would permit. This London fog and damp, thought Fern. No doubt, as Mr. Hastings' business grew more lucrative day by day, he would eventually consider sending his wife abroad to a spa or to a sunnier climate. It was possible, even though he seemed to spare little thought for the comfort of others, even for his patient, uncomplaining wife. Matthew Hastings' vision seemed to be bounded by his own comfort and seeing to the continuing prosperity of his business. Little else existed in his world, save the fluctuations of national and international affairs, and only then insofar as they might affect trade.

Fern's musings were interrupted by the rustle of skirts and shuffling of feet as the company rose from its knees. Mr. Hastings closed the Bible and put down his pince-nez.

"And now, to your duties," he commanded his flock. Mrs. Paddock, the cook-housekeeper, led the servants out, all save Bunting, who stood at attention awaiting the customary order. "Order breakfast to be served, Bunting, and bring me the morning post."

"Very good, sir." Fern stood hesitantly, a hand on the shoulder of each child, awaiting Mr. Hastings' decision as to whether he would allow his son and daughter to remain in the parlor for breakfast or dismiss them to the day nursery to eat with their governess.

Mrs. Hastings, noticing his air of abstraction, ventured to resolve the dilemma. "Shall the children return upstairs, my dear, or would you prefer them to remain?" she asked timidly.

"They must remain, of course, to hear our decision. Very well, Miss Saxby, you may go."

As Fern made to withdraw, Rosa, the housemaid, entered bearing a large tray laden with a tureen of porridge and a platter of scrambled eggs and kidneys. It was a relief to Fern to quit the pretentious parlor with its gloomy oil paintings and its ponderous, ornately carved furniture. Fern felt sorry for Lydia Hastings, trapped in that claustrophobic room with her domineering husband, unable to escape the pattern which marriage dictated, the undeviating pattern of husband, lord and master of his universe, while his wife was no more than his servant, trained always to listen and obey. Poor Mrs. Hastings, her lot is no better than mine, thought Fern, and possibly even worse. Marriage seems a deadly, stifling affair for a woman, for she gains nothing from it but her children.

Fern breakfasted alone in the nursery, her meal being served, not by Rosa, second in importance only to Mrs. Paddock, the cook, but by Clara, whose humbler position as kitchen maid would not be offended by having to serve a mere governess. Clara grinned as she set down the dishes.

"So you can eat in peace this morning, eh, miss? Miss Sarah and Master Robert been allowed downstairs for once."

Fern smiled. It was true, the children were rarely allowed to disturb Mr. Hastings' morning reading of the *Times* over breakfast. Though they were not permitted to speak at table, Mr. Hastings found their foot shuffling annoying and their manners distasteful, declaring it ruined his digestion. Today there must be something special he wished to impart to them if he was prepared to suffer their presence. Idly Fern wondered what it could be.

When the breakfast dishes were cleared away, Fern took out the schoolbooks from the bottom of the cupboard and laid them on the table. The grandfather clock was chiming nine. If Mr. Hastings had finished with the children, it was time for their lessons. Fern descended the stairs and knocked at the parlor door.

"Enter," Mr. Hastings commanded. He was relaxing in an overstuffed armchair while his wife and children still sat at the dining table, their white faces and tight expressions indicating that Mr. Hastings' news had not been pleasant.

Before Fern could speak, he rose from his chair. "Ah, Miss Saxby, the mistress would like to speak to you. Please be seated," he said, indicating a straight chair by the window. "And, children, return to the nursery. Miss Saxby will join you shortly." The children, rising obediently, shuffled quickly and silently out of the room.

Fern dutifully sat down, smoothing the skirt of her dark merino dress and folding her hands in her lap. Mr. Hastings went to follow his children, but paused in the doorway and glanced at the letters in his hand. "Oh, by the way, Miss Saxby, there is a letter for you among my mail this morning," he commented in tones of surprise. He held the intrusive letter toward her. Fern started in surprise. Who could possibly have written to her? She, with no friends and not a relative in the world. Never before in her life had she received a letter, save those that used to come at regular intervals from her parents in India, but that was long ago, before Afghan bullets had claimed their lives.

Even Mrs. Hastings' puffy face registered alarmed surprise at a governess's letter finding its furtive way into the master's correspondence. Fern took the letter from Mr. Hastings' outstretched fingertips and thanked him quietly. A quick glance at the neat, spidery handwriting on the envelope revealed no clue as to the sender, for it was completely strange to her.

Mr. Hastings cleared his throat noisily. "Now, remember, my dear," he addressed his wife, "tell Miss Saxby what has been decided and make arrangements accordingly. I wish everything to be clear-cut and orderly, as in business. No shilly-shallying or compromise, as is your wont, you understand?"

"Yes, Mr. Hastings, indeed," murmured Lydia unhappily. Fern felt sorry for the woman. Whatever unpleasantness Mr. Hastings had to communicate to his children's governess, he was deputing the task to his weary little wife to perform, and it was evident that Mrs. Hastings did not relish the prospect. A reprimand perhaps, thought Fern, some mistake or oversight on my part which has displeased him. As the master departed, closing the door sharply behind him, Fern forgot the letter on her lap and waited for Mrs. Hastings to begin.

The mistress's eyes shone unnaturally bright, Fern noted, as she sat twisting her fingers nervously in the folds of her skirt. As though she were feverish, or her eyes held unshed tears. As a good servant should, Fern sat in silence and waited to be addressed. At length Mrs. Hastings rose and crossed to the window, looking out at the square outside over Fern's shoulder.

"I . . . I really don't know where to begin, Miss Saxby," she stammered without looking down at her. "I don't, and that's the truth of it."

6

"Perhaps you could tell me what decision the master has taken, madam," Fern prompted.

The other woman's voice quivered yet more as she answered. "He . . . he has decided to send Sarah and Robert away to school."

It was a bald statement, terse and to the point, yet Fern's sympathy rose at once for Mrs. Hastings, for the fact she had just revealed meant far more to the wretched woman. Her children, the only joy of her life, were to be wrenched from her. Fern's dislike for Mr. Hastings grew more intense as she realized his unfeeling callousness toward his wife.

"Both of them?" she queried, aghast. "But Miss Sarah is only seven."

"I know. But Mr. Hastings feels that since Robert is now old enough to go to boarding school, it might be wise to send Sarah away as well. He feels they are not developing as they should. . . . Oh, not on your account, Miss Saxby, please don't misunderstand me. Mr. Hastings has said no word against you."

Her tear-filled eyes turned full on Fern now, anxious not to hurt. "It is not your fault at all, but mine, I fear. My husband feels that I indulge them overmuch and that they would be better removed from my influence."

Her voice caught on a sob as she spoke. Fern had to resist the urge to rise and comfort the woman, which would have betokened criticism of her master. Instead she tried to divert Mrs. Hastings from her misery.

"So I understand you will soon have no further need of my services, madam. Is that what the master wished you to inform me? Do not worry unduly on that account, for I am sure I shall be able to find another position soon."

Mrs. Hastings gripped Fern's hands between her own. "Oh, my dear, I would not lose you for the world if I could keep you here, but there is nothing I can do. I shall give you an excellent reference, of course, but . . ." Her voice trailed away in anguish. Making a firm effort to regain her self-control, she turned sharply away. "I shall do what I can, of course. No doubt Mr. Hastings will permit me to recommend your ser-

7

vices to others of our acquaintance who may be in need of a governess. We do entertain on occasion, as you know, and if the opportunity arises, I shall speak of you. . . ."

On occasion, thought Fern sadly. Mr. Hastings had long ago despaired of his wife as a hostess, and although Mrs. Paddock could be relied upon to provide a substantially appetizing if not inspired meal for his guests, his wife's social inadequacies left much to be desired. He could impress his business acquaintances far better over a meal in town.

"Well, now"—Mrs. Hastings wiped her eyes hastily—"I must begin the arrangements. The master wants me to order new clothes for the children, so if you would see that they are dressed in their street clothes, Miss Saxby, I shall take them to the dressmaker this morning."

"Very well, Mrs. Hastings. Shall they have their lessons this afternoon instead?"

"Oh . . . er . . . no, I think not. Mr. Hastings has not said what he wishes done then. Best leave lessons today. You may have the day off."

"Thank you, madam." Taking Mrs. Hastings' words as a dismissal, Fern rose and left the room, thrusting the letter into her pocket. Mounting the steep, balustraded staircase to the nursery, she found two disconsolate children sitting at the nursery table, their books unopened and their faces vacant. Poor little things, thought Fern, never the brightest or most rewarding of pupils, but amiable and anxious to please nonetheless, like their mother.

"Come, children, no lessons today," she said brightly, sweeping the books away from in front of them. "Your mamma is to take you to the dressmaker's instead, to buy you new clothes. Aren't you lucky?"

Robert looked up mournfully. "New clothes for school," he commented in a lackluster voice. "I don't want to go away to school, nor does Sarah."

Sarah's little white face stared beseechingly at Fern. "No, we'd rather stay here with Mamma . . . and Papa," she added quickly. "Please ask Papa if we can stay, Miss Saxby." The little voice was so plaintive that Fern could have hugged the child, but instead she spoke cheerfully.

"But you haven't really thought about it, Sarah. Just think, lots of playmates every day and all day. You haven't anyone to play with here, save Robert. Now you'll have lots of little girls your own age, and Robert will have boys of his age. You should be glad your father is so concerned for you. Come now, let me help you button on your boots while Robert fetches his coat."

She watched the two dispirited figures leave the house with their mother before returning to her room. A cheerless, sparsely furnished room, in strong contrast to the heavily overfurnished parlor, it was nevertheless a more congenial lodging than those the servants shared in the attic. On the second floor, far removed from the main bedrooms, it was yet close to the children's rooms and heated by a small coal fire in the hearth.

Fern seated herself on the edge of the bed and reflected. So, events would seem to decree yet another upheaval in her life. Soon she would be forced to leave this secure if monotonous existence, and what then? Two years ago had seen the first upheaval, when her father and mother had died suddenly and she had been obliged to leave her pleasant life at Miss Danby's Academy for Young Ladies in order to earn a living. She had coped then, so why not now? After all, at twenty-two she was no longer the immature miss she had been once, cosseted and indulged. Now she was both abler and wiser in the ways of the world. She would manage. Something would turn up. An advertisement in the columns of the *Times*, perhaps. That might produce a suitable position.

Suddenly Fern remembered the unexpected letter that remained still unopened in her pocket. She withdrew it curiously.

The letterhead indicated it was from Nathaniel Lennox, a solicitor in London. That was clear enough, but the text of the letter was puzzling: "If you would be so kind as to call at my office as soon as it is convenient to your good self, you will

hear of a matter which may be greatly to your advantage."
What matter? How could it be of advantage? puzzled Fern.

It was not far from Elton Square to the solicitor's office,
and as Fern threaded her way through the streets, among
fashionably dressed ladies and their frock-coated escorts
mingling with the shabby poor who scraped a living selling
matches or flowers and blacking boots, she wondered about
the letter. Could it be a legacy of some kind? Fifty pounds
would be extremely welcome just now, but who could possibly
have named her in a will, since she had no living relative in
the world? But if it were not a legacy, why should a solicitor
speak of a matter "to her advantage"? It really was most perplexing.

Mr. Nathaniel Lennox sat smiling benignly behind his wide
oak desk, his chins dimpling above his constricting high stock
and his fingertips arched together as he surveyed his young
visitor. The ordered regularity of his chambers with their
bookshelves lined with huge legal tomes lurched suddenly into
confusion to Fern's disordered mind, for his words were
senseless, crazy, and fantastic beyond all imagination.

"What is that you are telling me, Mr. Lennox?" she ventured at last, her breath seeming to catch helplessly in her
throat. "I cannot fully follow . . ."

"Yes, I admit it is a trifle overwhelming, but it is the truth,
Miss Saxby. There is no mistake. Mr. Thomas de Lacy, deceased, has bequeathed to you his estate in Yorkshire—subject to certain conditions, as I mentioned."

"But . . . but I have never heard of this Mr. de Lacy! There
must be some mistake!"

"None whatever, I assure you. I have checked most carefully. Though no blood relation of yours, Mr. de Lacy was
nonetheless distantly related to you, and anxious to redeem
what he considered to be an oversight in the past."

"An estate," murmured Fern, still too dazed to comprehend. "A sum of money, do you mean?"

"Money, as well as a mansion, a mill and several farms that
have quite a sizable acreage." He drew a sheaf of papers

10

toward him. "Would you like to know the precise figures at valuation of the mansion, the mill and the farmlands?"

"No, no. Let me think a little, Mr. Lennox. First, are you *certain* I am the person Mr. de Lacy intended to inherit? It seems so unlikely, as I have no relatives."

"I am certain, be sure of that, young lady. But the matter is a little more complicated. There is also another legatee to share the estate—a Mr. Bruno de Lacy, who again is distantly related to you."

A relative! A living relative—it seemed too good to be true. Fern's hitherto blank face broke into a smile. "Do explain to me, Mr. Lennox, I beg of you. How do these gentlemen come to be related to me?"

"It is a long story, dating from some seventy years ago, but I'll do my best," the old gentleman replied, drawing a blank sheet of paper toward him and dipping his pen in the inkstand. "At the turn of the century, or soon after, there was a Dorian de Lacy at Brackenroyd Hall, the only son and heir. He was to have married a young lady named Annot Radley."

"Radley? That was my mother's name!" Fern interrupted unthinkingly. "But I always understood her to say she had no kin. She did say her family had come from Yorkshire, but she rarely spoke of them."

"Well, Annot Radley bore Dorian de Lacy a son—your maternal grandfather. But she never married Dorian. She died suddenly," Mr. Lennox continued. "He later married a Sarah Ramsden, and it was his son and Sarah's, Thomas de Lacy, who bequeathed Brackenroyd Hall jointly to you and his grandson, Bruno."

"But why?" questioned Fern. "I do not understand."

Mr. Lennox shrugged. "I know it seems odd, for your claim through an illegitimate line would seem thin, but you did not know old Thomas. He was a very Christian gentleman, extremely conscientious and scrupulous, and it troubled him that had his father married Annot, then his elder half-brother would have inherited, and not he. Having lost sight of his half-brother, he resolved to reinstate his descendants if he could trace them. It took time, but I traced you. Thomas'

11

own son, George, being dead, his grandson, Bruno, inherits, along with you."

Mr. Lennox pushed across to Fern the sheet of paper on which he had been writing. She saw that he had written two neat columns, each one representing the line of descent from Dorian de Lacy.

Annot Radley   = Dorian = Sarah Ramsden
William Radley   Thomas de Lacy
Sophie Radley   George de Lacy
Fern Saxby   Bruno de Lacy

"I see," murmured Fern; then, pointing to the last name on the list, "And this Mr. de Lacy—Mr. Bruno de Lacy—we share a common great-grandfather in Dorian de Lacy. Does he know of me and of the terms of the bequest?"

"Oh, yes, and is quite content with the arrangement, for the inheritance is a substantial one." He beamed encouragingly at Fern. "Well, now, young lady, does the prospect appeal to you, of becoming an heiress and living high on the Yorkshire moors?"

Fern bit her lip dubiously. "To be quite honest, Mr. Lennox, I find it difficult to believe it is true. But if it is, it could hardly have occurred at a happier moment." On seeing Mr. Lennox's bushy eyebrows arch in question, Fern went on to explain. "It's a blessing, and that's a fact. You see, I find I am obliged to leave my present post and had no idea where to turn next to find work. Because money with which to live is vital."

"Indeed it is, my dear. Well, now, your problems would seem to be solved."

"It would be such a relief to leave the . . . restrictions of the household where I live. Oh, just to think of it! Breathing pure fresh air on the moors! Does the house have gardens, Mr. Lennox? Orchards, a lake perhaps?" Fern's eyes grew bright and enthusiastic as she reviewed the potentialities of this unlooked-for future.

"I have never actually seen Brackenroyd Hall, I'm afraid.

12

Mr. Thomas used always to come to London to transact his affairs with me. But I believe it is a fine house with all you mention in its grounds. On the edge of Brackenroyd village, I believe, not far from the river, with the moors above."

It sounded wonderful. But what of the other legatee, the grandson Bruno? Would he too wish to live in the Hall, or dispose of it and share the proceeds? she wondered. Pointing to his name on the list again, she inquired of Mr. Lennox if he knew the gentleman.

"Not personally, I regret, though no doubt the omission will be rectified in time. A fine, upstanding young man by all accounts, some ten years older than you, at a guess. He's a doctor, you know, and already earning himself quite a reputation in his field."

Mr. Lennox paused, toying with the pen between his fingertips. "But there is more to be discussed, Miss Saxby," he said tentatively, and Fern sensed that he found it difficult to pick his words with care. "As I mentioned before, there are certain conditions attached to the legacy, and these must be met before you can complete your claim."

Ah, yes, the conditions. Having held out a promise of heaven to her, what stumbling block was he now going to produce to make the vision fade? She felt a prick of anger and dismay at the thought of losing Brackenroyd Hall. She would not be cheated of it lightly.

"What are the conditions, Mr. Lennox?" she asked levelly.

"First, that on obtaining the Hall you do not sell it again, at least for five years after your marriage."

"Marriage? That is highly unlikely, Mr. Lennox. I have seen marriage at close quarters, and do not like what I see. It destroys the soul."

"Really?" The lawyer's bushy eyebrows arched again. "You surprise me, my dear young lady. Such a cynical view for one so young. I cannot say *I* have found marriage to be so destructive."

No, possibly not, she reflected, you have such a warm and kindly face. You, perhaps, would not sap a woman's happiness. You would not tear her beloved children from her.

13

Mrs. Lennox is a far more fortunate creature than Mrs. Hastings.

Mr. Lennox was studying her closely. "Are you quite determined against marriage, Miss Saxby?"

Fern looked up, puzzled. "Why do you ask?"

"Because I come to the other condition of Mr. Thomas de Lacy's will. In order to inherit and share Brackenroyd Hall equally with Dr. Bruno de Lacy, it is conditional that you and he must marry each other."

Fern sat aghast. Marry—and a man she had never even met? It was unthinkable! Ridiculous! The old man must have been crazed when he dictated his will. Mr. Lennox, watching the reactions on her face, seemed to follow the drift of her thoughts.

"It was a sensible enough solution on Mr. Thomas' part, my dear, if he wished to ensure that both legitimate and illegitimate lines of the family were secure. This way, your claim is valid and no one could ever contest it. I know the idea appalls you, as it would any sensitive young lady, but if you would like to go home and think about it for a few days, I believe the logic of the arrangement will become clear to you. Think it over, my dear, and let me know when you have decided."

Too numb to answer, Fern sat stiffly, clutching her gloves nervously.

Mr. Lennox murmured more persuasive words. "Just think of it, a fine young man, of very presentable appearance, with excellent manners and taste, I am told, and a respected doctor besides. A marriage partner many young society ladies would no doubt find highly desirable, I'll be bound."

A good catch for a governess, thought Fern, a chance I shouldn't sneer at—that's what he means. But the inheritance meant more than that. It meant escape from frustration and claustrophobia, escape from London's filth and poverty and drudgery, freedom to breathe and be one's own mistress. Was marriage to a stranger too high a price to pay for such bliss?

Impulsively Fern rose, stretching out her hand to the lawyer. "I thank you for your courtesy and interest, Mr. Lennox. I would not wish to take up yet more of your valuable time, so I will give you my answer now. I agree to the terms. If Dr. Bruno de Lacy is in agreement, I shall marry him as you request."

And Brackenroyd Hall will be mine, she thought ecstatically to herself as she retraced her footsteps to Elton Square. Whatever this Bruno de Lacy is like, handsome or ugly, human or demonic, I will not let my husband rob me of my inheritance!

Chapter 2

Matthew Hastings' change of attitude toward his children's governess was quite astounding when he learned of her sudden rise in fortune. Now he no longer banished her from his presence as quickly as possible, as an indeterminate thing neither quite gentle nor baseborn, but instead he became openly affable.

"Perhaps you would care to dine with us, Miss Saxby—this evening, if you would, when the Blandings come? We have never really conversed, have we? Let me see, now, your family are the Saxbys of Lincolnshire, are they not?"

But Fern declined his magnanimous offer, having no wish to be paraded with pride as Mr. Hastings' friend, the heiress of Brackenroyd. Lydia Hastings, however, was genuinely pleased at her governess's good fortune, relieved that the problem of her future was thus happily resolved and no longer presenting a problem to her conscience.

"You must let me help you choose new clothes, befitting your new station," she murmured anxiously. "Come with me to the dressmaker's when I take the children."

Fern, armed with the prodigious sum of twenty pounds that Mr. Lennox had pressed upon her once all the necessary papers had been signed, was glad to accept Mrs. Hastings' offer. The solicitor had said that Dr. Bruno de Lacy had given orders that Fern was to be furnished at once with all necessary funds for preparing for the journey, and a first-class railway ticket to Bradford.

"Dr. de Lacy will be writing to you himself shortly to make the final preparations," Mr. Lennox had said in his kindly, avuncular manner. "In the meantime, buy whatever fripperies a young lady needs, and do not hesitate to call on me if you require more."

Fripperies indeed. Fern smiled. Twenty pounds represented a half-year's salary as a governess, wealth indeed to one accustomed to budgeting carefully. It would more than pay for her few needs.

Lydia Hastings was touchingly helpful. "The violet wool gown enhances your fair coloring beautifully, and I think the gentian blue becomes you very well too," she would say in the privacy of the dressmaker's parlor, and the quick surreptitious dabs at her reddened eyes betrayed her misery. The children, Robert and Sarah, stood impassively, lifeless little waxwork figures, while the dressmaker's deft fingers measured and pinned.

What a sad duty for Mrs. Hastings, Fern thought, to be preparing her beloved children to leave her, while her governess prepared for a new life as a bride. These gowns were her wedding trousseau, Fern reflected, though Lydia Hastings did not know it. Fern had not disclosed to her employers that her inheritance entailed an unlooked-for marriage, only that she and a very distant relative, a doctor, were to share the bequest.

As the days slipped by, little Sarah and Robert seemed too bemused to register what was happening to them. Life had somehow slithered out of its familiar routine, for Father had decreed that lessons in the schoolroom were no longer necessary, and the household was in a state of upheaval, trunks everywhere and drawers and cupboards ransacked and emptied.

The departure of both children and governess was imminent. The atmosphere in the house was heavy with unspoken misery. It could have felt no more oppressive if they were funeral arrangements being planned, thought Fern, and she could feel no pang of nostalgia at leaving Elton Square. Mr. Hastings, however, seemed quite oblivious of the air of mournful silence in his household.

Then the letter came, crisp and practical. Fern stared at its strong, masculine handwriting, boldly self-confident yet with a trace of something remote, withdrawn, and intense in the firmly closed-in tails of the letters. Bruno de Lacy would seem, from his handwriting at least, to be more complex than his simple letter indicated. It told her the easiest way to reach Bradford by train, the most convenient train times, and assured her that he would meet her at the Bradford railway station.

"A Pullman coach, of course," Mr. Hastings dictated. "Second class would be most unseemly for a lady of your means. Yes, a Pullman will ensure comfort and privacy. I shall see you to the station myself."

Her trunk and smaller hand case loaded aboard the hansom cab, Fern turned on the step to bid farewell to Mrs. Hastings and the children. A momentary stab of pity compelled her to lean forward impulsively and kiss the older woman's cheek before climbing hastily inside. The poor woman looked so frail, so vulnerable in her misery, and Fern was obliged to force her mind to other matters.

Mr. Hastings seated himself cheerfully beside her and bade the cabman drive on. The dismal February afternoon dulled quickly into evening as they rode, and as the lamplighters touched the gas lamps into life, Fern could see in their flickering light the forgotten citizens of London still desperately seeking the means for supper. A forlorn flower seller sitting on an upturned box, her basket of limp violets on her lap and her threadbare shawl clutched about thin shoulders; a wizened man bent over his barrel organ, his equally wizened monkey holding out a pathetic tin cup to passersby as the thin, tinny music wailed on the evening air; the bootblack; and the rickets-twisted little boy trying vainly to sell his matches—all their cries vied with those of the street vendors selling baked potatoes or muffins. London's night air rang shrilly with the sounds of the poor.

It seemed odd to be setting out on a lengthy journey at so late an hour, thought Fern, but according to Dr. de Lacy's letter, the evening train was the most convenient of the day, necessitating no delay in making connections. It was odd, too, that the prospect of the journey and the unknown life ahead seemed to stir no expectancy within her, glad as she was to leave London and its claustrophobic atmosphere.

Luggage safely stowed in the guard's van and Mr. Hastings' final exhortations made as to securing a porter at the journey's end, Fern settled down in the Pullman coach.

The guard's whistle shrilled along the vast platform, and the train slid ponderously out from under the great dome of King's Cross station, out into the night and the unknown. As it chugged more and more rapidly and the clatter steadied into a regular rhythm, Fern began to drowse. Unbothered by other travelers, the nearest being two gentlemen at the further end of the coach, and soothed by the comfortable seats and upholstered head cushion, she remembered earlier days as a child when she had last traveled on a train, on a dearly longed-for day excursion to Brighton. It was on one of Mother and Father's infrequent home visits to England; tanned and handsome and laughing, they had appeared such benevolent gods to her child's eye. Gaily all three had gone down to the seaside for the day, and the indulgent parents had permitted her to ride on a donkey along the beach, to watch a Punch and Judy show on the sands, and to dabble her feet in the sparkling water. It had been such a glorious day of sun and buoyant laughter and freedom, one of the rare golden days of childhood she would always treasure, for she barely knew her parents after that. Her father, tall and resplendent in his captain's uniform, had borne Mother away again to India, and life had become a routine of lessons at the academy once more, until the day the terrible news had arrived. An Afghan raid, they had said. A marauding band in search of food or ammunition had crossed the northern frontier in the night. Papa had been very brave, they said, in defense of his bungalow and wife, but he and his few men and Mamma had all fallen victim to the Afghanis' bullets.

"Doncaster!" The guard's strident voice aroused Fern. Doncaster already? She must have been dozing, for it was now past eight o'clock. Fern sat upright and stared out into the darkness. Within an hour she would be meeting her future husband, and for the first time she felt a twinge of apprehension.

At Wakefield, Fern alighted, beckoned a porter, and followed his measured tread as he carried her luggage to the awaiting train that was to take her to Bradford. He helped her to mount the step into the coach and held out a grubby hand for his tip. As Fern gave him a coin, she became aware of a gentleman's eyes surveying her curiously, and as she seated herself opposite him, she saw he was looking from her to the label on her suitcase and back to her again.

He wore a clerical collar, she noted. Quite young, sandy hair showing beneath his top hat, a well-cut coat which had seen better days, and a now studiously averted thin face indicated that he was a harmless enough traveling companion. She sat back and watched the little station signposts as they flickered under their gas lamps—Ossett, Dewsbury, Batley—not far now. At Laister Dyke the young clergyman leaned forward.

"Forgive my impertinence, madam, but I see from your case you are traveling to Brackenroyd Hall. Allow me to introduce myself. I am Edgar Amos, vicar of Brackenroyd. I should be honored to see you safely to the Hall if you would allow me."

Fern looked up, pleasure irradiating her face. How pleasant to meet a future neighbor who seemed so friendly and welcoming! He was smiling a little diffidently, as though uncertain of the propriety of his action. Fern leaned forward with a smile, extending her gloved hand.

"How very kind of you, Mr. Amos. My name is Fern Saxby, and I am delighted to make your acquaintance, as no doubt we shall be near neighbors. Thank you for your kind offer, but there is no need to incommode yourself, for I believe Dr. de Lacy is to meet me at Bradford himself."

The young clergyman's sandy eyebrows had risen fractionally as Fern spoke, and she wondered why he should register surprise. His next words explained.

"Miss Saxby? Then you must be the new heiress of Brackenroyd, along with Dr. de Lacy? I am delighted to meet so charming a young mistress for the Hall, and sincerely hope your new life in the village will be a most happy and rewarding one."

"I have no reason to doubt it, sir." As she watched the comfortable smile settle over his bland features, she wondered what Mr. Amos was thinking. That she was not what he expected, that she must be a strange creature indeed to agree to marry a complete stranger? At least he knew something of Brackenroyd Hall and its present tenant. She resolved to try to glean something of his knowledge.

"The Hall?" he replied seriously in answer to her question. "Ah, yes, a fine building, constructed at the beginning of the century on the site of the old Hall, built in the sixteenth century. In fact, one wing of the old Hall still remains, and the new Hall was added to it, though I believe the old wing is now unused. Too cold and drafty, you know."

"And the De Lacys—have they always lived there?"

"Since the late sixteenth century, yes. They are a wealthy family of Norman descent, and the lifeblood of Brackenroyd village. Lords of the manor, as you might say, building cottages and later a mill for their tenants. Most Brackenroyd villagers even now still work in the woolen mill."

"And Dr. de Lacy—has he always lived at the Hall?"

"As a child he came frequently, but he lived mostly in Germany. His mother was German, you know, and as his father died young, she kept Bruno in her native country to be educated. He has only recently returned to Brackenroyd, on his grandfather's death."

The train rumbled to a halt at a small station. "St. Dunstan's," commented Mr. Amos brightly. "Nearly there, Miss Saxby. We shall be in Bradford in a few minutes."

Fern gazed out of the train window, anxious for her first glimpse of the great Yorkshire city, but in the darkness there was little to be seen save the occasional gas lamp. The train rumbled noisily into the great station, and Mr. Amos rose to hand down her suitcase before dismounting.

Few people other than those leaving the train loitered about the vast platform, for the February night air was chill and damp, but a greatcoated man, tall and impressive despite his gauntness, strode purposefully toward them. He doffed his hat, exposing his thick dark hair clinging damply about his temples, as he addressed Fern.

"Miss Saxby? I am Bruno de Lacy." His handshake was firm despite his few words, and he granted the young clergyman at her side only the curtest of nods.

Fern could not resist staring at him. He was uncommonly handsome in a dour sort of way, with no hint of a smile about his compressed lips, though the fullness of the lower lip indicated a generous nature. His dark eyes were surveying her intently.

Amos fidgeted slightly and excused himself. "Well, since the young lady is now safely delivered into your hands, I shall leave you, Dr. de Lacy. No doubt we shall meet again soon," he said, and disappeared quickly.

De Lacy's hand cupped Fern's elbow firmly. "The carriage is waiting, and the porter has seen to your trunk," he commented laconically. "Allow me to carry your hand luggage."

With a quiet, proprietary air he took the suitcase and led her to the waiting carriage and helped her inside. As the coachman whipped up and set off into the darkness, De Lacy sat silent at Fern's side.

"Is it far to Brackenroyd Hall?" Fern inquired timidly at last, fearful that he might resent her breaking his air of absorption.

"A half-hour's ride, no more."

He made no further effort to speak. Fern sat equally silent, wondering if he was assessing her appearance and bearing as

22

his prospective bride. She could not beat down the confusion which caused her cheeks to flush in embarrassment. For a long time no sound broke the tense silence save hoofbeats and the clatter of wheels.

At length he leaned forward and gazed out of the window. "Brackenroyd village," he said curtly. Fern could discern in the darkness only the glimmer of oil lamps in uncurtained cottage windows and the hulking outline of a great building, the mill perhaps. Then she spotted the spire of a small church, the one where Mr. Amos was vicar, no doubt, and she wondered why Dr. de Lacy had not offered a seat in the carriage to him.

"This is the way to the Hall," said De Lacy as the carriage turned off the cobbled street and began to climb a steeply graveled drive. The drive wound on and on, uphill all the way, until at last Fern could see the outline of the house starkly silhouetted against the skyline, right on the crest of the hill. She drew in her breath sharply. It was not only the strangely weird appearance of the vast building with its battlemented turrets which disturbed her, but also the uncanny feeling that she had seen the place before. And the half-recollection brought with it an unaccountable sense of sadness.

"Oh!" The sigh escaped her lips almost inaudibly, but De Lacy was quick to note it.

"What is it, Miss Saxby? Does the Hall disappoint you?" he asked with a wry smile.

"Oh, no, not at all. It was just an odd sensation that I have been here before, though I know I cannot possibly have done so. I seem to recognize it—that there will be a flight of steps and stone balustrades, a wide vestibule, and ..." She could remember no more, for the fleeting vision had dissolved. De Lacy was frowning slightly, as though he considered he had burdened himself with a half-witted girl.

Fern smiled as the carriage halted. "Silly, isn't it? Perhaps I am overtired after the journey."

"It is not an uncommon sensation, Miss Saxby. The French have a name for it—they call it *déjà vu*."

Found only in flighty, irresponsible females, thought Fern.

She wished she had never mentioned it to him. But as he helped her alight and mount the stone steps to the balustraded terrace, and a woman opened the huge front door revealing the wide, warmly lit vestibule within, Fern trembled again. It was exactly as she had visualized it. The woman smiled in welcome.

"Miss Saxby, may I present Mrs. Thorpe, the housekeeper," De Lacy said tersely, indicating the generously built, matronly figure. "Is there supper ready for Miss Saxby?" he inquired.

Before Mrs. Thorpe could reply, Fern intervened. "Indeed, I am not hungry, Dr. de Lacy, and should much prefer to go straight to bed if you do not mind. The hour is already very late."

He glanced at the oak grandfather clock in the corner, whose hands pointed to just after eleven. He nodded in agreement. "Very well. Good night."

At once he turned and entered a room off the vestibule. Mrs. Thorpe smiled and crossed to the staircase. "I'll show you to your room, then, miss. This way."

Fern mounted the wide, shallow steps behind her and followed her along the gallery, guided by the lamp in the housekeeper's hand. When at last Mrs. Thorpe opened a door and ushered Fern into a large, well-furnished bedchamber with a huge four-poster dominating the center of the room, Fern could feel only grateful relief. Sleep and rest at last. Her curiosity about the vast old house and its occupants could wait until morning.

"There's hot water in the jug, and a hot bottle in the bed," said the housekeeper as she fussed about, turning back the bedcovers and opening the doors of a huge press. "Leave your unpacking until the morning, and I'll send Cassie up to help you. If there's anything else you want, there's the bell rope by the fireplace."

Satisfied that Fern was comfortable, Mrs. Thorpe withdrew, leaving Fern to undress and wash. There was a low fire in the hearth, but the room was still chilly, and Fern was glad to pull her woolen nightdress over her head and climb into the downy depths of the great bed. How comfortable it was, a

24

feather mattress and blanket-covered stone bottle full of hot water on which to warm her feet. How luxurious, how vastly different from the plain narrow bed in the Hastings household, to be in this enormous four-poster with its brocaded hangings. As sleep crept over her, Fern mused idly as to the history of this bed. How many De Lacys had slept here, and what were their stories? Had there ever been a De Lacy bride before who had had no knowledge of her bridegroom before setting foot in the Hall?

Sleep came quickly, but with it came oddly tangled dreams of a tall, taciturn man with a thin, sneering lip and of a silently miserable woman who wept as her child was pulled from her arms. She was shabby and thin, gaunt misery in her eyes, but the vision seemed to have no substance, to hover vacantly in space. No house or landscape formed a frame to the picture. The only distinct impression was of the dark-eyed man's mockery and total lack of feeling as the woman, bowed and silent, finally yielded her child and turned away. Fern awoke before dawn, thin shafts of light entering the high window where she had left the curtains undrawn. She felt uneasy and not at all rested. Strange she had slept so fitfully when she had been so tired.

As the light grew stronger and sleep did not return, she rose, and pulling on her dressing gown, crossed to the window. Far below, down the hill, beyond the gravel drive which curled out of sight behind ancient oak trees, she could see the cluster of cottages that was Brackenroyd village. To the side of the house and sweeping up and away behind it rose a vast stretch of gray moorland where occasional sheep grazed in the hollows, out of reach of the sharp wind. She opened the window and breathed in the cold air. How clean and fresh it smelled! For the first time Fern felt glad. It was indeed pleasant to leave behind the fog and stench of London and be able to breathe clean, wholesome country air. As she closed the window again, a knock came at the door, and a housemaid entered. She bobbed a curtsy.

"Morning, miss. I'm Cassie. Mrs. Thorpe says I'm to help you unpack, once you've breakfasted." She laid a tray on the night table and began pouring a cup of tea. A bright-cheeked girl of about twenty, she looked happy enough in her work, thought Fern as she picked up the bowl of porridge on the tray and began to spoon up its steaming contents. She pulled a face. In North Country fashion, the porridge had been sprinkled with salt instead of the customary sugar. Hunger, however, overcame her distaste.

"I'll come back when you've finished," promised Cassie, and with a smile she was gone.

Fern sipped her tea thoughtfully. The strange, wistful feeling of the dreams came back to her, and she pondered again as to their meaning. The tall uncommunicative man—not Mr. Hastings—was probably Bruno de Lacy, about whom she evidently still felt a little apprehensive—and with reason, since she was soon to pledge her life to his. And the woman who wept—that must be Mrs. Hastings, for Fern did indeed feel great sympathy for the poor woman whose beloved children were being wrenched from her. Or was it she? For the woman in the dream was young and ethereally fragile, her face plaintive and vividly clear in Fern's waking memory. No, it must be Mrs. Hastings. Purposefully Fern brushed the dream aside, put down her empty cup, and set about unpacking her luggage. Cassie soon returned to help.

It was only when Fern had completed the task and stood by the latticed window surveying the Hall grounds below that she thought again about Bruno de Lacy. Even as she thought, his tall, gaunt figure appeared below, striding absently away from the Hall, upward toward the moor. Straining at the leash curled about his hand was a huge wolfhound.

Bruno's head was bare, despite the damp mists, and his appearance was decidedly disheveled. Cassie, bustling behind Fern, caught sight of her master through the window and sighed.

"There goes the master on his regular morning walk with Pharaoh," she commented as the figure receded rapidly into the mist.

"Where does he go?" Fern inquired.

Cassie shrugged. "Who knows? To the moor, happen to

think. He's a deep one, Dr. de Lacy, a very clever man, they say."

The mist played tricks with the figure fading into the distance, enlarging and distorting the shape till he seemed a giant with Cerberus at his heels. Fern shivered involuntarily. There was decidedly something very strange about Bruno de Lacy.

Chapter 3

Mrs. Thorpe's warm smiles as she conducted Fern on a tour of the Hall left the new young mistress in no doubt that the housekeeper at least welcomed her arrival. She bustled ahead of Fern, throwing open doors and cupboards proudly, confident that all was as a fastidious mistress would expect. Fern was overwhelmed by the beauty of the Hall, its vast rooms furnished with taste and heedless of expense.

"Mr. Thomas used to travel abroad as a young man, long before I came here," the plump matron enthused as she led Fern into the parlor. "Much of the furniture here he brought back with him."

From the Far East undoubtedly, for the room was filled with chinoiserie, embroidered tapestry screens, ornaments of jade, lacquered cabinets, and deep-red-enameled side tables. On the hearth, before an embroidered fire screen, stood huge vases filled with pampas grass and dried honesty, cheek by jowl with the gleaming brass fire irons. Fern sank into the depths of the sofa and sighed with pleasure. What a comfortable room, with its oak-paneled walls and gleaming chandelier, far more welcoming and cozy than the overstuffed pretentiousness of Elton Square. Mrs. Thorpe was hovering expectantly by the door.

"Would you like to inspect the kitchens now, madam? Or if you prefer to remain here, I'll send Cassie up to light the fire for you. Usually it is lit only in the afternoons when Mr. Bruno returns, but if it is your wish—"

"No, no, don't trouble yourself, Mrs. Thorpe. I think I too shall go out for a walk shortly," Fern interrupted as she rose. "Perhaps you would be so kind as to show me the rest of the house later?"

Mrs. Thorpe's plump cheeks dimpled. "But, of course, madam. You are the mistress now."

"I shall be—soon," Fern corrected.

"Mr. Bruno said I was to hand over the keys to you and treat you as mistress as soon as you came. The wedding was but a formality, he said."

Reluctant fingers slid to the bunch of keys dangling from a chain at her waist, or rather, where Mrs. Thorpe's waist would be if she had not been so amply built. Fern laid a hand on hers.

"Please—be so kind as to keep the keys, Mrs. Thorpe. Pray carry on exactly as you did before I came. From you I am certain that I shall learn much of the ways of skillful housewifery, for I confess I am totally ignorant and would be glad of your counsel. When my wedding is over, perhaps then I shall be ready."

As they talked, the women retraced their footsteps toward the vestibule. Turning a corner into a long, paneled corridor, Fern noticed a wide, arched doorway set into the corner, and a studded door. A quiver ran up her spine.

"What is that door? Where does it lead?" she asked the housekeeper.

Mrs. Thorpe spread her hands. "To the east wing, that part of the old Hall we never use now. Mr. Bruno keeps it locked. He goes there occasionally, but he tells me not to waste time cleaning it, for it is so damp with all those flagstone floors,

29

and some of it is crumbling. As I say, it's never used at all, save for Mr. Bruno's cellar."

"Cellar? For wine?"

"Bless you, no. Something to do with his work as a doctor, experiments or something; I never did quite catch on what it was, but he's a very quiet man is Mr. Bruno, and very clever."

In the vestibule Mrs. Thorpe left her, and Fern returned to her room to prepare to go out and inspect the Hall by daylight from the outside. Donning a small, veiled hat and ulster and pulling on her gloves, she walked down the steps, crunching the gravel drive underfoot and turning off the main drive along a flagged path before reaching the gate. The path wound between now barren flowerbeds and rockeries, rising gradually as it circled the house widely, and ending suddenly at an iron gate set in a high stone wall.

The lock creaked rustily at Fern's touch but opened easily. Beyond lay steeply rising rough turf and a pathway worn by countless feet. Clanging the gate shut behind her, Fern set off up the moor.

The path swept steeply across tough, wiry grass, between outcrops of black rock scoured into smooth gigantic monoliths by the searching Atlantic winds. Fern was entranced by the wild Pennine countryside, stark and majestic in its somber wintry mood, not on account of its beauty, for not even a poet could see beauty in the tough brown heather and wild, exposed wastes. But there was power, a kind of repressed strength and primitive appeal in these rugged gaunt mountains protecting the little village in the hollow far below, and in the fierce little brook gushing vigorously down its narrow rocky bed to join the river.

Not a figure broke the solitude of the landscape save an occasional browsing sheep that, startled at her approach, looked up with a distrustful, inimical stare. Fern, out of breath from her climb, and the wind catching in her throat, seated herself on an outcrop of rock to survey the scene. What an impressive countryside this was! Deep within her, something responded, low and vibrant, to the untamed majesty of the Pennines. It was as though their power evoked in her something she had once known and then lost, something she was over-joyed to rediscover. Coming to Brackenroyd was somehow akin to coming home.

Turning, Fern sought out the shape of Brackenroyd Hall. It was not difficult to discern, huge and brooding darkly against the skyline on the clifftop. From here it seemed to dominate and overwhelm the cluster of cottages and the church and mill in the valley below it, standing sentinel as the De Lacy family had done over its vassals for centuries. A shiver caused Fern to rise and resume her walk. The Hall was somehow an object of menace. Turning her back on it, Fern surveyed the view and made out at length the shape of a long, rambling building half-burying itself in the hillside. A strange edifice, neither church nor mill, but rather like a huge barn it stood, neglected and dilapidated, a no-longer-frequented house, per-haps. From a curl of smoke rising above a chimney, quickly whipped up and swept away by the wind, Fern concluded that the house was still inhabited after all.

It was cold up here on the heights, and Fern reflected that her London attire was hardly suitable for braving the gusty Pennine winds, which were laced with frost. Here and there a patch of snow still lay on the heather, and from the wind's icy, probing fingers it would seem that further snow was still to fall. Fern began to retrace her steps to the Hall.

Perhaps it was the wind's shrill rise and fall, or the crackle of her own footsteps on desiccated heather that drowned all other sound, but a sudden voice at her side caused Fern to leap in alarm.

"I see our moorland air has brought fresh color to your cheeks, Miss Saxby." Fern's startled gaze found Bruno de Lacy walking moodily at her side, his dark eyes regarding her penetratingly. She recovered herself swiftly.

"Indeed, it is fine, bracing air. I think I shall come to love Brackenroyd, sir, for it stirs deep feelings in me, a kind of familiarity almost."

He was looking at her oddly, and Fern remembered her re-mark on arriving at the Hall last night. He had looked at her equally oddly, almost mockingly then, when he had spoken of her sense of recognition as a common sensation.

"Do you think it is possible, Dr. de Lacy, that one can feel a sense of belonging where one knows one has never been before?" Fern inquired. "I could almost believe I know this valley and these moors—perhaps a kind of inherited memory through my ancestors?"

He stopped suddenly and faced her squarely, his gaze fierce and compelling. "No, I do not believe such things possible, Miss Saxby. Yorkshire folk are too full of common sense and practicality to have faith in any such nonsense." His voice was sharply emphatic.

"Yorkshire folk? But you . . ."

"I know what you would say. I am partly of German parentage and educated in Germany, but nevertheless one side of me is pure Yorkshire—and of you, too." He began to walk again, adjusting his long stride to suit Fern's shorter one. The dog, Pharaoh, unleashed, bounded among the lichen-spattered boulders.

For a time they walked in silence, Fern feeling she had been reprimanded for her foolishness and at the same time resentful of his superior ways. As they descended the pathway to the gate in the Hall's walls, Bruno spoke again carelessly.

"I presume Mrs. Thorpe has shown you over the Hall. If there is anything else you require in the way of amusement—a piano or embroidery materials or whatever a young lady desires—you have but to order it."

Fern was stung. Amusements indeed! "Thank you, sir, but I do not require diversions of the kind you mention. A library such as the Hall possesses suits me admirably, and a mare to ride would please me well."

He nodded curtly. "Malachi will see to a suitable mount for you. The library is, of course, at your disposal."

At the gateway he paused before opening the gate. "If I might presume, Miss Saxby, to call you by your Christian name, would you be offended? It seems a little . . . odd for a betrothed couple to be as formal as we are. May I call you Fern?"

Fern thrilled to the sound of her name spoken in such resonant tones, a sound as wild and untamed as the wind on the moors. "By all means," she said softly.

If only he were not so stiffly aloof and cold, she could quite like this man she was to marry. His tall frame and subdued manner bespoke strength, a power as repressed and formidable as that of the Pennine moors. Here was a man to lean on in time of adversity, a man in whom to place one's trust—if one could only penetrate his reserve. He had spoken of their betrothal; Fern resolved to press further.

"I think I can see the church spire there below," she said, indicating the gray tower amid the village trees. "Is that where we shall be married?"

"If you wish." How laconic he was!

"When?"

"When you are ready. At once, if you wish the banns to be published."

Fern felt a little mollified. He was not, then, anxious to delay the match lest he did not come to like her or because he resented her intrusion. In that case, she would not rush him. She too would be glad of a little delay while she came to know both Bruno and her new surroundings a little better. She glanced up at the leaden sky.

"It would seem that there is snow to come soon. Let us be married in the spring, when the winter is ended."

"Very well. I shall wait till you ask again."

They turned up the gravel path leading to the door of the Hall, the dog loping ahead of them. Bruno opened the front door for her and smiled, a fleeting curve at the corner of his lips which gave his saturnine expression a brief moment of humor.

"One would have expected your first excursion to be to the village, my dear, and not up on the barren moors. After lunch I must go down to see to matters at the mill. I shall take you down to the village and introduce you to some of our local worthies."

"Thank you. I shall be delighted."

That afternoon Malachi led out from the stables a beautiful

little gray mare named Whisper for Fern to ride, and a lively black stallion for his master. Bruno caressed its nose affectionately before mounting, though Fern could not catch the words he murmured in the horse's ear.

"Phantom and I are old friends," he commented as he swung a long leg over the saddle. "He was with me in the old days, in Vienna."

Strange to think of Bruno de Lacy in Vienna, that romantic city of music and gaiety. Somehow, in his taciturn, brooding manner he seemed to be more at one with this arid, bleak mountain country than with the waltzing beats of that far-off city. Together Fern and he cantered down the gravel drive, swinging sharply down into the cobbled lane leading into the village. Light precipitation began to cling to Fern's riding habit in the shape of miniature, coruscating snowflakes.

"Would you like to return?" Bruno demanded curtly. Fern shook her head. He was considerate despite his abrupt manner. As they rode past the inn, a cheery and red-faced young man at the door waved and smiled. Bruno reined in and turned toward him.

"Allow me to present to you Tom Rawcliffe, landlord of the Woolpack," Bruno said. Fern inclined her head, smiling. "This is Miss Saxby, Tom, new mistress of Brackenroyd Hall and my future wife."

Rawcliffe made a welcoming gesture, half-salute, half-wave, and grinned apologetically at his own gauche manner. "Glad to meet thee, miss. The Hall's been lacking a mistress this many a year, and it'll be grand to see a De Lacy wedding again."

"Thank you." Fern smiled over her shoulder as Bruno led her on down the cobbled street. Almost imperceptible twitches at the curtains of the cottages betrayed that other inhabitants were curious about the newcomer to the village, but no doors opened. Bruno had noticed. He grunted quietly. "Pennine folk are a cautious lot, as you'll find. They'll watch and size you up before they commit themselves, but their friendship is worth the having once you've earned it."

A suspicious race, then, he made them sound, but reliable

and solid once one had penetrated their reserve. Fern resolved to win their confidence, for they were her own folk, were they not, bred of the moors and the millstone grit which was her own heritage?

The gray-stone church was discernible to their left, surrounded by old oak trees. "We shall call on Amos after we have met the schoolmaster," Bruno remarked as he drew up before a low gray building, evidently the school, with the schoolmaster's house alongside it, for Fern could hear childish voices chanting, "Once seven is seven, twice seven is fourteen . . ."

In answer to Bruno's knock, a pleasant-faced young woman with smoothly coiled fair hair came to the door. From behind her skirts peeped a child, a girl with huge violet eyes and the same gilt hair.

"Bruno! How nice to see you," the young woman cried as she stepped aside to allow him to enter. Bruno smiled distantly. "Fabia, this is my betrothed, Fern Saxby. Fern, this is Fabia Armitage, the schoolmaster's wife."

Fern noted the young woman's appraising gaze as they nodded mutually and Fabia led the way into the shabbily furnished parlor. The child clung timorously to Fabia's skirt, and Fern was amazed to see Bruno bend to her, stroking her hair with one gentle finger.

"And how is my little Phoebe today?" he asked softly. "Still as timid as a little sparrow? But you grow more beautiful, like your mother, every time I see you."

Fabia laughed softly, a contented, happy sound. "She is well, I am glad to say, despite the influenza that struck so many of the village children recently."

Fern noted the quick, interrogative gaze that passed between Bruno and the young woman. She too held out her hand to the child gravely.

"How do you do, Miss Phoebe."

The child shrank away, alarm glistening in her huge eyes. Bruno rested his hand on her shoulder reassuringly and spoke across the fair head to Fern.

"I regret she does not understand you. Phoebe is deaf, and

consequently dumb. She is afraid of anyone who is not familiar to her."

Fabia's quick smile alleviated the sudden tension in the little parlor. "But she will come to know you soon, Miss Saxby, and no doubt she will care for you then as she does now for Bruno." She turned quickly to Bruno, and Fern could see the light of pure pleasure in her eyes. "You will stay to tea, won't you? I know Luke will be so disappointed if he doesn't see you, Bruno, and your charming bride. Lessons will be over soon."

Bruno shook his head. "I fear there is snow on the way, Fabia, and I must take Fern home soon. Moreover, there is business at the mill I must attend to. Tell Luke I shall come again soon."

"Very soon, Bruno. It does Luke a world of good to talk with you, for I fear I am no match for him. He needs the companionship of another clever man like you. And do bring Miss Saxby to visit us again soon." Her fingers rested fleetingly on Fern's arm as she bade farewell, and Fern felt glad. Here at least she felt she had found a friend. There was something so warm and hospitable, so unassuming and kindly about Fabia Armitage that one could not help but like her immensely. And Bruno's dark face, relaxed now into a warm smile, indicated that he too thought the same. For a brief moment Fern felt envious of the silent intimacy between him and the schoolmaster's wife.

But there was no sign of any such closeness between Bruno and Edgar Amos once they reached the vicarage, Bruno leading the two horses across the village green and tethering them near the lych-gate outside the church. Amos received them warmly enough and led them into his book-lined study, where paper and pens scattered on the desk indicated he had been working, perhaps on Sunday's sermon, thought Fern.

"You have, of course, already met my fiancée," Bruno said coldly, once they were all seated.

"A great pleasure," replied Amos, "and I hope you have settled in comfortably at the Hall. What do you think of your new home, Miss Saxby?"

"A most impressive house," said Fern uncertainly. It was difficult to convey how one felt, confronted by such an overwhelming edifice, and one whose atmosphere was incalculably strange and forbidding yet curiously familiar.

"Impressive indeed—and with a most impressive history, too," replied Amos. "I was working on some old records of the Hall still extant, going back to the mid-seventeenth century." He indicated the papers strewn before him on the mahogany desk. "A private piece of research, you know, a hobby I indulge when time permits. Perhaps you would come to peruse them if you are interested."

"Oh, indeed I am," Fern cried impulsively.

Bruno looked up sharply. "Perhaps it would be as well not to," he commented quietly. Amos' sandy eyebrows rose in question, and Bruno rose to leave, gathering up his coat. "Miss Saxby is perhaps of an ... imaginative turn of mind. She already believes she has some kind of inherited memory of the Hall, acquired no doubt in an earlier incarnation."

Fern was angered by the scornful tone in his voice but controlled her voice smoothly as she spoke. "You are very kind, Reverend Amos, and I should be most obliged if you would permit me to read your records at some time."

His blue eyes sought hers inquiringly. "Do you truly believe in reincarnation, Miss Saxby?"

Fern hesitated. She had never really considered the matter, but Bruno's sneer had roused her. "Who knows the truth of the matter? An intelligent mind remains open to inquiry and does not condemn out of hand. I should be glad to discuss the matter with you."

"You are most welcome here whenever you wish to call," Amos replied warmly, as he led his guests to the door.

"And you also at Brackenroyd Hall," Fern added, glancing sideways at Bruno's set face. Damn the man, how impertinent he was. She would invite whom she pleased to her home if she found their manner more to her liking than her fiancé's.

It was not a very auspicious way for their association to begin, she thought sadly as they cantered homeward in silence. Already Bruno and she were at loggerheads on her first day in

37

Brackenroyd. As they turned into the great stone gateway that marked the drive, she jutted her chin defiantly.

"I shall invite whom I choose to the Hall. I have a right to select my friends," she stated firmly.

He smiled wanly. "Indeed you have, and as mistress of Brackenroyd I shall not deny you the right. I could only wish your judgment better, that you chose more rational, logical companions than a superstitious creature like Amos, that is all."

Fern felt her cheeks burning with anger, and during afternoon tea in the lavish warmth and comfort of the dining room she could not bring herself to talk to him again. Mrs. Thorpe's hot buttered muffins and thinly sliced fruit cake, accompanied by strong Indian tea, helped to restore Fern's equanimity, but Bruno seemed abstracted, deep in his own thoughts as he sipped from the fine willow-patterned cup. After tea he disappeared, to the mill Mrs. Thorpe said, to conclude the business the afternoon's visiting had delayed.

The afternoon's freezing rain had now coalesced into delicate drifting snowflakes. Mrs. Thorpe offered to show her new mistress around the rest of the Hall.

"Though most of the bedrooms are now unused, of course, and the furniture draped until such time as we have guests again," she remarked. "It's many a year since the Hall had guests, Mr. Thomas being a very retiring and Christianlike gentleman who spent most of his time working or reading. He lost his wife when his son, Mr. George, was born, and when Mr. George went away to school, Mr. Thomas seemed to prefer being alone. Very shy he was, but as kind and considerate a master as anyone could wish. It's a pity Mr. Bruno didn't come home from Germany to keep the master company, for the old gentleman doted on him. Still, Mr. Bruno's home now at last, and to stay."

She looked at Fern appraisingly, and a sigh of contentment escaped her. "Aye, the Hall is a fine mansion, and I'm glad it's to have a young master and mistress to bring happiness back to it at last. It's seen far too much unhappiness in the past. But now is different. Reverend Amos will no doubt be calling often, and Mr. Armitage and all. Before long the house'll be full of company again."

Her warm face brightened at the prospect, and she ushered Fern happily into many bedrooms ornate with four-posters and Chinese rugs on parquet floors, all with marble-topped washstands and flowered ewers and basins, and all white-draped like spectral rooms awaiting ghostly occupants. Fern, while congratulating Mrs. Thorpe on their orderliness and cleanliness, nevertheless shivered again. There was undoubtedly an odd, forbidding air about the stately old Hall, but she forebore to question the housekeeper about the past's unhappiness. Instead she inquired idly about the dilapidated old barnlike house high and solitary on the moor.

"Oh, that's Fox Brow," Mrs. Thorpe replied as she relocked the last bedroom door. "Lovely old house in its time, but it's gone to rack and ruin since Mr. Stansfield died. Mrs. Stansfield still lives there alone, but she never receives company nor goes out, though it's several years since she was widowed. Pity. She was a very lovely woman, and no doubt could still have her pick of many a second husband, being still young, but she'd have none of it. They say she's gone a bit queer with grief, but I'm not one to gossip. It's for her to decide how she'll live, and nobody else's business."

It was clear from her firm tone that Mrs. Thorpe had done with Mrs. Stansfield, her duty done in putting the new young mistress into the picture so far as her neighbors were concerned. Though curious about the young widow recluse, Fern pressed no more.

They were passing the old iron-studded door to the east wing again. On an impulse Fern stopped.

"Have you the key to this wing, Mrs. Thorpe? I should like to see it."

The housekeeper's genial face became doubtful. "I have a key, though none but Mr. Bruno goes in there." On reflection, she seemed to decide it was the mistress's right to do as she pleased. Selecting a key from the bunch at her waist, she unlocked the door.

"There is no need to accompany me if you wish to attend

to other duties," Fern said, seeing the woman's perplexed expression. "I shall relock the door when I have done."

"Very well, madam." Mrs. Thorpe surrendered the key and pattered away. Fern pushed open the door, wondering what she could expect to find. A long flagstoned corridor led into a vast hall around which a high gallery ran. Windows set high allowed little light to enter, and since dusk was falling fast, the hall was steeped in gloom. Was it the cold air in here that caused that involuntary shiver along her spine?

Dust carpeted the expanse of stone floor, but footmarks back and forth indicated frequent use. Bruno on the way to the laboratory Mrs. Thorpe had mentioned, no doubt. Fern followed the track to a door in the corner, under the shadow of the minstrels' gallery, but the handle would not yield. Locked. No matter; perhaps it was as well if Bruno used this room as a dispensary. Doctors frequently had dangerous drugs and potions that it was safest to keep locked away.

As Fern turned to go, she caught sight of something in the shadows under the gallery, and peering closer, she could just discern a portrait on the wall, apparently of a woman. At that moment firm footsteps rang along the corridor leading back to the newer Hall, and a figure carrying an oil lamp approached. It was Bruno.

"Mrs. Thorpe told me you were here," he said curtly. "It is cold and damp. Permit me to accompany you back." His fingers touched her elbow, but Fern drew back.

"I was exploring, that is all. Pray tell me, who is the woman in the portrait, and why is her picture left here alone?"

By the light of the lamp she could see a young woman dressed in the style of some half-century earlier, her braided hair glinting golden and her pointed, wistful face expressing desolate unhappiness. Fern's sympathy was arrested at once by the girl's huge, saddened eyes. Bruno was staring at the portrait thoughtfully.

"She looks so sad, Bruno, and in some strange way oddly familiar. Who is she?"

"She is Annot Radley, your great-grandmother. The por-

40

trait was painted in readiness to hang in the gallery as soon as she became a De Lacy wife, which, as you know, she never did."

"Then why is her picture still here?"

"Grandfather Thomas would not dispose of it. I think it pricked his conscience, and he wished above all things to atone to Annot's son, though he never knew him, of course. Come, let us return." Again Bruno took her elbow, and this time Fern did not resist, for it was a reassuringly firm touch that helped to allay the shivering this hall induced in her.

"I wonder why she looked so familiar to me?" Fern queried idly as Bruno relocked the studded door to the old wing.

His tired features creased briefly into a hint of a smile. "No doubt because it was like looking in a mirror, my dear. You are remarkably like your great-grandmother."

Of course, that was it. Dismissing the thought, Fern inquired how matters stood at the mill.

Bruno sighed and answered absently. "Well enough, but there are many things I should like to change. I'll go again tomorrow and talk it over with Fearnley, the manager."

"Would you like me to come too?" Fern offered. "After all, the mill's affairs will be partly my responsibility too."

Bruno's eyes narrowed, and he looked at her directly, surprise in the dark, intent look. "Business management is hardly woman's work. I would have considered cooking or tending the plants in the hothouse were more to your taste, and I would not wish to trouble you unduly with matters you do not comprehend."

Fern's cheeks flamed. Again he was insulting her, belittling her as a woman of superficial thought; how like that unbearable Mr. Hastings he was! How insufferable he would be as a husband!

She spoke stiffly, but with control. "It is no trouble, I assure you. I should far prefer to occupy my mind with matters of business than my hands with mindless tasks." She was now outside her own door. Fern disengaged her elbow from his fingertips. "I shall see you at dinner. At what time?"

41

"At eight." He was gone. He too, it would seem, had no wish to prolong the conversation with her.

Half an hour before dinner, Cassie came up bringing hot water and fresh towels, complaining that she had extra work to do in the kitchen today. "Fanny's off ill—the kitchen maid. Got flu, Mrs. Thorpe says, so I've all her work to do as well as me own," she said as she laid the towels over the jug of hot water on the washstand.

"Poor Fanny," commented Fern. "Does Dr. de Lacy tend the influenza victims in the village?"

"Lor' bless you, no, miss. He's not that kind of doctor, isn't Mr. Bruno. Not one that cures illness, I mean. Mrs. Thorpe says he's a doctor of philosophy, whatever that may mean, and does very clever scientific work, but it's all Dutch to me. It's Dr. Briggs from up the far side of the valley who comes to sick folk. Will that be all, Miss Saxby?"

Over dinner in the dimly lit dining room, its oak-paneled walls receding into the gloom beyond the reach of the oil lamps and the candles on the table, Fern surveyed Bruno's dark, handsome features in silence. He seemed reluctant to talk, eating the brown Windsor soup and the superbly roasted sirloin of beef with an air of absorption. She wondered curiously what thought filled the mind of this strangely reticent man who seemed loath to allow anyone to invade the privacy of his mind. Problems of the business in the mill perhaps, or scientific problems currently occupying him in his laboratory, or was he mentally debating the wisdom of taking her to wife? It was already evident to both of them that they had little in common. Once the dessert plates were cleared away, he rose suddenly from the table.

"Allow me to pour you a glass of Madeira," he said, and Fern could hear the clink of glasses at the sideboard before he returned to offer her the glass. "Now I am going to work in my study. Good night, my dear." Abruptly he left her. Fern sighed and rose slowly, replacing the wineglass and her linen napkin on the table and crossing to the window. Outside, snow was still drifting down, silently and relentlessly. By morning the stark landscape would be softened and blurred

42

under the heavy blanket that was swiftly enveloping the house and hillside. Brackenroyd Hall seemed even more isolated and forbidding than ever. Fern let the braided velvet curtains fall into place again, deciding that though it was still only nine o'clock she might just as well go to bed, for it was evident Bruno would not seek her company again tonight.

Perhaps it was the chill of the bedroom, or possibly the strange air of unreality about the loneliness of the house after the hectic atmosphere of London, but whatever the reason, Fern slept badly, tossing fitfully until the small hours. The chill in the bedroom seemed to grow, the cold penetrating her bones despite the blankets and woolen nightgown. And strange dreams flickered in her mind.

Suddenly she sat upright, fear choking her. A gray mist seemed to be trying to force its way into her nostrils, and with it an alien, terrifying sensation. With returning wakefulness the menacing mist receded and Fern clung, gasping, to the bedpost. It was as though something had been trying to invade her body, to take possession of her. She shook her head firmly. What a terrifying nightmare!

But from the dream something still lingered—a wailing, piteous thing that held out its arms and sobbed plaintively. And with a sudden gasp Fern remembered. The woman in the dream the previous night who had wept for her child—it had not been Mrs. Hastings, after all. She had come again tonight—and there was no mistaking the face in the portrait in the east wing. The woman was Annot Radley.

Chapter 4

With a satisfied sigh Edgar Amos pushed back the chair from his mahogany desk and laid down his pen. There, Sunday's sermon was complete. With the contented feeling of a job well done, he rose and crossed to the study window. Snow still lay thick on the village green, graying and slushed by the hurrying feet of his flock as they busied themselves about their work, clogged feet tramping down the lane, at dawn mostly, to De Lacy's mill, and homeward again at dusk. From the window he could just see, beyond the church tower, the tip of the mill chimney belching its eternal cloud of black smoke. Only on Sundays was the Brackenroyd air clean and still; only on Sundays did clogged feet veer toward the church instead of the mill.

Amos' pale-blue gaze shifted westward, up from the village to the jutting crags of millstone grit rocks edging the moor and the stark outline of Brackenroyd Hall, silhouetted against the gray skyline. The De Lacy family had stood there, guardian of the vulnerable village at their feet, for countless generations, their decisions always affecting the lives of the stolid village folk below. It was a De Lacy who had always owned the land the tenant farmers worked; it was a De Lacy who, in this century, had built the mill farther downstream that had robbed the handloom weavers for miles around of their independence, forcing them out of business with his gigantic frames that could weave good Yorkshire woolens far faster than any human hand. They had given in at last, this proud, silent race, and in time they had come to realize that their standard of living had improved as a result; their admission that it was due to a De Lacy's acumen had remained tacit. Pride and independence were a heavy price to pay.

Amos admired the spirit of this dour race who had accepted him a few years back with warmth, if not with overwhelming welcome. Perhaps they had regarded a new young curate, unmarried at that, with a certain degree of native suspicion, but when the old vicar eventually died and Thomas de Lacy's patronage had been extended to young Amos as the new vicar, the villagers had continued the habit of depositing gifts of eggs and freshly baked bread in the rectory kitchen just as they had always done for his elderly predecessor. They asked no thanks nor wanted it. The silent gesture, unacknowledged by either side, was a mark of his being accepted and respected, as old Thomas de Lacy had pointed out to him, and Amos was glad.

He had missed old Thomas, a gentle, scholarly soul who had carried on conscientiously the family business he had inherited, leaving most of the daily running to the mill manager, Fearnley, while he busied himself among his books and papers in the Hall library. It had been Thomas' ambition one day to publish a history of the Hall, and Amos was proud of the old man's faith in him, that he had entrusted all his research to Amos as he lay dying.

"Carry it on for me, Edgar my boy, I beg you. If there is to be any monument to me. I wish it were this, that my papers were published. If you can find the time among your many parochial duties, I shall be eternally grateful to you."

Dear old Thomas, so loved and respected by all the villagers in their begrudging, taciturn way. Edgar had promised willingly to fulfill his obligation. He wondered idly whether the new master of Brackenroyd would ever win the admiration of Brackenroyd folk as Thomas had done. He was a strange fish, this Bruno de Lacy, with his penetrating dark eyes and stern Teutonic manner. One felt he was watching and calculating, unwilling to reveal himself until he had learned what one was thinking. That was due to his streak of Continental blood, no doubt, for Yorkshire folk were blunt to the point of rudeness, and they welcomed honesty in others. But this new master remained comparatively unknown to them, for in the two months he had been at the Hall he had communicated with the locals only so far as it had been necessary. He visited the mill and talked with Fearnley often, he nodded and passed the time of day with the villagers in passing, but with none had he appeared to form any kind of relationship. Amos felt a little slighted. Young De Lacy was reputedly academic and gifted, yet so far he had made no overture to the young vicar, who was, apart from Luke Armitage, the schoolmaster, probably the only other highly educated person in the district. One would have expected the new master to have sought Amos' company, yet he had not. It was Amos who made the first approach, paying a visit to the Hall after a deferential lapse of some days after De Lacy's return from Germany. His words of welcome and condolence left little apparent mark on De Lacy.

"You know, of course," the young man had said brusquely, "that my uncle wishes me to marry my distant cousin, Miss Saxby. When she comes, you will naturally conduct the marriage service."

Of course, Amos had known of old Thomas' wish. All the villagers knew, but since none knew the young woman, all still wondered whether she would agree. No such doubt seemed to enter young De Lacy's mind. Amos at once took a dislike to the dark stranger's self-possession and air of assurance. Such a manner was hardly calculated to win over the cautious villagers. De Lacy would have to strive harder to woo the valley folk than he would to win his bride.

The attractive Miss Saxby. Amos' thoughts dwelt pleasurably on the flaxen-haired young woman he had met by chance on the train, slender and tastefully dressed and with as warm a smile as he had ever seen. Now, she, if she had a mind to, could win the locals over with little effort; of that he was sure. Her gaze was direct and honest, a trait all Yorkshire folk admired, her wide blue eyes indicating intelligent interest. Amos hoped they would renew their acquaintance soon, husband-to-be De Lacy permitting, for there was promise of a worth-while friendship in that warm young face.

"You should be married, Amos." The bishop had said it time and again, implying that the incumbent of this village could hardly carry out his duties effectively unless he were cozily cared for by a warm and gentle wife. The ministrations of Amos' housekeeper, Mrs. Crowther, did not meet with the bishop's approval. "The sooner you find a young woman of breeding and tact who is fitted for the role of vicar's wife, the better," he had sternly admonished. Miss Saxby's pretty oval face flitted into Amos' mind, and he brushed the impious thought aside. It was easy for the bishop to propound, but how in the restricted round of parochial duties could one find such a wife?

The aroma of freshly buttered muffins preceded Mrs. Crowther's knock at the study door. Amos turned from the window, rubbing his hands in pleasure.

"Shall I set the tray here, Reverend?" the pudding-faced woman asked pleasantly, pausing by his desk. Amos agreed, and as he drew the heavy plush curtains together to shut out the gathering dusk, she poured the amber liquid into a china cup, handing it to him when he crossed to sit by the fire.

"There's rabbit stew and rice pudding in the oven for your dinner, so don't get lost in them books of yours and forget, now, will you, sir? It's time I were off home now."

Her words, though rough and rudely phrased, were kindly meant, he knew. He smiled appreciatively, biting into the buttery depths of a muffin as she withdrew. Her warning was not unfounded, for once he abandoned himself to the pleasure of working on old Thomas' notes, time no longer existed.

There was a ring at the doorbell, muffled voices in the little hallway, and then Mrs. Crowther reappeared, her face suffused in pleasure.

"Dr. de Lacy has come to call on you, Reverend. Shall I fetch another cup when I've shown him in?"

Amos rose suddenly, almost spilling his tea in surprised delight. He brushed the crumbs sharply from his threadbare worsted suit and stood, hands clasped behind his back before the fire, to welcome his exalted guest. Mrs. Crowther entered, bobbed an unaccustomed curtsy before announcing, "Dr. de Lacy, sir," and withdrew.

De Lacy strode into the small study and shook hands with the vicar with a curt, "Afternoon, Amos," and without waiting to be invited, he sank into an armchair, the one Amos had just vacated. Amos pulled forward another chair and sat gingerly on the edge. Mrs. Crowther reappeared with a fresh cup and saucer, which she placed silently on the tray.

"How pleasant to see you again so soon," Amos said a little uncertainly. De Lacy, so taciturn and unpredictable, was a little difficult to handle, but one would not wish to rebuff any advance he made. "Would you care for a cup of tea?"

Amos brandished the teapot invitingly, but De Lacy shook his head. "I did not come to stay, Amos, only to ask you if you would indulge Miss Saxby in a whim she has entertained these last few days."

Amos' sandy eyebrows rose. Miss Saxby did not seem the capricious type, but if he could please her and thereby please the master of Brackenroyd too ...

"Of course, my dear friend. Anything."

De Lacy was frowning. Amos wondered if it had been a mistake to presume to call this reserved young man a friend. De Lacy fidgeted restlessly.

"The fact is, I think she is bored with having to stay in the Hall. She wanders about and asks if she may come to the mill, but business is hardly a woman's concern. For a week she has asked endlessly about that ancestress of hers, Annot Radley, but since I do not know the story beyond what my grandfather told me, I cannot satisfy her curiosity. To be quite frank, Amos, I consider such curiosity rather morbid, but she insists.

I believe you have my grandfather's notes on Brackenroyd's history. Perhaps you would be so kind as to tell Fern the story or let her read the notes for herself. Then perhaps she will let the matter rest."

Amos smiled broadly, relaxing sufficiently to sit back more comfortably in his chair. De Lacy was not only more loquacious than he had ever known him, but he was taking the young vicar into his confidence too, and asking a favor of him. Matters were indeed taking a turn for the better.

"I should be delighted. Perhaps you would like me to bring the records to the Hall for Miss Saxby to read, since the weather is still so inclement? Tomorrow, if you wish."

"Then that's settled." De Lacy rose abruptly, picked up his riding whip from where he had dropped it on the desk, and strode toward the door. At the doorway he halted and turned. "One thing, Amos. I should not wish you to encourage Miss Saxby too much to talk about Annot Radley once she knows the facts. Already she claims to have dreamed about her, and I think she fancies she has some strange sort of relationship with the girl. Some odd notion about inherited memory, I think she said. Stuff and nonsense, of course, and I would not wish the notion to be encouraged."

He did not wait to ask whether Amos would agree to his request, as though he believed his order would be obeyed without question, thought Amos as he watched De Lacy mount his black stallion and ride off uphill into the gloom. From nowhere the great lumbering shape of De Lacy's wolf-hound materalized from the darkness and loped off in the sleet behind the horse. Amos shivered. If he had not been a man of the cloth, he might well have believed that the strange man on a black horse and the devilish hound following them were creatures from a netherworld. Closing the front door against the sleet, he hurried back into the cozy warmth of the study.

By mid-morning the following day an unexpected turn of mildness in the weather had almost melted the snows from the valley. Amos presented himself at the Hall, smiling at Fanny, the parlormaid, as he proffered his visiting card to be borne on a silver tray into the inner regions of the house. Although Miss Saxby had met him and indeed requested this visit, it was nonetheless etiquette to offer his card on his first visit to the new mistress of the Hall. Fanny, having seen service in greater houses in the West Riding, where she had rubbed shoulders with French maids and quickly learned their winsome ways, lowered her lashes demurely as she invited the vicar to step inside, flicking the ribbons on her cap, her heels clicking across the parquet floor before him.

In the drawing room Miss Saxby rose from her chair by the fire to greet Amos, and he noted that her fine features were somewhat drawn, as though she were fatigued or worried.

"A glass of wine after your cold walk, Reverend Amos?" she offered politely. "A glass of Madeira, perhaps?"

As Amos declined courteously, she nodded to Fanny to withdraw, then reseated herself by the fire, signaling Amos to be seated also. He drew a chair closer to hers.

"Mr. de Lacy is not at home this morning, Miss Saxby?"

She smiled wanly. "Indeed no, he is constantly occupied, either at the mill or engaged upon his own work in his study or the laboratory. I could wish he would tell me more of his work or allow me to be involved with business matters, but I think he does not feel it to be a woman's place." Her smile dimpled warmly. "Perhaps you could persuade him otherwise, Reverend, for I should very much like to use my brain a little."

Amos felt sympathy for the girl. She was undoubtedly intelligent as well as attractive. How presumptuous of De Lacy to discount her as useless. Courtesy bade him protect his new patron's actions, for like all the De Lacys since time immemorial, Mr. Bruno had agreed to see to the comfort of the village church incumbent.

"No doubt he considers this wintry weather unfit to take you down to the mill, Miss Saxby. Doubtless when the weather improves . . ."

"But that is not the reason for his silence in other respects, Mr. Amos. He will not talk of his research, nor of any other matter. I think he must by nature be a solitary creature, preferring his own company and thoughts."

By the nervous clenching and relaxing of her fingertips on the arms of the chair he could guess that she spoke against her better judgment. She obviously felt deeply about De Lacy's reticence to be tempted to speak of it with a comparative stranger, and Amos welcomed her confidence in him.

"Perhaps he is a little shy because he does not yet know you. Time will overcome that difficulty."

"Then why does he treat me like an imbecile?" Her pale face flushed angrily, and her eyes glittered with hard fire. Amos shifted uncomfortably. "Since my arrival nearly two weeks ago he has ignored me, offering me only childish pastimes to occupy my time," the girl went on. "He brushes aside my efforts to converse with him, he declines even to eat with me often. I think, to be quite honest, he considers me flighty, or even worse."

She relapsed into silence, knotting her fingers together nervously. Amos eyed her curiously. Worse? What worse could the master of Brackenroyd believe of her? She raised huge, sad eyes as she answered his unspoken question.

"I told him I had a strong affinity with this house, that I could sense an urgent communion with it, and when I told him that I even dreamed of Annot Radley, he stiffened toward me. I think he believes me mad. Do you think it impossible, Mr. Amos, to have a distinct feeling for one's past?"

Clearing his throat nervously, Amos smiled reassuringly. "No indeed, Miss Saxby. Here in the West Riding such feeling goes deep. I'll wager there isn't a man in the valley who doesn't feel as deeply for his heritage as you do. Such sentiments are common, and I think you are not unusual in that respect."

She sat up tautly, her eyes glowing. "But it is more than that, Reverend. My emotions are those of Annot Radley; I know it, though I do not yet know her story. Mr. Amos, tell me truly, do you believe in ghosts?"

Amos hesitated. Here was a tricky situation if he were to retain the respect both of the girl and of the master. "As a man of the cloth, my dear, I believe in the eternal life of the spirit, of course. But here, as you requested, I have Mr. Thomas' notes on Annot Radley. Let me leave these with you to peruse at your leisure." He saw her eyes gleam as her fingers closed about the sheaf of papers. "But do not let your mind dwell on poor Annot's story overmuch. Hers was a pathetic history, and I fear perhaps it would be a trifle ... unhealthy to dwell too long on such a morbid subject."

He rose quickly before she could engage him in further embarrassing discussion, murmuring that he must visit a sick child in the village. She followed him toward the door, the dull glow still gleaming in her eyes.

Amos tried to lighten the tension in the atmosphere. "Perhaps before long you and Mr. de Lacy will be holding a wedding party here. It is time the old house knew gaiety and laughter again," he commented brightly.

Her eyes softened. "Indeed, Mr. Amos. It is time the Hall knew peace and happiness," she agreed quietly.

The door burst open unexpectedly, revealing the tall figure of Bruno de Lacy, the wolfhound at his heels.

Amos, taken aback by the sudden apparition of the gaunt figure, uttered a strangled laugh. "Oh, Mr. de Lacy! I am so pleased to have the opportunity to see you as well as Miss Saxby."

Bruno's gaze flickered over him and beyond, to where Fern stood, motionless, the sheaf of papers in her hand. His eyes narrowed. "Are those the notes on Annot Radley?"

Amos nodded. "As I promised, copied from Mr. Thomas' own notes, verbatim."

"Give them to me."

As in a trance, Amos watched the tableau, the unmoving figures of the master and the girl, the one holding out his hand peremptorily in demand, the other holding tightly to the papers and glaring defiance. For some seconds neither moved.

"You hear me? Give them to me," De Lacy barked.

"Why?" The girl's face sprang into animation, her eyes dancing anger. "Why should I?"

"Because they will only encourage your romantic daydreams. This place has had an unsettling effect on you, it seems, and on reflection, I would prefer you to delay further investigation as to its history until you have regained your self-control."

Black eyes held fiery blue ones in their thrall. Amos could feel the charge that enmeshed their gaze and knew he was forgotten in the battle of wills. Then slowly he sensed the blue gaze weaken, the electric power of the black subjugating the girl. It was like watching a snake mesmerize a rabbit. Slowly she raised her hand and released the papers.

De Lacy took them and turned sharply to Amos. "As I told you, Miss Saxby has some strange notion concerning Annot Radley, which I prefer not to be encouraged for the moment. At some future date, perhaps it will be more opportune."

Chivalry dictated Amos' next words. "But, sir, you do not truly believe Miss Saxby's interest is unnatural? You yourself asked me to bring the notes."

"When I believed her interest normal and natural. Now I have reason to believe she is momentarily . . . unbalanced."

Amos was shocked. Such discourtesy, such uncouth unmannerliness, and such wild words!

The girl was nodding as if in satisfaction. "As I thought," she murmured, "he believes me mad."

"Not mad, my dear." De Lacy swung smoothly to face her. "I think, a little disturbed, perhaps, by the rapidity of recent changes in your life. Let us say I am concerned by the odd vivid dreams you have recounted to me. From my experience, I know such dreams to stem from an imbalance in the mind, which, in time, can be restored. It is only a question of patience."

Irritation prickled Amos at the man's arrogance. De Lacy stood, arms folded, in the center of the room, the high stock surmounting his well-cut frockcoat lifting his chin high and giving his curl-framed head a jaunty, high-handed look. With the massive wolfhound curled obediently at his feet, he looked every inch the dominating master of all he beheld, and Amos' instincts rebelled.

"Who is to say Miss Saxby is not correct?" he said evenly.

53

"It is not unknown for sensitive people to feel a rapport with their own past. It is not beyond the bounds of human belief that she does indeed recall something, the kind of inherited memory of which she speaks. An intelligent person does not dispute what he cannot disprove."

It was satisfying to see the girl's approving smile, but De Lacy was evidently angered.

"Equally it may be said that an intelligent person would not attempt to maintain that which cannot be proved. Let us discontinue a debate which is pointless."

The girl's voice cut in calmly, though Amos could detect a tremor, whether of anger or dismay. "You spoke of your experience, Bruno. What experience have you, may I inquire, of dreams and their relevance?"

Surprisingly, De Lacy turned a smile upon her. "It is too vast a subject to discuss at length now, my dear. Suffice it for now that my work in Germany with a brilliant young colleague named Sigmund Freud was in precisely that field. Little research has been done into mental conditions, and together we worked upon it for a time. Dreams, and especially in young females, we concluded, were an unconscious seeking for oneself, a search for one's own identity. Once the patient's mental confusion is resolved, the problem is solved and the dreams cease. This was our finding, but I am still researching on it. The rational, scientific mind cannot accept an explanation such as yours for dreams—an imagined rapport with the past. It is a primitive, almost superstitious explanation. To my mind there can be only some psychological reason for it, and once your problem is resolved and the dreams cease, you will have found yourself and be well again."

He called the dog, turning for the door. Amos recognized his movement as indicating that the conversation was now closed. He rose to bid Miss Saxby good-bye, and saw that her gaze rested on him thoughtfully.

"Where is Annot Radley's grave?" she asked quietly. Amos saw De Lacy's thick brows knit irritably. "Is it in the churchyard? I should like to see it."

Amos felt the color rush to his cheeks. "No, Miss Saxby, it

is not. Annot could not be buried there, for she was a suicide."

He turned away too quickly to see her reaction. De Lacy only grunted inaudibly in reply to his farewell, and Amos took his hat and cane gratefully from the waiting parlormaid outside the door. As he rode downhill again toward the village, he wondered whether De Lacy would reveal to the girl that the suicide's grave stood within a stone's throw of the Hall parlor, in a clearing of the copse in the Hall's vast park. If not, she would surely stumble across the little tombstone herself when spring sunlight tempted her out into the grounds. That wouldn't be long now, for already patches of ground were visible through the snow, and in the village's main street was already melting away.

Outside the Woolpack a lone figure leaned desultorily against the stone wall, his head drawn into his upturned coat collar for warmth and a seedy cloth cap topping his graying hair. Amos recognized Joss Iredale, the man whose little girl Amos was now on the way to see. Villagers had told him young Agnes was in a fever. At the sight of the young vicar the man turned and shuffled away toward the steep lane leading to his cottage, just as a buxom woman in a gray woolen shawl came hurrying downhill.

"Joss!"

He stopped and looked at her questioningly, his eyes hollow and bleared. Amos dismounted and approached. The woman caught hold of Iredale's arm, her lined face softened in pity.

"I'm sorry, lad, she's gone."

Visibly Iredale's figure slumped, and Amos felt a stab of apprehension. Not little Agnes, surely? The child was sick yesterday, but not mortally ill, was she?

Iredale turned vacant, misted eyes toward him. "I thowt as much. I knew it, vicar. Not content wi' our Nellie, we have to lose our Agnes as well. There's no justice, God help us, there's nowt."

His voice choked with emotion, Iredale broke loose from the woman's grasp and stumbled uphill toward the cottage. Amos stared disbelievingly.

"I must go after him, Mrs. Shaw, for the family will have need of me. I take it you have been with Mrs. Iredale?"

"Aye, vicar. The poor woman is near demented wi' worry. She loved that little lass, you know, the more so since she lost Nellie last year o' the measles. She never thowt as influenza'd kill Aggie, and she's afeared lest Joss takes it badly."

"Poor man," Amos agreed. "A willing worker and a fine family man, it will undoubtedly grieve him sorely. A terrible blow. Such misfortune. Are you going back to the house?"

Mrs. Shaw shook her head firmly. "There's nowt I can do now. Let 'em grieve in peace. But happen you could help, vicar. Another funeral in a twelvemonth is a great expense for a man on Joss's wage."

Amos looked at her inquiringly. "Ah, the old custom that the master of Brackenroyd should help, as a sign of his kindly patronage, you mean. You would no doubt like me to speak to Mr. de Lacy about it? So I shall. Doubtless he will agree, and Miss Saxby I am sure we can count on for sympathetic cooperation."

Mrs. Shaw's eyes narrowed, her lips tightening as she drew her shawl closer about her. "No point in asking her, vicar. She's a Radley."

Amos' blue gaze widened. "What on earth has Miss Saxby's lineage to do with it? She is a most kindly and agreeable lady and will be a fine mistress. Have you met her yet?"

Shaking her head, Mrs. Shaw pursed her lips tighter. "Nor wish to," she said tersely.

"Why ever not?"

"She's a Radley, like I said."

"And what is wrong with being a Radley? There have been no Radleys in the village for two generations, so you cannot have formed a dislike for any of them. What is all this about the Radleys?"

Mrs. Shaw's tense shoulders eased as she turned a forbearing smile upon the young vicar. "You're a stranger here, Reverend, so you wouldn't know. But for generations, long before I were born, or even my grandparents, the Radleys have always spelled trouble for Brackenroyd folk. That's why the old

56

Radley cottage is never used now, 'cept as a barn. There's trouble where there's Radleys, and specially when a Radley comes up wi' a De Lacy."

So that's it, thought Amos. The old story of Annot Radley and Dorian de Lacy had left its mark on local legend. Without knowing the details, cautious villagers knew only to avoid a Radley and De Lacy encounter.

"That's an old story, Mrs. Shaw, and one that has no bearing on present-day life. Put it out of your mind and be tolerant, as we should."

"Not where there's a Radley. There's an evil taint in the blood, my grandma told me, and everyone here knows it. No sooner does this Radley girl come to the Hall than trouble starts."

"What trouble, Mrs. Shaw?"

The woman's eyes flickered uphill toward Iredale's cottage. "Well, there's Aggie, for a start."

Amos protested. "You're not blaming the child's death on Miss Saxby, surely? Aggie had influenza."

"Aye. Well, others think differently, vicar. There's none i' this village who'll be happy while she's here, and we all hope as she don't marry Mr. Bruno. If she does, there's terrible grief for us all, mark my words. A Radley always spells evil."

Thunderstruck, Amos watched the woman's ample figure plod purposefully away. She couldn't be voicing the view of all the village folk, surely? If she were, then God help Fern Saxby in her attempt to begin her new life as mistress of Brackenroyd.

Chapter 5

It was nearing time for dinner. Soon the dull throb of the dinner gong would reverberate throughout the Hall's vast space, and for once Bruno had intimated that he would dine with Fern. Mrs. Thorpe's eyes had sparkled in anticipation as she relayed the news to Fern. No doubt, thought Fern bitterly, she thought the master was about to make a belated attempt to behave civilly, if not actually begin to woo his intended bride. At any rate, his company, however diffident, would be some improvement on his hitherto neglect.

Now, what to wear to impress him. The mauve-silk gown with the pretty lace at the throat, she decided, on surveying the wardrobe. And her hair coiled perhaps more softly, draped gently over the ears before being drawn up into pins. Yes. On surveying her reflection in the long pier glass, Fern felt satisfied. Becomingly feminine and yet demurely inoffensive, gold hair gleaming from her efforts with the hairbrush, by candlelight at the dining table Bruno must be just a little impressed. A dab of lavender water behind her ears, and Fern was ready.

As she laid her hand on the brass doorknob of the drawing room, Fern could hear deep voices, animated in conversation, beyond the oak panels of the door. Bruno sat in the great armchair by the firelight, speaking in low, urgent tones to a man seated opposite him, of whom only a fair head was discernible to Fern. She approached the two men with a smile. Bruno, noticing her, rose and laid aside his pipe.

"Ah, Fern, I should like you to meet Luke Armitage," he said warmly, indicating the seated figure, who now rose and turned to her.

By the fire's glow Fern saw a delicate-looking young man in his early thirties, his eyes warm and welcoming and his hand extended. His grasp was firm and his gaze direct, belying the fragile appearance, and Fern felt an instant liking for the man. Fabia's husband, and Phoebe's father. What a pleasant family they seemed. There would be agreeable company for her in Brackenroyd after all.

"Luke, this is Fern." Bruno's voice held such warmth that momentarily Fern wondered. Was it pride or pleasure he evinced? Or simply a residue of warmth that lingered from the conversation with Luke she had just interrupted, and which Bruno was so evidently enjoying?

"I am delighted to meet you, Miss Saxby," the schoolmaster was saying, and as he relinquished Fern's hand, he added, "and may I remark that you are as beautiful as Bruno and Fabia have both told me. Brackenroyd Hall will be graced with a charming mistress once more."

Startled, Fern looked quickly at Bruno. He had called her beautiful? As if embarrassed, he had already turned away and was busy arranging a chair for her. He waited until she was seated before sitting again and resuming his pipe. Luke leaned forward eagerly.

"It was very kind of Bruno to bring me to dinner, Miss Saxby. I do hope you are not inconvenienced by my unexpected arrival."

"Not at all, Mr. Armitage, I am delighted. Have you told Mrs. Thorpe to lay the table for three, Bruno?"

"Yes." He made no explanation of his omission to her as

59

the mistress, Fern noted. No doubt long bachelorhood had made him accustomed to doing as he pleased, warning only the servants. He had much to learn yet, as a husband. Still, she welcomed Luke's advent, however unexpected.

It was cozy by the fire's warm light, the candles yet unlit and the curtains undrawn. The men sat silent, but the silence was ruminative and companionable, and Fern did not wish to break it. The two men evidently shared a closeness which included intimate silence, and she was glad. Bruno could not be wholly cold and insensitive if he had won such friendship. The peace was shattered by Fanny's clattering entrance.

"Shall I bring more coal, sir?"

"No. Draw the curtains."

Brass rings rattled along bamboo canes as Fanny drew the heavy red-velvet draperies across the tall windows. Lighting a wax taper from the fire, she then lit three tall candles on the table, their glow reflecting on their brass holders.

"Is dinner almost ready, Fanny?"

"Yes, sir. I shall sound the gong immediately."

It was during dinner that Luke first mentioned hypnotism. He had been reading an article on hypnotism and mesmerism in a journal and was curious to know Bruno's opinion, he said. Fern saw the intense look return to Bruno's somber eyes.

"Both are induced states of trance brought about by different means. Most people can be hypnotized if they cooperate, but some are far more easily suggestible than others." Was it her imagination, Fern wondered, that his eyes flickered briefly over her?

"It was Mesmer who first experimented, was it not, in Vienna? I understand hypnotism can be used to good effect, as treatment for a sick patient?" Luke's light-blue eyes were lively with curiosity.

Bruno nodded. "Indeed. I have seen, and on occasion worked with, patients suffering from physical problems such as speech impediments. They have often benefited greatly from hypnotism. But its greatest use, to my mind, is in the treatment of nervous disorders. Someday, when the quacks stop using hypnotism as a music-hall entertainment, I hope it will be more widely used in this field. At the moment it is either distrusted or scorned by many."

Fanny's deft fingers removed the dessert dishes and laid out the decanter of port and glasses for the gentlemen. Reluctantly Fern rose to leave the gentlemen to their port, as was the custom, but as she was closing the door, she heard Luke's question.

"I had a reason for asking, Bruno. I wonder if you could help Phoebe?"

Poor little Phoebe, thought Fern as she returned to the drawing room. Was her muteness a result of deafness or of accident? Evidently Luke considered her plight not entirely hopeless if he was enlisting Bruno's help, but would hypnotism have any effect? Surely not, if the child was deaf and could not hear Bruno's voice.

Evidently Phoebe had remained the subject of the gentlemen's conversation, for they were still discussing her when they came to rejoin Fern. As Luke entered, she could not fail to notice the slight limp, the way he dragged a reluctant left leg after him. Bruno was in a contemplative mood, nodding in reply to Luke's comments and his dark eyes afire with interest.

"I think some effect could perhaps be achieved," he said at length. "We may even arrive at the cause of her disability, but at least no harm would be done. Bring Fabia and the child to tea with us tomorrow."

Luke's eager smile died suddenly. "There is a matter I had overlooked, Bruno. You know my salary as a principal teacher. A hundred and fifty pounds a year does not warrant luxuries such as the services of a specialist for Phoebe. I fear I may not be able to afford your fee."

Bruno's rugged face darkened angrily. "Between friends there is no question of fees," he snapped. "The experiment could well fail, in which case you are not beholden to me. I forbid you to mention money again."

Luke hung his head, a pink tinge coloring his pale face. Fern felt embarrassment for him, for while Bruno's intentions were friendly, his manner was abrupt and reproachful. She felt angry with him for his thoughtless unkindness, but her anger softened when he insisted on sending Luke home in the carriage. Aware of his friend's lameness, he would not consider his walking home, though he made no reference to the limp until Luke was gone.

"A childhood accident, a wagon ran over his leg while he was working at the mill. So he went back to school as a pupil-teacher," he explained laconically. Seeing that he was in no mood for further conversation, his look abstracted and distant, Fern bade him a quiet good night and went to her room.

It was a graceful staircase, wide and shallow, and as Fern mounted the stairs, fingering the carved balustrade affectionately, she reflected with pride on the beauty of her home. Mistress of Brackenroyd. She was a fortunate creature indeed to have inherited such grace and luxury, but still the suggestion of lingering unhappiness in the air troubled her. A ring at the front doorbell interrupted her musings, and Fern could hear Fanny's quick step hastening to answer.

A late hour for a caller. Who could it be? Out of curiosity Fern loitered on the gallery and saw Edgar Amos' sandy head below as he murmured to Fanny, and Bruno's quick exit from the drawing room.

"I regret troubling you so late, Dr. de Lacy, but the matter is urgent," Amos apologized, and Fern could see his nervous fingers clutching at his hat and the glistening droplets on his cape.

"Come in," said Bruno curtly, and the two men disappeared into the drawing room.

Fern hovered for a time on the gallery, filled with curiosity, undecided what to do. Eventually she went down again and crossed to the room, where deep voices could be heard in conversation.

"Do I understand you to say you are requesting me to undertake the funeral expenses?" Bruno's voice was demanding.

"Otherwise it will mean a pauper's grave for the child. Iredale would never live down the shame. And it has always been customary for the master to pay in the past," Amos' timid voice answered.

"Must I, then, for the sake of tradition, be prepared to pay for all my workers and their numerous dependents? It would seem a highly expensive precedent to set."

"For your workers, sir, not their dependents. Aggie herself worked in your mill."

"Aggie? I understand she was a very young girl?"

"Ten, sir. Ten-year-olds are allowed by law to attend school part-time and go to work part-time. Joss and his wife will miss her few shillings a week. And they lost their elder daughter last year from measles, and thus her income too. Joss's wage is barely enough to keep his younger children now, without Aggie's help."

"His wage is adequate, since the weavers' strike in this area last year. He earns a fair rate, the same as the others."

There was a pause, and Fern could visualize Amos' uncertain, blinking gaze while he awaited Bruno's agreement or refusal. If a child had died, a child who worked in *their* mill, Fern could not understand Bruno's hesitation to pay for the poor mite's funeral. With resolution Fern grasped the doorknob and walked into the room.

"Good evening, Reverend Amos. I have heard enough of your conversation with Bruno to understand that our help is needed in burying one of our child workers at the mill."

"That is so," Amos admitted with a quick, nervous glance at Bruno.

"Then have no fear that we shall honor our obligation. If you would be so good as to tell me where the Iredales live, I shall go to them myself tomorrow and assure them that the bill will be met."

As she stopped speaking, Fern turned a direct, challenging stare on Bruno. He stood silent, a thoughtful finger rubbing his chin.

"Will you permit me, Bruno?"

He spread his hands. "You will do as you think fit. I shall not presume to interfere."

Nor could he, she thought angrily. Joint legatees, they could each spend as they wished, but Amos was looking at her oddly.

"I think, Miss Saxby, if you will permit me to comment, that the offer were best coming from the master."

"I am mistress of Brackenroyd, Mr. Amos."

"That is so, but the villagers are queer folk." He was fidgeting with his hat, shifting uncomfortably, and his gaze refused to meet hers.

Fern was curious. "How do you mean? Please be plain, sir."

He hung his sandy head miserably. "They have strange ideas, superstitious almost, and they distrust a Radley. Your offer, though generously meant, could well be misconstrued, simply because you are a Radley. But since the hour is so late, let me leave you and the doctor to discuss the matter."

He made for the door, and Bruno made no comment as he rang the bell for Fanny to show the visitor out.

Fern hastened out after Amos. "I cannot understand your words, but I want to reassure the poor family their child will be decently buried. Surely there is no harm in my visiting them?"

For a moment Amos' bleak expression softened into a smile. "Perhaps your warmth and sincerity will make them forget the old stories," he said, and then turned to follow Fanny to the front door.

Bruno's face was blankly unsympathetic as Fern repeated her intention to go to the Iredales' cottage.

"If you insist, my dear, then I shall accompany you."

"There is no need for you to come."

He looked up sharply. "Indeed there is. You know so little of the villagers, and yet you will insist on interfering. I have warned you once that mill affairs are best left to me, and that includes the welfare of the workers."

"If you apparently care little for their welfare, then it is up to me to act," Fern retorted hotly. "If you—if we—paid our workers a better wage, there would be no need for us to have to appear charitable and bury their dead children for them."

Bruno's expression darkened. "Now you go too far. You know nothing, nothing at all, of weavers' work and conditions or their rates of pay. Nothing of their history, or of their recent strike. Though I admit your equal share in the mill, I will not permit you to make decisions as to its running. That is my province, and I would welcome your assurance that you will trust me and leave it to me."

Fern hesitated. He too was a newcomer to Brackenroyd, but undoubtedly, with Teutonic thoroughness, he had probably already acquainted himself fully with the state of the mill. But she was unwilling to relinquish her right to voice her opinion; it would be setting a dangerous precedent to let this dictatorial man tell her where she could or could not intervene.

"I should like to console the Iredales, nonetheless," she muttered fiercely at last. "And reassure them about Aggie."

"So you shall, if you wish. And I shall come too."

And he did. It was a gray, misty day that hung over Brackenroyd village as the carriage drove along the cobbled street and mounted the hilly lane to the Iredale cottage. Bruno helped Fern out of the carriage in silence. A woman, apparently a neighbor, answered his knock at the door of the tiny stone cottage with its slate roof. She turned at once and addressed the unseen occupants of the living room immediately inside the front door.

"It's t' master, Joss, t' master o' Brackenroyd, and his lady," she added dubiously.

Fern entered the low door, noting the cold stone-slabbed floor of the little room with its handmade rag rugs and deal table. A shawled woman, presumably Mrs. Iredale, glanced curiously at Fern, then crossed to a spindle-backed chair by the fire, arranged a calfskin over its rush bottom, and seated herself in silence. Joss Iredale, seated opposite her, laid aside a clay pipe he had been filling and rose to grunt a curt good day. His wife, ignoring her guests, riffled through a collection of balls of colored wool on the cupboard beside her and selected one to continue a half-done scriptural picture she had stretched over a coarse wooden frame. Fern, daunted by the cottagers' obvious uninterest, stood silent. Bruno cleared his throat while the neighbor stood curious, arms akimbo, by the door.

"Miss Saxby was most concerned about you, Joss Iredale," Bruno said, almost coldly, Fern thought.

"She's no need," Iredale answered gruffly.

"No, she's not," agreed Mrs. Iredale in a mutter.

Fern felt the time had come to speak for herself. Bruno's manner was far too peremptory.

"Do not take offense, Mrs. Iredale. I come only out of sympathy for you in your loss, and I would not wish you to worry unduly over the cost of the funeral. Dr. de Lacy and I would be honored if you would permit us to bear the cost."

Mrs. Iredale scowled but did not speak. Joss Iredale looked hesitantly from his wife to his master. A light footstep on the stone steps leading down directly into the little room from the upper floor interrupted the silent scene. Fabia Armitage, her blue eyes wide in surprise, stood on the lowest step.

"Bruno! I'm so glad you've come."

There was no doubting the genuine pleasure that irradiated her gentle face, and Fern saw the answering smile in Bruno's dark eyes as Fabia crossed the room, hands outstretched. Bruno gripped them silently. Fabia turned to the Iredales.

"There, now, I told you the master of Brackenroyd would honor the old tradition. Now you've no cause to worry."

Joss Iredale shifted uncomfortably, but his wife rose resolutely, clutching her shawl about her.

"So long as it's t' master who's offering, we'll accept. But we want nowt from *her*." And glaring fiercely at Fern, she turned and went into the little scullery. Fern saw her grasp the posser which stood next to a zinc dolly-tub and start pounding the clothes she was washing, suds spattering the stone floor angrily. She evidently had no more to say to her guests.

Fabia drew Fern aside, and while she talked, Fern saw Bruno talking quietly with Joss. It was difficult to hide the hurt she felt at the Iredales' rejection of her offer of help, but Fabia's words were soft and soothing. As they left the cottage together, Bruno suggested that Fabia fetch Phoebe now and drive up with them to the Hall.

"A pretty name, 'Phoebe,'" Bruno commented as they drove to the schoolhouse. "What does it mean?"

"'Shining one,'" replied Fabia with a smile. "It was Ellen Stansfield's suggestion when the baby was born, she was so shining-eyed and interested in everything around her. That was before Ellen was widowed and became so withdrawn."

"Names are so important," Fern said, anxious to share in the closeness that seemed to bind Bruno and Fabia. "Mothers must ponder for hours how to name their children aptly. No doubt Bruno's mother named him so because he was so dark."

Bruno was silent for a moment. "Then why did your mother choose 'Fern' for you, I wonder? A nostalgic reminder of happy hours in the countryside, perhaps?"

"No," retorted Fern swiftly. "She named me for what she hoped I would be. Fern is the Anglo-Saxon word for 'sincerity.'"

For a brief instant his dark gaze darted to meet hers, stared penetratingly, and then withdrew. In total silence they arrived at the schoolhouse.

Phoebe climbed eagerly into the carriage, taking a seat opposite her mother and next to Bruno. Fern noted how the child's hand slid trustingly into Bruno's and how he silently enfolded it, but she was still smarting from the Iredales' treatment and could not resist speaking of it to Fabia.

"They hate me, Fabia. I don't know why they should, but I could feel it."

"No, Fern, they do not know you. The villagers are very parochial in their outlook, and distrust all strangers. It will take them time, but their resistance will be overcome if you are patient."

"They accepted you, and you were a foreigner to them."

"That was many years ago." Fabia smiled. "And I was a curate's daughter, marrying their beloved schoolmaster. It was easy for me."

"And for Bruno." Fern's gaze slid to him, but it was as if he did not hear, buried in his own thoughts.

"Bruno is a De Lacy, hereditary lord of the manor," Fabia countered calmly. "Though a stranger, they will accept him because of his blood. Don't let them hurt you, Fern. Be patient, and you will come to love them."

"But that's just it," Fern burst out. "I *do* care for them. I feel one of them, I feel I belong, but they want to push me out, to dispossess me."

Bruno was listening now, his piercing gaze intent on her. Fern bit her lip and was silent. Now he would consider her hysterical indeed, judging by his thick, knitted brows.

"Well, Bruno, what do you think?" she challenged.

He shrugged. "I was thinking how you sound like a case I once treated, a man who thought everyone was determined to persecute him. The medical name for such a condition is 'paranoia.' Ah, here we are at the Hall."

The business of dismounting, entering the Hall, and ushering their guests into the drawing room absolved Fern from the responsibility of replying, fortunately, for she was too astounded and bereft of words to think coherently. Bruno was by now amused to watch Phoebe's wide-eyed reaction to the grandeur of the Hall, for it was the child's first visit.

"Don't touch, Phoebe," Fabia admonished the little exploratory fingers testing the texture of a china figurine. Fern noticed that Fabia raised her voice, and the child seemed to hear, for she withdrew her hand at once.

"Toasted scones and cream cakes for tea, Mrs. Thorpe has promised," Bruno said in a similarly loud tone. The child watched his lips and smiled. "And your papa will join us later. He has business in Bradford, I understand?" he added to Fabia.

She nodded. "He has to see the School Board in connection with the school's grant this year. He should be back soon."

Luke arrived as they were all seated about the table, apologizing as he limped into the parlor. Bruno indicated a vacant seat at the table. Fern noticed Bruno's genuine interest as he quizzed Luke as to the outcome of his meeting with the School Board.

"We are to have sixty pounds' grant, a slight increase over last year," Luke told him. "That will enable me to replenish a few books and slates." His keen gaze alighted on the newspaper Bruno had tossed on the sideboard.

"I see you have the Huddersfield *Examiner*. How is the war in the Sudan going? Has the Army put down the rebel Mahdi yet?"

Bruno pushed away his plate and sat back. "It seems Admiral Hewitt and General Graham have arrived at Trinkitat and are disembarking the troops. Their spies report that the Sudanese rebels are massing for an attack, so the general is awaiting the authority to advance."

"I see." Luke's lively eyes moved to Phoebe, busily munching Mrs. Thorpe's chocolate cake. "And my little Phoebe? Have you come to any conclusion about her?"

Bruno surveyed the child reflectively. "It would seem she is not totally deaf, so I shall attempt to hypnotize her after tea and see if I can discover the cause of her muteness. Tell me, Fabia, did she ever experience some shock as a small child, as a baby even? Some dreadful experience which could have caused her condition?"

Fabia's eyes took on a faraway look as she endeavored to recollect; then she shook her head slowly. "None that I can remember. She had to suffer a lot of teasing from the other children on account of her silence when she first began school, but the trouble must have stemmed from before that date."

Bruno rubbed his chin thoughtfully. "No sudden death of a beloved relative, or a physical accident?"

"Nothing of that nature. As a baby she would make the normal gurgling and cooing sounds all babies do, but even that ceased."

"Does she weep?"

Fabia nodded. "But they are silent tears, no sobs."

"Have you had her examined by a doctor?"

Luke cut in. "I took her to a specialist in Bradford once, but he was emphatic that there was no physical defect. Her lungs, vocal cords, and mouth are perfectly formed, and there was no reason for her not to speak."

"Which strengthens my view that the cause must be psychological," Bruno commented as he rose from the table. "Come, let us go to my study, and I shall see what hypnosis can reveal."

They all rose to follow him, and as Fern passed through the doorway, she involuntarily placed an affectionate hand on Phoebe's ringleted head. The child stiffened and pulled away, frightened eyes staring up at her, and Fern drew back sharply. It was as sharp a rebuke as the Iredales' abrupt rejection of her. Fabia's keen eye had seen the incident.

"I'm sorry, Fern, she did not mean to be rude. I'm afraid she is always cautious and rather suspicious of those she does not know."

Fern smiled to show her understanding, but the hurt lingered. How could the little one know how genuine was her sympathy and affection?

"Sit here, Phoebe," commanded Bruno, pointing to his own leather chair behind the desk, which he had turned to face the center of the room. An oil lamp on the desk threw a halo of light on the girl's fair head and Bruno's tall figure before her, while Luke and the women seated themselves in the shadows to watch.

Bruno turned to the adults. "Now, I must ask you all to be absolutely silent for the next few minutes. I shall talk to Phoebe, and whatever happens, I must insist that you remain silent. On no account are you to speak, or you will break the concentration. Moreover, it could be dangerous if you disturb Phoebe, for if she sleeps, she must be awakened only by my word. Are you ready?"

Luke and Fabia nodded, Luke sitting back relaxed and confident while Fabia sat nervously on the edge of her chair. Fern could see her fingers gripping deep into the upholstery of the arms.

Bruno dropped on one knee before Phoebe, his dark head now level with hers, and took her hands in his. Phoebe smiled shyly.

"Listen, Phoebe, can you hear me?" Bruno's voice was raised, though still kindly. Phoebe laid a finger on his lips. "Good, then listen, little one."

Bruno rose again and stood before her, his broad back to

Fern, and taking something from his pocket, he held it aloft. Fern could see something small and shiny on a chain.

"Watch this, Phoebe, see how it gleams." The child's eyes fastened on the shining object while Bruno's voice continued to speak. "Think back, Phoebe, think back to summer and warm days in the sun. Think how pleasant it is to be in the sun and watch the birds fluttering in the sky. Isn't the sun bright, Phoebe, doesn't it dazzle your eyes?"

The child's eyes flickered down from the object Bruno held, tried to find it again, and then closed.

"Sleep now, Phoebe, sleep peacefully in the sun's warmth," Bruno's voice urged, becoming quieter and firmer now. "Sleep deeply, little one, and do not wake until I tell you. Sleep, sleep, and dream of when you were a very little girl."

Luke and Fabia were watching and listening as if they too were entranced, soothed by the warm vibrancy of Bruno's voice. Phoebe sighed and stirred but did not open her eyes. From behind Bruno, Fern could see the child clearly, her downy eyelashes curving on her cheek and a peaceful expression on her cherubic face.

"Remember the orchard up behind the schoolhouse where you used to play before you started school," Bruno murmured. "Remember the apple trees and the sunlight flickering through the branches. Remember the sweet smell of the apples and the humming of the bees." Phoebe's expression was dreamily content. "You used to swing on the rope seat Papa made for you. You were very little then."

Fabia was nodding as she too remembered, but evidently Bruno was not satisfied. The child's memory of those years was peaceful; the trouble must stem from earlier.

"Now, think back, Phoebe, to when you were a baby, just learning to totter about the house and watch Mamma at her work." Phoebe's face remained content, a hint of a smile curving her lips. "And back before that, when you were a tiny baby in your cradle, when Papa and Mamma bent over you and made cooing noises to make you smile. Go back, Phoebe, back as far as you can."

Fern watched, fascinated. The child's face was still passive, but Bruno's was growing animated as he willed her to remember. His voice throbbed with determination.

"Go back, child, back. There must be a moment you recall which still offends you. Go back till you find it, Phoebe."

A restless flicker crossed the girl's face, but Bruno would not relent. "Back, Phoebe, back!" A frown rutted the childish forehead, and Phoebe began to roll her head from side to side, her eyes still tightly closed. Fern could feel the tension in the study grow until it became almost tangible. Luke sat upright, staring, and Fabia's knuckles were white with the force of gripping the chair.

"Don't be afraid, Phoebe, go back and face it." Bruno's eyes were staring wildly, his efforts frenetic to discover the fact that eluded him. "You are nearing it now, Phoebe, face it squarely!"

Phoebe's mouth sagged open, and a low moan issued from her lips. Fabia gasped, her fingers flying to her mouth to suppress a cry. It was the first sound the child had uttered since babyhood. Fern watched the scene as though from some remote viewpoint with a strange sense of detachment; Bruno, wild-eyed and farouche, willing the girl back to some far-off incident she obviously preferred to negate and forget, anxious parents sitting tense with worry, and herself, a stranger to this place and these people, witnessing the forcing out of an event in which she had no part. She could feel only pity for Phoebe, having to undergo such relentless harassing, and anger with Bruno for putting her unnecessarily to such torment.

"Back, Phoebe, back!"

Suddenly the child's eyes jerked open, and she sat bolt upright, her gaze roving over the adults in the room and registering only malevolent distrust of them. It was a terrible, baleful stare, and Fern was filled with horror. Phoebe's gaze went past Bruno and came to rest on Fern, and instantly her expression changed. Her eyes rounded and filled with fear, and her lips parted as she began to pant. Then, without warning, she began to speak.

"I didn't mean it to happen. I swear to God I didn't!"

It was not the words which electrified her audience, startling though they were. It was her voice. The voice emanating from the slight figure of the child was the full, throaty voice of a woman.

A strangled moan escaped Fabia, and Luke leaped to his feet, but Bruno stayed him, his gaze never wavering from the child. Phoebe rose slowly, still staring at Fern, and held out her hands. Then she flung herself at Fern's feet.

"Forgive me. I've wanted so long to beg you. Pray forgive me, Catherine, or I am accursed forever."

The enormous eyes, filled with pleading, suddenly closed, and the child fell limp on the floor. Fabia too fell senseless beside her.

Chapter 6

Fern was so preoccupied that night restoring Fabia and then calming the young mother's hysterical weeping until Luke took her and the child home that she did not know what happened to Phoebe. According to Bruno, once he was left alone with the child in the study, she had reverted to her silent, trancelike state, and he had then awakened her from her hypnotized condition normally. Apart from being sleepy, Phoebe showed no sign of distress, he said.

Fern did not discuss the incident of Phoebe's strange behavior with him that night. She was still too bewildered and benumbed with horror by Phoebe's unexpected outburst. It was not just that the child, a lifelong mute, had spoken at last, but the unnatural voice and strange words she had spoken. It was more than unnatural; it was supernatural, Fern was convinced—another sign of the disturbing atmosphere of Brackenroyd Hall.

Or was it some power in Bruno himself? Fern shuddered at the memory of his face contorted with frenzy, and pushed out of her mind the sudden notion that he could have some de-

74

monic power. Now she was thinking like a primitive, uneducated savage. He was a strange man, it was true, dark and secretive, and in some odd way restless and turbulent, but evil, no; surely the man she was to marry was capable of no malefic doing.

But it had been uncanny in the silent lamplit study, the way Phoebe, as if pushed back too far in time by Bruno's urging, had overstepped the boundary of her present life and revived an earlier one. Was it possible? Too tired and bewildered to speculate further, Fern began to undress and prepare for bed.

Sleep came reluctantly to Fern that night, doubt and the chill air of the bedroom combining to make her feel restless. Strange shadows, cast by the last dying flares of the fire, flickered beyond the curtains of the bed, leaping and fading by turns. In the gloom of the far corners it was easy to visualize phantom figures from the past who watched and waited, as though to see how the new mistress of Brackenroyd would conduct herself. At last sleep ventured to mist her drifting thoughts, Phoebe's words echoing in her mind. Catherine, she had called Fern. "Catherine, forgive me, or I am accursed." "Accursed"—that was an oddly archaic word, one a child was not likely to know. It was decidedly odd.

Dreams came, as they had done nightly since her arrival at Brackenroyd Hall, enveloping her in a hazy limbo world where pale faces gazed bleakly at her, but they were tangled, confused visions that were meaningless to Fern. The faces came, melted, and changed; cries turned to moans; and hands without substance reached out to her in pleading. Then a terrible, nauseous miasma enveloped her, reaching into her nostrils and threatening to suffocate her, and Fern awoke, trembling and struggling to push the mist away from her.

"No, no, I don't want you," she was crying out as she realized she was sitting up in bed, flailing her arms about her head in the effort still to ward off the menacing mist. The whole house was still and silent. Fern snuggled down again under the blankets, shivering. It was only a nightmare, and no one seemed to have been disturbed by her cry.

This time when she slept, the dream was clear. Annot

75

Radley, pale and thin and clutching a shawl about her, was walking in a woodland clearing by moonlight. She was glancing nervously about her, as though afraid of being discovered. Suddenly, from among the trees, a young man, elegantly dressed in frock coat and breeches and a silk cravat, strode toward her. Annot's anxious face softened.

"Oh, Dorian, I thought tha'd never come."

He enfolded her in his arms. "Now, Annot, you know me better than that," he said, a teasing smile curving his sensual lips. "I promised, didn't I, and I never break my promises to you."

Her face was buried in his chest, but she lifted her little pointed chin and regarded him seriously.

"Me dad's fair mad wi' me, Dorian. He threatens to send me away to me aunt's i' Nottingham. Says I've disgraced t' family's name."

Dorian's smile was sardonic. "*You've* disgraced the family name? It's surely little to be ashamed of, to be bearing a De Lacy child. My father, however, is probably justifiably furious with me, for fathering a child to a village girl."

"It's just as shameful for me, Dorian," Annot replied sullenly; then she clung closer to him. "What's to happen to me, love? Tha won't let 'em send me away, will tha? I couldn't bear parting from thee now."

Dorian's handsome face darkened. "My father has given me a choice. I may marry you, or return to London without my allowance. So I'll marry you."

The girl's upturned face grew radiant. "Dosta mean it, truly? Me, marry a De Lacy? Me father'll never credit it. Will thy parents truly let thee marry a lass from t' mill? Will they own me for a daughter? Oh, Dorian, could it really happen?"

"It will happen, there's no two ways about it. My father is insistent because he has his pride to uphold, though I must warn you that my mother does not really approve. They are to send for your father tomorrow to tell him."

"He were going up to t' Hall any road, to tell thy father tha should be horse-whipped. 'Appen he'll take a kindlier tone wi' thee when he hears tha's to make an honest woman of me."

"So he should. There's not many village folk who've captured a De Lacy. He should be proud. And being a Radley too, he should be especially proud."

The girl looked perplexed. "Why? What's being a Radley to do wi' it?"

He withdrew himself from her embrace and sauntered to the edge of the clearing. She could hear his voice only indistinctly, thrown casually back over his shoulder. "Oh, you know the old tale of the Radley blood being tainted blood. I don't know the details of the legend, but it's common gossip in the village."

Annot tossed her fair head proudly. "Aye, and that's all it is, gossip. There's nowt wrong wi' Radley folk. We're good hard workers, all on us, and just as good as t' next man. I'll have nowt said agen my folk."

Dorian turned, smiling at her display of pride. "True enough, Father says your father is one of the best workers in the new mill, now he's got over his disappointment of no longer being an independent hand-loom weaver."

"Aye, and that's no easy pill to swallow, I can tell thee. It near broke me dad's heart losing his independence. The cloth he wove were t' finest as ever went into Huddersfield Cloth Hall. He were proud of it, and rightly so. Still, he's got over it now, and he's a right good worker, one o' t' most loyal thy dad's got, but it wouldn't a stopped him coming up to t' Hall and demanding tha had a beating. It were all me mam could do to stop him giving me a right good thrashing."

"I'm glad he didn't, Annot. He could possibly have harmed my future son, and my father will forgive all if he has a De Lacy grandson to soften the blow. Possibly even Mamma will relent then too." He folded his arms about her again. "But come, Annot, we are wasting time. Let us lie here in the shadows and talk of when you come to live at the Hall."

"Me? Live at Brackenroyd Hall?"

"Of course. You must give up your work at the mill right away—after our two fathers have talked tomorrow—and move in with us. Then, at the right time, we shall be married."

77

"Not right away?"

"No, not yet. Papa suggests you could learn our ways a little first, and learn to know us all."

Annot laughed, a bitter little laugh. "I see. I'm to learn how to use the cutlery properly and talk nice, am I, before I'm fit to wed thee? They've to see whether I can be schooled right, like a pony for the master's children to ride. If I'm biddable and learn easy, I'll do."

Dorian's smile was amused. "Well, you must admit, little one, you could do with having some of your rougher points fined down. But don't worry, you'll become as fine a lady as Mamma or my sister, Sophie, I'm certain of it. Come, now, we're wasting time again."

And drawing her down into the shadows, he silenced her protesting mouth with kisses. Fern's vision of the embracing couple melted and vanished. Somewhere out in the night a dog howled at the moon, and Fern stirred in her sleep.

The vision shifted and changed. Annot was entering the door of a small stone cottage, and Fern recognized it as one of the little cottages near Brackenroyd church, those with a long row of windows on the upper floor. Fern had learned that this well-lit upper room used to contain the hand-loom weaver's prized loom in the old days before the mill came with its power looms and drove the independent weavers out of business. Annot stepped into the flagstone living room, where a woman was busy at the black-leaded oven range, stirring the savory-smelling contents of a large pan over the fire. On the deal table behind her a huge brown earthenware bowl held a mound of dough, left to rise. The woman looked up anxiously.

"Oh, Annot lass! Thy father's fair vexed tha were out so late. He's nobbut just gone out hisself to look for thee."

The girl smiled and sniffed. "Oven cake. I can smell tha's been baking oven cake, Mam. Where hasta hidden it? I could just eat a lump wi' butter on."

"Butter, is it? And where dosta think money for butter comes from, wi' thee giving up work an' all and soon an extra mouth to feed? Don't thee let thy father hear thee, vexed as he is."

"He'll not be mad wi' me long, not when he hears t' news."

"What news?" Her mother left off stirring the pot and straightened, wiping greasy fingers on her apron. "What news can there be to straighten this mess, I'd like to know?"

Annot found the oven cake, left to cool on a ledge in the back scullery. Clogs clattering down the two steps back into the living room, she broke off a piece and began to eat it, butterless. "How'd tha feel if I telled thee I were to be wed?"

"Wed? Who to? Who'd have thee now?"

" 'Appen Dorian de Lacy."

Her mother's eyes goggled. "Him? He'll never wed thee, tha great fool. His sort just take their pleasure o' the likes of thee and then wed some titled woman. The most thy father can hope for now is to get him horse-whipped—though that's far from likely—and 'appen a mite o' money to tide thee over."

Annot sat on the edge of the table. "Dorian says his dad's decided he has to make an honest woman of me, so we're to be wed. Me dad's to go up to t' Hall tomorrow."

"Never!" Mrs. Radley flopped into a spindle-backed chair, overwhelmed by the news. "Eeh, fancy that! Who'd a thought it? Our Annot mistress o' Brackenroyd. Well, I never did!"

It did not take long for Mrs. Radley's amazement to resolve itself into excited anticipation, but Annot's father was less eager to be mollified by his daughter's announcement when he finally returned.

"Art tha sure, lass? Canst be certain t' lad's not having thee on?" he grunted suspiciously, but on Annot's assurance that he was to be summoned to meet the master of Brackenroyd on the morrow to settle it, he abandoned his aggressive stance on the hearth, and seating himself, began to fill his clay pipe with shreds of black tobacco.

"Just think on it," murmured Mrs. Radley happily. "She'll be able to ring t' bell while t' maid fetches her tea to her, and ride about in a fine carriage just like Mrs. de Lacy does. What a grand life it'll be for her."

"Art satisfied, Father?" Annot asked.

"Mebbe. I'll think on it while I go down to t' privy," he replied, and rising and taking a large key from a nail by the mantelshelf, he went off through the scullery and out of the back door down the yard, his clogged feet clattering on the stone setts as he went.

"He'll be content once it's settled wi' t' master," Mrs. Radley pronounced confidently. "Shift thissen, Annot, side them dishes out o' t' way, and lay a place for thy father. When he's a bowl of this good stew inside of him, he'll think kindlier on it."

Fern's vision of the cottage parlor faded and was gone. Pictures began to flash before her eyes like the pages of a magazine, flicked rapidly by an unseen hand. There was Annot mounting the steps Fern recognized as Brackenroyd Hall; a pudgy-faced woman dressed in black, presumably the housekeeper, taking Annot's bundle of clothes to the kitchen and solemnly burning them all; a lady of middle age accompanied by a haughty young woman, both surveying Annot coldly, the one through gold-rimmed pince-nez and the other with an openly amused smile. The older woman turned away and left the group, the expression on her face registering disdain and extreme distaste.

Sobbing echoed in the bedchamber. Annot lay sprawled across the bed, knuckles pressed into red-rimmed eyes and her face contorted with weeping. Fern, sitting in the bed, could have reached out and touched her.

"They hate me! They despise me, but I'm just as good as them," the girl wept.

"Of course you are. Don't upset yourself," Fern soothed, but the sobbing continued.

"I hate 'em, and if it weren't for t' baby I'd go away. But I've noan got anyplace to go. What'll become of me? I hate 'em all, same as they hate me."

Fern reached out to pat the girl's convulsed shoulder, but touched nothing. Annot wept on, unaware of her. Then suddenly the door opened, and a shaft of light entered the room from a candle. It was Dorian, dressed in a brocade dressing gown, who carried it. He laid a finger warningly to his lips, his handsome face seeming Machiavellian in the candle's light.

"Hush, Annot," he whispered as he laid the silver candlestick on the night table and sat beside her on the bed. His hand caressed her shoulder. "Hush, love, or they'll hear."

She sat up sharply. "And what do I care? They've nowt but scorn for me and my common ways, and I doubt they'll interfere wi' what tha wants to do in t' middle o' t' night. After all, they'll say, tha's going to wed me any road."

His hand ceased its caressing, and his face grew gloomy. "Yes, Mamma and Sophie have accepted that."

"Well tha doesn't look too happy about it."

"It's not that, love, it's Papa. He considers it high time I settled down and married and stayed home to learn the running of the mill."

"Well that's summat, if he's glad on us wedding."

"But hang it, I'll have to stay here in Brackenroyd permanently, don't you see? Papa thinks my seasons in London are far too extravagant, and in any case, I should be here to learn the business. What a bore, to live here all the year round! I understood him to agree to continue my allowance if I married you, but I didn't realize I wouldn't be able to go to London. There's precious little I can spend it on here."

Annot lifted her tearstained face, and Fern could see the dawning suspicion in her blue eyes. "Dost mean tha only agreed to wed me for t' brass? Oh, no, Dorian, tell me tha loves me! Tha telled me tha did down in t' wood!"

He brushed aside her pleading hand impatiently. "Of course I do, silly. But I'm annoyed Papa sees this as a way to pin me down. And even Mamma, who's usually as indulgent as mammas come, seems to concur with him."

"Aye, if she's forced to have me as her daughter-in-law whether or not, she'll profit from it some road," agreed Annot bitterly. "Well, I wish her joy of it, because there's none for me i' this matter, seemingly."

"Come now, my love, you take too harsh a view of the

81

business," Dorian said smoothly. "You forget you'll have fine clothes and servants and a carriage—and here's something which will soon be yours."

From his dressing-gown pocket he withdrew a small object and gave it to Annot. Fern could see a heavily chased silver ring.

"What is it? A wedding ring?" asked Annot.

Dorian smiled. "No, a betrothal ring. It's been in the family for centuries, I understand. A De Lacy always gives it to his new bride, and I've just persuaded Mamma to part with it so I can give it to you."

Annot turned it over curiously. "It's got writing on it. What does it say?"

Fern thought she could detect a faint grimace on Dorian's face at this reminder of his fiancée's ignorance. "It has twelve raised points, each carved into a letter. It spells *Amor Aeternus*. That means 'Love Eternal.'"

The girl's face softened, a gentle light of happiness lighting her features. "Oh, Dorian! How lovely! I'll treasure it forever—that is," she added, "till the day I give it to our son for his bride."

"Our son? You seem very certain it will be a boy."

"Aye, well," Annot murmured, cradling against his chest, "in five months we'll know, one way or t' other."

Dorian slid the ring back into his pocket, shrugged off his dressing gown, and leaned over to pinch out the candle. In the darkness Fern could hear Annot's contented sigh.

When Fern again opened her eyes it was dawn, and the great bed was empty save for her own slender figure. She reached out expectantly, as though touching the coverlet where Annot had lain could confirm the reality of her presence in the night. Had she really lain there, sobbing and then consoled by Dorian, or had it been only a dream of unusual intensity and verisimilitude?

No, it was more than a dream. Fern was certain of it. Annot, whose life had once brought her to this very room, had somehow come back, crossed the barrier of time and of death to reenact the events of her life for her great-granddaughter to witness. But why? There seemed no reason for it—yet. Fern had the uneasy feeling that there was more yet to be revealed before the meaning became clear. And Bruno must be wrong, for it was undoubtedly some kind of race-memory, some link with the past which brought such vivid dreams, recollections, however one liked to name them.

She could hardly wait to tell him. Once he heard of the dreams, every detail of which remained indelibly clear to her, he must then at least begin to be convinced. She *must* convince him she was no neurotic.

As Fern washed and dressed, she glanced out of the latticed window. From the moorland path a solitary figure strode toward the house and paused below to look up. The look on his face was startling; a hunted, desperate expression glazed his eyes, which stared blindly upward. Fern drew back from the window quickly. It was Bruno, hatless and disheveled, his hair bedewed with mist. Behind him loped the wolfhound, Pharaoh. Suddenly Bruno turned away and strode around the side of the Hall, out of sight.

A few minutes later Cassie knocked and entered with the breakfast tray. Fern's curiosity was too great to be contained.

"Has the master breakfasted yet, Cassie? I see he walked out very early this morning."

"He's just come in, miss, in by t' kitchen door, soaked through. He's been out all night, seemingly, because his bed's not been slept in."

Fern snapped her lips shut. She had already overstepped the bounds of propriety in questioning Cassie about the master; curious as she was, she would ask no more, though she burned to know what he had been doing. Out on the moors all night in this freezing weather? Why? Then another thought crossed her mind. It answered the mystery of the dog whose howls had invaded her dreams—it must have been Pharaoh, chilled and miserable and longing for his bed by the kitchen fire.

"Did you hear a dog howl in the night, Cassie?" she asked, and then remembered the girl went home to the village to sleep and most likely had not heard it. But Cassie's usually amiable face had blanched. "Why, what's the matter? You look quite frightened."

"A dog in t' night? Not me, miss, nor do I want to hear it. Up on t' moor were it?"

"Presumably. But why does that frighten you?"

"Them's Gabriel's hounds, miss, so they say. Trouble to come to those as hear 'em. 'Scuse me, miss, have you done wi' t' tray?"

She could not leave the room quickly enough, so it seemed. Fern smiled. How ridiculously superstitious village folk could be. But she dismissed the thought quickly, for she was concerned about Bruno. His look had been so strange, and wild, that either he was disturbed by the strange happenings with Phoebe last night, or possibly he was ill. She hastened downstairs to find him and encountered Cassie just leaving his study. The girl laid a finger to her lips.

"He's fast asleep in t' chair, sleeping like a baby. I've lit t' fire, as he's still in his wet clothes, but I haven't the heart to wake him, he were so tired."

"Yes," Fern agreed reluctantly. "Let him sleep. I'll look in on him later."

But despite Fern's frequent peeping in on him, Bruno slumbered on all morning. Eventually the idea came to her that since she still had the key to the unused wing which Mrs. Thorpe had surrendered to her, she could look about there again, undisturbed. Satisfied that Bruno was still deeply asleep, Fern made her way to the ancient studded door.

Once again the chill air of damp and neglect struck her as she passed through into the stone-slabbed corridor, an atmosphere mingled too with sadness and decay. The dusty floor still showed signs only of Bruno's footsteps toward his laboratory. The door was securely locked, and Fern grew curious to know what lay within.

As she turned from the door, she noticed the dark wall beneath the gallery and the absence of Annot's portrait. Now, why should it have been removed? Undoubtedly it was by Bruno's order, but why? Fern felt a sense of perverse irritation. He had done it on her account, she was sure, and she would demand the reason just as soon as he awoke.

It was a relief to reemerge from the old wing into the warmth of the newer Hall. Odd, but it seemed always ominously cold in the old wing, a chill as of the grave. Fern shuddered at the silly notion and retraced her steps toward the study. Bruno was awake, seated at his desk. He looked up as she entered.

"I see you have been in the old wing."

It was a statement, not a question, and Fern felt resentful of the note of challenge in his voice. His face betrayed no wild signs of distraction or illness now.

"Yes, I have. How did you know?"

"There is dust on the hem of your skirt. Mrs. Thorpe is too able a housekeeper to permit dust elsewhere in the Hall, so it follows you have been in the old wing. Why?"

"Curiosity, that is all."

"But you found my laboratory locked. And I intend it to remain so, for it is dangerous for a layman to dabble there."

"Why have you removed Annot's portrait?" Fern's challenging look met a cool stare in return.

"For the same reason I appropriated the notes Amos brought, to discourage your obsession with the girl."

"Then you are deceived, Bruno, for I dream of her still." Fern's voice was almost triumphant.

"Still?" The thick brows rose in query. "Then your preoccupation with the subject is even deeper than I thought."

He looked down again at the papers before him, as if he had done with the topic, and Fern's protesting reply died on her lips. What was the use of arguing with him, since he was too cold and skeptical to begin to understand? He, devoid of feeling for any but himself—and possibly Luke and his family—could never understand her affinity with her past. Instead, she remembered his haunted look of the morning when he came home.

"You were out all night, I believe."

He looked up sharply. "That is no affair of anyone but myself. Do not seek to question me, Fern, for I will not be questioned."

"I was simply concerned for you. You looked so . . . strange, when I saw you through the window."

"It is nothing. I have many pressing matters on my mind. The mill, my experiments . . ."

"And Phoebe?"

His fierce look reverted to the papers before him. "Phoebe? No, to be sure. I shall isolate the cause of her trouble, but it will take time."

Fern was startled. "You do not mean to repeat an experiment like last night, surely? It was too much for her, and for Fabia."

"For Fabia, perhaps. She was a little startled, but the child is well and remembers nothing."

Fanny bustled in, apron and cap strings flying behind her. "Sir, the Reverend Amos begs leave to call on you."

Bruno rose from the desk, glancing at the mantel clock. "Amos, at this hour? He can scarcely have finished his lengthy Sunday sermon yet. Show him in, Fanny."

Fern could see by Edgar Amos' white, tight-lipped expression that he was tense, but whether with anger or with another emotion she could not tell. That he had come in haste was evident, for beneath his coat he still wore his cassock. Bruno nodded and waved him to a chair, but as Pharaoh uncurled his length from the hearth rug and came sniffing toward him, the young vicar remained standing.

"What brings you here so early, Amos?" Bruno inquired as he reseated himself behind his desk. Fern sat unobtrusively by the window.

"Dr. de Lacy, I have come to protest most vigorously on behalf of my parishioners Mr. and Mrs. Armitage about the incident here last night, and of which I understand you were the instigator."

Bruno picked up his pipe. Pharaoh began to growl at the vicar's angry tones, laying back his lips to bare his teeth. Amos twitched the hem of his cassock away nervously, taking a hesitant step backward.

"Weg, Pharaoh, still!" At Bruno's quietly spoken order the dog retreated sullenly to the hearth rug and lay down. "Forgive me, the dog understands only German," Bruno went on smoothly. "Now, please be seated, Amos, and tell me. Have the Armitages themselves protested?"

Amos sat gingerly. "No, they have not. But it is my duty, as a man of God, to protest on their behalf when you dabble with the unknown and bring them and their child into possible danger. They told me after morning service of what happened here last night, of their concern because they could not understand it, and I felt it was my duty to hasten here at once, to beg you not to repeat this experiment. You do not know what you are doing."

"But you do?" Fern had half-expected him to storm at Amos, but Bruno's voice was enigmatically calm.

"I know you succeeded in causing Phoebe to speak, but with the voice of a woman. I know there is something strange, something supernatural at work, and I entreat you not to experiment with an innocent child again. By dabbling so you could arouse elemental forces which you cannot control. There is much we do not know or understand, but to meddle with these supernatural forces can release evil powers which we none of us could combat. Evidently you have the power to evoke these forces, though I doubt you can control them."

Bruno's smile spread slowly. "You accuse me of witchcraft, is that it, Amos? You fear I may be a warlock or wizard, opposed to the strength of your church? You are talking rubbish, man, medieval superstitious rubbish. I am, as you know, a man of science, but I admit that science is not always concerned with absolute truths. In this fringe between the things we can understand and those we can't explain, between nature and the supernatural as you call it, lie many strange phenomena such as levitation, precognition, and hypnosis. What happened last night with Phoebe was certainly a phenomenon I have not encountered before, but there is assuredly a scientific, logical explanation of it. In time, I shall discover it."

87

"No good can come of it!" Amos' protest was almost a wail of despair.

"Good has already come of it. We have established that Phoebe is physically capable of speech. Now we must find what prevents her from speaking."

"It is not with her physical well-being that I am concerned, but her spiritual welfare," Amos shouted. The dog growled menacingly on the rug, but Bruno stilled him with a look.

"Forgive him, Amos," Bruno commented quietly. "Like many of us, he distrusts what he cannot understand."

Fern could feel her palms prickling. She felt acutely embarrassed by the hostility between the two men, but could not join the battle. After all, both men had valid points of argument.

"A little child such as Phoebe surely cannot come to harm, if such is your fear, if she is protected by her own innocence?" Bruno said after a pause.

Amos grunted. "Even the innocent suffer if evil powers are evoked. Innocence is no protection."

"I am not entirely convinced that malevolent powers were at work," Bruno went on, as if to himself. "Our view of the world is limited by the blinkers of our experience, and we must penetrate the fog of mysticism and superstition if we are to reach beyond. Possibly there is a scientific explanation for many so-called supernatural phenomena."

Amos looked surly. "It is possible, but not yet proven. All we know is that dabbling with these things produces dire results."

"And are you certain it was my presence which caused this ... manifestation, or whatever you may call it? Could it not equally well have been due to another's presence, say, Fern even?"

Fern's jaw dropped open in surprise. Amos too stared in bewilderment. Bruno lit his pipe slowly, as though savoring the moment.

"It is possible, I suppose," Amos admitted.

"No, no!" Fern cried in alarm. "You cannot blame me!"

"But you claim to have affinity with the past. If, as you

seem to believe, Phoebe's voice came from the past, why not attribute the reason to your affinity—and your presence?"

Fern was too stunned to answer, and since Amos was only blinking in embarrassment, too tongue-tied to come to her defense, she got up blindly and rushed from the room. Tears scalded her eyelids. How *could* Bruno blame her for the frightening event last night?

For almost an hour Fern paced her room, agitated and irate. It was this house that brought evil with it, she decided, its atmosphere which had affected Phoebe, or possibly Bruno himself in dabbling with unknown powers, as Amos stated. But not her, not Fern's fault, for she herself felt the power of this place, a victim of its strange emanations. It grieved her that either Bruno or Edgar Amos should believe her capable of bringing possible danger to Phoebe, although unwittingly.

At last she descended the staircase, calmer now, though still fretting, and saw Amos in the hall about to take his leave. He turned from Bruno, who reentered his study and closed the door, and saw Fern. His smile was weak and uncertain.

"I feel in need of a breath of air, and the sun is peeping out. Do you mind if I walk a little way with you?" Fern asked him.

"By all means, Miss Saxby. But do take care to wrap up well, for the wind is treacherously cold."

Fern fetched her ulster and gloves but chose to go hatless. The cold breeze whipped tendrils of hair loose from its neat coils, and Fern welcomed the unaccustomed feeling of freedom it gave her. Amos walked alongside in gloomy silence, measuring his stride to match hers. The gravel crunched beneath their feet as they walked. At length Fern broke the silence.

"Do you believe this occurrence to be of my doing, Mr. Amos?"

He shrugged his shoulders apologetically. "As the doctor says, you do claim an affinity with the past of the Hall. It is possible you are a contributory factor, though you may not realize it."

"Then you do believe Phoebe reverted to a former life? You believe in reincarnation?"

Blue eyes gazed at her blankly. "Who can say for certain? There is so much we cannot comprehend in this life. But I fear the consequences if Dr. de Lacy meddles. It is Phoebe's soul which is in danger—or her psyche, as he would term it. I am afraid, Miss Saxby. I sense danger, though I cannot explain it."

"And so do I." The words were out before Fern realized. They had reached the stone gate pillars surmounted by stone lions. Amos stopped suddenly.

"Go back to the Hall, Miss Saxby. It is bitterly cold, and you have no protection for your head. I would not wish you to catch a cold. Do go back."

Reluctantly Fern agreed. She would have liked to talk more with him, to try to clarify just what it was they both feared. Slowly she retraced her steps, then on an impulse turned off across the lawns, away from the direction of the moor.

A rose garden, now only a thicket of tangled thorny branches scoured by the winds, gave way to an enclosed garden bordered by a high yew hedge. Fern strolled through, unaware of the wind's keenness, and emerged into a glade of trees close by a lake. Beyond the trees a dark stump projecting from the ground caught her eye, and curiously she wandered toward it. Surely not a sundial, so far from the Hall?

It was a black-marble slab, with a few words carved in its glossy depth: "Annot Radley. Born 1798. Died 1815."

So Fern had found the poor creature who nightly invaded her dreams.

Chapter 7

The gong had already sounded for Sunday lunch by the time Fern regained the Hall, and Bruno was waiting in the dining room to place Fern's chair beneath her before taking his own seat at table. Fanny ladled out brown Windsor soup from the tureen and withdrew.

"I discovered Annot's grave in the grounds," Fern announced quietly. Bruno went on sipping a spoonful of soup. "Why did you not tell me it was there?"

"I supposed you would find it sooner or later. I could not prevent you," he replied coolly.

"If you could, you would have removed that too, like her portrait and the notes, I imagine." It slipped out. She had not meant to provoke him. Bruno sighed in sign of dissipating patience and then continued spooning his soup. For a few moments Fern ate in silence too.

"No doubt you think that removing all evidence of Annot will make me forget she ever existed, but it is not so. As I told you, I dream of her. I feel sure she comes back to me because she wants me to know something. It's not that I'm so obsessed when awake that I dream of her; it's more . . . more as if I were possessed than obsessed."

Bruno's spoon clattered noisily into his half-emptied bowl. "For heaven's sake, Fern, how long must this nonsense go on? You speak of possession now—influenced by all Amos' ridiculous primitive hysteria this morning about raising spirits, I've no doubt. How impressionable you are, a mere child at heart! Now, please cease this chatter about Annot before you too become hysterical. It's time, at twenty-two, that you became a mature woman, and especially if you are soon to become a wife."

Before Fern could answer, Fanny entered to remove the soup dishes and place a joint of roast sirloin before Bruno. As she laid the tureens of roast potatoes and carrots and Yorkshire pudding on the damask cloth, Fern watched Bruno's strong, dexterous hands as he deftly carved the joint. At last Fanny, her keen eye satisfied that all was correct on the table, bobbed a curtsy and disappeared. Bruno passed to Fern a plate of neatly sliced roast beef.

"You exaggerate, Bruno," Fern said calmly as she spooned carrots and potatoes alongside the beef. "I do truly dream of her, not wishfully, but it simply happens. And the detail of the dreams is so minute it can be no coincidence. I could tell you which cottage Annot lived in, the furnishings there, and a thousand other things I could not possibly have learned otherwise."

Bruno snorted disbelievingly. "It is no secret which is the Radley cottage. No one will live in it now, so disliked is the name, and Micklethwaite, who lives in the cottage adjoining, uses the Radley one as a pigsty. It is common knowledge, as you have no doubt heard."

"I knew no such thing. I have barely been into the village since my arrival."

"Village girls come to the Hall to work. You could have learned gossip from them."

Fern was irritated. "Do you think I have nothing better to do than make idle talk with the servants? I tell you I dreamed all this, but since you obviously do not believe me, let us leave the matter rest. What do you plan to do now about Phoebe?"

His dark eyes lifted from his plate, and a frown creased his brow. "Fern, it is not a wife's place to quiz her husband—or future husband—as to his actions. My affairs in my work are a private matter."

"Will you see her again?" She was not to be put down like a child so easily.

"I shall visit Luke this afternoon, to ascertain whether he is as disturbed as Amos represents over last night. Future course of action will depend on that."

"May I come with you?"

"No." It was a bold answer with no explanation. Fern felt hurt. He was cutting her out of not only the running of the mill, his work, and what he would do with regard to Phoebe, but now even out of his friendship with the Armitages, it seemed. He wanted her to share no part of his life. What a dismal prospect marriage to this man held out. No true union of minds, no affection, no companionship even. Inwardly Fern rebelled. Bruno, having now finished his dinner, sat back to await Fanny's arrival with the pudding, and as he sat in silence, he took an object on a chain from his pocket and began to swing it idly to and fro.

Fern's breath caught in a gasp in recognition of the object. It wasn't just that it was the bright shining thing he had swung rhythmically before Phoebe last night in the study; it was the heavy carving on a silver ring which brought back to Fern forcibly the vision of Annot and Dorian in the bedroom last night. Fern stared at it in fascination.

Bruno smiled wryly as he noted her rapt expression. Fern leaned forward in her chair.

"That ring—I have seen it before!"

He cocked his head to one side quizzically. "Yes, last night."

"And again—in the dream. Dorian promised it to Annot. Every De Lacy gave it to his new bride, he said."

"So you know the tradition. But he did not give it to Annot, but to the woman he did marry, my great-grandmother,

Sarah Ramsden. Someday soon it will be yours, Fern. I wonder where you learned about the ring?"

"I told you—in the dream. I saw it closely. It has twelve carved points which read *Amor Aeternus.*"

He frowned and slid the ring back into his pocket, just as Fanny entered with a huge steamed pudding and a bowl of custard on a tray. Fern waited until the door had closed again behind the maid before pursuing her advantage. Bruno was obviously impressed by her knowledge of the ring.

"So you see, from my dreams I am learning about Annot. She was brought to this house on trial, as it were, to be trained as a lady before the wedding could take place. I hope further dreams will reveal just why she became so unhappy that she killed herself."

Bruno pushed back his chair and rose from the table. "I want no pudding. Please excuse me. I am going now to see Luke Armitage."

Fern looked up at his face, but it was set and enigmatic. "Do you begin to believe me now, Bruno?"

He turned as he reached the door and his look was ominous. "I do not. Such detail as you have related is fully reported in old Thomas' notes, which Amos brought."

"But I have not read them, remember, you took them from me."

"They lie on my study desk. You could well have read them this morning while I slept. No, I am not convinced, Fern."

And before she could utter a startled denial that she could resort to such subterfuge, he was gone. Inwardly Fern fumed. How could he believe her capable of sneaking in and reading furtively while he slept! Pushing away her plate of pudding, Fern rose and ran out after him, burning in protest. He was in the hall, pulling on his caped greatcoat as she came up to him.

"And the ring, Bruno? How could I have known the wording on it?" she asked defiantly.

He turned and stared fixedly at her, his dark features solemn and implacable. "The dining table is eight feet in length. It would seem you have remarkably keen eyesight,

94

young lady. But the way you stared at the ring told me more."

He withdrew once again the glittering silver ring from his pocket, and again Fern stared at it transfixed. Bruno's eyes bored into her face. "It fascinates you, does it not, Fern? You are so suggestible, I could hypnotize you within seconds now."

She tore her gaze from the ring and glared at him. "You could not! I would not let you!"

He laughed, a hollow, mirthless tone. "You are so impressionable, my dear. There exists between us a rapport which I have never found before in a patient. We are very alike, Fern, you and I. Such a close affinity between hypnotizer and hypnotized does not occur often, but when it does, we recognize it, we medical men. It comes closely akin to hysteria in the patient."

"Again you accuse me of being hysterical," Fern cried, almost tearful in frustration. "But I am not. I am as sane and balanced as you are."

He picked up his riding crop from the hall stand, glanced at his reflection in the oak-framed mirror above, and strode toward the front door. In the passage he turned. A veil of angry tears was misting Fern's eyes.

"And this hysteria I spoke of, we know it has a sexual basis," Bruno added quietly, as an afterthought. The door opened, admitting a draft of icy wind, and he was gone. Fern stood aghast. For some moments she was too stunned to move. Had she heard aright? Anger and resentment gave way to a flood of shame and embarrassment.

She grew conscious of hot, sticky palms and of Fanny's approaching footsteps as she reappeared through the green-baize door leading down to the kitchens. Fern avoided the maid's curious gaze as she passed her to go to her own room. Two thoughts thundered in her brain: one, that Bruno believed her attracted by him, and two, that he had scorned her sufficiently to speak of a matter to which no member of polite Victorian society ever even remotely referred—sex. She did not know which insult to fume against most.

How dared he be so blatant! It was a measure of the man's

arrogance that he thought he could talk to her so coarsely and that he could believe her physically attracted to him. What a crude, ill-mannered oaf he was! Fern speculated how Lydia Hastings would have dealt with him, but in the presence of such a vapid, colorless woman he probably would not have felt the need to provoke with such crudity. In the Hastings household it was, as in any good Christian home, tacitly understood that sex was never mentioned, and even objects which could have a sexual connotation, such as the legs of tables and pianos, were discreetly draped. How, against such a background of polite prevarication, could Bruno be so monstrous as to speak to her of her sexual attraction to him!

Fern paced her room angrily, torn between fury and shame. Was he perhaps right in his judgment after all, and she was attracted to him? Scornfully she rejected the idea. It could not be true. He had nothing about him to appeal to a woman—no chivalry, no warmth, no tenderness. And how could one be drawn to a man who made it evident he found equally no appeal in her?

The dismal Sunday afternoon passed slowly, raindrops pattering incessantly against the windowpane. Fern declined Fanny's offer to bring up afternoon tea, and as the evening drew on she watched the great lumbering night clouds advance slowly over the mountain edge. Bruno still had not returned. Angered and disconcerted as she was by him, Fern felt the vast Hall empty and lifeless without his great vibrant presence.

Fanny came again to draw the heavy velvet curtains closed and replenish the fire, picking coals elegantly from the brass coal scuttle by the hearth with carved brass tongs.

"Will that be all, miss?" Fern nodded her thanks and dismissal, and Fanny bobbed and withdrew. With a sigh Fern decided to prepare for bed. Washed and nightgowned at last, she looked at her reflection in the dressing-table mirror. Hair unbound and the voluminous folds of the white nightgown ethereally pale in the candlelight, she looked young and defenseless, and inwardly she felt dreadfully alone. Her wide eyes stared back at her thoughtfully. Sleep was far away yet.

Rising, she donned her woolen dressing gown, and taking the candle, she went down to the library in search of a book.

As she reached the gallery she heard the front door open. Looking down over the parapet, she saw Bruno, greatcoated and hatless. The candle's light caught his eye, for he glanced up.

"Fabia has a mind to go shopping in Bradford tomorrow. I promised her you would accompany her. Malachi will drive you both down," he said quietly. Fern came down the stairs quickly, snuffing out the candle, and came to stand before him as he doffed his coat. Shopping, she thought, but with no money. Since sending her money in London, Bruno had offered no more, and she was reluctant to mention the omission. Having hung his coat on the hall stand, he turned to face her, his dark head silhouetted in the light of the solitary oil lamp. Fern shifted uncomfortably beneath his gaze.

"I shall furnish you with money." It was as if he had read her thoughts, and Fern was embarrassed. "I propose to allot you ten pounds per month, if that will suit you."

"It is generous, Bruno, thank you."

But already his eyes had lifted from her face and were turned toward the study. Having dealt with the matter of an allowance for her, he had already forgotten her. Politely he waited, but Fern was not ready to be dismissed.

"Were Luke and Fabia well? And Phoebe?"

"Perfectly."

"They were not disturbed, then, as Amos thought?"

"Not at all. He exaggerated, but then, he is a highly emotional man."

"Is Luke happy for you to continue your work with Phoebe, then?"

His eyes flickered down to her face, "He is, but I am not—yet. I deem the moment not quite ripe, and moreover, I sense Fabia was a little troubled, though she says nothing. But if you will excuse me, Fern . . ."

Already he was stepping around her toward the study. Reluctantly Fern bade him good night and remounted the stairs, her book forgotten. Perhaps, after all, Bruno was showing consideration, arranging a shopping expedition for her and Fabia, but his authoritative manner of announcing it, combined with his complete uninterest in her, would seem to deny it.

Fern slept a deep and dreamless sleep that night, and when next morning dawned bright and crisp with a mellow hint of spring in the air, she began to enjoy the prospect of the day's outing. Malachi drove her in the trap down to the village to call at the schoolhouse for Fabia, who was as excited as a child as she climbed into the trap and sat alongside Fern.

"Was it not kind of Bruno to suggest we spend the day in town?" she said happily as the trap made its way along the cobbled village street. Fern was watching the curtains twitch as they passed, and some women even looked up from scrubbing and donkey-stoning their front steps to stare dourly. No doubt, to them Fabia in her best gray flannel and Fern in deep-green velvet were hardly dressed for a workaday Monday morning.

"Luke has given me money to buy gloves for Phoebe and a length of flannel for a nightgown," Fabia was saying excitedly. "Poor little thing, she feels the cold so. I feel such a lady, driving into town with you to buy them instead of making them myself. Luke is so kind. And Bruno too—is he not the gentlest and most considerate of men? You and I are lucky indeed."

The village slipped away behind them as the trap mounted the moorland road up and away from Brackenroyd. The road that ran along the scar afforded a fine view of the valley below, and Fern gazed about her in wonder. The wind blew cold over the brow, and she drew the rug gratefully over her knees and Fabia's.

"Have you ridden along this road before?" Fabia inquired. "It gives one a splendid view of our valley. See, there is the Hall on the far ridge, and there Fox Brow, Ellen Stansfield's home."

Fern's eye was caught by the mill in the valley below, on the river's edge. From here it looked huge, ranks of slate-gray roofs marking out the textile-machinery buildings, blackened by the grime from its chimneys. Above it she could see the river's silver-gray ribbon threading between the curves of the mountainside till it flattened out in a vast gray expanse, hemmed by a wide dam.

"That's Bilberry Reservoir," Fabia explained. "And just above it, you can see Dr. Briggs's house."

The road twisted away from the valley and across the moor, across great tracts of winter-browned heather and through a tiny hamlet where chickens squawked in the roadway in protest at the trap's passing. Fabia was amused by the woman, her forearms white with flour from the baking she had evidently been wrenched from, who shooed the chickens fussily back into her yard.

"That's what I should be doing now, baking, and not jaunting off on a day's holiday." She chuckled happily. "Oh, I am so grateful to Bruno and Luke—and to you too, Fern."

Fern smiled. It was odd how often Fabia referred to Bruno's kindness. Evidently she saw him in a very different light from herself. Or it could be Fabia's own warmth and kindliness which elicited similar response in him, she reflected. Perhaps her own agressiveness was at fault that she had found no such gentleness in him yet.

"Phoebe is happy too," Fabia chattered on. "She is to have tea with Edgar. Funny, but they get on well together, which is odd when you consider how shy she is, and he too. But Bruno is her idol. She adores him and seems truly happy when she's in his company. I'm so glad, because she doesn't have a very happy time at school. The other children find her odd because she doesn't speak. At one time she was teased unmercifully, but now they just leave her alone. She's a very lonely child."

She relapsed into silence for a moment, pondering the problem. Fern instinctively reached for her hand in tacit sympathy. Fabia's back straightened.

"It's a pity she has no brothers or sisters, but it does not seem to be God's will. Nevertheless, I am glad she has Bruno. She seems to prefer adults' company."

Bruno's, and perhaps Edgar's, but not mine, thought Fern sadly. She still remembered the sting of the child's shrinking

99

from her touch. It was a hurtful memory, for it was said children were perceptive creatures.

"Bruno is optimistic he can help her," Fabia went on. "Now he knows she can hear, he is certain he can teach her a new method of communication recently devised, a means of conversing by sign language with the hands. He says it is being successfully used in Germany, and will be of great advantage to her until she learns to speak. He is so sympathetic, so kind . . ."

There, again, she was maintaining his consideration. Either there was a facet to his personality Fern had not yet discovered, or Fabia was besotted with him, and as she was obviously so in love with her husband, it was hardly the latter.

The trap jolted on, the horse's hooves clattering rhythmically on the road, and as Fabia relapsed again into silence, Fern drew in lungfuls of the clean, sweet air, pure and free from the smoke of the valleys, reveling in the sense of freedom the high moors gave her. Frowning hills, stern and rugged, overlooked vast undulations of heather-clad moor. The solitude and silence gave an air of powerful strength to the place. Mountainous and bare of habitation for miles, the moors were her native home, she felt, intoxicating in their solid majesty. After some miles when little was to be seen but dry stone walls lining the road and the expanse of Malachi's broad back, the road began to dip down, and an occasional farm or cluster of cottages was to be seen, and then it descended more steeply, and more houses came into sight, larger and more imposing, often with their own large gardens.

"We are in the outskirts of Bradford now," Fabia pointed out. "There, down in the valley, you can see the town."

And indeed Fern could see it, its great gray mass spreading in the very depths of the valley. The houses alongside the road were impressive, the solid mansions of prosperous merchants who had amassed their wealth from the area's woolen trade mainly. Fabia spoke of the town's history.

"Worsted, such as your mill produces, is manufactured here, and Bradford is renowned for it, though many mills do produce mohair and alpaca and silks too. Just see how many mills there are."

It was true, for they were riding by many gray, gaunt buildings, mills and warehouses, where men in clogs and aprons bustled about to the accompaniment of a background of whirring machinery. But soon the cobbled mill streets gave way to the broad clean streets of the town center. Fern recognized the railway station where she had first met Bruno.

"The church of St. Peter," Fabia indicated in Forster Square, "and there is our new town hall with its tower which is an exact replica of the campanile of the Palazzo Vecchio in Florence. There's the technical college—the Prince and Princess of Wales came to open it only last year. Almost all the buildings are but newly built. Is it not a fine town?"

Fern could not but agree, for its civic buildings were most impressive, and the many shops and banks and hotels were equally grand. Malachi, given orders to take the trap to an inn yard until they were ready to return, helped the ladies to dismount and drove off. Then the delight of shopping could begin.

Into every large emporium and small private shop in the main streets they went, exclaiming with admiration at the new French millinery in the Misses Drake's establishment, the caps and bonnets and headdresses for weddings, the gloves and cambrics and mantles, the sprigged muslins and luscious velvets. And finally they found the prosaic flannel Fabia sought. Having purchased that and some wool to knit Phoebe's gloves after all, she pronounced her errands completed and inquired what Fern required.

"I would like to buy gifts, for Phoebe and you," Fern said. Despite Fabia's protests, she insisted, and as Fabia firmly declined a pretty flower-patterned porcelain potpourri bowl, Fern persuaded her at last to accept some sewing silks, a sheet of pins, and new cutting shears.

"And for Phoebe, what shall I buy?"

"Really, she has no need of anything, Fern—beyond new clogs, that is. But of books and toys she already has sufficient, truly."

"Then I shall buy the clogs, and a length of muslin for a Sunday frock." And Fern was not to be dissuaded this time. As they both fingered the assortment of muslins in the emporium, Fabia sighed.

"Oh, look at that pretty violet-gray silk. It's exactly like a gown Ellen used to wear, before she retired into isolation. Poor Ellen. I think the wild Yorkshire countryside was alien to her. She came from Wiltshire, you know, and I think our moors frightened her a little. She changed so much after Arthur died."

"Did you know her well?"

Fabia shook her head. "I was new to Brackenroyd when she was widowed. Now she will see no one. Her old maid-housekeeper, Hepzibah, looks after her and occasionally comes to the village, but Ellen never goes out except in the evening, alone on the moors, and she runs home if she is seen. Bruno is the only person who can talk to her. He has an uncanny knack of getting through the barrier of those who are . . . handicapped in some way."

Like Phoebe, thought Fern. He can penetrate her cautious reserve, and that of the eccentric Ellen. If his manner is so efficacious with lame dogs, why does it not extend to ordinary people like me? Perhaps if he thought me helpless too, in some way, he would try. The bizarre notion of feigning the neurotic he believed her to be flashed through her mind. How foolish of her, to consider shamming madness in order to attract his attention!

To wind up a pleasant afternoon, the two ladies sipped tea from willow-patterned china cups in a little tea shop, nibbled hot toast and powdery sponge cakes. Finally the time came to return.

"It would be useful to have a little fob watch," commented Fern as they made their way to the inn yard.

"Then why not buy one?" Fabia replied.

Fern was shocked. "Did you see the price in that jeweler's? Thirty-eight and six for a lady's gold watch, and two pounds for a gentleman's. It's very expensive."

"But you are wealthy now. Two pounds is little enough on

your income," Fabia remarked calmly. "To us it would be a prodigious sum, two-thirds of what Luke earns in a week, but value is relative to one's income."

"True," Fern admitted. "But I am not used to wealth. Nor am I yet legally entitled to it."

"When are you and Bruno to be married?" Fabia inquired, tilting her head and gazing frankly into Fern's eyes. Fern hid a blush.

"I don't know yet. Soon, I expect."

And the thought of her marriage occupied Fern's mind throughout the homeward journey over the darkening moors. Bruno had made it clear he would not ask her to marry him again, but would leave the approach to her. The time had now come, it seemed, to make that approach. Until she was truly mistress of Brackenroyd, her position would remain as nebulous and ill-defined as it had been as the Hastingses' governess. Only as his wife would Bruno listen to her, take notice of her. Until then she was of no account.

In the village Fabia climbed down from the trap, promising to take Fern to the clogger's shop in the morning to order Phoebe's new clogs. Her face shone with happiness.

"It's been such a lovely outing, Fern, I've enjoyed it so much. I'm longing to tell Luke and Phoebe all about it. Thank you so much."

Fern envied the young woman's radiance, the light, eager step as she hastened indoors, waved, and closed the door behind her. She could visualize Luke's welcoming smile and the eager conversation that ensued. How lucky was Fabia, warm and secure in a happy marriage. Fern signaled to Malachi to drive on.

Brackenroyd Hall stood huge, sentinel-like, at the head of the drive, lugubrious and forbidding. No lights shone at the windows. Bruno must be out yet. As Malachi drew up at the wide, shallow steps, Fern waved to him to drive on around to the stable yard. It would be cozier to enter the Hall by a warm, lighted kitchen than by a desolate front vestibule. The pony began to canter under the arch into the stable yard, anxious for his feed and a warm stall. Malachi reined him in by the kitchen door just as Bruno emerged, caped and spurred, his tall figure silhouetted in the doorway against the lamplight within.

"Mein Herr?" Malachi murmured in query. Fern heard Bruno bark words of command in German, and the grooms-man nodded. Bruno turned to Fern.

"I wanted to talk with you, but that must wait now. I have business to attend to. Will you ride with me?"

Taken aback by his sudden desire to want her conversation and to have her company, Fern forgot her fatigue. "Gladly," she replied.

"Then change into a riding habit, quickly."

He strode off to the stables, Malachi following with the pony. By the time Fern returned, he was waiting in the yard alone, holding Phantom and Whisper by the reins.

"Mount up," he said tersely, and leaping into the saddle, he headed for the archway. Fern decided to ignore his lack of courtesy in not helping her to mount. She was too curious to know what he wanted to discuss, and what his errand was. Judging by his urgent manner, she thought it must be grave.

She followed him at a canter down the drive, and at the great stone gateway he turned, not down toward the village and the mill, as she had expected, but up toward the moor. That way lay nothing but Fox Brow, and then only the moors. What trouble could lie in that direction? Despite the steepness of the track, Bruno was urging Phantom on, and Fern was hard-pressed to keep Whisper up close behind him.

"Where are we going?" she called out at last, but Bruno's reply, thrown over his shoulder, was lost on the wind. Reaching the brow, he veered off the track across the heather, slowing a little. He was glancing back at her, to see if she was still with him, and then for no apparent reason he reined Phantom in to a canter. Fern rode alongside him.

"Is there trouble, Bruno? Can I be of help?"

She could see his expression in the gathering gloom only dimly, but it was clearly taut and resolute.

"Trouble enough. I've had Mrs. Pickering in my study this last hour."

"Mrs. Pickering?"

"The wife of one of my workers—*our* workers. You wanted to know the problems of running a mill. This is one of them. It's not just ordering and manufacturing and record keeping and buying and selling, but human problems too. Mrs. Pickering's family is half-starving."

"Because of the low wage we pay?"

He snorted. "The wage is uniform with what all the local manufacturers pay. It's Pickering himself. He drinks half his money away at the Woolpack. His wife tells me she stands at the inn door pleading with him for money for food, and many other wives are there after their husbands too. I'll not have it. I won't have starved families laid at my door. And since you are joint owner of the mill, I thought perhaps you too would like to help me persuade the men to see reason."

Fern was bewildered. Why, then, were they galloping up onto the barren moors at night? The Woolpack lay in the center of the village, and the men's cottages too. Bruno was watching her intently in the waning light as they rode. Before Fern could frame a question, her riding crop slipped from her hand.

"Oh, my crop! I've dropped it." Instantly Bruno reined in and dismounted, holding Phantom by the rein as he turned to stoop and search. Fern too dismounted to look. In a moment he found it and handed it to her in silence. Fern looked up at his face and saw the cool lantern in his eyes beginning to fade and be replaced by a light, a gleam of pleasure she had seen reserved only for the Armitage family hitherto. And then suddenly, without warning, high on a windswept hill, he stepped forward, dropping the rein and taking Fern in his arms. Without a word of preamble he kissed her, long and eagerly. Instinctively Fern responded. It was the first time anyone had ever kissed her, apart from Mamma, on the cheek, and it was an exciting experience.

His broad back under her fingers gave her a glow of delight. All her previous dislike of him, intense as it had been, melted with the passionate kiss. His touch evoked such a longing sensation that Fern was in ecstasy.

105

He stood back at last, his dark eyes raking her face. For a moment Fern could only gaze at him in wonder. How suddenly one could change one's whole view of a man, given the right motivation.

"Well, Fern, are you angry with me?"

"No, Bruno."

"Then how do you feel?"

"Reassured. I thought you hated me."

"Hated you? Hate is a primitive emotion."

"Well, scorned me, then. Now I can ask you what I decided today I would ask you. The time has now come, I think."

"Then ask me. What is it?"

"You said you would not marry me until I asked you, when I was ready. I am ready now, Bruno. Will you marry me, soon?"

It could have been imagination, but Fern fancied she could see the fire in his eyes die away. Once more the cool detachment took its place.

"Very well. I shall ask Amos to publish the banns at once. In a few weeks the wedding can take place. It is your privilege to name the date."

How cold, how unemotional he had suddenly become again! He spoke as if it were a legal or business transaction he was arranging, not a wedding. Fern began to feel confused and angered by his sudden, unforeseen changes of mood.

"Come, we waste time," he cut in sharply, taking her elbow to help her to remount. "We should be up on Thwaite moor by now."

He too remounted and turned Phantom's head toward the moor, up and away from Fox Brow. Sullenly Fern rode beside him, her mind turbulent and perplexed. Now she was contracted to him, this enigmatic, changeable, unpredictable creature. Of her own volition she had been misled into inviting him to be her husband.

Already he was spurring Phantom on ahead, his bride-to-be forgotten.

Chapter 8

The moon was venturing a pallid face over the horizon of crags before they reached the place Bruno sought. Fern caught a glimpse of the vast, expressionless surface of Bilberry Reservoir below in the valley as they galloped. Its inscrutability, and the silence and desolation of the moor, gave the moment a strangely unreal, dreamlike quality. Bruno, riding ahead, suddenly raised his hand and drew up. Fern did likewise, dismounting as he did.

He tilted his head slightly, listening. At first Fern could hear nothing but the moaning of the wind over the heather, but then other sounds drifted to her ears. Voices, men's voices, hushed but excited.

Bruno advanced slowly along the plateau to a ridge of gray crags, Fern following him. Beyond lay a hollow encircled by rocks, and within its bounds some twenty or so men crouched in a ring, their expectant faces illuminated by lantern light. All of them, cloth-capped and still wearing their working corduroys, stared fixedly into the center of the ring, where two gamecocks circled each other warily. Fern could see the light gleaming on the cruel steel spurs attached to the birds' ankles.

"Get at 'im, sithee," one of the men growled at his bird impatiently. Another laughed hoarsely.

"Tha's not fed 'im enough ale, lad. He's not fighting mad."

Bruno's sigh was angry. "So Mrs. Pickering was right," he muttered, as if to himself. "What's not spent on ale is wagered on cockfighting. I'll not have it."

Instantly he strode down the slope into the center of the circle, lifting the birds with a booted foot and tossing them apart. Both cocks' eyes glittered malevolently at the intruder but seemed to deem his spurred and booted feet a dubious proposition. Both retreated sulkily, while their respective owners, seeing the cape-clad figure that had swept down like a vengeful vulture in their midst, scooped up their birds and stowed them away in wicker baskets. All eyes stared fearfully at the master.

"Your cock may not be fighting mad, Enoch Drake, but I am," Bruno said quietly. "This is my land, and I will have no illegal activities here. You all know the law. You know that cockfighting has been illegal these thirty years and more. The magistrates would have no mercy on you if they knew, but I prefer to maintain the law on my land. I shall not tell them, provided you all give back the wagers you have laid tonight and give the money instead to your wives. There shall be no more cockfighting here. Take your birds and go, quietly."

Murmuring, the millhands rose and began packing their belongings. One, his corduroy jacket already grease-grimed and now bespattered with blood, growled in vexation. "I told thee we should a posted scouts on t' hill. Nobody'd listen to me."

Bruno turned on him. "Scouts or no, I would have found you and stopped this. Get home to your wife and children, Ben Pickering, and waste no more of your wages on ale and cocking. I'll hear no more excuses next time your rent is overdue."

The men moved off sullenly to tramp homeward across the moor, taking their lanterns with them. By the moonlight Fern could still see the evidence of their meeting, the strewn feathers and dark patches on the turf that marked the death of many birds. Their corpses were gone, no doubt to fill the village stewpots on the morrow.

Fern and Bruno rode home in silence, passing the gaggle of sullen-faced millhands on the way. Fern made no comment about the incident. Bruno was evidently unpopular with the men for spoiling their sport, but he had been right to protect the law and the village women. She felt grudging respect for his action, but still smarted to think how he had inveigled her into proposing marriage.

They rode on till the Hall came in sight, its gaunt turrets outlined against the moon. By night it wore a shrouded, secretive air, and with its windows all in darkness, it gave a sense of uneasy, waiting silence. Once again Fern felt that strange sense of familiarity mixed with apprehension.

"Who built the Hall, Bruno?" she asked as they cantered up the drive.

"Ralph de Lacy, Dorian's father."

Oddly, Fern shivered. It was the name "Ralph" that had caught her unawares, again with that strange feeling of half-recognition. "Ralph?" she queried.

"The last of many Ralphs in the De Lacy family tree. The name goes back for centuries. I rather think it was a Ralph—or Rafe, as it was spelled and pronounced then—who built the original old Hall."

Her gaze moved to the old wing, protruding until it half-buried itself in the cliffside. That was where Bruno's laboratory lay. Someday she must discover its secrets.

Once more in the stable yard of the Hall, Bruno helped her dismount. "Are you tired, Fern, or shall we talk over supper?" he inquired. She looked up at him, trying to gauge his expression, but it remained inscrutable. Well, she *was* hungry, and Bruno seemed to want to be forthcoming for once.

It being Fanny's evening off, Mrs. Thorpe served supper herself, with Cassie's somewhat gauche help. As she finally withdrew, Fern saw the older woman smiling contentedly to herself. No doubt she was glad to see what appeared to be dawning companionship and closeness between her charges, the new master and his lady.

After supper Bruno saw that Fern was comfortably seated in a deep armchair by the fire. He offered her wine, which she declined, and poured himself a glass of port. Then, taking up a position, feet astride with his back to the fire, he sipped the port in silence for a few moments. Fern waited to discover what he wanted to discuss.

"First, our wedding," he said at length. "Since you wish it to be soon, Amos shall read the banns at once. Shall you go to the church on Sunday to hear the first reading?"

"Indeed, I shall be glad to. And you too?"

"Of course, we must be seen together." He paused for a moment. "What kind of wedding would you like, my dear? The traditional white wedding, I presume?" Without waiting for her reply, he continued, "But not many guests, I think, since we have few friends and no relatives. A ball in the evening, perhaps, for the local worthies if you like."

That would be pleasant, thought Fern, a chance to decorate and enliven the Hall, filling it with gay company and laughter. That was what the old house desperately needed to chase away the shadows.

"Then I shall arrange the guest list and entertainment for the ball, and you the buffet and decoration. You must also visit a dressmaker to order your wedding gown and trousseau. The bill may be sent to me."

He was so practical and so prosaic about the affair, as if it were of no more consequence than arranging the delivery of some bales of wool, but Fern waited patiently to see how the conversation would develop. She would not hinder it by interrupting.

"We shall not go away after the wedding, for there is much to be done at the mill. Later, perhaps, if you feel in need of a holiday." For the first time he looked down at her. "Are you comfortable, Fern?"

"Perfectly, thank you."

"Then I beg you will join me in a glass of wine." And without waiting for her answer, he put down his glass of port on the mantelshelf amid the porcelain figurines and crossed to the sideboard behind her. Fern heard the cabinet door opened, and the clink of glasses.

"Canary? Madeira?" he asked.

"A small glass of Madeira, thank you."

In a moment he returned to offer her the glass and picked up his own. Then he seated himself opposite her, crossing his legs and leaning back in the chair.

"Now, let us talk. We know so little of each other, Fern, and I feel this must be rectified, as we are soon to be man and wife. Tell me about yourself. About your childhood, your family."

It was not easy to talk with those keen dark eyes leveled critically at her across the rim of his glass, but as Fern began, hesitantly at first, to speak of her parents, her schooling, the shock of their sudden death, and her change in circumstances, she began to feel more at ease. He did not interrupt to question, but occasionally nodded as he took a point and his somber eyes registered interest. Gradually Fern felt more and more that she wanted to open up to him, to establish an intimacy hitherto nonexistent. At last she reached the arrival of Mr. Lennox's letter and the new prospect of Yorkshire and marriage. Here she stumbled a little in embarrassment and fell silent. Bruno sat nodding reflectively.

"I see. And tell me, did you feel you had any *rapport* with Yorkshire before Mr. Lennox contacted you? Did your feelings of affinity with this place arise only when you came here?"

"They did. I had never had a chance to visit Yorkshire before, but it is with Brackenroyd only—the Hall and the village—that I have this feeling."

"Interesting," Bruno commented. "Now, tell me of your dreams—no, seriously, I do not mean to mock you. I honestly would like to know in detail what you have dreamed."

Fern regarded him earnestly. It was true there was no hint of mockery in his eyes, only an honest air of inquiry. Very well, then, if he was anxious to atone for his past disbelief, she would give him the opportunity. To meet halfway in compromise would be a better start to marriage than mutual distrust.

Every detail so far as she could remember of the dreams of Annot she recounted, and again Bruno listened thoughtfully as he sipped his port. When Fern had finished, she realized that without noticing she had drained her own glass while talking, and Bruno now rose in silence to refill it. Having done so, he sat opposite her again.

"And have you always dreamed, throughout your life?"

"I don't think so. I'm not aware of doing so before I came here."

"What else have you dreamed of? Other dreams, not connected with Annot?"

"Unimportant ones, I suppose. I forget them at once. Except last night's—I did have a silly dream then."

"What was it? I'd like to know."

"Oh, Mrs. Thorpe had a lot of colored balls of wool, and they were all in a tangle. I was helping her unravel them. And yes, there was a funny kind of gargoyle on the wall, and it had Malachi's face. I can't remember anything else, except that a dog kept barking."

"A dog? Any particular dog?"

"No. I never saw it in the dream. I just heard it."

"I see. Are you afraid of Malachi?"

Fern blushed. "No, I don't know him. You and he always speak in German, and I don't understand, but I'm not afraid of him. Why should I be?"

"Why indeed? He is quite harmless, I assure you, despite his bulky appearance and none-too-handsome features."

He fell silent, and remained so for some minutes. The clock on the mantelshelf gradually began to tick ominously loud in the vacuum, and as Bruno still did not speak, Fern wondered whether he had had enough of conversation and she should leave.

Suddenly he spoke. "Was it you or Mrs. Thorpe who needed help?"

"I beg your pardon?"

"To unravel the wool. Was it *your* wool, and Mrs. Thorpe was helping you?"

"No. I was helping her."

"And what colors were the wools?"

"Oh, I don't know. Red and blue, I think, and perhaps yellow."

"Primary colors. Are you afraid of dogs?"

Fern began to feel irritated. "No, I am not. I think I dreamed of the dog because there is often a dog barking at night near here. Cassie says it's Gabriel's hounds."

He laughed shortly. "Does she indeed? And do you know the legend of Gabriel's hounds?"

"No."

"Are you sure? It could be significant if you do."

"I tell you I do not. What is it?"

He leaned back thoughtfully. "This area is rich in Norse legend, since the Norsemen did come here, you know. It is one of their gods, Odin or Woden, who is said still to roam the Yorkshire moors with his dogs, the soul-thirsty Gabriel hounds. Perhaps you fancied it was your soul they were after, Fern."

Fern sat up angrily. "I did nothing of the kind, since I tell you I did not know the story. In any case, I don't believe it."

"Don't you?" His smile was frankly mocking. "I thought you believed in everything supernatural, communion with the dead, reincarnation, and all."

"And what if I do? We don't have to see and have proved to us all that we believe in. Edgar would agree with me in that."

"I'm sure he would." His smile lingered still, as though provoking her to go on.

Fern, angered by his cool scorn, went on. "You believe in the existence of electricity, don't you, because you've seen its effects. But you've never seen it. Does that make you doubt its existence?"

"Touché, young lady. You are quite right."

Now he was humoring her, as one would a petulant child. Fern rose, putting down her empty glass.

113

"I am tired. I think I shall go to bed now." He rose politely as she made for the door. In the doorway a belated thought came to her.

"Bruno, why did you say it was significant if I did know of the Gabriel's hounds legend?"

"Because in dreams we reveal what we truly are and worry about. You have told me much of yourself through your dreams."

Fern's eyebrows rose. "Do you mean you asked to hear of them only to analyze them and find out about me?"

"Yes. You are an excellent subject for research. When I have had the opportunity to consider it, I shall tell you the significance of the balls of wool and Malachi the gargoyle. Sleep well, my dear. I think you will dream well tonight."

Fern was so astounded and angered by his impudence that she slammed the door and marched furiously up to her room. The cheek of the man! Professing personal interest in her, and all the while he was only using her as a guinea pig for his research!

"I think you will dream well tonight." Now, what had he meant by that? That she was so incensed that a further dream would be born out of frustration and fury? Ah, well, she really was too tired to fret over his meaning any longer. The day in town and the ride over the moors must have really exhausted her, for her eyes could barely stay open.

Sleep must have come quickly that night. Either that or time suddenly sprang back with the rapidity of a recoiling spring. Fern was afterward never quite certain which. She only knew that in the darkness the door suddenly opened quietly, revealing a bulky figure outlined by the light of the candle in her hand. It was Annot, her eyes reddened and her face crumpled in misery. She put down the candle on the night table and flung her weight, increased now by advanced pregnancy, across the foot of the bed, where she began weeping noisily. Fern would have reached out to touch the shaking shoulders, clad now in finest merino wool instead of workaday serge, but the miserable figure had no substance.

Again the door opened. A chambermaid, trim in black

gown and starched apron and cap, carried in a jug of steaming water, which she set down on the marble washstand.

"Go away," Annot sobbed. Looking up through tear-fringed lashes, she saw the maid. "Oh, it's thee. I thowt it were Mrs. de Lacy, come to tell me off again. I can't do nowt right for her, Rose. She hates me."

"Not at all, miss. She wants you to be more ladylike, that's all. Breaking bread into your soup just isn't done in polite company. She only drew your attention to it in order to help."

The maid's tight lips confirmed her own disapproval. Annot sat up, reaching for the hem of her elegant gown to wipe her tearstained face. Rose clicked her tongue and fetched an embroidered handkerchief from a drawer.

"Then she shouldn't a told me so in front of all t' others. She could a said it in private, but I think she enjoys making a fool of me. Dost know what she said tonight, after dinner as we sat by the fire? 'Reach for the pole screen over there, Annot.' I fetched what she were pointing at, a little embroiderd thing on a frame perched on t' top of a pole, and put it by her. 'No, it's for you, your face is so red,' she said. Now, what were that meant to mean? How were I to know that ladies put it in front of them, to shield their faces from the fire? I thowt she meant me to do some stitching on it, though it were all done so far as I could see. She tittered and looked at the gentlemen as much as to say what a fool I were. No wonder Dorian don't talk to me much now."

"She meant well," Rose reassured as she poured water into the bowl. "And Mr. Dorian is kept busy by his father over the mill. I'm sure you're exaggerating."

"I am not! They hate me, all of 'em! I think even Dorian's sorry he let 'imself in for marrying me now. They all want me out. It's my bairn they want, all to themselves, but they shan't have 'im. I'll die first."

"Now, come, there's no point in upsetting yourself, though it's common in your condition. Let me help you prepare for bed."

"I'm ready for bed."

"Not without a wash you aren't. Don't you know all polite people wash before bed?"

"There's too much fuss over washing and scenting and curling, if tha asks me. If they paid more heed to being nice to folk, they'd do better. There's no honesty or a mite of human kindness in any of 'em. I'd much rather be back wi' my own folk."

"And that's where you'll end up if you don't shape. Now, come." There was a hint of compassion in the maid's voice. Annot rose reluctantly to let Rose help her undress, but even as the gown was lifted over her head with some difficulty she was still murmuring.

"They hide me whenever any of their grand friends come. They're ashamed of me, but I could stand all their scorn if Dorian stood by me. But he's grown cold, Rose, I know it. He no longer seeks me out. He wants no more of me."

Rose made no answer. Annot lifted huge eyes to her, mutely begging her to deny it.

"He'll not wed me, I'm thinking. I'm nearing my time, but there's still no word of a wedding. If it's a lad I bear, happen he'll have me then, eh, Rose?"

The maid compressed her lips, unwilling to be drawn into voicing an opinion. As she went out, Annot sighed, splashed some water on her face from the bowl, and dried herself. In the voluminous folds of her lawn nightshift the telltale bulge was less conspicuous. Annot surveyed her reflection in the mirror thoughtfully, then seemed to make a decision.

As she took up the candle and went out, Fern's curiosity mounted. She followed the spectral figure along the corridor to where Annot was tapping on a door.

"Enter," Dorian's voice invited. Fern watched the girl rush to his bedside, where the young master, already nightshirted, was about to climb into bed. She too, like Annot, saw the unwelcoming surprise on his handsome face. He looked very young and rather ridiculous with his tasseled nightcap flopping over one ear.

"Annot! What are you doing here?"

116

"Aren't tha—you—glad to see me? You never come to my room now." Her arms were held out invitingly.

"It . . . it isn't proper," he blustered, flapping his hands in bewildered uncertainty.

Annot shrank back, rebuffed. "That's not what tha used to say, Dorian."

He drew himself up proudly. "Father has made me see reason. We must wait till we're married."

Large eyes rose hopefully. "When, Dorian? When will t' wedding be? The bairn'll be here afore we say us vows, if we wait much longer."

His eyes flickered away in embarrassment. "I don't know. When my parents decide, I suppose. But get back to bed now, Annot, or you'll catch cold. And listen—there's a step on the stairs. It could be Father! Go, Annot, go!"

"Shall I come to thee later?" she whispered at the doorway, her pointed little face still alight with hope.

"No, I don't want you here. Go, quickly."

But it was the coldness in his eyes that daunted her. Fern could see clearly the misery in Annot's face as she turned, rejected and forlorn, to leave. Fern stood aside in the doorway to allow her to pass, forgetful of the wraith's insubstance.

Back in the bedroom again, Fern lost sight of Annot. She climbed into bed, and once again time seemed to lose its rational course. The wail of a newborn child pierced the night air and faded; fluid figures came and coalesced and vanished. Sounds filled the air, voices lowered on a sob and voices raised in dispute. Through all the confusion Annot's wraithlike figure, now slender again and bowed, moved slowly.

Fern rose from her bed and followed the forlorn figure of Annot downstairs. In the parlor the De Lacy family sat in solemn conclave, Mr. de Lacy behind the table, Mrs. de Lacy seated apart with her back half-turned, and Dorian standing downcast and irresolute by the window. Another gentleman, middle-aged and portly, sat beside De Lacy, his pince-nez focused on the girl who entered.

Fern stood behind Annot and felt the girl's vulnerable misery. The looks bestowed on her were solemn, critical, and

117

inimical. It was evident a family conference had been in progress up to her entrance. Only De Lacy senior granted her a brief smile.

"We have again been discussing the position, Annot, and wish you to know what we have decided," the old man said gently. His wife darted him an impatient look before cutting in.

"It is settled. Dorian is to marry his cousin Sarah. Her father, Mr. Ramsden here, is in agreement."

The old gentleman nodded, and Annot's face burned angrily. "And what of me, and of my bairn? What of thy promises that Dorian would wed me?" she demanded.

"Now, come, my dear, you must have seen for yourself by now that it would never work. Your way of life and my son's are very different," De Lacy began to point out.

"Tha didn't seem to take much account o' that before!" Annot exploded. "But I'll not stay where I'm not welcome. I'll take t' baby and go in t' morning. That's if Dorian is of a mind wi' thee."

Her look of appeal met Dorian's silent back.

De Lacy stirred to speak, but his wife was too quick for him. "You can leave the child with us. You are not in a position to support him, and you know he will be well cared for here."

"Not I. He goes wi' me. I'm not given chance to see him now while t' nurse keeps him to herself, so there'd be precious little chance of me seeing 'im if I left 'im to thee. He's my son, and I'll keep 'im."

"Now, don't be rash, Annot. He'd have far more opportunities with us than with you."

"I know it, and I'm grateful for the offer, Mr. de Lacy, but he goes wi' me."

"Let's discuss that tomorrow. But in the meantime, be assured that you will not suffer. We shall see to it that you have a regular income, small but adequate, so that you do not starve."

"There's no need o' that, Mr. de Lacy. I'll not be pensioned off. If Dorian no longer wants me, I reckon I'm well shut of him. I wish Mr. Ramsden's daughter joy of him, 'cause I no longer want him."

Dorian's face, pink and sheepish, turned briefly from gazing at the blank windowpane. Annot turned to go, her head held high, ignoring the flutters of protest.

Fern, full of approval of the girl's proud independence, followed her out. They were a thoroughly nauseating lot, the De Lacys; a haughty, disdainful mother, a well-meaning but malleable husband, and a weak, selfish son. Annot was well rid of them all.

Satisfied voices were congratulating themselves in the parlor. Amalgamation between the De Lacys and the Ramsdens was undoubtedly to the mutual benefit of their trade, both families being woolen-mill owners. No wonder Mrs. de Lacy wore a complacent smile as Annot left, a disreputable potential daughter-in-law now happily replaced by a wealthy one.

"That bitch'll not have my William," Annot was muttering as she climbed the stairs. "That Sarah Ramsden can toil for an heir for 'em, they'll not have my son."

Determination jutting her little chin, Annot took a cloak from her bedroom and went along the corridor to a farther room. She opened the door softly. Over her shoulder Fern could see a candle burning on a side table, a great wicker cradle, the low fire in the fireplace encircled by a huge mesh fireguard, and beyond the chenille-covered table a cot where a nursery maid lay sleeping.

Annot advanced stealthily to the cradle and bent over it. Then, cautiously, she lifted the sleeping child and bundled him in one of the cradle blankets and crept to the door. The baby stirred and whimpered, but Annot laid a finger to his lips, which he began sucking noisily. The sleeping maid did not move.

Out of the house and away Annot sped, Fern following close. Down into the village the girl ran, holding the child close to her breast. At the cottage alongside the church she stopped, knocking at the door imperatively. After a moment Radley appeared in his nightshirt.

"Annot, lass, come in," he said in surprise.

119

"I've no time, Father. Take t' baby and ask me mam to get 'im out o' Brackenroyd. Take him to cousin Ida's i' York, or somewhere safe. The De Lacys won't 'ave him, tha mun see to that. Promise me."

"Aye, we will. But what of thee, lass?"

"Don't fret for me. But take care o' William. That's all I ask."

And just as suddenly as she came, she was gone. Fern could feel no breeze though she saw how the wind ruffled the churchyard trees, bending them like eerie figures in the moonlight. Annot, to her surprise, was directing her steps back toward the Hall.

To the lake, that's where she was heading. Fern, knowing the girl's destiny, shuddered fearfully but knew that she could not change what was to happen. The girl's footsteps left imprints in the frost-speckled grass as she walked purposefully through the copse of trees and down to the lake's edge. There she paused and looked back to the house; then, sighing deeply, she dropped her cloak on the lakeside and stepped slowly in. Fern watched, petrified. Powerless to change fate, she stood as Annot's small figure slowly receded, step by step. At last, long hair floating on the water, her head disappeared. No sound broke the silence. Save for a few bubbles on the surface and a forlorn cloak at the water's edge, there was no longer any trace of Annot Radley.

Fern felt sick, nauseated by the De Lacys' inhuman treatment of the poor girl, which had led to this final, irrevocable act. Tears gushed to her eyes, tears of anger and frustration. Then, through the tears she saw a figure on the far side of the pool, watchful and silent. It was a woman in white, pale and spectral, and as Fern looked at her, her anger changed to horror. It was no living creature, she knew instinctively, but some spirit who came to witness a Radley's humiliation, a being somehow connected with Annot—and with herself, for the figure looked at her from hollow eyes, filling her with terror.

Fern shivered violently, the sensation of a foglike substance invading her nostrils and lungs returning with terrifying insistence as it had once before, choking and menacing. In a crazy

120

sort of way Fern felt drawn to the creature, though she was repelled by her, and felt she could not resist walking around the lake toward the fearful thing. But before she could move her feet, the vision began to fade, slowly, like morning mist dissipated by dawn sunlight. As the last vestige disappeared, a dog's cry echoed distantly, its howl lingering faintly and charged with foreboding. Fern awoke suddenly, to find herself in bed, the blankets over her head, but she was shivering like one in an ague. What—or who—was the frightening figure in the dream who came to watch Annot die?

She could not wait to tell Bruno of this latest dream, of how Annot was driven to her death. He listened intently.

"Now the story is ended, will your preoccupation with your great-grandmother cease, I wonder?" he asked at length.

"It is done, Bruno. You can restore her picture, and the notes if you wish. But there is still something amiss. Would you—to please me—have Annot's grave opened?"

"Opened? Why?"

"I don't know. I just feel there is some final ... mishap, of some kind, to be put right."

"She cannot be buried in the churchyard, you know."

"I know."

He sighed deeply. "Very well. If that will put an end to your obsession, I agree."

He was so reasonable, so patient, that Fern could not bring herself to tell him of the other creature, the one whose presence was far more terrifying than ever Annot's had been. He would think her even more neurotic if she spoke of this new visitation, and since the wedding was so near, perhaps it would be best to keep silent. With luck she would dream no more.

Bruno's expression was puzzled that night at dinner. "I had the gardeners dig up Annot's grave today," he commented at last over dessert. "She is now reburied, close by, and I think you need fret for her no more."

Fern laid down her spoon. "Then there was something wrong. What was it, Bruno?"

"She had been buried face-downward. Why, I do not know,

but it seems your misgiving was not unfounded. Now I hope you will be content."

Fern smiled her gratitude, though inwardly she burned with anger. Not at Bruno, but at the inhumanity of the earlier De Lacys. Not content with humiliating and maltreating Annot, they had subjected her to this final indignity. No wonder the poor child's restless spirit had roamed here, pleading to be restored to face her Maker, though denied a churchyard grave. Poor Annot. Poor maid, rest in peace now, Fern thought. The Radleys will come into their own soon. After the wedding, a Radley will inherit what you and your son, William, were denied.

She looked across the table at Bruno. A smile lighted his dark eyes, for he knew he had pleased her by indulging her whim about the grave. She smiled back. Marriage to this man would have its pleasant side, after all.

Cassie was bubbling with excitement as she helped Fern prepare to go to church on Sunday morning. "Tha mun look thy best, miss, to go to t' spurrings," she said excitedly.

"Spurrings? What's that?" Fern asked.

"Why, when t' vicar calls t' banns for thy wedding. We call it spurrings."

And it seemed as if all the village showed Cassie's excitement, for the little gray-stone church was crowded. Word had evidently got about that De Lacy banns were being read. Pale spring sunlight flickered into the gloomy church interior through the high arched windows. It was God's benison on their union, Fern thought optimistically, as, led by Bruno's firm arm, she took her seat in the high-backed family pew. The brass plaque on the end of the pew announced "De Lacy" proudly, affirming it as the seat of honor of the family who gave the village its patronage and protection. Curious faces turned, unobtrusively, to survey Fern and her straight-backed escort, the glint of inquiry in the villagers' eyes belying their stolid expressions.

"If anyone knows of any impediment why these two should not be joined together in holy matrimony ..." Edgar Amos' voice intoned, and for a moment there was an interrogatory

122

silence. Fern half-expected the ghost of Annot to sidle from the shadows to upbraid the De Lacy who now sat in the family pew; then she dismissed the silly notion. Annot now lay content in her woodland grave.

Outside the church porch afterward Bruno stood in the sunlight and chatted amicably with a still-cassocked Amos. Fern smiled at the villagers as they filed out past the group, though no smile was vouchsafed her in return. Only a few desultory, assessing stares flickered over her and away. Two elderly ladies in Sunday bonnets stood, heads together, whispering.

"Every inch a Radley, that one."

"Not so loud, Emily. She'll hear."

"Better-looking, happen, and walks well. What's that tha says, Nellie?"

"Lower thy voice, love."

"She'll never hear. And there's a sight more she'll never hear an' all."

"How dost mean, Emily?"

"About t' other one. He'll never let on to her about t' other."

"What other, love? What's tha talking about?"

"Tha mean tha hasn't heard? Well, I never! Fancy thee not knowing about her! I thowt all t' village knew. Well, come on, else us roast'll be burnt up in t' oven."

They moved down toward the lych-gate, out of hearing, but Fern had overheard. What did they mean? Another woman? Did Bruno have another woman on his mind? Then was their marriage only to carry out old Thomas' will, after all?

Fern felt the hot rush of blood in her throat. She stared at Bruno furiously, resenting the calm way he chatted with Amos, as if all was well and straightforward. Was he too, like Dorian once before, simply toying with her while all the time he loved another? She must demand the truth from him just as soon as they were alone.

Fern could not wait until Sunday lunch was over. Angrily she told Bruno what she had overheard outside the church and demanded an explanation. Bruno smiled indulgently.

"Rubbish. You should know better than to eavesdrop on

123

old maids' gossip. There's no truth in it at all. Speculation such as that passes idle moments entertainingly for such as the old Misses Hirst. I daresay Emily was simply teasing Nellie, pretending she knew more than her sister, that's all. Now, let's talk of our wedding plans."

Mollified, and satisfied that he was speaking the truth, Fern entered into discussion of the ball for the guests and the ball for the tenants and millhands which was to follow on the next evening. Luke, Bruno told her, had agreed to give Fern away at the wedding service, and Fabia to act as her matron of honor.

"And Phoebe should be a bridesmaid too," Fern suggested.

Bruno shook his head. "She will not. We have asked her."

Fern was surprised. "Little girls usually welcome the opportunity to dress up. Why not?"

He shrugged his broad shoulders. "It seems she has not taken to you, for some reason."

"You mean she dislikes me. I feel it, and yet I don't know why, for I like her immensely."

"Feelings need not necessarily be mutual. If she does not feel warmly toward you, for whatever reason, it would be better to accept it and leave well alone."

So that was that. Phoebe would not be a bridesmaid, but Fern still felt hurt that she could not communicate her warm feelings to the child, though Phoebe showed her love of Bruno openly. Still, as Bruno advised, best wait and let matters take their course.

The ensuing weeks were fully occupied for Fern with visits to the dressmaker to order her trousseau, with Fabia's help in the choice of materials and patterns, and to the shoemaker and the haberdasher in Bradford. Choosing shoes reminded her of her promise to buy clogs for Phoebe.

"The village clogmaker has the pattern for Phoebe," Fabia told her, and it was while Fern stood in his tiny shop, flag-stoned and low-beamed, that she saw the beshawled village women putting their heads together and whispering while they waited for the clogmaker to heat up new irons. She feigned not to notice, watching instead the clogger's slow, sure movements as he sought among his cardboard patterns, and then, having found Phoebe's, he brought forward a sackful of wooden blocks, roughly shaped.

"What'll it be, miss? Sycamore dost fancy, or alder or beech? All on 'em's hard-wearing."

Fern looked at him in bewilderment and heard the women's snickers. The old man's leathery face watched her with a kindly enough expression. "What does Mrs. Armitage usually order?"

"Beech, as I remember." He selected a block and swept his stock knife along its length, nodding in satisfaction. "New leather for t' uppers shall it be, or mill leather?"

"Oh, new, of course." Again the women behind sniggered. The old man explained.

"I'm only asking, as most folks prefer leather from t' carding machines in t' mill. That's waterproof, dost see, having soaked up so much oil."

"Oh, I see. Then I'll have that, and thank you for explaining. How long will they take to make?"

He paused for thought, calculations wrinkling his weathered brow. "I'll have 'em on t' stithy this aft. Tha'll not be wanting brass toe caps, I take it. Metal clips on tomorrow, and then t' irons; say Friday morning. Will that suit?"

Fern was glad to escape the little shop with its clutter of knives and benches, tanning horse and rollers, and array of metal and gas brackets. It was not its smoky closeness but the mocking smiles of the women she wanted to flee. They ridiculed her for her ignorance of what was vital to them; but why did she fear them instead of trying to befriend them? Their faces, gaunt from struggle and worry, wore distinctly hostile looks. And she had clearly heard the name Radley spat out in a tone of scorn and hatred as she left.

Chapter 9

Fern gazed out of her bedroom window, her heart seeming to knot with excitement. It was her wedding day. The first faint glow of morning sunlight was blushing through the fine veil of mist that blanketed the river, and the very air seemed to hold out a promise of fine weather. With luck the sun would shine on her nuptials, an omen of happiness and joy.

Already Brackenroyd Hall had taken on a festive air, groomed for the day. The dining room and the library had been decorated with hundreds of wax candles in silver sconces and in the chandeliers, mirrors gleamed in every alcove and recess to reflect their glow, and garlands of flowers hung from every vantage point. Tonight the ladies and gentlemen would dine and dance here in honor of the master of Brackenroyd's wedding. The servants, now greatly increased in number for the event, hurried busily about their duties in preparation; from below, Fern could hear their laughter and the clatter of dishes. A wedding had brought Brackenroyd Hall to life again, revived it to the bustle and joyful activity it had needed.

Gone now was its former gloom and silence. With its new-found activity Fern had felt her own spirits lift over the past week. Annot's memory now lay at peace, no longer troubling her sleep, and if Fern felt an uneasy twinge on recollecting the other, shadowy figure, she brushed it quickly aside. Of late no more dreams had troubled her. Sleep had been deep and restful. And after today, her nights should be always content and secure, with Bruno at her side.

She smiled to herself as she thought of the room she had had prepared for their bridal chamber, a grander and more spacious room than the one where she had slept hitherto. The finest tester bed in the house, with its fluted pillows and laven-der-scented hangings and coverlet, now stood there awaiting them, Persian rugs on the floor, chairs upholstered in gold satin, and tawny velvet curtains at the high windows. On the walnut dressing table candles in silver candlesticks waited to light their wedding night, glittering on the cut-glass bottles and pierced silver trays. Scented winter roses and hothouse hyacinths would make the chamber fragrant. The cheval mirror, supported by two gilt cupids, would reflect their union.

Her reverie was interrupted by an excited tapping at the door. She turned as Cassie entered, her eyes glowing and wisps of fair hair escaping from beneath her cap.

"We're fair throng down in t' kitchen, miss, wi' so much still to be done, but I were dying to see t' wedding dress, so Mrs. Thorpe said I could come and take a peek, so long as I didn't touch. That's if you didn't mind, she said."

Her mistress smiled, and crossing to the bed, she lifted the swaths of tissue which protected the creation. Fanny, as the superior maid, had been appointed lady's maid and would no doubt be vexed if she heard Cassie had been allowed to touch the gown. Nevertheless, Cassie's fingers stretched out despite herself as she cried out in admiration.

"Oh! It's beautiful! It's lovely! You'll be the bonniest bride t' village has ever seen!"

And indeed it was. Yards of creamy damask clustered over a satin undergown, the overskirt lavishly trimmed with cream lace, the bodice demurely high-necked and tucked. Fern declined to notice Cassie's work-roughened fingertips as she caressed the luxurious folds.

"And here is the cap I am to wear also," Fern said, turning to lift from the dressing table the little cream bonnet of silk, again trimmed with the lace and scattered with feathers. Cassie's fingers flew to her mouth in breathless admiration. Her sighs and squeals of delight were immensely satisfying to the bride. A light tap on the door preceded Fanny's entrance.

"Heavens above!" the maid exclaimed in horror. "What *are* you doing, Cassie?"

"It's all right, Fanny," Fern reassured her. "Go now, Cassie, back to your duties. Soon the dressmaker will be here, and she and Fanny will dress me. You shall see me before I leave for the church, I promise."

Madam Fixby, the dressmaker from Bradford, and Fanny were deft and sure in their buttoning and pinning, repinning and final stitching, but as they grew more and more excited as time passed, Fern felt herself growing oddly more detached from the frenzy. Bruno too would now be preparing to go to church, down in Luke Armitage's little schoolhouse. He had driven down early this morning while Fern was still in bed, leaving word that he would send Fabia back up to the Hall in the coach. The next time Fern would see him would be before the altar, where he and she were to plight their vows of constancy and love. . . .

Fabia arrived, aglow with excitement and more attractive than Fern had ever seen her in the new gown of palest blue silk Fern had chosen. Fabia leaned against the doorjamb, breathless in admiration.

"Oh, Fern, you look beautiful!" Fern looked at the reflection in the pier glass. Indeed, the froth of lace, the creamy luster of the damask, needed no enhancement with jewelry. The demure cap nestling on her piled gold hair was truly becoming. She felt as radiant as a bride should.

She picked up the little white Bible she had elected to carry, and cast a final look about the chaotic bedroom before she left. No more would she return to this room at night alone, a maiden, vulnerable and helpless. No more a prey to irrational dreams born of apprehension. By tonight she would be a wife. Bruno's wife. The thought was a very pleasant one.

Luke was waiting in the vestibule, and Fern warmed to the glow of admiration in his eyes as he helped her and Fabia into the coach. The sun, which had slipped briefly behind the clouds as they rode, burst out again magically as they drew up at the church, lighting its old gray stones and the few curious onlookers who clustered at the lych-gate.

As in a dream Fern let Luke take her arm and lead her into the gloom of the church. The pews were crowded, but Fern noticed no one but the tall breadth of the man who waited by the foot of the altar steps. His back, powerful and solid, made her surge with an emotion she could not define, save that it was a most pleasurable sensation. Edgar Amos, standing a head taller than Bruno at the top of the steps, seemed like a haloed saint where the sunlight from the high windows caught and held his sandy head. The whole scene was unreal to Fern, a tableau whose characters were but life-less puppets.

But music played, and Amos spoke. Fern heard her own voice speak words, and Bruno too, and then they were turning to go. Bruno's hand cupped her elbow, and slowly, slowly they were moving out. In Fern's ears rang the sound of Amos' voice.

"I now pronounce you man and wife."

So it was done. Now at last she was Mrs. de Lacy and mistress of Brackenroyd. Now nothing could ever take that away from her. She glanced up at Bruno, saw his stern, strong profile as he looked straight ahead, and was happy. A fine match indeed, as the old lawyer Lennox had said. Handsome, clever, rich—what more could one want of a husband?

Respect, perhaps; love, even? Well, that would come. There was all the time in the world now to win his esteem and affection. Fern bowed her head graciously to the villagers, acknowledging their cries, but whether the sounds were of affectionate congratulation or simply grudging admiration at the sight of a personable couple, one could not tell. Still, there was time enough too to win the villagers.

Bruno had never been more charming than tonight, she reflected later as their guests swarmed about the Hall, raising their glasses in toast to a lovely bride and exclaiming at Bruno's good fortune.

"Damn pretty wife you've got yourself," Fern heard one grudgingly admiring millowner remark to Bruno, his own jaded wife prattling incessantly to her daughter nearby.

"Indeed," Bruno rejoined, smiling at her proudly. Serenely Fern moved among her guests, poised and self-assured, smiling contentedly with her attentive husband at her side.

"Your wife adds grace and beauty to the Hall," Sir George Radborne commented to Bruno as he twisted the tips of his waxed moustache appreciatively. His lady wife bowed her head graciously in agreement. "An excellent mistress for Brackenroyd," Sir George added speculatively.

Bruno guided Fern through the throng of guests, introducing them to her with the utmost charm.

"I should like you to meet Dr. Briggs," he said, pausing to bow to an elderly bewhiskered gentleman, who rose, putting aside his wineglass to bow over Fern's fingers.

"Charmed, my dear. Brackenroyd must count itself favored to have acquired a mistress as delightful as yourself. May I present my wife?"

He indicated a fragile-looking lady seated on the velvet sofa, who bowed and inclined her head. Dr. Briggs murmured in Fern's ear, "Forgive her that she does not rise to meet you, Mrs. de Lacy, but I fear she is none too well. A bad chest, you know. But she was determined to come to your wedding."

"I am honored, Dr. Briggs."

"But if you would permit us, I must take her home very soon. You see how her color is mounting."

Indeed the lady did seem rather flushed and unduly bright about the eyes. Fern was at once concerned for her.

"You must take her in the carriage, Dr. Briggs. I shall ask Bruno to instruct Malachi to bring it around at once."

Bruno was quick to understand and act. Swiftly and unobtrusively Dr. Briggs and his wife left the reception, the doctor promising to send word of his wife's welfare in the morning.

130

The other guests, unaware of the lady's indisposition, continued their toasting and merrymaking throughout the evening. Fern was amazed how the mountains of food laid out on buffet tables, the legs of beef and mutton, the eggs and spring chicken and pigeon and game pies, seemed to disappear with bewildering swiftness. But it was warming to hear the lively chatter to the background of music.

"A governess, did you say?"

The shrill voice, raised in disbelief, cut through the general hum of conversation with the sharpness of a whip crack. Fern involuntarily turned toward the voice. A gaunt-faced woman, sparkling in diamonds and velvet, stood openmouthed as she interrogated her companion. Bruno touched Fern's elbow lightly and steered her away.

Fern tugged her arm free, her cheeks flushed with embarrassment, but before she could utter a word of protest, Bruno forestalled her.

"I know what you would say. But she is of no account and not worth the trouble to argue with. She is a snob."

"But one of your friends, I presume, since you invited her," Fern argued. "She does not think me worthy of you—or of Brackenroyd."

"She is no friend of mine. Simply the wife of one of the local magistrates, and since I invited most of the local dignitaries, she was included. Henceforth she will not be on our visiting list. Come, let us have a glass of champagne. I have not yet toasted my lovely bride."

Unresistingly, Fern let him lead her to the table. Despite her cheeks still flaming with anger, she felt warmed by his protectiveness. He raised his glass, his eyes resting on her over the rim.

"To you, Fern, the loveliest mistress Brackenroyd has ever known. May you find much happiness here."

"And you," Fern whispered. Bruno, inclining his head, kissed her lightly but lingeringly on the cheek. Fern's day of happiness was complete.

Carriages had been ordered for midnight, but by the time the last laughing guests had made their final congratulations

131

and farewells, the grandfather clock in the hall was preparing to strike one. Fern hung happily on her husband's arm, smiling and radiant. The footman closed the door behind the last guest.

"Shall I lock up now, sir?"

"Yes. It is time for bed. Come, Fern."

Together they mounted the wide, shallow staircase, Fern bemused with contentment. At the doorway to their bedroom, Bruno paused, opened the door, and stood back.

"Go now and sleep well, Fern. Tomorrow will be another busy day."

She looked up at him, startled. It was difficult to read from his expression just what he meant.

"Aren't you coming to bed?"

He shook his head, his eyes no longer alight, but dulled, as if with fatigue or worry.

"I have matters to attend to. It will be late before I retire, and I would not wish to disturb you. I shall sleep next door."

Fern stared, unable to hide the hurt, the disappointment in her eyes. His expression softened.

"Tomorrow we must tour all the tenant farms, to receive their congratulations, as is the custom. And in the evening we must attend the tenants' ball. You need to rest well and be re-freshed. Good night, Fern."

Abruptly he turned and left her, and hesitantly Fern went into the room she had prepared so lovingly. Fanny came, her pretty face now looking rather weary and hollow-eyed.

"Go to bed, Fanny. I can undress myself," Fern said. "Wake me early in the morning."

Alone again, Fern sat miserably on the bed, fingering its fine coverlet. How ironic for a new bride to be left to sleep alone, even if there was a door connecting her bedroom to the one where Bruno was to sleep. She rose and crossed to the door. From beyond she could hear his footsteps as he paced the parquet floor. Why had he left her alone? Surely not to work on his papers—was there some other reason he would not reveal?

Perhaps he sensed she had married him only for Brackenroyd. Or perhaps he loved another woman, as the two old sisters at the church had implied. Maybe he was tormenting her by his changeable ways, appearing affectionate one moment and cold the next, so as to confuse her. But why?

Fern turned away from the connecting door. She was not going to open it and beg his company. Slowly she undressed and prepared for bed. The sprigged dimity nightgown, specially bought for tonight, had somehow lost its charm, and as Fern hung her magnificent wedding dress away in the closet, she sighed ruefully. Bruno might be trying to teach her a disciplinary lesson in denying her his company tonight, but nothing could alter the fact that she was now rightfully and truly mistress of Brackenroyd. Nothing could take that away from her.

She lay in the great canopied bed, trying to find pleasure in planning what she could now do. Now she could alter or refurnish the Hall, now she could insist on taking a share in the responsibility of running the mill and the estate; but somehow these speculations brought less joy than she had anticipated. Somehow it seemed barren joy without company. The room grew chill as the fire burned low, and Fern felt lonely.

As the firelight dimmed and the room grew dark, Fern began to shiver. It was strangely, unaccountably cold. And the chill had a damp feel to it, clinging and unpleasant. She huddled lower among the blankets and closed her eyes tightly, willing sleep to come. But as her mind began to dull into the half-world between waking and sleeping, the damp chill seemed to grow into an insidious fog, wreathing its way into her nostrils and clamming her throat. Fern gasped for air, moaning.

"No, no, I don't want you!"

Recollection returned. Once before she had experienced this strange sense as she waited to see Annot's story reenacted. And then, as now, she had rejected the horrifying vapor that had threatened to invade her. Why did she fear the miasma so? Was it because its cold, clammy sensation made one think of death?

Terrified, Fern rolled out of bed and stumbled across the

133

room to the connecting door. There, her hand on the knob and her mouth already open to cry out Bruno's name, she paused.

It was the feel of death; she was certain of it. And yet, in some strange way the sensation was not one of menace. It was more of pleading, of entreaty. She had longed for company—but of the living, not the dead. But if it were the dead who came so persistently and urgently, there must be a reason. She had upheld, had she not, the power of the past even in the face of Bruno's scorn?

Fern made a momentous decision. She would fight the pervasive power no longer. Purposefully she climbed back into the great bed and lay back, relaxing the tension in her muscles and consciously baring her mind of antagonism. Brackenroyd held a strange, secretive air of past tragedy, part of which she had learned in Annot's story, but there was more that still haunted the gloomy old mansion, and its power would not be broken until the truth was known.

The chilly sensation returned, more slowly and insidiously now, less clamorous than before, as though it was aware of her new compliance. And this time as the haze filled her nostrils and throat it no longer brought with it the terror she had felt before. Closing her eyes and breathing slowly, Fern gave herself up completely to the invading mist, feeling it seep and spread throughout her body. A dizzying sensation made her mind reel; she felt as though she were spinning through a vortex, wheeling through space and losing count of time, being sucked down, down, through a black void.

Later, aeons later, it seemed, the strange sensations eddied and died away, and Fern lay bemused, her eyes still closed. When she opened them at last, it did not seem at all strange to find herself lying, not in the huge tester bed, but amid the long grass at the edge of a cornfield. She stared up at the deep azure sky above where the birds swooped and sang, and felt inexpressibly content. Leaning up on her elbow, she gazed downhill where the village lay, peaceful and broodily content in the summer sun. She had better return home before Mother grew angry at her absence.

Brushing the flecks of grass from her cotton skirts and gathering up the basket of eggs beside her, she began to descend the little track that ran down between the fields of ripening wheat and oats, noting as she did the thin, poor quality of the crops this year. Frost in May followed by the long drought in June had rotted many of the fields already; pray heaven the weather would not turn wet before harvest, or there would be little bread in the village again this winter.

In Brackenroyd's main street she passed a number of her neighbors, women outside their cottage doors busily plucking a chicken for the evening meal when their menfolk returned from the fields, or fetching their washing in from where it hung over fragrant rosemary bushes to dry. They all smiled or waved a greeting as she passed. At the gate of her home, right next to the little gray church, she turned in. Of course, Mother was at market today. The cottage would still be empty.

She dawdled in the garden, savoring the scent of Mother's treasured sweet briar roses from which she made her own toilet water and metheglin, admiring the tumble of honeysuckle framing the doorway. She loved the flowers in the little garden, the violets and gillyflowers, the marigolds and primroses, but not half so tenderly as she nurtured her own little plot of herbs in one corner.

Mother had been quick to spot her daughter's clever ways with herbs, years ago, and she had seen to it that the girl learned the arts of making simples and recipes from old Mother Uttley, whose wisdom and knowledge of cures for ills was known far and wide. Mother Uttley, her myopic old eyes peering closely but not unkindly as she supervised, had taught the little maid all she knew, and the girl was grateful that there was one skill she could now perform well.

The fragrance of her own plot filled her nostrils. Lavender, alive with humming bees, vied with sage and rosemary. Rosemary—dew of the sea, the curate had said it meant. What a beautiful name. Marjoram, sweet-scented geranium, its leaves smelling of mint; clove gillyflowers—all had their part in her life, either to preserve and make into jelly like the violets, or

135

to candy, like the rose-petals, or to form essential ingredients in her simples and compounds for treating afflictions such as the cough or a bellyache. Even her family, who considered her inept and slow at all else, acknowledged her now as a mistress of the art of making potions. The whole village found occasion to seek her help from time to time, and she was glad. No written recipes did she keep of her mixtures, nor did she use Culpeper's herbal, like they said Mistress de Lacy did up at the Hall—before she died, that was, God rest her soul—for she could neither read nor write, but she was proud of her one skill nonetheless.

Unlatching the cottage door, she went down the two steps into the flagstone-floored parlor. The fire was burning low, and she replenished it with firewood to keep the iron stewpot slung over it still at a simmer. Pulling off her white-linen cap, she let her hair fall about her shoulders, savoring the aroma of meat in the pot mingled with the scent of the herbs hung in clusters on the low beams. She seated herself on the high-backed bench, and as she did so, a marmalade cat crawled out from beneath, stretching her four paws delicately.

"Come, Tibb," murmured the girl. The cat leaped obediently onto her lap, kneading her knees with its paws before circling around and around and settling itself to sleep. It was a cozy room, wooden platters on the dresser nestling cheek by jowl with jugs of creamy milk and ale, pieces of salt pork hanging from hooks against the whitewashed walls, a leather bucket of water by the door, fresh-drawn from the spring.

The girl shifted the unwilling cat from her lap. As she lifted the basket of brown eggs from the floor and placed it on the oak table, a knock came at the door. A woman's flushed face peered around the edge.

"Oh, tha's come home. I'm that glad, as I wanted thee to make a salve for me, if tha would."

The girl indicated the high-backed bench by the window, and the woman eased her bulk gratefully onto it.

"It's our Will, he has a bad rash on his face, that spotty he won't go out. Canst make us an ointment that'll clear it? I've no wish to pay good pence to t' apothecary if tha can help.

He's starting to pick at them spots, he'll not leave the scabs alone. I fear he'll end up badly pockmarked, and it'd be a shame, such a good-looking lad."

He was quite handsome, the girl reflected as she took pots and jars from the press and took down the pestle and mortar from the dresser. But too vain for a fieldworker, though perhaps all youths were self-conscious of their looks. Will was ... what? Seventeen? Four or five years younger than herself, but already the focus of many a Brackenroyd lass's eye. Swiftly she pounded, milfoil and bugle, samile and a dash of wine, while the woman's eyes roved curiously around the parlor, missing nothing.

Strange, thought the girl, but people always seem to treat those with a disability as if they were simple or even weren't there. But perhaps it was not surprising, in the circumstances.

The door opened again, and a pretty girl entered, her dark eyes darting quickly from the girl to the woman.

"Oh, Phoebe, I just came to ask thy sister to make me a salve for Will," the woman said quickly, as though to explain her presence. The girl at the table looked up and met her sister's gaze. There was in Phoebe's eyes the hostile look, the guarded, distrustful look which had always been there.

"Oh, aye, that's all she's fit for."

The girl continued to pound in silence, as though she had not heard. The woman took it as a cue.

"Poor thing," she clucked, shaking her head sadly. "She's allus been a bit queer, hasn't she? Such a shame, thy mother being such a good woman an' all, to be burdened wi' a simpleton. Still, she has thee, and that's a blessing, Phoebe. Yon poor lass'll never get herself a husband, I'm thinking, but I doubt tha'll have any trouble in that direction."

Phoebe's smile was sardonic. "She's not so daft as she makes out, that one. She's sly, she is. Many folk mistake her quiet ways for gentleness or madness, but she's all there, if I'm not mistaken."

"Aye, well, thy mother dotes on her, and that's a fact. But folk often do favor the runt of a litter. Dost recall Mistress Sykes and her little clubfooted, squint-eyed lad? She near

137

died of a broken heart when he died, and he one of eleven too."

The girl never raised her eyes while they spoke across her, nor did she feel rancor at their words. It was true her mother was fond of her, and would be as fond of Phoebe if her sister's tongue was less vicious and hurtful. But why did folk always behave thus, shouting to poor old blind Hawthorne as if he were stone deaf instead of acutely sharp-eared, and talking of her in her presence as though she were a stone statue instead of only short of the one faculty?

She scraped the greasy unguent out of the mortar and scooped it into a little pot. The woman stopped prattling and came to take it from her.

"Thanks, love. Is our Will to put this on his face . . . tonight? Every night?"

The girl nodded vigorously. The woman turned to Phoebe. "Pity though, isn't it? She's a bonny lass, and very capable wi' her herbs and things. Pity she's not right." She tapped her forehead significantly.

None of the women had noticed the door open, nor the kindly faced woman in the doorway whose expression darkened as she overheard. They all started when she spoke, quietly but emphatically.

"My daughter is perfectly well, mistress, neither simple nor to be pitied. She is a gentle, well-behaved, and dutiful child, and a blessing to us all."

The visitor flushed. "I'm sorry, Mistress Radley, I'd no wish to offend thee. I were simply sorry for thee, one daughter so bright and clever, and the other—"

"The other just as clever, just as beloved, but the good Lord chose, for what reason we cannot tell, to keep her silent. That's all that ails the child, mistress, and I'd thank you to remember it."

Snatching up the pot of salve, the neighbor fled, her stammering protests silenced by Mistress Radley's firm manner. The mother stood by the door after she had gone, surveying her two daughters.

"I'll never know why it was the Lord chose to grant me just

the two daughters, the one who chatters overmuch and the other who has never spoken a word."

Phoebe turned and began to take down the plates from the dresser, while her sister cleared the table of her herbs.

"But I know this," Mistress Radley continued in a gentle tone. "I love thee both greatly, and I wouldn't have either of thee otherwise. Now, come, sharp about it, or thy father'll be home afore we've his supper ready."

Father came home from the fields, work-weary and aching, when the sun sank too low for work to continue. But despite his weariness, he found time to commend his wife and daughters for their care and concern for him.

"I'm a lucky man, wife," he grunted as he pushed his chair back from the table, patting his replete stomach in satisfaction. "Never had man a comelier nor a more capable wife, nor two bonnier lasses. I'll wager not King Charles himself is better cared for nor I am."

Mistress Radley chuckled softly. "That's true, husband. I'll wager Queen Henrietta Maria never made her husband a down mattress such as I made, or if she did, it were no softer nor warmer."

Phoebe yawned and said she was going to bed. Her sister sat by the fire, mending a rent in her homespun green kirtle. Her mother put the last of the platters away on the dresser, lit a tallow candle from the fire, and touched the girl's shoulder.

"Come, Catherine. Time for bed, lass, if tha's to be up early in t' morning."

Obediently she rose and put the mending aside. In the bedroom she undressed quickly in the dark so as not to disturb Phoebe, and climbed into bed alongside her. In the gloom she heard her sister mutter, "I wonder what goes on in thy mind, Catherine? I've seen that look in thy eye—tha's hiding summat, I know it. But what's the use of asking thee what it is—tha couldn't tell me."

Catherine lay back, smiling to herself in the darkness. Phoebe rolled over and propped herself up on her elbow.

"But I wish I knew what it were. Is it a lad, Kate? Hast thee a lad?"

Catherine closed her eyes, and Phoebe fell back with a sigh.

"What use if you had?" Phoebe grumbled on. "He couldn't get a word out of thee, no one can. No, it can't be a sweetheart, for who'd find joy in a dumb puppet? I would to heaven I knew what went on i' that head o' thine. I know one thing—tha's not daft, as the villagers all think. Tha's cunning, more like, knowing far more than folks think. What more didst learn from Mother Uttley, Kate? Did she learn thee how to make cows miscarry, or women even? Did she learn thee any spells?"

Catherine shook her head firmly, but Phoebe was growing excited with the idea.

"Tha can cure warts, and wi'out touching them who has the warts, too. Wouldn't it be just as easy to cure or harm someone else wi'out touching them, wi'out being near them, even? Was it you made Mistress Banforth miscarry last spring?"

Catherine sprang up, shaking with denial; she had no words to utter. She could hear Phoebe's laugh.

"Tha could have done it, Kate, for she beat thee in the contest for baking a cake at the fair. Tha were ill-pleased, I recall. But I didn't think as tha had the power to get thy revenge. Well, I never. Tha's in a fair way to becoming a witch, I'm thinking, after Mother Uttley's learning thee."

Catherine's fierce desire to deny the vile charge burst into anger. Involuntarily her hand rose, and she cracked it across Phoebe's cheek. Phoebe swore and grabbed at her hair, and the tussle would undoubtedly have become a fight if their mother had not entered to bid them good night.

In the darkness after she had gone, Phoebe burrowed down under the rough woolen blanket, muttering as she did, "Tha'd better take care, that's all I can say, Catherine Radley, if ever the witchfinder comes this way. He'll find thee out for certain."

Catherine turned to face away from her, trying to rid her heart of the dreadful feeling she had toward her sister. It was not charitable to hate, but Phoebe was so cruelly provoking. She must try to pray, to become calm and forget the hurtful lies, to realize it was difficult for anyone to understand when she was unable to tell them anything.

Phoebe had been so far from the truth in her wild guesses about her ability to cast spells, and yet so near the truth. She had seen something in Catherine's eyes which had betrayed her secret. Catherine's anger melted instantly as she remembered. It was difficult to keep the light out of her eye, the bounce from her step, when she felt so happy.

But she would hug her secret to herself for some time longer yet—how could she do else, when she had no voice to reveal her confidence? People would just have to guess at the reason for her happiness, and it was odd that Phoebe had been so quick to guess aright.

It *was* a lad—a man, rather. She had been up in the copse gathering firewood when he found her, and he had addressed her politely and with a warm smile that creased the corners of his eyes. He had taken her silence for maidenly modesty and been the more charmed, she could tell, and without invitation he had gathered and bound the wood for her, bidding her sit and rest on a fallen tree trunk while he did so.

"What is your name?" he had asked at last when she made to go. Shaking her head, she had turned and moved to the edge of the clearing. "No, wait, tell me," he had ordered, and there was urgency in his voice. "Then I shall find out for myself," he had said, following her to the edge of the wood. Then she had turned frightened eyes on him, fearful lest he accompany her into the village and set idle tongues wagging. He had grasped her wrist, sensing her fear.

"Do not fret, I shall not embarrass you. But I did not know Brackenroyd held so fair a maid, and now I have seen you, I must know more of you. Will you tell me who you are?"

Shaking her head, she had run down the crags, stumbling under the bulky weight of the firewood, hearing his voice behind her on the wind. "I shall find you, little one. And discover your name. We shall meet again."

Breathlessly she had fallen at last by the edge of the cornfield, hidden in the long grass. And there she had lain until it was time to go home, finding pleasure in recalling the deep timbre of his voice and the laughter lines about his dark eyes. And finding pleasure in knowing that he had found her desirable. She was certain she would see him again, for there was determination in his laughing words. There was a strength, a purposefulness about the handsome young man that made it inevitable.

He did not know her name. It was odd to realize now, in the stillness of the night alongside Phoebe's snoring figure, that neither did she know his. Everyone knew everyone in Brackenroyd, but he was a stranger, no common fieldworker or weaver. Strangely, she had not until this moment questioned who he was, but simply accepted his arrival in her life as inevitable. He was here, they would meet again, and he would still desire her.

A roseate cloud of happiness settled over Catherine as she neared the edge of sleep. Then, just on the brink, she started back into wakefulness. Somewhere out in the night a dog was howling pathetically at the moon, and in that instant she knew. With a sudden flash of insight she foresaw that the supreme happiness that would come with this dark stranger would be shattered at its zenith by the hand of death. It was to come. It was inevitable. Gabriel's hounds had sounded the knell.

Chapter 10

She opened her eyes, trying to banish the stab of apprehension and the prevision of tragedy brought on by the dog's cry. She stared about her in confusion. Dawn glimmered through a high leaded window, not a narrow cottage slit, illuminating a bedchamber of great beauty and taste. No Phoebe snored by her side; there were only the luxurious brocade hangings of the great bed.

It took some moments to orient herself. She was Fern, not Catherine. Fern Saxby, or rather Fern de Lacy now. And yet it was difficult to accept. But a few moments ago, it seemed, she had been simmering with frustration, yearning to deny Phoebe's accusations, and trying to quell her anger with thoughts of the man in the copse.

The man. Fern sat upright, startled. He had been the image of Bruno, tall and powerful of build, piercingly dark-eyed and black-haired. The same aquiline nose and dignity of bearing, he had been Bruno to the life, save that his was a kindlier, gentler expression. Was it all a dream, then, where Bruno, the last person in her thoughts before she slept, had played so prominent a part? Was it all a dream of wishful thinking, Bruno transformed to the sympathetic, understanding man she would like him to be?

It could not be. In the half-light of dawn she still felt more of Catherine in her than Fern, could still feel the mute girl's dismay and frustration. And she remembered the sensations of last night as she yearned for company and that dank, cold chill had enveloped her. It had been no dream. Catherine had come back, had possessed her body.

Hesitantly she rose from the bed, reaching for her dressing robe, half-minded to pursue her day normally as Fern and yet half-reluctant to dismiss the gentle Catherine. It was a hard choice to make.

"Bruno."

She had spoken his name before she was aware of it, and reproached herself inwardly. There was no need to call on his advice, for he would dismiss her silly dreams as yet more evidence of her instability. Nevertheless, she crossed to the connecting door.

"Bruno?"

There was no answer. Fern tried the handle, but the door would not yield. It was locked. Angrily she turned away. How foolish to think of approaching him when he was obviously so determined to keep her at arm's length.

Footsteps approached. It would be Fanny with early-morning tea, or possibly Cassie with jugs of hot water. Fern opened her bedroom door and saw Fanny, tray in hand.

"Put my tea down here, Fanny, and I'll take the master's in to him."

She ignored the girl's inquiring glance, taking from her the tray with its china pot and cream jug and the pretty patterned cup and saucer, and watched her set down the other tray on her nightstand.

Fern followed her into the corridor and waited till the maid had retreated downstairs, then tapped at Bruno's door. When no answer came, she entered quietly. Bruno lay sprawled, fully dressed and fast asleep, in a chair by the fire. But it was not the fact that he was dressed that startled her, but that his bed was still neatly turned back awaiting its occupant. He had not been to bed at all, and what was more, his breeches were mud-spattered, mud-caked riding boots lay on the hearth rug before him, and he still clasped a riding whip in his hand. Asleep, he looked vulnerable and carefree. Fern felt a maternal glow of affection and pride.

"Bruno, are you awake?"

She spoke softly, but he awoke at once, his sunny sleeping expression retreating rapidly into a clouded, suspicious look. He half-raised the whip in his hand before he mastered himself; then he dropped it to the floor and raised his arms to her. Fern would have run to them had not the tray in her hands impeded her. Slowly he lowered his arms and shook his head slowly, like one who has drunk too heavily the night before.

"God, what a night," he muttered hoarsely. "Such dreams, such nightmares."

Fern bit her lip, reluctant to speak of her own visions, but she saw the opportunity to score off him.

"Dreams are for those with a problem, you tell me, for those who have not yet found themselves."

He looked up sharply, his eyes glowing under their bushy brows. "And you think I have no problems? Did you in your sublime innocence believe you had the sole monopoly of problems? I too have mine, wife, and you are not the least among them."

His voice was so venomous, so full of spite and scorn, that Fern shrank. She banged the tray down sharply on the table beside him and rushed from the room, fuming with anger. How could one please such a man! He was cruel, unpredictable, and vicious! In his sleep he had looked so defenseless and human that she had been induced to feel a warmth for him she had not believed possible, but with a few malicious words he had killed off that feeling at birth. She felt cheated.

He appeared later in the dining room for breakfast, having changed now from his mud-stained clothes into a Norfolk tweed suit, but he still looked perhaps a trifle paler than usual, she thought. He ate morosely and with diffidence. Fern began to feel concerned; perhaps he was not well.

"Did you not sleep well last night, Bruno?"

"Why do you ask?" The words were sharp, brittle, and defensive.

"I noticed your bed had not been slept in. Did you ride out early this morning?"

"I did not. I rode all night. But I would prefer, madam, that you do not question me. What I do is my own affair and none of yours."

Fern was stung beyond endurance. It was useless to feel concern for this insufferable man. "Very well," she replied in level tones that belied the tumult inside her, "I concede that your affairs are private, and I claim the same right for myself. Henceforth I will not confide in you, nor expect you to do so in me. Is that how you would like it?"

He shrugged his shoulders. "As you will; it is of little interest to me. You have all you wanted now. You are mistress of Brackenroyd."

"You are right." She knew her eyes flashed fire and hoped he would register the extent of her anger and determination. "Quite right, I have all I want in Brackenroyd. It is mine now, equally with you, and no one can take it from me."

"No one but death," he countered quietly, and Fern felt the heat in her blood die into a chill. Death, he said. For a second or two she lay once again in a narrow truckle bed alongside Phoebe, feeling the threat of death overshadowing her happiness. With a wrench she returned to the dining table. Laying aside her damask napkin, she rose.

"Are we still to ride around the tenant farms this morning, as we planned?" she asked coldly.

"No need for you to go," he answered with indifference. "I shall say you are indisposed but that you will attend the tenants' ball this evening."

"As you will," Fern said, and swept back the heavy portiere that covered the doors. Outside she regretted letting him dictate the morning's program. Perhaps it was intentional to keep her from meeting the farmers this morning, to keep alive the locals' evident distrust of her. She would have done better to insist on going, to make their acquaintance and begin to break down resistance. In future she must take care to evaluate Bruno's schemes more carefully.

But there was still the ball tonight. There was still chance to befriend the farmers and start to win them over. And Edgar Amos would be there, so she would have one ally.

Oddly enough, Fanny came into the kitchen, where Fern was discussing the fare for the ball with Mrs. Thorpe, to announce that Reverend Amos was abovestairs.

"He said he called only to leave a message, but I thought perhaps you might like to be at home to the reverend, madam."

"Quite right, Fanny. Bid him sit in the parlor a moment. I shall come directly."

Amos rose quickly as she entered, and she could see that his keen eyes had noted something amiss, the way his sandy eyebrows twitched as though to rise in question before deciding it would be impolite. Calmly she bade him be seated again.

"I hope you will forgive my intrusion on the very first day of your wedded life," the vicar said. "I came really only to apologize, since I fear I shall not be able to come this evening. A sick parishioner has first claim always on my time."

"Which is as it should be, but I am sorry I shall not have your company."

He smiled uncertainly, though she could see he was pleased at the compliment.

"You see, I fear I have a long way to go to befriend the local people, and your guidance could be invaluable to me."

"I am at your disposal at any time, Mrs. de Lacy. That is, at any time other than today."

"I thank you." She paused a moment, considering how to speak. Then, impulsively, she rushed on. "Why do they hate me so? I know they do. I hear them. I heard them in the clogger's shop. They said the name Radley as if it were poison. Oh, Edgar, what have I done that they should hate me so?"

She was pleating folds in her skirt nervously as she spoke, hating herself for being so sensitive to their scorn and for pleading with a comparative stranger for help. It was foolish,

147

too; he would wonder why she turned to him and not to her husband.

He was looking at her sadly. "I do not know, Mrs. de Lacy, but I fear you are right. For some strange reason the name of Radley has always been loathed here, but not because of you. It existed long before you came. I never knew why, nor has anyone been able to tell me. Only, rest assured it is not you personally they dislike; now you are a De Lacy, possibly they will forget."

"But that is not enough! I want to know the reason."

He hunched his shoulders, spreading his hands in defeat. "There is much we would know but which is denied to us. We must learn to accept."

How weak he was, how ineffectual compared to Bruno. Instantly she regretted the comparison. Regaining her composure, she changed the subject.

"Do you have parish registers in the church, Reverend? How far back do they go?"

He nodded, evidently more at ease on this subject. "Indeed we have, and very interesting many of them are, too. I'm afraid I don't know how far back exactly records were kept, for many of the older registers have been put away in cupboards in the vestry and are somewhat dusty and dilapidated. In what period were you interested?"

Fern felt the muscles tighten in her throat, but she appeared calm as she spoke. "I believe there was once a Catherine Radley in the time of Charles I. I wondered if perhaps you might have a record of her birth . . . and death."

He was frowning dubiously. "I doubt that our records go back so far, but I shall most certainly check for you, Mrs. de Lacy. But another day, if you will permit, as I must be on my way to the sick lady now."

"Of course." Fern rose to escort him to the door. "By the way, who is the sick lady you are to visit?"

"Mrs. Briggs, the doctor's wife. She's very poorly, I understand, but then, she was always delicate, so we must not lose heart."

Poor lady, thought Fern after he had gone. She had looked

ill last night; it was to be hoped the indisposition was not serious.

In an effort to lighten her mood, and because the sun was shining again, Fern decided she would not stay indoors but go out in the cold fresh air. Perhaps she would find Fabia at home. She sent Fanny to fetch her cloak, electing to walk rather than ride. Nearing the schoolhouse, she saw Fabia and young Phoebe just coming out of the front door.

"It's so lovely, we decided to go and pick pussy willow—catkins, that is," Fabia said as she tied Phoebe's bonnet strings.

"May I come with you?"

"We'd be delighted, wouldn't we, Phoebe?" The child ventured a hesitant smile and took hold of her mother's hand. Fern fell in step beside them as they walked uphill toward the moors, leaving the village behind. She was grateful for Fabia's reticence, for she did not inquire why Fern was not doing the rounds of the tenant farmers with Bruno.

Above the village the fields stretched away into the purpling distance, interlaced by gray-stone walls, and here and there a copse or two. Pale-green buds on the trees seemed to glow with translucence in the soft spring sunlight, and Fern felt content and free up here. Fabia too was lighthearted.

"I know the best place for catkins—in Catsgrave Copse, down by the stream. Come, Phoebe, I'll race you there."

Laughing, they all ran. The heather sprang resiliently beneath Fern's feet, the breeze blowing back her hair and catching in her throat till she was breathless. They stopped, gasping, at the edge of a thick clump of trees, and Fern could see the glint of the sunlight on the stream rippling through the woods. Fabia was right. Heavy sprays of catkin hung, limp and yellow, in profusion.

Both women started forward, but the child hung back. "Come on, Phoebe, for we haven't much time," her mother urged, but the child still clung to her hand, pulling back. Fern waited, wondering. "Come on, Phoebe," Fabia pleaded.

The little girl began to whimper. Fern knelt by her side. "What is it, Phoebe?" she asked softly. The child's moans

149

ceased at once, her eyes growing round and suspicious. Fern touched her arm, but the child leaped back, her dark eyes now angry and hostile. Fern felt a shudder of fear run down her spine, for the eyes that glared were those of the other Phoebe. For a second Fern lay again in that truckle bed and saw the eyes and felt the tearing fingers at her face. The eyes were flashing still ... and they were the eyes of the child.

Numbly she rose and turned helplessly to Fabia.

"I'm sorry, Fern. I don't know what's come over the child," Fabia said in some embarrassment. "Perhaps she's sickening for something, in which case it would be as well to take her home."

She pulled a few sprigs of catkin from the nearest trees. It was a quieter, more thoughtful party on the homeward journey, and Fern began to wonder. They had all been so high-spirited just a few minutes earlier; was it her influence that happiness always seemed to turn sour so quickly? What was the malign influence she brought that caused the village folk to resent, even hate her, and a poor dumb child to fear her? The memory of those eyes recalled the night Bruno had attempted to hypnotize Phoebe, and the child's words.

"I didn't mean it to happen, I swear to God I didn't!"

Fern knew now, it was the other, older Phoebe who spoke, the one now dead for three hundred years. What had the other Phoebe done that she now repented?

It all seemed so clear now. Catherine was returning through Fern, and Phoebe through the child Phoebe—but to expiate or complete what?

Banishing useless speculation, Fern tried instead to talk to Fabia of other matters. How was Luke faring, she asked, and affairs in the school.

"He is somewhat hard-pressed at the moment, since one of his pupil-teachers has the influenza, but he'll manage," Fabia told her. At once the idea came to Fern.

"Then perhaps he would allow me to help for a time. I am not inexperienced in teaching."

Fabia tried to hide her pleasure behind a show of politeness, protesting it would consume too much of Fern's time, and she mistress of the manor too. But Fern would not listen. Besides, the idea had advantages; if she could not easily get to know the adults, the children of the village at least would be accessible. And in studying the faces of other children in order to learn their names and ways, perhaps she could shut out the picture of Phoebe's face, contorted with hate and fear.

Luke was more than grateful, and it was soon agreed that she should come to the schoolroom in the morning. "But are you sure Bruno will agree?" he inquired.

Fern felt resentment stiffening. "I agree, Luke. That is all that matters. Bruno's opinion does not enter into it."

She saw the surprise on his good-humored face and wished she had phrased her answer more diplomatically. He would feel sorry for his friend, married to a shrewish, self-willed woman, his bride of only one day. Still, this was as Bruno wished it to be. In time all the village would learn that each was independent of the other.

In fact, it was that same evening that the villagers were first made aware of it. The Hall once more was crowded with well-wishers for the master's marriage, but this time the guests were not the landed gentry but tenant farmers, the Hall servants, and the millhands and their wives. As before, the Hall shone with candlelight and decoration, and the tables were loaded with food just as generously as the previous night, but the toasts were drunk in ale and beer and not in wine. Fern wore, not a magnificent gown like last night's, but a decorous violet day dress, high-necked and beruffled, with a diamond brooch at the throat, which was a gift from Bruno.

"Be the gracious lady, Fern, charming but distant," Bruno murmured as he offered his arm to lead her down the staircase. Below, she could see the heads turn, and the subdued talk died away as they descended. The men nearest the stairs raised their heads in a sketchy salute to their master. Behind them she could see the wives peering curiously over their men's shoulders, appraising her gown and assessing the diamond before staring shrewdly at her face. Now, if ever, was the opportunity to meet them and attempt to disprove any preconceived notions they had about her. Mentally she rejected Bruno's advice to remain aloof.

"This is Fearnley, the mill manager," she heard Bruno say, and turned to greet the stocky man who was shifting uncomfortably.

"How do you do, Mr. Fearnley."

"Oh, aye," he grunted, growing pinker and obviously more ill-at-ease in the unaccustomed surroundings.

"I trust affairs at the mill are running well?" she went on, anxious to get him to talk on matters he knew about.

"Aye, none too badly."

"Perhaps I shall come in soon and see for myself," she said with a smile, and saw at once the way his gaze slid to the master. Bruno frowned.

"How is Mrs. Fearnley now?" he asked the manager.

"Fair to middling, sir. She's over t' influenza, but now t' bairn has it. He'll be right again soon, though."

"I hope so. I'll see you in the office in the morning."

Bruno turned away, leading Fern with him. He introduced her to several more people, but Fern found no opportunity to talk with them. Bruno was quick to intervene and to lead her away. Finally, exasperated, she dropped his arm. Bruno's dark brows rose in question.

"I wish to talk. I see Mrs. Iredale over there by the window, the woman who lost her child soon after I came. I want to talk to her." Fern had not intended her voice to sound so sharp, for several people were within earshot.

He shook his head. "Unwise, my dear. Come to the dais, where I will respond to their toast. A few more polite words with a few of them, and then we can leave quietly." He took her arm firmly.

"But I don't want to leave!" She shook off his arm, aware that now several more curious ears were straining to listen.

"Do as I say, Fern." His voice was low, but there was no mistaking the tone of command, the tone that implied he would not be disobeyed. Rebellion flared in Fern. She would not be dictated to like a child who does not know how to behave. She glared at him equally forcibly.

152

"I shall talk to whom I please. And I shall inspect the mill if I wish."

"Do you intend to make a spectacle of yourself in public, madam?" The voice, still low, was charged with icy anger, but Fern was not to be cowed. Her anger matched his.

"I do not, but it seems you will force it upon us both if you continue to dictate to me. Now, let go of me."

"I will not. We shall talk of this later."

Without another word he gripped her arm so fiercely that Fern could have winced with the pain. Forcefully he propelled her across the room to the dais, helped her to mount the steps, and then pulled out a chair for her to sit. Short of creating a scene by running from the room, there was little she could do. Defeated, Fern sank into the chair, but inwardly she fumed with rage. He would hear more of this later; he would not humiliate her thus again.

In a blur of anger she heard Bruno call for the beer tankards to be replenished, heard Fearnley's stumbling words of congratulation to the master of Brackenroyd and his lady, and the subdued cheer followed by silence as the throng emptied their glasses. The atmosphere was markedly different from last night's, when a gaily dressed company had chattered without restraint. Tonight's company, soberly dressed in their dark Sunday best, were emphatically more reserved, more subdued. Was it only that they felt a little ill-at-ease in the grand Hall, or was it more than that?

Bruno rose to respond to the toast, his quiet, authoritative voice betraying none of the anger of a moment before. The villagers listened in respectful silence, and Fern could see in their eyes no hate, no resentment of the master.

After he had done, he led her away. Fern went without protest. It had been a very tiring day; not physically, but emotionally she felt drained, too tired to argue more. At her door he left her.

It was Cassie who brought her late cup of hot chocolate, her eyes glowing.

"It were a lovely ball, miss ... madam. I'll always remember it." Her eyes misted in reminiscence.

"I'm glad you enjoyed it, Cassie."

"Shall I tell thee why, madam? 'Cos Tim Butley asked me out wi' him, on me next evening off. I'm that proud he asked me, 'cos every lass in t' village fancies Tim, they do."

Fern smiled at the girl's radiance, glad for her. To Cassie, marriage to a good worker like Tim must seem the ultimate in contentment. If only she knew what marriage was for a woman. Whatever stratum of society she lived in, it seemed it meant only blind obedience and submission, if continual warfare were not to ensue.

Two days married, and already so cynical! Fern could have laughed if the situation were not so tragic. Here she was, bound to a domineering man who evidently liked her no more than she liked him.

And yet ... As she undressed for bed, Fern mused about the laconic man with the dark ways she had married out of need. In some ways he was so attractive. If only he were not so silent, so uncommunicative, and so determined to rule her. Well, he would not. Tomorrow she would start work at the school with Luke, trying to live life her own way.

Suddenly the connecting door opened, and Bruno stood in the doorway. Fern pulled her dressing gown hastily about her, covering the delicate nightgown. He did not come forward, but stood there, seeming to fill the whole doorway with his height and breadth. He had not yet changed from his evening suit. Deliberately Fern sat in a chair with her back toward him.

"Fern," he said quietly, "I wish to make it plain that there must never again be a repetition of tonight's performance. However the situation may be between us, it must appear to others that there is harmony. Henceforth, therefore, I must insist that you do not cross me in public."

"Then do not make it necessary for me to do so."

He sighed deeply. "My dear girl, I am not anxious to dictate to you, as you seem to think, but simply to guide you. It is evident you do not know how a lady behaves when among others of a lower station. Tonight I only wished to save you from your own impulsiveness and ignorance."

154

"And how do you know how English people behave, living most of your life in Germany?" Fern flashed back.

"Because good manners and social etiquette are basically the same in both countries. I am not angry with you, Fern, only disappointed. But I believe there is a book I have heard good report of, which might help you. It's called *A Manual of Etiquette for Gentlewomen*. I shall order it for you when I go to town."

How dare he patronize her! Fern rose from her chair and faced him. "I am no common servant girl, to be schooled to become what you wish. No finer gentleman existed than my father, and I learned long ago that manners basically are consideration for others, something which you do not seem to comprehend. I would have done better to ignore you tonight, to inquire how that poor woman Mrs. Iredale fared."

"That would have been foolish, and you know it. Have you forgotten already how she resented your coming to her house?"

"Only because of some superstitious rubbish the villagers believe about the Radleys, and how am I ever to disabuse them of the idea if you try to prevent my talking to them?" She could not resist smiling as she went on to tell him her news. "But you shall not prevent me. Tomorrow I start to teach in the school, to help Luke. I shall get to know the children, at least."

To her surprise, he nodded and smiled. "A good idea. It will help to keep you occupied. Good night, Fern."

Stepping back, he closed the door, and Fern heard the key turn in the lock. So be it. She had no wish to have his company in her bed. And what was more, she felt she had scored a minor victory in refusing to capitulate. He had not argued long.

Fern slept a deep and dreamless sleep that night. In the morning she rose early, ate breakfast from a tray, and prepared to go down to the school. The morning was fine and clear, so she decided to walk, wrapping up well against the cold in a warm ulster and muffler. As she closed her bedroom door behind her, she saw Cassie outside Bruno's door.

155

"The master don't answer when I knock, madam. Shall I go in?"

"Give the tray to me. I'll take it in, Cassie."

Gladly the girl relinquished the tray and scuttled off. Fern tapped lightly at the door and went in. Bruno was not there. Nor had his bed been slept in. She put down the tray on the night table and left.

Curiosity nagged as she walked downhill toward the village. It was no business of hers, admittedly, since they had agreed to go their own ways, but where was Bruno? Neither last night nor the previous night had he slept in his bed. Was he sleeping elsewhere in the Hall, or was he out, and if so, where?

Outside the school, a gaunt gray-stone building, some boys played marbles in the small playground while a cluster of girls, the bigger ones holding the smaller ones by the hand, stood gossiping by the door. Fern smiled and spoke to them as she passed, but they only stared, openmouthed, too overcome to reply. She found Luke in his classroom.

"I'll show you your classroom," he said, leading the way to a smaller room with somber half-tiled walls and rows of iron desks. In the corner a huge iron stove belched intermittent gusts of smoke. Behind a single high desk on a dais, evidently the teacher's desk, stood a row of cupboards and a high blackboard on a swivel easel.

"In there you will find materials and chalk and all you require. The children's slates are in a slot at the front of their desks. The class monitor will be able to show you where everything is." Luke sounded abstracted. Evidently he had much on his mind, but Fern assured him she would be able to manage quite well.

"Arithmetic first, after prayers, then spelling and handwriting. After playtime, geography and drawing. This afternoon will be singing. I'm afraid we have no piano, but there is a tuning fork in your desk. Then, history and reading before school ends at four."

It sounded quite a heavy program, but Fern was looking forward to seeing the children. At last a whistle shrilled in the

156

yard. Looking out of the window, she could see the children lining up quickly into neat files, and then chanting a song as they marched in step to the rhythm into their respective doorways—the boys at the east door, the girls at the west.

She took off her ulster, hung it on the peg behind the door, and sat up at the high desk to await her charges. In a moment they came, no longer singing but marching silently to their desks, where they sat and eyed her expectantly. Row upon row of pale, solemn faces stared at her. Fern bade them good morning pleasantly and introduced herself, but not a flicker of emotion crossed their blank faces. Boys on one side of the room, of all ages, and girls on the other in neat white smocks over their dresses, they all sat uniformly still and emotionless. Fern felt dismayed. She was glad when a bell rang to summon them to the hall for prayers.

After a simple service consisting only of a hymn sung in lackluster voices, a reading from the Bible by Luke, and the Lord's Prayer, the class marched back to the classroom. Slates clattered out from the desk slots as Fern began writing sums on the blackboard. Not a child attempted to talk to its neighbor or disrupt the lesson in any way. It was unnatural. Fern found it hard to comprehend. But then she noticed the thinness of the little bodies, the gaunt, gray look, and some of them were even barefoot. Poor things, they looked too hungry and cold to think of mischief.

During the spelling lesson they began to appear more alive, possibly because the warmth from the stove was beginning to thaw out their cold little bodies. The morning passed without event, and at noontime she went to eat with Fabia in the house.

"Some of them even have no sandwiches for their dinner, Fabia, and some are barefoot. Are they really so poor?"

Fabia was careful. "The wages at the mill are not handsome, and most families have several children to feed and clothe. It is not easy."

"But I will not have them starve! Could we not give them hot soup, Fabia? If there are no facilities here, I could get

Mrs. Thorpe to make it at the Hall and send it down. They must have something nourishing to eat."

"Soup would be marvelous," Fabia said, and Fern could hear the careful note still in her voice. She was anticipating Bruno's opposition, perhaps. Well, if he was responsible for the children's hunger, through not paying their fathers sufficient wages, he was not going to interfere in her attempt to rectify matters.

"Then I shall see to it tomorrow, and clogs for the children who have none," Fern said stoutly. And she would, whoever might try to oppose her.

"There is one thing," Fabia said slowly. "The villagers may not welcome what you plan—they are a proud race and may well construe your actions as charity."

"Charity? What does it matter what one calls it? They surely will be glad to see their children shod and fed."

Fabia nodded. "They would welcome it, but you must be careful how you do it, for fear of offending them. They would sooner see their children cold and hungry than accept charity from ... from ..."

Her voice trailed away. Fern eyed her questioningly. "From a Radley, is that what you would say?"

Fabia nodded. "From the mistress of Brackenroyd is one matter, for they have been accustomed for centuries to protection from the master and his family. But from a Radley is another matter. I don't know why this age-old resentment of the name, but it is undeniably there. So I would caution you to take care."

Her advice was sensible, thought Fern as she returned to the school. A lone child sat at her desk in the classroom. There was something vaguely familiar about her face, solemn and wide-eyed.

"Have you had lunch?" Fern asked pleasantly. The child shook her head. "I seem to know you—have we met before?" The child stared without answering. "What is your name?"

"Elsie Iredale, miss."

Iredale. Fern could not remember one name from so many she had called out from the register this morning. Iredale. It was Joss Iredale who had lost a little girl just after she came—yes, this child here now had been lurking in the corner when Fern had gone to the cottage. She smiled.

"How is your mother now, Elsie? Has she recovered from the shock of your sister's death?"

A shadow crossed the child's face, and she scowled. "My mam says it's 'cos of you that Aggie died. She says when there's a Radley in t' village there's allus trouble, same as it's allus been for hundreds of years. There's a taint in thy blood, miss, me mam says."

Other children trooped into the room, relieving Fern of the obligation to reply. She felt shocked and hurt. The older people of the village were evidently passing on their distrust of her to their children. and the task of befriending them was not going to be easy after all.

It was during the afternoon's lessons that she became gradually aware that these were not all the same children who had been present during the morning. She still could not fit many names to faces, but the faces were different now; she was sure of it. She asked Luke when school at last was ended.

"You are right. Many of the older children go to work half-time and attend school half-time. Those from the age of ten up to thirteen work in the mill either in the mornings or in the afternoons and come to school half a day only."

"So that is why they look so tired! It is too much for them!"

Luke shrugged. "Unfortunately, in most cases it is an economic necessity. There is nothing we can do."

There must be something we can do, Fern argued inwardly as she made her way home. These poor, exploited children, made to work and freeze and starve without any hope of bettering their lot; it was appalling. Robert and Sarah Hastings, despite their father's coldness toward them, would never have to suffer the privations of these poor Brackenroyd children.

Over dinner she poured out her arguments to Bruno, who listened in impassive silence. At length he laid down his dessert fork and smiled at her in compassion.

"You want so much to be the benevolent mistress of Brackenroyd, don't you, Fern?"

"I can't bear to see their suffering!"

"Well, let me tell you, yours is not the way to overcome it. By your impulsive recklessness you could ruin all."

"You mean only to exploit them, to grow fat and wealthy from them, is that it? Well, I will not stand by and let you."

"Listen to me." His voice was icy cold. "You are young, inexperienced, and hotheaded. Let well alone, and do not interfere. I have told you that the mill and the welfare of the workers is my concern alone, and I repeat once again, do not meddle in what you do not understand. No, do not argue with me." He raised a peremptory hand to forestall her angry reaction. "You think you can change the world, but you cannot. Children of ten may work half-time—it is the law. I appreciate your concern for them, but you cannot, and *shall* not, change matters.

"Madam, I say it for the last time. Mind your own business."

Chapter 11

Edgar Amos squatted in the vestry among a pile of decaying registers.

"Drat those mice," he muttered as the ledger he was about to dip into crumbled into pieces in his hand. He laid it aside and withdrew another from the dark recesses of one of the huge cupboards.

The pale spring sunlight filtering in through a high window was suddenly blotted out by a shadow. Amos looked up interrogatively. A huge black shape silhouetted against the window made him start, till he recognized the voice.

"Amos?" It was the master, greatcoated and muffled against the chill breezes. Behind him lurked that great ugly dog. "I am on my way down to the mill. Will you walk with me?"

It was typical of the man not to explain his reason, but Amos agreed nonetheless. One did not readily offend one's patron, so he fetched a muffler and trudged along beside De Lacy, endeavoring to match the length of his stride. The dog sniffed suspiciously at his heels, and Amos wished the creature would not stare at him so malevolently from its great yellow eyes.

For a time they marched in silence. Amos was cold, and wondered if the master would broach the reason for seeking him out before they reached the mill, for it was not far. At the mill gates De Lacy stopped, staring at the waters of the river.

"Why are you not wearing an overcoat, Amos?"

The vicar smiled apologetically. "It is thin and fraying at the cuffs, but I cannot afford a new one."

"Then order one. Send the bill to me."

He would listen to no thanks. Strange, thought Amos, how the man could be so observant and concerned, and yet at other times so brusque, even callous.

"Soup is to be sent down from the Hall to the school today for the children," the master went on quickly. "I want you to see Luke Armitage, to tell him I sent it."

"That is exceedingly thoughtful of you, sir."

"Fern's idea, not mine. But the villagers would not accept it from her. You are to let it be known that it is the master's wish."

"Very good." Amos could not help feeling grudging admiration for the man. In an odd kind of way he was trying to protect his wife, but he was so gruff, so lacking in polish. His foreign upbringing, no doubt.

De Lacy turned to face him. "You're not a bad fellow, Amos. Intelligent and well-read. It's a pity you're in the church. It cannot be very satisfying for you to minister to a lot of primitive, superstitious people like the Brackenroyd folk."

"They are good people, sir, hardworking and honest." Amos was quick to defend his parishioners against a newly arrived foreigner.

"But superstitious, nonetheless. Was it not your great man of last century, Edmund Burke, who said that superstition was the religion of feeble minds? I agree with him. By the way, what were you doing in the vestry when I called?"

Amos was irritated by the change of subject before he

could retaliate, but did not show it. Instead he replied courteously, "Mrs. de Lacy asked me to see if I could find reference to a Catherine Radley in the seventeenth century. I was checking the records."

De Lacy's handsome face darkened into a scowl. "So, she is still besotted with her family history. She would do well to leave it alone."

The vicar saw his chance to score. "But was it not also Edmund Burke who said that a people not interested in its past was not worthy of its future? There I agree with him."

"Touché," the master admitted with a hint of a grim smile. "But to be interested is not the same as to be obsessed."

Without another word he turned and marched into the cobbled mill yard, but he could not rob Amos of a feeling of triumph as he retraced his steps toward the school. Just for once De Lacy had not got the better of him. The feeling of superiority in this encounter gave him a more charitable outlook toward his benefactor, and he mused as he walked that the master was not such a hard and heartless character after all.

Luke Armitage, the schoolmaster, smiled broadly when he heard of the master's gift of soup for the children. Amos felt content at being entrusted with news that brought such happiness, and the gray little valley seemed to glow under the benison of spring sunshine as he made his way back to the vicarage. A young woman was waiting on the doorstep. He recognized Lucy, Dr. Briggs's maidservant.

"Begging thy pardon, Reverend, but the doctor asks will you come at once. The mistress is very bad, sinking fast, the doctor says."

Poor soul. Amos half-ran with the girl up the hill to where the doctor's imposing stone house stood in its neat gardens, but it was too late. Mrs. Briggs lay still and white, her amiable features placid in death. Her husband and sister clung to each other, the one mute in shock, the other sobbing noisily.

"So sudden," the doctor said shakily. "A chill, and then, without warning, it became pneumonia. Nothing I could do. Nothing."

Amos performed his duties, consoling and making arrangements for the dead woman's funeral, and then left the family to mourn alone. His return to the vicarage this time was infinitely more thoughtful and less lighthearted than it had been this morning. Heavens! It was dusk already, and he had eaten nothing since breakfast. Mrs. Crowther would be flapping anxiously about him like a mother hen over her chick when he reappeared. Then he must notify the master of Mrs. Briggs's death and arrange for the burial. Ah, well, his research to find records of Catherine Radley could wait for another day.

Radley. An anxious thought struck him. It was highly likely that the villagers, shocked as they would be by Mrs. Briggs's demise, would shake their heads and venture to say, once again, that sudden death and the return of a Radley to Brackenroyd were no mere coincidence. Poor Mrs. de Lacy. She was going to find life here difficult for a long time yet.

It was not until the day of the funeral that Amos saw Mrs. de Lacy, and he was struck by her pallor, greater than was usual for one who was not actually a relative of the deceased. He was waiting outside the church door, despite the drizzling rain bespotting his starched cassock, to see the cortege arrive, and he could not help noting the young mistress's appearance as she dismounted from the first black coach behind the hearse. The master helped her and Mrs. Briggs's sister out, then Dr. Briggs, looking older and frailer than he had ever done. For a moment Mrs. de Lacy stared at the black-and-silver hearse, her black-crepe veil thrown back from her face, before lowering it and entering the church.

In the mild, misty rain the bearers lifted the highly polished coffin with its gilt mountings from the hearse, the four black horses with their black plumes, limp with rain, stamping their feet and snorting steamy breath.

Up the steps and into the church the bearers moved, slowly and majestically. Behind the coffin followed the family, in deepest black and the women heavily veiled. Amos took his place to begin, catching a brief glimpse of the De Lacys in their pew, both standing with heads bowed.

"I am the resurrection and the life, saith the Lord ..."
Amos spoke the words of the service, feeling the reverence
and solemnity of the occasion adding a new weight of importance to his little church. Dr. Briggs was evidently deeply
moved, his bulky frame shuddering slightly as though it were
a battle to restrain his tears.

"For man walketh in a vain shadow and disquieteth himself
in vain; he heapeth up riches and cannot tell who shall gather
them ..."

That would make a good text for a sermon to preach for
such as De Lacy. The rich man filling his coffers, but to what
end?

He was aware of thin cambric handkerchieves dabbing at
reddened eyes, of the gentlemen's shining top hats and silk
cravats, of the lurid patches of colored light on the mourners'
faces, cast by the stained-glass windows above. It was a melancholy occasion indeed, and he felt genuinely sorry for the
old doctor.

The service over, he led the file of black figures out of the
church behind the coffin. Rain was still falling on the sodden
turf and the heap of newly dug soil by the grave. At the gate
Amos could see the waiting coachmen and the horses stirring
restlessly, anxious to return to the dry warmth of their stables.
The mourners made a silent circle about the grave.

"For as much as it hath pleased Almighty God of his great
mercy to take unto himself the soul of our dear sister here departed," Amos intoned, "we therefore commit her body to the
ground...."

Dr. Briggs scattered a handful of earth on the coffin, and
while Amos spoke the final prayer, the other mourners cast
sprays of spring flowers. He saw Mrs. de Lacy sway suddenly,
as if to fall, but the master caught her elbow, supporting her
while the file moved slowly away.

It was not altogether surprising when Amos heard the next
day that Mrs. de Lacy was not at the school as she had been
the past week, but as the pupil-teacher was now recovered
and back at his post, she was no longer needed there. Still, it

might be as well to pay a visit to the Hall; the lady might be indisposed, and he must not neglect his pastoral duties.

Mrs. de Lacy was reclining on a chaise longue in the parlor when Fanny showed the vicar in, flashing him a quick smile with her pert dark eyes as she bobbed a curtsy and withdrew. Mrs. de Lacy laid aside a book she had evidently been reading and motioned him to be seated. She was still unnaturally pale, and her usually lively eyes were distant and cool. Amos sat in the leather chair next to the fire, rubbing his hands to the blaze.

"Are the children at the school eating their soup, Edgar?" Mrs. de Lacy asked in a lackluster voice.

"Indeed, and are relishing it."

"I am glad of it." The uninterested tone in her voice could only indicate either that she was not well or that she was aware that the gift of soup was her husband's gesture, no longer hers.

"How is Dr. Briggs?" she asked next. "I fear his wife's death has been a terrible blow to him. He must have loved her deeply."

"I have no doubt he did, but he is a very Christian gentleman. He will find solace in knowing they will meet again."

"In the hereafter, or in another life on earth?" The question was bald, but he could see the gleam of interest which now enlivened her eyes.

"Either is possible. Love is an abiding power."

"Then if you believe love can be reborn from one generation to another, is it not possible that hate, equally strong and enduring, can continue too?"

Her eyes glowed now, with the unnatural gleam of fever. Amos tried to parry her question, unsure how to answer.

"Is it this house that makes you think such thoughts, Mrs. de Lacy? Brackenroyd Hall has a powerful, intense, atmosphere. Evil memories are mingled with happier ones, and a sensitive person such as yourself could well suffer a kind of malaise, a sickness of the spirit, as a result."

"But I asked your opinion—can hatred linger on and come back?"

166

"Come back," he echoed thoughtfully. "You mean, like a ghost, *un revenant*, as the French say? I would prefer to think not. A body is laid to rest at death, and it is to be hoped the spirit remains at rest, in peace, forever."

Her eyes relapsed into an interior reverie. Suddenly Edgar remembered the reason for his visit. He sat forward to catch her drifting attention.

"I have found a reference in the parish records to the lady you inquired about," he said eagerly. At once Mrs. de Lacy sprang to life, her face registering rapt attention, and the gleam revitalizing her eyes again.

"Catherine? You found her?"

"Well, I found an entry for a Catherine Radley in the 1642 register. It was the only Radley of that name, although of course the name Radley appears frequently over the years."

"That is the Catherine I sought. What does it say of her?"

"It was very brief, an entry regarding her death." He raised his eyes ceilingward in an effort to recall the exact words. " 'Catherine Radley, departed this life Lammastide, the first day of August, 1642.' There was no mention of her age, but no doubt as I go back in the records, I shall uncover the date of her birth."

"It was 1620, for she was twenty-two when she died."

He regarded her in amazement, but she was cool and collected. There was no sign of feverishness about her pallid face, and yet how could she know? Before he could ask her meaning, the portiere across the door rattled back along its bamboo pole, and Bruno de Lacy stood there.

"Ah, deep in conversation, I see," he said, advancing to the fireplace and turning his back upon it, standing legs astride the better to enjoy the warmth. "What were you discussing?"

"Ah, whether love can surpass death, conquering it to be reborn," replied Amos, anxious not to betray the mistress's concern over this Catherine Radley. De Lacy would only sneer yet again.

"Philosophical speculation, which, unfortunately, can be neither proved nor disproved, and therefore a waste of time," the master pronounced. Amos saw Mrs. de Lacy's gaze fasten

167

on his handsome, dark features with an air of distaste. There did not seem to be an atmosphere of perfect connubial bliss in the Hall; perhaps he had best make his farewells and return to his study, where Sunday's sermon lay half-written on his desk.

Declining Mrs. de Lacy's invitation to stay for tea, he made his farewells and went out into the darkening April afternoon, glad for once to leave the Hall. It was, as he had said to Mrs. de Lacy, an oppressive, powerful atmosphere that clung to the very fabric of the Hall, but he had never been so conscious of it as now.

Fern sighed and sank back on the chaise longue after Amos' departure. Bruno offered her a cup of tea from the silver tray, eyeing her thoughtfully.

"You look tired, my dear. Are you not sleeping well?"

Fern put the cup aside and closed her eyes. "I sleep deeply, but I do not feel rested." It was true; deep sleep blanketed her mind, with no dreams to disturb her, but the lassitude by day was unaccountably strange.

"You've been overdoing things, with the school and the house to run. A change might be good for you, a month by the sea perhaps."

"No!" With a feeling near to panic, Fern sat upright. She could not leave Brackenroyd now. She was needed here; she felt it. Catherine needed her, though she had not yet come back.

"As you wish." Black eyes surveyed her levelly. "I shall go down to my laboratory to work now until dinner." Bruno laid aside the china cup and went out.

Fanny came to draw the curtains, light the gas lamps, and clear away the tray. Fern heard her skirts swishing through the doorway and the door closing. She lay, languid and limp, only her mind at work.

She *must* stay in Brackenroyd Hall, for Catherine's sake as well as her own. Somehow she felt intuitively that only by learning Catherine's problem could she resolve her own. It was imperative to stay, not to let Bruno drive her out, however oppressive and enervating the Hall's atmosphere.

The clock on the marble mantelshelf ticked on. It was nearing time for dinner, and she really must make the effort to raise herself and go upstairs to change for dinner.

Out in the corridor Fern had to pass the iron-studded door to the old wing. It was ajar. Bruno was down there at work in his laboratory. It occurred to Fern to go and warn him of the time, so, pushing the door open, she followed his dusty tracks to the old low-ceilinged hall and to the door in the corner under the minstrels' gallery.

That door too was ajar, but before Fern's hand could reach for the iron handle, a sudden chill came down over her, enveloping her like a dark cloak. She shivered. It could be the dampness of the age-old wing, or a sense of premonition ... or the feeling that came before with the advent of Catherine; but whatever it was, it was chilling to the very heart, and she felt afraid. Clutching her cashmere shawl closer about her shoulders, Fern paused, hand on knob, as the iciness grew, filling the murky shadows of the Hall. Opaque forms seemed to glow under the gallery, faint murmurs came to her waiting ears, and her fear grew into terror.

Fern pushed the door open sharply, anxious to see Bruno's reassuring shape, even though he might be angered at her interrupting him. But the low chamber with its wooden shelves and a bench was empty. She closed the door behind her, relieved that the menacing chill had not followed her in here.

But there was still that sense of weariness. She sank onto the stool beside the bench and breathed deeply, to quieten the thudding of her heart. On the bench stood a row of bottles and jars, all neatly labeled. Belladonna, digitalis, opium, laudanum, aconite, hemlock. Hemlock. For an instant she saw herself again in a flagstoned kitchen with a pestle and mortar, pounding a compound for a neighbor's abscess on the leg. Just as quickly the glimpse faded.

The door opened sharply, and Bruno stood there, scowling. "What are you doing here?" he demanded. There was hostility not only in his eyes but in his aggressive stance, feet astride.

"I came to fetch you for dinner." The excuse sounded as weak as her voice. His frown showed he did not believe her.

Fern felt angry with herself for sounding so guilty, and decided that, weak as she felt, attack was the best method of defense.

"Why do you have drugs here, Bruno? For what do you use them?"

The scowl darkened, his brows meeting in one long dark line. "For my work."

"But you are not a doctor of medicine. You told me your work is on the human mind."

"So it is. These drugs are capable of producing hallucination, and it is their effect on the human mind I am studying. Come, it is nearing time for the dinner gong."

She let him lead her away. This time the cold did not permeate her bones as she recrossed the old hall on his arm. It was only that night as she lay in the great four-poster that the thought suddenly came to her. How could she be so slow? It must be this strange weariness which had benumbed her wits, so that she had not thought of it before. The drugs in Bruno's laboratory—on whom had he been testing them? Unlike medical researchers with their corpses to dissect, he had no human brain at his disposal to experiment upon. The effect of hallucination on dogs or cats would be impossible to record, since they could not speak. So on whose brain was Bruno experimenting?

Of course. It was clear now. That was why he suffered Fern to come to Brackenroyd to share his inheritance. That was why he endured her as a wife. It was *her* mind he was tampering with! Hence, surely, the inexplicable lassitude, the tangled dreams. Fern felt fury mounting, chasing away the weariness and lack of interest. Then another thought struck her.

But were drugs the cause of Catherine too? No, no, that she could not believe. Catherine was no figment of a disordered brain; she was certain of it. Catherine was her own brainchild; no, more than that, *she was* Catherine.

How could she be so sure? Amos had confirmed it, had he not, by finding the entry in the records exactly as Fern had foretold? But the other dreams, the tangled balls of wool, and even the story of Annot—those, now she remembered it, had followed upon accepting a drink from Bruno before bed. That was how he had done it!

One doubt lingered. She could not thrust from her mind the memory of his eyes over the rim of a glass, warm and kindly, as he toasted his new bride on their wedding day. And that same night Catherine had come.

Torn with doubts and anxiety, Fern tumbled out of bed and tried the handle of the connecting door. It was locked. Out in the corridor she knocked angrily on Bruno's door, again and again. No answer came. To further furious banging, Mrs. Thorpe's anxious figure appeared. Fern turned on the plump woman in the arc of light thrown from her upraised candle. She looked curiously unfamiliar in dressing gown and gray hair fastened up in rag curlers. The woman's blue eyes sought hers in concern.

"Can I help you, madam?"

"I want to speak to Mr. de Lacy, but I cannot make him waken."

Mrs. Thorpe smiled wanly. "He is not there, madam. He is . . ."

"In his laboratory?"

"No, madam. He is out."

"Where?"

The woman's gaze shifted uncomfortably. Fern grew irritated. There was too much of a conspiracy of silence in this house.

"Where is he, Mrs. Thorpe? You must tell me. I am the mistress."

"Yes, madam. But I feel I should honor the master's confidence."

It was too much. Fern's patience snapped. "It is I who should have his confidence, Mrs. Thorpe, not you. I am concerned for his welfare, and I should know where he goes. Will you tell me?"

"Very well." There was distinct reluctance in the older woman's voice, but she gave in. "He rides often at night up the moors. He goes to Fox Brow."

171

"To Fox Brow?" Fern echoed in surprise. "That is where Ellen . . . Ellen . . ."

"Ellen Stansfield. Yes, madam."

Fern had to check her tongue, to bite back the impulse to ask why he went there. It was improper to discuss reasons with a servant. Thanking Mrs. Thorpe, she returned to her own room thoughtfully.

So it was to the young widow Ellen Stansfield that Bruno rode out every night. Fern could hear again in memory's ear the two old ladies outside the church.

"He'll never let on to her about t' other one." The other woman. It must have been Ellen all the time, and probably everyone in the village knew about it, except the mistress of Brackenroyd. Fern smoldered more and more. What kind of man was she married to? Not only did he drug her to use her brain for his experiments, but he betrayed her with another woman behind her back!

Her palms grew sticky as fury grew. She would not go back to bed until he came home; then she'd buttonhole him and have it out with him. And she would not be brushed aside by his cold, suave manner. This time they would have it out completely, openly, and honestly. She had had enough of his distant politeness, his urbane way of sliding out of matters he did not wish to discuss.

Odd, she thought, as she sat waiting in her dressing gown for dawn to bring him home, ironic even, that he has been using me while I thought all the time I was using him to validate my claim to Brackenroyd. All along we have been using each other under a thin veil of apparently respectable marriage. Both of us were frauds, but he at least knew what I was after. He never gave me the advantage of knowing what he sought from the marriage—a guinea pig in me, and a mistress in Ellen.

Before daylight Fern went to Bruno's room, withdrew the key from his side of the locked connecting door, and inserted it in her own side. Now she was mistress of the situation, she could dictate when she would speak to him, and this time he could not evade the answers she sought.

Her eyes were beginning to droop from sheer fatigue when at last she heard a movement in Bruno's room, and instantly she was alert. The first streaks of dawn were peeping through the gaps of the bedroom curtains. She sat still for a moment, listening and composing her thoughts.

He was not trying to creep stealthily, undetected, to bed, judging by the bumping sounds he made. Fern stood up, cold but determined, to challenge him now before he slept, now while he was fresh from his guilty rendezvous. Taking a candle, she grasped the key in the door, turned it, and opened the door, mentally girding herself to face the cold, uncompromising anger he would undoubtedly show at her demanding intrusion.

In the gloom beyond the reach of the candle's light she could not see him at once. There was no figure on the bed, no light in the room. Only a harsh, heavy breathing indicated his presence.

"Bruno?"

She held the candle higher, and saw the gleam of his eyes from the far corner. He staggered forward into the arc of light, and for a moment she thought he was drunk.

"Bruno, are you all right?"

He stared at her, and Fern's breath caught in a gasp. His clothing was disheveled and dirty, his black hair wildly disarrayed, but it was the wildness in his eyes that startled her— wide and staring, as if in disbelief, his mouth agape. At this moment he looked more animal than man, half-crouched as though about to spring. Fern stepped back involuntarily as a low moan escaped him, a piteous, haunted sound like a creature in pain.

"For pity's sake, what is wrong, Bruno?" she cried, but the moan changed to a growl, a sound so full of menace she was terrified. Then she saw the look in his eyes, fierce and intense, the pupils so enlarged they seemed to devour her, and her determination crumbled. As she stepped back through the door, slamming it and turning the key, she heard his weight crash hard against it on the other side, and his voice moaning and sobbing.

Shaking with fright, Fern slumped against the door. The other door—she must lock that too, in case he should try to reach her that way! Having done so, she sank on the bed, still shivering, and listened to the sounds from his room. After some minutes the moaning died away and there was silence.

It was hard to believe it had not been a dream. Bruno, always so remote and aloof, always so coolly in command—was it possible he could be that growling, half-wild thing beyond the heavy door who had seemed about to kill her? He must be drunk. There was no other possible explanation for his behavior.

He was sleeping now; she could hear his deep, stertorous breathing. Presently Fanny's footsteps approached, and Fern heard the clatter of the tea tray on the table outside the door. Fern composed herself for the girl's entrance.

"Morning, madam." Fanny's smile was bright as she poured amber tea into the china cup. "Mrs. Thorpe says I'm not to waken the master, as he has not slept. Will that be all, madam?"

"Tell Mrs. Thorpe I shall not be down until lunchtime, and after that I shall be going out."

"Yes, madam."

Fern had decided. First she would sleep, for she was exhausted, and later she would go up to Fox Brow herself, to meet Ellen Stansfield. If she could gain no answers from Bruno, perhaps she would learn from Ellen just what was going on.

It was a beautifully crisp, clear spring day when Fern at last made her way up the moorland path toward Fox Brow. She had dressed simply in a merino day dress and a hooded cloak, which now blew back from her shoulders as the mischievous breezes high on the moor whipped and played about her. Smoke curled from the low chimney above Fox Brow's dilapidated roof; its mysterious owner was evidently at home. Fern pushed open the latched gate and walked up the grass-grown path between neglected flowerbeds to the front door, its paint blistered and peeling.

Fern tapped at the door and waited, framing in her mind

the questions she must ask of this woman. But the person who came in answer to her knock was not at all what she had expected. Ellen Stansfield was undoubtedly once fair and desirable, but though still young, her beauty had fled.

"Come in, child, I have waited long for you." The voice was low and musical and with a warmth that touched a chord of memory. Fern followed the woman in, staring at the cloud of graying hair about the fine-boned head, admiring the graceful movement of her limbs. In the flagstoned parlor Ellen turned, her pale-gray eyes aglow but with a distance in them that made her seem abstracted, ethereal almost.

Fern stared, undecided now what to say. It seemed downright impertinence to accuse this gentle, vacuous character of duplicity, of alienating Bruno's affections. Ellen came closer, her thin gray gown seeming to float behind her, and she laid her fingertips on Fern's shoulder.

"I knew you would come, sometime. I'm glad you have come at last." The words trembled on the air, tenuous as gossamer. Again Fern felt the tingle of a half-remembered recollection, then lost it.

"I had to come, Mrs. Stansfield."

" 'Ellen,' please. Pray be seated." She indicated a well-worn armchair by the low fire, where a tabby cat glared at Fern before leaping down and surrendering the seat to her. Ellen sat opposite and held out her arms to the cat, who leaped gratefully onto her lap. She smiled at Fern. "Why did you come, child?"

"Because of my husband," Fern blurted out.

"You love him, do you not, and would like to know if he loves you?"

"I don't know ... Well, yes, I suppose so. I cannot understand him, but I know he comes to you at night. You must know him well."

"I do, indeed I do. He comes because he does not understand himself. But he will. Now you have come back to Brackenroyd, all will be resolved." There was a satisfied sigh in Ellen's voice, but Fern was puzzled.

"*Back* to Brackenroyd?"

The pale-gray gaze smiled on her again. "Oh, yes, you have come back, as I knew you would. You too have the gift, child, and if you do not know the reason yet, you surely will do so soon."

Fern began pleating folds in her skirt nervously, unsure how far to believe or trust this strange woman. But there was no one else in Brackenroyd in whom to confide.

"Bruno is strange, Ellen. Cold and unemotional, and yet he seems to have unaccountably violent ways at times. Why, only today I thought he would kill me."

Ellen smiled that faraway smile again. "Love takes us in strange ways, child."

"Love?" Fern sat upright, startled.

"It is a heat in the blood which cannot be cooled. It always appears fierce, sometimes even seeming like hatred in its violence, but it is still love in disguise. Indifference is more to be feared, for where there is coolness, there is no love."

"Are you trying to say Bruno loves me?"

"Did you ever doubt it?" The gray eyes met hers levelly. Fern sat clutching the arms of the chair in disbelief. Ellen leaned forward. "But you must have patience, child, for death must come before all is made plain."

"Death?" Fear clutched at Fern's heart. Already the villagers blamed her for the death of the Iredale child and Mrs. Briggs; surely there was not more to come?

"Death came once, long ago, and interrupted the play. Now the long interval is nearly over and the story can be resumed," Ellen was saying softly, gazing into the embers of the fire and stroking the purring cat in her lap. "Have patience, puss, it will not be long."

Fern rose to go, half-afraid of the eerie gloom where this half-mad woman murmured to herself and crooned over her cat like some medieval witch. Witch. That was it. The snatch of memory came back again—Ellen reminded her of old Mistress Uttley, who had taught Catherine the magic of herbs.

Ellen put down the cat and followed Fern to the door. "Do

not fret, child, all will be resolved, once death has visited Brackenroyd again. What you lost will be restored to you."

On the doorstep her thin fingers clutched Fern's arm. "Have you been to Catsgrave Copse yet?"

"No, that is, Fabia and I took Phoebe there to fetch catkins, but Phoebe would not go into the wood."

Ellen laughed softly. "That is not surprising. Phoebe will never go into the scene of her evil-doing, but you must go."

"To Catsgrave? Why?"

"Because that is where the story ended long ago and so must begin again. Have you not realized what its name means?

" 'Catsgrave' means 'Kate's grave.' Because that is where, Lammas night, many years ago, Catherine Radley met her end. That is where you must begin life anew, but only after death has come again."

Chapter 12

Fern refused to go to the dining room for lunch. She felt too confused, too puzzled and bewildered by her visit to Ellen Stansfield to face Bruno and possible interrogation.

It had seemed so clear before she had gone to Fox Brow. Bruno, it appeared, was being unfaithful to her, and added to that, he was planning some evil campaign against her. She was certain he had used his drugs on her, possibly to drive her mad with hallucinations or to render her physically weak, declining into ill health. Brackenroyd had been his goal, she believed, cheating her out of her inheritance by death or insanity, and she had hated him for it. Then the course had been clear—to fight rebelliously for her rights, for her inheritance and her husband.

But Ellen had undone all that, turning Fern's plans topsy-turvy. Fey, mystical Ellen was no husband stealer. And now that she too believed there was a kinship between Fern and Catherine, it put the lie to the idea of Catherine being only a figment of Fern's imagination fevered by drugs. And her

178

words had strengthened Fern's feeling that Catherine's story was still to be unfolded and fulfilled.

Fern shivered as she recalled Ellen's words. "Death must come before all is made plain." Whose death? Fern's own, or someone else's? Bruno's, perhaps? To her surprise, Fern felt a shock at the thought of Bruno dying; it was impossible that so much power and vitality, so much repressed strength as his should be cut off.

It would be wonderful to be able to believe Ellen, that Bruno did really love his wife. If he did, he had a very strange way of showing it, Fern thought begrudgingly. And yet, if he did . . . She brushed idle speculation aside. If he did, he would say it and show it as other men did. Until then, she would not entertain the possibility.

But still she had a desire to see him. Mrs. Thorpe shook her head apologetically.

"He left straight after lunch. He was going down to the schoolhouse to see Phoebe, madam."

"Phoebe?"

"Yes, madam. He gives her a lesson most days, how to talk with her fingers, Mrs. Armitage says. Very clever man, Dr. de Lacy."

Fern had forgotten Bruno's intention to teach Phoebe the sign language of the dumb. Apparently he had not thought it important to mention to his wife that lessons were in progress—no more than she had told him of her teaching with Luke until after it had been arranged. For a newly married couple, there was little communication between them,

She must see him, if only to try to bridge the chasm that yawned between them, to try to establish some kind of amicable contact. Fern blotted out deliberately the impish thought that she wanted to see some telltale light of affection in his dark eyes.

Putting on her cloak, she followed him down to the schoolhouse. Fabia's blue eyes clouded as she answered the door.

"He's left, Fern. He was going to the mill. I'm so sorry you've missed him."

Not to be deterred, Fern trudged on toward the mill.

179

Crossing the cobbled mill yard to where a high double door emitted the noise of clanking machinery, she stopped and stared inside.

Even a layman could guess that this was the weaving shed, for a row of great iron looms hurtled and clanged, the shuttles flying so fast it made one dizzy to watch. Women in clogs stood, gray-faced and blank, before the great looms, and children too, some of whom Fern recognized from the school. Some of them, she noticed, had bowed legs, the result of rickets, and all of them looked weary and lifeless.

A man came striding toward her. Fern recognized Fearnley, the manager. He doffed his greasy cloth cap and jerked his head toward the next shed.

"Too noisy here. Come in t' mending shop," he bawled.

She followed him into the shed, where more women sat at tilted tables, poring over pieces of wool fresh from the looms. Fern could see they were examining the stuff for tiny flaws, repairing and drawing up those they found with extreme care. As they worked, men staggered in under the burden of yet more rolls of greasy cloth.

"From here t' stuff goes on to be milled and scoured," Fearnley told her with pride. "Would thee like to see, mistress?"

Assuming she would, he turned to lead the way, across the yard and into the scouring place. Lengths of wool in long iron troughs were being soaked in boiling-hot liquid and forked along mechanically till they reached great rollers, which squeezed the cloth.

"That's to get rid of t' grease," said Fearnley, "and in t' next room t' wool is dried."

In the drying room was a huge iron chamber where hot air was being blown through by a fan. The lengths of damp wool passed slowly over a series of lattices until it emerged dry at the far end. Outside the door Fern could smell the noisome vapor which arose from a series of vats.

"Grease from t' scouring, and sulfuric acid that is," Fearnley said, "to make into oil, and what's left t' soap manufacturers buy. No waste here. Wouldst like to see t' teasing shed

180

now, or t' scribbling room? Or there's a load of fine cloths I can show thee in t' warehouse, meltons and worsteds and t' like?"

"Thank you, no, Mr. Fearnley, not now. I came only to find my husband."

"Oh, t' master's been and gone, half-hour sin."

"Do you know where he went?"

"Oh, aye. He were concerned over t' flow of t' water in t' river. He's gone up to t' reservoir to have a look."

Bilberry Reservoir—that was far away, too far to go on foot. Bruno was doubtless on horseback, so it was impossible to catch up with him now. Fern smiled her thanks and turned to go.

Catsgrave Copse; she could go there. It was not far, and the April afternoon was mild and sunny. Ellen had warned that a visit to Catsgrave—to Kate's grave—was essential.

It was a relief to escape from the thunderous clatter of the mill, with its powerful odors of grease and acid and its slimy stone floors, to the fresh, clean air of the moors. Fern breathed deeply, enjoying again the feeling of freedom that walking the crags always conveyed. She looked along the valley to where Bruno had gone, and in the mist she could just detect a glimmer of sunlight on the waters of the reservoir.

Farther along the crest she turned down toward the copse, led toward it by the bubbling moorland stream which wound its way down and eventually through Catsgrave. Fern followed its curving path to the edge of the copse, and paused.

Despite the mellowness of the afternoon sunlight and the luxuriance of the catkin-laden trees, the copse had a desolate air she had not noticed before. It was unnaturally still, no branches moving in the breeze. And no birds sang. Fern shivered. Perhaps it was the gray clouds slowly looming up from the east that stilled the birdsong, for they sensed the rain to come.

Just inside the wood there were a number of stepping-stones across the stream, and Fern noted as she stepped carefully across, the hem of her gown lifted high, that even the waters made no sound as they rippled past the stones. The farther bank rose steeply to a small clearing, and here Fern stopped.

Tree trunks rose high all around, and in the deep-green and silent gloom the place had the air of a cathedral, only lacking in its sanctity. Fern sat on the grass, leaning against a fallen trunk.

This time Catherine came swiftly, a quick inrush that pervaded Fern's body without the fearful chill that had brought terror. Fern felt her gentle presence taking over and resigned herself contentedly to the usurper, for this was what she had sought. Too long had she waited for Catherine to return.

With her coming the birds suddenly found their voices again, trilling softly through the trees. A shadow fell across the faded blue of Catherine's gown, and she looked up. He was there, his black eyes dancing with happiness as he held out his hands to pull her to her feet.

"Cathy, my love, have I kept you waiting? My mare cast a shoe, and I had to take her in to the blacksmith and walk up."

No matter, she thought inwardly, for a glimpse of your beloved face I would wait a century. She held him back at arm's length to admire him, the broad strength of his body clearly revealed in the fine white shirt and dark-green breeches he wore. How soft and luxurious his shirt felt beneath her fingertips, far removed from the coarse smocks the villagers wore. Suddenly she felt ashamed of her own cheap, workaday gown, the faded cotton which was a hand-me-down from Phoebe.

"Cathy, I swear you grow more beautiful each time I see you," he was saying, drawing her close again to murmur in her ear. "How I failed to notice you in the village before I went away to London, I'll never know. Perhaps you were only a chrysalis then, a green young thing not yet grown to the beautiful butterfly you are now."

She nestled close, savoring his words. In all her life no one had spoken to her thus. Up to now she had been only a butt for criticism and scorn on account of her silence. Only now did she yearn for words to tell him how she loved him too.

"You are enchanting, Kate, and I would not have you otherwise. No, I know you would say you wish you could speak, but why yearn to be a chattering wench when you are so perfect as you are? We have no need of words, you and I, for we understand each other."

He cradled her close, and Catherine felt a glow of contentment and peace such as she had never known. That he loved her truly she did not doubt for a second; had he not, after their first chance meeting, sought out her name, as he promised, and waylaid her again, and again?

And he had told her his name. It had been a shock to discover he was Rafe de Lacy, son and heir to the lord of the manor. Only his constant reassurances that the gap between them was of no account had soothed her. He had sworn he would wed her and no other woman, but Catherine was glad she had no words to tell her family. They could never believe a rich landowner's son had honorable intentions toward a village wench.

Only Phoebe suspected that something new had come into Catherine's life, for she questioned sharply about her sister's sparkling eyes and lightness of step. But even Phoebe had lost interest in Catherine in the last few days, for she had found a beau of her own, a soldier invalided out of the king's army after a stray musket shot had injured his leg. Now she was too preoccupied to notice Catherine's frequent absences.

"Do your family know of me yet, Cathy?" Rafe's voice, tender and warm, invaded her musings. Catherine shook her head dubiously. Rafe smiled.

"Do not look so solemn, sweetheart, there is no sin in keeping it secret yet awhile. But I have told my mother about you."

Alarm leaped into Catherine's eyes. Mistress de Lacy would be sorely angered and might wreak her vengeance on the Radley family, perhaps even depriving them of the strip of land that was their livelihood. Rafe read her misgivings and pulled her down on the warm grass beside him.

"Have no fear, sweeting, for she is glad. She approves my choice, for your family is respected as honest and hardworking, and since my father's death she is anxious for me to wed and give her grandsons to bear the De Lacy name. Yours is good stock, Kate, and she and I will both be happy when you bear my sons."

Catherine reddened and buried her face in his welcoming arm. Rafe laughed, that youthful, buoyant laugh that never failed to fill her with happiness and optimism, and with his free hand he wound tendrils of her unbound hair about his finger.

"Your hair is spun gold, my lovely Kate. I adore your hair, as I worship you. See, I almost forgot—I brought a gift for you."

She looked up shyly as he held out his palm. On it lay a glittering silver ring.

"I had it specially made for us, Kate, with a message on it which betokens what exists between us."

She gazed into his dark eyes inquiringly.

"It is in Latin, and it spells 'Love Eternal,' for our love will outlast time, will it not, beloved?"

She nodded, gazing in wonder at the strange carvings on the ring's surface, then lifted her face for a kiss. He gave it, lingeringly and tenderly, then caught hold of her pointed chin.

"Now it is your turn. We are betrothed now, Kate, and you must give me a gift in return for the ring. I know! I will have a tress of your gold in exchange for my silver."

From his belt he withdrew a hunting knife, and before Catherine could protest, he cut off a curl from the nape of her neck. It lay, glistening in the sunlight, in the broad palm of his hand.

"I shall never, never part with this, Kate, I swear. And when we are old and gray we shall look at this curl and remember how our love began."

A tear hovered on Catherine's lashes. He was so gentle, so loving and kind, that she could never thank God enough for sending him into her life. A distant call on a hunting horn would have passed unnoticed, but Rafe sat up, alerted.

"I must go. Forgive me, Kate, but I must hasten. Will you meet me tonight? The old barn near the crossroads would be easier for you to reach than here?"

She hesitated. Until now they had met only by daylight,

184

here in the copse. The barn was too close to the village for comfort. But still, Rafe was unheeding of prying eyes. He saw no need for secrecy, so let it be. She nodded shyly, pouring love through her eyes.

He squeezed her close. "Tonight, then, soon after dusk. I shall not be late this time."

And he was gone, leaving her feeling bereft and the afternoon a shade grayer for his going. Catherine felt as though the whole encounter had been a magical dream. Could she truly believe her ears, that he had declared his love for her and that Mistress de Lacy actually welcomed the union? God was indeed merciful. And she had a silver ring as token of their betrothal—but no, it was not in the pocket beneath her kirtle. He had taken it with him. In the haste of his leaving, Rafe had pocketed it again. But no matter. Tonight he would give it her again. Catherine reclined against the tree trunk to enjoy the last of the afternoon sunlight before it would be time to go home and milk the cow for supper.

As the shadows lengthened, Catherine rose and wound her way upstream out of the woodland glade, skipping lightly across the stepping-stones and climbing uphill to the crags that edged the moor. Curling her hand above her eyes to shade them from the dipping sun, she could see the outline of the Hall against the skyline, its Tudor white walls and black timbers cradling against the moor's edge. Her thoughts lingered on her beloved, who by now was no doubt within those walls among his family, and her heart raced to think of him possibly speaking of her there now. She, a common villager, one day to enter that gracious Hall as Rafe's bride—it did not seem possible. She could not resist walking closer to it, to try to visualize the golden future he had promised.

Drawing closer, she could see beyond its walls the formal design of its grounds, the symmetrical knot gardens and precisely clipped yews bordering the gravel walks, so unlike her own garden, where plants grew in profusion, spilling over untidily and unrestrained. Cautiously she inched around the upper side of the Hall, where the great wing jutted out to bring itself in the hillside. On that side lay the stables and the mews, and the smell of new-mown hay drifted out deliciously to her nostrils. Impulsively Catherine opened the low iron gate in the wall and crossed to the barn. Inside, the scent of the hay was sensuous and soothing. She climbed the loft ladder and lay, luxuriating, in the warm depths of the hay.

The peace and stillness and warmth lapped about her like a comforting blanket, and Catherine must have drifted into sleep. Later she stretched self-indulgently and sighed, opening her eyes. A candle burned low in its holder by her side. Through parted bed hangings she could see the embers of a fire in the hearth and a paneled mahogany door. She sat up with a start.

Fern was in her own bed in Brackenroyd Hall. It was April 1883, cold in the small hours of the morning, not a summer evening in a barn. She furrowed her brow, trying to recollect. As Fern she had gone to Catsgrave Copse, but try as she might, she could not remember returning to the Hall again. It was confusing. Previously she had come back from that other life and continued this one where she had left off, but this time there was a gap in her memory. It was disturbing. What had she done in the forgotten interval? Had she seen Bruno as she intended, and if so, what had she said to him?

Bruno—Rafe—they were so alike in feature and yet so different in nature, the one so cold and unfathomable, the other so loving and candid. The one could make a woman seethe with anger and frustration, while the other evoked love as sincere as his own in return. Now, if only Bruno ...

Sleep slithered over her again, wiping out the cares of Fern and bringing back the rapture of Catherine, surreptitiously creeping from her cottage at nightfall to keep her tryst with Rafe. "Yon lass is prattling down at the pump again, I've no doubt," Mother had remarked when Phoebe was not back at dusk. Catherine was glad Phoebe was not about, because Phoebe would not have let her sister go without much curious questioning.

The barn near the crossroads was dark and musty, not half so warm and inviting as that up at the Hall. Catherine lifted the latch and entered cautiously, hoping he was already there, his arms held out and a smile on his young dark face to welcome her. She wished she could whisper his name into the gloom.

A rapid scuffle and swishing in the hay alerted her to someone's presence, but no one spoke. A rat, perhaps? She sidled forward into the darkness, tingling with a mixture of hope and apprehension, but no one came to meet her nor spoke a word of welcome. She stopped, frightened. If not Rafe, then who or what had she heard?

As her eyes accustomed to the gloom in the musty depths of the great barn, she looked cautiously about her. Bulky outlines of bales of hay stood silhouetted against the walls, the rungs of a ladder ascending into the invisible loft above, the gleam of a hay fork carelessly cast aside when some farmhand had hastily left for home. She was alone. Catherine turned to go back outside, regretful that once again he was late for their rendezvous.

From behind the door a pair of eyes glowed with menace. Catherine uttered a shriek, and the eyes moved toward her. It was a man, a stranger, and his outstretched hands were no less menacing than the eyes, predatory and intent. She shrank back, terrified, catching her foot against the pitchfork and almost stumbling. He leaped forward with a snarl, and Catherine, terror-stricken, lost track of reason. Unthinkingly she groped for a weapon to fend him off, snatched up the pitchfork, and closed her eyes, holding it before her. She felt his weight against it, felt the heat of his breath brush her cheek, and pushed, desperate to keep the creature away. When no resistance came, she opened her eyes. The eyes still stared, but lifelessly. He was transfixed to the doorjamb, and as she watched in horror, his body slid slowly forward and lurched to the ground athwart the pitchfork.

Catherine stared, petrified and disbelieving. The approach of footsteps jerked her into life, and stepping across the body, she ran out into the night. Rafe came striding jauntily, a smile lighting his handsome face. Catherine, unable to tell him of the horrible nightmarish event in the barn, flung herself into his arms, weeping hysterically.

He cradled her tenderly, trying to calm her sobs. "Come, now, sweetheart, what's amiss? Has your mother been scolding you? Whatever it is, it cannot be so terrible, surely? Come, my sweeting, let me comfort and caress you, and you will soon forget."

She broke away from him, shaking her head violently, till her hair tumbled over her face, clinging in tendrils to the tear-soaked cheeks. She must show him so he could understand the reason for her distress, but she could not face the ugly sight again herself. She gesticulated furiously toward the barn, and as he cocked his dark head questioningly to one side, she began pushing him toward the barn door. He smiled in good humor.

"You are in a hurry, sweetheart—but it should be my place to urge you into the barn. Come, then."

He held out his hand, and Catherine saw his puzzled look when she shook her head and backed away.

"No? Then what? Ah, I have it—you would prefer the copse, is that it? It was always your favorite spot. If ever I lost you, Kate, I should know to find you there. But come quickly, we are wasting time. Tomorrow I must go to London for a few weeks, so let us make the most of precious moments."

His black eyes glowed with affection, and his arm snaked lovingly about her waist. Catherine, sickened at the mental picture of the foul thing within the barn, leaned against his warm strength and let him lead her away. How could she explain, even to Rafe, the corpse there, that the man had been about to attack her? And nothing on earth would induce her to go back there, to lead Rafe in to show him the grisly sight. In her present state of turmoil she could not even think clearly. Gratefully she clung to Rafe's reassuring warmth as they went into the wood.

Rafe was comfort, he was love and loyalty and all that she so desperately needed at this moment. Shivers of terror ran through her body at the memory of the man in the barn, and maybe Rafe was misinterpreting her tremors, her responsiveness, but all she wanted now was forgetfulness, oblivion, ecstasy to wipe out the agony. At no time in her twenty-two years had she felt the need of words as sorely as now. But Rafe more than made up for her inability, his torrent of words expressing love and passion so fiercely that her mind was wiped clear of all else. She sank to the grassy bank beneath him, lost to memory and to suffering.

Time seemed an eternity. When at last she opened her eyes, all emotion spent, she felt now only relaxed and content. All terror and guilt had fled. She rolled over and was startled to find she was alone. Beyond the bed drapes the connecting door yawned wide.

Fern felt dizzy and had to jerk her wits together. She was Fern now, not Catherine, alone in her bed in Brackenroyd Hall. But she slithered the bedclothes back and stared down—she was naked, and the door to Bruno's room stood agape. Surely ... No, he could not have come in here. She would certainly have awoken.

She lay back, trying hard to reorient her mind to the present, but half of it was still luxuriating in the bliss of moments ago. Catherine in her copse, filled with love, while Fern battled to understand.

Bruno could not have come into her room. He had made it plain he did not want her as his true wife, of one flesh, so what reason could he have for opening the door? But she lay naked, her nightgown lying on the floor alongside the bed. She frowned, puzzled and uneasy.

The drugs in his laboratory. Could he have drugged her and then stripped her? No. She had taken great care to accept no more drinks from his hand. But he was a clever man; he could have found some other means to drug her, in her food, perhaps. Anger burned at the thought of it. No man of integrity would drug his bride in order to ravish her. No, not Bruno. He was a man of strength and determination. He would not stoop to surreptitious methods.

In an unguarded moment Fern almost felt regret that he had not. To be made love to by Bruno would be ... would be ... She brushed the daydream aside, irritable with herself for her weakness. Picking up her robe, she draped it about her

189

shoulders and crossed to the door. Bruno lay asleep on the bed in his dressing gown. Silently she withdrew the key from his side of the door, inserted it on her own side, and locked the door.

It was only as she was about to climb back into bed that she saw the gleam of silver under the light of the bedside candle. It was the ring, the one Bruno had used to hypnotize Phoebe, the one Rafe had offered her last night and then forgotten.

She picked it up. A hollow laugh escaped her lips as she read the words on it. *Amor Aeternus*. Love Eternal. So Bruno *had* been into her room while she slept.

But what had he done when he came? Fern felt a mixture of shame and joy at the thought of what he might have done, and was angered with herself. At last, as dawn was breaking, she could bear the indecision no longer. She rose, put on her night robe, and opened the door to his room. He still slept as soundly as a child. She advanced to the bedside firmly.

"Bruno, I want to speak to you."

He stirred and rolled over, a half-smile lifting the corners of his lips. His eyes opened, dark and still bemused with sleep, and he looked up at her with tenderness. Fern bit her lip, undecided how to ask the question that burned within her.

"Did you come to my room in the night?"

The question was sharper, more staccato than she had meant it to sound. He evidently read the hostility in her tone, for the smile fled and his eyes darkened.

"Do you need to ask?"

Embarrassed, blushing with shame, she blundered on. "I am confused. I cannot remember clearly." She could not confess to him that she barely distinguished between Fern and Catherine, that she never quite knew when she changed places, so quickly and easily she seemed to slide from one to the other now. "I found the door open when I awoke, and I seem to remember . . . but I cannot be sure . . ."

He was sitting up now, curiosity in the depths of those eyes, and a sardonic twist to his lips.

"What do you think you remember, Fern? That your husband came to you, as a husband should?"

She hung her head, ashamed at herself, then jerked her head proudly upright. "You made love to me, did you not?"

"And if I did? Your response was most gratifying. But why do you seem so confused, for you were anything but confused at the time."

Fern glared at him. "You knew—you must have known—that I was unaware of what was happening! You took advantage of me!"

"Really?" His thick eyebrows shot up questioningly. "Then your response was remarkably warm in the circumstances."

"You treated me like . . . like a woman of the streets!"

"And you reacted like one."

Fern gasped, stung by the cruel retort. But she was totally unprepared for his next move. He rose leisurely from the bed, crossed to the marble-topped washstand where lay the contents of his trouser pockets. He picked up some coins and returned to her, holding out two golden sovereigns.

"I think perhaps you would consider this adequate payment in the circumstances?" His black eyes bored fiercely into hers. Fern felt fury boiling. She dashed his hand away so that the coins clattered across the parquet floor and rolled under the bed. Then, without thought, she dealt him a fierce blow across his cheek, watching the skin redden over the bone, but he did not move.

She ran from his room, tears burning her eyes. It was clear that as she had lain savoring the caresses of Rafe, she had unwittingly received those of her husband, and she hated him for it. But no more. Never again would he come to her bed; she would see to that. As her rage cooled, Fern dressed for breakfast. When at last she was ready to go downstairs, she heard a sound by the door. Turning, she saw a sheet of paper protruding from under the connecting door.

Curiously she picked it up and read the words in Bruno's firm, upright hand: "Madam, the village will expect an heir to Brackenroyd within a year of our marriage."

She stared at the note, aghast at its coldness and bald statement of fact. No words of atonement or of affection, simply a terse statement as if it were a business letter. "Madam" indeed!

Brackenroyd would wait long for its heir, she resolved. A very, very long time.

Chapter 13

"I'm sorry, madam, the master's gone away."

Mrs. Thorpe's smile was apologetic as she placed the break-fast dishes before Fern, conscious that it was embarrassing for her to know more of the master's movements than the mistress did.

"Gone? Did he say where?"

"Something to do with the dam, he said. Bilberry Reservoir is giving him cause for concern, so he was to go and see the reservoir commissioners. He'd be back in a few days, he said."

"I see. Thank you, Mrs. Thorpe."

Fern was both irritated and disappointed. No doubt after their last encounter Bruno was loath to face her again and so had deemed a message via the housekeeper politic, but it was hurtful to learn of one's husband's movements only through a servant. And she was sorry he was gone. After the terrifying experience of Catherine in the barn, she had need of his company, of his reassuring strength. He was so like Rafe in appearance, and yet so unlike in character.

The Hall too seemed unaccountably desolate without his vibrant presence. Fern wandered disconsolately from room to room, restless and undecided what to do. Last night's events had quite unsettled her, the jumbled dream of Catherine's tragic mishap in the barn aggravated by the strange way Fern had awoken, recalling the comfort of Rafe's arms—or were they Bruno's?

With a pang Fern realized she was aching for the feel of those arms about her again. For all her irritation and anger against Bruno in the past, she needed his reassurance now, and despite herself, she missed him.

Throughout the day Fern's sense of disquiet persisted, and by night she lay restless in her bed, conscious that Bruno no longer lay in the next room. His absence caused an ache which, though she knew it to be irrational and groundless, nevertheless tormented her. However she reasoned with herself that she hated him, distrusted him, feared him even, still she longed for his return.

Sleep brought no peace. She lay crouched in a truckle bed in a corner of the cottage, listening to Phoebe's screams reechoing about the rafters of her little room, wide-eyed and terrified.

"Don't take on so, Phoebe," Mother was murmuring soothingly. "Tha'll make thissen ill, carrying on in that fashion."

"Ben, Ben!" Phoebe sobbed, her face scarlet and contorted with hysterical weeping. "He were to have wed me. What shall I do now? Oh, Ben! Who could a done this to thee!"

She crouched by the hearth, rocking to and fro in her agony and heedless of her mother's attempts to console. Catherine lay numb, stricken with horror. The man in the barn, the man with the menacing eyes and grasping fingers—he had been Phoebe's lover, the swain she had been so proud of. Remorse and guilt flooded Catherine. To have killed a man was sin grievous enough to ensure hell in the hereafter, but her sister's lover!

"Come, now, lass, give over yelling like that—canst see how tha's frightened thy sister?" Mother was urging the grief-stricken Phoebe. But for half the night she sat crooning to the girl while Catherine lay silent, overcome by the enormity of

194

her crime. Useless to confess, to try to explain. Phoebe would never forgive, even if she could understand the reason which had driven Catherine to it.

Even Mother, with all her warmth and kindliness, would be loath to believe the truth, even if Catherine were to express by dumb show that she was the cause of Ben's death, the more so as there was no way Catherine could mime his menacing approach to her. No, best to stay as she had always been, dumb and unobtrusive. Perhaps in time she could find some way to atone to Phoebe.

Gradually Phoebe's wracking sobs and screams gave way to silence. In time she became withdrawn and sullen, and Catherine could see Mother shake her head sadly behind the girl's back.

"It's shock, tha knows. It takes some that way," she murmured to Father. "But she'll get over it, given time. It's a new lad she needs."

"It's a bit more work she needs to occupy her idle hands and give her summat to think about," Father retorted, but not unkindly. Catherine watched her sister fearfully, lest her sharp eyes detect the guilt that Catherine felt certain was stamped all over her face.

Not even in Rafe could she confide the truth, for he was less able to understand her signs than her family. He was content to accept her as she was, wordless and trusting. And now that she had Phoebe's work to attend to as well as her own, there was no opportunity to see Rafe for a time, even after she heard he was back at Brackenroyd Hall.

Phoebe began to go out again, down to the village pump for water in the evenings. And Catherine noticed how the group of girls clustered about the pump ceased their gossiping whenever she approached. But it was not long before the usually garrulous Phoebe had reinstated herself with them, and then it was on Catherine's approach that the sidelong glances were cast her way. Catherine was still riddled with guilt and afraid. Did her guilt show in her expression?

Then rumors began drifting to the Radley cottage.

"Witchcraft? What flummery! Never heard such nonsense

in my life!" exploded Mrs. Radley when a neighbor sat whispering by the hearth. "That lad died 'cause he had a pitchfork stuck through him, and there's nowt supernatural in that. Some tramp, happen, or some gypsy who was stealing from the barn, that's who did it, if tha asks me."

Catherine sat silent but apprehensive at the table, her fingers shelling peas while her ears strained to listen.

"But that's what they're saying, Mistress Radley," the neighbor defended herself. "I'm only telling thee what they're saying in t' village."

"Who says? And who in t' village is capable of witchcraft, I'd like to know? These are dangerous times we live in, neighbor, and to accuse anyone of witchcraft is a certain way to send that body to their death."

"Well, there's old Mother Uttley . . ."

"Who's done nowt but good for us all. Why, she cured thee of a toothache not a month gone."

"Aye, but them as can cast good spells can happen cast evil ones too."

"Fiddlesticks. Tha's no cause to speak ill on Mother Uttley, so leave the poor creature alone. Besides, she's learned our Catherine a useful potion or two. Our lass has learned a lot from her."

"Aye, that's what they're saying."

Mistress Radley's eyes grew wide in disbelief. "Tha's not saying, surely . . . Tha can't believe . . ." She glanced quickly across to her daughter. "Catherine, leave t' peas, there's a good lass, and fetch in some milk from t' cowshed. I shall need some for t' baking in a minute."

Catherine rose obediently but lingered outside the cottage window, opened for the sake of a cool breeze on this hot afternoon.

"Who's been saying such cruel things, neighbor?" Mistress Radley was demanding in a fierce whisper. "Who'd dare say owt agen my Catherine?"

"Well, to be honest, mistress, it was your Phoebe."

"Phoebe? Never!"

"I heard her wi' my own ears. She reckons as Ben was

lured to his death by an evil spirit, and there's precious few hereabouts as know how to cast spells. Then she said as Mother Uttley was ill abed that night and so couldn't a harmed him. So that left only . . . only . . ."

"I'll not have it," Mistress Radley shouted, and Catherine trembled at the rage in her mother's voice. "They'll not say a word agen my poor girl, blighted as she is, but good and pure for all that. They'll not threaten my poor lass!"

"It's Phoebe as says it," the neighbor stammered. "I'd not have repeated it else. But there's some as is anxious to report the matter to the authorities. Tha knows how they hunt witches out."

"I know. I've heard of them witchfinders and what they do. They'll not come pricking and ducking my innocent lass, and I'll thank thee to put the lie to this evil rumor. Good day to thee, neighbor."

Catherine shrank back behind the corner of the cottage as the neighbor emerged, her foot crushing a patch of her beloved mint-scented geranium and sending up the pungent aroma to envelop her. A sweat of fear banded her forehead. So by mischance the villagers had guessed the culprit, Ben's murderer, but for the wrong reasons.

Witchcraft, they said. Catherine shuddered. It was unbelievable. Phoebe must believe her filled with spite or jealousy to want to occasion her lover's death, and by such stealthy means. Oh, it was so cruel! To be justly accused of murder was one matter, but to be wrongfully accused of devil's work for malicious reasons was more than heart or soul could bear. Catherine felt giddy with fear and horror. She stumbled across the green to the sanctuary of the church.

Torment wracked her. Even in the sepulchral gloom of the deserted church she could find no peace. The faces of the saints enshrined in stained glass seemed to frown down on her and it was in vain that she tried to pray for guidance. Guilt weighed heavy on her soul, dragging her down to inevitable hell fire. Catherine moaned in agony.

Two village women came down the aisle bearing clusters of flowers for the altar. On seeing Catherine, they glanced ner-

197

vously at each other. In the somber silence their whispered words carried clearly to her ears.

"That's her. Never think it to look at her, wouldst tha?"

"Fancy having the nerve to come into church after what she's done. Face of an angel and soul of a devil, that one. Who'd a thowt it?"

They gazed up at the altar as if they half-expected an avenging God to crack a thunderbolt down on the sinful maid, and Catherine could only stare helplessly at them. If these women who had known her all her life could believe such evil about her, what chance would she have of convincing the authorities that Ben's death had been only a tragic mistake? Again the dizziness enfolded her, the vivid colors of the stained glass swimming and merging in the shafts of sunlight.

Rafe! Oh, Rafe, come to me, help me! she cried inwardly. Through the eddying mist that threatened to submerge her, she heard a woman's voice.

"She'll get her deserts. Tha knows what t' good book says: 'Vengeance is mine, saith the Lord.' He'll see to it she pays for what she's done."

"Aye," agreed a vindictive voice. "Soon as t' witchfinder gets here, she'll suffer. I hear as pricking t' devil's mark and t' ducking stool never fails."

"She hasn't t' devil's mark, has she?"

"Oh, aye. Phoèbe says it's clear as day, just under her left armpit. And that cat of hers must be her familiar, I reckon."

Oh, no, it was too cruel! A mole interpreted as a condemning mark, and a hairless pet like Tibb as a familiar spirit—how credulous people could be! Catherine felt desperate, alone, and terrified in her mute world. Oh, Rafe! For pity's sake, help me!

She opened her eyes. In her hand a candle glowed, and with the other she was rattling a doorknob. Fern steadied herself, fighting to hold on to a time and a place. She was here, in Brackenroyd Hall, in her bedroom, and struggling to open the door to Bruno's room. And her voice was crying plaintively for help. Footsteps came scurrying in the corridor, and someone knocked peremptorily at the door.

"Are you all right, madam?" It was Mrs. Thorpe's voice. Fern opened the door to her wearily.

"Is anything wrong, Mrs. de Lacy? I heard you calling for the master. He's not home yet, remember." Her welcome face, framed in rag curlers, expressed concern.

"It's all right, Mrs. Thorpe. A bad dream only. I had forgotten the master's absence."

The housekeeper's anxious face softened. "He'll be back in a day or two. Now, can I make you a hot drink to help settle you?"

"No, really, thanks. I'll be all right now."

"Very well, then. Good night, Mrs. de Lacy."

After her slippered feet had scuttered off down the corridor again, Fern blew out the candle and climbed back into bed. She felt disturbed and somehow guilty, as if Catherine's guilt had rubbed off onto her. But then, she *was* Catherine, with only an interval of time separating her former life from her present one. Nevertheless, she felt remorseful. She had deserted Catherine just at her moment of greatest need. She must endeavor to return as soon as she could.

But throughout the rest of the night Fern could not sleep. She tossed restlessly, thinking of the villagers and their hatred of the Radleys. "Tainted blood" they had called it, the only relic of the story of Catherine that had come down to them. Poor Catherine, all these centuries unjustly condemned as a witch, shadowing the lives of all succeeding Radleys like a menacing cloud.

In the morning Mrs. Thorpe searched Fern's face anxiously. "You look very pale, madam. Are you sure you're not sickening for something?"

"I slept badly, that is all. Perhaps fresh air will revive me. The day is warm and sunny, so I think I'll ride out on Whisper. Please ask Malachi to saddle her up for me."

It was a mild and beautiful May morning as Fern rode down to the village, undecided what she would do when she arrived there. As she drew up by the village green, Edgar Amos was standing sunning himself by the lych-gate.

"Good morning, Mrs. de Lacy. I was just thinking of you. Quite a coincidence you should ride by."

"Of me? Why?"

"That old register where we found Catherine Radley's death quite intrigued me. I've just been reading it again. Curious, but there seem to have been quite a number of deaths in strange circumstances just about that time, the summer of 1642. Come, I'll show you, if you're interested."

Dismounting and tying Whisper to a fence rail, Fern followed him into the vestry. Specks of dust rose from the ancient ledger as he opened it, hovering in the sunlight that fell from a high window. Fern read the faint, spidery script with difficulty.

On Julye xii William Brygg was drowned at Park Mylne as he crossed over a narrow bridge. A soden tempest of wind blew him into the water, and the water was unnaturally greate.

Jennett, wyfe of John Marsden, as she comed from ye pasture from milking, ye xxi daye of Julye, was struck by a thunderbolt and died.

Agnes, wyfe of Richard Littlewoode, within xi dayes of she was delivered of a child, rose out of hyr childe bedde and went privily to a little well not halfe a yarde deepe, and there drowned the childe.

All these deeds by instigation of the devil, and more yet we wot not of, perchance.

Fern straightened up from poring over the ledger. Amos was watching her, his fair head cocked to one side speculatively.

"What do you make of that, Mrs. de Lacy?"

She shrugged. "Some poor old parson who was unduly superstitious, no doubt."

"Or a wave of hysteria swept the village. It was a bad year for the village. The crops failed, owing to storms, and the register lists a number of stillbirths. These events would frighten the villagers. It was the era of witch-hunting then, you know, when Matthew Hopkins, the self-appointed witchfinder general, was terrorizing the south."

"What do you make of it, then?"

He frowned. "Taking into account the hatred that has always been felt against the Radleys, the ancient belief in their tainted blood, and the curt way in which Catherine's death is reported simply as 'departed this life,' I think it was she who was suspected of witchcraft."

"And her death? What caused that?"

She would discover, sooner or later, how Catherine died, but the question was of burning importance. She hoped Amos would not notice the eagerness in her voice.

"I don't know." He rubbed his chin thoughtfully, his gaze clouded and far away. "There are more records I've not yet read. Perhaps I shall find the answer there, and then I'll let you know."

He followed her out of the church into the sunlight. At the gate he cupped his hands to help her mount, then shaded his eyes against the sun to watch her ride off. Fern felt choked by the dust in the vestry, the claustrophobic air of the village, the knots that bound about her heart, and longed for air to breathe freely. The moors. That was what she wanted—the vast space and freedom of the moors.

Up and up she urged Whisper, up over the crags on the crest of the hill and away across the vast expanse of moor, where there was only solitude and strange silences, across an endless succession of heather-clad undulations which melted in the purple distance into the sunlit sky. Up here she could breathe again, here where it seemed as though a person could ride for days without seeing a human face or hearing a human voice. The moors held a terrifying power, even on this fine day, for she remembered how in the gloom of winter their dark, frowning presence had dominated the landscape.

Near the lapping waters of the reservoir she dismounted and let Whisper graze on the short, springy turf. Fern stared across the rippling, expressionless waters and felt miserably alone. Here, in the high free air, the burden of guilt seemed to weigh less heavily, but she longed for Bruno to come back, for his nearness to allay the suspicion of fear and impending tragedy that darkened her mind. She needed his strength, his reassuring rationalism, to try to extricate herself from the turmoil of Catherine, who was more in her than Fern. Differentiation between herself then and now was becoming increasingly difficult and less definable. She felt she would go out of her mind unless help came soon.

In the distance a thin wreath of smoke coiled up into the air. Fox Brow. Ellen was at home, alone but for old Hepzibah. Impulsively Fern resolved to go and see the young widow. Perhaps she, in her half-crazed world, could understand and help.

Ellen's door was already ajar when Fern dismounted. Fern hesitated on the step. Ellen was close to Bruno, his friend and confidante—would it be wise to reveal one's doubts and anxieties to her, especially when one's doubts included that close friend?

Ellen's light voice called from within, "Come in, Mrs. de Lacy. I have been expecting you."

She was sitting by the table, her hands composed in her lap. Her eyes searched Fern's face curiously.

"You are troubled, I can see. Sit by me and let me guess at what distresses you."

Fern sat opposite her and felt the gray eyes raking deep, as if searching out her soul. It was a soothing sensation, that someone cared and wanted to help.

"You have the gift, as I told you once. By its means you have discovered the reason for your unhappiness—and that of all the Radleys. Now you come close to the answer, as no Radley has done before."

"What is the answer, Ellen?"

"Love. There are many great and powerful cosmic forces which only the mystics can understand, but the most universal, the most potent of them all, is love."

"Love?" Fern was bewildered.

"It is energy, psychic energy. Love of one's fellow men, the

202

consciousness of becoming one and the same person with another, that is the ultimate power of the universe. Forgive me my philosophical wanderings, but it is the one truth I have learned. You too are learning it now, I believe."

"You mean ... I love Bruno?" Fern's voice was hesitant, reluctant to mouth the words.

"Did you ever doubt it? And your family inheritance, else you would not be at one with your past as you are. But you are still blind. You have yet more to learn."

"What must I learn, Ellen?"

"Patience, understanding. I think you do not yet see how Bruno suffers."

"He suffers?" Amazement rang in Fern's voice.

"Oh, yes, my dear. His is a battle to find himself."

Fern sat perplexed, thinking over Ellen's words. To find oneself. That was the very problem Bruno had once said she had to resolve before she would find peace. And if Ellen was right, he was faced with the same problem himself. It had never occurred to Fern that Bruno, the dark, taciturn man of strength, could have a personal difficulty such as this.

"You forget, my dear, that he is of mixed parentage, and so of mixed heredity. The Yorkshire part of him, wild and unrestrained and imaginative, is at variance with his Teutonic blood. He sees himself as cool and rational, analytical and precise, as a scientist should be, and he cannot easily reconcile himself to the passionate, irrational moods that overtake him from time to time."

"Bruno?" Fern thought Ellen must be speaking of some other man.

"Oh, yes, he suffers as a result. He is a soul in torment, Fern, but through your love he can find himself again, as he was meant to be. You must have patience, for you have found yourself, and he is still to attain that. It will not be long now, though the worst of the suffering is still to come."

Ellen's eyes were misted now, remote and sad. Fern felt she could foresee the tragedy, but something stilled her tongue from questioning.

"It will ... work out right, won't it, Ellen?" Fern's voice was faint with apprehension.

"This time it will; it must." Centuries of hope and sadness lay in Ellen's tone. Slowly Fern rose to go, filled with a new determination.

"Thank you, Ellen. I shall remember what you have said."

Somehow, thought Fern as she rode back toward the Hall, somehow I must resolve the problems of both Catherine and Bruno. And somehow the two problems seemed one, inextricably linked though separated by three hundred years and more. In an inexplicable way she knew that the solution of the one problem would inevitably resolve the other. Tonight she would welcome Catherine's advent and the unfolding of the poor maid's unhappy tale.

But Catherine did not come. By morning Fern felt utterly drained and exhausted from willing her to come, but in vain. She felt afraid, too, afraid that Catherine was slipping away from her, and only by a tenuous thread was the unhappy creature still bound to her. She could not fade away now, to vanish into a limbo of lost souls, forever wandering and wretched. Fern was fretful and sick at heart.

All day she carried the burden of desolation and aimlessness with her, unable to set her mind to anything. By nightfall it seemed too much of an effort to dress for dinner, with Bruno away still.

Mrs. Thorpe tapped at her mistress's door. "The master is home, madam. He's gone down to his laboratory and says he will not take dinner tonight."

Fern's heart leaped into life. Somehow, with Bruno now in Brackenroyd, Catherine seemed a little closer. Despair and lethargy fell from her shoulders. She dressed quickly in a delicate filmy gown and went down to meet Bruno.

The heavy oak door to the old wing swung open as she neared it, and Bruno emerged, bowed and hollow-eyed. On an impulse Fern drew back into the shadows of the corridor until he had closed and locked the door. Then, as he turned to go toward the dining room, she moved forward into the light of the gas lamp on the wall. He stopped suddenly, a light coming sharply into his dark eyes, a look that was at once fierce and compelling.

"Beloved," he murmured.

Instantly she flung herself into his outstretched arms, happiness and warmth suffusing her. His arms enclosed her tightly; then he kissed her. Fern welcomed with delight the feel of his mouth hard on hers and the bittersweet taste of his lips, then drew slowly away.

"I've missed you, Bruno."

The soft words had an effect she could not have anticipated. At once he stiffened and his eyes grew cold. He stood erect and formal, and Fern was bewildered by the sudden change.

"What is it, Bruno? What's wrong?"

He hesitated. "I don't know. I am not myself today. Please forgive me."

It was then that she noticed the gleam in his fingers. It was a frond of hair, a blond tress not unlike her own. He must have been carrying it when she met him.

"What is that, Bruno?"

He looked down at it with an air of surprise, as if he had not seen it before, then raised it to the light of the lamp and examined it, a hint of a smile softening the line of his mouth.

"Where does it come from, Bruno?"

"I don't know. I found it in a little box in the study."

"Then why do you have it?"

He shrugged. "For some reason, I find it interesting. I shall replace it in the box."

In his study she watched him take out a small ebony box from a drawer, opening it to reveal a velvet-lined interior. He laid the curl inside, tied with its faded ribbon, and closed the lid gently. Something in the way he moved his broad, muscular hands over the lid, tenderly and slowly, made Fern ache to recapture the closeness there had been between them in the corridor only moments ago. She moved closer to him.

"There is something nostalgic in a family heirloom, is there not?" she murmured softly. He drew himself up sharply.

"I have no time for sentimentality." His voice was cruelly

sharp, accusing in its denial. For once Fern was not angered by his sudden change; only a pang of pity touched her that always, always he seemed to feel the need to defend himself, to retort and deny. Ellen was right. One needed patience to understand this man. His eyes held a distracted, almost hunted look. Fern took his hand shyly and led him back into the corridor.

"Come, let us go in to dinner, and then we shall go to bed early. You look tired."

He drew his hand away. "I do not wish to eat, nor have I time to sleep. Tomorrow I must go to see the magistrates; the commissioners will not listen to reason about the reservoir."

"You work too hard, Bruno. The problem of water supply is not so pressing that it cannot wait. The mill has functioned quite well up to now."

He sighed and passed a hand across his brow. "You do not understand. I have told you before that you do not understand. I am not concerned with the mill, but our safety. The reservoir dam is in need of repair, and I must get the commissioners to act before it is too late."

"Tomorrow, Bruno. Tonight you must sleep."

He turned on her suddenly, his expression almost savage. Fern involuntarily took a step back. "Tonight I must go to Fox Brow," he hissed softly.

"Fox Brow?" echoed Fern. "To Ellen Stansfield? Why do you go there so often?" He did not answer. "Why, I asked you? Every night almost since our wedding you have gone there, I know."

He was turning away, her question unheeded.

Fern grew angry. She grasped his arm and glared at him. "Why must you see Ellen Stansfield every night, and not your wife? Is she your mistress?"

Fern never saw his arm rise, only the color that flooded his cheeks and the fire in his eyes. But she felt the fierce sting of his fingers on her cheek. Disbelievingly she stared, her hand to her face. Bruno glared at her, anger and hatred staring from his black eyes; then he turned suddenly and strode away, leaving her alone in the empty corridor.

Angrily Fern turned back along the passage. As she neared the studded door to the old wing, she noticed the keys still dangling from the lock. Bruno had evidently forgotten them when she came upon him unexpectedly.

The sting of his hand still hot on her cheek and the bitter-sweet taste of his mouth still fresh on her lips, Fern turned the key over furiously and opened the door, taking the bunch of keys with her into the darkness beyond.

At the far end of the stone passage a solitary lamp burned, piercing only a part of the intense gloom of the old Hall. Her footsteps echoed hollowly as she crossed toward the laboratory, ringing mournfully in the desolate atmosphere. Tonight the old Hall had the air of an empty tomb, and a frisson of fear went down Fern's spine. Would she ever find Catherine again, to play out the last, tragic scenes of her pitiful life? The fear that she might not gave Fern a terrible, unbearable sense of loss. She picked up the oil lamp, and by its light tried the keys in the lock of the laboratory door.

The second key opened the door. In the circle of light thrown by the lamp Fern could see the bench and shelves, the gleam of bottles and jars. On the bench lay an empty glass. She picked it up and sniffed the dregs cautiously. The smell was familiar. A tentative taste on the tip of her finger confirmed it. It was the bittersweet taste of Bruno's lips. Hemlock, belladonna, laudanum, opium—of all the bottles arranged there, from which ones had he concocted a mixture to drink . . . and why?

Fern relocked the door after her, replacing the keys in the lock of the heavy door to the main house where she had found them, before going down to a solitary dinner. Mrs. Thorpe came in as Cassie was clearing the dishes away.

"Begging your pardon, Mrs. de Lacy, but was supper not to your liking?" she asked anxiously.

"Perfectly, Mrs. Thorpe. I was not hungry, that is all."

The old lady's eyes searched hers. "Are you quite sure you are well, madam? It's not like you to leave your meal hardly touched."

Fern saw her questioning eyes, the speculative stare, and

recognized the unspoken suspicion. Was the mistress of Brackenroyd pregnant already? That was no doubt the gossip belowstairs.

"I am simply tired, that is all. I shall go to bed soon."

"Very well, madam. The master has gone out with Pharaoh, so I have just put away his things in the study. I hope he will not mind."

"I'm sure he won't. What things?"

"Papers, files. Oh, and that little lock of hair." Mrs. Thorpe's eyes misted with nostalgia. "Old Mr. Thomas used to take that blond lock out of its box sometimes and wash it in brandy, to keep it bright he said."

Despite her weariness, Fern was curious. "Did he say whose hair it was, Mrs. Thorpe? An old sweetheart, perhaps?"

"Dear me, no. He said it had been in the family for ages, hundreds of years he said. And he said a funny thing. He said Brackenroyd would never be happy until its owner came back. I never could understand old Mr. Thomas, but he was a very kind and clever man."

Mrs. Thorpe smiled at the memory, and left, leaving a faint scent of lavender water in her wake. Fern rose wearily from the table and had to clutch at the edge for support as a wave of dizziness washed over her. She slumped into a chair by the fireside and felt distinctly nauseated.

She was trembling with apprehension. What on earth was wrong with her? Could the suspicion clearly showing in Mrs. Thorpe's eyes be true after all, that she was carrying Bruno's child? It was unthinkable, to be bearing a child whose conception she could not even remember. Nor could she be certain it had ever taken place. Exhaustion—that was much more likely to be the reason. Or the effect of Bruno's potion she had tasted down in the laboratory. But, no. A tiny fingertip taste could hardly have such drastic effect, when Bruno, having drunk the glassful presumably, had walked out on the moor tonight apparently unaffected.

Or maybe he was affected by the drugs. How was she to know when his behavior was different from usual, when she did not really know the man? But he did change personality often and inexplicably—had this always been due to drugs?

It was odd to remember how she had suspected him of drugging her, while all the time he must have been administering the drugs to himself. But why?

Speculation was cut short by the discreet knock and entrance of Fanny. The maid bobbed a curtsy.

"Begging your pardon, madam, but the Reverend Amos is here and wishes to see you. Mrs. Thorpe says I am to inquire whether you feel well enough to receive him."

"Of course, Fanny. Please show him in here."

Edgar Amos' eyes sparkled as he strode in and crossed to the hearth. "Forgive me, Mrs. de Lacy, for intruding so late in the evening, but I have just discovered among the late Mr. Thomas' notes a story I knew would intrigue you. I had to come and tell you at once."

"Pray be seated, Edgar. Fanny, a glass of wine for the reverend. Madeira, Edgar, or Canary?"

"Madeira, excellent, thank you." He waited until Fanny had handed him the wine, bobbed, and left the room. Then he leaned forward eagerly, putting the wine aside.

"Your Catherine de Lacy was a witch. Or at any rate, the villagers believed she was. Mr. Thomas unearthed accounts—which I can verify, as he states his source in the notes—which told how the villagers suspected her and began to amass evidence against her."

Fern stared at him and felt no emotion. What he told her she knew already. All that concerned her now of Catherine's story was its ending, how she died and how her relationship with Rafe fared. Edgar Amos watched her face curiously.

"Are you not interested, Mrs. de Lacy? I thought you would be."

"You tell me what I already know, Edgar."

His sandy eyebrows shot up. "You knew? Were there other notes of Mr. Thomas' here in the Hall?"

She shook her head wearily. "Tell me, Edgar, does the account say anything of Rafe de Lacy?"

"No, not really, except to mention that he was lord of the

manor at the time and unable to prevent the witch-hunt against one of his villagers, as he was absent from Bracken-royd. Curiously enough, he seems to have returned here on the date given in the parish records as the date that Catherine departed this life."

Fern leaned forward, a gleam of interest revived. "The parish records neglected to state the cause of her death. Does Mr. Thomas' account reveal what happened?"

"He does not state the manner of her death, I'm afraid, but the persecution she suffered leaves one in little doubt. The villagers were unable to try out the usual test for a witch, of getting her to repeat the Lord's Prayer to see if she falters, because it was useless in the case of a dumb girl. Perhaps out of fear or respect for her father they did not duck her in the river either, nor prick the witch's mark she is reputed to have had on her body, but they harassed and tormented her nonetheless."

"So you are in little doubt how she died?"

"What would a poor dumb creature do in such circumstances, unable to run away and fend for herself? I think she probably committed suicide like Annot, for her body does not lie in the churchyard."

Fern felt anger for Catherine flood through her veins, bringing back life and purpose in place of the lassitude of a moment ago. She rose and crossed to the fireplace, to pull the bell rope.

"There you are wrong, Edgar. Catherine did not kill herself. Would you do something for me?"

He rose quickly. "Of course, Mrs. de Lacy."

"Then pray accompany me to Fox Brow."

"Now? It is late, and darkness has fallen. Is it Mr. de Lacy you seek, for I will gladly fetch him for you."

"No, Edgar. It is not Bruno I seek, but Catherine. I must go now, before it is too late."

He was staring at her, openmouthed. "Catherine? Do you mean Ellen, Mrs. de Lacy, Ellen Stansfield?"

Fanny appeared in the doorway. Fern turned to her, forgetting Amos for the moment. "Please fetch my cloak, Fanny, and tell Mrs. Thorpe not to lock up until I return. I am going out with Reverend Amos."

The maid bobbed and withdrew. Fern turned again to Amos. "I meant what I said, Edgar. I need Ellen's help. If Catherine will not or cannot come to me, then I must go in search of her."

Chapter 14

With lamplight gleaming from one uncurtained window as they drew near, Fox Brow had the appearance of a squat, one-eyed monster crouching on the cliff edge. In the moonlight its shape was only indistinctly visible.

"Ellen is still up, at any rate." Amos seemed embarrassed at their late visit, and then Fern remembered that he had probably never visited the house before, since Ellen was reported to receive few callers.

Fern waited while Edgar stepped down from the trap and turned to help her down. As she stood poised on the step, a faint, far-off sound came to her ears.

"What was that?" There was an edge of fear in Fern's voice.

"I heard nothing," Edgar replied after a moment's pause.

"I thought I heard a cry."

"Just the wind over the moors, I expect. Come, Mrs. de Lacy. It is cold out here."

Fern hesitated, transfixed. She could have sworn she heard it—a faint voice calling "Catherine" in a long, drawn-out, despairing cry. She pulled herself together. He was probably right. The wind could sound deceptively human, and especially at night.

It was old Hepzibah who came to the door in answer to Amos' knock. The door opened only inches, restrained by the heavy chain, and Hepzibah's suspicious face, wreathed in rag curlers, peered out at the visitors.

"Mrs. de Lacy wishes to see Miss Stansfield. You recognize me, do you not, Hepzibah?" Amos said gently.

"Aye, Reverend, but we weren't expecting company at this hour," the old woman replied gruffly as she unlatched the chain. "Coom in."

She shuffled ahead of them into the parlor. "H's t' vicar and Mrs. de Lacy."

"Come in and warm yourselves by the fire." Ellen's silvery voice betrayed no surprise as she waved her visitors to the vacant chairs by the fire. It was a cozy scene, lamplight and firelight casting a mellow glow over chintz covers and chenille tablecloth and the frail figure of the woman with a cloud of prematurely gray hair about her gentle face.

"Shall I mend t' fire for thee?" Hepzibah asked.

"No need of more coal tonight. Get yourself to bed, Hepzibah."

The old woman grunted and withdrew. Ellen turned to Fern. "Do you come in search of your husband, my dear, for I fear you have missed him. He was here, but he left half an hour ago."

Fern shook her head. "Do not misunderstand me. I want to see Bruno, yes, but first I must find someone else."

She could see from the corner of her eyes the wondering look on Amos' face as he sat quietly, just beyond Ellen's line of sight. He might think her crazy, but what matter? Finding Catherine—and Bruno—was a problem so urgent that now they seemed a matter of life and death to her.

Ellen's gaze was mistily remote. "He still seeks himself, poor man. But the time is not far off when he will arrive at the truth."

"Bruno?" Fern prompted softly.

"He was like a man crazed with fear—or hate, or some other violent emotion."

"Tonight?"

The soft, misted eyes turned on Fern. "Aye, tonight. He talked of wild things, meaningless jumble. I could make no sense of it. He was like a man possessed, or drunk."

Amos cleared his throat apologetically. "I too have seen him in that condition, I'm afraid, Mrs. de Lacy. I did not wish to alarm you with undue fears, but I do wonder if Dr. de Lacy does not perhaps, um, imbibe more than is good for him."

"Not drink, but drugs," said Fern quietly.

Amos was startled, but Ellen showed no reaction. Fern leaned toward the older woman and took her hands. "Tonight I found the emptied glass in his laboratory. Did you know he took drugs, Ellen?"

Ellen nodded slowly. "I knew he used to, when he first came here, for he told me about it. His work was concerned with the human mind, he said, and the causes of hallucination."

"So he took drugs himself?" Amos queried.

"One could not measure the effect of them on an animal's mind, so it was necessary to use a human subject for experiment, he said."

Fern remembered how she had suspected him of drugging her, how he had interrogated her about her resulting dreams. She stared at Ellen, who shook her head again in mute reply.

"What better subject than himself, he decided, for he could best gauge the results on himself." Ellen's eyes clouded in bewilderment. "But he told me some weeks ago he was discontinuing the experiments. They were having side effects he found unpleasant, he said. I thought he had stopped."

"He has not. I found the evidence tonight."

"Then there must be another reason."

"He could have become addicted, perhaps," Amos interjected, but it was an explanation Fern could not accept. Bruno was too stubborn, too self-willed to allow himself to become dependent on a prop.

214

Suddenly Ellen withdrew her hands from Fern's, and rising, walked slowly to the table. "Now I think it becomes clear. Dr. de Lacy has been discovering something of the truth about himself—so much I have gathered from his ramblings—and he does not like what he learns. It would seem he tried to discontinue the drugs because it was by their means that he was finding out."

"Then why is he taking them again?" Fern asked hesitantly.

"Because he is strong. Though he dislikes it, he will find out the truth. It gives him pain, of that I am certain, and I think it also brings him fear."

The atmosphere was tense. Amos tried to lighten it with a staccato laugh. "What devilish secrets can the poor man have in his past that he does not like to recall? Some foolish misdeed in his youth, perhaps? But then, what man in Christendom hasn't committed some trifling misdemeanor he would prefer to forget?"

Ellen did not seem to notice the vicar's presence. "But then, it was not primarily about Dr. de Lacy that you came, my dear. Have no fear, his problem will be resolved very soon now. I feel it."

"Are you sure, Ellen?"

She nodded sagely. "As soon as he comes to terms with his Yorkshire blood instead of trying to deny the wild and passionate part of himself. He has been brought up in Germany, taught to think like an objective, reasoning creature, and he believes it wrong to be a slave to one's feelings. But one cannot deny what is in the blood. Heredity will have its way."

She was sitting now at the table, chin resting on cupped hands, a halo of lamplight about her head. Fern went to sit in the spindle-backed chair opposite her.

"It was not about Bruno that I came, but Catherine. I cannot reach her, Ellen. You must help me."

She saw the woman's eyes soften in answer to the pleading in her voice. Amos pulled his chair nearer the table. A coal settled noisily in the hearth, and the firelight grew dimmer. In another room a clock began to chime softly, but whether it struck ten or eleven, Fern did not notice. Her gaze was fixed on Ellen's translucent face. Ellen did not speak, but Fern could feel the atmosphere in the little room thickening, and she knew Ellen was mentally in communion with her, willing Catherine to return. For both of them the intrusive vicar did not exist.

Shadows gathered about the corners of the room. The old clock on the draped mantelshelf ticked relentlessly on, seeming to grow louder in the silence that fed the growing tension. Amos cleared his throat nervously, but the two women were unaware of him.

"It's getting cold," he said in a brittle voice at last. "Are you sure you wouldn't like me to put more coal on the fire, Mrs. Stansfield?"

Ellen's eyes did not waver from Fern's. It was true, the room was becoming very cold, the chill seeming to climb from Fern's feet to her knees. For a moment she began to doubt the wisdom of what they were doing, but the die was cast. Catherine *must* be reached. . . .

She felt the muscles in her back and her neck begin to stiffen with tension, and the shadows in the corners seemed to move nebulously and start to take shape. The nape of her neck prickled, and she heard Amos cough. Fear began to gnaw her, and she started to pant in shallow, panicking breaths. Ellen's hand reached forward to close over hers, and her touch was as cold as death.

"Do not fear." Ellen's voice was faint and musical, like a distant harp.

For the first time Fern saw Amos' face, white and tight with fear, his pale eyes staring. It was as if he saw something terrifying in the shadows. A strange, soft moaning sound pervaded the house, a sound infinitely pathetic and hauntingly tragic. Fern closed her eyes and willed Catherine to come, to take possession of her body. She was near now; Fern could tell by the terror in the air, the terror Catherine had felt before her death, a terror so powerful it had persisted through the centuries and kept the restless spirit wandering in search of exoneration.

You are near, Catherine, I feel it, so near. . . .

Suddenly the door crashed open, and Hepzibah rushed in, her face blanched and her rheumy old eyes popping. Instantly the charged atmosphere reverted to normal, and Amos rose unsteadily. Fern could have wept with frustration.

"What's going on, Mrs. Stansfield?" Hepzibah demanded, her body shaking so violently she had to clutch the back of Amos' vacated chair for support. "Summat's up, and I can't understand it, such fierce cold and funny noises. I don't hold wi' such goings-on, and though I nivver interfere as a rule, Mrs. Stansfield, I'm that shaken I mun speak. Summat wicked's about to befall us. I can feel it!"

"It is gone now, Hepzibah. Go back to bed, my dear. All is well. Nothing will happen to you." Ellen's voice was reassuringly firm, and Hepzibah let herself be cajoled back to bed, muttering emphatically that no sleep would come to her that night after what she had experienced. Many prayers would be necessary to chase away the malign influences. Fern, however, could barely control her vexation, fighting to keep back the tears. Amos was still tense and bewildered.

"I don't know what was happening in this room a few moments ago, Mrs. de Lacy, but I too would like you to know that I do not approve. Table-rapping and suchlike have become fashionable pastimes with the gentry, I believe, but if that is what you and Mrs. Stansfield were up to, a séance of some kind, I should point out that it is a very dangerous practice."

"It was no séance, Reverend. Mrs. de Lacy has a natural affinity with her past," Ellen said quietly.

"Well, whatever it was, it will bring no good," Amos averred emphatically. "I am not one to deny the psychic abilities of some people, but I do not hold with tampering with unknown forces."

"The forces are not unknown to Fern and me," Ellen countered, firmness latent in her mild eyes.

"Nevertheless, one can inadvertently release powers one is unable to control. Admittedly, I have no direct experience of such matters myself, but I have colleagues of the cloth who have been hard put to it to exorcise the evil influences which

217

have been evoked in this way. I think it is time I escorted Mrs. de Lacy back to the Hall."

Fern had never seen him so forceful, but there was no doubt that fear directed his words. He was shaking still, his blue eyes widened till the whites gleamed in the lamplight. His fingers trembled as he helped her put on her cloak.

Ellen accompanied them to the door, standing on the threshold while Amos helped Fern into the trap. The pony whinnied restlessly. A bank of cloud, thrust by a rising wind, scurried across the moor and obliterated its light.

Fern's cloak flapped about her as they drove away. "The wind's getting up," Amos remarked in a voice aimed to sound calm and natural. And indeed it was. Across the moor Fern could hear it rising and howling, then sinking to a mournful moan before gathering fresh breath to howl again. By the time they reached the Hall, heavy raindrops were spattering the wide flight of steps. Amos seemed distinctly relieved when, having seen Fern into the Hall, he was able to stride away down the drive in the direction of the church.

Cassie brought a cup of hot chocolate as Fern prepared for bed. She looked pinched and cold, and her hand trembled, rattling the china cup in the saucer as she placed it on the night table. Fern climbed into bed and sipped the hot liquid gratefully. There was a chill in her bones which had begun in Ellen's little parlor and which it seemed would never be driven from her body again.

"Aren't you going home tonight, Cassie?"

"No, madam. Sometimes I stay t' night if t' weather's bad. Mrs. Thorpe lets me sleep in t' kitchen. It's nice and warm there."

"But it's only just begun raining. Couldn't you have gone home before, at your usual time?"

The girl hesitated before answering, plucking nervously at her starched apron. "Aye, well I could, but I didn't want. It were cold—very cold considering t' time o' t' year—and them dogs were howling, and I were scared."

"What dogs, Cassie?"

218

"Them hounds, madam, them Gabriel hounds. Surely tha must a heard 'em when tha rode out wi' t' vicar."

Fern cast her mind back to when they arrived at Fox Brow, when she was dismounting from the trap and thought she heard a voice cry out. It must have been the same pathetic sounds Cassie heard.

"Tha heard 'em once, Mrs. de Lacy, 'cause I remember thee telling me. Didst not hear 'em tonight? They mean death, tha knows."

The girl's face was pallid and her eyes wide. She too could feel the tension in the atmosphere. It pervaded not only Ellen's house but also the Hall and Brackenroyd village, it seemed. And it was unusually cold, as she said, unnaturally cold for a May night.

Fern patted the edge of the bed. "Sit a moment, Cassie, before you go down again."

The girl hesitated, mindful of constant exhortations not to presume familiarity with one's betters, but her need for company and consolation overcame her misgivings. She sat warily on the very edge.

"Have you taken chocolate in to the master, Cassie, or is he already asleep?"

"No, madam, he's not come home."

So Bruno was still out there on the moor, wandering in the rain and the wind. Where could he have gone after leaving Fox Brow? He must be troubled indeed to forgo the warmth and comfort of his bed. No doubt Pharaoh was with him.

"Of course, it must be Pharaoh you heard crying, Cassie."

"Pharaoh?"

"The master's wolfhound. If Dr. de Lacy is still out walking, the dog is probably miserable in all that cold and rain, and howling for his bed of straw by the fire."

The girl looked only half-convinced, but she did manage a weak smile. Fern patted her hand reassuringly.

"Go down and sleep now, Cassie. All is well."

At the doorway the maid turned. "I hope as how tha'rt right and all's well, but I fear it's not. I can feel evil in t' air, thick like I could touch it wi' my hand. I'll not sleep till that wind and cold has gone."

"Say your prayers, Cassie, and no harm can come to you. Blow out the lamp and go now, and sleep."

Fern was anxious to be rid of the girl, for she sensed it too. Excitement quivered in her. The air was pregnant with shadows, with emotions she knew could only mean that Catherine was close. It was as if the wraith hovered patiently outside the latticed window, mutely entreating Fern to let her in. Whatever magic Ellen and she had worked between them in their silent communion in Fox Brow, it had evidently succeeded in bringing Catherine close again. Fern tingled with expectation.

Shivering, she rolled over in the bed, and her knees encountered an averted back. Instantly the other occupant of the bed sprang upright.

"Don't touch me, hellcat. I fear thy touch worse nor thy silence." It was Phoebe, her eyes flashing fury in the light of the moon that glimmered in through the low window. She lay down again, curled suspiciously on the far edge of the truckle bed.

For a moment there was silence in the little room; then Phoebe began muttering in the shadows. "It's all thy fault, tha knows it is. None i' this village comes owt for thee now, for all are afeard of thy powers."

Useless to deny, impossible to repudiate, Catherine was forced to lie helplessly listening to her sister's vicious words.

"It were thee as killed my Ben. I know it. I saw thee coming from t' barn that night. I saw thee in Rafe de Lacy's arms. Tha were jealous I had a lover too, so tha killed him. But tha'll not escape, Catherine Radley. I'll see to it tha's punished for thy sins.

"Tha'll not have thy lover, I swear it. Tha's robbed me, and I'll rob thee likewise."

A sob of fear caught in Catherine's throat. There was such vindictive determination in Phoebe's voice that Catherine knew she would do no less than she had sworn. It might well be that she had poisoned Rafe's mind against her already, for

Catherine had had no glimpse of him since that terrible night, even after he had come home. Somehow she must see him again, to try to convince him that her action had been only in self-defense. But how? For the thousandth time Catherine cursed her blighted tongue, which would not curl itself about the words she needed.

Phoebe was still murmuring, plotting aloud the scheme she knew Catherine could not divulge. "They all begin to believe me that tha'rt a witch, and before long I'll convince 'em. Thy Rafe'll not come near thee then."

It would not be hard to do, thought Catherine. The crops had failed this summer after unexpected fierce hailstorms, Mistress Arnley's third had been stillborn only last week, and poor Jennett Marsden had been killed by a thunderbolt as she came home from milking. Unnatural events indeed, to be explained away only by the presence of an evil spirit in the village, and the local folk would be only too glad of a scapegoat. Already, as Phoebe said, they were half-convinced Catherine was the culprit. No longer did any of them come asking for Catherine's help for a toothache or a wart. It was evident they all feared and distrusted her.

The first glimmer of dawn light was filtering through the little window when the footsteps came tramping toward the cottage, heavy steps ringing when they reached the cobbled yard. Catherine heard voices and her father's angry demand.

"What the devil brings thee here so early in t' morning, Arnley?" he was bawling through the open window.

"Thy lass, Catherine. We've had enough of her mischief. We've talked it over and decided to make certain."

"Certain? Certain of what, tha meddlesome creature? My lass is as good and virtuous as they come, and I'll not have thee say otherwise."

By this time Father had evidently put on his breeches, for Catherine heard him open the cottage door to argue with Arnley. Phoebe was sitting up now, listening intently, her dark eyes agleam.

Mother was in the little flagstone parlor too, her voice angry and plaintive.

221

"Just because the lass is different, tha's no cause to say she's wicked. What hast got against our Kate?"

There was a shuffling of clogs on stone and a few muttered prompts from Arnley's companions. "Well, there's all t' strange happenings of late. Jennett Marsden for one, crops ruined for another, and now my missus is heartbroken over our son."

"It's no fault of our Kate's if tha has only two wenches and t' first lad were stillborn. That's God's will, and tha were best to accept it. Tha'll happen have another lad soon."

"But it's not chance that thy Catherine looked at my missus only t' day afore and scared her half to death. It were t' evil look, thee just ask my missus."

"Flummery!" Mistress Radley was furious. "And Jennett Marsden—did our Kate look at her too? And at t' crops in t' fields? Is that all tha can say against t' girl?"

Another man's voice cut in. "What of soldier Ben's murder, Mistress Radley? A pitchfork doesn't rise up in t' air and pierce a man lest it's by witchcraft. We all know Kate were jealous of Phoebe having a swain, she so quiet and mouselike that no lad followed her."

Phoebe leaped from the bed, pulled a shawl over her nightgown, and went out. Catherine followed, fearful of what her sister would say to augment the accusations mounting against her.

Phoebe stood in the doorway of the little parlor, the group of men near the outer door having moved just inside the room. They stared at the girl, and seeing Catherine just behind her, shrank back farther toward the corner.

"Tha'rt right," Phoebe was saying eagerly, "my sister is a witch. She killed Ben Pickering."

Mother moved forward to clutch Phoebe's arm. "What art saying, lass? Thy own sister." Her eyes stared helplessly from a blanched face.

"Aye, Mother, and I can prove it."

From under her shawl Phoebe withdrew an object which she held forward for all to see. Over her shoulder Catherine could see a piece of wax, crudely shaped into the figure of a man. And transfixing its body was a bodkin, such as all the village women used to fasten up their hair.

"Where didst find it?" Father's voice was barely a whisper.

"Under her bed."

The figures in the shadows drew back yet farther. Fearful eyes turned from the wax effigy toward Catherine, and she saw their terror, their accusing hatred. Even Mother turned to stare incredulously at her.

"It were thee as made t' tallow candles last week, Kate," she murmured reluctantly. Catherine longed to cry out, to deny, to explain that Phoebe had taken the leftover tallow when the task was done. But most of all she felt bewildered, unable to believe that Phoebe had taken the tallow willfully, to incriminate her. She stared helplessly at her sister, who returned the stare with a mocking, defiant smile.

Catherine's confidence waned. Phoebe would win now. Rafe would never dare to consort with an acknowledged witch, and even if in the eyes of the law Catherine was not proven to be a witch, the village would forever believe it. For a moment she felt a new, unknown emotion, a hate so powerful against Phoebe that she inwardly cursed her for her lying, vindictive tongue. Would that the girl were cursed with dumbness as she was, so that she could never lie again!

In the tense air of the little room, the faint mew of a cat broke the silence. From under the settle where she had been sleeping, Tibb came out, stretching her paws and arching her back daintily. The villagers watched in silence as the cat, staring around haughtily for a moment at the intruders, sought out her mistress. Catching sight of Catherine by the door, she crossed leisurely to her mistress and began rubbing herself luxuriously against Catherine's skirts, purring with pleasure. A murmur rippled through the onlookers.

"Her familiar," Catherine heard someone whisper.

"Aye, it seeks to be fed," another replied.

"The witch's mark—she'll give it food from the witch's nipple."

Mistress Radley, confounded by all the terrible evidence against her child, found her tongue at last. "Get thee all hence, home to thy families. There's no cause to come here making mischief. I'll not have all this wicked gossip, dost hear, Arnley? I'll thank thee all to be gone and let us about our work. T' sun's up already, and there's no water fetched from t' well yet. Get thee away home, neighbors, and let's have done wi' all this nonsense."

Arnley shuffled uncomfortably. "Much as we'd like, it's not so easy done, Mistress Radley. That there wax figure has proved all for us. Now we mun put thy lass to t' test."

"Test? What test?" Catherine heard the hollow tremble in her mother's voice. "Tha's surely not thinking of ducking our Catherine, art tha?"

"Nay, mistress. We've talked to t' vicar, and he'll not have us duck her nor prick t' witch's mark neither. He reckons that's only for t' proper authorities to do."

"Thank God t' reverend has a bit of sense at least," muttered Mistress Radley. "What then?"

"He'll let us weigh her."

Father, silent up to now, took a step forward. "Dost mean to weigh her against t' parish Bible?"

"Aye."

"But tha can see how slight she is, nobbut a slender little thing. Your hefty Bible is bound to outweigh her. That's no true test."

"It's fair notwithstanding. It's known as witches can never outweigh t' Bible. T' vicar says we can do it after t' evening service. So tha'd best see thy lass is at t' church, Mr. Radley. Tha surely can't object to a fair test."

Radley stood dumb, aware that a refusal would only incriminate his daughter more. Arnley, his ultimatum delivered, signaled to his companions, and they all shuffled out. As if in a trance, Catherine heard their footsteps fade away across the yard and down the lane until silence settled over the cottage once more.

Little was said of the occurrence, but all day the threat of the evening's trial hung heavy in the air. Mother and Father seemed incredulous, unable to believe that anyone should question their daughter's virtue, she who had freely given so much of her skills to help others. And Phoebe too was silent, but whether because she felt she had already said too much or because she was content with her victory, Catherine did not know.

The July sun was still high over the western horizon when the time for evening service came, and the little church was sultry. Catherine sat with her parents and Phoebe, her heart tilting for a second when she saw Rafe enter and sit alone in the De Lacy pew. He did not look her way, not then or throughout the service.

The vicar hastened away into the vestry once the service was over, as though reluctant to be part of what he knew was to follow. Catherine sat, head bowed, while men clattered the great iron scales to the lectern where the great Bible lay. From the corner of her eye she could see Rafe still sitting as though in silent prayer.

"Now, then, Mistress Radley." It was Arnley who stood before them, holding his hand out for Catherine. Quietly she rose and followed him. Every eye in the church was fixed upon her as hands helped her to seat herself in the great iron pan of the scales. It dipped to the stone floor beneath her weight.

"Now for t' Bible." Reverent hands grasped its bulk carefully, struggling to transfer it from the lectern to the other pan. As they did so, Catherine felt herself rising slowly till her feet were clear of the floor. The Bible's massive weight had proved her guilt.

"Didn't I tell thee?" she heard the excited whispers. She looked up, not to see her parents' or Phoebe's reaction, but to the De Lacy pew. Rafe was leaning against the pew in front, eyes lowered and his face as pale as a sheet. For God's sake, speak now, defend me, or I am lost, she prayed fervently.

"There's no doubt now," Arnley was saying. "Catherine Radley is a witch. God's Holy Book does not lie." Catherine stared beseechingly at Rafe, who rose, stumbling, and made for the door.

Don't desert me, oh, for pity's sake, come back and help me in my need! She screamed silently, but his great shape only lumbered out through the door and was gone. She could

225

barely believe it. Even he, who had sworn undying love for her, had turned his back on her.

Fury gathered within her. Nowhere on this earth was there truth and honesty; no love was pure and strong; no man was to be trusted. If he had no faith in her, then no man alive would ever believe her. Silently she cursed Rafe de Lacy for his treachery. May he wander forever, tortured and suffering as she was now, never to find peace if he did not come to her.

"Art satisfied?" Father was saying gruffly to the group of villagers who clustered about Arnley. "Can we take t' lass home now?"

Arnley eyed the other before nodding. "We mun decide what's to be done. In t' meantime go home."

Catherine felt her mother's urgent hands pushing her toward the door and out into the evening sunlight. Phoebe followed with her father, murmuring as they left the porch, "See, she does not weep, as one might expect. They say witches cannot weep."

"Hush, Phoebe. Tha's said enough," Catherine heard her father retort. To the door of the Radley cottage was but a few yards, and she was relieved to enter the little parlor, out of reach of the villagers' malevolent, distrustful eyes.

"There's mischief afoot; I can sense it," Mistress Radley muttered to her husband. "There's no trusting them when they're in this mood. Lock and bar t' door, Father."

"They'll do no more, saving happen to report to t' authorities. They done do no more themselves."

"Bar t' door notwithstanding." Mother's lips were set in a tight, determined line. "Dost know what night it is? It's Lammas eve, or witch's feast, and a night them out there might well have a mind to do mischief."

Father locked the door without further protest. Phoebe followed Catherine into the little room where they slept, mocking her while they undressed. "They're locked out, and tha'rt locked in, sister. No moonlight meetings for thee in t' woods tonight, neither wi' a coven nor a lover."

Footsteps clattered up the staircase. Mother and Father were going to bed with the sun so as to be ready to rise with the sun for the day's work. Silence soon settled over the

Radley cottage, but Catherine could find no sleep. Inwardly she boiled in a ferment of vexation, anger, and hatred. They all feared and scorned her, the villagers, her own family, and Rafe, whom she had loved and trusted above all.

Gradually anger dwindled to despair. What was there left to live for now? Deep regular breathing from Phoebe's thin curled frame indicated that she was sleeping. A sudden thought struck Catherine. The wax figure, Rafe's stumbling steps and pallid face—had Phoebe in fact shaped the little figure in order to curse Rafe, thus causing his apparent sickness?

Catherine reproached herself. What a wicked thought. Rafe, sick or not, had deserted her, and she could not blame Phoebe for that. Rafe's was the crime, and may he suffer long and miserably for his perfidy.

Such unnatural hate in her heart made Catherine restless. At last she could lie still no longer, and rising stealthily so as not to disturb Phoebe, she put a shawl about her shoulders and looked out of the little window. Under the moon's pale light, which robbed everything of color, she could see the sleeping village street, the gaunt outline of the church tower. Not a soul stirred nor a light showed. Cautiously she unlatched the door and pulled it silently closed behind her.

Up, up toward the moor, where the air was free and she could breathe, anything to lessen the dead weight that threatened to choke her. Catherine's thin mules made no sound on the cobbles as she turned off from the main street and struck uphill.

Brackenroyd Hall's great windows lay blank and expressionless too, she could see as she reached higher ground. The rambling old building had an air of death and emptiness. Somewhere within its thick stone walls lay that faithless Rafe de Lacy, and again she cursed him. If only he would appear now, tall and broad in the moonlight, striding out toward the copse to meet her as he had done so often before. But long as she stared, no figure came.

The copse, that was where she would go, and ease the ache in her temples with the cool waters of the stream on whose bank they had lain and loved. She could see the outline of leafy branches silhouetted against the craggy skyline beyond.

Voices and footsteps below in the valley came to Catherine's ears. She turned and listened. Clogged feet were running on the cobblestones, and men's voices called out.

"Where is she, then? Witches' sabbath, is it? Well, we'll find her."

"There'll be no more spells cast i' Brackenroyd. We've had more nor enough of her cursing."

The footsteps grew in volume, marching down the street in a vengeful, rhythmic stamp. Catherine froze, her palms sweating and nausea trembling in her stomach. They were seeking her, and God knew what they would do when they found her. To flee to the moors was useless, for she would be easily spotted, a running white figure in a nightgown in the pale light of the moon.

The copse. That was the only place where she could find shelter to hide. She crouched amid the undergrowth and prayed, her mouth dry with fear.

The footsteps grew duller as they left the street and crunched over grass. From afar a dog howled, and Catherine felt the sweat prickle on her skin. The Gabriel hounds—that betokened death. She closed her eyes and prayed, but the steps came nearer, crashing up the hill through the bracken, closer and closer, growing in volume until the sound was like thunder in her ears.

"There's evil in her black blood, and we mun put a stop to it," Arnley's voice cried, so close that Catherine felt faint with terror. The footsteps were almost on her now, thundering, roaring.

A hand grasped her shoulder. "For heaven's sake, mistress, wake up! The house is shaking, and it seems like all hell has been let loose!"

She opened her eyes weakly, and the misted figure of Mrs. Thorpe hovered before her. "Go away," she protested, but the housekeeper only shook her again.

"Mrs. de Lacy, please wake up! There's the most terrible storm raging, and Pharaoh has come home without the master. I'm worried for him. Please wake up!"

Chapter 15

For a dizzying few seconds Fern thought the thunder of footsteps still threatened to discover her hiding place. Then slowly
she realized that real thunder cracked and reverberated over
the Hall, lightning darting in at the windows and cutting
across the light of the candle Mrs. Thorpe held in her hand.
Another resounding bang and vivid flash brought her to her
senses.

Mrs. Thorpe brought her dressing robe from the chair,
"None of the servants can sleep in this dreadful storm; I wonder you sleep so peacefully, madam. I'm afraid for the master
out in all this."

Rain was pelting wildly against the windows, hurled by a
buffeting gale. Mechanically Fern rose and pulled on the robe,
mentally screaming to return to Catherine. The girl's terror
was bringing her close to death, and it was unthinkable to
desert her now.

A bell clanged below. Mrs. Thorpe started. "Whoever can
that be at the door in the middle of the night? Surely no one
is fool enough to venture out in weather like this?"

She scurried away, and Fern followed. From the gallery she watched the housekeeper open the door to admit a dripping, apologetic Edgar Amos.

"I'm so sorry to trouble you, Mrs. Thorpe, but Dr. de Lacy sent me."

"Is he all right?" Fern heard Mrs. Thorpe ask anxiously.

"He is safe, but he appears somewhat disturbed. He came galloping into the village in all this rain, shouting to everyone to get up and leave. He made me ride Phantom back to warn you to get ready to receive them."

"What is wrong, Edgar?" Amos looked up at the sound of Fern's voice and bowed slightly.

"He seems to fear some catastrophe, Mrs. de Lacy. He was rather agitated and shouting something about it being all his fault. At any rate, he was determined to evacuate the village and send everyone up here. Two farm carts laden with women and children are not far behind me."

"Lord bless us!" exclaimed Mrs. Thorpe. "Then we'd best prepare. Cassie, make up the fire in the servants' hall and get some soup on the stove. They'll be half-drowned in this weather."

Cassie, lurking in the background to listen, rushed off. Mrs. Thorpe took Amos' sodden cloak and hat.

"Mrs. Thorpe, I shall put on a cloak and go down to the village," Fern said. "Keep Phantom ready at the door. There is no time for Malachi to saddle up Whisper."

Amos stared up at her. "You don't mean to go out in this, Mrs. de Lacy? I'm sure I don't know what the doctor fears, but I do think he is being unnecessarily hysterical."

"It is not for you to criticize the master. I am sure he knows what he is about," Fern retorted as she turned to reenter her room. Pulling off her nightgown and donning a woolen dress and riding cloak, she thought quickly. Either there was trouble imminent or Bruno was ill, as Amos hinted. Either way, he needed her help.

Mrs. Thorpe was still in the hall, opening the door again to admit the women and children who tumbled wetly from the carts. Fern snapped orders quickly as she passed her.

"If the servants' hall becomes full when more arrive, open up the old Hall and light a fire. Feed them and give them what dry clothes you can find. I shall return soon."

Malachi stood at the bottom of the steps holding Phantom. Without a word he cupped his hands for Fern to mount. She swung lightly into the saddle and then had to wait, reining in the restless horse, while Malachi shortened the stirrups. Phantom was evidently nervous, the whites of his eyes standing out against his black mane. He too sensed the disquiet in the air.

His great, powerful body reared and plunged forward and galloped off down the gravel drive, the heavy rain beating into Fern's face. The wind still raged, whipping off the hood of her cloak and blowing her hair wildly about her, till the rain soaked it and made it cling damply about her face.

At the foot of the drive two more carts were turning in to the Hall. Fern recognized the sodden figure of Fabia sitting huddled between the others. She reined in sharply.

"What is happening, Fabia?"

Fabia's white face looked up. "Bruno and Luke are rousing the rest of the villagers and trying to find Phoebe. She disappeared while we were gathering the children. I wanted to stay and look for her, but Bruno was adamant I must come up here."

"Did Bruno say what was wrong?"

"He's crazed, Fern. I think he's gone out of his mind. He's raving about the storm being all his fault, an elemental reaction to his past sin. He says the villagers will die for his misdeeds unless we escape to the Hall."

Fern paled. "What sin? Did he say?"

"Not so I could understand. Something about his faithlessness long ago and how he had tried to deny it but now he knew he must atone before it was too late. Fern, I'm afraid. I fear for him—and for Phoebe."

"Don't worry. I'll find them both. Go up to the Hall and wait. Which way did he go?"

"He was heading along the main street, knocking at all the doors, and was going on to the mill."

Fern swung the horse about and rode on down the cobbled

lane that led to the village street. A sodden figure leading a band of bedraggled villagers stumbled toward her. In a fierce crack of lightning she saw it was Fearnley, the mill manager. He waved and gesticulated when he caught sight of Fern.

"Get back, mistress, get back to t' Hall! The master says as t' dam is going to burst!"

She heard his words clearly enough, borne on the whipping wind as she galloped by, but did not stop to argue. If he was right, there was little enough time to find Phoebe.

And what of Bruno? Suddenly she felt no fear for his safety, only a fierce exultation that swept over her. Fabia and Amos might not understand his apparent raving, but to Fern it was clear. Somehow, miraculously, he had come to learn of his treachery to Catherine so long ago, either by means of drugs or by dreams that tortured his sleep so that he was forced to walk abroad at night. No matter how he knew. It was enough that he too was obliged to remember, and to suffer as a result. For a split-second it was Catherine who rode into the village, exulting that her curse on Rafe had had its effect.

Fern reined in on the green before the church. Another vivid flash of lightning ripped through the black sky. The whole main street was deserted, cottage doors left ajar and rain washing in rivulets down the street. There was not a sign of Luke or Bruno or any soul left in Brackenroyd. It seemed that everyone had fled to higher ground, either to the Hall or to Fox Brow or possibly up to Dr. Briggs's house.

A rending crash of thunder split the air, and then immediately another brilliant shaft of lightning, illuminating the rain bouncing on the shining slate roofs and revealing for a moment the eerie stillness of the village, forlorn and abandoned like some shunned ghost town. Fern, soaked to the skin and shivering, sighed and turned Phantom about.

"Phoebe!" she cried out, but her voice was whipped from her by the wind and tossed up among the branches of the churchyard trees, which bent low under the weight of rain. As she urged the horse forward, a faint sound came to her ears, almost lost in the clop of hooves and the wind's roar. She stopped quickly and strained to listen. Was it wishful thinking, or did she hear a child's cry, shrill and terrified, above the roar of the storm?

She slid from the horse and led him by the reins to the schoolhouse gate.

"Phoebe! Are you there, Phoebe?"

No answering cry came from the shuttered cottage, but Fern saw the door of a shed alongside open a crack. Letting go of the reins, she ran to the shed, pushed open the door, and saw a cowering white figure crouched on the floor.

"Phoebe! Thank God you're safe! Come with me, and we'll go to Mother, up at the Hall." Fern's arms were outstretched to the child, but Phoebe only shrank farther, whimpering. "Come, little one, there is nothing to fear," Fern coaxed, but as she approached the child, Phoebe shrieked.

Impatiently Fern grasped her arm and began to drag her outside. Phoebe struggled to break away, and Fern's grasp grew tighter. This was no time to argue.

As if by a miracle, the storm had lessened in intensity. Dull reverberations in the distance now and again indicated that it was moving away, but rain still lashed ruthlessly. Fern tried to cover the child under the folds of her own sodden cloak, but Phoebe still fought to get free.

Phantom—where was he? At the schoolhouse gate Fern looked about for the horse and saw him pawing the ground restlessly under a churchyard elm. A far flash of lightning sparked, and Fern saw his huge eyes widen, the whites staring, and he reared into the air, whinnied in fear, and began to canter away.

"Phantom! Come back!"

It was no use. The last flash had been too much for him. Now all he sought was the shelter of his stable. His hooves clattered wildly along the lane uphill toward the Hall.

Phoebe was still whimpering and scratching. Fern grasped her resolutely and marched her along the lane in Phantom's wake. Holding the drenched child like a half-drowned rat, her dark curls glued about her pointed little face with rain, Fern hurried along the lane, aware of rain trickling down her neck and squelching in her thin shoes. Suddenly another sound came to her ears.

A long, low, ominous rumble made her stiffen. It was not the sound of distant thunder, but lower and more menacing. Involuntarily she found herself grabbing Phoebe up in her arms and running off the side of the cobbled street and up the steep grassy bank.

Phoebe's weight caused her to stumble, gasping for breath, but Fern seemed to sense instinctively that unless she reached higher ground they would never return to the Hall.

She continued to stagger up the slope, her feet slithering and sliding on the soggy grass, till at last, devoid of breath and her heart thudding with effort, she stumbled and sprawled on the slope. Phoebe rolled from her arms.

The distant rumble was growing and becoming louder, a roar now that was becoming a crescendo of sound, cracking and hissing as if all hell were let loose. Fern's heart almost stopped in terror as she recognized its significance. The dam! Bruno had been right after all—Bilberry Reservoir, swollen by the torrents of rain till it could contain no more, had burst the dam! In moments the wall of water would gush down the valley and submerge the village. Fern leaped to her feet and grabbed Phoebe's arm.

"For God's sake, Phoebe, run! The dam has burst, do you hear me? Run!"

Only for a second did the child pause, her head cocked to one side, and then she moved, scrambling up the slope ahead of Fern. Fern followed close behind the diminutive figure in the drenched white frock that clung to her thin little body. They were still far from the top when the waters came.

The little figure ahead turned at the sound of the wrenching, crashing, tearing clamor behind. Fern saw her eyes widen in disbelieving terror and turned, holding the child's trembling shoulders. A massive black wall of water was bearing down the valley, trees torn up by the roots projecting from its inky surface. Thundering, it crashed into Brackenroyd, sweeping down the main street in horrifying fury, tossing the carcasses of cattle and sheep among the cottages and hurling timber in its path. Fern watched aghast. The black monster reached and devoured the long-abandoned Radley cottage like matchwood, and swirled on through the churchyard and the schoolhouse. She shuddered as the shed where Phoebe had hidden broke up and disappeared in the monster's maw.

"Higher, Phoebe, we must get higher!" They scrambled farther up the slope. Fern glanced back at the roaring menace, which, having swept on down the valley, was growing ever deeper over Brackenroyd. Bodies both of animals and of people swirled in the flood; bales of hay bounced along in the torrent alongside dye vats and looms and unrecognizable wreckage of timber. With a sick thudding of her heart Fern realized the mill must have gone. Pray God Bruno and Luke had not been there.

Suddenly Phoebe uttered a scream. Fern looked up in time to see the little figure stumble and totter, lose her footing on the steep slope, and start to roll downhill. Fern lunged forward to grab her, but the child was falling too quickly. Impulsively Fern threw herself after her, terrified lest she should fall into the ever-rising flood.

The little body gathered speed as she fell, and Fern could not keep up with her. She saw the waters coming closer, closer, and still Phoebe's headlong fall continued. Fern cried out as the little white figure splashed as she reached the water. "Phoebe!"

There was a tree still standing at the water's edge, not yet engulfed, and Fern saw with relief that Phoebe's struggling little shape was clinging to an outstretched branch.

"Hold on, Phoebe! I'll help you!"

The water was surging about the child, threatening to tear loose her grasp on the branch. Fern threw off the saturated cloak and waded into the water, feeling it sucking about her skirts. Phoebe's terrified face, encircled in clinging tendrils of black hair, stared at her beseechingly.

"Help me!"

Fern was too distraught to wonder. Reaching the child and grasping her about the waist with one arm and the tree with

235

the other, she struggled to regain a foothold on the slope, but the water tugged mercilessly at her skirts. Inch by inch she pulled herself along the branch, burdened by Phoebe's weight and the sucking current. Mercifully she felt solid ground under her feet and managed to pull herself and the child clear of the flood. Already it had risen several feet, high as they were. Exhausted, Fern scrambled a few feet higher to level ground and sank to her knees.

"You go on, Phoebe, I'll follow."

The child, dripping and shivering, shook her head and crouched by Fern. With a desperate effort Fern struggled to rise and stumble on, holding Phoebe by the hand. The child's teeth were chattering, and the hand was numb with cold. They must regain the Hall and warmth quickly.

At the stream, swollen by rain, Fern paused. It was impossible to cross here, or they would be swept down into the valley again. The copse! By Catsgrave Copse there were stepping-stones, and there they might still be able to cross safely. She struck out for the higher ground. Phoebe struggled on gamely beside her.

Reaching the copse at last, Fern looked back. The waters now were far below and seemed to be growing less deep. No doubt the reservoir, having disgorged all its millions of gallons of water into the valley, now lay empty, and the torrent was flooding on down through all the unsuspecting villages below Brackenroyd. Fern felt pity in her heart. Bruno's vigilance may well have saved Brackenroyd, but what of the poor creatures down the valley?

A despairing nausea clutched Fern as she sought the stepping-stones. Her head ached and she felt giddy with strain. The stones were still there, though the water now gushed over instead of around them.

"Can you manage to cross, Phoebe? Hold your skirts clear and step carefully."

The child nodded and stepped out. With bated breath Fern watched her anxiously, and breathed a sigh of relief when Phoebe at last turned on the farther bank. A wave of faintness swept over Fern again.

"Go on up to the Hall, Phoebe. It's not far. I shall follow you in a moment."

Phoebe hovered hesitantly, reluctant to leave her. Fern waved her on sharply.

"Go on, do as I say. Get out of those soaking clothes at once. Your mother will be very anxious about you."

The final words had the effect she sought. Phoebe ran off into the darkness. Glad of a respite from struggle, Fern sank to the soggy ground and leaned her back against a tree. The waves of dizziness and nausea were coming more quickly and severely now. Just for a moment I'll rest, she thought wearily, and then I'll have the strength to go home. If only this sick sensation would go away . . .

Unresistingly she leaned back against the tree; then to her ears came the vague sound of thunder, rumbling on and on and ever louder. Dimly she was aware that it was no longer the storm but the drumming of running feet. Suddenly the bushes parted. Arnley stood there, his coarse linen smock gleaming in the moonlight and his expression one of savage triumph.

"She's here, lads! I've found the witch!"

Hate glittered in his eyes, and she felt too sick and weak to protest. Other feet came running, until a crowd of faces gathered about him, pale and menacing in the moonlight, peering at her, half-fearful and half-malicious.

Before she buried her face in her hands, she could see by their malevolent looks that their fear, bred out of superstitious ignorance, meant ill for her. Well, so be it. She had done wrong in killing, even though in self-defense, and punishment was no more than her due.

For some moments no one moved or spoke. Then suddenly she felt a sharp pain on her shoulder. In surprised disbelief she stared at the tear in her sleeve, and the dull gash that showed blackly beneath. She looked up at her persecutor and saw that it was Arnley who had thrown the stone.

At once the others followed his lead.

"Drive the demon out of her!" another cried as his arm raised in the moonlight and came swiftly down. She felt an-

237

other piercing pain, this time on her hip, and instantly it was followed by another on her breast. Incredulously she stared, from her tormentors to the wounds and back to their hate-filled faces. More of them were scrabbling for stones in the undergrowth. Arnley bent and straightened again with a large piece of rock in his hands.

"Death to the devil's creature!" he roared, and Catherine sank to the grass, stunned by the violent pain in her forehead. A warm moistness collected on her temple and dripped slowly down her chin. She put her fingers to her head and could not believe the gash, wide, open to the bone beneath. Dimly she heard voices shrieking abuse and hatred and felt the thudding blows to her body, but somehow they brought no more pain.

"She'll do no more of the devil's work!" a voice cried, but it was faint and far away. Then a sudden hush fell, followed by a flurry of footsteps. Catherine lay still, aware only that they had fled and that her life's blood was oozing from her.

Strange she could feel no animosity, no hatred for them, only for Rafe, who had deserted her. She lay sprawled in the grass under the tree that had witnessed their joyful meetings so often, and thought how bizarre it was to see only her own body, spattered and drenched in blood, and feel none of the emotion which used once to flood her veins.

Only disillusionment, and a strangely cold, detached revulsion for the traitor she had once called lover. And then suddenly, as if thought had conjured him up from the night mist, he was there, bending over her.

"Catherine, beloved, I heard the cries down here from up on the brow. What is it, sweetheart? What have they done?"

There was remorse as well as anguish in his dark eyes as he bent closer to examine her. A shudder of distaste shook his broad shoulders.

"Dear heaven, what have they done to you!"

Aye, she thought wearily, turn from me once again, as you did before. What matter now? Too late, too late for accusation and recrimination.

He knelt, burying his face in her shoulder, but not before she saw the brightness—could it be tears? A tinge of compas-

238

sion penetrated the blank emptiness within her. She raised a feeble hand to his face.

Don't ... weep ... for ... me. The words had to remain unspoken. It was a desperate effort even to think them, for a black mist eddied about her, swallowing her for a second and then receding, though hovering persistently near. She was aware of his face close to hers, his great eyes probing hers and trying to infuse in her the will to live.

"God forgive me, Kate, I never thought it would come to this. I knew they thought ill of you, but not this, never this." His voice caught on a sob. "I should have come to you. Forgive me, beloved. I should have come to you. Forgive me, beloved. I should have come, but at first I thought it best to wait until the gossip died, and then in the church I felt so ill. Oh, God, my Kate, can you ever forgive me?"

Suddenly he leaped up. "I'll take you home to the Hall and send for the physician. You shall not die, Kate, I will not let you!"

But the moment he lifted her from the ground, agony ripped through Catherine's frame, and she moaned. At once he put her gently down again. She knew he had seen the awkward jutting of broken limbs and the bright flow that soaked the grass beneath.

The swirling mist was growing more insistent now, thickening before her, until Rafe's face was only a blur. Death was slow in coming, and the pain was agony. Through the encroaching fog that seeped into her nostrils and clogged her throat till every breath was penance, she could hear Rafe's voice, receding on a constant cry.

"Forgive me, Catherine! I will atone, I swear it! I shall come to you again, beloved, and this time there will be no parting. Come back again, Catherine. Forgive me."

There was a fleeting instant when she was aware of hovering, of pausing on the brink of eternity, and then suddenly she was free. She seemed to be floating somewhere among the branches of the tree where Rafe knelt below, sobbing over a prostrate figure in a tattered, blood-soaked gown of white muslin, and as she felt herself being drawn inexorably away, she found a voice.

"I forgot, dear Lord, I forgot! I laid a curse upon him, to suffer eternal torment! I should have recalled the curse before I died, God forgive me! Let me go back, just for an instant, to erase the curse!"

But no one heard. From afar she saw Rafe rise from his weeping, already smitten with the misery she had wished upon him, and prepare to lift the pathetic little body. Catherine cried out in vain for a second of eternity to return to atone, and her soul knew hell. Forever now she would have to wander in limbo, remorse-ridden and helpless. Her soul would never know peace.

In a vast black void she reviled against the injustice of it all. No one had ever known the truth and come to defend her. No one had cared—or so she had believed until it was too late. Now she knew Rafe loved her, and she knew she would love him until the end of time. Bitterly she sobbed, screaming to get back but sentenced to wander helplessly in time and space that had no ending. Eternity was terrifying.

And then suddenly God relented. A whirling through space and the cool, sweet smell of rain on the moors, and she was home. She opened her eyes slowly, disbelievingly. Interlocked branches of a tree overhead, the springy feel of grass beneath her—it could not be true. Hope rose again in a heart too long accustomed to pain and frustration. Slowly she became aware of a new vitality beginning to throb in her veins. A shadowy face bent over her.

With a surge of joy she recognized his face, hard lines of anxiety and anguish about his eyes. His lips were moving, muttering words of pain. A fierce light suddenly illuminated his black eyes when he saw she was gazing at him.

"You've come back! Oh, beloved, you've come back to me!" There was savage joy and triumph in the words, and she felt new life in knowing she was so loved. But he was not wearing his leather tunic and breeches; instead he tossed aside the tall hat in his hand and pulled off his greatcoat to envelop her tenderly.

Another tall figure came crashing through the undergrowth, a huge hound following at his heels.

"Malachi, go fetch the trap. The mistress is well but weak." The broad-shouldered figure did not move until a few words in German, snapped in a hoarse voice, caused him to nod and lumber away quickly.

She stared up at the beloved face, careworn and fatigued. The mist was clearing from her brain now. Bruno, of course. But it was Rafe's face, full of remorse and contrition, mingled now with joy. He knelt again and cradled his arms about her.

"Catherine, forgive me. I have waited long."

It was unbelievable! Bruno spoke with Rafe's love and concern in his voice. And he had called her Catherine. She stared in bewilderment and tried to struggle upright, but he restrained her.

"Lie still, my love. You have a bad bruise on your temple." His fingers caressed her forehead, smoothing away the sodden hair from the weal. It was as if time had suddenly spun backward. Consciously and deliberately she lifted the curse on him, inwardly and in silence. No more would he suffer the pangs of eternal torment.

The care lifted from his eyes, and the harrowed look vanished. His lips brushed her forehead lightly.

"Soon we shall have you home and safe, beloved, and then I shall never let you from my sight again. So long I have waited. Too long to risk losing you again."

Fern found the strength to speak at last. "How did you find me here?"

"Phoebe told me where you were."

"Phoebe?"

"She came running to the Hall as I was leaving again to look for you. When I asked her where you were, I expected her to reply in the sign language I had taught her. To my surprise, she spoke!"

"What did she say?"

"One word—Catsgrave. It was a miracle, but now her silence is broken, she will learn to speak very quickly."

Fern kept silent. No need to tell him Phoebe's first words

had been spoken to herself, a plea for help when Phoebe feared death. It was enough to know that yet another curse had been lifted.

The rain had stopped, and the clouds rolled away to reveal a crescent moon. By its light she saw Bruno's anxious glances uphill toward the Hall.

"Malachi will be back directly with the trap, and when I have you safely home, I must go and look for Luke."

"For Luke? Wasn't he with you?"

"I sent him on down the valley to warn the villagers in Heatherfield. He hasn't come back."

"Poor Fabia, she must be distraught with worry. Her husband and her child both in danger."

"Phoebe is safe now, and Fabia knows she owes the child's life to you. You have her undying friendship and devotion."

Fern answered coldly. "I owed it to Phoebe. It was no generous gesture, but a debt."

To her surprise, he did not ask why, but simply nodded. "I know, but now it is done. It is I who am still in your debt."

"For what, Bruno?"

Dark eyes regarded her soberly. "You know well, my love. I forsook you in your need."

"Then you remember?" It seemed impossible that Bruno, the clinical, the detached, the disbeliever, could remember that other life. But he did—and he had called her Catherine.

At that moment, Malachi reappeared. Only when Bruno had lifted her carefully into the trap and covered her with rugs and Malachi was whipping up the horse did Fern speak again.

"When did you discover . . . about the past, I mean?" she whispered. Bruno's hand tightened on hers.

"I don't really know when it began. When I first met you at Bradford station, I think. I remember feeling a distinct jar of half-recognition when I saw you talking with Amos. And then, when I realized I couldn't possibly have seen you before, I dismissed it from my mind."

"*Déjà vu*, I think you called that feeling once."

"Yes. I dismissed your feelings about the Hall as female hysteria, evidence of an unbalanced mind, as I recall."

She smiled wryly. "You did. But when did you have further feelings about the past—and me?"

"Not for some time. And then, when the odd strange dream occurred, of a girl in olden days and her pure and lovable simplicity, a girl with your face and silken hair, I began to think I must be ill. The dreams frightened me, for I always awoke with a feeling of terrible dread and remorse, and I didn't know why."

"So you tried to ignore the dreams?"

"Dreaming had had no part in my earlier, well-ordered life. Everything in Germany was so straightforward, so rational. Dreams, I felt, were a self-indulgence, but there was no indulgence in the dreams that made me wake in a sweat. I could not explain them, and as a man of science I believed there had to be a logical explanation for everything."

"So what did you do?"

"Since you were the focal point of my dreams, I tried to avoid contact with you. I buried myself deeper in my work, or at least I tried to, but I found it difficult to concentrate."

"You took drugs."

"To further my work only. My research was into their effect on the human mind, and I could use only my own brain for experiment."

"You never drugged me. Once I thought you did."

"Because you too were dreaming?"

"They were not dreams. I saw Annot's story and I relived Catherine's. Because I am Catherine."

His hands tightened so hard about hers that Fern winced. His expression by starlight was one of deep pain again, and she felt pity for him.

"I know," he answered hoarsely. "At first I thought the dreams only hallucinations caused by drugs, and tried to ignore them. But the pain they evoked drove me on. In time I came to use the drugs to learn more, and the more I learned of the past, the more I suffered when I realized my guilt. But I could not stop. I had to know the ending."

"And the ending is now, Bruno. Or the beginning."

He looked away from her, down over the fields to the valley below, where only chimneys and the church steeple broke the surface of the waters enveloping the village. His voice was hollow with regret.

"Brackenroyd has suffered tonight. See how it is, broken and humiliated. It is all my fault, Catherine. A De Lacy wronged the valley and is not worthy to be its master."

Fern spoke softly as the trap turned up into the Hall's gravel drive. "And tonight a De Lacy atoned by saving the lives of the villagers. But for your vigilance they would all be lying drowned there now."

He shook his head. "Others will have died down in Heatherfield. Ellen prophesied that death would come."

Fern eyed him curiously. "How did you, always so remote, so aloof, come to befriend Ellen? You went so often by night to visit her."

He was gazing into the distance, up to the moors, as he replied. "It was part of the fantasy that haunted me. For some inexplicable reason, I found that as soon as I came here, even before you arrived, I was drawn to Fox Brow, again and again. It was as if I knew I must be there when the time came. But I did not know the reason. I tried to dismiss the lure of Fox Brow as a silly, irrational notion, but somehow I still found myself wandering up there at night."

"Do you know the reason now?" she asked quietly.

"Yes." He bent close over her, his face almost touching hers. The trap was drawing up by the Hall steps, and figures were crowded in the doorway. "Yes, beloved. It was from the brow that I—that Rafe—heard the cries when Catherine was stoned to death. Only from there could I watch Catsgrave for your return."

Mrs. Thorpe hurried down the steps to meet them. "Thank the Lord you're safe, Mrs. de Lacy! Come on in. I have hot water ready to ladle into the bath for you."

Bruno lifted Fern and carried her in. In the vestibule Edgar Amos was standing surrounded by a group of villagers, still bemused at the suddenness of the night's events. Fabia was clinging to Luke's arm, her eyes, brilliant with joy, betraying her relief on seeing Fern.

"Dear Fern, I am overjoyed," she said softly. "Luke has returned safely, and you saved Phoebe. Tend her well, Bruno, for we have need of people such as the De Lacys in the valley."

Bruno smiled and began carrying Fern up the great staircase. A woman's hand restrained him. It was Mrs. Iredale.

"Mrs. Armitage is right, master. But for thee and Mrs. de Lacy, we'd all be dead. The village'll come to life and prosper again wi' thee and her to care for it, that it will, I'm certain."

Bruno nodded. "We'll do our best. Already the water is falling. Soon we'll rebuild the cottages and the mill, and life will start afresh. We'll talk of it tomorrow. All will be well again in Brackenroyd. I promise."

The murmuring voices of the villagers and the grunts and nods of approval and thanks warmed Fern's cold bones. Mrs. de Lacy, they had called her. She was no longer "that Radley woman," the creature with a dark taint in her blood. Grudgingly, slowly, they were warming to her. In time she would be accepted, one of them, and the true mistress of Brackenroyd.

Kate's spirit was at rest now. No more would Catsgrave Copse be haunted by a tormented soul. And the Radley cottage was swept away, the last evidence of a curse that had blighted the village for three hundred years. Contentment enveloped Fern as she lay, tended by a joyously tearful Cassie, in the big tin bath of hot water before the fire.

Tucked up in bed at last with a stone-hot-water bottle at her feet, Fern inquired about Bruno.

"He's belowstairs, madam, seeing as all the villagers are seen to. Oh, madam, I'm so glad tha'rt alive and well! I thought them Gabriel hounds had sounded thy death cry."

"Not mine, Cassie, but I fear some people down in Heatherfield were not so fortunate."

"Aye, and but for t' master it'd have been all of us an' all. He's a fine man, is Dr. de Lacy."

"Indeed he is. Go down and ask him to come up, Cassie. Then, if Mrs. Thorpe no longer needs you, go to bed."

"Yes, madam." In the doorway the girl paused awkwardly. "And bless thee, madam. There's not so many like thee." Swiftly she was gone, pink with embarrassment.

By candlelight Fern snuggled down under the bedcovers, content as she had never been. It was no surprise when the connecting door to Bruno's room opened and she saw his broad figure in a dressing robe outlined in the doorway. She held out her arms to him. He came forward slowly and stood by the end of the bed.

"How do you feel now, Fern? Does your head ache?"

"No. I am tired only."

He turned back toward the door, and she felt a keen sense of disappointment. But he reappeared in a moment and closed the door behind him. In his hands he held the little box.

"Your lock of hair, Catherine. It has waited long for its owner to return."

She smiled and laid the box aside on the night table; then, opening the drawer, she took out the silver ring and offered it to him. His mouth lifted in a wry smile.

"*Amor Aeternus.* Love Eternal," he murmured as he gazed at its lettering. "Let me now place it on your finger, as I should have done long ago."

Fern gave her hand eagerly. "Will you always call me Catherine?" she teased.

His expression at once became serious. "I think not. We were all at fault, Phoebe and you and I, but the past is best forgotten. I shall call you Fern, for the name suits you."

"You like it? You did not seem to once."

" 'Fern' for 'sincerity.' Your mother chose well, for it suits you admirably. Oh, my love, forgive me. I should have recognized your sincerity long ago. Can you ever forgive me for the way I treated you?"

For a second she paused. Was it Rafe or Bruno speaking, and to Catherine or Fern? No matter. It was all one now, and life held out promise and hope at last.

His dark eyes raked hers, evidently misinterpreting her hesitation. "Fern . . . say you will forgive and forget. I love you. I have waited so long."

There was such humility and pathos in his eyes that Fern held up her arms in compassion and love. She too had waited an eternity for this moment. So much suffering, but it had all been inevitable. She knew it now. History would not be disinherited.

His eyes glowed with such love and joy that she knew the connecting door would remain closed and locked, tonight and always, for he would remain by her side, as he had sworn.

With a fierce surge of exultation Fern welcomed his arms about her. Soon new life would come to Brackenroyd. As Bruno had once wished, the villagers would have their heir to Brackenroyd within the year.

MALLORY KEEP

MALLORY KEEP

Aileen Armitage

PAN BOOKS

This edition published 1999 by Pan Books
an imprint of Macmillan Publishers Ltd
25 Eccleston Place, London SW1W 9NF
Basingstoke and Oxford
Associated companies throughout the world
www.macmillan.co.uk

This title first published in Great Britain 1998 by
SEVERN HOUSE PUBLISHERS LTD of
9-15 High Street, Sutton, Surrey SM1 1DF
Originally published in 1977 in Great Britain under
the title *The Devil in Crystal* and name of *Erica Lindley*.
This title first published in the U.S.A. 1998 by
SEVERN HOUSE PUBLISHERS INC of
595 Madison Avenue, New York, NY 10022.

British Library Cataloguing in Publication Data

Armitage, Aileen
  Mallory Keep
  I. Romantic Suspense novels
  I. Title
  II. Lindley, Erica, 1930-. The devil in crystal
  823.9'14 [F]

  ISBN 0 330 39657 9

Typeset by Palimpsest Book Production Ltd,
Polmont, Stirlingshire, Scotland.
Printed and bound in Great Britain by
Mackays of Chatham plc, Chatham, Kent

"How long have I beheld the devil in crystal?
Thou hast led me, like a heathen sacrifice
With Music and fatal yokes of flowers,
To my eternal ruin. Woman to man
Is either a god or a wolf."

Webster, *The White Devil*

CHAPTER ONE

'What a surly devil'
—T. W. Farrar, *Eric, or Little by Little*

The salt sea wind blew coldly against my face, penetrating my thin coat, causing me to shiver despite my struggling with my heavy box up the steep cliff path. The sky was darkening rapidly and everywhere there was silence, save for the whine of the wind and the crash of breakers on the rocks below.

A sudden explosion of birds startled me. Their wings beating and their hoarse cry as they scattered from a ledge below made me pause and stare down towards the beach, silver-pale and mournful in the dimming light. Then I saw figures, shadowy shapes moving silently along the beach, a half dozen or so of them, and I felt afraid.

This barren stretch of Yorkshire coast was an alien world to me, a girl city-born and bred in the great metropolis and but newly arrived in this desolate spot. Barely half an hour could have elapsed since I had descended from the train and persuaded the carter to carry me and my few belongings to Mallory Keep, and only a few minutes since he had helped me down at the foot of the hill, declaring the path too steep and narrow for him to go further.

Perhaps it had been presumptuous of me to expect some kind of conveyance to be awaiting me at the station, sent by my new employer, Miss Fairfax. In London it had been different. I must remember now that I was only an employee, or companion, not likely to be offered the symbols of status that the Fairfax family undoubtedly enjoyed.

The shadows below blurred, snaking in and out among the rocks. Still I felt timid, unused to country ways. No doubt I was behaving stupidly to be afraid of them, but I couldn't help reflecting that in the city a group of men moving so quietly could not possibly be about lawful business. One would be foolish there to deliberately encounter such a group by dark. I stood close by the low stone wall, not daring to move, lest movement betrayed me.

I strained my eyes to stare down into the gathering gloom, but I could see the shadows no more. Like mist they had melted and gone. For a few minutes longer I clung to the wall, until I was certain they were there no longer.

With a deep breath I took up my box again and resumed my climb, watching now instead for the outline of Mallory Keep to appear on the skyline as the carter had emphatically assured me. Had I really seen furtive figures on the beach, I wondered, or were they merely spectres of my overtired imagination, the result of moving light on the water's edge and my own hearsay knowledge of Yorkshire's ancient history? Spectres of the past. It amused me, while I toiled uphill, to believe that I felt some kind of affinity with this stretch of coastline between Whitby and Scarborough, with its rocky chalk cliffs and miles of heather moorland behind. In my breast there was a trembling of excitement and anticipation I had never felt before, and I relished the salt tang on my lips.

No sooner had this new sensation of excitement replaced my former fear, than I was suddenly bereft of my wits yet again. I was dimly aware of a sound as of approaching thunder, and then the sea gulls exploded again in a shrieking, enraged storm of flapping wings, and a great black shape suddenly engulfed the sky ahead of me. I dropped my box in alarm and shrank back against the wall, raising my hands to ward off the huge black phantom which plunged, snorting, over me. It was a man on horseback who almost careered into me, his rearing horse and enormous cloaked figure filling the night sky like some avenging angel of destruction.

'What the devil are you doing here?' he demanded angrily, reining in the plunging creature and turning to inspect me with a savage stare. 'Who are you?'

'My name is Amity Lucas. I am looking for Mallory Keep,' I replied nervously. His bulk and furious glare daunted me, and I remembered my aunt Cecily's advice that a gentle answer always turns away wrath.

'Are you then? Why? What is your business there?' The voice was still harsh and uncompromising, the dark eyes just as probing.

'I am to be companion to Miss Fairfax,' I replied, jutting my chin high. I had no reason to be ashamed of my mission, nor of being here alone on the cliffs. And to be truthful, I was just a little resentful of his curt, demanding manner.

I saw his eyes withdraw suspiciously under the craggy brows, and his fingers slide as if to shelter within his waistcoat. A distrustful gentleman this, I mused, whoever he was.

'The devil you are,' he muttered as though to himself, and spurring the horse on he ignored me completely. I watched the black shape of horse and rider plunge on recklessly down the rocky slope of the path until they were lost to view in the dusk. Then taking a deep breath, I picked up my box to continue my uphill struggle.

The wind blustered about me as I neared the top of the cliffs, taking my breath away and blowing whisps of my hair loose from its pins. I would present a rather dishevelled appearance to my new employer, I knew, but at the moment, reaching the safety of the Keep before utter darkness fell was my prime aim. I had no wish to be out alone on these treacherous cliffs when night came.

Almost as if imagination had conjured it up out of wishful thinking, the silhouette of what was unmistakably Mallory Keep rose before me. Grey, gaunt and turreted, it rose against the skyline, not a glimmer of light enlivening the blackness of its many windows. Around it, like some threadbare necklace about the neck of an aging crone, stood a hedge of bare thorns, all leaning to one side as if yielding to the biting lash of the sea wind. In the middle sat the solid stone Keep, imposing and awe-inspiring in its grim implacability.

I shivered. It was not as I had expected; it seemed too cold and haughty to promise a warm welcome. I gripped my box firmly and approached the weather-beaten oak door.

The bell clanged dully and distantly within. For a few moments there was complete silence, and I began to wonder if the old mansion was untenanted after all, and I had come to

7

the wrong house. Slow, shuffling steps within and the grating of a drawn bolt reassured me someone lived here. At least I could enquire where my employer was to be found. At any rate, I was anxious to enter or leave quickly so as to suffer no longer the blind gaze of the crumbling stone gargoyles above me.

The door creaked open. By the light of a lantern she held high, I could see a woman, her cap-covered head cocked curiously to one side. The housekeeper, I adjudged, by her dark gown and the bunch of keys clattering at her waist. Her stare was probing though not inimical.

'Aye?' The note of question in her voice was mixed with curiosity.

'Good evening,' I began in my most pleasant tone. 'I am Miss Lucas. I am looking for Miss Fairfax of Mallory Keep. Could you direct me?'

'This is t'Keep. Miss Fairfax is up in her room. Come in.'

She turned and left me standing there, undecided whether to carry in my box or wait until someone should send out one of the menservants. But somehow I felt from her manner that civilities might be more than I could expect. I struggled to lift the box into the vestibule. The woman stood watching me unconcernedly.

As I straightened up from my efforts, I heard voices from the back of the house. A girl's high-pitched cry came from an open door at the end of a stone-flagged corridor.

'I know nowt about it, I tell thee. They don't tell me owt about their affairs.'

The housekeeper jerked her head in the direction of the voice. 'Hold on a minute. I'll be back,' she said to me. She shuffled off quickly towards the door, and as she thrust it open I could see two young people framed by candlelight, a fair-haired servant girl in cap and apron leaning over the deal table, and a young red-faced man in a roll-necked jersey and cloth cap.

'What's all t'fuss about?' demanded the housekeeper. 'I can hear thy jangle from t'front door.'

The girl scowled. 'It's no but Ben. He's just come in to see me,' she muttered.

8

'Oh, aye? Well, put t'kettle on t'hob to boil. There's a visitor as'd like a cup of tea, no doubt.'

Before the housekeeper pulled the door shut and came back to me, I saw the gleam of interest in the girl's eyes. No doubt there were few strangers to this remote house high on the bleak cliffs.

I was still thinking of the warming prospect of a cup of tea when the housekeeper led me towards a broad flight of shallow stairs. 'Up this way,' she said. This time I decided to relinquish my baggage as I followed.

The stairs were uncarpeted, though bordered by a fine balustrade, and the corridors at the top were cold and drafty. It would seem that Miss Fairfax cared little for creature comfort, for there was little light either. I kept close to the guiding oil lamp in the housekeeper's hand. She stopped and knocked at a doorway. A low voice within called, 'Come in.'

Inside the door the housekeeper pulled back a heavy chenille curtain covering the opening, no doubt against the keen drafts that penetrated everywhere. The room was in darkness. She addressed an unseen person.

'Miss Lucas is here, madam.'

'Ah, yes. Bring her in, Mrs. Garner.'

'Shall I light t'candles, madam?'

'Just the one on the table. Come in, Miss Lucas.'

As I moved forward, Mrs. Garner bent to light a wax taper from the low fire. A dim shape rose from a chair and I heard the rustle of a silk gown as the lady moved to stand by the window. I stood by the table expectantly as Mrs. Garner lit the solitary candle in its iron candlestick, wondering all the while at the youthfulness of the voice from the unseen lady. Somehow I had expected Miss Fairfax to be an elderly spinster such as usually advertised for a companion, but the musical voice of Miss Fairfax indicated someone still young.

Mrs. Garner stood back, her grey hair under the cap gleaming in the candle's gentle glow. 'Shall I bring up t'tea, madam?'

'If you please. Miss Lucas, pray be seated.'

Her hand waved me delicately towards a chair, but Miss Fairfax herself still remained barely visible, a dark shape against the uncurtained window, far from the candle's light.

9

She was tall and slender, that I could see, erect and with a proud tilt to her head. But of her face I could see little, only a profile which indicated a good-looking young woman.

I sat, folding my hands in my lap and waiting to be addressed by my employer. For a moment there was silence, only the measured tick of a clock on the high oak mantel breaking the quiet. No doubt Miss Fairfax was looking me over, taking in my travel-dusty coat and gown, my unkempt hair under my best bonnet. I wished Mrs. Garner had permitted me to tidy up before thrusting me into Miss Fairfax's presence. I sat upright, defiant almost, awaiting my mistress's words.

'You are young, Miss Lucas.'

'I am almost twenty, madam. I wrote so in my letter.'

'So you did. I had forgotten.'

Again she relapsed into silence. I had expected questions as to my journey, how long I had been trevelling, whether I was weary or would like to go to my room to wash. But she simply continued to look at me hard and long, until I began to feel uncomfortable. She seemed to sense my discomfort, for she turned away to look out of the window.

'Tell me about yourself, Miss Lucas.'

'There is little more to tell, other than what I wrote.'

'Tell me again.'

'I live – lived – with my aunt and uncle in Clapham, for my mother died when I was a baby and my father worked a tea plantation in Ceylon until his death four years ago.'

'You had a good education?'

'My father sent money regularly to my aunt to ensure it. I attended an academy for young ladies until I was sixteen.'

'When your father died?'

'Yes, of a tropical disease. My aunt and uncle are not wealthy. Uncle Leonard is a clerk in a tea merchant's office, and Aunt Cecily has several young children. It was necessary for me then to go out to work.'

'In a dressmaker's workshop, you said.'

I lifted my head as I answered. I felt no shame for having to work with my hands. 'Yes, madam. I learned the crafts of cutting and sewing, of embroidery and appliqué. I was happy at Madame Bertrand's salon.'

'She speaks well of you. Why did you leave?'

I hung my head. I had had no wish to leave the dreary little back room in a London side street, where Hetty and Agnes and I had stitched and cut by feeble candlelight till our fingers ached and grew raw, but circumstances had forced it. Aunt Cecily was unusually fertile.

'My aunt's house in Clapham was not very big, madam, and she had need of all the rooms as her family increased.' I thought of my seven little cousins, three and four in a bed, and Aunt Cecily's despairing look when she learned that the eighth child was on its way and baby Septimus would have to yield up his cot to a newcomer. Much as she appreciated my few shillings a week board, she needed my room more. Not that she ever complained. Aunt Cecily, like our dear Queen Victoria, regarded subservience and maternal devotion as the highest female virtues. It was Uncle Leonard, stern patriarch of the family, who finally suggested I should vacate my room and earn my keep elsewhere.

'I see,' Miss Fairfax murmured. 'Then there was no disagreement either with your employer or your family. Do you get on well with people, Miss Lucas?'

Hesitantly I answered. 'I think so. I had occasion to meet few in my work, since I was mainly in the back room, but madame did ask me sometimes to soothe a ruffled customer. They were mostly ladies of some means, merchants' wives and the like.'

'And children? And animals?'

An odd question, I thought privately. She had written that there were only adults in the Fairfax household.

'I have no experience with animals. I was fond of my small cousins, especially little Benjamin.'

'Why?'

'He was a cripple, but a delightful child.'

Miss Fairfax turned quickly. 'He limped? Did he not repel you?'

Irritation pricked me. 'Why should an unfortunate disability repel me? On the contrary, I found him a most attractive child, happy and extremely likable.'

I fancied I heard a faint hiss, as of a sigh, before Mrs. Garner tapped at the door and came in with a tray. She laid it

11

on the chenille-covered table and looked at Miss Fairfax, rubbing her hands on her apron.

'Shall I pour, madam?'

'No, thank you. I shall do it.'

Mrs. Garner nodded and withdrew. Miss Fairfax came forward at last into the light where I could see her. Her hair was thick and dark, parted in the centre and framing the delicate paleness of her face. She was beautiful, so far as I could see, for she still kept her face slightly averted, but I could see the high forehead and finely chiselled nose and full lips.

Her voice came softly from her lips. 'So, disfigurement does not frighten you, Miss Lucas?'

'No, madam.'

'Then what of this?'

She turned suddenly towards me, taking up the candle from the table and holding it aloft. As she did so I saw her full face, the beauty of its symmetry marred by the ugly red weal that ran down her right cheek, from eyebrow almost to chin. She was young, not yet thirty, I guessed. Defiantly she stood there, eyes ablaze as though challenging me to shrink or cry out.

It took a determined effort not to let my eyes betray the shock I felt. Nothing she had said had prepared me for this, the fierce jagged scar that stood out so starkly against her otherwise perfect pale skin. Resolutely I looked back at her challenging face, willing my features to remain composed. After a few seconds of tense silence she spoke.

'Do I not sicken you, Miss Lucas?'

I felt a stab of pity for her. From her tone it would seem others had found her repelling, and she was daring me to admit it. On the contrary, I could feel only compassion for the young woman.

'Not at all, Miss Fairfax. I am only sorry that you have been stricken thus, for it must cause you much anguish.'

'Do not pity me, Miss Lucas. I cannot bear pity.' She replaced the candlestick on the table with a clatter, shaking off droplets of wax on to the tablecover. When she spoke again, the fire in her voice had cooled.

'Do I understand you aright, Miss Lucas? You would be

12

content to remain at the Keep as companion to me, despite my disfigurement?'

'Completely content, Miss Fairfax. If I suit you, I shall be very happy to stay.'

Without warning, the door burst open, and a towering, bulky shape filled the doorway. A man, with dark, undisciplined hair flying wild about his face and angry eyes, strode into the room. I recognized him as the rider on the cliffs who so nearly rode me down.

'Regina,' he snapped, ignoring me utterly, 'what is this I hear of a companion?'

Miss Fairfax smiled for the first time, and her face, despite the scar, came alive.

'My brother, Miss Lucas. May I present Damian Fairfax, Master of Mallory Keep.'

I proffered my hand but he disdained to see it, turning instead to his sister. 'Why is she here, Regina? I knew nothing of this. We want no strangers at the Keep. You know how I hate strangers.'

'She is here at my invitation, Damian. I have need of feminine company. You would not deny me that, surely?' Her voice was gentle though not pleading. Her brother grunted and turned to stare at me fixedly for a moment. From the doorway, a great evil-looking hound with yellow eyes prowled in and sniffed about Mr. Fairfax's feet before coming to sniff at my shoes.

A prickle of fear ran up my spine, for I am rather afraid of large dogs. For a moment I stood stock-still, fearful to breathe, and then in an effort to conciliate the animal, I reached down to touch his great shaggy head.

'Don't do that, Miss Lucas. You will regret it.'

I looked up quickly. Mr. Fairfax was scowling at me.

'Caesar owns to only one master. Everyone else is a potential enemy, so if you care for your safety, do not attempt to touch my dog.'

He bent to scratch behind the beast's ear as if to prove his words, and in so doing I saw the man clearly in the candlelight. He was broad shouldered and with thickly tangled black hair that curled defiantly about his brow. His face showed strength in the firm set of his lips and long, straight

13

nose, but in the furrows of his brow I could detect anger mixed with sorrow. His manner had already shown me that he was an impatient man, uncaring of common courtesy.

Suddenly he straightened. 'Very well, Regina. But if she stays, see that she keeps out of my way. Already she has startled my horse on the cliff path so that the beast nearly threw me. Keep her if you must, but keep her out of my sight.'

He glared at me, and then without another word he strode out of the room, the shaggy hound lurching out after him. Miss Fairfax sighed and seated herself opposite me.

'Then that seems to be settled. There is only Uncle Eustace now whom you have not met, but he is elderly and stays much in his room. Other than Mrs. Garner and the staff, there is no one else. Do you think you will be content here, for we do not entertain?'

I felt more misgivings than I cared to admit even to myself but I smiled to reassure her. 'I think I shall be quite content, Miss Fairfax. There is beautiful countryside around here to be explored, and I can fill my spare time quite admirably with painting and sewing. I shall not trouble your brother.'

She smiled faintly. 'Please do not mind my brother's ways, Miss Lucas. He is an admirable man, but he dislikes women. It would be as well to do as he says and avoid him as far as possible.'

'Indeed I shall.' And I meant it. I had no wish to encounter the surly, scowling Mr. Fairfax again, without good reason.

'Then shall we take tea now? I fear we may have let it go cold.'

She lifted the woollen tea cozy from the teapot and poured out tea into china cups. I watched the candlelight glow on the amber liquid as she poured, and accepted the cup gratefully. Tepid though it now was, the tea was welcome refreshment after my long journey.

Miss Fairfax rang the bell when we had finished, then crossed to the window.

'There is a heavy mist coming up off the sea. The local fishermen will not be going out tonight, I think,' she murmured.

Fishermen, of course. What I saw down on the beach must

have been a group of men going fishing. Before I could comment on it, Mrs. Garner arrived in answer to the bell.

'Leave the teacups, Mrs. Garner. Just draw the curtains and then take Miss Lucas to her room to prepare for dinner.'

I rose as the heavy chenille curtains swung to, clattering their brass rings along the bamboo poles. Mrs. Garner led me out and along the corridor. Miss Fairfax's voice called after me. 'Dinner will be at eight, Miss Lucas.'

I followed Mrs. Garner along uncarpeted corridors, wide and cold, her slippered feet shuffling along the floorboards, and wondered that so huge and imposing a residence as Mallory Keep should be so sparsely furnished. When at length she showed me into a room and left, a quick survey of my bedroom confirmed the view.

A large bed with brass rails and a patchwork quilt dominated the panelled room. Around it spread an expanse of linoleum, with a hand-pegged rug before the fireplace where a low fire glowed. A huge wardrobe and a marble-topped washstand stood near the window. I dipped my fingers in the water in the flower-patterned ewer. It was stone cold. The Fairfaxes were stoic people indeed if they washed in cold water in the depths of winter.

I shivered and looked out of the window, but could see little but the thick mist that eddied about the garden. Someone had brought up my cases while I was taking tea with Miss Fairfax, so I began to unpack.

I chose a grey wool gown for dinner. Indeed I possessed no elaborate evening dresses, but in any event I deemed the grey wool suitable for this sombre house with its chilly atmosphere. Probably there would be only Regina Fairfax and myself at dinner, judging from what she had said about Uncle Eustace, and Mr. Damian Fairfax had made it abundantly clear he would not seek my company.

By the time I had dressed, my hair now brushed and combed, and my appearance far more presentable, the bell for dinner had still not sounded. I surveyed my reflection in the dressing-table mirror critically. Smooth fair hair becomingly outlined my neat features, though I could have wished I possessed Regina Fairfax's straight nose in place of my

15

slightly retroussé one. I debated whether to wait in my room or go down in search of the dining room. I could hear no footsteps or clatter of dishes. I stood by the uncurtained window and traced my finger idly on its steamed surface. Regina, I wrote first, then Damian and Eustace, the names which would shape my future here in Mallory Keep. On a whim I added my own name, Amity.

Still no sound from downstairs. I decided to go and investigate. The rest of my unpacking could wait.

A solitary oil lamp on a night table glowed in the corridor, lighting its dusty length. A door at the further end opened and a bent figure emerged, candle in hand. He straightened at my approach.

'Good evening, my dear.' The voice was remarkably youthful considering the furrowed lines of age about his pale blue eyes. His bushy eyebrows reminded me of the woolly caterpillars I had sometimes seen on the cabbage leaves in Aunt Cecily's little back garden. He was oddly dressed, an embroidered waistcoat showing beneath his frock coat contradicting the carpet-slippered feet and the tasselled nightcap topping his sparse hair. It must be Uncle Eustace, at whose eccentricity Miss Fairfax had hinted.

'Good evening, sir.'

He nodded genially. 'I don't think I know you, my dear. Are you real, or yet another of the pretty wraiths that haunt the Keep, I wonder? It becomes increasingly difficult to determine these days.'

I smiled. 'No wraith, sir, but Miss Fairfax's companion. My name is Amity Lucas.'

Again he nodded, but there was an air of perplexity in the soft gaze. 'You must come and see me again, Miss Friendship. I shall look forward to that.' He must have noted my look of surprise, for he added, 'Amity means friendship, you know. Gemini, I should guess.'

'I beg your pardon, sir?'

'Your birth sign. You were born about the end of May, were you not?'

I was startled, for he was correct. 'Indeed, sir, on May the twenty-seventh I shall be twenty.'

He nodded again sagely. 'I knew it. There is an unmistak-

16

able charm about you, typical of the sign. I shall look forward to our meeting again.'

He turned and reentered his room, leaving me open-mouthed. Downstairs I found Miss Fairfax, still in her drawing room, though she had evidently changed, for she now wore a beautiful gown of dove grey silk moiré.

'So you've met Uncle Eustace,' she remarked with a wry smile when I told her of the encounter. 'A pleasant old fellow, but vague and only half with us, I'm afraid. Take no notice of the rather odd things he may say. He's really quite harmless.'

The dinner bell rang. Dutifully I rose as Miss Fairfax did, and followed her to the door. More lamps now glowed in the gallery as we descended the wide oak stairs, and I could see the many portraits gazing down from the minstrels' gallery. Proud gentlemen with swords at their sides and powdered and bewigged ladies watched our progress with a haughty stare.

'My ancestors,' Miss Fairfax remarked as she noted my interest. 'Generations of Fairfaxes who have lived at Mallory Keep. My father is the last on the right there.'

'And Uncle Eustace?'

'He is not a Fairfax, but my mother's brother. Damian's will be the next portrait to be hung, when he agrees to have it painted.'

The dining room was a cosy sight, lamplight illuminating the damask-covered round table and the glow of deep red velvet curtains. A muslin-capped maid, tall and thin-lipped, stood with hands clasped awaiting her mistress's order to pour soup out of the jug into flower-patterned bowls. It was a simple meal of cold beef and vegetables, followed by steamed pudding, but my famished stomach did justice to its amplitude.

During the meal Miss Fairfax talked amiably of the Keep, its distance from the neighbouring village, and thus the infrequency of visitors.

'In fact, apart from delivering food and essentials, the villagers rarely call here,' she remarked, 'save for the few who are employed here. Some, like Ellen, the parlour-maid, who has been serving us dinner, and Ethel, the housemaid, live in here, and others, like Rosie, the chambermaid, live in the village and come in daily. We do not employ a large staff. Many of the rooms in the Keep have been shut up to reduce the need.'

Though she did not say it, Miss Fairfax's words implied that the family had come down in the world. It was no shame to be impoverished, and maintaining the Keep would tax the pockets of the wealthiest, I fancied. She seemed to realise she had betrayed too much.

'Do not mistake me, Miss Lucas. The Fairfaxes are an old and respected family. We have been in this part of Yorkshire for centuries, and our history is a noble one. We have always upheld the monarchy, even in Cromwell's day, and we have suffered much for our loyalty.'

'I do not doubt it, madam.'

Instantly her proud face softened. 'Pray do not call me madam, but Regina, if you will. I have need of a friend such as you. May I call you Amity?'

I smiled in pleasure. It was heartening to be thus welcomed by a stranger. 'Indeed, I should deem it an honour.'

She smiled and sat back, relaxed now and content, the scar on her face half-hidden in shadow. Sympathy for the woman welled in me, for I could sense the loneliness in her, isolated in this chill house with only a sour-tempered brother and half-crazed uncle for company. Like little cousin Benjamin, there was infinite appeal in her vulnerability, and I warmed to her immediately. I was fortunate indeed to have secured a position as companion to such a young and sensitive woman, instead of to some peevish, cantankerous old maid.

Regina pushed back her chair and rose from the table. 'It is growing late, Amity, nearing nine, and I'm sure you must be very fatigued after your long journey. Much as I should like to continue our conversation, I must let you go to bed. Tomorrow we shall talk again.'

Gratefully I bade her good night and climbed the stairs to my room. Someone had evidently been there during dinner, for the bedcovers were turned back and my best woollen nightgown lay draped across a chair by the fire. In the downy depths of the bed lay a stone hot water bottle. There was a knock at the door.

A girl came in carrying a jug of hot water. I recognised her as the girl I had seen when I first entered the Keep, talking to a young man in a jersey.

'Hot water, miss,' she said laconically as she placed the jug on the washstand. I could see the curious look in her sidelong glance. 'Is there owt else tha'll be wanting?'

'Thank you, no.' She bobbed a curtsy and made for the door. 'What is your name?' I added.

She turned. 'Rosie, miss. Rose Pickering. I'm t'house-maid.' Red fingers rubbed dry on the coarse serge of her skirt, missing the stained apron.

'Ah yes. You live in the village.'

'Aye, and if tha's got all tha wants, I'll be off home now to me mam.'

'Good night then, Rose.'

I drew back the curtains before climbing into bed, rubbing the steam from one small pane to look out, but there was little to be seen. No wonder Rose was in a hurry to get home, for the mist lay thick and heavy over the Keep now and the cliff path would be more treacherous than ever.

Or perhaps she was in a hurry to meet her follower, the sudden thought struck me. That fellow, Ben, below with her, was handsome in a gruff way, and she had told the housekeeper he had come in to see her. It was a mellowing thought, that a romance could be blooming in the wastes of this gaunt old house. Young love could have a warming, humanising effect on its bleak austerity.

I went to stand by the fire, warming my hands at its glow before undressing to put on the nightgown someone had so thoughtfully placed there to warm. Perhaps it would be best, though, to go in search of the water closet before undressing. Regina had mentioned that it lay at the end of the corridor.

Taking up a candle, I lit it from the fire and went out. The lamps in the corridor had been extinguished now, so I was glad of the candle's flame. I turned right, away from the staircase, and walked slowly along the corridor, inspecting each door as I came to it, but not venturing to open it in case it should be someone's bedroom. The end of the passage was blocked by a stout, nail-studded door which I found to be locked. I turned to retrace my steps.

A faint swish ahead startled me. I raised my candle higher.

'Is someone there?'

No answer came from out of the darkness, only a soft shuffle. I walked slowly on until I reached my own door. It was still ajar as I had left it.

I moved further down, towards the stairs. To my relief I discovered the water closet, its door open to reveal the yellow porcelain bowl within.

A few moments later, I went back to my room and found the door now closed. Going in, I found no one there. Surely Rose had not returned, since her duties were done. Then who had come to my room in my absence? Regina, perhaps, out of duty, to see I had all I required. I put down the candle and began to undress.

It was only as I stood at last in my nightgown that I noticed that I had left the window curtains still undrawn. I hurried across to draw them before leaping into bed, my feet tingling with cold on the bare linoleum floor. As I did so, I saw again the faint lettering where I had written names in the steamed glass earlier. I smiled as I made out the indistinct words – Damian, Regina, Eustace. Then the smile froze. I bent closer to the small pane.

Where I had written my own name there was only a clear patch, someone had vigorously erased the word. Of Amity there was no trace. But underneath, in crisp, newly printed letters, stood another name.

Rachel.

CHAPTER TWO

'Devils are not so black as they are painted.'
—T. Lodge, *Margarita of America*

I must have slept a deep and dreamless sleep in my new bed, all memory of Clapham driven from my mind by fatigue, for the next thing I knew it was morning. I opened my eyes and looked about me, trying to get my bearings.

Of course. No longer a chintz counterpane on a narrow bed in a tiny bedroom in Aunt Cecily's house, but a patchwork cover on a great double bed in this large room of Mallory Keep. And a maidservant bringing me morning tea. This was luxury indeed. It must have been her knock which had awakened me.

Rosie put down the tray and went to draw back the heavy curtains, and I stretched contentedly as I watched her. She looked attractively fresh in a clean calico gown of grey with its crisp white apron and cap. Pale wintry sunlight flickered in through the thorn trees and cast soft shadows on my bed.

'T'mist's all but gone, miss,' Rosie said in a tone of satisfaction. 'Just a haze out at sea now.'

I climbed out of bed and pulled on my robe, anxious to see the view from my window. Rosie poured out tea. The clink of the china was a deliciously luxurious sound.

Beyond the denuded thornbushes I could see an expanse of gardens sloping down to a cliff edge, and beyond it a grey waste of sea. Evidently there was a bay below the cliffs, for I could see a headland to the south encircling a stretch of rocky beach. I questioned Rosie.

'Aye, miss, that's Manacle Bay down t'cliffs from t'Keep. That's Carnelian Point tha can see.'

What strange, attractive names, I mused, evocative of the coast's history. Manacle, the handcuffs of bygone prisoners, and carnelian, the semi-precious stone sometimes known as moss agate. I stood gazing out of the window, entranced at the prospect of living in this magical place.

'Wilt drink thy tea before it goes cold, miss? Then I'll bring thee hot water.' Rosie prompted me. I was turning to go when my gaze fell on the windowpane where last night I had traced my finger in the steam. Out of curiosity I turned to Rosie.

'Rose, is there a Rachel in Mallory Keep?'

She cocked her fair head to one side, a tendril of hair falling loose from her cap. 'Not as I can think of, miss.' She tucked the curl back as she probed her memory further. 'Not one o't'maids, 'cos I know 'em all. And there's precious few servants here now, not like my mother's day. No, no Rachel here, miss.'

'No matter. Did your mother work here, Rosie?'

'Aye, over twenty years since, when old Mr. Thomas Fairfax, Mr. Damian's father, were alive. She left when Mr. Thomas were killed.'

'Killed?'

'A riding accident. Horse threw him.'

'How unfortunate. Was that long ago?'

' 'Appen twenty year sin, afore I were born. Miss Regina were only a young girl and Mr. Damian no but a little lad. I'll get thy hot water now, miss.'

She bustled away, leaving me to sip my tea and reflect on what she had said. The poor children, Regina and Damian, being robbed of a father so young. And what of their mother? It would appear that she too was dead.

I wondered again about the writing on my window-pane. Evidently it was not Rosie who had erased my name and written Rachel, even assuming the child could write. Her innocence had been obvious when I asked her if she knew of such a person. Curious. Still, it was unimportant. Exploring my new surroundings was far more pressing to me now than idle curiosity.

The chance of freedom to explore came more quickly than I had hoped. Today I had expected Miss Fairfax to demand my companionship, but when Rosie returned with the jug of hot water she was at pains to apologise for her mistress.

'Miss Regina begs as how tha'll excuse her this morning, miss, she'll be busy wi' t'bailiff. She asks if tha'll mind eating breakfast alone and then happen tha'd like to walk out in t'gardens, seeing as how it's fine weather. She'll join thee at lunch, she says.'

I smiled to ease the girl's embarrassment. It had been an effort to remember the message and deliver it tactfully. 'Pray tell Miss Regina I shall be delighted to have the opportunity to look around the grounds. I shall be quite content.'

'Shall I bring thy breakfast up on a tray then?'

'If you would, please, Rosie.'

She soon returned with a bowl of porridge, bacon, kidneys on toast, and a pot of fragrant coffee. I sat eating while she cleaned the grate and relaid the fire. I could not help but admire the deft way in which she twirled paper into corkscrews and arranged them geometrically with pieces of kindling. When she finally scrambled up from her knees, her white cotton apron was no longer immaculate, and there was a smudge on her rosy cheek. She glanced at the clock on the mantel.

'Lord bless us, look at t'time. I'll have to shift. I've not done t'master's fire yet. He'll be raging if he's about,' she muttered as she gathered up the pail of ashes and her brushes. I bit back the desire to question her as to whether her master was perpetually bad-tempered.

'Is Mr. Fairfax up then?' I enquired. If he was, I wanted to avoid meeting him when I went out.

'Not seen him, but that means nowt. He might not have gone to bed yet,' Rosie answered as she gathered up the last of her tools. 'I'll be back to make t'bed and clean thy room later,' she promised, and she was gone.

Not have gone to bed yet? I was puzzled. Was Mr. Damian in the habit of staying up all night, I wondered? And if so, why? I ate the last of my toast and dismissed the question. Undoubtedly Mr. Fairfax was an unaccountable character.

As soon as I was washed and dressed, I put on my bonnet and coat and prepared to go out. I was excited at the prospect of exploring. All was quiet in the Keep as I opened my door, save for the far-off clatter of dishes.

Quickly and quietly I walked along the corridor towards the main stairs, but softly as I trod, the quick ears of Uncle Eustace must have heard me. His door opened as I passed, and his stooped figure, wrapped in a worn dressing robe, emerged. The nightcap still drooped over one bright eye.

'May the twenty-seventh, at what time?' he asked. His small head cocked to one side and the lively eyes made me think of an inquisitive London sparrow.

'I beg your pardon, sir?'

'At what time of day were you born? And where?'

'Oh. In London. Tea time, I think my mother said. About five o'clock.'

'Excellent. Now I can draw up your natal chart.'

I stood puzzled as he disappeared back into his room. Natal chart? Ah, astrology of course; he wanted to cast my horoscope. I smiled indulgently as I continued on my way.

Reaching the front door uninterrupted, I opened it and went out, hopping its creaking hinges would disturb no one, and especially Mr. Damian.

My footsteps crunched on the gravel path as I rounded the house to the lawns behind. From here I could see it was a larger mansion than I had been able to see by night, a long colonnaded terrace running along the length of the main block, and in which my room was located, overlooking the grounds. At each end projected a wing, the western one furthest from the cliffs, and an eastern one whose windows were clouded with dirt. It would appear this wing was unused, probably owing to the high cost of upkeep. A pity, I mused, since it lay near the cliffs and probably afforded a much better view of the bay.

For a time I walked about the gardens, saddened to see the neglected shrubs and grass-grown borders. It must have been very beautiful here in its heyday, but on a chill February morning, its air of neglect, combined with the dead barrenness of winter, lent the place no attraction whatsoever. A small arbor, now dilapidated and crumbling, was a pathetic vestige of a once splendid garden.

I retraced my steps towards the front of the house, then on

an impulse decided not to go out by the main gate with its gaunt stone pillars. I searched along the thorn hedge until I found a small iron gate leading out onto the cliff path.

Beyond it I paused. Uphill or down towards the village, I debated, and chose the former. The village I would explore later.

The wind blew gustily about me, whipping my skirts tightly about my legs and impeding movement, but as I neared the rocky edge I could see that the wind had also cleared away the last traces of the night's sea fog.

The view was magnificent. A huge grey circle of sea lay trapped within the bay, a restless surge of swelling waves that broke in frothing wreaths on the cliff-bound shore. It must be high tide, for there was no beach visible, only the rocky bases of sheer cliffs, save for a small jetty where the village lay at the southern end of the bay.

I trod carefully as I continued uphill, since the path was perilously close to the cliff edge, disappearing altogether in places. Extreme care was needed if I were not to plunge two hundred feet or so onto the rocks below. I stepped aside onto the springy brown turf.

From here the village of Mallory appeared minute, a clutter of tiny red-roofed houses perched dangerously one atop the other in an effort to cling to the steep hillside. So close-packed were the little houses that I could scarcely have believed it possible that there was space for any streets between them, had I not myself driven through the narrow lanes only last night. It was almost impossible to believe that here I was, two hundred miles from home, in a setting vastly different from any landscape I had ever seen before.

I breathed in the pure, fresh air deeply, resolving that I would enjoy this new life far from London's fog and filth. A whole new world beckoned, inviting and exciting. I turned to look back at the Keep.

There it stood, stark and impregnable as a fortress on the cliff top, its castellated outline dark and sombre despite the pale sunshine. So engrossed was I that I did not notice that I was not alone on the cliff path until I felt a sniffling at my feet.

A little white terrier patched with brown was darting playfully at my skirts and away again, as though inviting me

25

to throw a stick or join in some other game with him. I looked up the path and saw a gentleman, evidently his owner, striding towards me.

I drew back on the turf to leave the path clear. He wore a black cape overcoat and top hat, and as he drew nearer I saw that he also wore a clerical collar. He doffed his hat politely, revealing crisp, grey hair.

'Madam, pray forgive my dog. He is unaware of the necessity for introduction.'

I could not help smiling. 'He is a friendly fellow.'

He smiled too, his grey eyes creasing at the corners in a way which indicated a kindly nature. 'Come here, Patch,' he ordered the dog sternly. 'Make your apology to the lady.'

Obediently the dog ran to sit before me, cocking his head to one side as though enquiring whether I would forgive. I could not resist bending to pat his head, thinking the while how different he was from the brutish hound of Mr. Damian. The gentleman seemed pleased, for his smile creased his eyes again.

'If you would permit me, madam, to introduce myself to atone for Patch's oversight, I am Hugh Parmenter, vicar of St. Matthew's yonder.'

He was pointing down in the direction of the red roofs of Mallory village, and there I could just discern the squat grey tower of a church. He had offered me his credential of respectability, for he knew as well as I that our informal meeting would be irregular in normal circumstances. Casual conversation between a lady and a gentleman who were strangers to each other would be unthinkable.

I offered my gloved hand. 'Amity Lucas, sir, newly arrived in Mallory to act as companion to Miss Fairfax at the Keep.'

'Indeed? I am charmed to meet you, Miss Lucas.'

He took my hand with the lightest of pressure and I could see the gleam of surprise in his grey eyes. He recovered quickly, waving one arm in a sweeping gesture towards the bay.

'It is no doubt, then, your first view of our little bay? Your first visit to Yorkshire, perhaps?'

'Indeed, sir. I have never been out of London until yesterday. I am most impressed by the magnificent view here.'

He smiled with proprietary pride. 'The coast hereabouts has many such bays and coves – perhaps you have heard of Robin Hood's Bay, Renswick Bay, or Carnelian Bay? Or the Emperor's Bath and Devil's Punch Bowl?'

I shook my head. 'I knew of none, sir, I fear, until I looked at a map when I learned I was to come here. But I hope to rectify the omission soon, for they have delightful names.'

'And an interesting history all,' he remarked. 'Like the whole region, the moors behind you, and the old abbey there, the place is steeped in history.'

I turned as he pointed inland. So entranced I had been by the view to seaward that I had not looked this way before he pointed it out to me. A vast expanse of moorland covered in dry brown heather and rutted by ravines stretched for miles as far as the eye could see. On the horizon lay the jagged outlines of a ruined building with roofless arches, no doubt the abbey he had mentioned.

'Malvaux Abbey was destroyed in the time of Henry VIII,' my kindly informant said, his eyes misted as he gazed towards the ruin, as though reaching back through the mists of time. 'The worthy monks were turned out to beg or starve, and the magnificent abbey was torn apart. Since that time when, so the locals will tell you, a curse fell on the land, there has been much tragedy in this area.'

I looked at him questioningly. 'Tragedy? For the village folk?'

'For all who live hereabouts. The fisherfolk in Mallory village, the farmers, and most of all perhaps for the Fairfaxes, who have always lived here. Do you know the name Mallory means ill-omened?'

I did not, for I had learned little Latin. I felt a shudder in my spine, despite the sunlight, and tried to counteract the atmosphere by a bright reply.

'The village looks pretty and pleasant, and no doubt is a hive of activity. Surely the villagers no longer believe such ancient superstition.'

He smiled wryly. 'Belief such as theirs is instilled in them from birth, and it is hard to counter.'

'Not even with faith of your kind, Reverend?'

'Do not mistake me. Mallory folk are God-fearing and

27

industrious. They work hard to wrest a living from the sea and attend church regularly, but ancient beliefs die hard nonetheless.'

I heard his sigh, and then he paused. Turning to me again he added, 'Do you know, there is in my churchyard a very old stone, a great monolith they call The Devil's Arrow. My parishioners regard that obelisk with almost as much awe as they do the church altar.'

'The Devil's Arrow,' I breathed softly. 'What an evocative name! Your countryside seems to abound with attractive names.'

'It has an attractive story too. Tradition has it that the devil, enraged at seeing a church being built, hurled an arrow at the workmen, but it fell short.'

'And what is it really?'

The Reverend Parmenter shrugged. 'Who knows? An ancient sepulcher, perhaps, or a Druid monument. Such huge stones, over twenty feet high, have been regarded as an object of reverence and awe for centuries. Even now, people believe in 'holy stones'. Perhaps pagan rites were once performed near it, and then, with Christianity, men probably built their own sanctuary near it. But you understand what I mean about old beliefs dying hard.'

'Indeed I do.'

Even as I was answering him I became aware of another figure on the landscape, a dark man in a cape-coat hurrying across the heather towards the Keep. And even before I saw the lurching shape of the hound behind him, I knew it was Damian Fairfax.'

'Your employer, I believe,' the reverend remarked, nodding in his direction. 'He does not appear to wish to come and speak to you.'

'He is not my employer, but Miss Fairfax.'

Damian Fairfax hurtled on, staring ahead, but his black eyes glazed as though he saw nothing but his inner thoughts. I am certain he did not even see us.

'A strange man, Mr. Fairfax,' Reverend Parmenter said quietly. 'A strange family.'

Defensively I turned. 'He is a withdrawn gentleman, I understand, not fond of company. But he is not obliged to

28

speak to me simply because we meet on a morning walk.'

'I beg your pardon, Miss Lucas, I meant no offence.' His voice was genuinely apologetic, and as I turned downhill towards the village, he fell into step beside me, he on the outer edge of the cliff path and picking his words with as much care as he picked his step. 'You are to be commended on your loyalty to your employers.'

I bowed my head primly in acknowledgment.

'But I assure you I intended no criticism. It is the general opinion hereabouts, for the family has a checkered history. The villagers regard them with awe.'

'With suspicion, do you mean?'

'Well, they are withdrawn, as you put it. Miss Regina never appears in the village since she suffered an accident some years ago, nor her uncle. Mallory folk do not understand this, and naturally they are wary of what they do not understand.'

'Have you seen Miss Regina since her accident, sir? Is she not one of your parishioners?'

'I have not, nor is she one of my congregation. None of the Fairfaxes are.'

'Then if you saw her, and how tragically she has been disfigured, you would understand her reluctance to put herself on public view.'

'I had gathered as much from my parishioners who work at the Keep. But the Fairfax inclination to shut themselves away is not restricted to Miss Regina. Her parents and grandparents were the same.'

A vision came to my mind of generations of remote Fairfaxes in lace and powdered wigs. Without conscious thought the next question sprang to my lips.

'Do you know of a Rachel in the family?'

He glanced up at the sky and his brow furrowed. 'Rachel. Rachel Fairfax. No, I do not recall the name. But I have records of the names of all the Fairfaxes, and indeed quite a store of books on local history, if you are interested. You would be very welcome to peruse any of them at your leisure.'

'You are most kind, sir.'

'I shall be more than delighted to show you. You know, every inch of this coast has a story to tell, and most of them fascinating tales. Did you ever hear tell of Nicholas Post-gate?'

'I do not think so.'

'He was a seventeenth-century priest, hunted as a recusant. He was caught hereabouts and hanged, drawn and quartered at York.'

'How dreadful!' I cried.

Reverend Parmenter pointed inland across the moor. 'Over yonder, in the Littlebeck Valley, lies a pool which recalls the story yet. You see, the man who gave Postgate away, a local exciseman named Reeves, found himself ostracised by the countryfolk here. He found it so unbearable that he finally drowned himself in that pool. People call it Dead Man's Pool, and they swear no trout will swim in it even now, though the rest of the valley teems with trout.'

We had passed the little gate in the thorn hedge and now arrived at the main gate to Mallory Keep. I had spent so much time in this entertaining gentleman's company that I felt I must return to the house, leaving the village to explore another time. I gave my hand to the Reverend.

'Sir, you have been most kind, and I have enjoyed hearing about Mallory immensely.'

He bowed over my hand. 'Then I trust this may be the first of many such meetings, Miss Lucas, for I too have enjoyed your company. Pray do me the honour of calling on us at the vicarage very soon. My wife would be delighted to meet you.'

Calling to Patch, he strode on down the path, and I turned up the gravel drive to the house, feeling agreeably content. If the rest of Mallory folk were as pleasant and welcoming as their amiable vicar, then I would certainly enjoy life here.

There was a round-faced young housemaid crossing the vestibule as I entered. She was pretty though snub-nosed, and she bobbed a curtsey when she saw me.

'Miss Regina is in her drawing-room, miss. She asked as you'd come up when you came in.'

I thanked the girl and asked her name.

'Ethel, miss.' She blushed prettily and scurried on her way.

Upstairs I went to my own room first, to divest myself of my bonnet and coat. Then, as I was closing my door after me, I glanced along the corridor towards the unused east wing. To my surprise I saw that the nail-studded door separating the wing from the main block stood open. Odd, I thought. I know that door was locked last night. Perhaps the servants were in there cleaning.

I must not keep my employer waiting. I hurried along to Regina's drawing-room and, as I neared it, the door opened. A stocky young man turned in the doorway to speak.

'I'll see to them fences at once, then, miss. Good day to you.'

As he turned, I recognized him. It was the young man in a roll-neck sweater who had been talking with Rosie last night when I first entered Mallory Keep. Now, no longer wearing a cloth cap, I could see he had sandy hair that frizzed defiantly about his ears. He was young, in his late twenties perhaps, soberly dressed in dark grey jacket and trousers. He looked at me and nodded, no sign of recognition in his set features.

As I laid my hand on the doorknob, I turned to look back at him. He was standing at the head of the stairs and watching me, his keen blue eyes alight with curiosity. I opened the door and went in.

Regina was still sitting behind a large oak desk. As I came in she pushed away a sheaf of papers before her, leaned back in her high-backed chair, and stretched her arms above her head with a deep sigh.

'Oh, it's a relief to have all those problems ironed out. Ben Jagger is a very efficient bailiff. I don't know what we'd do without him.'

I seated myself in a chair by the window. The sunlight fell across Regina's desk, showing up every scratch and inkstain on its worn surface. I couldn't help reflecting that a bowl of flowers would help immensely to brighten the drab cheerlessness of the room. 'He seems very young for the position,' I remarked.

'He took over when his father died two years ago. A Jagger has always been bailiff to the Fairfax estate.'

'What did he do before his father died?'

'He was a fisherman, like most of the village men. He still

31

has his boat and goes out occasionally, but managing the estate takes up most of his time now.'

'There must be a great deal of work to be done.'

'Indeed there is,' she laughed ruefully. 'Our tenants have constant troubles; poachers, foxes stealing chickens, wandering cattle or dogs threatening the lambs.' She rose from the desk and crossed to stand by the window. It was a habit with her, I realised, to stand with her back to the window so as to keep her scarred face in shadow.

'What a worry it must be to you.'

'Oh, I am lucky to have a man like Ben Jagger upon whom I can rely utterly. I can cope.'

And I felt she would. Regina Fairfax was a woman of strength and capability, one could sense it in her. But why didn't her brother take on the load? Before I could stop myself, my impetuous mouth had framed the question.

'Why doesn't Mr. Damian manage the estate? It seems a burden more fitted to a man's broad shoulders than to a woman's?'

I saw her mouth set in a firmer line before she answered. 'He cannot.'

She turned to look out of the window, and I realised that the averted back indicated that I was to question no more. I shut my mouth tightly to prevent any further indiscretion, but Regina seemed to reconsider. Perhaps she felt her answer had been too abrupt. Without turning she went on speaking.

'My brother used to manage the estate at one time. Now, however, circumstances have changed. He does not feel he can cope with it any longer, so for the last year or two I have done it. Not perhaps as efficiently as others could, but we survive.'

'I am sure you are doing the job admirably. The people hereabouts must have great respect for you.'

She half-turned, and I could see the bitter curve at the edge of her lips. 'Respect? Ah no, my dear Miss Lucas, suspicion, perhaps, and hatred, but never respect.'

I was aghast. Why should the villagers hate her? What could Regina Fairfax ever have done to them to cause such bitterness? Sharply I bit my lips to stop another impudent question. Regina was gazing into the far distance.

'Mallory means evil-omened, Amity. Did you know that?'

'Why, yes, I met a gentleman on the cliff path today who was telling me something of local history and legend.'

'And did he tell you that the Fairfaxes are hated because they are believed to be the cause of the curse which lies over the land?'

'Why on earth should they believe that?'

She shrugged. 'Who knows why they believe the strange things they do. Ancient beliefs are handed on and accepted without basis or proof. But that is why we have difficulty in getting servants to work here. They hate and fear Mallory Keep.'

A shudder ran through me, that feeling so intense and terrible could envelop a family, and yet they had to struggle to survive there. Regina, as though sensing the shudder, turned brightly.

'But there, let us talk no more of silly gossip. Let me tell you only that Damian is not really well enough to run our affairs. He has not had a happy life, you know, as our parents died when we were quite young. And then, a year or so ago, he suffered a terrible shock. He has not yet recovered, nor will he, I feel, for some time yet. That is why I cope. And that is why I ask you to bear with him if you should happen to meet. But for the most part, avoid him as he asks. He is best left alone to work out his problem.'

'Of course, I understand. And I thank you for entrusting me with your personal affairs.' I felt happy, despite her anxieties, that she felt she knew me well enough already to confide in me. I resolved to help this proud, courageous girl as best I could.

'Now, what shall we do after lunch, Amity,' Regina said with a smile. 'I was going to suggest we walk in the grounds, but I see the sun is disappearing behind a cloud. I think it is going to rain, so shall we talk and perhaps sketch a little instead? You could sketch the latest London fashions for me, for I fear I am far behind the times.'

'I could do more. I could make you a gown in the latest style if you wished it.'

Regina clapped her hands in delight. 'To be sure, you are yourself a couturiere, I had forgotten! Oh, I would love that above all things, but would you mind? After all, you are employed as my companion, not my dressmaker.'

'I should be very happy. You choose the material once you have seen my sketches.'

And so the afternoon passed pleasantly, despite the drizzling rain outside. We sat at the drawing table, heads bent together while I drew and Regina watched. Although my sketching was not professional, Regina was entranced by the designs I drew, the tight-fitting bodices and wide-flowing crinoline skirts, the full sleeves and lace trimmings. Finally she pronounced one sketch her favourite, the skirt layered in three sections and the wide sleeves with their tightly cuffed undersleeve would be sure protection against the Keep's drafts, she laughed. In silver grey and violet wool, that was how she visualized it.

'You must go into the town and seek out the material for me. You will, won't you?'

'To be sure. But won't you come too, to choose it?'

She coloured slightly. 'No. I haven't left the Keep since . . . since. . . .'

'Then of course I shall go for you. I only hope I make the right choice.'

'I am certain you will. Oh Amity!' She clasped her hands and smiled happily. 'If only you knew what it meant to have a friend! I am so glad you came to Mallory Keep. You will stay, won't you?' Before I could reply she rushed on. 'Please promise me you will stay, whatever happens. I couldn't bear it if you left now. Please don't let anyone frighten you away.'

'Frighten me? Who would want to do that?'

She looked down at her hands. 'Forgive me, I prattle nonsense. Uncle Eustace bewilders some people because he seems a little strange, and Damian could frighten you with his outbursts, but I think you could weather that. I just don't want to lose you. Not yet, so soon.'

I covered her hands with mine. 'It would take more than Uncle Eustace or your brother to drive me away, Regina, have no fear.'

She withdrew her hands, evidently embarrassed by her display of vulnerability. 'Then choose my wool for me, Amity, and some tiny pearl buttons for the bodice. And now

34

I think it is time to dress for dinner.' She rose from the table and went to stand by the fire, gazing down into t .e hearth.

I glanced at the mantel clock. It was more than an hour till dinner, but I realised Regina wished to curtail an interview where she perhaps felt she had revealed herself too suddenly to a comparative stranger. I gathered together the leaves of my sketchbook and was rising to go when the housekeeper tapped and entered. Regina looked up.

'What is it, Mrs. Garner?'

The woman looked from her mistress to me and back again before answering. I could see she fumbled for words.

'It's the master, madam. He'll not eat.'

'Is he awake then?'

'Yes, ma'am. But he won't eat afore he goes out again.'

'Did he eat yesterday?'

'No, ma'am. That's why I came. It's a bad sign when he's like this.'

'I'll see to it, Mrs. Garner. Go back to the kitchen and see to dinner for Miss Lucas and myself. I'll see my brother.'

'Very well, ma'am.'

Mrs. Garner shuffled out and Regina followed, her brow furrowed. I could see I was forgotten as I went out after her, following her slowly up the staircase. She walked quickly ahead of me, past my door and on to the end of the corridor where she opened the studded door to the east wing and went in.

So Mr. Damian's room was there in the unused part of the house, I mused. Odd that he should choose to sleep in a deserted wing. Before I could speculate further, a voice distracted me.

'Ah, Miss Gemini. Do come in. I was just working on your chart.'

I was outside Uncle Eustace's door, which stood open, and inside I could see him seated at a desk, books and papers spread out under an oil lamp. I entered and stood just inside.

'Close the door. Come and sit down.' He jumped up briskly and went to pull out a chair for me. I did as I was bidden. If the old gentleman wanted a chat, well there was still an hour to go before dinner. On the desk between us,

35

cluttered with books and papers, I could see *An Introduction to Astrology*, by William Lilly, lying alongside a dusty copy of Raphael's *Prophetic Alphabet Almanack*. The old man's watery blue eyes sparkled at me over the top of a pair of gold pince-nez, and his wispy grey hair seemed to stand out from his scalp in electrified excitement.

'I've finished the chart. There,' he pronounced, pushing in front of me a sheet of paper on which there was a large circle intersected by six lines. In each of the twelve segments so formed there were symbols and figures. Uncle Eustace's woolly grey caterpillar eyebrows were raised expectantly.

'Do you make anything of it?'

'I'm afraid not. Astrology is an unknown science to me, sir.'

He drew back the paper with a satisfied smile. 'Yes, it is an acquired skill. Anyone with an elementary knowledge of mathematics can cast a chart, given the right ephemeris, but the real skill lies in the interpretation of it.'

It looked very complicated. Even the symbols were strange to me. Uncle Eustace pointed to the chart and explained. It was a map showing the exact positions of the planets in the heavens at the moment of my birth, he said. Each segment of the circle was called a house, or sign of the zodiac.

'The Sun was in Gemini, and the ascendant – that is the star rising over the eastern horizon – was Virgo. So you have the Gemini qualities of a quick, clever brain and adaptability combined with Virgo's analytical and loyal qualities.'

'I see.' To be truthful, I did not see, but perhaps it would become clearer as he went on. He did go on, speaking of the Moon in one house and Mercury in another and Venus in another, until I began to feel quite bewildered. I think he had forgotten I didn't understand a word of astrology, for he rattled on excitedly as though he believed me to be following intelligently.

'Yours is an air sign, of course, which means you are lively and unpredictable. But the dual sign of the twins also means that you can be changeable and sometimes moody.'

That was not true, I thought hotly. Angry sometimes, yes, but moody, never! Uncle Eustace was peering at the chart again.

'Jupiter is in your eleventh house,' he announced with an air of satisfaction.

'What does that signify?' It was all nonsense, I thought privately, judging by his last pronouncement.

'It is a very good sign for friendship. You should settle happily among us here.'

'I am sure I shall.'

'But there is Uranus in aspect, and I'm afraid Mercury is in retrograde. But don't let that worry you.'

'Is there cause to be worried? What do they mean?'

He looked at me over the top of the pince-nez. 'Mercury placed so indicates delays of some kind, to your plans possibly, and Uranus indicates unexpected happenings. Nothing serious though, I think.'

I smiled. 'Everything here is new to me, so any event will be unusual if not unexpected. And delay is of no importance, since I am in no hurry to do anything.'

He was staring at me earnestly over the gold rims and from under the shaggy brows. Now the light had gone out of his eyes and there was a sad, pleading look.

'Do not harm Damian, will you? He means well despite his manner.'

I stared at him disbelievingly. 'Harm Damian? What do you mean? Why on earth should I?'

'Mars is in bad aspect, though the position of Venus would indicate a basic desire for peace and stability. But Mars is in bad aspect. . . .'

I stood up quickly. 'I have no feelings of dislike at all towards Mr. Fairfax, and whatever your stars may tell you, I would not dream of harming him. I think it is time to dress for dinner.'

As I was turning to go I heard his voice behind, low and lugubrious. 'That was what the other one said. Even with her Sun in the eighth house.'

I turned in the doorway. 'I beg your pardon, sir?'

'In the eighth house, the house of death. Death was coming, but still she did not believe.' Pale eyes looked across at me. 'You will not harm him, will you?'

'Of whom are you speaking? Who would not believe you?'

'Rachel. God help us, it was a black hour when she came to

37

Mallory.' His old face was grey under the lamplight, his eyes haunted as he spoke the name. 'Swear you will be a true friend to us, as your name implies, Miss Amity. Damian could bear no more suffering.'

I stammered some words I could not remember once I had closed the door on Uncle Eustace, and fled to my room. My mind was racing. Rachel. That name again. Who was she, and how had she caused Damian to suffer? And whose death had been imminent? Reluctant as I was to probe into private Fairfax business, I resolved to ask Regina at dinner. After all, if someone called Rachel had once brought trouble to this house, I had no wish inadvertently to do the same. Knowledge would be the best prevention.

CHAPTER THREE

'Dream of the devil and wake in a fright.'
—R. H. Barham, *Jackdaw of Rheims*

Try as I might, I could not find occasion, either during or after dinner alone 'with Regina, to question her about the mysterious Rachel. Regina chatted amiably about current London fashions, quizzing me closely about new vogues and materials, and seemed reluctant to be diverted into talk of the past.

Understandably, I thought afterward. She had spoken of the family history only insofar as she felt a stranger ought to be acquainted with it. I had no right to press her further, presuming upon a friendship as yet barely begun. I had to be content to wait until a more favourable opportunity to pursue my questioning.

After dinner Regina played the piano for a time, and then retired to bed quite early. Since there was no one else about, and I had no further duties, I decided I might as well go to bed too. I closed the piano lid and turned out the oil lamps in the drawing room before going to my room.

The bedroom was decidedly chilly, despite the low fire in the hearth. The curtains were moving gently, and I realized the window had been left open, probably by a forgetful Rosie after airing the room. It was as I was leaning out to pull in the casement window that I heard a voice below in the garden.

"Take care, I tell thee. Tha mun be careful not to let her know owt."

It was Ben Jagger's voice, low but urgent. The voice of a woman murmured a reply. I stood stock-still and silent, made curious by Jagger's forceful tone.

'I know,' he said irritably, 'but she's shrewd, that one.

She has quick eyes and she'll not miss a trick. So tha mun take very great care wi' her. Keep her in t'dark. What t'eye don't see, t'heart don't grieve over. So just thee take heed of what I say.'

'Aye, Ben, I will. She'll learn nowt from me.' Their footsteps crunched away along the gravel path. That was Rose Pickering's voice, I recognized it clearly. So she and Ben Jagger did have an affair going, it would seem. And what did they have to hide? From Regina? It appeared so. I closed the window carefully and sat on the bed wondering what mischief the couple were up to. Was the bailiff cheating his mistress in some way? It would be a thousand pities if he were, for Regina evidently held him in high esteem and leaned upon him greatly.

Perhaps the rogue was taking advantage of his mistress's dependence on him to deceive her in some way, over the accounts possibly. The thought angered me. But it was no use speculating wildly on the variety of possibilities. The best course would be simply to report to Regina what I had overheard and let her take what action she might choose.

No time like the present. Regina could not have gone to sleep yet. I knocked at her door and heard her call 'Come in.'

I entered half-apologetically. Regina was seated at her muslin-draped dressing table, already in nightgown and robe. She was brushing her hair, loosed from its pins, falling in a black cascade over her shoulders. She turned, brush in midair. "Oh, I thought it was Rose. Come in, Amity.'

I breathed quickly. 'It was about Rose I came to see you.'

In a few words I told her of the incident. While I was still speaking she turned back to look in her mirror and continued brushing her hair. When I had done she sat silent. I began to feel uncomfortable.

'Well, there it is. I thought it best you should know. I'll go back to bed now. Good-night, Regina.'

I turned to the door, feeling stupidly clumsy. In the repetition the story sounded silly and trivial and I wished I could learn to restrain my impulsive nature. As I was closing the door Regina spoke.

'I am grateful to you for your concern, Amity, but do not

40

let the incident trouble you. All is well. Forget what you heard, and sleep well.'

'Very well. Good-night.'

'And one thing more. If you should chance to see the door to the east wing is open, please do not go in there.'

'Of course not.'

She hesitated. Her gaze, meeting mine through the mirror, dropped. "It is only that it is not safe, you understand. The wing has not been kept in good repair. Beams and rafters are unsound in parts and you could meet with an accident. The place is very old, riddled with passages, some of which we know of and others we do not. Floors anywhere could even cave in, so that is why I say this. You do understand, Amity?'

'To be sure. Good-night and sleep well, Regina.'

I undressed for bed quickly, since my room was still chilly. Odd, I thought, that Regina had dismissed the incident so coolly, for it must have been her whom Rose and Ben were discussing. Which other woman in Mallory was shrewd and therefore to be kept in the dark? Surely not Mrs. Garner. But of course. It could have been someone in the village. Rose's mother, perhaps, who was to be kept ignorant of their affair. How stupid of me not to have thought of that earlier.

Just as I was about to climb into bed, I heard the sound of heavy footsteps in the corridor outside. They pounded unevenly, as though lurching and blundering. I hesitated. The thought crossed my mind that it could be Uncle Eustace, and that the old man might be ill. I pulled on my dressing gown and went to the door.

Near the head of the stairs stood Damian Fairfax, crouched over the banister rail. By the light of the lamp illuminating the staircase I could see his face, his eyes staring and his features contorted. Alarm filled me. Either he was ill or intoxicated, and in either event I felt I should help him.

But I had been warned to avoid him. For a few seconds I hovered, undecided, in my doorway. He seemed to sense my watching eyes, for slowly his black head swivelled towards me. The look in his eyes was one which terrified me, for I have never seen such an expression in the eyes of any but the desperate, like the poor creatures ground down by poverty slinking in the courts of London's back alleys. It was a look at once mournful and angry, full of misery and hatred. I made up my mind. He needed help. Just as I began to move towards him his lips curled into a sneer.

'You come to haunt me, woman? Leave me be, for pity's sake. Must you always bedevil me?'

I stopped dead, thunderstruck. He turned and lurched down the stairs, tripping and stumbling. I held my breath, convinced he would fall, but he reached the vestibule and stumbled to the door. Out he ran, into the night, leaving the cold wind to blow in through the open door. A manservant I had not seen before appeared from below stairs and closed the door quietly.

Back to bed I went, bewildered by the venom of Damian's words. His resentment of an intrusive woman in the household I could understand, but surely I did not deserve the hatred in his voice. I must confess I felt just a little resentful as I settled down to sleep.

Sleep came slowly, and when it did, it was a fitful and restless sleep. Strange dreams haunted me, visions of long, crumbling passages, dusty and deserted, save for a woman who flitted before me, always vanishing around the next corner. My feet seemed to sink into a sea of treacle as I sought to run, and a feeling of panic pervaded my mind. What it was I feared I did not know, but the endless corridors enveloped in gloom frightened me. From out of the shadows I seemed to see a vision of Damian Fairfax's haunted eyes filled with hate, and cries of anguish echoed along the dusty passages. The more I tried to flee, the deeper I sank into the treacle sucking at my feet.

I awoke abruptly, beads of sweat standing out on my brow. I was shaking and filled with a feeling of foreboding. I sat up and stared around the darkened room. Not a sound or a movement disturbed the still night.

Suddenly I stiffened. Just as in my dream, a howl of anguish filled the night air, far away but unmistakably poignant. It was in the Keep, I was certain. Ears strained, I sat tense in my bed, and then – yes, there it was again!

Trembling, I rose and put on my robe. Out in the corridor all was still. Neither Uncle Eustace nor Regina had come out in answer to the cry. I held my candle aloft and looked in both directions.

The door to the east wing stood open. Even as I recalled Regina's warning, the cry came again. It was from the forbidden wing. Resolving to ignore Regina's prohibition in the interests of humanity, I pushed the studded door further open and went in.

Almost at once I was struck, not so much by the gloomy, neglected air of this part of the house, but its atmosphere – chill, dank, and ominous. I moved forward slowly, footprints in the dust ahead of me indicating the presence of someone else.

All was silent now. I paused and raised my candle high. Nothing was to be seen, only a row of closed doors. Feeling apprehensive and a little guilty, I decided I had better return to my room, for whoever had cried out was silent now.

Even as I turned to retrace my steps, something hurled past my face, something small and alive, for I felt its fur skim my cheek. And I heard its shriek, enraged and almost demonic in the still air. In my terror I dropped the candle which went out at once, and covering my face where the thing had touched me, I ran. I could hear the thing hissing and spitting somewhere behind me, and I could not reach the door swiftly enough.

At last I reached it, slamming it behind me, and leaned panting and terrified against its nail-studded strength. I made my way back into my own room, but still no one in the main block of the house had stirred.

How silly I had been, I reproached myself as I tried to recapture sleep. To become nearly hysterical over what had probably been a cat disturbed from its sleep, was foolish in the extreme. I was letting the stark, cold atmosphere of the old Keep get the better of me. By morning, in the cold light of day, I would laugh at my unreasoning fears, but until dawn came I still could not help lying awake, strangely disturbed.

Although I was up early, Uncle Eustace was in the corridor already, fully dressed, when I left my room in the morning to go downstairs to breakfast. He was counting aloud the two pairs of his shoes left outside his door last night to be cleaned.

'Four. Good. And there are the right number of pictures

on the walls, and oil lamps. I count them every day, you know. Can't be too careful. Servants are very untrustworthy these days. Why, one of my socks did not come back from the wash last week.'

I smiled gently. Regina was right, the old gentleman was mildly eccentric.

'They don't like us, you know,' he went on confidentially. 'Think the local curse is due to the Fairfaxes. I'll be bound it was the villagers who killed Thomas Fairfax.'

I looked at him curiously. 'Regina's father? But it was a riding accident, surely?' I countered.

He shrugged, his mild eyes blinking. 'Who can tell? His horse came home alone, and when a search party went out they found his body at the foot of the cliffs. It was believed that his horse threw him on the cliff path and he fell to his death below. But who knows what really happened?'

Uncle Eustace was reentering his room. He turned in the doorway. 'Won't you have breakfast with me? Regina will not miss you. She very rarely breakfasts downstairs. Always in her room when she wakes. Virgos need plenty of sleep, you know. They work hard and well, but need much rest.'

I accepted, and followed him into the cluttered, untidy room. He shifted a heap of books and papers from the small table on to his desk, and then rang the bell. Rose came.

'Breakfast for Miss Lucas and myself here, please, Rose,' the old man told her. I saw Rose's curious glance at me before she went. She was still eyeing me oddly when she returned with a huge tray of porridge, tea, and toast. Uncle Eustace began pouring tea graciously.

'Yes, you and Regina should get on well, since you have a Virgo ascendant. But she'll have no truck with any psychic affinities you may show.'

I laughed. 'I am no psychic, sir, I fear. On the contrary, I'm a very practical, down-to-earth person. The vogue for spiritualism and consulting mediums holds no appeal for me.'

He put the teapot down and stared at me, his blue eyes now intense and serious. 'Perhaps not, but you have psychic abilities nonetheless. It is in your stars, young lady. You may

44

not have realized your potential ability yet, but it is there notwithstanding.'

Rose finished clearing the hearth, bobbed a curtsey, and withdrew. As soon as the door had closed behind her, Uncle Eustace put down his cup and leaned across the table, so that his lined face was only inches from my own. 'Have you not heard the cries of the tormented?' he demanded in a whisper.

'Cries?' I repeated. With a shudder I recalled the distant howls in the night. 'What cries?'

'The moans of those in suffering. If you have not yet, then you surely will.'

'I heard – I think I heard – someone cry out last night. I believed it was someone ill, or in pain,' I admitted reluctantly. It seemed childish now in the cold light of an April morning.

'From the east wing,' he said. It was a statement, not a question.

'Well yes, I think so.'

He nodded in satisfaction. 'Then I am right. I too have heard them, but I also have the gift, you see. Like me, you are attuned to the sufferings of those who have been associated with this place.'

I put down my teacup. I was becoming so jittery at his words that the china cup was rattling in the saucer. 'Whose cries, sir? What was it I heard?'

He darted a quick look about the room before answering in a sibilant whisper. 'The monks of the monastery, of course. Those who died starving, when Malvaux Abbey was destroyed.'

'In Henry the Eighth's time, do you mean, at the dissolution of the monasteries?' He nodded vigorously. I thought rapidly. 'But the abbey is some distance from the Keep – a mile at least – so why should the monks be heard here?'

'Ah,' he wagged a knowing finger at me, 'because many of the stones from the ruined abbey were used to build part of the Keep. And the unhappy memories stored in the stones lie in them yet.'

I knew his next words before he spoke them. I could have spoken them in unison with him. 'The stones from the Abbey were used to build the east wing.'

I shivered, reached for my spoon, and began eating the hot porridge to chase away the chill which enveloped me. Uncle Eustace began spooning his too, sucking each mouthful noisily. By the time I had finished eating mine, I had recovered something of my poise.

'Regina warned me to keep away from the east wing,' I remarked chattily. 'She said Damian dislikes women, and also that the wing is unsafe.'

'Indeed it is. Some of the spirits who haunt the wing are less godly than the poor monks. Every stone has soaked up its share of tragedy, and you, with your sensitive mind, could awaken one which could bring you tragedy in its turn. Be warned, my child. Do as Regina says, and keep away from the east wing.'

I was beginning to feel just the slightest bit cross with the old man. He had summed me up completely wrong, I felt, and it would be as well to help him get rid of the idea that I was some kind of ghost-raiser. I debated inwardly how to phrase it politely, for I genuinely liked Uncle Eustace. Before I had arrived at a satisfactory conclusion, he was speaking again.

'It would be as well to humour my niece too, you know, for she is a determined woman. Damian is a good fellow too, though he has his cross to bear. His bark is far worse than his bite, but it would be as well to avoid him for Regina's sake.'

'For Regina?'

'She is a very possessive woman. As his elder sister she virtually brought Damian up herself, and she resents the intrusion of others. That is what caused the trouble over Rachel. And that is why you should keep away from the east wing.'

Rachel again. I leaped eagerly at the chance of discovering more about her, and at the same time to divert Uncle Eustace from his talk of ghosts. This time I leaned anxiously over the table.

'Do tell me about Rachel. Who was she?'

Uncle Eustace's eyes misted over in recollection. 'She came here. She loved Damian, and he her. But there was terrible trouble. She died, you know.'

He relapsed into silence, his mind obviously reaching back

46

and his expression becoming melancholy. I had not the heart to press him, but waited hopefully for more. Poor Damian. I began to understand now why he was so vulnerable and sensitive. It must be terrible indeed to love and then to lose one's love.

'Well now, have you finished?' Uncle Eustace leaped up and began stacking the dishes on the tray. 'Two bowls, two cups, two saucers, two plates, two knives, two spoons,' he counted methodically. 'Can't be too careful, you know.' And as he carried the tray carefully to the side table near the door, I knew he had forgotten all about Rachel.

When I eventually went downstairs, Mrs. Garner was standing in the vestibule.

'Miss Fairfax said to tell thee as she'd be busy all morning once she comes down. She'll see thee at lunch,' the house-keeper told me. So now I had the opportunity to go down to explore the village.

Spring sunlight glinted on the wave crests, and April mildness enveloped the countryside in a pleasant haze. As I descended the hill towards Mallory village, I could not help but admire the way the tiny fishing village had survived the wind and the sea, its cottages clinging precariously to the steep cliffs, cosily tucked in, one above the other, with a honeycomb of passages between. It looked too fragile, its connection with the land too tenuous, and yet it had thrived here for centuries. It would be interesting to explore this network of galleries, passages, and steep steps.

'Morning, miss.' A stocky figure overtook me, passing close by my shoulder. It was Ben Jagger. He nodded as I returned his greeting and strode on ahead. By the time I passed the church and entered the village I could see him no more.

One could tell, by the dark, worn state of their stones, that the cottages in Mallory were very old, but it was evident that their owners took great pride in them. Every one gleamed with fresh paint, so that their doors and windows stood out from their aging walls like bright eyes in an old man's face. A fisherman's wife knelt at her front doorstep, scrubbing the step and then brightening it with ochre donkey stone. Another was polishing the iron bootscraper beside her front door with black lead. Neither woman spoke, though both nodded to me curtly. A proud folk this, I deduced, though not easily approachable.

It was a delightful village, and I was entranced by it; what was evidently the main street was little more than a narrow cobbled track, winding its way down to the water's edge. I resisted the impulse to explore the many intricate side-paths and galleries, and headed straight down to the sea.

The road ran straight into the sea, a small jetty to the northerly side of it. The last two cottages in the street were mounted on high stone bases, forming a kind of bastion. I stood and looked across the bay, where many small fishing craft lay at anchor, to the cliffs on the far side. Now, at low tide, I could see a number of caves holing the cliffside at varying levels, from rocky beach to near the summit.

Turning to walk along the little jetty, I was startled to see a figure I had not noticed before. It was a man, hatless and windblown, leaning on the low stone parapet and staring into the pebbly shallows. By his shape and wildly tossed black hair, I knew him at once for Damian Fairfax, and I hesitated.

He had his back towards me, but he could turn at any moment and see me. The air of dejection about him, almost of misery, as he leaned on his elbows, evoked my sympathy. Poor man. In view of what I knew about him, I could forgive his uncouth manner, could almost wish to go to him and lay my hand comfortingly on his sleeve. But I could not betray the confidences of Regina and Uncle Eustace. Damian must not learn that I knew of his tragic loss.

Moving as unobtrusively as I could, I edged back to the corner and round into the main street. It is difficult to remain inconspicuous in a wide crinoline, but I succeeded. I could climb the steep road to where one of the myriad passages turned off, and there I could lose myself to view.

Halfway to the turning, I became aware of quick footsteps behind me. I did not glance back until a voice addressed me, and I knew it was he.

'Miss Lucas. Good morning.'

A distant nod, or a cool glance, and then he'll pass on by, I thought. But I was wrong. He shortened his step to match mine and fell in beside me. 'May I be permitted to walk with you?' he asked politely.

I looked up at him in surprise. The angry, brooding look in his great, dark eyes was gone, though they still seemed somewhat clouded. What beautiful eyes they would be, I reflected, clear and untroubled by misery. I realised with a start that I had not answered his request.

'To be sure, sir.' I was relieved to see that the huge hound was not loping after him.

For a time we walked in silence. I was marvelling at the sudden change in his manner, and wondering whether Regina would be angered that I had contravened her request to avoid her brother. But it had been none of my doing; I had done my best.

After a time, he glanced at me from under his great shaggy brows. 'Do you think you will enjoy living in Mallory, Miss Lucas?'

'I see no reason why I should not, sir. Your sister is kindness itself to me, and I love this beautiful, wild countryside. I think I shall be very happy here.'

He grunted. 'You like the Keep?'

'It is a fascinating house, steeped in atmosphere.' I temporised, I knew, but it would not be strictly true to say I did like it, unreservedly, after the experience of last night.

Damian's laugh was loaded with world-weary cynicism. 'Atmosphere? The devil it is! Its influence has affected us all; and you too, Miss Lucas, will soon lose your bright-eyed optimism in Mallory Keep. It is a cursed place, and soon you will feel its constraint clamping on you, stiffening your smile to a grimace and deadening the music in your voice to a moan.'

I stopped and stared, wide-eyed. His words struck fear into me. He turned and gripped my shoulders, his brilliant eyes boring into mine.

'Take warning, Miss Lucas. Go away, back whence you came, before the curse overcomes you too. Go, before it is too late.'

The fierce grip of his hands on my shoulders pained me, but the pain was less than the terror he engendered in me. It was not so much the words he spoke, as the unfathomably

49

intense look in his eyes. I stared, petrified, like a rabbit ensnared by a snake's magnetic gaze. Suddenly he loosed his hold on me and strode on up the road.

For a moment I stood there, stunned, watching his disappearing figure. Then my stupefaction gave way to annoyance. I hastened afte him with difficulty, since the road was steeply cobbled and his pace far greater than mine. At last I caught up with him, panting from my exertion.

'Sir, by what right do you dismiss me? I am employed by your sister, may I remind you,' I stammered breathlessly.

He turned huge, sad eyes upon me. 'By no right, but out of compassion, I have seen the Keep destroy all, one by one. I would not wish to see you suffer needlessly.'

I could find no words. He had robbed me of my righteous indignation by his sudden concern. What a capricious, changeable creature he was! I sighed deeply.

A tremor of a smile touched the corners of his lips. 'Have no fear. You can escape the evil of the Keep if you leave quickly. Others would not be warned. They stayed, they suffered.'

Before I could think, my lips had framed my next unplanned words. 'Like Rachel? Was she one who suffered?'

I knew at once I had said the wrong thing. The soft light in his eyes smouldered instantly into a bright flame of fury. I could have bitten my wayward lips with annoyance. But I was unprepared for his sudden howl of anguish, the way he threw back his great shaggy head and let out a roar like a wounded animal. Net curtains in cottage windows along the street twitched curiously.

He glared at me, malevolence and hatred glittering in the black orbs of his eyes. 'Do you come to torment me more, you she-devil?' he roared. 'Is it not enough that I suffer agonies, my soul damned to eternity? Leave me, get out of my sight!' And with a sound suspiciously like a sob, he turned and ran from me, up the cobbled street and out of sight.

Feeling very subdued and cross with myself for my impetuous, careless words, I slowly retraced my steps towards the Keep. How very clumsy of me to touch him on a wound still so raw that I reawakened his suffering so acutely.

I felt deeply penitent, and wondered how to make amends. To avoid him as he wanted, and to explain and apologise to Regina, that would be the best I could do in the circumstances.

But I had no intention of leaving Mallory Keep, despite Damian's dire warning. Maybe I had not begun my life there in the most auspicious way, maybe I had committed errors inadvertently, but that was no reason to give up and run away. I would stay, and I would endeavour to correct my mistakes.

Passing the lych-gate of the village churchyard at the edge of the village, I stopped. I was curious about the little church where my friend on the cliffs was vicar. I pushed open the gate and went in.

The state of the graveyard surprised me. The old tombs, their stonework pitted with age, were overgrown with weeds and half-smothered in a dense undergrowth of tall bracken and giant willow herb. The path to the church door was thick with dried mud and grass penetrating the cracks, and the guttering on the church eaves hung broken and rusted from crumbling brackets. It was a sorry sight, this neglected little country church.

The only part which appeared tended and cared for was a little clearing about a huge stone obelisk. It was a tall narrow block of close-grained stone, more than twenty feet high. Smooth and rounded it rose, except for the topmost six feet or so where it was furrowed to the tip. I recalled Reverend Parmenter's words about the 'holy stone' and the villagers' primitive reverence for it. It would appear he was right, for here the ground was well trodden and the grass verges kept neat. It was another insight into the kind of people among whom I had come to live. Age-old beliefs were evidently stronger even than their Christian faith. No wonder they believed utterly in the power of a curse.

A sombre mood enveloped me as I went to leave the shabby, overgrown churchyard. I scarcely noticed the dark-robed figure under the shadow of the lych-gate.

'Good morning, Miss Lucas.' It was the Reverend Hugh Parmenter, a wide smile lightening his genial face. 'Do you come to explore my church and churchyard? It is somewhat neglected, I fear, but full of interest and anecdote for all that.'

'Good morning, sir. I hope you will forgive a trespasser.' I smiled, but it was with effort, since my mood was heavy.

'With all my heart, when the trespasser is an enchanting young lady. Will you not come into the vicarage and meet Mrs. Parmenter? I told her about you, and I know she would love to talk to you. We have so few newcomers to Mallory.'

'Another time, Reverend, if you will permit. I am expected soon at the Keep, for it is nearing time for lunch.'

He drew out a watch from his fob pocket. 'Dear me, is it so late? I must hurry. Perhaps you will be an addition to our little congregation on Sunday?'

Assuring him that I would be among that number, I made my farewell and went on uphill. Soon I had left the village behind, looking impossibly tiny and insecure in its grip on the cliffside, and was climbing the cliff path once more.

Grey banks of cloud were beginning to darken the sky. I felt the sea breeze whipping my mood of solemnity from me, and by the time I neared the top, I had regained my former equilibrium. Watching the sea gulls swooping and darting between the rocks, I began to feel almost content again.

The gentle April sunshine was obscured now by the clouds. By the time I entered the gateway of the Keep, raindrops began to spatter. I lifted my face, welcoming their cool freshness and feeling the optimism that began to throb in my veins. I loved the clear, bracing air of this coast, the wind and the sound of the waves. How different from London, and how beautiful!

Even the birds were different. In London I had known only the pert sparrows and robins and the occasional gull from the river, but here in the garden were a whole variety of birds I had never seen before. I stepped off the gravel drive on to the turf so as not to frighten them away by the noise of my crunching footsteps.

Tiptoeing thus, I rounded the house, past a dilapidated arbor towards the door. So expertly did I move, quietly, almost furtively, I came so close to one bird that I could almost have stroked it before it took flight.

I nearly jumped out of my skin in alarm when a man's voice

spoke, so near it sounded at my elbow. I realised then that there was someone in the arbor, probably sheltering from the shower.

'Dost agree, then? It's all right by thee?' That was Ben Jagger's husky voice.

There was a low-murmured reply I did not catch, but it was the lighter note of a woman's voice. I began to tiptoe on, anxious not to let my presence be known, lest they thought I was deliberately eavesdropping. Moreover, it was embarrassing to be obliged to overhear the couple. I was certain in my own mind that it was a lovers' tryst. Just about now, Rosie would be temporarily released from duty while she had her midday meal in the kitchen.

Ben's voice went on. 'Then it's up to thee to see all is well within. Tha mustn't let suspicion be roused.'

I stopped. The words had an odd ring to them, sly and surreptitious. Was it only a rendezvous they were discussing, or something less innocent? Curiosity aroused, I stood still, the birds about my feet forgotten. The woman's voice spoke softly again.

'No,' Ben said emphatically. 'Tomorrow will 'appen be too late. And tha knows there's no fishing hereabouts of a Sunday, never has been.' After a pause he went on. 'Tonight then? Tha'll see to it for tonight?'

There was movement in the arbor, the scraping of a chair and a rustle of skirts. I fled noiselessly to the door into the Keep, not wishing to be discovered.

I stood in the vestibule, breathless, pondering over the significance of Ben's words. Ought I to seek out Regina and tell her at once, in case he was planning mischief? I hesitated to do that, remembering her reception of my last account about Ben. But if I kept silent, how could I explain or atone later, once the mischief was done?

I took off my bonnet and stood shaking the droplets of rain from its trimming. Mrs. Garner appeared from the direction of the kitchen door, a letter in her hand.

'Oh, Miss Lucas. I thought it were t'mistress coming in. I've a letter for her.' She turned back again through the kitchen door. Almost at once the front door opened and Regina entered. She smiled at me.

'Ah, back from your walk, Amity? Did you like our little village?'

'Delightful.' I was looking at her thin wrap and the book she carried. 'Have you been out long?'

'Only for a short stroll in the grounds. The rain drove me in.'

'It's quite heavy now. Your wrap must be soaked.' I went forward to help her remove it, but she took my hand.

'No, I'm quite dry. I've been sheltering while I read my book. The roof of the old arbor is still quite sound.'

I was so startled, that I withdrew my hand from hers, and I saw the puzzled look in her dark eyes. How like her brother's eyes they were, piercing and compelling. I turned away to veil my face lest my too expressive features should give me away. Regina in the arbor? Then it was she and not Rosie making plans with Ben Jagger!

'Mrs. Garner has a letter for you,' I said as casually as I could. At that moment the housekeeper appeared again. 'It must have come while you were out.'

Regina took the letter and opened it. Mrs. Garner, having announced that lunch would be served in a few minutes, shuffled away again. I was about to mount the stairs to my room, leaving Regina to read in private, when I heard her quick intake of breath. I turned on the stairs. She was holding the single sheet of paper in her hand, her face drained of colour, save where the scar stood out.

'Is anything amiss, Regina?'

She recovered herself quickly. 'No, no. Please do take off your wet coat before you catch a chill, Amity.' But despite her words I could hear the sharp note in her voice, anxiety perhaps? And I saw her fingers tremble as she refolded the letter.

I had reached the top of the staircase and turned along the minstrels' gallery, under the row of expressionless Fairfax portraits, when I heard the front door open again. Looking down I saw Damian's large frame blundering across the vestibule, a trail of muddy footmarks behind him. The ubiquitous manservant appeared quietly and closed the door his master had left standing wide to admit the blustering rain.

54

Regina was still standing where I had left her. She reached out to touch Damian's arm as he passed.

'Damian, there is a letter. I must talk with you.' She glanced at the manservant, indicating, I realised, that they must talk in privacy. Damian stopped and looked at her with irritation.

'Letter? You always deal with correspondence. Why bother me with it?'

'It is important. Please, Damian.'

'Not now. Leave me alone.'

He shook off her restraining hand and went to climb the stairs. I drew back, but I heard Regina's cry.

'Damian, it is from Richard Fairfax!'

There was silence for a few seconds. Then Damian grunted. 'Richard Fairfax? Impossible! He died many years ago. Let me go.'

'It is from him – see the signature yourself.'

I heard the rustle of paper and then that terrible howl again. Damian's cry rang among the rafters of Mallory Keep.

'Richard Fairfax is dead! Why can't he stay dead? Even from beyond the grave they come back to haunt us!'

There was such terrible pathos in the pitiful cry that I fled to my room and heard no more.

CHAPTER FOUR

'The Devil will come, and Faustus must be damned.'
—Goethe, *Dr. Faustus*

The lunch gong sounded. As I made my way downstairs, undecided whether I ought to burden Regina with my company at a time when she was so obviously disturbed by the arrival of the letter, I heard voices from her drawing room.

She was talking in a low, controlled voice, with an occasional interruption of 'I just don't understand it,' and 'It can't be true,' from Damian. Evidently she was endeavouring to explain and pacify. No doubt it was all capable of explanation too, but Damian in his self-absorption and grief was just incapable of accepting. Poor Regina. She had need of all her self-control and quiet capability to cope with this household.

I lunched alone. Ellen, the tight-lipped parlourmaid, explained tersely that her master and mistress were busy and would lunch upstairs. I listened to the rain pattering incessantly on the windowpanes while I ate, and was obliged to admit that further exploration of the countryside would be out of the question this afternoon. If Regina were to remain occupied, I should have to find some other way to pass the time.

I sat in a window seat and busied myself over a tapestry frame for an hour or so, but the dimming light of a rain-laden sky finally obliged me to stop. How quiet and lonely it was in the Keep. I thought of the months, years even, that Regina must have sat alone thus, and could fully understand her need for a companion. The gloom of this house could easily turn the most optimistic and sunny-natured person into a despondent soul.

56

Dinner proved to be a solitary meal also. This time I was offered no explanation for Regina's absence, and as Ellen cleared my dessert dishes away, I prompted her.

'Miss Regina gave me no message for thee, miss.' Her pursed lips emitted a few more reluctant words, 'But I reckon as she's too busy to think on it. She's off in t'morning.'

'Off?' I repeated, not understanding.

'Aye, she's off to town.'

'Going away, do you mean?' I could not help the disbelief in my tone. Regina, who herself had told me she never left the Keep, going away? I stared at the maidservant incredulously.

'So she says.' Ellen's lips clamped shut. She evidently thought she had let out enough, if not too much. I deemed it wiser not to pursue my questioning, but to wait until I saw Regina.

There were many thoughts to occupy my mind during that long, rainy evening. Questions for which I could find only flimsy answers flitted in and out of my brain. Why did Regina meet Ben in the arbor, and what was the significance of tonight? Why did the name of Richard Fairfax, whoever he was, fill her with alarm and Damian with rage? Somewhere in these answers lay the reason for Regina's quitting her nunlike seclusion to go out tomorrow, I felt sure.

The clock on the high oak mantel chimed nine. I stretched, rose, and made my way upstairs. On the gallery I paused to peer at the Fairfax portraits in the dim light. One, a family group I had not noticed before, arrested my attention. I lit a candle from a lamp on the table outside the drawing-room door.

A man, tall and dark, and with the unmistakable Fairfax features of Damian, stood behind a wicker garden chair where a fragile woman was seated. Her hair, black and sleek as a raven's breast, was echoed on the heads of the two solemn-faced children who knelt by her, their hands clasped in hers on the red silk of her lap. I knew them at once. There was no mistaking the piercing stare of Damian, and the cool, penetrating gaze of Regina.

'Thomas Fairfax and family' read the inscription on the brass plate beneath. I surveyed the portrait thoughtfully. At first glance it seemed a perfect family group, and I reflected sadly on how beautiful the child Regina was, how lovely the woman should have been, but for that terrible scar. How, I wondered? No birthmark, that was certain, for the face of the child Regina up there was unblemished.

The mother's eyes, on closer scrutiny, had a wistful, faraway look, as though her thoughts rested on other matters. Her husband's gaze was darkly critical, as though he doubted the artist's ability. And the boy Damian's eyes held the dark fire that I had seen myself, sometimes smouldering, sometimes erupting into passionate anger. A strange family, I felt, far deeper and more complicated than the surface would depict.

I moved on to the next portrait. As I raised my candle higher, so as to see better the face above the tall full-length portrait of a man, my heart thudded for a second. I don't know whether it was my fanciful imagination, or a trick of the flickering candlelight, but I could have sworn the handsome face creased into a smile. And such a smile. It was the kind of radiance that reaches from deep within to light up a face with warmth and humanity, the kind of smile that melts one's natural reticence into unconditional friendship. I would have liked this man, had I known him, broad-shouldered and relaxed, his sympathetic young face framed, not with the Fairfax black hair, but with unruly fair locks rebelling into curls despite the bear's grease pomade. He was young, no more than twenty or so.

I was bending to decipher the name on the frame when the drawing room door opened and Regina appeared. Beyond her shoulder I could see Damian seated by the fire, slumped deep in the armchair, his glowering expression illuminated by the firelight. Regina closed the door and came to me.

'Amity, I must talk with you. Are you busy?'

'Not at all. I was just looking at your family portraits.' I indicated the fair youth beside her.

'Ah, my uncle. He was not at all like my father, was he? Come, let us go to my bedroom, I need your help.'

Her room was cosy and warm, the firelight reflecting on polished brass hearth dogs and fender. Regina turned up the lamp burning low on the table, and went to open the doors of her vast mahogany wardrobe. Within hung rows of gowns and capes of every colour and fabric.

'Help me choose, Amity. For years I have worn the same gowns, since it mattered little here in the Keep what I wore. But tomorrow I must go to York.'

I refrained from comment, nor did I mention that Ellen had already told me. The tone in which Regina conveyed her news indicated its importance.

'Today we received a letter which renders it necessary for me to leave the Keep,' Regina went on. 'I do not relish the prospect, but it is imperative. You see, I fear we may be the victims of some kind of confidence trick, and it is essential I discuss the matter with the family lawyer in York as soon as possible. So what am I to wear, Amity? Examine my gowns and select what you deem suitable, if they are not yet too out of date.'

It was not difficult. Among the dresses I found a beautiful violet wool gown with a matching coat, perfect for the city, and on the shelf above, a little black hat with a veil. With a little rearrangement the veiling could be disposed so as to becomingly conceal Regina's face and spare her unnecessary embarrassment. Carefully I explained how I could, with a few stitches, alter the hat so as to bring it into the latest style.

Regina was not deceived. I saw the quick leap of understanding in her eyes. 'You are so kind, Amity, and I would be most grateful. Will it take long?'

'If you have needle and thread, I can do it now.'

From a corner cupboard she produced a satin-lined workbasket from which I selected my needs. As I seated myself by the lamp to begin work on the hat, Regina pulled out more gowns from the wardrobe and tossed them on the patchwork counterpane of her bed. Then she took off her grey gown and stepped into the violet wool one.

'So many buttons,' she commented as her fingers contrived to fasten the many tiny buttons into their rouleau buttonholes. I laid aside my sewing and rose to help her. That done, she surveyed her reflection critically in the mirror.

'I think the waist needs easing. I am not as thin as I was.'

'I can alter that too in a moment. And there is a stitch undone on the hem,' I replied, and was rewarded by the

59

warmth of her smile. She waved a hand towards the bed.

'There are gowns far and above my needs in the wardrobe, Amity. If you can make use of these in some way, unpick or adjust them, they are yours if you wish.'

'Oh, Regina, no, really!'

Her smile vanished. 'Have I offended you, Amity? Oh, I am so sorry! I did not wish to patronize.'

I rose to reassure her. 'No, truly. It is only your generosity which overwhelms me. I shall take them and am grateful to you.' In an effort to relieve the sudden embarrassing tension which had sprung up between us, I went on. 'How shall you travel tomorrow?'

'By coach. I leave early in the morning.'

'Would you like me to come with you?' I made the suggestion timidly, anxious not to venture too far. Even so, I was startled.

'No!'

She turned away sharply and began wrenching at the tiny buttons of her gown, undressing with abrupt, angry movements. I lowered my gaze to my sewing.

'I am sorry, Regina. I did not mean to intrude.'

Instantly she turned again and came to me, standing before me with penitence on her troubled face. 'Amity, forgive me. You are kindness itself, and I am unkind in return. This is a matter I must handle alone, but how thoughtless of me not to realise that you would enjoy a day in the city while I am occupied. Of course you must come, and look around the shops.'

'I could buy the material you wanted,' I suggested, eager to leave the Keep in the expectation of a day in town. 'And here is your hat. Try it and see how it looks now.'

It looked charming, and Regina was pleased. Its veiling hid the scar effectively. 'It was my riding hat once, though I no longer ride now. That reminds me. There is my riding habit somewhere. Do you ride, Amity?'

I told her I had ridden, slowly and decorously, in the park while I was still at the academy. Regina nodded. 'Then you shall have my habit so that you can ride out here. We still have a horse or two.'

There it was again, the indirect reference to the Fairfaxes

having come down in the world. I ignored it tactfully and thanked her again while she searched in the wardrobe. At last she stopped.

'Ah, now I remember. I shall ask Mrs. Garner to fetch the habit for you later.'

A discreet tap at the door made her turn as Rosie entered, her fair curls clinging damply to her forehead. I realised she must have been out in the rain. She bobbed and looked from me to her mistress.

'Begging thy pardon, madam. I've a message for thee,' she murmured hesitantly. I was quick to sense the diffidence in her voice and realise that my presence was an embarrassment. Rising, I crossed to Regina, holding out the violet gown to her.

'There, I think you will find the gown fits well now. If not, call me and I will see to it.

'Thank you. And take the gowns with you.' I gathered them up from the bed and passed Rosie, aware of her great watchful eyes on me. As soon as I had closed the door behind me I could hear her voice, low and urgent, but I could not hear the words.

Uncle Eustace was standing on the gallery, candle in hand, gazing fixedly at the portrait of the fair young man. As I passed him the old man shook his head.

'He's come back, Damian says. Strange, for I never saw his ghost. But Damian says he's come back.'

'Who is he?' I asked softly.

'Richard Fairfax. He was Damian's uncle, you know, his father's brother. I always understood he died, oh, more than thirty years ago. Perhaps his spirit is restless too. I must go to Damian. He is very distressed.'

The old man shuffled off ahead of me, past my door, and up to the door of the east wing. I took the gowns into my room and then came out again, too curious and puzzled to settle down to sleep yet. I followed Uncle Eustace to the studded door and stood watching his shambling figure under the arc of light from his candle.

'Two, three, four, five, six.'

I could not help smiling. Even now the old man was counting something, keeping a check on errant servants, it

61

would seem. But then, when he stopped at a doorway and knocked quietly, I realised. It was the doors he was counting. He had knocked at the seventh. As I watched, the light disappeared as Uncle Eustace went in and closed the door.

So the seventh room along the east wing was Damian's. Even as I was digesting the information and turning to go, a sound came to my ears. It was a crunching, grating sound, far away, but heavy and prolonged. And it came from somewhere in the east wing. I was straining my ears to listen, when footsteps approached. I turned to see Mrs. Garner coming towards me, lamp in hand.

'Madam says as I'm to fetch thee her riding habit,' she said tersely her gaze scrutinizing my face.

'No need to bother tonight, Mrs. Garner. I'm to go to York tomorrow with the mistress, so there is no hurry.'

'Might as well get it now, since it's so close.' She passed me, walked beyond the studded door and along the passage, and I followed. At the sixth door she stopped and turned the handle.

'This is t'Rose Room. Was a guest room once, never used now. T'master doesn't like folk coming in here.'

I recognised the hint and stayed by the door while she went in, but I could see, when she set the lamp down on a table and crossed to a wardrobe, that it had once been a very beautiful room. The fireplace of rose-pink marble and curtains of deep rose velvet were thick with dust now and laced with cobwebs. The silver-backed brushes and jars on the pretty draped dressing table were as filmy with dust as the fine chiffon drapes over the great four-poster bed. How sad and neglected it was.

Mrs. Garner was coming back towards me, the habit in her hands. 'There's a riding stock with it too, miss,' she said as she gave them to me. Before I could thank her, the door of Damian's room opened and he appeared. When he took in the open door, and the housekeeper and myself standing there, his dark face grew thunderous.

'What are you doing here? Get out, both of you,' he roared. Mrs. Garner turned pale, biting her lip in shame. I hastened to explain her innocence.

'Miss Regina gave orders . . .' I began, but he cut me short.

'No one gives orders to enter that room. Do you hear me? Get out!'

Mrs. Garner snatched up the lamp and fled, and I had no alternative but to follow the retreating light, unless I cared to remain here in the darkness with a furious, unpredictable man. I followed the light. Regina could explain to her brother later.

The housekeeper went straight along the passage to the stairs. I stopped at my door and was just going in when Rosie opened the door of Regina's room. Regina's voice pursued the girl.

'Do you understand, girl? He must do as I say.'

'I gave him your message, but he said it must go on, whether or no,' the girl retorted hotly. 'Don't blame me, madam, I only brought t'message.'

'Very well. Now go home, Rose. Good night.'

I closed my door, but I heard Rosie's sob as she passed. What, I wondered, had provoked an angry scene between maid and mistress? This old house was full of unanswered questions.

Sleep came swiftly and I slept undisturbed until dawn. Rosie brought hot water for my toilet and then breakfast on a tray, but I noted how unusually subdued and uncommunicative she was.

'Is Miss Regina awake?' I asked her as I ate.

'Yes, miss. She's ordered t'coach to be round t'front in half an hour.' Her blue eyes slid from me, their frank brightness dulled to an almost surly refusal to be held. I finished eating, pushed aside the tray, and began to dress for the journey. Rosie picked up the tray and left the room without a word.

Cooper, the coachman, made sure his mistress and I were comfortable in the coach, warm rugs tucked about our knees, and we set off on the first lap of our journey. We were to stop for lunch at Matton, Regina told me, before continuing to York, where we were to stay for two nights. The turreted outline of Mallory Keep soon disappeared behind us as the coach rumbled up over the moor.

A mile or so from the Keep we passed a ramshackle little farm where a child of seven or so was swinging on the gate and watching our approach solemnly. Paint flaked from the gate, and the hinge creaked rustily, but Regina waved to the boy as we passed. He did not wave back nor acknowledge her gesture in any way, his dark eyes simply watching, staring from a tanned face specked with freckles like a thrush's egg. Regina smiled wryly.

'Little Eric does not remember me, I fear. I was there at his birth, and helped his mother to nurse him when he was ill with the measles, but he does not remember.'

She stared out of the carriage window over the rain-soaked fields, and I recognised the sign of withdrawal. Regina evidently wanted to be left alone with her thoughts, so I kept silent, watching the countryside unfold as the carriage lumbered on. It was a comfortless scene, flat moorland bare of trees and depressingly grey under its mist of April rain.

From time to time a farmstead or village came into sight, grey stone cottages surmounted by red-tiled roofs and sometimes surrounded by orchards of budding apple trees, but still Regina sat silent and deep in thought. Finally we descended a slope into a valley, crossing a narrow river by a stone bridge, and travelling on along the bank. My mistress awoke from her reverie at last.

'The Derwent Valley, Amity. Soon we shall reach Matton.'

By Matton the rain had ceased and the sun was beginning to peep shyly out from behind a bank of cloud. Matton was a quaint old town with two Norman churches standing above a lush grass slope to the river. Over lunch in the inn, while a waiter hovered obsequiously to attend Regina's every move, she seemed to make a determined effort to become more sociable.

'Soon we shall pass Kirkham Priory. That is a place which never fails to fascinate me, because its history is so similar to Mallory's,' she told me.

I pricked up my ears. The history of Mallory interested me too, and I was eager to learn more. 'Do tell me, Regina. In what way?'

She dabbed the trace of custard on her lips with a napkin. 'Well, like Malvaux Abbey, the Priory was closed by Henry VIII in the Dissolution, and the lands granted to a certain family. On that land the family built a house, Howsham

Park, using in its construction quantities of stone from the old Priory.'

'I see,' I murmured. 'Just like the east wing of Mallory Keep.'

'Precisely. Because Howsham too was cursed as a result of the sacrilege.'

'Cursed?'

'To the effect that all the male heirs of the estate would perish young.'

I laughed uncertainly. 'And do people believe the curse really has power?'

She shrugged. 'It may be only coincidence, but all the Banburghs did, in fact, die young, and the male line died out. One, a boy of twelve, was thrown from his horse and killed on the mossy steps of the ruined Priory. His father died of heartbreak, so they say.'

She called for the bill, so there the conversation ended. I found myself curiously anxious to catch a glimpse of the Priory as we passed, as if in contemplating its curse I could find an explanation to the curse which overhung Mallory. The lunchtime conversation had revealed to me that Regina herself seemed to believe in the power of the curse, however she might deny it.

Cooper, wiping the froth of his lunch ale from his lips with the back of a calloused hand, helped us into the carriage and climbed back on the box, cracking and hollo-ing to the horses. I sank back in the corner facing forward so as to catch a sight of the Priory as soon as I could.

The river wound on through fertile meadows, twisting and turning so often, and the road with it, that the scene changed frequently from one miniature tableau to another. Beautiful glades embowered with tall trees, their leaves pale-tipped with buds, bordered both river banks. Suddenly, with a final twist, the road came to a stone bridge spanning the river, and on the far slope, on a plateau, stood the grey ruins. I leaned forward.

'That is Kirkham Priory,' Regina said quietly.

It was a stately ruin, partly mantled with ivy, with a wide, pointed archway beyond which I could see sloping meadows and the mossy remains of a stone cross. Above the arch rose a tattered wall with two high windows, and in the spandrils above were four coats of arms. Stony faces stared down from the wall and unrecognisable, defaced figures in niches stood eternal sentinel. I felt a shiver. Beautiful though the mouldings and carvings of the Priory must once have been, the place had the same unmistakable air of poignant sadness as Mallory Keep.

I sank back into my seat. Regina, opposite me, was watching the receding ruins with a thoughtful air.

'You see,' she said softly. 'They are alike, Kirkham and Mallory.'

The memory of Kirkham's haunting sadness lingered with me all the time as we drove on in silence. I wanted to argue with Regina that if the Keep seemed tragic because of a curse, then it should be Howsham Park and not the Priory which held such an air of tristesse. But I held my tongue. In the late afternoon Regina remarked that we were travelling near Stanford Bridge, but the strange atmosphere of the Priory still haunted me. I could feel no interest in King Harold and the place where, just eight hundred years ago, he had been obliged to fight and kill his own brother Tostig.

It was nightfall when at last we reached York. By now I was sleepy and only dimly aware of the gateway into the city though its high battlement walls, and the cobblestones under the carriage wheels which caused it to rattle most uncomfortably. At the inn Regina had selected, I accepted without question her suggestion that we share a bed to save cost.

We dined, then climbed into the high old bed, both too tired to talk. I fell asleep almost immediately. It was far into the night when I awoke. I lifted my head from the pillow. Regina was murmuring something.

'*Quam . . . salve . . . nos. . . .*' I could make nothing of what she was saying, and as I was about to speak to her, I realised. Latin. I could remember only a few words of the tongue from the smattering Miss Dobson had taught us at the academy, but I knew it was Latin. Strange. I lay down again.

Regina fell silent, and in a few moments her deep, steady breathing indicated that she was asleep. Within minutes I joined her.

In the morning we parted; Regina to consult with the

lawyer, and I to explore York. My mission was to purchase the materials for Regina's new gown for which she had given me money, and she and I were to meet again at the inn in the evening for dinner. Tomorrow we were to journey home again.

York proved to be sheer delight. I began by returning to Bootham Bar, the gate through the battlemented medieval city walls by which we had entered the city last night. As I walked, I was entranced by the city's bright, creamy stonework, unblackened by smoke and grime as London was. The towers of the Minster dominated the scene, but I determined to savour its beauty last of all.

Bootham Bar fascinated me with its castellated turrets and narrow slit windows, and even its ancient portcullis still remained. At the Bar I climbed the stone steps to the top of the walls and surveyed the scene with delight. Red tiled roofs glowed in the sunlight which had chased away yesterday's rain. I could see the imposing twelfth-century Micklegate Bar, and I shuddered to remember from my history books the noble heads which had hung spiked above there, dripping blood on the cobblestones beneath.

I stared through the frowning gateway at the castle and recalled the story of the massacre of the Jews there in 1190. I wandered down the delightful narrow street named Stonegate, where medieval houses with overhanging upper storeys and quaint little windows still stood, down the cobbled shambles where butchers' shops, with their slaughterhouses behind, still traded.

Antique shops selling curios, and old timber-framed houses, plastered and ochre-washed, were a delight to the senses. I found in one little shop exactly the shade of material Regina had wanted and asked the elderly lady behind the counter to be sure to deliver the parcel to the inn by dusk. I was pleased with my purchase. From the sum of money Regina had given me I had ordered the material, buttons, hooks, and thread, and still I had nearly half the money left. I was glad to be able to prove myself thrifty. Regina would appreciate that.

In order to economise further, I decided to lunch lightly, deciding that hot tea and a meat pasty in a small tea shop

67

would tide me over comfortably until dinner. Moreover I thus had more time to explore York.

The city's crowning splendour, the Minster, was the greatest joy of all. I stood entranced in its lofty dimness, listening to the sound of its great organ filling the raftered ceiling with solemn music, and felt transported.

So enraptured was I with the magnificent solemnity of the age-old Minster that I barely noticed the touch on my elbow. So many sightseers like myself were strolling in the aisles that I gave little attention to the unintentional touch of a passerby. It was only when the handsome face of a tanned young gentleman obtruded itself between me and the high altar that I realised he was speaking to me.

'Begging your pardon, ma'am,' he said gravely with a hint of humour in his light blue eyes, 'I guess you were so absorbed you did not hear me. I'm real sorry to disturb your concentration.'

'I beg your pardon?' I stammered. It was not only the unexpectedness of being addressed by a strange gentleman, but the tall breath of him and the soft drawl in his deep voice. It was as though Adonis had stepped down into this holy place. He was without doubt the most personable young man I had ever encountered. And almost simultaneously I felt a stab of recognition. I felt I knew this man, and yet I knew I had never seen him before.

He smiled at my dumb stare. 'Forgive me. I only wanted to return your glove. I was looking around your lovely old Minster and I saw you drop it back there.'

He was holding out my kid glove and I took it gratefully. That pair of gloves cost me a whole week's wages last year. I smiled shyly.

'Thank you so much. You are very kind.'

He bowed slightly and moved away. With a feeling almost of disappointment, I watched the tall figure recede to the south transept door, pause, and look back. I looked away quickly. It would not do to be caught watching him, as if I were interested in him. Guiltily I glanced sideways from under lowered lids. He was leaving. I saw the grey frock-coated figure emerge into the sunlight, adjust his top hat on his fair head, and disappear.

Somehow I found the Minster less absorbing now he was gone. Though his coming had shattered my reverie, he had in some way brought such a radiance and atmosphere into the place that it seemed suddenly vacant without him. With a sigh I decided it was time I turned my steps in the direction of the inn. By now Regina's business might be concluded and she would be looking for me.

Regina was awaiting me so that she could order dinner. She was still remote, I noticed, for even the arrival of the parcel and the delicious material I had chosen for her failed to arouse her interest. She stayed moody and withdrawn throughout our evening meal. I decided after all not to recount my meeting with the stranger with the unusual accent. Moreover she might consider the incident unladylike.

After supper she announced that she would go to bed at once. 'Tomorrow you will travel home as we arranged, but I regret I must stay on for a day or two. This business appears to be more complicated than I expected,' she said wearily.

'I am so sorry. Shall I give a message to your brother, Regina?'

'Only that the business is protracted, but I shall return as soon as possible. Do not alarm him by hinting at any complications, mind, only say that legal affairs tend to be tedious.'

'I shall. Are you sure you do not wish me to stay with you?'

She smiled, a tired little smile. 'Thank you, no. Now that I have overcome the obstacle of meeting people again, I shall cope. Good night, Amity.'

She rose from the table with the slow, laboured effort of an old woman. I watched her go with concern. Either the effort of facing the world was taking a far greater toll of her strength than she would admit, or the affair with the solicitor was causing her great worry. In either event I should have to wait for Regina to confide in me when she felt the time was ripe. Intrusion of unasked help on my part would only evoke resentment.

As I lay down beside Regina's sleeping figure that night, I thought again of the Adonis in the Minster. Strange that I had felt I knew him, and stranger still that I had felt such a sense of disappointment at losing him. I laughed away my silly romantic ideas and settled down to sleep.

The journey home passed quickly. Only at Kirkham Abbey did I purposely look out, and again I felt the same sense of tragedy as at the Keep. Mallory, of evil omen, I recalled. And yet, oddly enough, I was looking forward to returning there.

Rosie, all pink and flustered, opened the door to me. 'Thy room and the mistress's are all ready and warm,' she said, her eyes sliding past me to the carriage at the foot of the steps.

'Miss Regina is not coming back for a day or two, Rosie. Where is the master, that I may tell him?'

Mrs. Garner's plump figure glided from the baize door to the servants' quarters. She came to stand between Rose and me.

'Go fetch Miss Lucas's tray, Rosie, there's a good lass,' she said to the girl, who obediently left. Then she turned to me. 'T'master's not here, miss. He's out.'

'When do you expect him back?'

She shrugged. 'Who can say? Let me take thy coat, miss. Rosie'll fetch thy supper up to thy room.'

'When did you last see Mr. Damian?' I went on, not to be dissuaded.

'Not since thee and Miss Regina left.' She was going away, carrying my coat. I followed her.

'Do you mean he has been out for two days, Mrs. Garner? What about his meals?'

'Happen he's out, happen he's not. We've not seen him. We leave food in his room and he eats when he feels like it.'

'And has his food been eaten?'

'Some of it. He's a light eater, is t'master.'

I watched in shocked disbelief as she shuffled away. It seemed incredible that she neither knew nor cared what her master was doing. Poor man. That he was sick I was certain, but even his surly, unkind manner should not make his servants so uncaring about his welfare.

And what was he doing, shutting himself out of sight for two whole days? He could be ill somewhere, lying in need of help for all anyone knew. I hastened to his room. At least I must deliver Regina's message.

The east wing was still and silent. As I moved along, counting the doors to the seventh, I thought of Uncle Eustace

70

and his passion for counting. There was no answer to my knock on Damian's door, nor any sound from within. Perhaps the old man could tell me where he was.

I was about to go back when something made me pause. It was the damp, mournful chill of the east wing. Sadness impregnated the place, the stones of the wall and the very air itself. Like Kirkham Priory, this old wing built from the abbey ruins held its tragedy captive within the stone. My senses, attuned to the atmosphere, seemed on the brink of unlocking the stone and releasing the suffering, and I felt afraid. I grasped the handle of the sixth door and entered the Rose Room.

The dusk of evening was calling, but even in the half-light I could see what a beautiful room it was. Before I had seen it only from the doorway, but now I saw not only the pink marble fireplace carved with a rose leaf design and the gilt and enamel clock upon it, but also the soft-piled carpet and the fleur-de-lys wallpaper and the pink-upholstered chaise longue. From a plaster medallion in the centre of the ceiling hung a gilt chandelier.

I turned back towards the door and caught sight of an oil painting, a portrait, above a carved table on which stood a large silver vase. It was of a beautiful young woman whose dark style of beauty was enhanced by the Spanish costume she wore. Deep lustrous eyes looked down at me from a pale oval face with full, petulant lips. One white shoulder protruded provocatively from the crimson lace of her gown. In the fading light the slumbrous eyes seemed to follow me as I moved towards the table.

The silver vase stood alone on the table. On its lid I read one word. Rachel. Of course, it was she whose stare followed me. I felt an intruder. It was as I was opening the door that I saw the black cat uncurl itself on a chair in the corner. It glared at me, arched its back, and hissed. Quickly I closed the door after me and returned to my room, all thought of Uncle Eustace forgotten.

Scrawling a hasty note for Damian, to tell of Regina's delay in York, I returned to push the note under his door. Then I returned to eat the sandwiches and cake on the tray which had appeared in my room in my absence.

In the morning I came downstairs to find Ben Jagger talking to Rosie in the vestibule. I could hear their voices before I saw them.

'Isn't she back then? I must see her,' Ben was saying urgently.

'No, only Miss Lucas is back. T'mistress has to stay away a day or two,' Rosie replied.

'But I must see her soon. We've already been delayed two days.'

'Then tha'll have to get on wi'out her,' Rosie replied. 'Get on wi' it, I say. She'll not mind.'

Some matter of the fallen fencing, I surmised as I descended the stairs with a smile. But I saw the sudden look that passed between them and the way Ben stiffened as he greeted me. Why were they always on the defensive with me, I wondered. For some odd reason they did not seem to trust me.

Two days passed, two days of ennui and frustration during which I saw neither Damian nor Uncle Eustace. Then as I was sitting one afternoon in Regina's drawing room, tacking together the pieces of her gown I had begun in order to surprise her, I heard the crunch of carriage wheels on the gravel drive. With a leap of gladness I realised Regina was home.

Hastening downstairs to meet her, I flung open the front door, too impatient to await the servants answering the bell. Regina was mounting the steps to the house, her face grave and pale. Behind her someone was raising the carriage step and closing the door. I went forward, arms outstretched to greet her. She allowed me to embrace her, then stood back.

'Allow me, Miss Lucas, to present Mr. Richard Fairfax.'

I turned from her to offer my hand to the gentleman who followed her. Then my hand stopped in mid air and my mouth fell open. The handsome face without a smile took my breath away, for it was my Adonis of the Minster.

CHAPTER FIVE

'The devil whispered behind the leaves.'
—R. Kipling, *The Conundrum of the Workshops*

Without a flicker of recognition he took my hand, but the solemn coldness in his eyes struck chill into my heart. Whatever warmth I might have thought I had recognised in his glance in the Minister was certainly dissipated now. Vaguely I heard his greeting as he bowed slightly over my hand, and my own voice murmur the conventional reply.

'If you would follow me, Mr. Fairfax,' Regina said coolly, indicating the parlour. His fair head bowed in acknowledgment and I recognised that I was not included in the invitation. Regina and he had business to discuss, evidently, the business which had taken her to York in the first place. As I climbed the stairs again, I glanced back and saw the tall breadth of his figure following Regina's slim, erect frame out of sight. It was only on the gallery, before the assembled array of Fairfax portraits, that it came to me.

Of course Richard Fairfax was familiar to me. Was it not his portrait on the gallery I had once gazed at in admiration? I stared at it again now, puzzling as to why something seemed odd.

The date, that was it. The date on the portrait of the flaxen-haired young man before me was 1835 – before our Queen came to the throne. Nearly thirty years ago. And yet the young man downstairs with Regina was only in his late twenties, only a few years older than the identical man gazing down at me solemnly from the gilded frame. If the Richard Fairfax below in the parlour was the same man, Regina's uncle, it was incredible.

By my reckoning he must be nearing sixty.

Uncle Eustace was hovering outside his door, pince-nez dithering precariously on the tip of his nose.

'Mars in conjunction with Uranus,' he muttered excitedly. 'Undeniably a sign of conflict.'

'Indeed,' I concurred.

'So glad you agree. Then we must be right. Watch out for storms, my dear.' So saying, he scuttled back into his room and closed the door.

I ate dinner from a tray, alone in my room, anxious not to intrude on Regina's privacy with the stranger. Nevertheless I speculated as to who he was and the reason for his sudden appearance at Mallory Keep. I did not have to wonder long, for as I prepared for bed there was a knock at the door. Expecting Rosie, I called out cheerily.

'Come in.'

It was a pallid Regina who entered, her face tense and thin-lipped.

'Forgive me for disturbing you so late, Amity.'

'You are welcome, Regina. I have missed you.'

She smiled thinly and seated herself by the low fire, spreading her slim fingers before its warmth. 'Mr. Fairfax has left now. He is to stay at the inn in the village.'

'Then he is not leaving Mallory yet?'

'No.' She paused, as if to consider how to continue, then turned and looked at me anxiously. 'Amity, I hesitate to burden you with our problems, but I feel it is important you should know something of the situation so as to know how to conduct yourself.'

I moved towards her, hoping to lessen her obvious embarrassment. 'I am honoured you should wish to confide in me, Regina. It is no burden, I assure you.'

'Then let me tell you briefly. My father's brother, Richard Fairfax, disappeared mysteriously many years ago, and as time passed the family believed him dead. Now this young man appears, claiming to be Richard's son.'

'Strange that neither father nor son has been in contact with you before now,' I murmured.

'Indeed. He tells me his father went to America and began farming. He there married and had two sons, of which he is

74

the elder. It is only now, he claims, that he is able to come to England to trace his family.'

Regina's face was still pale and tense in the firelight. I could not help wondering why she, lonely and vulnerable as she was, was not delighted at the prospect of discovering a relative, and a young handsome one at that.

'Why are you so troubled, Regina?' I asked at length as she sat silent. 'Perhaps he could be useful to you. Perhaps he knows about estate management from his father and could provide help for you when you so much need it.'

I had meant no implied criticism of Damian's failure, but I sensed I had said the wrong thing when I saw Regina's face redden with anger. She turned on me fiercely.

'He means more than to help at Mallory, Amity. I think he means to take it from us.'

I stared helplessly, lost as to her meaning. 'Take Mallory from you? But how can he?'

'Because his father, if my uncle *was* his father, was the elder son and the rightful heir. Mallory should have been theirs, not ours.'

'Oh, Regina!' It was all I could say, bewildered as I was. She rose slowly and crossed to the door.

'I shall fight to keep what is ours, Amity. I have worked long and hard for Mallory and will not let go easily. But the lawyer says if Richard Fairfax's case can be proved, we shall have to relinquish it.'

'Yes, I see that. How unfortunate.'

'Unfortunate?' She laughed bitterly. 'It will be a tragedy after all our struggles. But that is the curse upon us – tragedy always. I must let you sleep now. I came only to tell you that when Mr. Fairfax visits us again, as he undoubtedly will, to view the estates he regards as his, you must remember not to warm to him as a friend. He is our enemy, Amity, so beware. The man had undoubted charm and one could easily fall victim to it.'

'Indeed he has,' I murmured involuntarily, but she did not hear for she was already closing the door behind her. As I climbed into bed, I felt full of pity for Regina. She had worked hard to maintain Mallory, and there was little doubt she would lose it soon. Richard Fairfax's resemblance to the man in the portrait made his claim a highly tenable one, and in my opinion, undeniable. I made up my mind to dislike him intensely for what he was doing to Regina.

The next morning, Sunday, I decided to go to morning service in the village church. It would be pleasant to see the Reverend Parmenter again and hear him preach a sermon. I remembered from the church notice board that the service was at ten. At nine I sent Rosie with a note to Regina, asking if she would care to accompany me. The walk down the cliff path to the village, in bright spring sunlight, might help to dispel her cares, I felt.

Back came Rosie with a note written in Regina's crisp hand.

'Thank you, no,' it read. 'I am not in the habit of attending that church, nor any other. Regina.'

I shrugged and prepared to set off alone. Odd, I thought, but I would have believed the Fairfax family, old and respected as it was, to have been a pillar of orthodoxy and convention. Apparently I was wrong, since they were non-churchgoers.

As I arrived, a straggle of villagers were entering the lych-gate and strolling up the weed-grown path to the church. They all glanced at me covertly and looked away. Inside the doorway I paused, then chose not to go to one of the box pews near the front with brass nameplates upon them, one of which would probably bear the name of the Fairfax family, but to sit in an empty pew towards the back. In the dim church, shafts of sunlight from the high, stained windows cast lurid colours over the small congregation. The old man in a cloth cap and tobacco-stained white moustache looked spectral, shrouded in green light; the child fidgeting in front of me positively feverish in the crimson glow over her thin face. There was a smell of mint humbugs in the air, and I heard the thin-faced girl sucking noisily.

Throughout the service and the sermon no one looked at me, at least not openly. I sensed every person felt uncomfortable, perhaps because of wearing their Sunday best, the unaccustomed suits instead of smock and corduroys, the tightly-bodiced Sunday gowns in place of print dresses and aprons. Whatever the reason, there was an uncomfortable atmosphere in the quiet little church.

When the service was ended, I sat still for a time, letting the village folk leave first. By the time I emerged into the sunlight I expected them all to have gone, but I was wrong. A knot of people, mostly men, were congregated about the Devil's Arrow. As I passed by I could feel hostile eyes upon me. It was as though they were protecting their age-old 'holy stone' against me.

'Good morning, Miss Lucas. I am glad to see you here.'

I looked up eagerly, surprised at the warmth of the voice. It was Hugh Parmenter, the smile on his lips matched by that in his eyes. As he spoke, the knot of men behind him began to break up slowly and disperse. I know it was a stupid notion, but I couldn't help thinking that it was as though they no longer feared for their precious stone, the power of the church was there to protect it from my evil eye.

The reverend and I fell in step, strolling together down the path to the lych-gate. At the gate I remarked, irrelevantly, that I had invited Miss Fairfax to accompany me, but she had declined. Reverend Parmenter nodded thoughtfully.

'Yes, that is natural. The Fairfaxes are a Catholic family, you know. Have been for centuries.'

I looked up in surprise, but refrained from comment. There had been no evidence of it at the Keep – no crucifixes, no holy water or statues. And Regina's note had said she attended no church. Still, it was no business of mine. I parted with Reverend Parmenter cordially, promising to take tea with him and Mrs. Parmenter very soon.

It was too glorious a day to return too soon to the gloomy atmosphere of the Keep. I resolved instead, once I had arrived at the gate, to go on along the path and turn off across the moor towards the abbey. On a day such as this, a solitary walk amid sanctified ruins appealed to my romantic nature. Presently I turned inland, leaving behind me the expanse of white-capped waves frolicking in the bay.

Before me the heather moor spread itself out under the periwinkle sky, vast and uninterrupted, save for one small wooded valley. I was enjoying the fresh mildness in the air, the salt smell of the sea, and the spring of turf under my feet; and as I began to descend the hollow I heard the trickle of water. A small stream running towards the sea had carved its path through the moor over the centuries and it afforded now a shady, pleasant spot. I was crossing the few stepping-stones when I saw the man.

He sat, dark and morose, on the far bank, the gleaming knife in his hand whittling a twig. A farmhand, by the look of him, in working clothes. He merely glanced curiously at me and carried on whittling. I reached the bank and went on.

The roofless arches of the old abbey stood out against the sky, grey and moss-spattered. I was surprised, as I approached, to see how large a ruin it was. Of the original cruciform shape, the choir, most of the north transept, part of the nave and the western front still stood. Lancet windows in three tiers, the moulded columns and tooth ornamentation told me it was early English architecture, as also did the keystones with their carvings of a lion, a ram, and a dragon. On a pillar in the north transept, I could see the traces of a Latin inscription, now no longer legible. Along one wall of the nave still clung some of the ruined pillars of the erstwhile cloisters.

I strolled between the cloister pillars, enjoying the sunlight and reflecting on the tranquillity of the monks who had once walked here, deep in prayer and meditation. Tranquil, that was, until the autocratic Henry VIII swept away the last vestiges of their peace and piety, driving them out of their haven to beg or starve.

Strolling thus, lost in thought, among the ruins scoured by the biting east winds off the sea, I felt at peace. It was as though I could recapture from the stones the tranquillity which once had permeated Malvaux Abbey, and for the moment I could forget the tensions and anxieties of Mallory Keep.

I mounted the crumbled step of a doorway which had once connected the cloisters with the junction of nave and transept. As I came into the main body of the Abbey, treading carefully over moss-covered stones, my feeling of solitude was suddenly shattered, for there, at what had once been the choir steps, knelt the cloaked figure of a man.

His head was bowed, deep in prayer, but from the breadth of the muscular shoulders, and the black curls flickering in the breeze, I could recognise Damian Fairfax. I drew back silently behind a pillar, unwilling to disturb his meditation. As unobtrusively as I could, I crept back into the cloisters.

Churchgoer or not, my master evidently still felt the need to worship in a Catholic abbey. Far be it from me to intrude on his private prayer, even if we had been on friendly terms, he and I. Disliking me as intensely as he did, discovery would probably incur his furious wrath, so as quietly as I could, I put a distance between the abbey ruins and myself.

It was as I neared the woodland copse near the stream again that I heard the cry, long-drawn-out and pitiful. I halted for a moment. It came from the copse, an agonised cry. I hastened forward anxiously. It sounded like a child in pain.

Half-stumbling down the grassy bank towards the bubbling stream, I saw it was no child but a rabbit, its ears laid back and its eyes wide with terror. It lay on its side alongside the cruel grey glint of steel. A hind leg hung, almost severed from the body, in the vicious jaws of a gin-trap. My hand flew to my mouth, half to stifle the cry of alarm, half to hold back the shock of nausea that rose in my throat. City-born and bred as I was, the cruelties of life such as the rabbit now endured were unknown to me.

I looked about for help. To my surprise a pair of grey eyes under a cloth cap were watching me levelly, and I recognised the man who had been whittling a stick when I had passed this way earlier. In my need, ignoring the proprieties, I spoke to him.

'The rabbit – it's in pain – can you free it?' I asked anxiously, pointing to the wretched animal. I saw surprise in his eyes melt into amusement.

'Aye, I can,' he grunted.

'Then please do, as quickly as you can.'

He leapt nimbly down the bank and began prising back the steel jaws of the trap. The rabbit lay silent now and still, but its twitching eyeballs showed it still lived.

'Poor thing,' I said jerkily. 'How cruel.'

He uttered a wry laugh. 'Cruel? Nay, it's necessary, Miss Lucas. That'll make a fine dinner for my brood, that it will.'

I was staring in disbelief. Of course that was how all the rabbit stews I had ever eaten had been obtained, but somehow it had not mattered when I had not seen the poor creatures die. But the thought was driven out by another. The man had addressed me by name. And a sneaking suspicion quickly followed the thought. Had he been spying on me?

'You know who I am?' I said as he straightened up from the trap, leaving the mutilated animal lying motionless beside it.

'Aye, miss. Tha'rt at t'Keep.'

'And who may you be, may I ask?'

'Ramsden, miss. Live up at Keep Farm, on t'moor.' His arm waved vaguely across the heather inland. 'And tha's no need to fret over t'rabbit. I'll kill him clean and easy now.'

He bent to the inert creature, dead already, so far as I could see. But before his hand touched it his head turned and the grey eyes fastened on me. 'That's what happens to unwary creatures as wander where they oughtn't,' he said softly, and I realised from his tone and the curious gaze that he was giving me a warning. 'Them as trespass get hurt,' he said crisply.

The angry retort never reached my lips, the remark that the poor rabbit had every bit as much right in the copse as he, for a huge dark shape suddenly thrust itself between Ramsden and me. I drew back instinctively when I recognised Caesar. The wolfhound bared its teeth and began to growl, not at me, I was relieved to note, but at the man bent over the rabbit. Ramsden froze.

A thunder of footsteps and a bellowing cry cut across the clear moorland air. I looked around. Damian Fairfax, his cloak billowing behind him like outspread black wings, came running towards us. As his gaze fell from us to the trap at our feet his dark eyes blazed angrily.

'Back, Caesar!' The dog slunk back and Ramsden straightened slowly. 'What the devil are you up to, man?' Damian roared. 'Haven't I forbidden you to set gin-traps? Does your greed always overcome your obedience? Remove it, man, and set no more or I'll let the dog at your throat, so I will!'

As Ramsden stepped to one side to deal with the trap, the

rabbit's torn body was exposed to Damian's view. With a strangled sound that was half-moan, half roar, he swooped down on the wretched creature and lifted it tenderly. Cradling it close to his chest, he turned to go. As he did, his sorrowful eyes alighted on me.

'I did not think you capable of this. I had thought better of you,' he rasped, and strode off to cross the stream, the dog after him. Anger filled my eyes with tears, anger born of frustration and misunderstanding. How could he believe me capable of conniving at the rabbit's torture?

'He oughta join his like up there at t'Abbey,' grunted Ramsden, 'and to the devil wi' 'em all.'

The two men disappeared, the cloaked figure of the one up the further bank and the cloth-capped figure of the other along the stream among the trees, the trap in his hands. I was alone by the lapping stream with only a bloodstain the size of a handspoon as evidence of what had just taken place.

Though I followed the direction Damian had taken with the wounded animal, I did not see him again before I reached the Keep. Regina was a little testy when I apologised for my lateness at lunch.

'No matter,' she said crisply. 'Mrs. Garner has kept the stew hot in the oven.'

It seemed a deliberately cruel twist of irony that it was a rabbit stew Ellen served up to us after the brown Windsor soup. My stomach quailed at the scent of it, and in my mind's eye I could see again the twisted, pain-wracked creature in the copse. I pushed my plate away and smiled apologetically.

'I'm sorry, Regina, I'm afraid I can't eat it.'

Her eyebrows rose. 'Not sick, are you? I do hope not. You have a healthy enough glow in your cheeks.'

'No, no, I'm quite well, thank you. It's just that – I saw a rabbit in a trap today. I've never seen one before.'

'A gin-trap? Damian will be angry. He hates them and has forbidden their use on the estate.'

'I know. He came and took the rabbit.'

'And no doubt will nurse it till it either recovers or dies. He's a tenderhearted man, my brother.'

Not quite the view I held of Damian Fairfax, but I did not argue. It had been an unexpected glimpse of another side of

81

his character, but I was still smarting from his mistaken belief that I had something to so with the animal's capture. And puzzled too, as to why Ramsden seemed to be trying to warn – or threaten – me.

'Damian will surely punish whoever set that trap, if he finds him,' Regina remarked as she polished off the last of her stew.

'He knows the man. His name is Ramsden and he lives at Keep Farm,' I told her.

'Ah yes. A stubborn man,' Regina nodded. 'You remember the boy, Eric, swinging on the farm gate the day we went to York? His son. The wife is amiable enough, but Ramsden . . .' She shook her head, wiped her mouth with her napkin, and rang the handbell for Ellen.

I ate the steamed pudding and custard without difficulty, having acquired quite an appetite during my morning excursion, for all except rabbit stew, that is. Regina had relapsed into silence again, bent on her own thoughts, so I ventured no remark as to the thoughts that puzzled me – why Damian knelt at prayer alone in the abbey ruins, why Ramsden saw fit to warn or threaten me, and my misgiving that Damian believed me Ramsden's accomplice in the trapping of the rabbit.

It was at dinner that night that Regina told me that she was to introduce her brother to Richard Fairfax during the evening. Damian had not been at home when Mr. Richard came yesterday.

'Mr. Richard is staying at the inn in the village. You will probably not see him tonight, but if you should chance to meet, remember to keep him at a distance as I asked. I would prefer you to keep to your room tonight.'

I understood her request. No doubt she anticipated angry words between Damian and his cousin. Nevertheless, out of curiosity, I could not resist tiptoeing to the minstrel's gallery when I heard the doorbell clang. I wanted a discreet glimpse of the devastatingly handsome American cousin.

He entered jauntily, his tall frame and suntanned face lighting up the gloomy vestibule, and his cool, quiet voice vibrating life into its stillness. He chatted in friendly tones to Ethel, the pretty little housemaid who took his hat and cane, and I could see the pink pleasure on her snub-nosed face before she led him to the parlour. As I returned to my room I was almost bowled over by the hurtling figure of Damian, heading for the stairs. His dark features were clouded and sullen.

Uncle Eustace had been right, I mused. Storms were imminent. I resolved to hide away in the writing room and occupy myself by penning a long-overdue letter to Aunt Cecily and Uncle Leonard.

At first my pen flowed easily, following up the earlier descriptions I had given my aunt and uncle of the house and its occupants and relating my visit to York, but after some time my pen faltered. It was difficult to try to explain to them the strange atmosphere of the Keep and the uncommunicative nature of the family. They never seemed to tell one another of their movements nor discuss their feelings, Uncle Eustace closeted with his astrolabe, Damian roaming the moors by night, and Regina left to cope with the family problems alone as though she were the man of the household. Silence spread between the Fairfaxes like a cancer, insidious but menacing.

Aunt Cecily would never understand. She would be puzzled as to why I should find their remoteness remarkable. To her it would seem only the natural aloofness of the well-born towards their inferiors, and she would urge me to get on with my work capably, in order to earn their esteem, and not criticise the behaviour of my betters but to learn from them while I had the opportunity.

Dear Aunt Cecily. Complaint was not in her amiable nature, as Uncle Leonard well knew and took advantage of it. I lay aside my pen, cupping my chin in my hands, and gazing absently about the room while I reflected on my aunt's way of life, wondering how she was faring in her advanced state of pregnancy. After a time I rose and went to inspect the rows of books inside the glass-fronted cabinets.

Volumes of philosophy and poetry nestled against tomes of natural history and travel. A thick coating of dust over them all indicated yet again how the Fairfax rank of servants had been depleted, for it must have been years since a duster flicked over these books. Idly I withdrew a volume of Pope, sneezed violently when I opened its pages and was about to replace it when I saw the corner of a dog-eared exercise book tucked behind. I pulled it out, curious to know if it were some long-forgotten schoolroom workbook of one of the Fairfax children, Regina or Damian as a child.

No name embellished its cover, only the date, some seven years ago, so it was no ancient relic after all. Mildly disappointed, I was about to return it to its dusty shelf when some words in the angular, childish script arrested me.

'So dark, so noble of brows, so broodingly handsome and severe, like some great avenging angel he stands.' I recognised it at once, the description of Damian Fairfax. I seated myself again at the desk and read on under the lamplight.

'He is just as arresting as I remembered from the first occasion I saw him, and just as unaware of me. Today in church he stood, head bowed and deep in worship, whereas I forgot my piety and had eyes and thoughts only for him. My brother scolded me after Mass for my inattention, but I care not. I shall be noticed, I swear it, or my name is not Rachel Longden.'

Rachel. The name sprang at me from the page. I was startled, for knowing she was dead, it was as if I was listening to a dead girl's voice. Shaken, and feeling a little guilty, I prepared to read on, for I confess I was anxious to know the rest of the story.

A low hissing from somewhere above me made me start. Looking up above the lamp in the direction of the sound, I could see nothing at first in the shadows. Then I fancied I saw a shadow move on the bookshelves. I rose to go forward.

The dark shape uncurled and sprang, passing my head by inches. A low cry escaped my lips as I shrank back, and simultaneously the door opened. Uncle Eustace stood there, and I saw the black cat slither past his ankles and out into the darkness of the corridor.

'Ah, there you are, my dear,' Uncle Eustace murmured. 'I was looking for you. Regina and Damian are still in the parlour with the gentleman, and I heard raised voices when I passed. The gentleman is undoubtedly a Leo, by his face, so that is not to be wondered at. So I looked for you instead.'

'You've been downstairs?' I asked in surprise.

'Outside, to be precise, to the stables. I went to see to my cat.'

'Your cat? A large black one?'

'Dear me, no. A plain domestic tabby. It's my little job, you know, to care for the stable cats, and Jemima has just kittened, so I have to see all is well. A black cat, you say?'

'Yes – it was here. I've seen it before in the east wing.'

'Have you now? That's rather unfortunate.'

'Why?'

'Well, don't tell Regina about it, at any rate. You see, some of the maids have spoken of a black cat in the east wing, guarding the Rose Room, they say. But there is no such cat. They say it's a wild cat, an evil spirit, but Regina grows angry when she hears such gossip. She'll think you're as superstitious as the village girls.'

'But I *did* see it – it tried to scratch me.'

'That's just what the maids say. An evil spirit who tries to attack anyone who touches Rachel's possessions. Curious.'

I sighed. 'Why were you looking for me?' Since he evidently wasn't going to believe me, I must discover his reason before he forgot.

'Ah, yes. Oddly enough, it was about the Rose Room. Coming from the stables I was counting the bedroom windows in the east wing,' I couldn't resist a smile. I wondered if Uncle Eustace could ever move from one spot to another without counting. It seemed as indispensable to him as a walking stick to a lame man. 'And there were lights burning in the sixth room. The Rose Room. No one ever goes there but Damian, and he's in the parlour.'

'And what do you want of me?'

He smiled, a shy, winning smile that creased his old face like crumpled parchment. 'Only to go and see why there are lights in there. Perhaps it is only that lamps were left burning inadvertently.'

He knew as well as I that it was unlikely. Regina's housekeeping was of the thriftiest, and oil lamps were not left to burn unnecessarily. Nevertheless I agreed. The cat had unnerved me, and I was anxious to prove that all was normal and quite explicable.

Uncle Eustace padded along behind me until we reached

his door, and there he stopped to watch me go on towards the east wing. I pushed the studded door open. Why was it that a chilly blast always seemed to strike one's face on entering this forbidden part of the Keep?

As I moved quickly and quietly along the stone-flagged floor, its coldness striking through the soles of my thin slippers, I felt a prickle of apprehension. Suppose the black cat was still stalking me, awaiting the chance to leap at my face again? I pushed the thought of its outstretched claws from my mind, and counted the doors.

The sixth. I turned the knob and pushed the door open slowly, standing back lest the creature was crouching there. Uncle Eustace was right. Two oil lamps glowed, one by the bedside and the other behind the door. I went inside.

The second lamp stood on the table below the portrait of Rachel, and alongside, the vase I had noticed before gleamed brightly. I turned aside to cup my hand over the bedside lamp and blow it out, then returned to the table. Rachel's proudly beautiful face stared down at me, as though resenting my intrusion. For a fleeting second it was the cat's malevolent stare I saw, and I felt angry with myself for my unreasoning stupidity. I was growing as superstitious as Uncle Eustace had said the maids were, in their ignorance. I quickly looked away from the portrait.

Then I noticed the little kneeling-bench half-tucked under the table, a prie-dieu I think it is named, such as used to be used in private chapels and oratories. Perhaps Damian knelt here to pray, making Rachel's room into a shrine, her portrait into an altar. That was why the bedroom still remained as it was when she last slept here, no doubt, her silver-backed hairbrushes and pots of lotions still on the dressing table. And her gowns still in the great wardrobe too, for I remembered a glimpse of them when Mrs. Garner had fetched out the riding habit. Perhaps the poor bereft man kept all in readiness in the crazed notion that in this way he could keep her alive, or even in the desperate hope of her return.

It saddened me to think of him here, nourishing such fierce passion for a dead woman. Grief had turned his mind indeed, to diminish his religious belief into such sacrilegious worship.

I traced my finger reflectively over the surface of the crystal vase with its figured cover, and without conscious thought I raised it. Inside there was a fine grey powder. I dipped my fingers in it curiously, inspecting my fingertips in an effort to determine what the substance might be.

A hiss of indrawn breath behind me startled me out of my wits. I wheeled about to see Damian's cloaked and booted figure filling the open doorway, his face pale with rage, his eyes staring till the whites showed, and his hand clenched about his silver-headed riding crop. I stood mute, guilt reddening my face.

Suddenly, without warning, he raised his hand. The crop flew down across my arm, making me wince with pain.

'She-devil! How dare you enter here! Get out!' he roared, his eyes wild and his face no longer human. As I hurried to pass him to reach the door, he fell before the table, moaning as he replaced the lid on the crystal vase.

Fleeing along the corridor, I suddenly realised, with a shock of horror, what the vase contained. It was an urn, and the powder was Rachel's ashes. I rubbed my fingers furiously on my skirts, like Lady Macbeth, anxious to be rid of the incriminating evidence that I had defiled his temple. And as I ran I swear I heard the distant sound of a woman's laughter, soft and mocking, drifting along the chilly silence of the east wing.

CHAPTER SIX

'Your adversary the devil, as a roaring lion,
walketh about.'
—The Bible, 1 Peter

It must have been raining heavily during the night, for when I arose in the morning the sky was leaden, and from my window I could see that the grounds were sodden. Necklets of crystal raindrops hung tremulously from the branches of the thornbushes and huge puddles laced the gravel walks.

Now only a fine drizzle was falling, peppering the panes so that at first I did not see the figure walking below. When I did, I recognised the tall figure of Richard Fairfax.

I was puzzled. Why was he here on the grounds of Mallory Keep so early in the morning? I watched his long, easy stride as he crossed below me and the way he turned his face up to meet the rain, almost as though he welcomed its touch. Once again I felt pleasure in the sight of him, but drew away from the window lest he should see me watching him.

Rose knocked and entered with my morning tray. 'Morning, miss,' she said gloomily. Today she no longer seemed country fresh and lively, for her face looked grey and drawn, as though she had not slept well. But I was too curious about Richard Fairfax to concern myself overlong with Rose's appearance.

'Thank you, Rosie,' I said, seating myself on the bed and pouring out tea. 'I see Mr. Fairfax – Mr. Richard Fairfax – is out in the garden.'

It sounded a casual, conversational remark, but I was anxious to probe. Rosie might well know why. I was not disappointed.

'Aye, he's just leaving. Been here all night, Mrs. Garner says.'

'Indeed' I tried to sound offhand, but it was difficult to keep out of my voice the ripple of excitement I felt. Regina's distrust of the man, and the fact that Uncle Eustace had overheard Damian's anger in the parlour last night made it most unlikely that Richard Fairfax had been invited to be a guest at the Keep.

'It were fair teeming wi' rain last night – I know – I got soaked going home,' Rose told me wearily. 'Miss Regina asked him to stay, seemingly, rather than go back down to t'village.'

So I was wrong. Perhaps Regina's distrust had waned. Perhaps Mr. Richard's charm had won her over after all. But my feeling of pleasure faded when I remembered that he was now on his way back to the inn. He was not to stay at the Keep. That was unfortunate. The gloomy old house could well benefit from his vital presence.

'Will that be all, miss?' Rose asked, trying hard to stifle a yawn.

'Thank you, yes.' I'd have liked to question her further to discover what else Mrs. Garner might have revealed about the visitor, but it was not seemly to question the servants. With luck Regina might tell me more. As soon as I had washed and dressed I went to find her.

I found her in the writing room. Today her recent air of absorption had vanished and I found instead she had a quiet air of determination.

'I shall be busy this morning, Amity. I have letters to write, one to our solicitor especially. Will you be content to read, or go out riding if the rain clears? There is a break in the clouds and the sun may shine soon.'

'Of course, if you're sure I can't help you.'

She smiled grimly. The scar showed vivid against the pallor of her cheek. 'No, I must tackle this myself. It is the matter of Richard Fairfax, of course.'

'I see.' But I didn't see. Though he had been a guest overnight, her present demeanor indicated that Regina was still dead set against him. I hovered at the doorway while Regina seated herself at the desk and sighed.

'He plans to take Mallory from us, Amity,' she said, and there was infinite weariness in her voice.

'Oh no, surely not. Did he say so?'

'Not in so many words. But last night he told Damian and me all about himself. He told us of his life on his father's farm and how he always planned one day to come and find his relatives here, having heard so much about Mallory from his father. And he was at pains to let us know that his father was the elder son.'

'That may not mean what you fear, Regina.'

'Oh, he is too clever to say straight out what he plans, too charming to threaten. He's a handsome devil and makes full use of his charm. He was smiling and sunny throughout. Damian was furious.'

I could believe it. Though he had little concern for the estate himself, he would not easily yield what was his.

'I'm afraid he shouted at Richard, called him a cheat and a thief.'

'How did Mr. Richard react?'

'He denied, very quietly and pleasantly, that he had any wish for Mallory.'

'Well there you are,' I said.

She laughed, a hollow, unconvincing laugh. 'Do you believe that? It's one more mark of his cleverness, to lull us into a sense of false security. I must write to ask Mr. Boyd, the solicitor, to come here quickly. Something must be done if we are to save the Keep.'

She picked up the pen. Taking it as a gesture of dismissal, I left her. She was right, the clouds were receding and revealing a patch of blue sky. I would take her advice and go for a gentle ride across the moor.

The mare Cooper led out from the stables for me was a pretty grey who whinnied as if with pleasure at the prospect of a canter. 'Miss Regina used to ride Twilight regular one time,' Cooper grunted. 'She don't get much exercise now.'

The mare, I presumed he meant. Though she looked amiable enough, I still felt a trifle apprehensive as I mounted her sidesaddle, aided by Cooper's cupped hands. My riding lessons had been a long time ago. Cooper watched me critically as I turned her about and rode off under the arched gateway.

'Her name's Twilight, don't forget, miss,' the ostler called out after me. An apt name, I thought, for the dusky grey. Murmuring her name, I urged her on to a canter across the lawns and down through the thorn hedge to the cliff path.

Along the path I slowed her to a walk until we reached the moors stretching inland. There I turned her westward, towards the abbey ruins. For no reason other than curiosity, I had a desire to visit again the spot where I had seen Damian on his knees. For him, evidently, the place held the same fascination as it did for me. But I did not know the reason.

I did not need to make use of Regina's silver-headed riding crop, for Twilight needed no persuasion to canter across the rain-soaked heather. It was an exhilarating ride, and by the time we had ridden through the copse by the stream where I had met Ramsden, the sun had peeped out and the clouds were receding fast.

The ruins were bathed in spring sunshine when I dismounted by the cloisters. Twilight seemed happy to graze contentedly, so I left her untethered while I strolled towards the choir. It was so tranquil, so peaceful amid the ancient stones. Doubtless it was this solace, this rest from turmoil, that had brought Damian here.

And not only Damian. With a start I realised I was not alone, for a tall figure stood silent in the shadows of an archway. Just as I saw him he evidently sensed my presence, for he turned quickly to face me. With a lurch I recognised Richard Fairfax.

He was coming towards me. There was no possibility of pretending I had not seen him nor chance of ignoring him. He approached with a grave smile.

'Good morning, Miss Lucas.' As he doffed his hat and bowed slightly, sunlight glistened on his fair head. Solemn blue eyes regarded me seriously. 'You enjoy old churches, evidently, since I met you first in York Minster,' he said.

'There is an atmosphere here which intrigues me,' I replied calmly, my tone belying the excitement I felt at seeing him again.

'Then perhaps you would allow me to accompany you while we explore. That is, if my presence does not intrude on your mood of contemplation.'

He proffered his arm invitingly, and I took it. His forearm felt muscular and strong beneath the broadcloth and again I felt a shiver of excitement. We turned and walked companionably along where the aisle would once have been, and out of the main doorway.

'There is an air of strength and sadness here,' he remarked as we came out on the crumbling steps. It pleased me that he was a man who could sense atmosphere. Such sensitivity was usually regarded as a feminine trait rather than masculine, and it was gratifying that he could admit to such sensitivity.

He asked me if I knew of the abbey's history, so I told him what I had learned of the monks dispossessed by Henry VIII, and how some of the stones had been used to build part of the Keep. On mentioning the Keep I felt guilty. It was not for me to talk of my employers' home, the home this man threatened. I withdrew my hand from his arm.

To my surprise he stopped walking and turned to stare at me quizzically, his lightly tanned face tilted to one side. 'Do you like your employers, my cousins Damian and Regina?' he asked.

The directness of his question startled me. An English gentleman would have understood my reticence, but not this handsome young colonial. Whether he understood our ways or not, I must answer.

'Regina is kindness itself to me,' I replied. 'She made me a gift of this riding habit and crop.'

He inclined his head. 'And Damian? What of him?'

'I – I barely know him, for we seldom meet,' I prevaricated.

'But he is an odd fellow, you sense it too,' Richard Fairfax stated quietly. 'I had expected a welcome from him for a long-lost cousin, but instead he accused me of trying to steal what was his. I have no wish to take Mallory Keep or the estate, only to find my kin now my father is dead. But Damian would not believe me. I wonder why he is so distrustful and suspicious. Do you find him agreeable?' I made no answer. 'Your silence does you credit,' he went on, 'whether it is natural caution or loyalty to your employers. But I am curious to know more about my cousins.'

'Why?' I prompted. Perhaps he would reveal his intentions.

'My father had told me of Thomas, my uncle, but I did not know I had cousins until I visited Mr. Boyd, the solicitor. I expected to find only Uncle Thomas, not knowing he was dead.'

'Because of the curse,' I murmured, thinking aloud. Richard Fairfax looked puzzled.

'The curse? What curse?'

Briefly I told him of the legend as Reverend Parmenter had told me, of Thomas's fall from the cliffs, and the curse which was said to haunt all the Fairfaxes. Instead of looking surprised or apprehensive, his face brightened into a smile.

'The Fairfax curse. Why, that's wonderful! Here I was, trying to soak up some of the atmosphere of history which my country lacks, and I find my own family has a tradition of its own. You don't know how happy that makes me.'

I stared curiously. Happy, to learn of a curse? The man was as eccentric as Damian. Suddenly his smile faded. He turned and looked about him.

'Do you get the feeling we're being watched?' he demanded of me.

'Why – no.' I had been too absorbed in Richard Fairfax to notice anything else.

He shrugged. 'Perhaps it's the talk of the curse, or I'm growing superstitious. We seem to be in a graveyard, where the old monks buried their dead, I imagine.'

So that was what the mounds indicated, I thought. No headstones marked the resting places of the monks. Unless the fallen masonry littered about between and half buried in the hillocks had once been their headstones. I seated myself on a slat, inspecting Regina's riding crop, while Richard stood and stared into the distance across the moor.

I was admiring the silverwork on the crop's head, the ornate initial R traced on its surface, when Richard drew my attention to the path worn by passing feet.

'There would seem to be many visitors to the abbey ruins,'

he remarked. 'The path comes from down there, the cluster of trees in the hollow. Pilgrims, do you think?'

'I have come that way myself on foot,' I replied. So I had, the day I met Ramsden. 'The path continues inland along the stream's bank. I have not heard of any pilgrims.'

He turned to me and smiled. 'I'm probably quite wrong about pilgrims, but it is great to explore and speculate. I feel such a – a kind of affinity with this stretch of England, my patrimony, as you might say.'

Regina was right then. He did feel he belonged here, or this place belonged to him. I made a resolution that, however I might enjoy his company, I must beware of him for her sake. However tempting, I must abjure the delight of his companionship.

My heart sank at his next words. 'It is time I was returning to the village, I fear. I have enjoyed talking with you, Miss Lucas, and trust we shall do so again soon. May I escort you to the Keep?'

Remembering my resolve, I shook my head. 'Thank you, no. I shall ride home later, but for a time I shall stay here to enjoy the view.'

As he came forward to take my hand to bid me goodbye, I suddenly remembered Uncle Eustace's words. A Leo he said Richard Fairfax was, if he was not mistaken. On impulse I asked.

'What is your birth sign, Mr. Fairfax? I mean, what date is your birthday?'

How stupid and irrelevant, I reproached myself instantly. But Richard Fairfax only smiled.

'August the eighth. I'm afraid I don't know what sign of the Zodiac it is.'

'Leo,' I said with conviction. I hoped Uncle Eustace was right.

'Why, how clever of you. I do believe it is. Goodbye, Miss Lucas. We shall meet again soon.'

'Shall we?' I hardly dared to hope it, but despite my resolve I did hope it.

'Regina has invited me to stay on at the Keep for a time. I'm on my way to the inn to collect my baggage. For a time at least then, goodbye.'

He strode away between the hillocks, his long legs cleaving a trail in the heather and the sunlight gleaming on his head. I sighed contentedly. It was reassuring to think of his broad strength and friendly smile to relieve the gloom of the Keep.

Alone again, I let the peace and solitude of the ruins work their magic on me. Sitting in the warm sunshine, absorbing the atmosphere, I must have fallen prey to its soporific effect. I was very nearly about to fall asleep, sitting up as I was, and had to make an effort to rouse myself to go in search of Twilight. As I made to go through the arched doorway through the abbey, I could swear I saw just a glimpse of a figure retreating behind a pillar. A woman's figure this time, a whisk of skirt flitting out of sight.

Surely I was not dreaming on my feet. I walked around the pillars cautiously, but no one was to be seen. Though I spent several minutes exploring, I could find no one. I was alone in the ruins.

Odd, I thought, as I took up Twilight's reins and re-mounted. Richard had sensed we were not alone. Had he been right? But why were we being watched? And by whom? No human being could have been spirited away so completely and without trace.

No human being. I shivered as I urged Twilight into a canter, away from the abbey. I was becoming as superstitious as Uncle Eustace, to think I could have seen a ghost. For a moment I wished I had accepted Richard Fairfax's offer of accompanying me home.

Regina was in the vestibule when I entered the Keep, supervising Ethel who was laden with blankets and sheets.

'Now remember, Ethel, make up the bed and then light the fire to air the room well. Make haste now, for Mr. Richard will return soon.'

Ethel sped upstairs and Regina turned to me with a smile. 'Poor Ethel, she's rather cross at having to do Rose's work, but the wretched girl hasn't come in this morning.'

'I am glad to hear Mr. Richard is to stay after all,' I said. 'I do hope that means you mistrust him less.'

'Not at all,' replied Regina calmly. 'I simply felt it would lessen the gossip. After all, a Fairfax should stay at the Keep, or the villagers would imagine all kinds of mischief. Moreover,' she added as I went to go upstairs, 'it will mean I can keep an eye on him here. If he plans anything, I could not know of it from a distance.'

She moved smoothly away in the direction of the parlour, leaving me to wonder. How very cool and practical she was. And how much I still had to learn about the way her mind worked.

Changing out of the riding habit and into my best grey gown, I debated what to do next. Perhaps if Regina were still busy I could return to the writing room and have another discreet glimpse into the notebook hidden in the book shelves. From the dead Rachel's memories I could perhaps learn more of my inscrutable master, Mr. Damian.

As I was about to close my bedroom door behind me, I heard a flurry and a click. Glancing up towards the east wing I realised someone had closed the studded door hurriedly, as though anxious not to be seen. Curiosity overwhelmed me. Not Damian or Regina, evidently, for both had a perfect right to be in the forbidden wing; neither would hide away quickly.

I tiptoed quietly to the door and opened it. The dusty corridor stretched away before me, deserted and silent. I moved forward a few paces, then stopped when I saw the black cat crouched near the door of the Rose Room. It looked up at me momentarily, its eyes baleful and malevolent, then turned its attention to the floor, and it began licking hungrily.

Nausea sprang to my throat when I recognised what it lapped with such satisfaction. Large droplets of red substance glistened in the gloom, and I recognised blood. I turned sharply back, slamming the nail-studded door after me.

As ever in this house, questions seethed in my mind. Whose blood? Had the cat, whose savagery I knew for myself, attacked someone? And whom? Visions of Regina's scarred face floated before me. Had someone else now been marked by the cat whose presence seemed more than natural?

Gathering my courage I moved slowly back towards the

door. As I did so it opened suddenly, and Rosie, cloaked and with damp hair clinging to her face, hurried past me. I recovered quickly.

'Miss Regina has been looking for you, Rosie,' I said to the quickly retreating figure heading towards the main staircase. She paused but did not turn. 'She has need of you to prepare a guest room.'

Her voice came back to me, strained and diffident. 'I've been delayed. I'll go to her straightaway.' And she hurried downstairs. But from the brief glimpse I had had of her as she passed me, I had seen she was not marked. The cat had not attacked her, at any rate.

For once I did not have long to wait for answers to the questions that troubled me. Unwittingly, at lunch, Regina answered two of them. She was chatting about Damian and his lifelong concern for dumb creatures.

'Though he takes little concern in the running of the estate, he does insist that no gin-traps may be laid by any of our tenants,' she told me. 'Snares he will permit, provided they cause no pain. And he is very hard on poachers who defy him.'

I nodded. I remembered his encounter with Ramsden in the copse.

'But he really carries his concern too far. Do you know, he even brought home an injured rabbit and insists on nursing it himself in his room. I tried to persuade him to leave it in the stables, but he would not.'

Of course! The bloodstains I saw were those of the hapless creature. They were near Damian's door, and the hind leg had been nearly severed. I still shuddered as I remembered the cat's relish as it licked at the floor, especially when I remembered what Uncle Eustace had said. There was no such cat, he said. Only an idle rumour of the maids, about an evil spirit guarding Rachel's room. Nevertheless I was relieved that the blood had no more sinister significance.

Regina's tone changed slightly as she went on, changing the subject. 'By the way, I believe you rode out up to the Abbey again this morning? Do you find its historic atmosphere interesting?'

Though the words were spoken lightly, I could detect, I

thought, a deeper significance beneath. And how did she know where I had ridden? In a flash I knew. Rosie had told her. Richard had been right when he sensed we were watched – Rose had been the unseen watcher, and Rose had reported to Regina.

And yet she had been back here at the Keep when I rode back, hiding in the east wing corridor. She could barely have had the time to get back so quickly, even if she had run all the way. And I could hardly have missed seeing her on the barren moorland. More questions now puzzled me. But Regina was awaiting an answer.

'Indeed I do find it an interesting spot,' I replied coolly. 'And I was not alone. Mr. Richard was there admiring the ruin too.'

Her eyelids did not flicker as she murmured 'Indeed?' I guessed she had known that too from Rosie. But why? Why should Regina, who professed to like and trust me, set a maidservant to spy on me? I decided to mention Rosie's name, to watch her reaction.

'I see Rose did turn up this morning after all, though somewhat late. I told her you had need of her.'

'Ah, yes.' This time Regina's eyelids did flicker before she went on. 'She was delayed. Her mother was not well. But she has now completed the preparations for Richard, so all is well.'

After lunch she went to her room, declaring she had a slight headache. It was suspicious of me, perhaps, but I guessed she wanted to avoid further talk of Rose. I felt a little unhappy that she might have set the girl to spy on me. After all, what was there to hide? And I felt hurt that, after all her talk of trust, she could not trust me enough to tell me the truth.

However, now that Regina was in her room, the coast was clear for me to return to my illicit reading in the writing room, for no one else was likely to disturb me there. Uncle Eustace rarely left his domain, and Damian was probably completely absorbed with ministering to the sick rabbit.

As my fingers slid between the books to withdraw the exercise book, I could not resist glancing about me to make sure that the wretched cat was not watching me once more, ready to spring at me as it had done when last I ventured to probe into Rachel's diary. But I was alone. I seated myself by the lamp and began to read at random.

'Such power, such suppressed strength I can sense in him! I have made up my mind. Others have found me desirable, and so shall he. I shall not rest until I have him completely in my power.'

The poor girl had evidently fallen wildly in love with Damian from the very outset. That she had succeeded in gaining his love I knew, for his tormented grief was still evident for all to see. I settled myself more comfortably to read on. Guilt niggled me just a little that I was spying on their love, but curiosity and sympathy brushed guilt aside.

I turned over a few pages. 'It is not so difficult,' the childish hand scrawled, 'I told him I had great need of his help for I am so troubled. He was kind and patient, encouraging me to confide. So I whispered my woes, my fears that I am wicked and sinful, and I saw the sadness cloud his beautiful dark eyes. He told me I am not wicked, else I would not fear it. He bade me come and talk whenever I wished.'

I smiled sadly. Poor little thing, to fret so over her probably very minor misdemeanors. Evidently she wished for perfection so as to be worthy of him. The next few words disabused me of this idea.

'So now I have the freedom, both of him and of my family, to visit him and talk as often as I wish. Now is my chance. A low voice and husky, tremulous words affect him visibly. It will not take long.'

The scheming little minx! But I could not help being amused. It was a typically feminine wile, to pretend distress to attract a man's attention. I turned a few more pages. A quick dip into the little book here and there would have to suffice, for I had no way of telling how long I would remain undisturbed.

'He is patience personified as he listens to my girlish confidences, patience combined with fortitude, for I am certain it demands much of his self-control not to attempt to console me. I muster tears to my eyes, gazing at him mournfully as I bewail my sins, and now and again I even sway as though physically affected by my woes, weak and in need of help. I can see his dark eyes moisten. Soon he will raise a hand to comfort, and then he is mine.'

I flicked over a couple of pages. Here the handwriting grew large and angular in its excitement.

'At last! Success is mine! He is mine! It needed but the balmy gentleness of a June evening and birdsong in the copse to complete the idyll, and he yielded to me. I should have thought of it before. Who, and especially a man from the cold, bleak northern moors, could resist the beauty of our Kentish countryside on a soft June night?'

Kent. I was mildly surprised. Somehow I had visualised the growing passion of Rachel for Damian as taking place here on the wild Yorkshire moors, not in the far southern meadows of Kent. I read on, anxious to learn of their first kiss.

'My father would be furious were he to know what occurred in the hedgerow of his beloved Daisy Lea. Damian touched my face to reassure. Within moments he was touching my hair, my neck, my lips.

'What followed was bliss. He was not to know, as I guided his trembling fingers, that I had been tutored well before. Frenzies of passion shook him, and he whispered words of undying love such as I had imagined for weeks.'

My fingers trembled too as I laid the book aside. My cheeks burned with embarrassment, for I had read more than I intended. A first, tremulous kiss I had anticipated, but Rachel's words implied that far more had befallen. I felt like a spy, a voyeur on some forbidden scene. A footstep in the corridor outside made me leap guiltily, snatch up the book, and hastily replace it at the back of the bookshelf.

Sitting there, tense and shamefaced, I heard the footsteps approach, bustle past the door, and die away down the corridor. A door slammed and once again the Keep reverted to silence. For a few minutes I sat wondering, and then curiosity overcame guilt. I retrieved the dog-eared little book from the shelves and read eagerly.

'Without a shadow of a doubt he is mine, inflamed with passion for me! Together we have lain as lovers in the stillness of the night, and shall do soon again! I have won! Whatever allegiance he has sworn to others, it is refuted now and forever. Triumph is mine!'

I was puzzled. Rachel's words were those of a woman who has beaten a rival, not words of love. It was her pride that was satisfied, not her feeling for Damian.

Regina. Perhaps it was Regina she had beaten, exulting in having snatched Damian from his sister's possessive grasp. That would account for Regina's apparent dislike of the dead girl. But why should Regina be so jealous of her brother caring for another woman? It was very puzzling.

I let the book lie idly in my lap while I lay back in the chair and tried to visualise the scene. Kent, hot summer nights, and clandestine meetings in the orchard between the abrupt, wild-eyed Damian and the sultry black-haired beauty of the portrait. I must have dozed, for dusk was falling when I awoke. Replacing the book, I went upstairs to dress for dinner.

Richard would be at dinner. For once I abandoned my usual dark gown and selected a silver-grey satin one from among those Regina had given me. Mentally I tried to deny that I wanted to look my prettiest because a handsome young man would be there, but innate honesty compelled me to admit it. Would I have taken such trouble to brush my hair till it glistened, or pinch my cheeks and lips to acquire a becoming glow, had he not been there?

He was sitting by the fire with Regina, his long legs sprawled across the hearth rug towards the fire when I went down. Damian, to my surprise, was also seated there, slouching moodily and listening to Regina and the guest converse.

'My dear, how enchanting you look!' She held out her hands to welcome me. Richard leapt to his feet, a slow smile touching his lips, but Damian sat unmoved. Regina turned her bright smile on Richard. I was pleased to see that she too had put on a pretty gown, the one I had just made for her. It fitted her trim figure admirably, and its violet shade became her colouring. She almost seemed to have forgotten the scar as she talked in a lively fashion.

Richard listened attentively and replied with grace. It was surprising how a gentleman's attention could restore a woman's confidence, making her blossom, and I watched

Regina with pleasure. Like him or not, she undoubtedly was deriving benefit from his presence.

When the dinner gong sounded, Regina took Richard's arm. 'Damian, pray lead Amity in to dinner,' she directed her sulking brother. Damian rose and held out his arm to me coldly. I laid my fingertips on his forearm, conscious of the intense dislike directed at me. But now I was not alone. Richard was here to share part of Damian's misanthropy. I glanced at him, his fair head bent towards Regina's dark one to listen, and felt a bond with him.

Ellen poured the soup. Regina leaned across the table towards Richard. 'Do tell us about America, Richard. Tell us about your life there. I regret I am very ignorant about your country, though I do know you have had a civil war there.'

I saw Richard's smile fade quickly. For a moment he paused before answering. 'What shall I tell you, Regina? I grew up on my father's farm in Virginia. I was an only child, for my mother died at my birth. Now my father is dead too.'

'What kind of farm?' It was Damian who spoke, unexpectedly and harshly. I saw Regina's quick flush of embarrassment, for Damian's suspicion was evident. Richard answered calmly.

'A fruit farm. The Shenandoah Valley is lush grassland and very fertile. Father also kept some sheep on the Appalachian foothills, though most other farmers there raised turkeys.'

'And did the war have any effect on you?' Regina's tone was deliberately calm to allay the tension in the air.

'Yes, ma'am. The dividing line between the north and the south, the Unionists and the Confederates, ran right through our valley. There was always fighting.'

I could see the horror in Regina's eyes, the thought of how she would feel if warring were to take place over her beloved Mallory lands. Despite her cousin's evident reluctance she pressed him.

'Did you see the fighting? Was your farm harmed?'

Richard's cornflower blue eyes darkened to the murky shade of the sea when a storm threatens. He pushed away his soup plate and sat back.

'My father was ambitious for me. He sent me away from

the farm to study in Baltimore. He wanted me to become a doctor. It was last spring, while I was away taking my final examinations, that General Sheridan sent his troops into the Shenandoah Valley to punish the people, to lay waste the land and loot and plunder. Our farm was burned to the ground, the fruit destroyed, and our sheep slaughtered. I heard of the general's campaign, but could not get back across the lines in time.'

I stared at Richard, aghast. How terrible to find one's home destroyed and feel powerless – more than that, feel guilty for being absent too. My sympathy went out to him, the more so since he did not seek sympathy.

Damian picked up the silver carving knife and fork and began attacking the joint of roast brisket Ellen had placed before him. He severed a couple of thick slices and laid them on a plate which Regina passed to me.

'So, having lost your farm you came here,' remarked Damian. Though his voice was low there was venom in his tone. Regina passed the next plate to Richard. Ellen, placing the tureens of boiled potatoes and carrots before us, stared at Richard. Regina gave her a sharp look, and the maid hurried back to the sideboard to fetch the gravy boat. Richard did not speak, and Damian continued hacking the joint savagely. I watched the juices, pink with blood, trickling from the joint, and held my breath.

'What a tragedy,' said Regina, helping herself to potatoes. 'And I believe you said your father is now dead too. He must have been heartbroken to see his life's work ruined.'

Richard laid aside his knife and fork. 'It was not heart-break that killed him, ma'am. He did not have time to feel the pain.'

Damian stabbed the carving fork viciously into the joint and pushed the meat away. 'What does it matter what he died of? You lost your father and your farm and decided to come here, isn't that so?'

'Indeed. I had no wish to remain in the valley I had once loved so well. There was nothing now to keep me there. I came to find my family, that is all.'

'And a new livelihood in Mallory estate.'

'No. I have a livelihood as a doctor.'

103

Regina cut in quickly. 'I am so sorry about your father, Richard. How did he die?'

The coldness of the haunted look that came over her cousin's face evoked my pity. It was evident he did not care to remember what he was obliged to tell us now. The meal lay forgotten in front of him.

'Father's sympathies were with the Confederates. On occasions he took part in irregular cavalry missions, harassing Sheridan's troops. When the Unionists ravaged the valley, they made short shrift of those they discovered.'

'What happened to him?' It was my own voice, an involuntary whisper. He turned a wretched face towards me.

'They hanged him. When I rode in two days later and searched the ruins, I found him at last, strung up on one of our own apple trees. The rooks were picking his body.'

Not a sound, not a movement stirred the room. I saw the wide eyes, and Ellen, arrested like a statue, by the sideboard. Pity flooded me. After a few seconds, Damian snarled.

'Ha! You think to arouse our sympathy, do you? Then think again, cousin. You shall not take Mallory in place of your lost patrimony!'

'Hush, Damian!' It was Regina who spoke, soothing and remonstrating together. 'The matter is in the hands of the lawyers. Mr. Boyd will be here shortly and no doubt some agreement can be reached.'

'No compromise!' Damian shouted. 'Mallory is ours and will remain so! This foreign interloper shall have none of it!'

Richard rose quietly. 'Nor do I wish it. I told you I came in search of my family only. If you prefer, I shall leave Mallory Keep now and never cross your threshold again, nor shall you ever hear of me again. If that is what you wish, speak now and I shall go.'

I stared helplessly at Damian's thunderous face and Regina's troubled one and felt the bottom had dropped out of my world.

CHAPTER SEVEN

'For here's a young and sweating devil here
That commonly rebels.'
– Shakespeare, *Othello*

How we reached the end of that miserable meal I cannot remember. I only know there was an embarrassed stiffness in the air, an atmosphere almost tangible in its potency. I noticed that Richard declined the stewed fruit and custard. Damian's outburst had robbed us all of appetite.

After dessert, Regina laid aside her napkin. 'Now, Amity and I will leave you gentlemen to your port,' she annouced, pushing back her chair. Richard rose at once to pull out her chair and help her rise. Damian making no move, I rose unaided.

Damian glowered at Richard. 'I do not wish to drink,' he muttered.

'Nor I, as it happens,' Richard replied smoothly. 'With your permission, cousin Regina, I should prefer to retire early.'

'But of course. And Amity, what shall you do?' Regina's dark eyes betrayed her concern. I knew she did not wish me to stay with Richard while she was occupied with Damian, but it seemed clear she wanted to converse alone with her brother.

'I think I too shall retire early.' It was the last thing I wanted to do, to sleep, when every fibre of me was taut with tension. But I saw relief in Regina's eyes as I said good-night and withdrew, leaving Richard to make his salutations.

Rose was hovering by the green baize-covered door to the servants' area, a silver tray on the table beside her. I saw the two glasses and the decanter of port.

'You are here late, Rose,' I remarked. 'If you are waiting to serve the gentlemen's port, they have decided not to take it tonight.'

'I want to see t'mistress,' Rose replied, twitching her apron nervously. 'I mun see her soon.'

'Can't it wait until morning? I think she is still talking with the master and Mr. Richard.'

'No, it can't. I'll wait a bit.'

I shrugged and moved on up the stairs. There was no sound of a door closing behind me. Richard had evidently decided to stay.

Outside the writing room I hesitated, deliberated, and went in. Curiosity led me back to the dog-eared little book on the shelf, and by the light of the oil lamp still burning on the chenille-covered table, I read.

'They are sending him away!' the erratic handwriting protested in alarm. 'He told me today that he has been discovered. Now, in disgrace, they are sending him away, back to the cold north. What shall I do? I cannot lose him now!'

The handwriting grew smaller and less volatile on the following page. 'He does not seem to care what happens to him now. I expected tears, but he walks hollow-eyed and silent. He grows cold, I fear, and that I cannot tolerate. I will not give him up. I shall follow him to the ends of the earth, whatever my family may say. He is mine, and even the grave shall not part us.'

Such devotion, I thought, and yet she spoke no word of love for Damian, only of possession, as though he were a treasured trinket. As I went to turn the page a sudden voice outside the door startled me. It was Regina.

'Very well then, Rose. Come and I shall write a message to him. It will only take a moment.'

I barely had time to leap to my feet and rush towards the only hiding place in sight before the door opened. I pulled the heavy velvet drapes together and stood, frozen, hoping Regina would not notice the movement. Fortunately the room was lit by the solitary lamp on the table.

I heard rustling, and then the scratching I recognised as pen on paper. I also heard Rose sniffing as she waited. I hardly dared breathe in the silence lest they heard me. At last I heard crackling. Regina folding paper, I guessed.

'Here, give this to Ben at once, and tell him above all else he must be silent as the grave. There are inquisitive minds in the Keep, as you know. Make haste, now.'

'Aye, miss. Tha'll see to t'east wing, then?' I heard Rosie's fading voice as she retreated.

'Of course. Now be off with you.'

The door closed as I heard two pairs of footsteps receding. Hesitantly I ventured out from the curtains, the book still clutched in my hand. For the moment I had lost interest in its contents, curiosity aroused in me as to why Regina should have secret arrangements with the bailiff and a maidservant. And how was the east wing involved?

I knew without a shadow of a doubt that I was one of the inquisitive minds she was anxious to elude, and probably Richard was the other. Did Damian know of whatever intrigue she was up to? Loyalty to Regina told me I should forget what I had overheard, but curiosity, always my greatest fault according to my aunt, was uppermost.

'Curiosity killed the cat,' Aunt Cecily would pronounce solemnly, 'and it is not a sign of genteel breeding to ask so many questions, Amity. I know some people say an enquiring mind is a sign of intelligence, but still, it is not ladylike. You really must learn to control yourself.'

So, making a firm effort at self-control, I reseated myself by the lamp and began to read. But even Rachel's tearful outpourings, about how desolute the village was now Damian was gone, failed to hold my attention. My mind kept wandering to the east wing and wondering about its significance. Why was Regina anxious to keep strangers away from the disused wing, and what was she to 'see to' there, as Rosie put it?

At last, unable to concentrate on the plaintive Rachel's words, I put the book back on the shelf, and making sure there was no one about in the corridor, I went back to my room. It was only as I was divesting myself of the pretty gown I had put on for dinner, in a vain effort to catch Mr. Richard's eye, that I made a sudden decision.

I would go and investigate the east wing. Not just the

corridor where Damian slept, and the Rose Room with its strange cat guard lying still and silent, but the corridor beyond. Feeling guilty but excited, I pulled on my own dark merino gown. It would be less conspicuous in the half-light than the gleaming evening gown.

I was glad of its warmth when I entered the chill air beyond the studded door, carrying the candle from my bedside table. Swiftly and silently I moved along the passage, passing the door of the Rose Room apprehensively, lest the black cat should be lurking in the shadow. Damian's door was slightly ajar, and I could hear the sound of deep breathing within and felt relieved. He was sleeping soundly.

I edged on to the far end, past several more doors. By the light of the candle I could see a flight of stone steps leading up to a door on a gallery to my right. The dust did not lie so thickly on the steps, I noticed, and then I realized that footprints from the gallery down to the last door in the corridor indicated frequent passage. This last room and the one up on the gallery seemed to be in constant use, despite the crumbling state of the winding stairs.

I tried the handle of this last door. It yielded silently. I held the candle aloft and saw a small room, not so large as my own, and with dust-sheets over pieces of furniture. I went in and raised a dust-sheet curiously. Beneath it lay an old-fashioned wicker cradle, and I realised this was probably once a nursery. To investigate further in safety, I closed the door quietly.

Under other dust-sheets I found old velvet-covered chairs and a tall cheval glass, as old-fashioned as the oak-panelled room with its great stone fireplace. Both the chamber and its furnishings left one in no doubt that this wing was far older than the rest of the Keep.

A scratching sound near the fireplace startled me. Raising my candle higher, I could see nothing. A mouse in the wainscoting, probably. But when I heard footsteps approaching I was truly alarmed, and blowing out my candle, I darted under the dust-sheet covering the tall looking-glass. I had no sooner concealed myself than the door opened and a soft swish of skirts told me that it was a woman who came in.

Scarcely daring to breathe, I was nevertheless aware of a

perfume, a mingled scent of lemon and rose water, and I recognised it as Regina's scent. I heard her cross the small room towards a fireplace, pause, and then I heard a whirring sound. To my amazement, she spoke.

'Are you there?' My heart thudded in alarm, for I believed she knew of my presence, but another voice murmured. 'Good,' said Regina calmly. 'Then do your work as swiftly and silently as you may. You need not fear for my brother. I have given him a sleeping potion and he will sleep soundly. Nevertheless, it is imperative you be silent.'

A voice grunted assent. 'Before you go,' Regina went on, 'let me show you how the mechanism operates. See, this leaf here. Press it, that is all. You know how to operate it from within. Now go and bid the others to take extreme care.'

Footsteps moved, and then the whirring sound again. Then Regina left the little room and I emerged from under the dust-sheet, wondering at what I had overheard.

A secret passage, I thought, as I relit my candle with a lucifer from the box I had fortuitously picked up from my bedside table and placed in my pocket. I felt my heart thump with excitement. I remembered Regina's talk of secret passages when I had first come, but I little thought them to be still in use. Moreover, I was burning with curiosity to know why she should make use of such a passage.

It must have been Rose or Ben to whom she spoke, and I knew already she had some kind of clandestine business with them, but what, and why? I stared at the great stone fireplace, the direction from which the sound had come, and wondered.

A leaf, she had said. Great scrolls of vine leaves looped around the fireplace, carved in the stonework. Intrigued, I fingered each left in turn. None of them seemed to differ from the rest.

Turning my attention to the oak panels on each side of the fireplace, I tried to detect where one of them seemed movable, since the sound I had heard was undoubtedly the sound of a panel sliding aside. Once again they all seemed alike. Disappointed, I returned to the vine leaves.

My fingers probed gently. One leaf, the third from the left end of the mantelshelf, seemed smoother than the others. I pressed it gently. Again I heard the whirring sound, and a panel at the side of the fireplace began to move, slowly and ponderously. I stared in excitement, watching the gap grow into a space some four feet high and eighteen inches wide before the sound ceased.

All was silent in the darkness within. Advancing cautiously, my heart thumping with anticipation of I knew not what, I held my candle out to inspect the interior of the opening.

It was a tiny room, no more than six feet square, with wooden floorboards and stone, windowless walls. Disappointment surged in me, for there was nothing to be seen, not a chair or anything.

A priest's hole, without a doubt. Old houses in England frequently contained such discreet hiding places for Catholic priests in the old days of religious persecution, and the staunchly Catholic Fairfax family undoubtedly had helped such hunted priests. Sometimes the poor unfortunate creatures, I had heard, had lain and starved in such places, unable to escape while the tormentors lingered, and many had died agonising deaths.

But others had escaped. I remembered once reading of an old mansion whose priest-hole had been connected by a secret passageway to the house's stables, and the account of the number of priests whose lives had been saved as a result. This tiny room in which I stood must have such a secret exit, for Regina's companion of a few minutes ago had not come or gone by the nursery door.

I held by candle close to each wall in turn, but could find nothing. Then I turned my attention to the floor. A notch in one floorboard soon gave the clue – of course, a trapdoor to a passage below. Before raising the trap, I realised I must close the panel into the nursery, if I was not to be discovered. I found a small lever which, when I pulled it, caused the panel to whir back into its original position. I hoped fervently it would work as smoothly again when I returned.

Raising the small trapdoor, I saw a flight of toughly hewn stone steps leading down into a dark void. Gathering my courage and clutching my skirts I descended slowly.

There were only eight steps, and below, a passage cut from

the rock. I followed it cautiously, and felt a slight breeze ruffle my hair. I shaded my candle with my hand and moved carefully on.

The passage was long and narrow, descending gently as I walked. On I went, expecting at any moment to find a door or steps which would lead me into the Keep stables. But on went the passage, dropping more rapidly now, and dwindling in height until I had almost to crouch at times.

The passage curved suddenly, and I saw to my surprise that it was joined by another before continuing. I hesitated, wondering which of the two directions to take, and decided on the further one, for the nearer one seemed to have come roughly parallel to my own. Perhaps there would be other intersections further along. To make certain I did not mistake the way on my return, I stooped to pick up a piece of rock, and with it I scratched a mark on the exit of my passage.

After a time the way began to rise again, and I began to feel a little nervous. By now I must be far beyond the stables, beyond the grounds of the Keep too. But underground I had no means of telling in which direction from the Keep I was travelling, and I began to feel confused and apprehensive. Suppose Regina's companion discovered me and was angry. Suppose it was a stranger who did not know I was her friend. I had been reckless to venture into this place alone and without telling anyone, for the way was slippery and uneven. If I were to fall and hurt myself, I might never be found.

The shiver that ran up my spine was not only of apprehension. It was cold down here, dank and clammy. I was glad at least that I was wearing my warm merino gown and not the flimsy one I had worn to dinner. But even so, the damp air struck coldly.

I stopped suddenly. Two things impinged on my senses at the same time – I heard a sound, far-off and indistinct, but nonetheless I was sure it was a voice, and at the same moment my nose registered a scent. I sniffed. It was tangy – salt, like seaweed. The sea, of course! My passage was leading towards the beach!

And it was not far away, I could tell by the way the candle's flame began to dance jerkily in the breeze. I crept forward, and as I rounded the next curve of the passage the flame was suddenly extinguished. For a moment I stood, confused and frightened, and then my eyes grew accustomed to the dark. Ahead of me I could see a dark grey circle of light. The end of the passage was in sight.

I felt my way along the wall until the passage broadened out sharply into a cave. And the noise I could hear was the splash of sea waves close to hand.

And voices. I stiffened sharply, clinging to the rock wall in an effort to remain invisible as men's voices came closer, accompanied by a thumping sound and the flickering light of winging lanterns. I thanked Providence for my dark gown as I closed my eyes and listened.

Crash! A man's voice sword loudly. 'Mind where tha' drop them cases, man! Tha damn near had my foot then.'

I opened my eyes. Two figures stood silhouetted in the cave entrance. I fancied the voice was familiar but could not place it. I was far more concerned that they should not see me.

A third figure joined the silhouette tableau. 'Get a move on, then, Ramsden. We haven't got all night, tha knows.' I recognised instantly the voice of Regina's bailiff. So it was Ben Jagger with whom she had some kind of clandestine business. I prayed all the harder that I would remain undetected, for he and Rose had been warned to keep me in ignorance of whatever was going on. And I fancied the dour redheaded bailiff could be ruthless if occasion demanded it.

'Now get off to Keep Farm as fast as tha can, and take care,' I heard Jagger admonish.

'Aye.' And Ramsden, the man I had met in the copse, turned to go. Not, as I had expected, towards the cave entrance, but towards me! I froze against the rock face, half-crouched, and grateful for the pile of rocks that lay between me and him. As he passed, I could see by the light of his lantern that he led a mule, its back loaded with packs and its feet strangely noiseless. Then I saw that its hooves were bound with cloth.

Man and mule passed close by me, heading towards the passage where I had come. My mind raced. If Ramsden was heading for Keep Farm, a mile inland, then that must be where the intersecting passage led.

112

'Now it's time tha went,' Jagger said to the remaining man. 'Call Rose down. Tell her I'm off.' The man nodded and went out, leaving Jagger to pace the cave. Fortunately for me he seemed deep in thought, and when the slight figure of a girl came running breathlessly into the cave he picked up a lantern which stood on a rock ledge.

'Make haste now. Were all clear?'

'Aye, Ben. Nowt in miles.'

'Come on, then. Take this.'

The two figure passed by me towards the passage and I could see that each carried a package. I listened, my heart thumping, until their footsteps had faded, leaving me only the sound of the sea outside.

For long moments I crouched there, too fearful to move lest one of the others outside should return. But time passed and no sound came but the even rhythm of the waves, crashing and breaking. At last I plucked my courage to emerge from my hiding place.

I could not go back along the velvet-black passage without a light. I tried several times to relight my candle, but the lucifers in my pocket had somehow become damp. My gown was damp from where I had clung to the wet rock face.

There was no other way but to go out on to the beach and scramble up to the cliff path. Cautiously I picked my way out over the rocks, clutching my candlestick and useless candle. Not a soul was to be seen. With a huge sigh of relief I looked for the easiest way up the cliff to the path that would lead me back to the Keep.

There was no easy way, but I found a slope less steep and jagged than the surrounding area and began my climb. It was difficult and painful, for I kept slipping on the loose stones and catching my ankle against sharp points of rock. Despite the cold and my soggy gown, I soon began to perspire with the effort of the climb, panting for breath but determined to keep going.

I made it at last, reaching the level of the familiar old cliff path with great relief. But at the same moment a curious prickle started between my shoulder blades. I had the uncanny sensation that I was being watched.

It was a clear night, though no moon shone. Looking about

113

me I could see no one, only the odd wheeling, screeching gull whose sleep I had disturbed on my climb. I recalled the night I arrived in Mallory, and how the gulls had taken to screaming flight while I had watched dim shapes on the beach down there. I knew now it must have been Jagger and Ramsden who, as tonight, were engaged in some nefarious activity. But even now I did not know what it was.

Stumbling along the cliff path in a hurry to reach the warmth of my bed, I deliberated how I was going to explain away my ringing the doorbell at such an hour. I dreaded the inscrutable stare on Mrs. Garner's face, and realised that perhaps, through her, Rose and Ben Jagger would come to hear of my being out on the cliff at night. And perhaps they would guess . . .

A clatter behind me startled me out of my wits. I turned, terrified, and saw the huge black shape of a cloaked figure on horseback bearing down on me. The path being barely wide enough for him to pass me, I shrank against the low stone wall furthest from the cliff edge, barely able to suppress a shriek of alarm. The cloak flapped wildly nearer, the black horse's eyeballs staring like a demon's. It was Damian, I was sure of it, just as he had galloped down on me that first night. Not sleeping after all, as Regina had said, but awake and here, and doubtless furious. . . .

I could almost feel the great black stallion's hot breath on my face. I closed my eyes, near to fainting. The creature plunged, a great strong arm came down and circled round my waist, lifting me clear of the ground and up on the horse's back.

'Fool!' a voice roared in my ear, and I cringed. The arm held me fast, and timid as I was of my precarious situation, I tried to loosen the tenacious hold. Somehow the thought of Damian's touch was distasteful to me. This man, so unpredictable of mood and given to violent outbursts of temper, terrified me. I wriggled hard.

'Sit still, can't you? We'll be home in a second.'

It wasn't Damian's voice. In amazement I turned to stare. Instead of the scowling black eyes and taut lips of Damian Fairfax, I was staring at the set, fair features of cousin Richard!

114

It was more than relief that flooded my veins. It was a warm, secure feeling that all was well. I did not stop to question why Richard Fairfax should be out on the cliffs at such an hour, or on Damian's horse. It was enough that he was here, strong and vital and so reassuring. I let myself sink back against the warm strength of his body, and was distinctly disappointed when, having cantered up the gravel drive, he swung out of the saddle and lifted me down.

Ignoring me completely, he marched up to the door and rang the bell, repeatedly and insistently. Unlike me, he evidently did not fear explanations.

Mrs. Garner appeared at last, with sleep-dulled eyes and her hair in rag rollers.

'Why, Mr. Richard! And Miss Lucas!' she exclaimed, opening the door wider.

Richard pushed it open and marched in. 'Miss Lucas is soaked. I think a hot bath is called for, Mrs. Garner.'

Her eyes widened. 'No, no, it's really not necessary,' I interpolated quickly, reluctant to cause a fuss with all the boiling and fetching of pails of water in the middle of the night. 'I'll get straight into bed with a hot water bottle.'

Despite his protests and Mrs. Garner's offer to see to the bath, I managed to escape and get safely to my room. My bed felt like a feather heaven after that cold wet cave, and though I wanted to lie and think, to wonder why Richard was on the cliffs, what Jagger and Rose and Ramsden were up to, where Regina fitted into all this – I could not. Sleep overcame me within minutes.

I did not see Richard Fairfax the next day until he, Regina, and I gathered in the dining room for lunch. I had resolved not to mention last night's encounter unless he did, and wondered how on earth I was going to explain my nocturnal sortie if Regina were to hear of it, either from him or from Mrs. Garner. Richard, however, did not mention it. He chatted politely and Regina answered distantly, as though preoccupied. I kept my eyes downcast to my plate and remained silent.

'I walked down into the village to watch the fishermen put out this morning,' Richard remarked. No reply came from either of us, and he went on. 'The villagers seemed rather

115

agitated, and I gathered from snippets I overheard that there was a revenue cutter cruising off Carnelian Point last night.'

I glanced up quickly, awareness of the implication of his remark beginning to glimmer in my brain. Regina helped herself to more potatoes.

'That is not unusual, cousin Richard. The revenue men have had to keep a close eye on this coast for many a long year.'

'Smugglers, eh?' said Richard with a smile.

'Once there were, a thriving colony hereabouts. Little enough occurs nowadays, I imagine.'

Little enough, but nevertheless it did still happen, I realised, and if I was not mistaken, that was what Ben Jagger and his fishermen allies were up to last night. Mules, packages – yes, that was it!

Then I remembered Regina in the nursery, talking to someone in the priest hole. She must have known of the venture, colluded in it, and I was certain of it when I recalled her earlier conversations with Ben Jagger, like that time in the arbor when they spoke of 'tonight'.

I could laugh at myself now for my slowness of mind. To think I had suspected Regina of having an affair with her bailiff! The next question that crossed my mind – but why? Why should Regina collaborate with the village folk in smuggling, she who in every other respect appeared so law-abiding and honest? It didn't make sense.

But now I understood many other things which had puzzled me – why 'inquisitive' folk such as Richard and myself had to be kept in ignorance, why Rose had lingered long after she should have gone home, to give urgent messages to her mistress. And the strange sounds of shuffling, and the woman's laughter I had heard echoing in the east wing – of course, they had been moving the smuggled cantraband, and the voice was Rose's, she stood lookout, just as she did on the cliffs last night.

Satisfied I had solved part of the problem which had been perplexing me, I turned my attention back to the conversation between Regina and Richard.

'Have you any plans for the afternoon, Regina?' Richard

was asking politely, refolding his linen napkin and inserting it in the silver ring before him. 'I thought perhaps we might ride together and you could show me around the estate.'

Regina shook her head firmly. 'This afternoon I shall be occupied with business, but you ride of you wish. Take Damian's horse, Vulcan, again, to survey your domains.'

I saw his look of surprise. So Regina did know that Richard had been out in the night and on Damian's horse. I wondered whether she also knew about me. She had a very efficient intelligence service, it seemed.

Richard adroitly ignored the one implication of her remark to take up the other. 'Mallory is not mine, Regina, nor is it likely to be. I would not wish us to become enemies over a quarrel which does not exist. Mallory is yours, and shall stay so, as Damian says.'

'That remains to be seen, and it is that which occupies me today. Mr. Boyd, our lawyer, is coming from York, and I expect him shortly. Thereafter I may know better how we stand.'

As she rose from the table, Richard rose too, moving swiftly round the table to take her hands. 'However it may turn out legally, I hope we may still remain friends, Regina. To have family means more to me than possessions.'

I rose to slip away unobtrusively, but before I closed the door I saw the colour that suffused Regina's cheeks, making the scar stand out darkly. Whatever defences she might try to build up against her cousin, surely she could not help but succumb to his charm, I thought. I at least was convinced of his honest desire to be a friend.

Some time later, as I passed the drawing room on my way out for a walk in the spring sunshine, I saw, through the open door, Regina and two men seated at the table. Mr. Boyd and his clerk, I adjudged, for the younger man was producing a sheaf of papers from a portfolio to pass to his senior. Their two heads bent close together over the table, the one large and rounded with greased blond hair, and the other small and shrivelled with a grizzled tonsure, made me think inadvertently of a melon and a grapefruit. And Regina's smooth black coiffed head was a ripe Victoria plum.

Ellen came to the door and I heard Regina call to her.

117

'Bring tea for us, Ellen, and then make sure we are not disturbed.'

'Yes, ma'am.' Ellen passed me with a hint of a smile, reaching the green baize door just as Rosie emerged, without her apron, and wearing a thick black woollen shawl over her slim young shoulders.

An idea seized me. 'Are you going down to the village, Rosie?' I asked her.

'Ay, miss. It's me afternoon off.'

'Then I'll walk down with you if I may.'

A light in her eye indicated suspicion or defensiveness, I could not tell which, but she evidently guessed my intention.

'I'll meet thee at t'side door, then. Us servants can't use t'front door,' she replied, turning away to re-enter the servants' area.

As I made my way out and round to the side of the Keep, I wondered if she had appeared in the vestibule intentionally to intercept me. But there was no reason for her to do so, I argued with myself. She had not known of my presence in the cave last night. But if she had wanted to discover what I knew, it must have taken her by surprise that it was I who contrived our tête-à-tête.

She was standing at the edge of the gravel path, nudging the turf with her toe when I reached her, her shawl drawn now over her head and only her worried little face visible. She turned to walk down towards the thorn hedge and I fell in beside her.

'What do you do on your afternoon off, Rosie?' I asked companionably.

'Oh, help me mam to do t'baking as a rule,' she murmured. 'We bake t'bread for t'family for t'week.'

'Are there many of you in your family?'

'Me mam, me, and three brothers.'

Her father was dead, evidently. 'What do your brothers do?'

'Fishermen, all on 'em.'

'I see.' I was learning that this was the way all the coast folk spoke, tersely, and with an admirable economy of words. No waste, no time for frills. It was the way they lived, thriftily and diligently. I was certain there was warmth under the

118

brusque exterior, and I was beginning to understand and respect their way of life.

Except for the smuggling. Somehow it seemed out of character for rough, honest folk to stoop to illegal trafficking, and I wondered at it. I skirted round the problem, debating how to broach the subject without giving too much away of what I knew. I picked my way down the rocky path as carefully as I picked the words I would use.

'Dost like Yorkshire?' Rosie interrupted my thoughts sharply. 'Dost like living here?'

'Yes, I do, Rose, but it's a strange place, very different from London.'

'Strange? How is it strange?' I could see the interrogative gleam in her eye. We were nearing the topic close to both our hearts.

'It's so – wild, and your ways are different from ours.'

'And tha doesn't understand 'em.'

'It's true, I don't. But I hope I shall come to understand.'

'And meantime, don't probe into what tha can't comprehend, miss. It's safest that way.'

'What do you mean, Rosie?'

'Folks can come to harm by meddling. Tha can get caught up wi' things tha cannot cope wi'. Best leave 'em alone.'

'Yes, Rose, you're right. And I could say the same to you.'

'What dost tha mean?' She glared at me, half angry, half alarmed. 'Art tha warning *me*?'

'It seems possible you could be getting involved in a matter you cannot handle,' I said cautiously. Her look was hard, challenging. I wanted to help without angering her.

A sudden hiss of indrawn breath made me forget my words completely, and I saw Rose stop suddenly and stand, pale and wide-eyed, staring down the path to the village.

'What is it, Rosie? What's wrong?'

'Oh, miss, I mun hurry!'

She darted off ahead of me, running and stumbling, and I was hard put to it to keep up with her. Below in the village I could see uniformed men walking up from the jetty towards the Silent Inn. Customs men, I guessed by the uniform, looking for contraband, and I understood Rose's agitation.

She raced downhill along the cobbled main street, past the

119

inn and up a small side passage to a neatly kept cottage with donkey-stoned steps. I ran after her, coming to a stop breathlessly behind her as a motherly grey-haired woman opened the door to her.

'Come in, lass. Who's that with thee?'

'Miss Lucas from t'Keep. Come in quick, miss, and shut t'door.'

The woman closed the door and turned questioningly. 'What's up, Rose?'

'T'preventive men, mam, they're at t'inn.'

'Go down t'yard and tell Sam, quick.'

Rose crossed the flagstoned floor to a rear door leading out into a yard. Her mother turned to face me.

'You Miss Fairfax's friend, then?'

'Her companion *and* her friend, I hope.'

She nodded, wisps of hair falling loose from the tight bun at the nape of her neck. 'Miss Fairfax has need of friends. Sit thee down there at t'fireside then, and I'll make us a pot o'tea.'

She busied herself drawing a humming kettle from the old black lead range and pouring its contents into a large brown earthenware teapot. In a moment Rose returned, her face still set and pale.

'Sam says all's well, and to see tha's got all safely stowed here.'

As she spoke a shadow crossed the window, momentarily blocking out the sunlight, and a heavy knock sounded on the cottage door. My heart thumped as I saw the two women exchange a startled look.

'Open t'door, Rose.'

Rose did as her mother bade, and as her slim young hand raised the latch, I heard Mrs. Pickering's gasp. She was staring at a wooden cask close by the scullery door. Instantly I realised the reason for her alarm. My heart sank as Rose stood back to let the two men in.

CHAPTER EIGHT

'Tell truth and shame the devil.'
—Shakespeare, *Henry IV*, Part I

'Can we come in?'

Two burly figures pushed past Rose, stooping to enter under the low stone lintel. Both broad and overwhelming in their uniform, the red-faced one doffed his cap at the sight of me.

'Afternoon, miss.'

Rose's stupor vanished. 'As tha can see, officer, we are entertaining a lady of quality today. Miss Lucas, from up at Mallory Keep, has obliged us by coming to take tea wi' us.'

Mrs. Pickering was still staring stupidly at the cask, unable to gather her wits as swiftly as Rose. Pity overwhelmed me. In a trice she would be caught, apprehended. Without stopping to reason, I moved.

'Indeed, Mrs. Pickering, but I fear we have talked so long that our tea may have gone cold in the pot. Please pour it out now, for I swear I am parched with thirst.'

As I spoke, I crossed the little room, keeping my voluminous skirts between the red-faced officer and the cask. As I reached it I turned, spreading my skirts wide, and sank down to sit on it as though it were a stool. To my relief my skirts draped over it completely.

'To be sure, miss. I'm right sorry,' said Mrs. Pickering, recovering her wits at last. 'I'll pour it now. Wilt take a cup wi' us, officer?'

'Thank you, no. We've work to do. Excuse us, miss, but we must have a look around.'

The younger, fair-haired customs officer looked decidedly disappointed at his senior's refusal. I fancied he liked the

121

look of young Rosie and would have welcomed the opportunity of becoming sociable with her. However, he took his disappointment stoically and began a systematic search of the little room. Pulling out drawers in the great mahogany sideboard against one wall, he made the china ornaments on it rattle precariously.

'Take care, lad,' Mrs. Pickering warned ominously.

The older officer prowled about the room, opening the iron door of the range oven and poking with his stick into the far depths of the fireplace.

'Tha'll find nowt there,' Mrs. Pickering remarked. He grunted and came over towards me. 'Art comfortable there, Mrs. Lucas?' my hostess asked.

'Beautifully,' I replied. 'And I've no intention of moving till I've had my tea.'

The officer took the hint, passed me by, and went out into the stone scullery. As Mrs. Pickering poured the dark brown liquid from the teapot and handed me my tea in a willow-patterned teacup, I could hear the clatter of iron pans in a stone sink. Mrs. Pickering snorted.

'He'll find nowt in my pans but a good beef broth for our supper tonight.'

The officer returned, jerking his head towards the back door. 'Have a look down t'yard, lad, and then we'll be off.'

The younger man darted out, returning a few moments later with an apologetic smile. No one had spoken in his absence. 'Nowt there but a fisherman flat on his back snoring in t'shed,' he said.

'That'll be our Sam, drunk again,' remarked Mrs. Pickering. 'I'll flay t'hide off his back when he wakes.'

Rose ventured forward, lowering her eyelids demurely at the young officer as she spoke. 'Shall I wake him, mam, and bring him in here to sleep it off?'

'Tha'll do nowt o't'sort! How much work dost reckon I could do i'my kitchen wi'that great lump of a lad stretched out i'my way? Let him lie where he is. It'll do him no harm.'

The older officer turned towards me. 'Then I reckon we'll be off. Sorry to have troubled you, miss.'

'Not at all, officer. Good day to you,' I replied with a smile. As the door closed behind them I saw the tension recede from the two women's faces, their taut expressions fading and their stiff attitudes softening. Mrs. Pickering nodded to me brusquely.

'I'm obliged to thee, Miss Lucas. Tha'd no call to help us but tha did, and I'm grateful.'

'Don't mention it,' I replied, my casual air belying the relief I felt. Rosie came shyly to my side.

'Mam's right. We're grateful, miss.'

'Then pour me another cup of tea, I beg you. I spilt most of this one in the saucer in my anxiety.' They both laughed nervously. Rosie poured a fresh cup and brought it to me.

'Then tha'll not tell on us? That cask o'brandy were for t'vicar, tha knows. Tha'd not rob him, would tha?'

'No, Rose. But I must tell you that I do not approve of dishonesty. Though I could not let you be caught this time, I would not help again if you persist in such wicked behaviour. I wonder that your mother permits it.'

Mrs. Pickering was staring at me, her eyes hard with challenge. 'What does a lady like thee know of it, may I ask?' she demanded harshly. 'Tha's never had to struggle to stay alive like us. It's devilish hard work to keep a family clothed and fed wi'out a man to provide. Since my Sam were taken by t'sea I've had to make what I could, how I could, for my children to eat. But then, what can a lass like thee know about hardship?'

'But they're all grown and working now, Mrs. Pickering, providing for you. Surely there's no cause for thievery,' I replied. Rose turned away, refilling the teapot with water from the kettle.

'Aye, well 'appen there's more to it than that,' Mrs. Pickering muttered. 'Best leave well alone, Miss Lucas, lest harm befall thee. I'd hate to see that happen.'

'Are you trying to frighten me?'

She stared into my eyes, her face close to my own. I could smell onions on her hands, remaining, no doubt, from preparing the evening broth. 'It would be well for thee to be frightened, lass. There's many wiser than thee hereabouts who stay deaf and dumb. Thee take heed and follow suit. Hear nowt, see nowt, say nowt. That way things'll be healthier for thee.'

123

I drained my cup and rose to put it down on the scrubbed deal table. The woman followed me to the door, but the girl stood silent by the fireplace.

'Tha'll not speak to Miss Fairfax about what tha knows, wilt tha, miss?' Mrs. Pickering demanded as she held the door open wide.

I bit back the quick response that since Miss Fairfax knew of and seemed to be implicated in their nocturnal activities, there seemed to be no harm in it. Instead I shook my head.

'I'm not saying as we're not grateful to thee, 'cause we are, and we'll think of it, if ever it comes to it, that tha did us a good turn. And I hope as tha'll call to take tea wi' us again.'

And suddenly I was outside on the scrubbed steps, the fresh-painted door shut firmly behind me. I was in a reflective mood as I climbed the cobbled main street up past the churchyard. The prevention men were still about; I could see two uniformed figures emerging from the Silent Inn, and I thought wryly that the place was aptly named, judging by their abject faces. They had learned nothing there.

I glanced through the lych-gate and wondered idly if I might not walk in the grass-grown churchyard for a little while, to pass the time before I was expected back at the Keep. It had sometimes entertained an idle hour in the past to wander in one of London's little churchyards and read the inscriptions on the graves, musing on the histories often revealed. A mother often lay in the grave where numerous offspring had led the way, many still babes in arms, and I had speculated as to how a woman could bear to give birth so often, only to lose so swiftly. There were many whose lives were far more hapless than mine.

Just inside the gate I turned aside to walk around the outer fringe of the graveyard. The headstones were mostly small and unpretentious, the blackened stone often making it difficult to read the words upon them. The one thing I noted was how often the same names appeared – the Redferns, the Pickerings, the Jaggers, the Ramsdens, and the Horsfalls, all names I had heard spoken, for they still lived in Mallory. Only of Fairfax was there no sign. Wherever the Catholic Fairfaxes lay, it was not here in the village churchyard.

By a straggling weed-grown path I went nearer to the church, from the further side I had not seen before. As I rounded the ancient grey stone of the church towards the front entrance, I saw the great mass of the Devil's Arrow rising before me. And I stopped. At its base were two men, one bending, and the other crouched on his haunches.

It was with a start of pleasure that I recognised them, the only men who had spoken kindly to me since I arrived in Mallory. The crouched figure was the Reverend Parmenter, gazing in concentration at something in his hand. The other, dressed for riding and leaning forward to inspect, was the tall figure of Richard Fairfax. He evidently heard my footfall on the gravel, for he straightened and smiled at my approach. A tremor rippled through me. I could still sense the warm strength of his hold on me last night on horseback on the cliffs.

'Good afternoon, Miss Lucas,' he said with that slow, easy drawl I found fascinating. 'I hope you are enjoying your walk.'

The vicar rose, beaming. 'Ah, Miss Lucas! A lovely day for a stroll, is it not? One feels the summer is almost here.'

He held forth his hand, not to shake mine, but to reveal what he held in his palm. 'And my day is made the happier since I have found this,' he added, his amiable face aglow with contentment.

I inspected the wriggling beetle with distaste. The Reverend turned to Richard. 'I am indeed indebted to you, sir, for drawing my attention to this specimen. Just think, I have sought long for just this to complete my collection, and there it was all the time in my own churchyard. Thank you kindly, Mr. Richard. I am delighted also to welcome another naturalist to Mallory, and I earnestly hope we shall spend many hours together.'

Richard laughed in deprecation. 'No naturalist I fear, sir, but I was brought up on a farm and came to know the creature well. Like you, I find them fascinating.'

'And beetles? Do you collect them?'

Richard shook his head, the fair curls gleaming in the sunlight. 'Our beetles back home are not the same as yours. Some we must destroy to protect the crops.'

'A farm, you say. Shall you return to work your farm one day?'

Richard turned away sharply, and I felt a pang of embarrassment for the pain the vicar had unwittingly caused him. 'We no longer have a farm. I am a doctor now.'

The words sounded curt and coldly spoken, but I knew it was from grief and not from anger that he spoke. The reverend must have sensed the tension, for he changed the subject quickly.

'Then between your interest in natural history, Mr. Richard, and Miss Lucas's in local history, I hope I may have the pleasure of your company frequently. Have you been exploring more of·the locality today, Miss Lucas?'

'I have been taking tea with Mrs. Pickering,' I answered evasively.

'Indeed? Then you are honoured, for as a rule the coast folk are slow to take to strangers. Mrs. Pickering must have formed a warm liking for you to invite you into her home.'

I declined to tell how I came to be there. Instead I replied simply. 'The customs officers came to search the village. They came into the house while I was there.'

'Did they now?' But the vicar wasn't really listening. Over the top of his head I saw Richard's keen gaze levelled at me. He was evidently thinking of last night, of finding me on the cliffs. If he had seen the fishermen's stealthy activities, he must be thinking that I was in league with them.

The Reverend Hugh was peering into his palm as he spoke again. 'What did Mrs. Pickering have to say to you, my dear?' His tone was casual, almost as though he wasn't interested in the answer. But I remembered the cask I had sat upon to conceal, the one Mrs. Pickering had said was intended for the vicar.

'She told me to hear nowt, see nowt, and say nowt.'

Throwing back his grey head the vicar chuckled. 'Such a pithy way they speak, do they not? But a wise maxim nonetheless. Not to interfere where there is no understanding the cause or the motive – yes, a sagacious attitude. Despite their rough, uncouth ways the coast folk are really a shrewd race. Well, if you excuse me, I must go and see to my beetles.'

126

As he began to turn away, Richard stepped forward. 'Would you mind very much, sir, if I left my horse tethered where he is for a time? I should like to accompany Miss Lucas on foot.'

The vicar waved his free hand airily. 'By all means. Let him crop as much grass as he will; the churchyard will benefit, overgrown as it is. I must do something about replacing Baxter the verger, poor old soul, for he's getting far too old to keep the place tidy. The weeds utterly defeat him.'

I watched his retreating figure, thinking how true to his own words he was. If he knew of the villagers' nocturnal lawbreaking, he was, as Mrs. Pickering put it, saying nowt. He was not so amiably naïve as he appeared.

My musing was cut short by Richard's firm grip as he cupped my elbow. Once again I found his touch pleasurable. 'Shall we walk down to the jetty and see if the customs men have gone?' he suggested. I acquiesced with a smile. I didn't mind in the least retracing my steps in such pleasant company.

Long before we reached him, I recognised Ben Jagger's red hair glinting in the sunlight as he bent over an upturned wooden crate. He was wielding a long slim-bladed knife over a heap of glistening fish. He paused in his rhythmic movements as Richard addressed him.

'Have the revenue men gone, Jagger?'

Jagger's blue eyes stared into Richard's equally blue ones before replying, his look dark and distrustful. 'Aye. No but a few minutes ago.'

We followed the direction of his knife, pointed out to sea. There in the distance was the revenue cutter, just rounding Carnelian Point and heading south.

'Did they find anything?' Richard asked, but Jagger's attentions were again on his fish, the knife sliding smoothly in and ripping up thin gleaming bellies. As he gutted them and tossed the entrails in a pail, raucous gulls wheeled and shrieked close by his head, anxious to get at the banquet.

'Nowt,' he answered laconically. An elderly man trudged wearily across the pebbled beach, carrying a lobster pot and a live crab. 'They found nowt, Joss Baxter, did they?' Jagger called out.

'Not they.' The old man's rheumy eyes flickered over us warily. I was fascinated by the writhing movements of the creature in his gnarled hand. Hand and crab, both looked so ancient as to date from primeval times. A terrier came dancing along, yapping at the old man's heels. I recognised Patch, the reverend's dog. The old man surveyed the terrier, put down the lobster pot, and scratched the wisp of grey hair on his head.

'Patch, oh aye. Tha's made me think on. I'm to take a lobster up to Mrs. Parmenter today, am I not? I'm right glad I seed thee, Patch.'

The old man stumbled away, the dog barking after him. Jagger had turned his back on us to continue his fish-gutting. Richard pulled my elbow gently.

'Come, let us take the cliff path and go up across the fields.'

I was not displeased, for the roughness of the path afforded me every opportunity to avail myself of Richard's helping hand. We climbed in silence, arriving at last breathless at the more level ground. I flung myself down on the grass to rest a while, and Richard stood gazing out over the shimmering sea. It was a delectable day, the slight mist over the blue-grey waters casting a mellower atmosphere than I had seen on this rocky coastline, and my handsome companion towering tall and broad above me. I was completely content.

'The cutter is quite out of sight now,' he remarked.

That reminded me of the smugglers, of last night, and of my encounter here on the cliffs with Richard. I must explain to him, exonerating myself from the smugglers' activities.

'No doubt you wonder, Mr. Fairfax, why I was out here alone last night,' I began. He neither moved nor answered, continuing to gaze out into the distance. 'Ever since I came here I have been aware of unusual occurrences, and last night I was moved to go and investigate.'

'Tell me no more,' he said abruptly, turning to me and holding out his hand. 'Come, let us go on.'

'But I must explain . . .'

'No need. Remember your friend's wise words – hear and say nothing. We have already been amply warned, you and I.'

I stared at him. 'Do you think we are being threatened?' I asked incredulously.

'Let us say, warned. Do not pry, dear Miss Lucas, and that way you will come to no harm.' He offered his hand again and I rose obediently. I had meant to tell him so much more – of the sounds in the east wing, of dead Rachel's shrine, the cry of a woman's voice, of the diary in the writing room, and of the fearful cat that lay in wait.

But his set features indicated that for him, at least, the subject was closed. A cloud drifted slowly across the sun, blotting out its brightness, and for me the day lost its sparkle. A gulf was widening between us, and I knew I had inadvertently caused it.

As we turned inland from the cliffs, striking out across a field where sheep grazed, I wondered at his reluctance to hear or talk of the odd goings-on in Mallory. Was it because he knew of the smuggling and condoned it? Surely he was not part of it! And the other strange happenings in the Keep – he surely could not know of them, sleeping so far from the east wing as he did.

A loud caw overhead made me glance upwards. A lone bird flew erratically hither and thither, and hard behind it flew a large body of birds, silent and purposeful, following its every move.

Richard was watching them too. 'Rooks,' he murmured indistinctly, and I knew what he was thinking. I had a vision of a lifeless figure on a tree, pecked and mutilated, while the countryside around lay devastated and silent. I shivered. Suddenly Richard grasped my arm and pointed across the field.

The solitary bird had landed on the springy turf and stood watching its pursuers as they too alighted and formed themselves into a perfect circle about him, about twenty yards across. Having taken up their positions, every one remained motionless and mute, just staring at the bird in their midst.

'A rooks' court!' Richard breathed, gripping my arm more tightly. 'I have heard of but never seen one. Stand quiet and watch.'

'What is it?' I whispered, excited by the tension engendered by the birds' strange silence.

'The one in the middle has offended their code in some way. Perhaps he's an intruder – like we are in Mallory. Watch.'

I stood close to Richard, hardly daring to breathe. For long minutes the circle of birds remained as motionless as a tableau, only the offender in the centre fluttering occasionally and uttering a few feeble squawks of protest. Still no bird moved. Finally the helpless bird in the middle pivoted about slowly, staring in fascination at each of his accusers in turn. Now I fully expected them to rush in to attack, but still not a bird stirred.

Without a sound the lone bird tottered and fell. The silent circle remained a moment longer, then all suddenly took flight and wheeled away, far into the distance. I could not believe it. There had been such an atmosphere a moment before, charged with tension and menace, and yet they had all flown away without even approaching the culprit.

Richard had let fall my arm and was walking towards the bird. He knelt and picked it up slowly.

'What happened, Richard? Did they frighten it unconscious?'

He shook his fair head. 'It is dead.'

'Dead? Impossible! They never touched it!'

'They had no need. The power of fear is terrible.'

'It is unbelievable! Though I have read of such things, of primitive tribes who can kill their enemies by magic, by making them believe they have the power to kill from a distance. But who would believe that birds have such power!'

'Only rooks, so far as I know. I always hated rooks.'

He laid aside the lifeless creature and rose to rejoin me. The homeward walk was accompanied by silence, both of us deep in thought over what we had witnessed. I could not help wondering about Richard's reference to the intruder bird being like us. Was he suggesting that similar danger lay ahead for an intruder in Mallory? I was, I must confess, glad to reach the door of Mallory Keep.

For once the door stood open, no doubt on account of the sunny mildness of the day. Richard and I went into the vestibule and then stopped short, arrested by the sound of

130

raised voices coming from the parlour, whose door likewise stood ajar.

'But Damian, one must accept the facts,' Regina was saying patiently. I could see her looking out of the window, her back to us.

'Be damned to the facts,' her brother roared. I could not see Damian, but I could imagine his handsome dark face contorted with anger. 'Boyd is a fool. I don't care wnat he says.'

'Hush, dear, he'll hear you.'

'Let him hear! I'll be damned if I'll do as he suggests.'

'Then we must give up our claim to Mallory.'

'That we shall not! No puffed-up little upstart from America is going to steal my patrimony.'

I saw Richard stiffen and his tanned face blanch. He walked away purposefully, up the stairs and out of sight. I remained where I was.

'Then we must accept Mr. Boyd's suggestions, Damian,' Regina went on reasonably. 'If the one suggestion repels you, then we must sell some of the land.'

'Very well,' Damian grunted. 'We'll sell Keep Farm.'

Regina turned from the window and I drew back out of sight. 'Oh, not Keep Farm, dear. One of the others, perhaps.'

'No, Keep. I dislike Ramsden intensely.'

'Because your rabbit died? We must have better reasons than that.'

'Because I object to his sneaking, furtive ways. Because he poaches in my woods and I see him creeping about at night by the shore. What the devil's he up to, I'd like to know. I'd be glad of a reason to be rid of him.'

'I still think it would be better to retain Keep and sell another farm.'

'Keep or none.' Damian's tone was stubborn, petulant, like a spoiled child's.

'Then none it shall be. It is I who manage the estate, remember, with Jagger's help.'

'And none too well either, it seems. I did not know we had such entails upon the estate.'

'I did what was best. You did not wish to be bothered.

131

Very well then, let us discard the idea of selling land and consider Mr. Boyd's other suggestion.'

'That I marry? Never! You understand, I'll hear no more of marriage!'

As Damian's voice thundered across the room, I saw his huge shape advance towards Regina. I felt afraid for her. I had seen the passion in his eyes before, and I thought his emotions could one day carry him too far.

'Come now,' I heard Regina's gentle tones, 'let us sit and discuss the matter reasonably. Close the door, will you, Damian? There is a draft.'

The door closed, and I went upstairs to my room. Why should Damian marry, I wondered; how would that help their claim to Mallory? Perhaps the problem was simply financial? Some land must be sold to pay off debts or else Damian must marry an heiress? Whatever the reason, it appeared that he was adamantly refusing. No doubt his grief for Rachel precluded the possibility that another woman could ever replace her in Damian's heart. Poor man; despite his unpredictable manner, and the indifferent way he left Regina to carry all responsibility, I pitied him.

Uncle Eustace was on the gallery, hastening back to his room. His old eyes were asparkle with pleasure.

'I have decided to come down for dinner tonight,' he told me proudly. 'Mr. Beckwith says I have remained alone too long, and that I should rejoin the family. Pray tell Regina to have a place set for me.'

'To be sure. We shall be happy to have your company. And I daresay Mr. Richard will also be pleased.'

'Ah, Richard Fairfax, yes.' The rheumy eyes grew misty as thought invaded the old man's brain. 'Richard, back from the new country. Mr. Beckwith urges me to meet him again.'

'Mr. Beckwith?'

'My very dear friend. Now I must go and prepare. And by the way, the auspicious time of year is about to begin for you, Miss Lucas.'

'It is?' It was gratifying to hear promises instead of threats.

'But of course. It is your natal time, and we always prosper best at that time of year when we were born. Did you not know that?'

Not only had I been in ignorance of it, but I had also forgotten the passing of time, so occupied had I been in the mysteries of Mallory. But he was right, and my birthday was only a week away.

'Gemini-born people are at the best from mid-May to mid-June,' the old man was saying musingly. 'Their greatest benefits of the year usually fall then. And one's fortune goes in seven-year cycles too, you know, so every seven years one's fortunes are at their peak. How old did you say you were?'

'Twenty next week, sir.'

'Then next year will be your happiest, just you see. Next year your fortunes will be at their highest.'

And that would not be very high, I thought in amusement. Now my fortunes depended on those of the Fairfaxes, and as the family seemed in trouble, it was unlikely I should prosper. The way matters were progressing, I was more likely to lose my position.

He shuffled off into his room to prepare for dinner, and I made my way to my bedroom. Once again I dressed and coiffed my hair with care. I was just putting a dab of lavender water behind my ears when a knock came at the door. I called out 'Enter,' expecting Rosie to come in.

It was Regina, already dressed for dinner, wearing a gown of the prettiest sapphire blue tarlatan which suited her dark colouring admirably. But for that scar she would be a handsome woman indeed, slim and graceful, proud and refined. She sank on to the edge of my bed and sat for a moment in silence.

At last she spoke, hesitantly and with effort. 'Amity, I have no friend but you to confide in. Forgive me if I burden you again.'

I turned on my dressing stool, hands clasped in my lap to indicate patient attention. Again she groped for words.

'You know Damian and I have problems to resolve over the estate. I cannot find it in myself to hate Richard as I thought I would, but we must take care not to befriend him. Though he denies it, I think he still plans to take Mallory from us. He watches us, critical of all he sees.'

'Oh, I don't think so!' I interjected.

133

'Yes he is, I can see it. And I know I have not managed the estate expertly, but I did what I could.'

I said nothing. I don't think I was expected to comment. After a few seconds' pause she continued.

'The problem can be solved, but Damian and I cannot agree on the solution. I would have him marry, but he would prefer us to sell some of the land.'

'If marriage is distasteful, then why not sell land?'

'Because he would have us sell Keep Farm, and to that I cannot agree. I would not anger Ramsden for the world.'

No, of course not, since she and he were in league over the smuggling business. Ramsden could betray her activities to her brother, to the world. I kept silent.

'You see, we are indebted to Ramsden – I cannot explain how – but deeply indebted, and I would not rob him of his livelihood,' Regina struggled on.

It would be dangerous to make an enemy of Ramsden, I thought, remembering his calculating appraisal of me as I crossed the stream, while he sat whittling a stick with a sharp knife. Those black eyes held menace. I could see Regina's problem.

'Then if the sale of land is impracticable, what of the solution by marriage you spoke of?' I asked. 'How would Damian's marriage solve the problem?'

'Because Mr. Boyd says our title to the estate would be stronger than Richard's if Damian had an heir,' Regina replied quietly. With a hollow laugh she added, 'It would be a case of possession being nine parts of the law, I imagine, the possession being thoroughly established if there was a Fairfax son.'

I turned away thoughtfully. I pitied the woman Damian married if her sole duty would be to provide him with a son, for of love there would be little in this marriage. Rachel's memory would prevent that.

Regina rose and came to my side, resting a slim hand on my shoulder. 'I do not ask you for advice, Amity, only for a patient ear. I cannot reveal my thoughts to Damian in full; you know how – irascible – he can be. Nor can I confide in Richard, or Uncle Eustace. There is no one else.'

'Cannot your bailiff advise on the land?'

134

I saw her start. 'Ben Jagger?' she said questioningly. 'No, I cannot talk to him. To tell the truth, Amity, I fear he may be using me.'

It was I who started now. She, whom I knew to be in league with Jagger, speaking of being used by him? Then I understood. Regina was quick-witted, and Rosie was loyal to her. Regina knew I had guessed, even seen, what was going on, and she was trying to convince me of her innocence, trying to pretend she didn't know of their nocturnal activities on the cliffs and in the secret passage from the east wing.

I tried to look innocent and remarked casually, 'By the way, you mentioned Uncle Eustace. That reminds me, he says he's coming down to dinner tonight.'

Regina's face registered annoyance. 'Oh dear, and Richard will be there too. It could prove embarrassing.'

'It is to see Richard he is coming. He says his friend Mr. Beckwith advises it.'

'Beckwith? Again? Oh no!'

I looked up at her questioningly. Regina clicked her tongue, a frown marring the smoothness of her forehead. 'I'm sorry, Amity. There is no Mr. Beckwith. It's an imaginary companion Uncle Eustace produces from time to time. It's months, a year or more since he spoke of him last, but whenever he reintroduces this Beckwith it's a sign he's going to have one of his attacks. No, don't be alarmed. Nothing serious, just a little more eccentric than usual, that's all.'

She made for the door, pausing in the doorway. 'I'll go and order Ethel to lay another place, but be a dear, Amity, and try and persuade Uncle Eustace to stay in his room. He's sure to question Richard most embarrassingly, and may try to enliven the conversation with talk of ghosts in the east wing, one of his favourite topics. I know! Suggest he dine upstairs alone with you. He'd enjoy that.'

I nodded, my heart sinking with disappointment. I'd far sooner dine with Richard than a meandering old man, pleasant as he was.

'Bless you,' said Regina warmly. 'How nice it is to have a friend in the Keep. Now I'll try and persuade Damian to dine alone too. He's very moody at the moment. That rabbit died, you know, and it's quite upset him.'

135

She left me sitting disconsolately, thinking that my lavender water would now be wasted. I could understand her wanting to get Damian out of the way for dinner, for his brooding anger could erupt into another argument. But if she succeeded, it would mean she would have Richard all to herself in the cozy warmth of the dining room, with candlelight and wine. I felt very envious.

It was as I was going to Uncle Eustace's room that I noticed the door to the east wing stood open. I approached it curiously. From along the corridor I could hear voices, or to be more precise, a voice, a man's voice. I crept forward, my curiosity causing a tingling in my veins.

The door to the Rose Room was open, and I now recognised the voice as Damian's, but he spoke words I could not understand. It was the pathos in his tone that drew me onward until I could see him, kneeling before the portrait of his dead love.

'*Mea culpa*,' he moaned, and then throwing his shaggy head back he cried, '*Fiat voluntas tua*.'

Latin, just as Regina had murmured in bed that night weeks ago. Their Catholic upbringing, I guessed, did not desert them utterly, although they no longer practised their faith. I backed away slowly, unwilling to disturb Damian's prayers. As I reached the studded door I heard him cry out suddenly.

'The Lord shall smite thee with madness and blindness,' he bellowed, and I heard him rush out and into his own room, slamming the door. That phrase I did recognise. It was from the book of Deuteronomy. In my memory I could hear again my uncle Leonard's voice intoning the words at family prayer. Poor Damian. He was suffering badly.

Uncle Eustace was delighted to dine alone with me instead of downstairs. 'I can show you my paintings,' he said with pride, throwing back the hessian cover over an easel.

'I did not know you were a painter, sir,' I remarked, surveying the motley collection of strange figures against a sombre grey background.

'Beckwith suggested I begin,' the old man smiled with

136

satisfaction, 'and young Mr. Richard fetched me some oils. What do you think of it?'

I hesitated, cocking my head to one side as if to appreciate the work more fully, but in reality I was unable to find words to commend the rather childish angularity of the figures and the violently primary colours. 'It is striking,' I said at last.

'Glad you like it,' Uncle Eustace nodded. 'They are my ghosts, you know.'

'Your ghosts?' I stared again. There was a woman in emerald green with black hair, and a man in a black robe, and a dark woman with a crown on her head.

'Those whose spirits linger here, and some who live here still,' he amended. 'There you are, my dear.'

He pointed to a fairylike, fragile girl-child in the picture, all yellow and green. 'And Regina,' he said, pointing at the figure with a crown. 'So queenly, so autocratic.'

'And which are the ghosts?'

The old finger indicated the emerald green woman. 'She's the wicked one who'll never leave here.' His old eyes looked infinitely sad. 'Vicious and spiteful, just like a cat.'

I shuddered, remembering the cat in the Rose Room. And then I recognised the green woman's black hair. It was Rachel, I was sure of it.

'And this one?' I indicated the man in black.

'Mad, for all his priestly robes,' Uncle Eustace replied.

I nodded. A monk, of course, one of those from the ancient abbey who remained by the old stones, trapped as Uncle Eustace had once told me.

'Damian,' he said. 'Shall we dine in your room?'

'By all means, if you wish. Which is Damian?'

'He, of course.' He pointed at the mad monk.

'I don't understand. You said that was the mad monk. One of the ghosts here, is he not?'

The old man's watery eyes became a sea of infinite sadness. 'There are some whose spirits haunt the world before death, and Damian is one. He is mad, you know, crazed.'

'With grief. But he is no monk, sir.'

'With grief, aye, and remorse. He has lost his soul for her and wanders the world, eating the bread of sorrow and supping the water of affliction. A monk, no, but do you not know what happened to Damian, then?'

'No, sir, I know nothing of what chanced before I came here.'

'To understand Damian's madness then, you must know, my dear. He was a priest, a Catholic priest.'

I stood, open-mouthed. 'And then he lost his faith and left?' I ventured weakly.

'Good heavens, no! He was unfrocked because of Rachel.'

CHAPTER NINE

'The devil was sick, the devil a monk would be.'
—Motteux, translation from
Rabelais, *Gargantua and Pantagruel*

Uncle Eustace's revelation eddied round in my brain, making no sense at all. Damian a priest, unfrocked on Rachel's account? Surely, no. There was some mistake. I regarded the old man's amiable face closely. Already his mind had reverted to his painting and he was prattling about the intricacies of mixing the oils.

It was not true, I decided, but some figment of the old man's wandering, senile brain. His mind was so cluttered with half-remembered memories, with ghosts of long-dead monks and deceased inhabitants of this gaunt old house, that he could no longer separate fact from fantasy. That must be it.

But other memories teased me, the recollection of Damian muttering in Latin in the Rose Room, quoting from the Bible, and his aversion to women. His dislike of me I had attributed to grief over Rachel, but it could be the Catholic celibate's renunciation of women which was responsible.

As it transpired, I did not have much time to weigh up the truth of the situation, because when at last Uncle Eustace decided to leave my room, events began to move swiftly. No sooner had he declared that he must return to talk with Mr. Beckwith, and bidden me a stately good night, than a knock fell on my door.

'Come in.' I expected it to be Regina, come to say good night, but it was Mrs. Garner's ample figure which entered. She glanced about my room quickly.

'Oh, I heard voices. I thought perhaps Miss Regina was with you, miss. Do you know where she is?'

'I'm afraid not, Mrs. Garner. Mr. Eustace was here, but he's just left. Can I help you?'

A guarded look came over the housekeeper's eyes. 'It's the mistress I want really, miss. I'll go see if she's in the writing room. She'll not be with Mr. Richard, that's for sure, and Mr. Damian is out.'

She looked so agitated that I rose in concern. 'What's the trouble, Mrs. Garner? Are you sure I can't help?'

'Well, I'll come back if I don't find the mistress.'

So saying, she turned quickly and left. Within a few minutes she was back, her anxious face registering apology.

'It's no use, she doesn't seem to be in the house. I wonder can you suggest what I should do. Mrs. Ramsden, up to Keep Farm, sent her servant lass down to tell Miss Regina that her little lad was ill.'

I recalled Regina's interest in the freckle-faced child swinging on the farm gate. Eric, I remembered she called him.

'Did Mrs. Ramsden want the mistress to come, Mrs. Garner? If so, I could go in her place. I am quite accustomed to sick children.'

It was no less than the truth. Many a time I had helped Aunt Cecily to nurse one or more of her brood through an attack of whooping cough or chicken pox.

Mrs. Garner hesitated. 'Aye, I think she'd want the mistress to come. Miss Regina is that fond of the boy that she'd be upset at him being ill.'

'Then I'll go now. Tell Cooper to saddle up Twilight for me, and you can tell Miss Regina when she returns that I am seeing to the boy until she comes.'

The housekeeper's face still showed signs of doubt. 'Mrs. Ramsden'll want the mistress here, but I doubt her husband will, if he's there. He's no fondness for the Fairfaxes, hasn't Ramsden.'

'But I'm no Fairfax. I'm sure he'll accept me if I come to help this boy.'

'Aye, happen.'

Impatiently I began to change into my boots and riding

140

habit. What a cautious, suspicious lot these folk were, to distrust offers of help even for an ailing child. Really, this was carrying reserve too far.

Mrs. Garner was in the vestibule when I came down, Cooper hovering by the front door, cap in hand.

'Think on then, Miss Lucas,' the housekeeper reminded me. 'Ramsden's no respecter of gentry. He could show you the rough side of his tongue. Take no notice of him if he speaks harshly.'

'Indeed I won't,' I assured her firmly. Though I did not like the look of the surly eyed man in the woods, I was not going to be frightened by him.

Outside the front door Cooper had brought up Twilight and another horse, a roan. I realised he intended to ride with me, and I baulked at the thought. Coping with Ramsden would be enough for me without the taciturn ostler.

'There is no need for you to come, Cooper,' I told him sternly. 'I am quite happy to ride alone.'

He eyed me quizzically. 'T'mistress'll expect me to go wi' thee,' he remarked coolly.

'No matter, I'm telling you to stay here and attend to your duties. I prefer to ride alone.'

Shrugging his broad shoulders the ostler began to lead the roan around to the stables. I watched him disappear out of sight around the end of the house before setting off at a canter down the drive.

The crunching gravel gleamed dully pale in the light of the moon which was just rising above the thornbushes. I could hear the distant roar of the sea behind me as I wheeled Twilight about to face inland and go up over the moor. As we rose over the heather I could discern the white stones of Malvaux Abbey ruins away to my right, and the dark line of trees bordering the stream that led inland towards the Ramsden farm. Following the line, I rode purposefully on.

Twilight was beginning to pant by the time I made out the outline of the low farm building and the light streaming from a lantern-lit window. The farm gate, where I had once seen the child Eric swinging, stood open, and I rode straight on up to the farmhouse door.

By the time I alighted, the door was opened by a harassed-looking woman, her greying hair escaping in wisps from her linen cap. I guessed her to be Mrs. Ramsden. At the sight of me her expectant expression faded, but she came forward nonetheless.

'I telled Sarah to fetch t'mistress,' she said, catching my reins as I dismounted and tethering the horse to a rail.

'Miss Regina was absent. I came to offer my help until she comes,' I replied, making for the door. She followed me without murmur, and once inside, led the way through the trim little parlour where a log fire burned, to a far door.

'He's in here.'

The boy lay pale and motionless in a great double bed I guessed to be Mrs. Ramsden's own. On a bedside table a lantern glowed, illuminating the moist pallor of his skin and the dark, shrunken circles of his eyes. I laid a hand on his forehead. He was indeed in a high fever.

'How long has he been like this?'

'Since yesterday morning. He'll not eat nor drink. And there's spots on his chest.'

Pulling back the heavy woollen blankets I saw what she meant. Measles, and a bad case of it too. Already his eyelids were beginning to crust, and he whined feebly when I gently turned his head to inspect the rash creeping up behind his ears.

'Remove the lantern to the further side of the room,' I told his mother, 'the light troubles his eyes. And take off some of these heavy blankets.'

'I mun keep a fever warm,' she protested.

'Do as I say. And fetch cool water and a cloth.'

Muttering, she went out. Quickly I rolled down the blankets and unbuttoned his calico nightshirt. He no longer whined, for he seemed to be almost unconscious. In a moment Mrs. Ramsden returned with a bowl of water and a large linen handkerchief. She watched me in silence as I dipped the handkerchief in the water and began to bathe the scorching little body.

'We must get his fever down,' I explained as I worked. 'Have you had a doctor to the boy?'

She shook her head. 'Can't afford doctor's bills. It's for Miss Regina to say.'

142

I did not question her. At that moment I was more concerned with the child. As I patted him dry with the rough towel Mrs. Ramsden had brought, his dark eyes opened wide. He stared at me, unrecognising, and after a moment he cried out feebly in alarm.

'Never fear, lovey, it's Miss Regina's friend,' Mrs. Ramsden coaxed. 'Miss Regina will be along herself to thee soon.'

Apparently reassured, Eric closed his eyes again, but not before a vague sense of recognition had disturbed me. Where had I seen that dark and haunted look before?

'There, let him sleep now,' I said when I rose, my task done. 'And make some good nourishing broth. Perhaps you'll be able to persuade him to sip a little in the morning. But in truth I think he needs a doctor, and I'm sure Miss Fairfax would agree.'

'She'll be here presently. She'll decide,' the woman answered laconically. She turned towards the door to the parlour, holding it open for me. I dried my hands and followed. In the parlour her set expression softened a little.

'I'm grateful to thee, Miss Lucas. It's no time for a lady to be out alone, and I appreciate thy kindness in coming.'

I smiled in deprecation, but the smile dried as the outer door was flung open and Ramsden staggered in. From the glazed look in his eyes and the rakish angle of his cloth cap, as well as his unsteady gait, I guessed he had been drinking.

The glazed look focused on me and a frown grew between his bushy brows. 'What's she doing here?' he demanded of his wife, jerking a thumb in my direction.

'The boy's sick. I sent to t'Keep and it were Miss Lucas who came.'

The frown deepened. 'We want no help from t'Keep,' he barked, 'neither from t'Fairfaxes nor from her.'

'But Seth, t'lad's sick,' Mrs. Ramsden began.

'No matter. Dost know what they're saying in t'village? They say as t'Fairfaxes are going to sell Keep Farm – *my* farm – wi'out a word to me. Dost think I want traitors like them, or their friends, in my house? I'd be obliged if tha'd leave, Miss Lucas. We've no call for thee here.'

'But Seth, tha's foregetting . . .' his wife shrilled in protest. Ramsden stilled her tongue with an angry wave.

143

'I'm forgetting nowt. It's them Fairfaxes as have forgotten what they owe us. They're in our debt, not we i'theirs. And this is how they want to repay us, by selling our livelihood over our heads, and in secret too. Traitors, that's what they are. Neither them nor their friends are welcome here.'

The fiery gleam in his eye frightened me not a little. I was about to deny the rumour, to tell him that Regina and Damian had decided on another course of action rather than sell Keep Farm, but I hesitated. It was not for me, a paid companion, to discuss my employers' private business matters which I had been told in confidence. Instead I turned to Mrs. Ramsden.

'I shall not embarrass you further by staying. But do keep the child cool not cold, mind you. And I think he should have the services of a doctor as soon as possible.'

I heard Ramsden's derisive snort as his wife led me out to where Twilight stood tethered. She held the reins while I mounted, then waved as I turned about.

'Thanks, and good night,' she said, and as I rode away I heard her voice calling after me. 'Get thee home swiftly, miss. There's restless spirits haunting the moors of a night. God speed thee.'

I pondered over her words as I turned out through the farm gate and away over the moor. A kindly wish, or a warning? In the moonlight the abbey ruins stood out palely clear, and I shivered at the thought of restless spirits anchored there by suffering. Twilight's hooves clopped dully over the springy heather as we mounted a knoll, and I started. Dark figures moved slowly and noiselessly between the skeletal arches of the ruins.

I reined the horse in and sat motionless, too frightened to move. Beneath me I could feel Twilight's restless twitch, as though she too were nervous. My first impulse was to flee as swiftly as I could, but logic persuaded me that that way I would only draw attention to myself, a lone rider on a vast, open stretch of moorland.

But would ghosts notice a woman riding alone? Firmly I told myself these could not be spectres I saw down there, flitting silently between the roofless arches of the abbey. Live

144

human beings they must be, but what could they be doing up here in this desolate place at nearly midnight?

My old enemy, curiosity, began to prevail. Touching Twilight gently on, I rode slowly towards the line of trees bordering the stream that lay between me and the abbey. Once within their shadow I could watch unseen. I was glad of my dark riding habit that rendered me less conspicuous in the pale light of the moon.

Reaching the shelter of the trees at last, I slipped down from Twilight's broad back and led her softly towards the bank of the stream. From here, where the ground fell away sharply to the water's edge, I could see nothing. I tethered Twilight loosely to a tree and moved forward alone.

I found the stepping-stones across the stream, the spot where I had first seen Ramsden. Again in my mind's eye I could see his stare of animosity and the purposeful way he whittled the twig with a gleaming knife, and I shivered. Ramsden was not a man to trifle with. I was a fool to be still out here alone at night with men such as he about. Still, I knew I would not sleep in peace until I knew what was going on in the ruins. Too many unexplained mysteries in Mallory teased me to allow the chance of resolving one of them to pass.

So as to keep silent, on the further bank I climbed the slope almost on hands and knees. On a night as still as this the sound of a twig snapped underfoot could carry clearly and warn of my approach. Cautiously I came to the edge of the trees and stood behind a broad tree trunk.

I could hear their footsteps now, crunching on fallen bits of masonry. No ghosts these, whose footfalls rang on the night air. My courage rising now, I peeped out, just as the moon retreated behind a bank of cloud.

They were only just discernible, a line of hazy figures returning into the central nave of the ruins. One by one they disappeared from view, till only two remained, close together as though in conversation. I strained my ears to catch a murmur of voices, but still and open as the place was, I could hear nothing. Then the two figures broke apart, the one leading the way after the others who had gone inside. The second paused for a moment, a slim black shape in a robe.

I started. Either it was a man in monk's robes or the ghost of a monk – or a woman. Whichever it was, it looked slowly about and then followed inside. The abbey ruins looked deserted. I held my breath and waited.

Long seconds I waited, minutes even, I could not tell how long. But no figures reappeared. I dared not move lest one of them should suddenly reappear and discover me, so I stood, tense and frustrated, still not knowing what was going on. But thoughts and queries kept flashing through my brain. The idea of ghosts I rejected absolutely – I had heard their movements. A robed man, then, but who? I recalled Uncle Eustace's revelation about Damian. Could it be he, in his priestly robes?

No, I decided. Even if Uncle Eustace had spoken the truth, I knew enough of Damian Fairfax to know he was a solitary man, given only to his own company. He was highly unlikely to come up here with a band oi others.

A woman, then? I reviewed the possibilities. I knew Rose Pickering went out at night – I had seen her on the beach with the smugglers. Of course! Why had I not thought of it? Perhaps the figures in the abbey had been smugglers, and Rosie with them. It would make sense of Mrs. Ramsden's warning, since Ramsden was one of the gang.

I shifted uncomfortably. I was growing cramped, keeping still so long. Why had the figures not yet re-emerged from the shadows of the ruins? I wondered what they could be up to in there for so long.

Smugglers did not seem a rational explanation, I decided at last, for there was no reason they should be here, so far from the beach, when they had underground passages to keep their missions secret. Well, if not smugglers, then there was no reason for Rosie to be here. And that left the question – who was the woman?

Without conscious thought the next idea flashed into my mind. Regina was not to be found when the Ramsden boy fell ill tonight. She was out. My curiosity could bear the suspense no longer. I left the shadow of the trees and moved in close to the abbey ruins.

A flutter agitated my stomach as I came near to the old stones and thrill shivered on my spine as the moon came out again, showing up the bleached ruins like a skeleton against the deep azure sky. There was no doubt of it, the moor was a frighteningly vast and ominous place to be in at night, and close by the legend-ridden abbey the atmosphere was at its most menacing. I was a fool, and Aunt Cecily was right. Curiosity would kill the cat yet.

By the crumbling nave wall I hesitated, hardly daring to venture round it for fear of what I might see. When at last I gathered the courage to lean forward to peep around the corner, my mouth fell open in amazement. There was no one there.

Nothing. Not a soul, nor a sound. The ruins were as deserted as they had been for centuries, only the moon and I playing eavesdropper on its privacy. I could not believe it. I had seen at least ten figures enter here, and now there was no sign of them. And they could not have left the abbey from the further side, for in the open miles of moorland surrounding it I must perforce have seen them.

I shivered involuntarily. It was just not humanly possible, and if not humanly, then how? Fear gathered in my veins like a festering sore, burning and immobilising me. I thought of the anger and misery of the ghosts of long-dead monks, their vengeance pent up for so many centuries. At last sheer terror galvanised me into action. I picked up my skirts and fled headlong towards the trees, splashing through the stream, heedless of stepping-stones, and flung myself on Twilight's neck.

'Oh for heaven's sake, take me home!' I implored the animal. She twitched her ears nervously as I fumbled furiously with the reins, flung myself into the saddle, and turned her about. She too seemed glad to leave this mournful spot as she gathered speed to gallop across the moor.

The distant roar of the sea came closer as I rode on, the turreted outline of Mallory Keep growing larger and more distinct as I neared the cliffs. I had never been so glad to see the place, its gloomy darkness seeming even comforting for once. I skirted the side of the house to go in by the stableyard.

Under the stone archway to the stables I nearly leapt out of my skin. In the shadows, waiting and motionless, sat a figure on horseback. For a moment I thought it was Damian, and I dreaded the whiplike lash of words I was sure he would utter, but then to my relief I saw the bareheaded rider was fair. With a lurch of pleasure I recognised Richard. I reined in.

'You startled me,' I said with a smile. 'You really should not frighten a lady so. It is lucky I am not given to having fits of the vapours, or I swear I should have had one now.'

He slipped down from his saddle and I could see that he was booted and spurred and wearing a cloak. he too had evidently been out. Coming towards me, he held out his arms to help me dismount, and willingly I leaned down to him, feeling the warmth and strength of him as he lifted me.

'Where have you been?' His voice was cold and sharp. In the moonlight I could see his eyes were equally cool and demanding, and I felt piqued.

'You question me like some truant schoolchild,' I remarked sullenly. 'What has my business to do with you?. The pleasure I had felt in his arms a moment ago had completely vanished.

'I ask you for your own good,' he snapped in reply. 'Where were you?'

'Visiting a sick child.'

'Where?'

'At Keep Farm. The Ramsden boy.'

'Alone?'

'Yes, alone. Cooper would have come with me but I bade him stay. Now why are you questioning me?'

'Was Ramsden at the farm?'

'He came in while I was there. Now what is all this about? It is late and I wish to go to bed.'

'Did you go near the abbey?'

His eyes held fast to mine, piercing and devastatingly clear. I looked down before answering, hesitating how to reply.

'No. Why should I?'

'You're lying.'

Anger smouldered in me. How dare he interrogate me like some miscreant! I turned on him furiously. 'Who do you think you are, sir, to waylay me and subject me to such uncivil behaviour? And to slander me too? I will not be treated in such a way. Stand aside, sir, and allow me to pass.'

148

He stepped aside, a mocking smile on his lips. 'I will not detain you longer, Miss Lucas, for it is evident I shall not learn the truth from your lips. I know you were at the abbey ruins tonight. I saw you there. But since you deny it, I know I can never again expect to hear the truth from you. Good night.'

He turned abruptly and strode away, leaving me to lead Twilight into her stall alone. Anger and humiliation burned in me as I went into the house and climbed the stairs, humiliation that I had been caught out in a silly, useless lie. And vexation that I had thoughtlessly occasioned this rift between Richard and myself, when it would have been far wiser to invoke his help.

Impetuosity had been my undoing again. Furious with myself, I pulled off my riding habit and prepared for bed. I must seek Richard out in the morning and try to undo the harm I had done. But first I must see Regina and tell her about the Ramsden boy. I pulled on my warm dressing gown over my nightdress, took up the candle, and left my room.

The whole Keep was in darkness, except for the lanterns burning in the corridors. I tiptoed to Regina's room and tapped at the door, once, and then twice, but no answer came. I tried the knob. The door yielded easily.

Inside, the room was in darkness. I entered quietly so as not to startle her awake, but by the light of the candle I found the room empty. Not only was Regina not abed, but the bed had not yet been slept in. The counterpane had been neatly folded back by the chambermaid, and I could see the edge cf Regina's pink nightdress protruding from under the sheet. I put my hand into the bed. The nightdress lay over a now stone-cold hot water bottle.

The clock ticking on the mantelshelf indicated a quarter to one. I shrugged. There was no point in waiting for Regina. The news would have to wait until morning. Warily I made my way back to my own room, climbed gratefully into bed, and blew out the candle

It was morning almost as soon as I had closed my eyes, or so it seemed. Daylight was streaming in through the window, slanting across my bed and prizing my reluctant eyes awake.

I sat up with effort and tried to focus my eyes on the mantel-shelf clock. Almost eight already? I wondered why Rosie had not wakened me with early tea as usual.

Regina. I must give her the message about young Eric. Stumbling from bed, I pulled on my dressing gown and went in search of her. With luck she would still be in her room.

But she wasn't. Rosie knelt at the hearth, shovelling the ashes into a pail. She looked up, her cheek soot-grimed where she had evidently swept back a fair curl.

'Where's the mistress, Rose?'

'Gone down to breakfast.' Rosie turned back to her work. After a moment's hesitation I decided I would, for once, flout convention and go downstairs as I was, dressing-gowned, in order to deliver my message the swifter.

Regina was already seated at the table in the dining room; with a silver paper-knife she deftly flicked open the flap of a letter. As I advanced towards her I noticed that someone was seated by the window. It was Richard, and I felt a pink tinge of embarrassment colouring my cheeks.

'Forgive me, Regina, for coming down undressed, but I have a message for you,' I apologised weakly, sitting in the chair next to her so as to render my déshabillé less conspicuous.

'One moment,' she replied, raising a hand to silence me. I sat quiet, waiting while she ran her eyes quickly over the contents of her letter. Should I, I wondered, in view of the importance of my message, insist on interrupting? But habit dies hard. I was the servant, she the mistress. Dutifully I sat, hands folded in my lap and eyes downcast to avoid meeting Richard's look, until she had finished and laid the letter aside.

'You have a message for me, you say,' Regina remarked with a smile. 'Well, it seems I have one for you too. Exchange is no robbery.'

I was opening my mouth to tell her about the boy, but her words startled me. A message for me? In that letter? I had assumed it was from her lawyer over the Fairfax claim. Who could be writing to her with a message for me? Regina must have noticed my dumbstruck look, for she smiled again.

'Let me put you out of your agony. Now, don't become

anxious, but your uncle has written to me to ask if you might be allowed to come home for a few days. Your aunt is not well after the birth of her child.'

'Aunt Cecily? She has had the baby?'

'A little girl, it would seem. Here, read for yourself.'

She passed the letter over to me and I heard the rattle of cutlery as she began helping herself to food. I was dimly aware of her inviting Richard to join her at table, but did not look up as he seated himself opposite me. I was engrossed by my uncle's neat copperplate script.

'I would hesitate, madam, to incommode you by my request, but my wife is not recovering as swiftly from her travail as one might wish. The child is well but delicate, and I would appreciate my niece's help in nursing both mother and child for a few days. There is no other female relative in the family upon whom I can call to perform this service.

'If, therefore, I might prevail upon your charity to release Amity from her duties, I should be eternally grateful to you.'

Poor Aunt Cecily. My heart flooded with sympathy for her. I must go at once, if Regina would agree. I looked up at her.

'Of course you must go at once, Amity. I shall give orders to Cooper to drive you to the station for the afternoon train. That will give you time to prepare and pack what things you need.'

'Thank you, Regina. I'm most grateful.'

'Do you have sufficient money for the fare?'

I flushed, feeling the colour creep up from my neck. Richard rose from the table and crossed to the sideboard to help himself to scrambled eggs and kippers. I was grateful for his tact, for his apparent unawareness of this private conversation between mistress and servant.

'I don't think so.'

'Then I shall advance your first quarter's salary. Now that is settled. What is your message for me?'

Guiltily I looked at her expectant face. The unexpected recall to London had quite driven the Ramsden child's illness from my mind. Briefly I told her of Mrs. Ramsden's call for help last night and how I had gone in Regina's place. I saw Regina's skin grow pale, the scar standing out livid against the pallor.

151

'Was he very sick?'

'He had a high fever. I did what I could.'

'What exactly did you do?' It was Richard who spoke, his clear eyes regarding mine levelly.

I told them, and also how I had urged Mrs. Ramsden to fetch a doctor. 'But she insisted she must wait until you came,' I finished, looking at Regina apologetically. Somehow, in retrospect, my actions seemed inadequate.

Regina folded her napkin and rose from the table. I could see she was still very pale and tense. 'I must go at once. Why on earth did you not tell me sooner. For heaven's sake, illness is no matter to trifle with.'

I stared. True, but it was not her child, I thought. Regina was behaving strangely. She moved towards Richard and laid a hand on his shoulder.

'I need you, Richard. Will you come?'

'Of course.'

Pushing back his chair, he left his kippers unfinished and followed her to the door. For a moment I felt envy, jealousy even. What closeness seemed to exist between them, where few words were sufficient. Gloomily I sat there for a few moments after they had gone, conscious of having failed Regina. Then I decided to go and wash and dress before taking breakfast.

As I came downstairs again Regina was in the vestibule, dressed and ready to go out. She was looking anxiously about her.

'Where is Richard? Have you seen him?'

Mrs. Garner shuffled across from the baize door. 'He is outside, madam, holding the horses ready.'

'Ah, good.' She made to pass me, without a word. I could not help speaking.

'Do you still want me to go to London, Regina, or would you prefer me to remain a little longer.'

The very look she gave me cut into my heart. 'Go, by all means. You may perchance be of more use to your aunt and uncle than you can be here.'

Tears leapt to my eyes. 'Regina, I'm sorry. I did not mean to cause harm. Please let me make amends if I can.'

152

'There is no need. Richard will do what he can.'

So saying, she swept out. Through the doorway I could see Richard's tall, lean figure silhouetted against the morning sky and the effortless way he swung Regina up into the saddle. Only then did I remember. Of course, Richard was a doctor. How could I have forgotten that, seeing how often this man invaded my thoughts!

If only I had remembered that, perhaps I could have enlisted his help for the child last night, when I encountered him by the stables. What a stupid, forgetful fool I was! Now my forgetfulness had succeeded in bringing him and Regina yet closer together.

It was with a feeling of despondency that I breakfasted and then returned to my room to sort out what things I needed to take with me to London. I hoped Regina and Richard would return before I left, for I loathed the idea of leaving under a cloud of disfavour. I felt I was misunderstood by them both, and longed for the opportunity to clear the air. But by lunch time they still had not returned. I felt oppressed and unable to eat.

'Miss Regina left this package for you,' Mrs. Garner told me as I left the dining room after scarcely touching the poached fish. I could tell by the feel what the contents were. Sovereigns.

'Thank you, Mrs. Garner. At what time will Cooper take me to the station?'

'In half an hour.'

'Any news from Keep Farm?'

She shook her grey head. 'If they're not back, I reckon the lad's real poorly. I hope as how he'll be all right.'

'Many children get over measles,' I reassured her brightly. 'I'm sure he'll recover quickly.'

'Aye, well I hope you're right. It'll be a sad day for the Fairfaxes if that lad dies.'

I looked at her quizzically. 'I hope he will not die, Mrs. Garner. But why is it so significant to the Fairfaxes?'

She looked at me sideways, a curious assessing look. 'You don't know? Well, it's not for me to say. I can only tell you that it'll alter all our fortunes if harm comes to that boy. And I'd not want to be in your shoes if it does.'

Her mystifying words were still ringing in my ears when Cooper finally drove me away down the long gravel drive. And I had the whole of the long, monotonous journey to London to ponder over recent events and to wish desperately that I had not had to leave Mallory. If only there had been time to explain to Regina and to Richard. And time to try to find out what on earth was going on. For all I loved Aunt Cecily, I could have wished she had chosen any other time to need me. Now was the worst possible time to have to leave Mallory.

CHAPTER TEN

'The devil's riddle is mastered.'
—Swinburne, *The Triumph of Time*

London seemed depressing despite the bright sunshine that illuminated its dusty, noisy streets. As I was not expected, there was no one to meet me at the station, so I hired a hansom cab to drive me out to Clapham.

The unpretentious little street where my aunt and uncle lived looked more dismal and shabby than I remembered it. The neat little terrace houses, with their discreet lace curtains maintaining a respectable air of privacy, and the neatly clipped hedges of privet, gave me a feeling of claustrophobia. Before I descended from the cab to enter my aunt's house, I was already longing for the freedom of the cold, pure air of the moors I had left behind.

Little Millicent, the eldest of my little cousins, a pale, shy child of eleven, was stirring a pan of stew on the great kitchen range when I came in. She dropped the ladle to fling her thin arms about my neck in joyful greeting..

'Father will be home from the office soon, and I can never please him,' she explained timidly. 'He is so accustomed to Mama's cooking, and I fear mine is not up to her standard. And he always complains that the tea is overdrawn.'

Taking me by the hand, she led me upstairs to where Aunt Cecily lay abed, pale and wistful looking. Alongside her in a cradle I could see the baby, a pretty little pink thing with gilt hair. My aunt held out her hands with a welcoming smile.

'Amity, my dear, I am so glad to see you. I feel so guilty having you brought home like this. Really. Millicent has been coping very well, but your uncle was insistent that you should come.'

155

'And I'm glad to be here, Aunt,' I reassured her as I bent to kiss her cheek. 'Miss Fairfax was anxious that you should be restored to full health as quickly as possible.'

'So kind,' Aunt Cecily murmured. 'But I'm not ill, you know, just very tired. A few more days in bed and I'm sure I shall be well enough to take over the household again. It's just that the little ones are too much for Millicent on her own.'

She looked so worried and apologetic that I forgave her at once. Mallory and its problems could wait until Aunt Cecily was well again.

There was genuine welcome in Uncle Leonard's greeting when he came home from the office, and it was gratifying to see his satisfaction as he ate Millicent's stew – to which I had added suet dumplings – and sipped a cup of fresh tea.

'That's better, Millicent,' he nodded approval at his daughter. 'Fresh and strong and not overdrawn. Just the way I like it.' Millicent's answering smile slid from her father to me, conspiratorial and happy.

In the succeeding days I found myself too busy to brood over Mallory and its inhabitants. Running up and down stairs to see to Aunt Cecily, feeding the new baby and the other two not yet at school, getting the older ones fed and dressed for school, washing, polishing – the day seemed too short to fit in all that had to be done. In retrospect I could appreciate the pampered life of leisure I had been enjoying at Mallory Keep.

On the third evening I was sitting at the table in the parlour, darning a pile of socks by the light of the oil lamp. Uncle Leonard, relaxed in his armchair and contented now he had eaten well and all the children were abed, stretched his slippered feet towards the fire and lit his pipe.

'I'm glad you're home, Amity,' he remarked quietly. I looked up in surprise, my darning needle in midair. It was unlike Uncle to express any feeling openly. 'The house seemed all wrong with your aunt ill and everything awry,' he went on. 'Millie did her best, but it wasn't the same.'

I went on darning, hearing his contented puff on his pipe and the clock ticking steadily on the chenille-covered mantelshelf. After a few moments he spoke again.

156

'Were you happy in Yorkshire? Did you get on well with your mistress?'

His tone was casual, yet I knew he genuinely cared. Uncle Leonard was a religious man who made no move without consulting his conscience, and he would be saddened if he believed I was unhappy in my new life.

'I am happy, Uncle. Miss Regina is kindness itself, and does me the honour of calling me her friend.'

'Indeed?' There was no mistaking the gratification in his voice. It was an honour indeed for a lady of quality, such as Miss Fairfax, to befriend a member of the lower middle class such as I. Uncle, conscious of his lowly standing in the rigidly defined class structure, a clerk in a tea merchant's office barely aspiring to the lowest rung of middle classhood, felt reflected pride in my new friend's magnanimity. 'She seems a very charitable lady, to free you from your duties thus in order to help at home. I must be sure to write and thank her when you return,' he mused, puffing still on his pipe. A cloud of heavy smoke hung suspended over his thoughtful head, no draft of air able to penetrate the heavy chenille curtains at door and windows to waft it away.

'And Mr. Fairfax? Is he also an agreeable person?'

I hesitated. Agreeable was the last word one would use to describe Damian Fairfax. I decided to parry the question.

'Mr. Fairfax is a rather remote person, keeping to his own rooms most of the time. In fact, I hardly know the gentleman, Uncle.'

'Ah, a studious gentleman, no doubt.' Another puff of smoke rose to join the cloud above him. He had evidently found my answer satisfactory. It would seem I had fallen into a cultured, refined family and my uncle would be happy on my behalf.

He asked a few other desultory questions about the kind of countryside where Mallory was, the farms and the fishing, but he was less interested in my answers than he had been in the Fairfaxes. As the fire grew lower and my pile of darning diminished, I could see Uncle Leonard was content at the way events had turned out. I was ensconced in a respectable family, landed gentry at that, and he had nothing with which to reproach his conscience.

157

A few days later a letter arrived from Regina, but addressed to my uncle, not to me. I had to wait until his return from the office that evening to learn of its contents.

'It is very brief, but to the point,' Uncle Leonard remarked as he laid the missive aside without offering to let me read it. 'Miss Fairfax apologises for her brevity, saying she is very occupied, but assures me that you must stay as long as you are needed. There is no hurry for your return.'

Irrationally, I felt disappointed. My presence was not being missed at Mallory, and worse, I did not know what was going on there, for Regina sent no news at all. That night, long after the rest of the family were asleep, I lay listening to the gentle breathing of the baby – I had brought her into my little room to make sure Aunt Cecily had a good night's sleep – and pondered over Mallory.

I wondered still at the significance of the moonlit figures at the abbey ruins. Were they the smugglers from the beach – but if so, why so far from shore? The ruins must be at least a mile inland. And did Richard think I was one of them? He surely did, having seen me there that night as well as the night I had eavesdropped on the smugglers in the cave. A frisson of pleasure rippled through my veins as I remembered how he had swept down on me, on horseback, and gathered me up on the saddle. I could still feel the warm strength of his arms about me.

Sternly I reproached myself for my romantic silliness. Why should my mind dwell so fondly on the fair-haired man who had never evinced any interest in me beyond dislike? My confined days in a young ladies' academy had rendered me vulnerable and foolish when at last I was thrown into the company of men. Until recently, Uncle Leonard had been the only male occupant of my word; safe, unobtrusive, unmenacing. Now there was Damian Fairfax, who sent shudders of fear and incomprehension through me, and Richard Fairfax, who made my impressionable heart tremble from the very first instant I had set eyes on him in York Minister.

The baby stirred and whimpered. Quickly I rose to soothe her and make her comfortable. The little thing gurgled, and I swear she smiled before closing her deep blue eyes again to sleep. Dear little thing, as yet unnamed. I felt a wave of sympathy and protective love for the child, unwanted as she had been by her parents. But I knew my aunt and uncle had welcomed her when at last she came. In a moment of self-pity I wished I felt as wanted, not just needed.

Climbing back into my narrow chintz-covered bed, I curled up again and reverted to thoughts of Mallory, wondering how close Regina and Richard had become during my absence. Involuntary jealousy clouded my thoughts, and I had to remind myself forcibly that I had no right to feel so. Regina and Richard were well-born, scions of an ancient family, while I was but a poor servant, poles removed from their level. But still the envy gnawed.

On Sunday Aunt Cecily made a rather tottery appearance in the parlour, supported on her husband's arm. She looked radiant, to be up and dressed once more and returning to normality at last. A soft glow of pleasure suffused her gentle face.

'Oh, how pleasant it is to be downstairs again, and how beautifully clean and shining everything is!' she enthused, as Uncle Leonard lowered her into the armchair. 'Oh, Amity! How meticulously you have kept house for me!'

It was worth all the days of sheer hard work and sleepless nights with the baby to see her genuine pleasure and gratitude. And her unexpected appearance gave me a glow of hope. Soon I might be able to return to Mallory.

Once Uncle Leonard had taken the older children to morning service as befitted a respectable middle-class family, I scrubbed and peeled the vegetables for dinner while a joint of sirloin beef was roasting in the kitchen range. Aunt Cecily kept an eye on the little ones playing about her feet in the parlour.

'Now, Septimus, don't snatch!' she was admonishing her youngest son who was endeavouring to capture his older sister's rag doll. I stood in the kitchen doorway, taking pleasure in the family scene. For all Aunt Cecily's constant child-bearing and difficult economic circumstances, she was a supremely contented woman. I felt a sense of guilt at my own restlessness, my hankering to be off and away, back in the gloomy strangeness of Mallory Keep. One day, with luck, I too might experience the calm and contentment that seemed to settle over my aunt like a comfortable old blanket. But not yet. Youth and impatience held the prospect far away.

Aunt Cecily recovered rapidly once she was able to join in family life again. As the days passed she grew stronger and I grew more hopeful. The baby, whom by now they had decided to name Violet, was putting on weight and filling out into a truly bonny child. Mother and baby both thriving so, I began to chafe at the leash which held me there. Soon, I hoped, Uncle Leonard would deem the time ripe for my aunt to take over the running of the household again.

My release came unexpectedly. The post arriving earlier than usual one morning, Uncle Leonard paused on his way out of the house to open his mail. Glancing quickly at the grandfather clock in the hall, he frowned.

'In three minutes I must be at the end of the street or I shall miss the tramcar,' he remarked as he slit open the first letter. 'Oh, from Mallory Keep.'

I held my breath as he read silently. At last he refolded it, replaced it in the envelope, and put it down. 'A Mr. Richard Fairfax writes to say your presence is needed.'

'Miss Regina's cousin,' I informed him. I had made no mention of the rival claimant to the estate to my aunt and uncle. 'I wonder what is amiss?'

'He does not say. But as all is well here, you had best prepare to go at once in case there is trouble. I'm glad you came, Amity. We are grateful to you. But I must go now.'

With an avuncular peck on my cheek he was gone, leaving Richard's letter on the hall table. The other unopened letters he had taken with him.

I picked up the envelope with the letter inside. Much as I should have liked to, I could not bring myself to take out the letter to read exactly what Richard had written, for I was curious to detect his tone. But I had to satisfy myself with looking at his large, sprawling script on the envelope, the very size and boldness of his lettering betraying the breadth and freedom of his mind, and I felt happy. He had written to ask me to come back.

So he could not dislike and distrust me too much. I pushed away the thought that he might have written only because Regina had asked him to do so. She would have written herself. No, it was Richard who wanted me back in Mallory. I sang as I washed the breakfast dishes and prepared to leave everything in the little house as orderly as I could before leaving.

'I'm so glad,' Aunt Cecily said when she heard I was going. 'I thought your uncle might detain you overlong in his concern for me. But now I can cope, with Millicent's help, and I think it would be wise for you to return to your position quickly. Good positions are not easy to find nowadays.'

She smiled as I rode away in the hansom cab, she and Millicent waving from the doorstep, and the twitching lace curtains about betraying that the neighbours were standing by their potted aspidistras to watch my departure. I smiled. People were the same everywhere. Both here in Clapham and in the wilds of Yorkshire, curiosity was a human trait which I found endearing, perhaps because, as Aunt Cecily so often said, I was a victim of it myself.

The journey northward passed without incident, I being too excited at the prospect of seeing Mallory Keep and its occupants again to take much notice of my travelling companions on the train. It was only as I was descending from the train at the journey's end that one traveller forcibly caught my attention.

He was alighting on the platform from the next coach to mine, a tall young man in grey frock coat and hat. Only for a fleeting second did our eyes meet, but in that instant I sensed a flash of recognition, of looking into dark, intense eyes I had looked into before. But there was no answering recognition in his eys. His gaze rested on me for only a second, then he turned away.

I must have been mistaken, I decided, for there was nothing familiar about the tall figure striding away towards the ticket collector. It was his eyes, black and penetrating that had given me that strange sensation, and it was not similarity to Damian's eyes, dark and piercing though they also were. A trick of the light, an illusion. I was becoming fanciful, my head peopled with those I wanted to see at the Keep. I dismissed the stranger from my mind and handed in my ticket at the barrier.

With relief I saw Cooper, the coachman, standing beyond the barrier. He doffed his cap at the sight of me.

'T'carriage is outside the station,' he said gruffly.

I handed over my small bag gratefully. It was thoughtful of Regina to send the carriage down when she did not know just when I would be arriving. I smiled at Cooper, aware of the pleasure I felt at hearing his flat-syllabled Yorkshire tones. It was like coming home.

'Drive straight around to the stables,' I called out to Cooper as the carriage crunched its way up the long drive of the Keep. It would be cozy to go in by the kitchen entrance, I thought, where the fire would be made up high in the range ready for supper and the appetising smell of cooking filling the air.

Dusk was falling as the carriage turned in under the stables archway and clattered to a halt in the cobbled yard. Cooper climbed down and opened the carriage door to hand me out. As I descended, I saw the tall, broad figure of Damian Fairfax emerging from a stall, leading Vulcan by the reins. The horse whinnied at the sight of me, and his owner grunted.

'So you've come back.' Hardly a welcome, but I managed a smile. Damian flung himself into the saddle. 'God knows why you should come back,' he muttered as he turned his mount about. 'One is fortunate to escape this place and its curse. Only a fool would come back.'

He cantered off under the archway, leaving me open-mouthed. I was accustomed to his graceless ways; perhaps I should have known better than to expect a greeting. Shrugging, I went into the kitchen.

A cozy glow of light from candles and the fire met me as I entered. Mrs. Garner was at the great deal table, her back towards me and her sleeves rolled up as she kneaded a mixture of what I took to be pastry in a big crockery basin. Across the table from her sat Rosie, and behind her Ben Jagger leaned nonchalantly on the back of her chair. He glanced up at my entrance, his sandy eyebrows rising, and

162

then he reached for his corduroy jacket thrown on another of the ladder-backed chairs.

'Time I were off, I reckon,' he muttered. Mrs. Garner nodded and Rosie got up from her seat. She smiled shyly at me.

'Evening, Miss Lucas.'

Mrs. Garner turned round, raising her floured hands in surprise. 'Bless my soul! Miss Lucas! We weren't expecting you yet,' she said, rubbing her hands vigorously on a towel and reaching for the kettle. Ben Jagger grunted as he passed me towards the door.

Mrs. Garner called after him. 'You'd best manage the estate as best you can till the mistress is about, that's all I can say. Good night, Ben Jagger.'

'I'll make some tea,' the housekeeper added to me. Rose followed Ben outside into the yard.

'There's no need, Mrs. Garner. I'll go and tell Miss Regina I'm here,' I said, making for the door. 'I don't want to delay you when you're preparing supper.'

She glanced at the unrolled pastry and she shrugged. 'Waste of time cooking, it is, with no one to eat it but Mr. Richard. Mr. Damian's gone out, and Miss Regina's neither eaten nor spoken these three days.'

I turned anxiously. 'Is the mistress not well then? Is that why Mr. Richard called me back?'

The housekeeper's eyes narrowed. 'Oh, it were Mr. Richard as called you, were it? I wondered. No, Miss Regina's not ill exactly. Not in the body, that is, but she's not herself. Shock, I reckon.'

Frowning, I moved towards her. 'Shock? What do you mean? What has happened to the mistress?'

Mrs. Garner shrugged as she picked up the wooden rolling pin and began bettering the piece of pastry on the table. 'She can't accept it, I reckon. But fate's fate. You can't escape God's will. Like the vicar says, you have to accept humbly and carry on.'

'Accept what, Mrs. Garner? I don't understand!' I could have throttled her in my impatience. She looked up, rolling pin poised in midair.

'You don't know? Well, of course, you couldn't know

163

down there in London, could you? It was little Eric Ramsden. He was taken very bad.'

'I know I was there. It was measles, but Mr. Richard and Miss Regina nursed him, did they not?'

Mrs. Garner shook her head. 'They nursed him well enough, morning, noon and night they were up at Keep Farm, sometimes all night. But it were no use. The little fellow got worse. His eyes went first, then he got a terrible cough. Mr. Richard said it were pneumonia. Poor little fellow, him only seven years old and all, and the Ramsdens' only child.'

My heart was leaping in agitation. I must be misinterpreting what the housekeeper was saying. 'You mean . . . the boy didn't recover?'

'Nay. He died on Monday. He was buried by the vicar yesterday.'

Oh no, poor Regina! Unaccountable though it was, I knew she was devoted to the boy. She must be heartbroken. Mrs. Garner laid the circle of pastry over a large dish and began trimming the edges.

'Mr. Richard went to the funeral, but neither the master nor the mistress. Miss Regina took to her room when he died, and hasn't spoken to a soul since.'

'And she hasn't eaten either?'

'Nay. She locked the door. And to think I used to grumble about getting the master to eat. Now she's as bad as him. Well, maybe now you're back you can get her to eat. I'm afraid she'll pine away else.'

The door to the house opened and Richard came in. Seeing me, he came across and took my hands. I trembled with pleasure. Perhaps we had parted in misunderstanding, but soon I should be able to clear the air with him, for his welcome was apparent. But that could come later. I gripped his hands in return

'Amity, I'm glad you're back.' His voice was low and husky. 'Regina needs help.'

'Where is she? I'll go to her now.'

'That's why I came down. Mrs. Garner, she's not in her room. I've looked everywhere. Do you know where she is?'

The housekeeper's face wrinkled further in thought. 'I

don't know for sure. But it's likely she's in the old chapel, the state she's in, though she's not been in there for years.'

'The chapel? Where is that?'

'In the east wing. But mind how you go, because the steps are rotten and some of the masonry is falling. I'm only saying she *might* be there, mind. She used always to go there once when she was troubled, but that was in the old days when they were still Catholics.'

She stopped suddenly, as if aware that she was revealing too much of her employer's private affairs to comparative strangers. Richard was already making for the door, pulling me after him.

'It's right at the end of the wing, on the left,' the house-keeper added as an afterthought just as the door was closing. Richard marched on, letting go my hand in the vestibule to pick up the oil lamp from the hall table.

'Put your bag in your room and we'll go straight to the east wing,' he commanded as we mounted the stairs. Obediently I did as I was told, then followed the halo of Richard's lamp-light in the direction of the east wing.

The cold air struck us as soon as we passed through the studded door, and I was glad I was still wearing my merino ulster. There was complete silence, save for our footsteps, as we passed by the Rose Room and Damian's bedroom. At the far end of the corridor Richard raised the lamp. In the arc of light I could see to the left a spiral stone staircase descending into the darkness.

'Take care,' Richard warned as he led the way down, reaching up his free hand to help me. 'Mrs. Garner was right. Some of these steps are crumbling badly. Give me your hand.'

I was glad of his aid for there was no balustrade edging the spiral. Below us a black void yawned, silent and unwelcom-ing. And there was an air of menace, a musty smell of decay that put me in mind of a graveyard. I recalled the ghosts of ancient monks linked with these rotting stones, and I shud-dered.

At last we reached the bottom, an unevenly flagged pas-sage on whose dank floor something moved, scuttling from the light. Rats or mice. I was so filled with distaste that I felt sure the fastidious Regina could not have come to such a noisome place, especially not alone. I tugged at Richard's sleeve.

'She's not down here, Richard. The chapel must be upstairs, in the corridor near Damian's room. Let's go back.'

The sickly-sweet stench of decay and putrefaction all about us was invading my nostrils and clogging my throat until I felt quite nauseous. I longed to escape it. Richard laid a finger to his lips and cocked his head to one side.

'Listen!'

And then I heard it too, a long, low moan like a creature in pain. I trembled. I had heard that piteous sound emanating from the east wing once before. Uncle Eustace was right. These ancient stones still held spirits captive, spirits who could find no rest. I clung to Richard's arm.

'There is someone down here – can't you hear it too?' Richard demanded. 'It's from that direction, beyond that door.'

He walked on towards a great wooden door studded with iron nails. I followed close, anxious not to let go of him. He was right. The moaning sound was louder. The source of it lay beyond the door.

Before I could stop him, Richard had turned the iron knob and thrust the great door wide open. In the centre of the room, in the circle of light thrown by a solitary candle, a woman's figure lay prone on the floor, a huddled white splash with streaming black hair.

'Regina.'

Richard strode forward, putting down the lamp on the stone block before which Regina was sprawled. I stood stock-still, mesmerised by the strange scene – and half afraid of what Richard would discover.

He took Regina's shoulder to raise her head. Her body was instantly galvanised into life. She leapt up, tensing herself into a crouched position, her eyes staring wide at him.

'Get away! Don't touch me!'

Richard's hand withdrew slowly, but Regina crouched, watching him warily. He knelt down by her, and his voice was full of patience.

166

'Come, Regina, let us take you upstairs. It is cold and damp here. You will make yourself ill.'

Again his hand rose in a gesture of offering, but Regina shrank further into the shadows.

'Don't touch me!' she shrieked. Her great black eyes, encircled by a ring of staring white, glared malevolence. Her fingers curled as though in readiness to attack. Involuntarily I thought of the cat in the Rose Room.

I moved a step forward, into the arc of light from candle and lamp. Regina's gaze turned to me suspiciously and then sprang back to Richard. He rose slowly from his knees.

'Will you come, Regina?'

'No! Get out! I hate you!'

'It's no use, Regina. Grief will not help. He could not live, you know.'

She moaned again, a long, agonised cry that sent shivers up my spine, and flung herself again on the floor. Then I saw that the stone block before her was some kind of altar, for there was a wooden crucifix above it on the wall, only just visible in the half-light. I felt helpless. I wanted desperately to help Regina in her grief, yet felt guilty at invading her sanctuary.

Richard pulled my sleeve. 'I cannot help – she will not listen to me. You try to reason with her. I'll wait upstairs.'

And he went. Regina lay for a time whimpering softly, and then she sat up, her gaze turning accusingly to me.

'Why don't you go too, and leave me in peace?'

I stretched forward a timid hand. 'I want to help you, Regina.

She thrust my hand away, rose to her feet, and glared at me, her lips drawn back in a sneer. In the candlelight her scar stood out starkly against the white skin. The hate in her eyes and the scorn made her look repulsive.

'You? Help me? That's ironic, after what you've done!'

'I? What have I done?'

'You let him die!'

I was bewildered. 'The boy, you mean? I did what I could. Oh Regina, I share your sense of loss, but I'm sure I could have done no more for him.'

'You could have told me.'

'I did – as soon as I could.'

'Not soon enough. Richard could not save him. Or perhaps he did not want to.'

I stared in horror. 'What are you saying, Regina? Richard is a doctor, sworn to save life where he can. Of course he did all in his power, I'm certain of it. But be reasonable, Regina, come.'

I held out my hand again, and again she shrank from me, her eyes glittering with distrust and dislike. 'You fool, you gullible fool,' she muttered. 'How far can I believe your seeming simple ways?'

She turned to look at the crucifix on the wall, then turned slowly again to face me. 'Experience has taught me to believe no one, neither you nor he with all his charm. I have been deceived before.' Her voice was cold now, empty of feeling. I stepped closer.

'Come upstairs, Regina. You are taking this too hard. Come up and rest.'

My voice was low and coaxing, but it seemed to sting Regina. Her face burned with anger.

'Don't try to mollify me! I know what you're up to! You're in it together, Richard and you – you wanted the boy to die!'

'Regina! How could you say that? It's not true! Why should we want him dead?'

'Because you knew! And you knew if he was gone, then Mallory would be lost to us. Damian and I would have nothing left.'

A glimmering suspicion began to creep into the mystified blankness of my brain. I seized Regina by the shoulders.

'What are you saying? What had the Ramsden boy to do with Mallory?'

Her voice was ice-cold now, lifeless as she stared at me. 'You know already. He was my nephew, our only hope of clinging to Mallory.'

'Your nephew? I don't follow.'

But I did. Almost before she spoke the words, I knew. 'He was Damian's son.'

CHAPTER ELEVEN

'What a mischievous devil Love is.'
—Samuel Butler, *God Is Love*

Bewilderment numbed my wits. All I could do was to stare at
Regina, dumbstruck. With her black hair tumbled about her
shoulders instead of in its usual neat coil, and her eyes staring
wildly at me, she looked as crazed as I had seen Damian look.
I began to suspect a streak of insanity in the Fairfax blood.

But if grief had driven her mad, could I believe her words?
I spoke gently.

'Damian's son?'

She swung away sharply, her hair flicking like a soft black
curtain between us. 'Yes,' she replied sulkily.

'And his mother – was it Rachel?'

My words had an electrifying affect. Regina spun round to
face me, her eyes blazing. 'Don't speak that name! Here,
above all places, where the Fairfaxes lie in honour, never
mention that name!'

She snatched up the oil lamp and moved quickly away
from me, towards the further wall. Until now the edges of the
room had been in utter darkness, but by the light of her lamp
I could now see there were stone shelves running along the
wall, and on them great stone rectangles. I moved up close
behind Regina. She held the lamp aloft, and I could see the
carvings on the stone boxes. Then I realised. They were
tombs, the resting-places of the Fairfaxes.

'She was no Fairfax,' Regina was muttering angrily, 'only
an intruder here. But the boy – he was ours. By rights he
should be lying here now if he was not to live and inherit
Mallory.'

'Here, in the chapel?'

'This is the crypt. The chapel is upstairs. For centuries the Fairfaxes have worshipped and been interred here in the Keep. Damian and I will lie here one day.'

'Then why did you not bring little Eric here, if he is Damian's son?'

She rounded on me sharply. 'Because he was a bastard for one thing, and for another, because Damian did not know.'

I gasped. 'Did not know the boy was his son? But how could he not know?'

Her eyes narrowed in suspicion. 'You ask many questions, Miss Lucas. Did Richard bring you down here to find out what he did not know? Are you spying on me, you and my cousin?'

'Indeed not, Regina. Why should we?'

'Because Richard stands to gain Mallory. Now the boy is dead . . .'

'But Richard does not know, no more than I did, about the boy.'

'Then why did you come? And how did you know where to find me? No one has been down here in years, ever since Damian and I . . .'

Her voice tailed away, but I knew she meant since she and her brother had lost their faith. And now I began to understand why. Damian had loved and lost a woman who bore his son, though strangely he did not know of the child. And Regina – why had she too lost her faith? I surveyed her curiously. Her eyes were vacantly staring. Reluctantly I came again to the conclusion that the Fairfaxes were an unbalanced strain.

'Go away,' Regina said in a flat, expressionless voice. 'It is your fault he is dead. Go back up to your Richard, but mind you tell him nothing. Damian must never know.'

I picked up the lamp she had replaced on the stone, leaving her standing in the circle of candlelight. At least she seemed more composed than when Richard and I had found her there.

As I climbed the spiral staircase, I remembered suddenly the haunted look in the eyes of the child, the night I had gone to Keep Farm. And I remembered how I had found the look somehow familiar – it was the same haunted look I had seen in his father's eyes. Only then I had not known Damian was his father. Outwardly there had been no resemblance between the saturnine, dark-countenanced Damian and the freckle-faced boy, other than the look of fear in his harassed eyes.

Richard was awaiting me at the top of the staircase. As the circle of lamplight fell on him, sitting on the top step, I realised he had been sitting for some time in the dark, having left the oil lamp in the crypt. Rising, he looked at me questioningly.

'Is she all right, Amity?'

'She is calmer now. I think she will come up soon. Best to leave her now.'

He turned to walk beside me along the east wing, back towards the main house. 'Did she explain her state? Why she is so upset over the boy?'

'In part. I cannot tell you more.'

He nodded. 'I hoped she would confide in you at least. That is why I sent for you. No one else could come near her, and I was anxious for her health. For some reason she still distrusts me.'

'And me, I fear. She blames me for the child's death,' I said, anxious for reassurance that I was not at fault. He did not fail me.

'You were in no way at fault. I have already explained to Regina, while we were nursing him, that nothing more could be done. You did just what I should have done that night. No one could do more. Regina is unjust, but I suspect grief has clouded her judgment.'

'Grief,' I remarked sadly, 'seems to bedevil this house. Regina grieves for Eric, Damian for Rachel . . .' I stopped. I was clumsily about to add Richard, whose witnessing a flock of rooks in a field recalled agonising memories of a father he also mourned. But he did not notice my abrupt stop, for he latched on to my final words.

'Rachel? Who was she?'

He had stopped walking and was looking down at me, his blue eyes curious, and his fair head tilted to one side in question. Realising we were outside the Rose Room, I laid a

171

finger to my lips to signal discretion. Once again my impulsive tongue had led me too far.

There was a sound from the Rose Room, a rattle, and then the door suddenly burst open. Damian stood there, his burly frame filling the doorway, his dark face thunderous, and his eyes blazing.

'What are you doing here?' he demanded in a shout. 'This wing is private. No one comes here but Regina and myself. Get out, both of you!'

Richard looked as if he was about to speak, to explain, but I tugged his sleeve to lead him away. I knew from experience that explanation or apology to Damian was useless. Reluctantly Richard followed me.

We had passed the studded door on to the minstrel's gallery when Damian swept by us, cloaked and spurred and evidently on his way out. We watched in silence as he hurried downstairs and out of the front door, slamming it behind him so that the great solid block of oak shivered in its framework.

'A strange man, my cousin,' Richard remarked drily.

'Stranger than you know,' I murmured. On a sudden impulse I turned to him. 'You do not know of Rachel, you say. Come, let me show you.'

Turning back whence we had come, I went back through the studded door into the chill of the east wing, Richard close behind me. At the door of the Rose Room I stopped.

'Has Damian locked the door?' I said aloud, testing the knob. He had not. Taking the lamp from Richard's hand, I led the way inside. 'See,' I said, holding the lamp aloft, 'this was Rachel's room and there is her portrait.'

Richard stood in the middle of the room, looking about thoughtfully, his hands deep in his trouser pockets. Finally his gaze came to rest on the portrait, his blue eyes regarding the haughty black ones of the black-haired beauty.

'She was very beautiful,' he remarked. 'Was she Damian's wife?'

'I think not,' I replied, remembering how Regina had called the Ramsden boy a bastard. But that piece of information I could not divulge. 'I believe, however, that she was his lover, for he grieves deeply for her still.'

172

'Understandably, for she was very beautiful, though not the kind of woman who appeals to me.'

I looked at Richard curiously, wondering but not daring to ask what kind of woman he preferred. I indicated the panelling beside the fireplace.

'And behind there is a secret chamber, with a passage leading from it down to the caves on the beach.'

'Indeed? That is not unusual in old houses, and particularly the houses of Catholics. A priest hole, no doubt, with its own escape route. How did you come to learn of it?'

I told him of that night, when Regina gave orders to someone in that chamber, and how I later found my way down through the passage to the cave.

'Idle curiosity?' Richard asked with a smile. 'I thought you were in the conspiracy when I found you on the beach.'

'I guessed you would believe so, and was anxious to clear myself.' Neither of us spoke the thought that was evidently in both our minds, that though I might have no connection with the smugglers, Regina apparently had. Another irrelevant question came into my mind.

'Are you also a Catholic?'

'No.'

'But you are a Fairfax.'

'That is true, but my father did not practice the faith nor have me baptized in it.'

'You know that Damian and Regina are – or rather, were – Catholics?'

'I never thought about it. Were, you say?'

'Until Damian fell from grace. Now neither of them practice the faith.'

Richard's eyes narrowed in interest. 'How did my surly cousin fall from grace, as you put it?'

'He was a priest, and was unfrocked on account of his liaison with Rachel.'

'A priest!' There was no hiding the shock on Richard's face. 'Now *that* I did not know. My cousin exhibits none of the qualities one usually associates with the priesthood.'

'Possibly grief changed him,' I suggested. 'I have heard him in here, obviously very distressed. He must have loved

173

her very deeply to be still so grief-stricken after all this time. It must be about eight years since she died.'

'A long time to remain heartbroken,' Richard agreed.

A sound outside the door made me look away from him sharply. Richard heard it too, a rustling, shuffling sound and a strangled moan. He took the lantern from me and, crossing to the door, opened it and looked out. I followed him. At the end of the corridor the shadowy figure of a woman was just passing through the studded door to the main wing. She was lost to view as the door closed behind her. I shivered, remembering the distant laugh of a woman I had heard once in the night, and Uncle Eustace's talk of ghosts.

'I had forgotten Regina was still down in the crypt,' Richard said as he closed the door of the Rose Room behind us. 'She must have just come upstairs. I wonder if she overheard us talking of their private affairs.'

I felt distinctly guilty at the thought, but relieved to think it had been no ghostly apparition. How silly of me. No sooner was I back in the gloomy chill of Mallory Keep than I was immediately affected by its brooding atmosphere. I was glad Richard was near to maintain my customary practicality.

'I hope she did not hear,' I said as we walked back towards the main wing.

'Because your employer would not appreciate your talking to me, of all people, of what does not concern you?'

I was stung by his words. I felt the blood rush to my cheeks. 'I did not mean to betray them, and well you know it! I was only trying to explain to you why Damian, at least, is not always as reasonable as he could be. And Regina too. At the moment she is unapproachable because she too is distressed.' My words exploded angrily. He evidently took my fury for a protestation of innocence underlined by guilt, for he simply smiled at me, a wry smile that was devoid of humour.

'Or is it a plea for me to be charitable? To forget my claim in a welter of sympathy for my poor desolated cousins?' he asked quietly.

I stopped in the doorway to stare up at him. His expression was calm, his eyes cold. 'What do you imply?' I asked in

174

stammering tones. 'Are you suggesting I have some ulterior motive in telling you of their troubles?'

He took my elbow and walked on towards my bedroom door. 'It is not impossible. I know my cousin Regina well enough by now to know that she has a clever, scheming mind. Her apparent distress and your charming explanations could well be part of an elaborate scheme.'

Anger bubbled in me, both that he could disbelieve Regina's very real distress and that he could believe me capable of collaborating in any underhanded scheme. I wrenched my elbow from his hand and turned to glare at him.

'Just what are you saying?' I demanded angrily.

'Only that I suspect you have been set by my cousin as bait for me, a charming and pretty bait I admit, but a distraction nonetheless.'

'To what end?'

'To deter me from taking Mallory. To play on my sympathy.'

'You have, if I may say so, a suspicious mind that does you no credit, and the manners of a bumpkin.'

He spread his hands and smiled. 'You may say so, for it is true. I was not raised to the fine ways of a gentleman, but to speak honestly what is on my mind. A farm is no place to breed fine gentlemen, and what I have encountered in life has made me suspicious. If you find my manners uncouth, I am sorry, but I note you did not deny my challenge.'

We were outside my door now. I drew myself up to my full height, still a clear eight or nine inches below him, and answered haughtily.

'I have no need to deny. A clear conscience is my safeguard, though I regret that Regina cannot clear the name you dishonour.'

He tilted his fair head to one side, a mocking smile on his lips. 'You would not deny she would do anything to keep Mallory from me, surely?'

'And with justification! Mallory was hers and Damian's long before they ever heard of you! What right have you to threaten them?'

'I did not intend to when I came. It is only now, having

seen how neglected the estate is, that I think I should accept the responsibility and try to restore it. I cannot avoid my duty.'

'Duty?' I glared at him, scornfully. 'You use a fine motive to cover base covetousness, sir.'

A frown furrowed his broad brow. 'It is not a task I relish, I assure you, but I know my farming training could help to rescue what is left of Mallory and to deter those who seek to destroy it.'

'Who seeks to harm Mallory – other than you?' I said sharply. Disappointment barbed my words, for I had believed him a man of integrity. It is always disillusioning to find one's idols have feet of clay.

'Regina leaves too much for her bailiff to decide.'

'Ben Jagger has been invaluable to her, she told me herself. She could not have continued to run the estate without his help. She does not need your help.'

'So she told me. But I fear the time has come when I must take over.' There was cold determination in his words. Anger got the better of me.

'You had best be warned to leave well alone, or I shall find it necessary to tell Regina of your plans.'

He smiled quizzically. 'Your loyalty is a little belated. It did not prevent you telling me of your employer's private affairs, which doubtless she would have preferred to be kept silent. If you regard me as her enemy, then remember you have played into the enemy's hands by convincing me of my cousins' incapability of managing Mallory.'

'How?'

'By proving they are both mad, whether because of grief or whatever reason. But now it is clear I *must* take over the estate.'

He leaned forward, brushing my cheek with his hair as he bent to turn the knob of my door.

'Good night, Amity. You must be tired after your journey.'

Angered and hurt, I was not going to be dismissed so lightly. But as I stiffened, refusing to go through the door into my room, he simply made me a slight bow and walked on towards his own room. Defeated, I had no choice but to go in and prepare for bed.

I heard the grandfather clock in the vestibule distantly chime midnight, and still I did not sleep. There was too much unrest in this gloomy old fortress of a house for sleep to come easily. Like the spirits of the past haunting the east wing, I too felt uneasy and not at peace.

Shuffling footsteps outside my door suddenly made me sit bolt upright. I was not the only inhabitant of the Keep whom sleep eluded. The steps retreated, but I could hear them still in the distance. I got out of bed and pulled on my dressing robe.

It was Uncle Eustace who loitered there on the minstrel's gallery, a candle in his hand and the tasselled nightcap askew on his head, gazing up at the portraits.

'One, two, three, four, five,' his thin voice came to me on the still air. I smiled. He was eternally vigilant against predatory servants, checking the family portraits now to ensure they were all there.

'Good evening, sir,' I said quietly, so as not to alarm him. He raised the candle as I advanced and peered at me from under his caterpillar brows.

'Ah, it's you, Miss Friendship. You are still with us then,' he remarked with an amiable smile. 'I haven't seen you for some time, and I was beginning to think I had imagined you too. Regina keeps telling me I grow confused, but I'm glad you are real after all. I like you. I don't like some of the others I see.'

'I have been away, sir.'

'Then I'm glad you're back. Perhaps you will help me.'

'To be sure, if I can.'

'I wanted to see if Mr. Richard's portrait was still here, for I thought I had seen him in the east wing. Now did I imagine him, or is he still here on the wall?'

He raised the candle to inspect the last portrait. The image of Richard Fairfax's sober face stared down at us, and I saw the perplexed look that crossed Uncle Eustace's face.

'Dear me, that's very odd. I could have sworn . . .'

'Do not fret, sir, you are not imagining things,' I hastened to reassure him. 'Mr. Richard's son, who is also named Richard, is here as a guest. And they are as alike as two peas.'

It was pleasant to see the old man's frown fade and the smile reappear.

'And is he real, my dear, or do you imagine him too? For you are psychic, you know. I told you once before.'

'He is real, sir, I assure you. I have felt his hand on my arm.'

'Then that's all right. Tell me, was I right about your horoscope? Has it turned out as I predicted?'

I felt too ashamed to confess I had forgotten what he had predicted, so I said nothing. Uncle Eustace seemed to forget his question as he began to shuffle back towards his room, but as he retreated I heard the quavering voice.

'Conflict. Stars in such conjunction make it inevitable, more's the pity. Severe conflict, but it will amend in time.'

He disappeared into his room, the circle of candlelight with him, leaving me in darkness. I had to grope for the knob of my door.

For ages I sat on my bed, fuming with anger and deeply hurt by Richard's words. I had meant no betrayal of my employers, only to help them, and yet betrayal was how Richard saw my actions. I was furious. To think I had been so eager to return to Mallory Keep, to see him again! I almost hated him for his blindness. Uncle Eustace was right. There was nothing but conflict in my life, with Damian, with Regina who held me responsible for the boy's death, and now with Richard. Life could be so cruel, mocking one with malicious turns of fate, just as one looked for contentment.

There were no warning footsteps outside my door to forewarn me of the knock that came, low and urgent. I jumped as a voice followed the knock.

'Amity, are you awake?'

It was Richard's voice. I ran to open the door to him eagerly. Perhaps he had come to apologise for his hurtful words, for wrongful accusation. I could not help a smile of welcome.

His tanned face was darkly sober by the light of the candle he held, one hand cupping it against the draft along the corridor. 'Do you hear?' he asked quietly.

178

'Hear what?'

He raised a hand and listened intently. So did I, but I could hear nothing. All was silent in the Keep.

'Come.' Richard's tone of command brooked no denial. I followed him to the door of the east wing. 'Now listen.'

Now I could hear – it was the same distant shuffling and bumping sound I had heard once before, weeks ago. I nodded. 'I hear it. I have heard it before.'

'I am going to investigate. We know Regina has gone to her room and Damian is out, so whoever is in the east wing is there without sanction. I shall find out who it is.'

'I'll come with you.'

'No.' His hand gripped my elbow. 'You must stay here. If it is the smugglers using the passage from the Rose Room, they may resent my interference. I want you to stay, and if I am not back within half an hour, wake Regina and tell her. You understand?'

I understood. He suspected Jagger of nefarious activities of which Regina was being kept in ignorance. I watched Richard go through the studded door, closing it behind him. I went back to my room to wait as I was bidden.

It was deathly quiet. I felt apprehensive for Richard, for I too distrusted Ben Jagger. On the mantelshelf my clock seemed to tick slowly as I waited impatiently. After twenty minutes Richard still had not reappeared, and I could bear the waiting no longer. Taking up my oil lamp, I went out along the corridor to the east wing.

Once again the chill struck me as soon as I passed through the door. Ahead of me there was nothing but darkness and silence. I moved forward cautiously, on towards the Rose Room where I was sure Richard had gone. When I reached it I found the door standing open, but no one inside. It was dark and silent as a tomb.

Richard had come here, I was certain, for the door was open. But where was he now? Had he followed the smugglers through the secret chamber down the passage to the beach? Holding the lamp aloft, I could see that the door in the panelling into the chamber was closed. It was hardly likely he would have closed it behind him.

As I hesitated I heard the sound again, the scraping sound

179

Richard had heard. And it came not from this room but from out in the corridor. Moving silently out again into the passage, I listened. The sound came from the far end, from where the spiral staircase led down to the crypt.

Against my own better judgment, I approached the top of the stairs. Here the air was yet colder and more menacing, and the sickly smell I remembered of death and decay was oppressive. Fear ran in my veins, fear both of this nauseous place and fear for Richard. No good could come to him if he were down there.

I pushed my loathing of the place to the back of my mind. Richard could be in need of help. Summoning my courage, I began to descend the stone steps with care.

Regina had been right. Some of the steps were broken and crumbling, and it took all my concentration to climb safely down, no rail to the outer edge, nor Richard's strong hand to prevent a fall. It was as I neared the pool of darkness at the bottom that I felt the furry thing hurl itself at my legs. With a stifled shriek I could not repress, I flattened myself against the wall. Though I never saw it, I knew it was that devilish cat again.

Then there was silence, profound quiet one could have severed with a knife, it was so tangible. I reached the bottom and moved towards the crypt door, my nerves tingling with apprehension. Much as I disliked the horrible place, I must go in. Richard might be in danger.

The only sound to cut into the stillness was the creak of the hinge as I pushed the door open with a trembling hand. To my relief the crypt was empty and in darkness. I held the lamp high to make sure there was no one there, and in doing so I caught sight of something lying on the floor, over by the stone block where we had found Regina.

I crossed the chamber towards it and bent to see what lay on the slabbed floor. It was an iron candlestick, denuded of its candle, such as Richard had been carrying. I laid it on the stone slab thoughtfully.

It would seem that Richard had been here, though the Keep had many such candlesticks scattered about its many rooms. This was not necessarily his, and if it were, where was the candle? And then another question worried me. If

Richard had decided for some reason to discard the candle-stick, would he have just dropped it on the floor?

Perhaps there had been a struggle. Perhaps Jagger and the other smugglers, angered by his intrusion, had overpowered Richard and taken him prisoner. But then, I reasoned with myself, why should the smugglers come here to the crypt when their secret passage led from the Rose Room?

My gaze swept the stone shelves about the chamber and the great stone coffins upon them. It was an unnerving thought, to think I was alone in this gloomy place, save for the company of these long-dead Fairfaxes, the powdered and bewigged creatures whose portraits graced the minstrels' gallery. Only now they were no longer painted, pretty creatures, but mouldered bones and dust. I shivered and turned to leave.

Then I stopped. In a corner I noticed bulky shapes which were not rectangular, coffin-shaped, and I went back to inspect them more closely by the light of the lamp. Kegs, they were, barrels and banded boxes. So the smugglers *had* been here to hide their booty. It must have been an arduous task to transport these heavy kegs and boxes down the spiral stairs from the secret passage in the Rose Room, but it would account for all the bumping, scraping sounds Richard and I had heard earlier.

It was while I was bending over the boxes that I suddenly had the strangest feeling. I could swear I could feel eyes on my back. I swung round, raising my lamp, and fear rising in my throat. There was no one there. I was alone. Nevertheless I could feel my heart thudding in my chest and made up my mind to leave this gruesome place without further delay.

But before I could take a step towards the door I heard footsteps, heavy, uncertain steps from outside in the passage. Someone was coming down the spiral stairs. As I watched I saw through the open door a ring of light appear at the foot of the stairs, a lamp held alongside a pair of trousered legs.

Richard! I was about to rush forward in relief when another shape arrested me. It was the lumbering figure of Caesar, Damian's wolfhound, loping along towards me under the lamp. I drew back in alarm, cupping my hand over my own lamp and blowing it out lest Damian should find me

181

here in the sacred sanction of the Fairfaxes. Half-crouched against one of the cold, clammy stone coffins, I waited, certain I would be discovered.

At the doorway to the crypt Damian stopped. The hound padded on past him and entered the chamber. Instinctively I shrank back further against the coffin, fearful lest the creature should scent me and possibly attack me. I remembered Damian had once warned me of the brute's hostile ways with all but himself. But the dog did not come towards me. In the centre of the chamber he suddenly stopped, laid back his ears against his great, shaggy skull, and let out a fearful howl. Then in a half-crouching position he backed towards the door.

'Here, Caesar, come out of there!' his master snarled. The dog slunk out rapidly. Every movement of his great body indicated abject terror. But before I could wonder at his strange behaviour, I was startled by Damian's next move. Without a word he pulled the heavy door shut and I heard the sound of a key grate in the lock. Then his footsteps faded away along the passage.

Utter blackness now enveloped me, as if someone had just thrown a heavy blanket over my head. For a moment I was so stunned I did not think to run to the door and beat on it, crying to Damian to let me out. And by the time I had recovered my wits there was total silence outside. Damian was by now upstairs again, too far away to hear my cries. I groped in my dressing-robe pocket. I was unlucky. The lucifers were no longer there, and I had no means of relighting my oil lamp.

A feeling of near-hysteria pulsed in my veins. For as long as I could remember I had had a fear of enclosed spaces, claustrophobia, Uncle Leonard had called it. It dated since the time when, for some childish misdemeanour, I had been locked in a store cupboard, in my kindergarten school. For a long time afterwards I had even been afraid of the dark, pleading with my aunt to allow me one small night light by my bed. Now, in this dark, dank chamber my childhood fears rose involuntarily to the surface again, and it was all I could do not to scream in terror.

I crouched, the blackness in the crypt so dense it seemed to

182

invade my nostrils and choke me. Never before in my life had I felt so filled with fear and panic. And then, as though to increase my utter terror, came the sensation once again that I was not alone, the feeling I was being watched. It was a ridiculous thought, for no one could see in that unfathomable darkness.

Only a cat. I remembered the wolfhound's shrinking from this place, in just the way a dog will back away in fear from a cat, and I was certain. That diabolical creature from Rachel's room was in here with me, no doubt watching my human weakness impassively. But though I could sense the baleful eyes, I could see nothing in the place, only the velvet blackness which threatened to envelop and asphyxiate me.

My palms grew clammy and I could feel my head beginning to spin. In a detached corner of my brain I told myself I was about to have what Aunt Cecily called a fit of the vapours, and I made a determined effort to pull myself together. But I was losing. My hands grasped the damp stone flags as I struggled to stay upright. I could feel unconsciousness about to claim me, to absolve me from the terror that clutched me. As I hovered on the brink of the vortex I heard a grating sound and then, blessedly, light flooded the crypt.

With a cry of relief I stared at the origin of the light. A hole appeared to gape in the stone floor, behind the great block of stone, a circle filled with light from a candle and the dark shape of a man's head.

At that moment it would not have mattered who the man was – Damian, Ben Jagger, Ramsden even – I would still have felt and acted the same way. As it was, it was Richard who was subjected to my rapturously happy embrace. I could not have been happier.

'Oh, Richard! Thank God you've come!' I cried as I hugged him. He was trying to keep the guttering candle outside my feverish embrace, but I could see he was astonished nonetheless. He showed no alarm at having been leapt upon unexpectedly in the Fairfax vault.

'What on earth are you doing here?' he asked quietly. 'I thought I told you to stay where you were. Come now, back to bed.'

'I followed you when you were gone so long. Then Damian locked the door and I couldn't get out.'

'I see.' He thought for a moment. 'Stay here and I'll go back down the passage. It connects with the other to the Rose Room, I think. I'll find the way round and unlock the door from outside.'

'No, I'll come with you. I couldn't bear to stay here alone a moment longer.' I clung tightly to his arm.

'Very well. Step carefully now, for the light is nearly gone.'

The candle did begin to sputter as I followed him down the rough-hewn steps into the hole. Below, in a roughly carved tunnel under the vault, I could feel only immense relief at being released from the tomb of the dead at last. Holding Richard's hand, strong and reassuring, I followed him along the winding passage, sloping up and around until at last we came to the wall.

'Ah yes, here's the priest hole,' said Richard touching the wall and leading me inside. The candle sputtered its last gasp as we emerged into the lamplit Rose Room.

'What happened?' I asked breathlessly as I followed Richard out into the corridor. 'Did you follow them? Was it the smugglers?'

'Explanations later. Time for bed now,' he replied tensely, leading me firmly by the hand. Beyond the studded door we came face to face with Uncle Eustace, padding along in slippered feet and his tasselled nightcap askew over one ear.

'Oh, good morning,' he said brightly, as though it were an everyday occurrence to meet us at night emerging from the forbidden east wing.

'Good morning, sir,' Richard replied. 'It is indeed near dawn, I think.'

'And I hope it will be a fine, bright day for you, Miss Amity,' the old man said with a smile. 'Many happy returns, my dear. Have a happy day, Miss Friendship.'

He padded away towards his room before I could register his meaning. Of course. Things had been happening so swiftly of late I had lost count of the date. But not Uncle Eustace – he counted everything. He was right. Today was the twenty-seventh.

At my doorway Richard stopped. 'Sleep well for what is

left of the night, Amity,' he said soberly. 'We'll talk in the morning. Good night.'

And then a twinkle enlivened the tired blue eyes. 'Your birthday, is it? Then let me be the first to salute you, with all my very best wishes.' And so saying, he bent towards me. A stupid witless fool I must have looked, standing there limply while the most handsome man I had ever met took me in his arms and kissed me. No avuncular kiss such as Uncle Leonard used to bestow on my birthday, but a firm, lasting kiss on my lips.

I shivered, feeling the same drifting, fainting sensation I had felt when I almost fainted in the crypt. But no terror accompanied it this time, only pleasure and a rippling excitement, and I wanted to go on.

But when he stood back from me, a smile curving his lips as his soft voice again drawled 'Good night,' I felt angry.

I rushed into my room, rubbing the offending kiss furiously from my lips. What did he take me for, to reprimand me and scold me and then kiss me as if I were as easy to approach as a kitchen maid? Evidently he felt no respect for me at all. I began my birthday miserably, unable to sleep.

CHAPTER TWELVE

'The Devil's awa' wi' the Exciseman.'
— Robert Burns

Heavy-eyed and heavy of spirit, I came down to breakfast in the morning. Richard was already helping himself to porridge from a steaming tureen on the dining table, looking as tanned and bright of eye as if he had slept well. I hesitated in the doorway, ashamed to face him. He caught sight of me and smiled.

'Come and eat, Amity. Regina is feeling better today, more like her old self, and has promised to join us for lunch. Come, sit by me.'

He rose to pull out a chair for me so I had little choice. But from embarrassment I remained silent while spooning porridge into my dish. I was aware of his speculative stare. Was he, I wondered, perhaps regretting his rather ungentlemanly behaviour towards me early this morning?

'You look a little pale this morning,' he remarked at last. 'A little stroll down to the village would help to restore the colour to your cheeks. We shall take the air together after breakfast.'

It was a command, orders from a doctor to a patient, I fancied, rather than a desire for my company. Nevertheless I would go with him. I wanted to know more about last night and what Richard had discovered.

It was beautifully warm and sunny as Richard and I made our way down through the gardens to the gateway in the thorn hedge that led out on to the cliff path. At first Richard walked beside me at a respectful distance, but as the path narrowed and became steeper he drew my arm through his.

'One must take care here, for the stony surface makes one's feet slither,' he explained. I made no answer. Angry as I might have been with him, I still welcomed his arm.

'Tell me about last night,' I urged him. 'What did you find out?'

'Well, as I reckoned it might be, it was Jagger in the east wing. But not in the Rose Room. I followed the sounds and found they came from the crypt. Jagger and that ferret-faced man from the farm were supervising some other fellows in removing barrels and boxes.'

'That would be Ramsden from Keep Farm. He was with Jagger that night in the cave.'

'They spoke of the cave. It seems it fills with water at high tide, therefore they must remove the contraband to a place of safety, immediately after it is landed. So they bring it to the crypt, knowing the Fairfaxes never go there as a rule.'

I looked up quickly. 'But Regina . . .'

'Yes, that is why they were anxious to remove the stuff last night, because she had taken to coming there.'

'She must have seen it earlier, when we found her down there. But what I was going to say was that Regina evidently knows of their activities already. It was she who opened the secret door in the Rose Room.'

'She does not know all, evidently,' Richard's voice was grave. 'After the others had finished and left, I overheard Jagger and Ramsden talking. They were boasting of how little she knew and how clever they were. My guess is that Regina is told only a fraction of what they do. I was sure Jagger was deceiving her, and what I overheard strengthens that conviction.'

I felt dismay for Regina, knowing how she had trusted Jagger. If Richard were right, she would feel bitterly betrayed.

'Shall you tell Regina what you learned?'

He shook his fair head slowly. 'Not until I can prove it. She will not believe me otherwise, but no doubt accuse me of lying to gain Mallory for myself.'

I eyed him thoughtfully. Yes, that was probably what Regina would believe, and how was I to believe otherwise? The clear, candid look in his eyes as he gazed out over the sea

187

allayed the sudden suspicion. Somehow I could not believe Richard Fairfax capable of deceit.

The breeze was tugging playfully at my bonnet strings, but I was scarcely aware of the beauty of the day. I gazed down at Manacle Bay, to where the high tide lapped in frothing white waves at the cliff's foot. The cave was hidden beneath the waves.

'Surely contraband is usually landed directly at the jetty and brought into the village,' I said at length. I was remembering the day I had drunk tea while seated on a cask in Mrs. Pickering's cottage.

'When the coast is clear, probably, but if the revenue men are about then the cave and its passages are more discreet.'

'Especially if the booty is to be carried inland. I remember one of the passages leads to Keep Farm.'

'That figures. Some of the stuff is to be sold and the rest kept here for their own use. That's what they were removing last night.'

As Richard spoke we reached the bottom of the cliff path and turned towards the main village street. We were nearing the lych-gate of the church, his arm still closely linking mine.

'Where did they take it? Did you follow them?' I asked. 'You haven't told me yet.'

'I'll show you.' He pushed open the lych-gate and led me up the grassgrown path towards the church. 'Yes, when Ramsden and Jagger left the crypt, I followed. It was in my haste to find the flagstone covering the steps down that I dropped the candlestick, and snatched up the candle before it went out.'

'They did not hear you?'

'No, I followed at a safe distance. Fortunately the passage twists and turns so I could remain close enough to hear most of what was said. Did you know that Ramsden pays no rent for Keep Farm? I wonder how many other rents never reach Regina.'

I hesitated before answering. 'I think there could be a good reason for that. Regina is in the Ramsdens' debt for a past favour.' I could not bring myself to betray Regina's confidence over the child, but it was necessary to explain something of her indebtedness.

188

We were by the great stone obelisk, the Devil's Arrow, when Richard stopped. 'Poor Regina. Both Ramsden and Jagger seem to have a hold over her. No wonder she cannot make the estate prosper,' he said quietly. 'If only that fool cousin of mine, Damian, would pull his fuddled wits together instead of leaving all the care to her . . .'

'He can't,' I said abruptly. 'Why have we stopped here?'

'Because this is where the trail ends,' he said with an enigmatic smile. He looked amused at my puzzled look. 'This where the passage ended.'

He pointed to the Devil's Arrow, or rather to a clump of bushes immediately behind it. 'There is a boulder covering the entrance, then the passage runs sharply down. I followed only as far as here, so I don't know where they went, but my guess is into the church. No doubt the vicar has an abundant supply of whisky and geneva gin sitting in his vestry right now.'

I was sure he was right, for the vicar was in the conspiracy with the villagers. The cask I had sat upon in Mrs. Pickering's cottage had been destined for him.

From the churchyard I could see down over the red roofs of the closely-huddled cottages to the sea. It was clear to me that contraband could easily be passed from cottage to cottage, across the tiny passages and yards, to reach the sanctuary of the church without the prying eyes of revenue men ever noticing. And the alternative route underground made secrecy even more secure. No wonder the tightly packed little houses wore such an inscrutable air of conspiracy and complacency.

And the Devil's Arrow. I looked at the towering obelisk with new insight. It was no age-old respect for an ancient religion which had made the fisherfolk stand close guard around it that Sunday I was here, but suspicion and fear lest I discovered the entrance to their underground passage. I realised then how little I had come to know the village folk. Although I had kept their secret when I sat on the cask of brandy, I still had not earned their trust. I looked up at Richard. He was surveying the landscape thoughtfully, a speculative frown rutting his tanned forehead.

'It is well-contrived, with the church as hiding place if the booty is landed at the jetty when the coast is clear, and the cave and passages to the Keep as an alternative,' he remarked.

'And a passage inland to Keep Farm,' I added.

'Yes. And even overland goods can be conveyed discreetly along the valley where the stream runs. Pack horses would be hidden among the trees. The villagers are indeed well placed for their little game.'

A sudden suspicion crossed my mind. 'You are not going to betray them to the revenue men, are you, Richard?'

He laughed softly, and I loved the way his eyes creased at the corners and his whole face took on a radiance as brilliant as the May sunshine. 'Indeed, no. Who am I to presume to judge them? Good luck to them, say I, but I must find out how Jagger is deceiving Regina. As their ringleader, he knows the full extent of their profit, and my guess is that he keeps Regina in the dark.'

'Why?'

'To maintain power over her.'

'You think she is in with them – for profit?'

He shrugged. 'How else can she afford to keep Mallory running? No doubt it goes against the grain with her, but she is obliged to collude to keep Mallory.'

I turned to face him squarely. 'And you want Mallory, you told me so. If you betrayed the smugglers, Regina would not have money. Mallory would be yours. How can one be sure you are not tempted?'

His smile faded. His voice was rough when he spoke again. 'Yes, I want Mallory, but not that way. By fair means I shall have it, not foul. But who is this gentleman approaching? Is it the vicar?'

Turning to look towards the lych-gate I saw the Reverend Parmenter's cassocked figure approaching, preceded by a flash of black and white. His terrier, Patch, bounded joyfully about me then crouched and barked interrogatively at my companion. Richard smiled and offered a hand to sniff. Patch, reassured, licked the hand and raced back to join his advancing master.

The vicar's smile was warm, but I could see that the

190

interest in his shrewd grey eyes was for Richard, not for me, as he offered me his hand. I shook it gravely.

Richard bo..ed slightly. I could see the two pairs of eyes, the grey and the blue, held the same assessing look. The reverend held out his hand.

'And I am delighted to meet you again, sir. I have seen you walking abroad, looking at our abbey ruins and moorland, and once down in the village. Do you find our stretch of the coastline attractive?'

'I find it very interesting,' Richard replied in a guarded tone. The vicar's eyelids flickered, but he held Richard's gaze steadily. I felt ignored as the two men sized each other up.

'It seems you have a taste for the outdoor life. I have seen you often taking the air, both on foot and on horseback.'

'I was reared on my father's farm.'

'Do you intend to return to your farming life, sir?'

I saw Richard's quick look at the vicar's amiable face. 'I doubt it, sir. I find this part of England has its attractions.'

The reverend's gaze transferred to me. 'Indeed, you are right,' he remarked. I wondered whether he believed Richard found me to be one of the attractions, and I blushed. 'The coast is rugged but beautiful hereabouts,' he went on. 'The countryside is rich in legend, but the folk are reserved. Even after all my years here, they still have not completely accepted me.'

Richard smiled charmingly. 'You surprise me, Reverend. I would have believed they both admired and trusted a gentleman such as yourself.'

The vicar shook his head slowly. 'Respect me I believe they do, and trust me to a certain extent, but there is a limit to their trust. A proud race, these Yorkshire folk, and suspicious. They have to have one's trustworthiness proved to them. You will see.' His expression brightened. 'But I think you will have little difficulty, sir. With your knowledge of the farming life, you already have something in common with them. It will take a little time, but you have more to your advantage than your cousins.'

'Indeed?' Richard's fair eyebrows rose in question. 'Do you imply, sir, that the locals have little regard for my cousins? Since the Fairfaxes have been the squires of Mallory for so many generations, surely they have the villagers' loyalty?'

The Reverend Parmenter's smile had faded fractionally, but he quickly recovered himself. 'I am sorry, I did not intend any such implication, sir. Though I must add that respect is not one's by inherited right, but must be earned. Now that you mention it, however, I must confess that the local folk have little truck with the Fairfaxes these days, beyond being their tenants. They never could quite understand them.'

'Why is that?'

'Well, you must remember that the Fairfaxes are Catholic, worshipping at their own chapel in the Keep. They do not come down amongst the villagers to christen their children and bury their dead. That puts a distance between those already removed by birth and wealth, and their tenants.'

'Is that all? Is there no other reason?' Richard persisted.

'Well, your cousin Damian has never shown great interest in their affairs. They felt disappointed when he left the village to . . .' The vicar hesitated. 'To do what he felt he must,' he finished.

I could understand the villagers' dismay when the squire they expected to be able to turn to for help and guidance forsook them to minister to strangers far away. Richard seemed to be thinking the same as he watched Patch prancing around the obelisk.

'And my cousin Regina?' he asked quietly.

'Miss Fairfax is respected for her efforts, but as a woman with little knowledge of country life she has her limitations,' the vicar replied. He was right. Regina herself had admitted she would have wished to run the estate more efficiently. If Richard was right, I felt angered that Jagger, whom she trusted, evidently did not serve her well. The bailiff did not help her standing with the locals if he was betraying her.

'I think they could have forgiven his leaving Mallory,' the vicar went on thoughtfully, 'but his return did not mollify them. Though I have no actual knowledge of the events, not yet having come here at the time, I am told he came back with a woman. The villagers could forgive a man's need to serve

192

his church, but not his abandoning that too, to fulfill his baser desires. But, as I say, I know nothing of that. It is only hearsay.'

Richard prodded a tuft of grass with the toe of his shoe. 'Have the Fairfaxes always been disliked?'

'Not always. My predecessor was very interested in local history, and he wrote a pamphlet on the history of the Fairfaxes. Mostly it was fact, but some of it mere supposition, I fancy. From it I gather that, generally speaking, the family and the locals lived at peace with each other.'

'A truce only, not in amity,' Richard remarked.

'Do not mistake me, sir. There were times when the Fairfaxes were true leaders and highly respected.'

'And on others?'

The vicar's expression saddned. 'According to my predecessor, on other occasions they were hated. He even hinted at worse.'

'What did he hint?'

'That hands had been raised against the family. You know the belief of the old religion, that when hard times fall on the land, the spilling of royal blood is the only way to placate the anger of the gods?'

'I had not heard of it,' Richard said.

'Oh, yes. Some believe that that is why King William Rufus was killed in the New Forest – to appease the gods and restore the crops which had failed.'

'What has the legend to do with the Fairfaxes?'

'In truth, nothing. But as centuries-old rulers in this area, my predecessor evidently thought that they sometimes fell victim to the locals' ancient beliefs. It is true that unexplained accidents did occur.'

I spoke before I could stop myself. 'Like Mr. Thomas's fall from the cliff?' I asked. 'Your uncle,' I added to Richard in explanation. 'It was a mystery how he came to fall.'

'Well, I would not like to claim that his death was attributable to the villagers,' Reverend Parmenter said hastily. 'The last incumbent merely implied that unexplained accidents to the family could perhaps be due to the ancient belief.'

I looked up at the stone obelisk. 'And the locals do hold old beliefs, you told me once.'

193

'Yes, they are a strange, stubborn folk. Of Norse descent, and proud of it. One can guide them but one cannot force them.' The vicar turned brightly to Richard. 'But you need have no fear, sir, they will come to like and respect you, I am sure of it. Just give them time.'

Richard took my elbow. 'Well, we shall continue our walk. We are making Miss Lucas's birthday visit to the village.'

'Indeed? My felicitations, Miss Lucas.'

Richard paused as we were about to leave. 'I wonder if you would permit us to look round your lovely old church, Reverend. I am interested in old English churches.'

I had a sudden vision of my first sight of him, the sunlight casting a coloured halo about his fair head in York Minster. The vicar smiled apologetically.

'Tomorrow, perhaps, I could show you around, Mr. Fairfax, but now I am due to visit a sick parishioner. It must be nearing noon, so I must hurry or I shall be late for lunch. Mrs. Parmenter likes us to be punctual for meals. Tomorrow, then?'

As the vicar's black-robed figure disappeared around the side of the church towards the vicarage, Richard drew out a silver watch from his breast pocket. 'A quarter to twelve,' he remarked. 'Regina will expect us for lunch at one.'

'There is still time to walk down to the village,' I replied, taking his arm again. I was enjoying our close companionship and reluctant to return home too soon.

We set off down the cobbled main street, past the neat cottages, all of which bore a deserted air about them. Not a single housewife was to be seen scrubbing her steps or cleaning the windows, and not a curtain moved as we passed.

'The Reverend Parmenter interrogated me well, I fancy,' Richard remarked at length. 'He did an efficient job, though with all politeness. It was evident his shrewd mind was busy assessing the new situation.'

'With a new claimant to the Mallory estates you mean? Yes, I think you are right. And what is more, if I am not mistaken, I think he was putting a proposition to you.'

Richard glanced at me sharply. 'You are a quick-witted young lady, for I had the same impression. What did you make of it?'

I looked up at his fair, earnest face. So he had interpreted the drift of the vicar's conversation in the same way that I had. I decided to speak openly, to watch Richard's reaction.

'I feel he was telling you of the villagers' dislike of the Fairfaxes who now control Mallory, and implying that a *new* Fairfax, who understood their problems and could deal with them, would be infinitely more acceptable.'

'That I would be welcomed as squire, in fact. Yes, that is what I read into his words.' Richard's tone was quiet and matter-of-fact. There was no hint of bragging or pride. Before I could frame my next question we reached the bottom of the street where it turned along the jetty, and Richard exclaimed in surprise.

'Ah, no wonder the village is quiet. Look!'

Along the little quayside, between the steep cliff and the low sea wall, dozens of women in canvas skirts and white sunbonnets were working silently at trestle tables. Mountains of fish surrounded them, and the sunlight glinted sharply on the metal knives the women wielded, deftly slitting and gutting the silvery fish. It was a picturesque scene, sunlight dappling the waves beyond the wall, and the many hues of the women's workaday print dresses flooding the scene with colour.

Movement replaced sound, I noticed, and that was odd. Sparkling fish scales gleamed as the women tossed the gutted fish into wicker creels, but no one spoke. A gathering of women, of whatever class, usually meant chatter. Why not now? And then I saw why. Beyond the wall, on the narrow stretch of shingled beach, Damian was sitting, arms curled about his knees, staring out to sea and lost in thought. He was too close to them to permit them to speak freely.

One of the women straightened, put down her knife, and wiped her hands on her coarse apron. She muttered a few words, picked up a creel of fish, and turned to walk towards us. Under the white sunbonnet with its protective neck-flap I recognised Mrs. Pickering. She nodded to me as she approached, and I saw her curious eyes linger on Richard.

'Good morning, Mrs. Pickering,' I said with a smile. 'You are very busy today.'

'Have to get t'fish salted afore t'men come back with

t'next catch,' she replied, indicating the contents of her heavy creel.

'Where is it salted?'

'Saltersgate Inn, up over t'moor, on t'York Road.'

'Mrs. Pickering, this is Mr. Richard Fairfax, kin to Mr. Damian.'

She nodded. 'I've heard of thee.'

Richard smiled. 'Charmed to meet you, ma'am.'

'Foreigner, aren't tha? Like that other fellow.'

'I'm from America, but my father came from here.'

'Aye, belike. Well I mun get on. I've eight miles to walk. Good day, miss.'

I could not help noticing that she bade farewell to me, a servant of the family, and not to Richard. It was an indication, I felt, of the locals' reluctance to accept him – yet. Mrs. Pickering's plump figure trudged away up the hill.

'I think we shall not disturb my cousin,' Richard remarked after a moment. 'Shall we return?'

'If you wish.' I was reluctant to leave the scene of peaceful activity in the village. The day was so glorious, and the atmosphere so unlike its usual hostile secretiveness, that I wanted to linger. I was enjoying my birthday outing.

After a few minutes I turned. 'Very well, you are right. We shall be late for lunch if we do not go.' Richard's hand cupped my elbow firmly as we climbed the cobbled street. As we reached Mrs. Pickering's cottage she emerged, carrying the creel and closing the door after her. A sudden thought came to me.

'You spoke of another foreigner, Mrs. Pickering,' I said. 'Who is he?'

She shrugged her broad shoulders. 'Don't know his name. Staying at t'Silent Inn, he is, and asking a lot o' questions. Young chap, dark, looks Spanish or summat.'

Noting her scathing look, I smiled. 'Do you think he's a spy, a customs officer perhaps?'

She reddened. 'Doubt it. He asks about t'family mainly. I mun be off now.'

She padded away up the street. I heard Richard's soft laugh. 'Mrs. Pickering is a lady of ample girth, but I think she has grown stouter in the last few minutes. What do you say – a roll of silk about her waist and under her kirtle, or a pig's bladder filled with rum or gin? No wonder she blushed at the mention of the preventives.'

'You know a great deal about the ruses of smugglers – if you are right,' I commented.

'I have seen smuggling and gunrunning before,' he replied quietly. And I knew he was thinking of the war-torn days in the Shenandoah Valley and those ravening crows. I changed the subject quickly.

'What do you intend to do about Jagger?'

Richard considered before he answered. 'I think I shall begin by checking the accounts he renders to Regina, if he will permit me. It is evident he is accumulating money, for he told Ramsden he would soon have enough to buy a cottage and get married.'

'To Rose Pickering. He and she are keeping company.'

'Jagger said he would have enough by the time they had completed the next job – a big job, he said. I wonder if that was to be another smuggling coup. Somehow I had the feeling it was not that. We must watch him and see what he plans.'

I noted the way Richard tacitly assumed that I would help him. In the circumstances, if he was not planning to steal Mallory, I saw no reason why I should not help. In any case, curiosity drove me to want to know what happened next.

We turned off the main street along the cliff path, and as we did so I caught sight of a small ship rounding the headland and turning into Manacle Bay. Richard raised his arm to point.

'The revenue cutter. Mrs. Pickering left with her booty only just in time.'

We watched as the boat came ashore and several uniformed figures leaped onto the beach. Damian's diminutive figure rose and went to meet them. After a few moments' conversation the group turned and walked up the jetty, past the watching women, and into the door of the inn.

'I wonder what my cousin has to do with the customs men,' Richard said, and as we turned to continue our uphill climb he remarked quietly, 'A strange fellow, cousin Damian. Secretive, morose, and it would seem, unscrupulous.'

197

'He is not betraying the villagers, I am sure of it,' I replied with some heat. 'I think he is unaware of their activities.' I was remembering the night I heard Regina saying she had given him a sleeping potion. That was surely to keep him unaware of Jagger's movements in the east wing.

'I was not referring to that,' Richard said calmly, 'but to his abandoning of the priesthood in order to bring his mistress here. That's what the vicar said.'

'That's not how it was! He's not unscrupulous, as you think. Weak maybe, but not without scruple.'

Richard was smiling in amusement. 'You are very quick to defend a man who it seems is never anything but churlish towards you. How was it then, Amity, if I am wrong?'

'She pursued him here. He did not bring her.'

'She was Rachel, of course. And how do you know? Did Regina tell you?'

I felt the flush suffuse my cheeks. 'No, not exactly.' I was filled with shameful embarrassment. My impulsive defence of Damian had led me into trouble.

'Then how do you know?'

The searching gaze of Richard's blue eyes made it impossible to lie. Overcome with confusion, I was forced to confess.

'I read a diary belonging to Rachel. It was behind some books in the writing room.'

'I see.'

To my surprise he made no further comment, either about his cousin or about my behaviour. I expected him to judge me, to censure me, but he remained silent as we neared the gate in the thorn fence.

Inside the grounds he let go of my arm and I wondered whether it was from dislike or simply that I no longer needed assistance. The only sound as we walked was the crunch of gravel underfoot and the occasional cry of a swooping sea gull. I felt miserable. I wished he would say something, so I knew how he felt.

Reaching the front door I made up my mind. I would not go in with him, nor to lunch, while he kept me at a disdainful distance, not knowing whether he despised my actions.

'I'm going round to the kitchen,' I said abruptly, and left him on the doorstep. Once in the stable yard, out of his sight,

198

I loitered. I felt wretched. My sunny birthday outing had suddenly become chill and clouded. I looked up at the sky. The sun had indeed disappeared behind low grey cloud, and a blustering breeze was blowing up.

The yard was deserted. From the direction of the kitchen I could hear the clatter of pans on the iron range and Mrs. Garner's voice raised in reproach. Through the half-open door of the stables I could see Vulcan and Twilight in their stalls mournful-eyed and evidently patiently awaiting the ostler bringing their bran. Of Cooper there was no sign.

Vulcan whinnied, and the whites of his eyes shone out of the gloom of the stable. He snorted and pawed the ground, and I saw Whisper turn her head to stare at him. I wondered if it was the sight of me which had disturbed him, and thought irrelevently, like master, like beast. I moved forward and leaned on the lower door. Vulcan quietened and watched me.

Pushing open the lower door I went inside. 'I'm sorry, old boy, I haven't got your dinner,' I said brightly, taking my opportunity to attempt to befriend the animal. I came close to his stall, but not too close. And then I saw he was not looking at me, but beyond me, towards the door.

He was watching for Cooper, I decided, too intelligent to think I was going to feed him. Moving along to Twilight's stall I stroked her velvet nose and murmured a few words. She nuzzled my arm affectionately.

And then, without warning, a sudden feeling of chill came over me. It was not just the darkening sky outside and the approach of rain, not just the thickening gloom in the stable. It was a cold sensation of fear, of menace. My neck prickled, and slowly I turned around.

There was no one there. Although I had heard no footsteps in the yard, I fully expected to see someone in the doorway watching me. But I was alone with the two horses, and Vulcan was still staring towards the door.

I must get out of here, I resolved, before the chill sensation engulfed me. I was becoming a silly, near-hysterical thing, imagining danger where none existed. But to me it was real. The air of menace was as powerful as in the oppressive east wing of the Keep.

It was as I took hold of the lower stable door to pull it shut after me that something made me look down. On the back of the door was something small and dark, fastened in place by a hay fork.

I recoiled, my stomach heaving, as I recognised what it was. A tortoiseshell cat, a piece of fish still hanging from its jaws, was pinned to the woodwork, transfixed by the fork. Its eyes were staring wide, evidently surprised at the moment of death by unexpected attack. And that attack could not have taken place so very long ago, for blood was still seeping down the woodwork from its innards and congealing in a sticky puddle on the cobblestones.

Clutching my mouth to try and stem the retching in my throat, I ran from the stables and into the blessed warmth of the kitchen. Pushing past a startled Ellen and Mrs. Garner, I ran through the kitchen and out, making for my room. I could speak to no one. The one thought in my mind was that whoever had wrought such a nauseous deed had only one intention in mind, to warn the Fairfaxes. Something terrible lay ahead for one of the family, I was certain of it, and the cat's horrible death was but a premonitory signal.

CHAPTER THIRTEEN

'. . . . half-devil and half-child.'
– Kipling, *The White Man's Burden*

I could not go down to lunch, for I still felt too nauseated every time I recalled the revolting sight of the cat. Even when time came for dinner I still could not face the thought of eating. But I had to go down. Regina would expect me.

One thing was certain, the murdered cat was not the one that haunted me in the Keep. My cat was black and lithe, a creature I was beginning to believe was only the product of my own mind, since no one else ever seemed to see it. But the tortoiseshell cat in the stable was plump and all too obviously of real flesh and blood. I shuddered again at the vision of its mutilated corpse.

And the piece of fish in its mouth. That indicated that someone had fed the animal to induce a sense of false security before ramming it with the pitchfork. And who but someone from the village would come with fish. I remembered the newly unloaded catch the womenfolk had been busy gutting on the quayside.

I must go down to dinner, if only to warn Regina of what had happened and of my suspicions. Cooper might not have told her of the cat's death, and a warning to the family would be of little avail if they never came to hear of it When the gong sounded I made my way downstairs to the dining room.

When I entered, Richard was pulling out a chair for Regina to be seated. I was relieved to see that my mistress now looked calmer and more composed than when I had last seen her, and the colour was returning to her cheeks. Richard came to draw out my chair next, but he neither smiled nor

201

spoke. He looked preoccupied as he seated himself next to Regina. Ellen came in with the soup tureen.

'Let's not wait for Damian, though he promised to come down for dinner,' Regina said, nodding to the parlourmaid to begin pouring. 'I expect he'll join us later.'

For a time we all spooned soup in silence. Then Regina turned to Richard. 'Your thoughts are far away, cousin? What have you been doing all afternoon?'

'I'm sorry, I was thinking,' his low voice drawled in reply. 'I've been in the writing room, reading.'

'Reading Jagger's accounts?'

'Yes. I'm obliged to you for letting me read them.'

'And do you still think I'm being cheated?'

Richard laid down his spoon. 'It is not easy to say. The accounts certainly raise questions which I'd like Jagger to answer.'

'Indeed? They seem straightforward enough to me. The accounts balance.' It was reassuring to see the gleam of interest on Regina's face in place of the hollow, gaunt look of misery. I would have to await an opening in the conversation later to talk of the cat.

'It's not the figures I question, but rather the omissions,' Richard said quietly. 'Though I know little of current prices in England, the amounts received for sale of livestock seem on the low side. And there are gaps where farm rents do not appear to have been paid.'

Regina picked up the handbell and rang for Ellen to serve the next course. 'Times have been hard. Jagger got the best prices he could for our livestock,' she said.

'And the farm rents? Do none of your tenants pay rent?'

'Keep Farm is the only exception. The others do.'

'But there are no entries for the past two years. Did Jagger not collect them?'

'No. The farmers have had poor crops, and for various reasons he said they were unable to pay.'

'Did you not press them?'

Regina's expression hardened. 'One does not harass loyal tenants, especially in hard times.'

'Did you go to see them yourself?'

'No.'

I felt a rush of pity for Regina. She was too proud to explain to her cousin that her disfigurement had meant her total seclusion.

'Then the rents could have been paid but never entered in the accounts, for all we know,' Richard went on. 'I think we should question Jagger.'

Regina coloured, but she kept silent as Ellen entered and removed the soup bowls. Ellen brought a covered dish to the table from the sideboard.

'Turbot, fresh from the sea this morning,' Regina said with satisfaction. 'Rose brought it up for us.'

My stomach quailed, but I fought it down. After Ellen had brought the vegetables and potatoes and left us, Regina turned to Richard.

'Leave Jagger to me, cousin. I do not wish him to be harshly interrogated. He and the other villagers have been very loyal to us.'

Richard smiled wryly. 'Not so very loyal if he has indeed been cheating you, Regina, but I bow to your judgment.'

'As indeed you must, since Mallory is still mine until proven otherwise. But I am grateful for your concern nonetheless.'

The tone of her voice indicating that the subject was now closed, I saw my opportunity. As casually as I could manage, I introduced the topic that was nagging me.

'I understood there were no cats in the Keep but I saw one dead in the stables today.'

'No, there are none in the house,' Regina replied firmly. 'For all his fondness for animals, Damian dislikes cats for some reason. The stables are another matter. Cooper no doubt feels they are necessary there to keep the rats at bay.'

'This one had been killed. Stabbed by a pitchfork.'

Regina shuddered. 'Ugh! How distasteful! But there is no need to concern yourself over a stable cat, surely?'

'I felt it might be a warning,' I said lamely. I was conscious of Richard staring at me, and felt acutely embarrassed. I wished I hadn't mentioned the wretched animal.

'A warning?' Regina repeated in surprise. 'Really, Amity, you're becoming as superstitious as Uncle Eustace with all his talk of omens and signs. That reminds me, he was asking for you this afternoon. I said I would ask you to go and visit him after dinner.'

'To be sure I will,' I agreed. And I was glad there was no more talk of the cat. It had been a silly mistake to allow myself to become so obsessed with its death and the possible significance. To my relief, Damian came in at this point and the subject was forgotten.

The master of Mallory flung himself into the chair next to me without a word of apology to his sister for his lateness. So close to me, I could sense the angry discontent and misery exuding from him. Ellen followed him in and fetched the soup from the sideboard.

'No soup, just the fish,' Damian growled, then, ignoring Richard and me, he addressed Regina. 'Damn customs officers. They kept me talking in the inn all afternoon. I'm famished. Haven't eaten since yesterday.'

I noticed Regina's colour fade as she stopped eating. 'Customs officers? What did they want?'

'Lot of damn silly questions about whether I knew anything of contraband being carried hereabouts. Told them they were barking up the wrong tree. No smuggling hereabouts to my knowledge.'

'Quite right,' said Regina smoothly. 'But why did it take so long?'

'They kept on. Local squires often finance vessels for the smugglers, and I think they suspected me. Ridiculous. I told them we had not enough money for our own purposes, let alone to finance enterprises of any kind. But they were persistent devils – had I heard or seen pony trains going over the moor or craft landing on the beach by night.'

'What did you say?'

'That I'd seen nothing of the kind, of course. They finally let me go.' He forked a chunk of fish into his mouth.

Regina passed a tureen to him. 'Then eat well now, Damian, for you must be starving. I'll send Ellen for more.'

The turbot lay uneasily in my stomach. I declined the stewed apple and custard afterward, and finally Richard and I rose to go.

'Don't forget Uncle Eustace,' Regina reminded me as Richard opened the door for me.

'No. I'll go to him shortly,' I promised.

'Come and talk with me for a while in the writing room before you go,' Richard invited. I hesitated. Perhaps he was going to scold me over Rachel's diary, but in the end I agreed. I was weak where he was concerned, I decided. I liked being in his company.

The writing room was cosily inviting, velour curtains drawn, the oil lamps lit, and a fire glowing in the hearth. I seated myself on the velvet sofa and waited for Richard to speak. He stood, his arm along the oak mantelshelf, gazing into the fire.

'Tell me about the cat,' he said quietly.

I recounted the story, how I had sensed unease in the stables and Vulcan's disquiet, and then discovering the animal impaled on the stable door. Richard listened without looking at me.

'Perhaps it showed lack of taste on my part, to speak of it at the dining table,' I said at the end of my tale, 'but at the time I thought it was some kind of warning, and Regina ought to know.'

'I am of the same mind,' Richard said, crossing the room and seating himself beside me. 'From what I have learnt of the villagers, it seems it could well be their way of giving a warning. To Damian, if I am not mistaken.'

'You think so?' I was relieved beyond measure to think I was not being stupid after all. 'You really think so?'

He nodded thoughtfully. 'The vicar told us how Damian is already disliked for abandoning his folk, and then betraying his calling by bringing a woman here. And today the fisherfolk saw him with the excise men.'

'But only being questioned,' I interjected.

'For all they know he could be in league with them. We know he knows nothing of their activities, but they do not. After all, he is Regina's brother, and she knows all.'

'Should we warn Damian then?'

Slowly he shook his head. 'For the moment, best to observe and draw judgment. We could be wrong. Better to watch him and all that goes on before taking hasty action we might regret.'

Rising, he walked over to the table and picked up a book

which lay under the lamp. I recognised the cover at once. It was Rachel's exercise book diary.

'To that end, to discover and learn before acting, I too have been reading this diary,' Richard said as he came back to join me. I could not help staring at him in surprise. So he had not been silently reproachful after all!

'You found its hiding place?' I gasped.

'It was not difficult, since you had told me it was behind some books. After Jagger's accounts this made interesting reading.'

I felt my old enemy, curiosity, rising to the surface. I wondered how much more of Rachel's story he knew than I did, and I was eager to learn that part which I had not yet had chance to read.

'How much have you read? Did you read it all?'

'More or less. The gong sounded before I reached the end, but I had learned enough. Cousin Damian is to be pitied rather than scorned, I think, knowing now what befell.'

'I read that she planned to follow him to Yorkshire. What happened then? Poor thing. It seems she was very much in love with him.'

Richard's eyebrows rose. 'Poor Rachel? I fear you are mistaken in pitying her, Amity. She was a cunning, devious creature. She never loved him, but wanted only to attract him because he was a priest and therefore a challenge. Forbidden fruit is the sweetest, so they say.'

'It seems she succeeded in doing that, since he was unfrocked on her account.'

'Oh yes, she revels here in her triumph,' he said, his slim fingers tapping the book. 'Her vanity was satisfied once he was seduced and disgraced. But her triumph turned to dismay once she discovered she was pregnant.'

'So that's why she followed him.'

'Of course. Her family would renounce her, she believed, so she ran away before they found out. Now that Damian was free of the church, she was sure she could get him to marry her.'

I reflected on Richard's words. 'But he did not marry her. Why not, I wonder, for he loves her still.'

'That I doubt,' Richard replied flatly. 'According to

Rachel's own words, he would have nothing to do with her when she arrived here. She says he sulked in his own room, refusing to come out.'

'Just as he does now.'

'She evidently hoped to charm him once again when she could be alone with him, but she blames Regina for not being able to do so. Regina stood over him like a protective mother hen over its chick, refusing to let Rachel near him. She tried to drive the girl away, but Rachel would not go.'

'Where else could she go, poor thing?' I interrupted. 'Alone and pregnant. I am surprised Regina could be so hard on her.'

'I think my cousin doubted it was her brother's child. Rachel says she called her a slut and a whore, and Rachel hated her. She envied Regina's cool poise, and her beauty and her domination over Damian.'

'Her beauty? Then Regina was not scarred then?' The words erupted from my lips without thought, but Richard did not notice my thoughtlessness. He shook his head.

'Regina's beauty was not marred until Rachel marked her.'

My mouth fell open. I thought of the cruel scar down Regina's cheek. 'Rachel did *that*? Oh no!'

'Read for yourself.' Richard placed the shabby book in my hands, already open at a grubby page. My eyes followed the erratic, excited handwriting until I came to it.

'I could not help myself. Regina has been so cold, so unfeeling and unreachable until today, but when I told her I felt my time was near, I could see the scorn and hatred glittering in her black eyes. She told me I had brought harm and suffering enough to the house, and the sooner I and my bastard left, the better it would be for them all.

'I begged to see Damian, for I doubt he even knows of the child, she keeps him so well hidden. She laughed at me. I would never see him, she said, never call him husband, for I was not fit for him. I had already destroyed him, a man of God, and I would wreak no more evil on the Fairfaxes.

'Who do they think they are, these Fairfaxes, with their pride and coldness? I hate them, Damian too, for his weakness, and would do anything to damn their eyes for their

207

callousness to me. Staring at Regina with her beautiful face and haughty eyes, I could bear it no longer. I seized the oil lamp from the table and rammed it into that proud face. The glass broke, cutting her cheek, and the flame seized her lace collar. I watched it blaze, enveloping her beauty in licking flames.

'She fell, screaming, and I fled. I locked myself in my room, frightned at what I had done. But I am glad. No more will that proud woman taunt me. I shall have him yet.'

My hand trembled a little as I laid down the book. Richard was watching me.

'You see. There is no pity or repentance.'

'No. She seems rather to glory in her evil. But I feel she had provocation. There is no accounting for what a distraught woman may do, and a pregnant woman at that.'

Richard sat down by me, his hand closing over mine. 'You are a sympathetic soul, Amity, anxious to see both sides of a question. But if you read more of Rachel's thoughts you would find she was utterly self-centred, conscious of no one's desires but her own. She was more than wilful. She was wicked.'

I was so absorbed with the warmth of his hand on mine, and his quiet words close to my ear, that I did not notice the door open. I did hear a rustle of silk, and on looking up I saw Regina standing there. A smile of quiet satisfaction lifted the corners of her lips.

'I am glad you recognise her wickedness, cousin, but I would prefer that you did not read private papers,' she said calmly, holding out her hand. Richard surrendered the diary. 'Amity, have you visited Uncle Eustace?'

'No,' I said guiltily, rising to my feet. 'I am going now.'

Before I reached the door Regina had turned again to Richard. 'You will never know the full extent of that girl's evil, cousin. She brought tragedy to Mallory Keep.'

'De mortius nihil nisi bonum,' Richard remarked quietly.

'You are right. We should not speak ill of the dead, but even in death she would not relent. She swore she would gain her revenge.'

I closed the door after me and heard no more. Upstairs on the gallery I was dismayed to see Caesar, Damian's wolfhound, snuffling at Uncle Eustace's door. I had to pluck up my courage to approach the hound.

'Away, sir,' I said sharply, and to my relief the dog shrunk off towards the east wing. I wondered if his presence indicated that his master was with Uncle Eustace. I tapped timidly at the door. No answer came. I knocked again, this time more loudly.

Hearing no answer, I opened the door and peeped in. Perhaps Uncle Eustace had tired of waiting for me and gone to bed. But no, an oil lamp still glowed on the table, and by its light I could see the old gentleman still dressed, sitting in his armchair by the fire.

'Good evening, sir.' I closed the door and crossed the room to him. He did not move or speak. When I came near I saw that his eyes were closed. Reluctant to wake him if he was dozing, or disturb him if he were only deep in thought, I stood patiently beside him for a moment. There were papers in his gnarled hands, papers with the strange astrological hieroglyphics I had seen him draw before. And on the easel beside the table hung a still-wet canvas. Uncle Eustace had not been idle today.

Going closer to the easel I inspected his latest work of art. It was still in the same style as his earlier works, clear, sharp colours, and gauche, simple figures. I recognised the black-haired woman in emerald green from his earlier painting, the one I believed was Rachel. And this time I was certain it was she, for her beautiful head and shoulders rose from the supple body of a cat, a black cat.

I shivered, remembering my cat of the east wing, and was convinced Uncle Eustace had seen it too, and connected it with the dead girl. Was the animal her restless spirit, or a creature set to guard her earthly abode, I wondered, and was anxious for the old man to awaken so I could ask him what he thought.

Other figures dotted the canvas, a man in a riding habit, tall and fair. That could be Richard. And my eye was drawn to another figure, evidently a dark man whose face was hidden because he was floating, face downward, as though in water. A semicircular archway over him separated that portion of the picture from the rest.

A branch tapping at the window caught my attention. The wind outside was gusty and growing stronger, and the curtains were still undrawn. I crossed to pull them and caught sight of a flickering red light. Straining my eyes to see out into the darkness, I realised the light was away up on Carnelian Point. At that moment I heard a moan behind me and heard the rustle of paper. Uncle Eustace was waking.

I waited quietly, within his vision, while he stretched and rubbed his knuckles in his eyes. A slow smile of recognition spread over his wrinkled features.

'Good evening, Miss Amity. Have you been waiting there long?'

'Not long, sir. I am sorry if I visit you too late. I should have come sooner, as you asked. Would you prefer to see me in the morning?'

His caterpillar brows rose. 'Did I ask to see you? Now I wonder why. I'm afraid I can't for the life of me remember.'

'No matter,' I hastened to assure him. It was inconsiderate of me to visit him so late and expect him to be coherent. I felt guilty seeing his bemused expression as he racked his brain in an effort to recollect. 'No matter, sir. It is pleasant to see you and talk to you.'

He smiled amiably. 'What were you looking at out of the window, my dear?'

'A light on the Point. I was wondering what it was.'

'A light? Is there a swell on the Bay?'

'I imagine so. The wind has risen tonight.'

'Then it will be one of the fisherwomen warning the menfolk that the sea is too rough in the Bay. They will know then to land down the coast a little, so as to avoid being washed on to the brigg.'

I could not see the brigg from the Keep, but I remembered the arm of needlelike rocks reaching out to sea to the north of Manacle Bay. In weather like this, it would be far safer to come ashore south of the Point.

'I see you have been busy today, sir,' I said, indicating the easel. 'Is it finished?'

'Not yet, my dear. I felt rather tired today. Perhaps I shall finish it tomorrow.'

He rose from the armchair and shuffled across to me. I

could not help noticing how the slippered old feet, usually so sprightly, dragged wearily across the floor. He stared dully at the canvas for a moment. Feeling I had kept the old man from his bed overlong already, I was about to bid him good night when he spoke.

'Do you like my paintings?'

I hesitated. 'They are certainly very colourful and full of activity, sir. But I fear I do not always understand them.'

He appeared puzzled. 'But they are very simple pictures. What do you find difficult to understand?'

'Well, sir, I feel I can recognise some people I know. But who is the half-cat and half-woman creature? And what is the significance of this man who appears to be drowning?'

He cocked his grizzled head on one side and rubbed his chin thoughtfully. 'The sphinxlike woman is Rachel, I remember. She always reminded me of a cat, so stealthy and cunning. And under her beauty was a vengeful malice, sheathed like a cat's claws, but just as terrible when she raged. And I fancy I have seen her as a black cat, haven't you?'

His mild blue eyes stared directly into mine. It made me uneasy to think he too had seen the evil black thing. I changed the subject quickly.

'And this man face downward?'

Uncle Eustace frowned. 'Now I remember. That is why I wanted to see you. You must look to the man, help him, don't let them harm him. I cannot help him, but I know that you, with your unselfish kindness, you will help him, won't you?'

'But who is he, sir?'

The frown deepened. 'I cannot remember, my dear. I know I saw him, or at least I think I did, and he needs help. Did I see him, Amity? Or is he another visitor from the past? When one grows as old and confused as I, it becomes very difficult to distinguish the past from the present or even the future. I wish I could remember, but I am so tired.'

'Then I must let you go to bed, sir. Good night and sleep well.'

As I was leaving, I saw him pull out his tasselled nightcap from his pocket and put it on, sinking once again into the armchair by the fire. Out in the corridor I found Richard gazing up at the portrait of his father. Resolute features of a fair young man looked down on its image. Richard smiled as I neared him.

'I can understand how Uncle Eustace mistakes me for the returning spirit of my father. It is like looking into a mirror. How is the old fellow?'

'Tired and confused. He is about to go to bed.'

'Then I won't disturb him to say good-bye. Tell him for me that I shall see him on my return, in a week at the most.'

'Are you going away?' I wished I did not betray my every emotion so patently. The dismay and disappointment were obvious in my tone.

He took my hands. 'For a few days only, to see my lawyer in London. But while I am away I want you to take care. Don't go investigating alone. Just sit quiet and watch events till I come back.'

I nodded, but despite the warmth of his pressure on my hands, I felt suddenly desolate. The thought of this gloomy old house and its secretive occupants, and the air of foreboding which had seemed only to deepen since Uncle Eustace had spoken to me, seemed almost intolerable without Richard's vibrant, reassuring presence.

'It is a good time for me to go, since Regina tells me that she is to have company tomorrow,' Richard added.

'Company? She never entertains,' I said disbelievingly.

'Perhaps having you and then me has given her the confidence to meet people again. She tells me a Mrs. Marchbanks and her daughter are coming from York.'

'I wonder she did not tell me. Though of course there is no reason why she should,' I added quickly, aware of the inadvertent note of censure in my voice. My employer was not obliged to tell me of her plans.

'Good night then, Amity, and au revoir. I shall be away early in the morning.' For a moment his grip tightened on my hands and he came close. But as I felt my heart begin to thump in anticipation, he suddenly let go and turned away. I was a long time falling asleep once I reached my bed, for a jumble of emotions and questions troubled my mind.

In the morning Regina breakfasted in her room. I passed

212

the morning listlessly. the sky was still leaden and the house was desolate and without company for me. I was glad when Regina came down to lunch, cheerful and brisk and showing no sign of being cross with me over last night.

'There are two ladies coming to take tea with Damian and myself this afternoon,' she told me over the braised beef. 'You are welcome to join us.'

'Friends of yours?' I enquired. I was curious. I had seen no friends of the family nor heard of any.

'Acquaintances, rather,' she replied her eyes not meeting mine. 'Mrs. Marchbanks is the wife of a wealthy millowner in York. Her daughter Dorothea will accompany her.'

I saw the tall, broad-boned woman in the vestibule as I came down to tea that afternoon. She was florid and flat-featured, though her afternoon gown was well-cut and of good-quality material, I noted with professional interest. Ellen was entering the parlour carrying a printed card on a silver tray. Behind the tall lady a fair-haired young woman in a pink hat was standing staring about her, wide-eyed. She was pasty-faced and freckled, heavy-bosomed but evidently wearing tight stays, for her waist was incredibly tiny.

Ellen returned and led them into the parlour. I waited a few moments before descending the stairs to join them. I wanted to give Regina time to make her introductory greetings. When I entered the parlour the ladies were already seated, Regina beside them on the sofa, and Damian was standing stiffly by the window. He looked uncomfortable in a neat grey jacket and trousers and with his unruly hair for once tamed. He was staring gloomily at the ladies. Regina, I noticed, sat so that the scarred side of her face was farthest from her guests.

'Mrs. Marchbanks, may I present my friend and companion, Miss Lucas,' Regina said with a smile. The lady nodded briefly in my direction. The younger woman ignored me completely and I could see from under lowered lids she was covertly assessing Damian. I wondered at her interest as I seated myself on an upright chair at a discreet distance from the group.

'I regret my uncle is unable to join us,' Regina remarked conversationally. 'He is not feeling himself today and is obliged to rest in his room. He hopes you will forgive his absence.'

'To be sure,' Mrs. Marchbanks purred.

There followed some desultory conversation about the atrocious weather for the time of year, and the muddy state of the moorland roads over which Mrs. Marchbanks' carriage had been obliged to travel. Not once did the pale-faced girl either speak or raise her eyes.

'Do come and sit down, Damian, and I'll ring for Ellen to bring tea,' Regina coaxed her brother. He slumped silently into an armchair, and I could see the older woman's keen eyes travel over him thoughtfully.

'Do you farm many acres, Mr. Fairfax?' she asked him crisply. Damian's dark eyes glared at her.

'Much of our land is under pasture. Less than half of it is farmed,' Regina answered for him in an agreeable tone.

Mrs. Marchbanks was not easily deterred. Again she fired a question at Damian, and again Regina answered. I was wondering at the questions the lady put to her hosts, rather too private, I thought, for polite tea-party conversation. It indicated a lack of breeding on the lady's part to pry so openly.

Ellen brought in the tea and Regina poured it for her guests. I noted Mrs. Marchbanks' outstretched little finger as she sipped, and the robinlike brightness in her eye as she surveyed the room and its furnishings, her hostess's gown, and the quality of the china.

'Do you ride, Miss Marchbanks?' Regina asked, turning to the younger woman. The girl blushed and looked to her mother.

'Don't be shy, Dorothea, my dear,' her mother reproved. It amused me the way Mrs. Marchbanks made 'Dorothea, my dear,' rhyme in a tone of great affectation. 'My daughter is so reserved, Miss Fairfax. Really refined, she is. Go on, Dorothea, tell Miss Fairfax that you do enjoy a ride.'

'I enjoy a ride, Miss Fairfax, now and again.'

'I'm so glad. It is one of my brother's favourite pursuits, is it not, Damian?'

Damian grunted assent.

'Of course, we have little opportunity of riding in York,'

214

Mrs. Marchbanks went on. 'Now here in the countryside, and with all this farmland, it must be a positive delight to go riding.' She beamed at her hostess who smiled in return.

Suddenly it came to me why Mrs. Marchbanks was here and posing questions, why her daughter simpered in silence and discreetly inspected Damian. Of course! Why else was Damian put on show in respectable attire and with his hair groomed? Regina was trying to engineer the marriage of her brother and this whey-faced girl.

The Marchbanks were a wealthy family, she had told me, and the Fairfaxes needed money as well as an heir if they were to keep Mallory. And Mrs. Marchbanks no doubt welcomed the prospect of marrying her pallid daughter into a family with age-old lineage, a family whose name was renowned and respected. It made sense. And Richard was away, unaware of the latest move to keep him from taking Mallory. No wonder Regina had maintained an air of sweet reasonableness with him yesterday, with this new trick up her sleeve. I gazed at my employer with admiration. She never gave in.

When I deemed it time to leave them, I rose to make my farewells. I was conscious that Damian's moody gaze followed me as I went out. Perhaps he was envious of my freedom to leave, while he was obliged to stay and endure the female company he so evidently detested. Poor soul. Despite his unlikable qualities, I could feel only pity for him.

I had resolved not to go down to dinner in case the Marchbanks' ladies were invited to stay on, but when I heard the wheels of the carriage crunching away down the drive, signalling their departure, I still decided against going down to dinner. Regina and Damian must have much to discuss after the introduction of the prospective bride to her groom.

So I dined alone, seated by the fire in my room, listening to the rain pattering on the window. Perhaps later I would go and visit Uncle Eustace, to see if he felt brighter now. I looked up as Rose came in to remove my tray. The girl's face was set and unsmiling.

'Is anything wrong, Rose? You don't look as happy as usual.'

215

'There's nowt wrong wi' me. But Miss Regina's finding fault wi' us all.'

Of course. The girl was resentful of Jagger's accounts being checked. Doubtless he had told her all about it.

'Don't worry, Rose. All will be well, I'm sure of it. Miss Regina is anxious to do her best for us all.'

Rose grunted as she pulled the door to with her toe. I wondered whether she knew her sweetheart had been cheating her mistress, and doubted it. Though she evidently connived at his smuggling activities, I felt she would draw the line at robbing Regina. There was in her a basic honesty and straightforwardness which would make the idea anathema to her.

The house was so still and silent, and the firelight and the rain's rhythm on the windowpanes so soporific that I think I must have dozed off for a while. I came to with a start. Something had disturbed me. The clock on the mantelshelf was showing a quarter past ten.

It was too late to visit Uncle Eustace now. Time to prepare for bed. I was just rising from my chair when I heard the sound again. It was a scratching sound, and it came from the door. I stood stock-still, unwilling to go and open the door. I feared it was Damian's hound, for I had seen him at Uncle Eustace's door last night, and I had no wish to encounter that great brute face to face.

The scratching stopped and I heard a low sound, as of someone muttering outside. I went nearer the door and listened. It was Damian's voice, cursing the dog.

'Get away, you brute, back away, damn you.'

For a moment there was silence and I imagined master and dog had gone on to the east wing. Then to my surprise there came a low but urgent tap on my door. As I hesitated, the tapping began again.

'Miss Lucas, are you awake?'

Damian's tone was so high-pitched and strangled that I felt obliged to open the door to him. He leaned against the doorjamb, his eyes staring wildly, his stock askew and his hair tumbling about his face despite the pomade. I stood back from him, a little afraid of his wild appearance.

'What is it, sir? Is something wrong?'

'May I come in?'

Without waiting for my answer, he strode past me, across to my bed where my nightgown lay spread out ready. I felt acutely embarrassed as he stared at it for a moment before turning to me.

'Regina wants me to marry that bovine wench of Marchbanks!'

So I had guessed correctly. I clasped my hands before me and stood dutifully waiting for his next words. I felt he expected no comment from me, only an audience to whom he could express his frustration. I was right. He began pacing about the room, muttering to himself.

'I can't do it, I won't! I swore I would never marry, but if I must, it shall not be to that pale milksop. I would rather not marry at all, but Regina says I must if we are to keep Mallory. Damn Mallory! It has brought us nothing but worry and pain, and I would to God we could be rid of it!'

I moved forward instinctively in a gesture of comfort. 'You surely can't mean that, sir. Regina has worked so hard to protect your birthright.'

He turned his smouldering black eyes upon me. 'Can't I? If you only knew the misery this house has known. No happiness ever ventures within its gaunt grey walls, for it is an accursed place, as its ill-omened name implies. It is a house of tragedy, Miss Lucas, surely you have felt it.'

'But, sir, it is yours and Regina's, and surely you want to keep what is yours? A house can be made happy by the people within it.'

Despite his wry smile there was bitterness in his voice. 'You are an optimist, I see, but the Keep will change you too. But you are right. I cannot disappoint Regina. Our patrimony means much to her. That is why she insists I must marry and produce an heir, but it shall not be with that Marchbanks chit. If I must, then it shall be to a woman of my choosing.'

'I am sure your sister will agree.'

He came a step closer to me. 'I have chosen, Miss Lucas, and I have told my sister.'

I could smell the bear grease on his hair, he was so close. Despite my feeling of revulsion at his proximity, I smiled.

217

'Then all is well, sir.'

His next move took me by complete surprise. His huge hands rose and clasped firmly on my shoulders. I was pinioned, unable to draw back.

'I think you understand me a little, Miss Lucas, and how I suffer. Though you do not know the reasons, you know I am restless and troubled in mind.'

'I know a little, sir.'

'And I feel I know you. A brave little soul, you would make no demands on me nor presume to intrude on my privacy. I fear the night for it brings restless spirits that torment my soul, and I fear I am not myself in those hours of darkness. But you would not haunt me unless I sought you out.'

'Indeed not, sir.' I was beginning to feel apprehensive about the drift of his words, though I could not understand them. One thing was certain. I would not seek out Damian Fairfax by night or by day for that matter, for the truth was that his strange, unpredictable wildness frightened me. I wished he would let go of my shoulders.

Suddenly he did. Dropping to his knees he flung his arms about my skirts, holding me in a terrible embrace. I could not move.

'Then marry me, Miss Lucas. For God's sake say you will marry me. At once, without delay.' His voice was a sobbing moan, half-buried in my skirts.

Struggling to free myself, I cried out. 'I cannot, sir! I do not love you!'

At once he rose to his feet, his black eyes glittering. 'Nor I you, Miss Lucas, but what matter? I need you, Regina needs you! For God's sake, have pity on us and marry me. Think on it and tell me in the morning that you will.'

He half ran from my room, leaving me shaking like the last quivering leaf of autumn, destined soon to be cut down by winter's icy blast.

CHAPTER FOURTEEN

'Needs must, when the devil drives.'
—Old Proverb

Morning dawned grey and gusty, the wind chasing the clouds like hunted animals across the leaden sky. I felt sapped and hollow-eyed when I went down to breakfast, having been robbed of sleep by the tumultuous thoughts that had kept me awake after Damian's unexpected proposal.

My initial revulsion had gradually changed to resentment as I tossed in my bed. Marriage to a brooding, melancholy husband was unthinkable, but I knew his action was prompted only by necessity. They were trying to make use of me, Regina and he, to help save Mallory, and I felt angered that they probably expected me to submit and agree with demur. It would be a fine match for a mere servant, to be allied to a noble name, far above my wildest expectations. I sensed Regina's managing, analytical mind behind the move and rebelled inwardly.

How could she presume so on our friendship! But then I knew how much Mallory meant to her, and to save it she would stop at nothing. But I was determined not to be sacrificed to attain her goal. I sought for reasons to give her to explain my refusal.

Regina was already at breakfast, and I noticed how her keen gaze raked my face. She smiled brightly as she offered to pour me a cup of tea.

'Good morning, Amity. the weather looks most unpromising, does it not? I hope you enjoyed the company of our guests yesterday.'

'It made a change to have visitors. But I think Mr. Damian did not care for their company.'

A veiled look came over Regina's eyes. 'No. Mrs. and Miss Marchbanks will not be calling again, nor shall we return their call. The meeting did not transpire as I had hoped, but still, matters will turn out right, I am sure.'

I knew she was fishing for information, whether Damian had approached me. Too weary to attempt to be devious, I told her.

'Damian has proposed marriage to me, if that is what you mean.'

She put down the teapot with a cry of delight. I was irritated by her feigning surprise, and could not resist snapping the next words.

'But I shall refuse him. He does not care for me nor I for him. It is unthinkable.'

She stretched a hand across the table to cover mine. 'Not so unthinkable, Amity. You and I are like sisters already, are we not? And you are of a good family and well educated.'

Although you are only a servant, she implied. I felt the heat creeping up my neck. Pulling my hand from hers, I attacked my bowl of porridge.

'Nor am I a fool, Regina. I have no wish to be used as a brood mare to provide the heir Damian needs.'

They were dreadful words for a lady to use, but Regina remained surprisingly cool.

'I will not deceive you, Amity. We need you and would be grateful if you would agree. You will not stand to lose by marrying a Fairfax.'

There, she was saying it openly, that I should be glad of the good match. Secretly I could wish it was Richard Fairfax I was asked to marry, and not his strange, wild cousin.

'I am not a Catholic, Regina.' Excuses rushed to my mind. The prospect of Damian was unbearable.

'No matter, for neither are we now.' Regina's voice was coolly logical. I could not argue. Suspicion still lingered in my mind that she had waited until Richard was away to plot to outwit him. I wished he was here now, he who had warned me to take no action during his absence.

I pushed my empty bowl away and began sipping the hot tea. 'How long have you been planning this, Regina?' I asked. Her cool eyes surveyed me over the rim of her teacup.

'Did you employ a companion only to provide a wife for Damian if all else failed?'

'What nonsense you talk, Amity.' There was distinct amusement in her tone. 'At the time you came I had never ever heard of cousin Richard. There was no need for Damian to marry.'

Of course. Lack of sleep was befuddling my wits. But I did not give up. 'Then you accept that Richard is your cousin and the true heir, not the bogus claimant you once thought.'

She put down her cup carefully. 'Mr. Boyd's enquiries in America confirm what our eyes already told us. Richard is the image of his father's portrait, but I needed proof to be sure. There is no doubt now. Hence the need for urgent action. Damian must be married, and at once.'

She leaned forward, her eyes bright with determination and the scar prominently red against her pale skin. 'So I implore you, Amity, be the friend I think you are. Save us, save Mallory, and I shall be eternally in your debt. I have no other friend in the world but you.'

The bacon choked me. I could not eat with Regina's eyes so pleading and at the same time so forcefully willing me to accede. I tossed aside my napkin and rose from the table.

'Think on it, Amity. Damian will not prove too hard a husband. Left to his own devices he is harmless. You will scarcely know you are married. For pity's sake, say you will marry him.' Regina's voice pursued me as I fled, almost colliding with Ellen who was bringing in fresh buttered toast.

Impetuously I hastened to my room, put on my ulster, and went out to walk. I needed the bracing wind to clear the cobwebs in my brain and help me to think. I crossed the lawns, making for the gate in the hedge of thorns which would lead me to the cliff path.

Before talking to Regina it had been quite clear in my mind that marriage to Damian was out of the question, but now, her pleading words still ringing in my ears, I could not feel the same resolve. Regina needed me, and no one else could help her. How could I let down a friend?

Yet on the other hand, how could I link my future to that of the strange man who was her brother? And in doing so, I would foil Richard in his plan to gain Mallory. He, if anyone,

221

had proved himself my friend, and in helping one friend I should be betraying another. Oh, the choice was impossible!

Gusts of wind whipped at my skirts and pulled my hair loose from its neat coil as I descended the path towards the village. As the red roofs of the cottage came closer I could see fishing nets spread out to dry in the wind. The fishermen were ashore today then, it seemed. I loitered on the path, tasting salt on my lips and hearing the screech of gulls, and thought of how the village folk disliked and feared Damian Fairfax. I knew they scorned him for his fall from grace from his church, and his weakness, since it was because of a woman. I knew too that they found his black moods and sudden rages incomprehensible and totally alien to their phlegmatic, imperturbable natures. And he was to be feared too, since he had been seen in company with the enemy, the customs officers.

The cat. I recalled the slaughtered cat in the stable and felt pity for Damian and Regina. I was certain the cat was a warning. Would a marriage, I wondered, soften the villagers' attitude towards the Fairfaxes? Once again I felt my resolution waver. And then I knew; if there was any way I could help Regina in her struggle, then I must help.

As I turned back up the hill I tried to force out of my mind the revulsion I felt towards Damian. I tried to ignore the thought that I would prefer any other man in the world to be my husband. But I could not ignore it. I could picture Richard's surprise and dismay when he returned, and as I conjured up the vision of his frank, open face, I shivered. In that moment I knew what I really wanted. I wanted Richard.

For a moment a great longing and feeling of loss swept over me just like those vast grey rolling waves sweeping over the shingle in the bay below me. For a moment I let myself surrender to the longing and aching for his tall, vibrant presence and the reassuring warmth of his voice, for the leaping pleasure I derived from his nearness. And then I took myself firmly in hand. Wilful daydreaming! I must banish such romantic, silly dreams and concentrate on a practical approach to the problem which faced me.

Even if I had foolishly allowed myself to fall in love with the handsome young American, I must not let it blind me to my duty. My duty was to my employer and friend. But before I could begin to reason out my own argument with some attempt at cool logic, my attention was distracted by movement on the beach below.

It was Damian. I recognised his tall, broad figure and loping stride, even if I could not distinguish his face from here. And for proof it was he, I could see the ubiquitous hound Caesar ambling behind him. I stood back from the cliff edge so that he should not see me watching him, but the move was unnecessary, for he stared down towards his feet as usual, no doubt lost in thought.

But just as I moved, another shape caught my eye, a figure in grey, almost indistinguishable from the rock ledge where he crouched, several feet above the level of the beach. Whoever it was, he too was watching Damian Fairfax in secret.

He did not move, only squatted motionless until Damian and the hound had passed along the shingle towards the village. Then the man, rising and looking around to ensure he was alone, leaped nimbly down the rocks onto the beach and began walking in the direction whence Damian had come. I was glad he did not look up, for I feared the wind flapping at my skirts would have made me as noticeable as a lone scarecrow in a barren field.

I saw him reach the end of the beach where the cliffs circle round the bay and project out to sea to form the brigg. Here, at the entrance to the cave, he paused and looked about him again. Then he turned and disappeared into the cave.

I was curious. It could have been one of the fishermen smugglers keeping a watchful eye on his untrustworthy squire, but he was not dressed in the usual woollen jersey and sealskin cap the fishermen wore. He looked more like a gentleman, so far as I could tell, fairly well-dressed but bareheaded, for I had seen his dark hair. Why should he enter the cave if he was a stranger to the village? I was still curious as I made my way on up the path, and more than a little protective towards the unconscious Damian. If he was being spied upon, then he was still in danger, and he did not even know of the warning of the cat.

I do not know whether it was a misguided sense of nobility or pity or duty that dictated my next move. All I know is that when I returned to the Keep and went down to lunch, and when I saw Regina's questioning eyes across the dining table, I made a sudden, unreasoned resolution. Perhaps it was Uncle Leonard's teaching over the years, that a sense of duty well done can be infinitely more satisfying than indulging one's own pleasures. Whatever the reason, when Regina spoke, the decision was already made in my mind.

'Have you thought over the matter I put to you, Amity? Will you consent to marry Damian?'

I did not hesitate. 'If you think it will help, Regina . . .'

I did not need to finish the sentence. Perhaps I am unduly sensitive, but I fancied the light that leapt into Regina's dark eyes was of relief rather than pleasure. Nevertheless she leaned across the table to cover my hands with hers.

'I am so glad. Thank you, Amity. I shall endeavour to see that you do not regret it.'

Before I could remark that I failed to see how marriage to an impecunious companion could improve the Fairfax straitened circumstances, Regina had reverted to her usual practical self.

'The wedding shall take place as quickly as possible. I must speak to Reverend Parmenter. Perhaps the ceremony can be performed within the week. No need for fuss. No guests, plain costume. The quieter and more unobtrusive the event the better.'

Because of the difference between Damian's standing and my lowly status? I wondered. But I took no offence, for I am certain Regina meant none. She was right. If it had to be done, then the quicker and quieter, the better.

Trying hard to maintain the same cool, practical air as Regina, I remarked on the stranger on the beach.

'I am sure he was a stranger,' I said. 'He was certainly not one of the village folk.'

'At the cave, you say? But perhaps that is to be expected. Visitors often come to see the caves and search for ammonites, especially in the summer.'

I let it go at that, omitting to mention that the stranger had been secretly watching Damian, while I watched him. I shuddered at the thought of Damian. I wondered how soon Regina would inform him that I had agreed to become his

224

bride, and hoped it would not be for a while. I still had to try to soothe my conscience over Richard.

Mercifully Damian did not appear at dinner. Later, as I prepared for bed, Rose came in to my room with hot water. She was pale and tight-lipped, and I noticed the angry way she slammed the ewer down on the marble-topped washstand.

'Is there something wrong, Rosie? You seem upset tonight?' I enquired in a kindly tone. She jerked the curtains so fiercely that the rings clattered along the bamboo pole noisily.

'Nowt I can't manage,' she snapped.

'Is it Ben? Or have you been having words with Mrs. Garner?'

She sniffed and wiped her nose brusquely with the hem of her grubby apron.

'Not Mrs. Garner. She never finds fault.'

'Ben then? A lovers' tiff?'

She dabbed again at the betraying tears. 'We were to have been wed this summer, and now he says we can't. I'm that disappointed, and I know me mam will be furious. He thowt he could manage to buy us a cottage this year, he says.'

'Oh, dear.' So that's what Richard's intervention in Jagger's little game meant for Rosie. I felt sorry for the girl.

'Have you seen him today?'

She shook her head vigorously so that the curls danced. 'Not since Wednesday. We had a right old barney, down in t'stables. I've not seen him since. He were furious wi' me.'

So that was it. She was upset lest her impatience had driven her lover away. Wednesday. The stables. That was the day I found the dead cat. I looked at Rosie curiously.

'Did you see a cat in the stable, Rosie?'

She turned quickly on me, blue eyes flashing. 'That weren't me, it were Ben, honest. He's got that fierce a temper when he's roused. I won't harm a fly, I wouldn't but the cat sprang at him and he were mad. He didn't mean it, I'm sure.'

'What happened, Rosie?'

'We was talking, Ben and me. The cat had just had kittens, and I think she thought as Ben were after her little ones. She jumped at him, scratched him. Ben picked up the hay fork.

225

He hates cats. He said the master would thank him 'cos he hates cats too.'

'Mr. Damian?'

'Aye. He hates cats. Always raging that we've put one in his room, but we haven't. He swears there's a black cat there. We take no heed, Mr. Damian being a bit odd like.'

Having turned down the bedcovers, Rosie left me. I was relieved to learn that the dead cat had a harmless significance after all, but still shuddered at Ben Jagger's venom. Staking a cat like that was a measure of his potential brutality. Rosie's delayed marriage could be a blessing in disguise for her after all.

I had just climbed into my nightgown, thoughtfully placed by Rosie near the fire to warm, and was about to blow out the lamp when I heard the footsteps outside. I paused to listen. The shuffling steps hesitated and then stopped.

Uncle Eustace, perhaps. I was considering whether to go out to see if I could help him in any way, when to my surprise my bedroom door was thrown wide open. I gasped in alarm at the sight of the huge figure filling the doorway, then alarm gave way to embarrassment. It was the master, Damian, and I was clad only in a nightgown. I reached for my dressing robe, debating whether I should protest at his invasion of my privacy.

But Damian Fairfax seemed completely unaware of the impropriety of his action in coming into a young woman's bedroom. He took his slumbrous stare from me for a second to brush back with his leg the great hound that was trying to follow him in.

'Out, Caesar. Get out.'

The dog slunk out and Damian closed the door. I stood immobile, the dressing robe held high to my neck to cut off that probing stare.

'Mr. Fairfax, sir? Is something wrong?'

He slumped into the chair by the fire, shaking his shaggy head.

'Not now. Regina tells me you have agreed,' he muttered.

'I have, but that does not warrant your coming to my room, sir.'

Those great mournful eyes rose to meet mine. 'I mean you

226

no harm, Amity. I come only because I find a moment of calm in your company. I have known no peace these many years.'

In the face of the sorrow in his voice I could not bring myself to lecture him. If he meant me no harm I could not force him to leave. Seeing his stare now probed the embers of the fire, I hastily pulled on my robe and fastened it, then walked across to stand by him.

'I shall endeavour to serve you well, sir, if only because of your sister's kindness to me.' My voice was as cool and detached as I could make it, despite the turmoil I felt, for I did not want him to think I cared for him. He simply looked up at me, a thin smile just lifting the corners of his lips.

'I only ask that you be there, gentle and understanding. I ask no more, for I know how hurtful love can be. Oh Amity, love is so cruel! It demands all, a complete and utter possession, and possession is destruction. I know.'

'Oh, surely not, sir!' I was shocked by his definition of love. It was not as I had imagined it to be, all selflessness and devotion. He was wrong. he must be wrong.

'I tell you I know, Amity. I loved but once, and now I have lost my soul's right to eternal life because of it. Such is the power of love's destruction.'

I knelt beside him. 'You are wrong, sir. You have been unfortunate in your experience, that is all.'

'I loved, Amity, and therefore I sinned. So mortally that I can never obtain redemption for my soul. I am doomed to wander for eternity in search of the absolution I shall never obtain. I denied my profession for love of a woman.'

'She led you astray. She never loved you. It was she who sinned, not you. Your fault was weakness, sir, but we are all weak. That is no irredeemable sin.'

I stopped suddenly, biting my lip in vexation. I had let impetuosity rule me again. Now he would ask how I knew of Rachel and her intentions, and who was I to presume to judge. But he did not. He simply looked at me, his rugged face gaunt and tired.

'You speak just like my sister, but you are both wrong, I fear. I have knelt on cold stone by the hour praying for guidance and forgiveness. I have offered Mass on the sacred

227

ground of the old Abbey, but I know in my heart that I can never escape the retribution which must follow. Rachel told me, before she died.'

'Told you what, sir?'

'That I would never be forgiven for denying her and our child who died. She said the boy's death was a sign of God's anger, and that I would be forever doomed. And she swore, she cursed . . .'

His tired voice died away. Kneeling still, I gripped the arm of his chair, desperately anxious to calm and reassure him.

'What did she say?'

'She swore she would always possess me, till the day I died. If she could not have me, then no one else would ever have me. Her memory would obsess me and hold me in her thrall forever.'

I gasped. 'You surely do not believe that?'

Lugubrious black eyes turned slowly to me. 'I know it. From that moment I have never been free of Rachel. She haunts me day and night.'

I shivered. To think I had believed the Rose Room to be a shrine in memory of a beloved Rachel, and all the time it had been a prison, full of memories to keep him captive. I wondered why Regina had not obliterated all trace of the girl to lessen his suffering.

'I don't know what I would have done without Regina,' he murmured, as though talking to himself. 'I think I would have married Rachel but for her. It was she who recognised Rachel's cunning. She is very shrewd, my sister.'

So that was it. I had been wondering why he did not marry Rachel once he was unfrocked and learned the girl was pregnant. Had I read more of Rachel's diary I might have learned it was Regina's doing which had prevented it. I began to understand why Rachel had hated Regina so.

'I did not believe Regina at first,' Damian went on quietly. 'Rachel seemed so innocent, but Regina was not deceived. She always said she was wicked and cunning. I was forced to believe it when I witnessed for myself the extent of Rachel's venom.'

He stopped, and I wondered what it was he saw. After a moment his curiosity was satisfied and he continued.

228

'Did you know that Rachel caused that hideous scar on Regina's face. It was terrible. My sister was so beautiful. Rachel was a fiend.'

'What did she do, sir?' I heard the hesitant tremor in my own voice. I had no right to pry.

'The lamp was on the table. Rachel's face grew ugly with anger when Regina told her emphatically that child or no, marriage was out of the question. Rachel snatched up the lamp and threw it in Regina's face.'

My hands flew to my face as though to ward off the flame. 'And it burned her so badly?'

He nodded. 'The flame caught the lace collar of Regina's gown. It blazed up, hiding her face and hair. I could smell the hair scorching and the charring flesh. By the time I flung the table cover over her head to smother the flames, the damage was done. From that day Rachel was kept locked in the Rose Room for fear of what else she might attempt.'

'And she stayed there until she died?'

'She was brought to bed of the child very soon after. Regina found sufficient forgiveness in her heart to tend her at the confinement. The baby died, as I told you, and Rachel contracted a fever. She died a week later.'

It was a tragic tale. I thought of Rachel, dying full of hatred for a weak lover and his possessive sister, and felt pity for her. It was a terrible wound she had given Regina, but I felt the Fairfaxes had not come out of the incident completely innocent. The girl had some reason for her grievance, though not for laying a curse on Damian. If she knew him as I now did, she would know that he would believe it and remain forever obsessed by her. For all his weakness, I felt deep compassion for Damian.

'Regina said we should keep the Rose Room just as it was, and keep Rachel's ashes there, to serve to remind us of human frailty and what it could lead us into. She believed the reminder would preserve me from temptation in the future.'

Anger pricked me. What right had Regina to set herself up as judge of her brother? It was a measure of her possessiveness. She wanted to keep him away from women and keep him to herself. Perhaps that too, I thought more soberly, was understandable, since she had always protected and guarded

229

him in a mother's place. It would not be easy for her to let go.

A large hand clasped over mine on the arm of the chair. Despite my sympathy for him I shuddered at his touch. When he spoke, Damian's voice was urgent.

'So you see I have need of your gentleness, Amity. Day and night I am tormented with remorse, but at night the suffering is worst. Stay by me in the night and hold off the devils that haunt me.'

'The devils, sir?' I was alarmed.

'Wherever I go they are there. If I pray at the Abbey I can feel their presence. Sometimes I have even seen them flitting into the shadows when I turn to look.'

The smugglers, I thought privately. But I would not mention what he obviously did not know.

'And here in the Keep too,' he went on. 'The ghosts of the monks remain with their abbey stones here, and I feel their reproachful gaze upon me, a fellow priest who has committed mortal sin. They died for their faith; I betrayed mine. And always, she is there.'

'Rachel?'

'Aye. She haunts me as she swore she would. I see her sometimes, watching me and waiting. Waiting until I join her in eternal punishment. Oh Amity! I see that cat wherever I turn.'

'A cat? A black cat?'

'That is Rachel. Regina has never seen her, but I do, and she is as vengeful as ever. Caesar shrinks and runs away when she appears. How did you know she appears as a black cat?'

'Because I have seen it. It nearly tripped me on the stairs, and sprang at me once.'

I was unprepared for his cry of anguish. He drew his hand from mine and buried his face in his hands, with a strange sound halfway between moaning and weeping.

'So she is real and not just a figment of my imagination! And she hates you because she fears you may release me! Oh God, I am undone! I cannot escape!'

'Be easy, Mr. Fairfax, sir, please be calm!' I was agitated, unsure how to cope with a man so disturbed, and in my room at this hour of the night. After a few moments he looked up, and I could see how his eyes glistened with tears.

'Help me, Amity.' His voice was a croak.

'How can I help, sir?'

'Let me stay. Do not send me away tonight. Please let me stay, just to sit here by the fire. I shall be calm if you are close.'

'I don't know, sir. Miss Regina would not approve.'

'She will not disapprove. Go peacefully to bed, Amity, for I shall not disturb you. I shall sit quietly here and maybe even sleep a little if you are near. It is a long time since I slept.'

How could I refuse the pleading in his voice? In great embarrassment I went to bed, still in my dressing robe, but the agitation clamouring inside me gave me no peace. Quite apart from the impropriety of the situation, I was afraid of Damian Fairfax. Though he seemed chastened, I knew his capricious changes of mood. Even if he sat aloof all night, I was compromised. I felt trapped. Now I would have no choice but to marry him. I tried not to think of Richard Fairfax and how I could possibly explain all to him on his return.

It was nearing dawn before I eventually slept, fitfully and briefly. When I awoke, Damian was gone. he must have crept out quietly, out of consideration for me, for I had not heard him leave. I wondered how long he had sat there, whether he had come close to look at me lying asleep, and I shivered. But now he was gone and the sun was shining in through my window, and I could feel only a sense of profound relief.

But as I dressed I began to feel gloom descending on me again. The sunlight outside seemed only to enhance the cold unhappiness that permeated Mallory Keep, enveloping all its occupants in brooding and self-preoccupation. I too was falling victim to it. The thought occurred to me that even as wife to the master of Mallory I should still be as powerless as I was now, and in time no doubt I would become like Damian and Regina, hopeless and defeated. My natural optimism seemed to be waging a losing battle against the oppression of this gaunt old house.

Regina, with her dominating personality, would never relinquish her control to her brother's wife. Last night, after hearing Damian's account of Rachel's death, I was beginning to form a fresh opinion of Regina. Her protectiveness towards her weak brother had seemed understandable before, but now it took on the unhealthy appearance of being selfish greed rather than protectiveness. A mother refusing to let her child go, keeping him from all women – until expediency directed otherwise. I was being permitted to have a little claim on him only because Regina was forced to let him take a wife. If only she had married herself, then perhaps she would not behave so unnaturally. Matters, I felt, would not go easy between Regina and me once Damian and I were wed.

But I had no choice. I had to go through with it, but already I was regretting the impetuous nature Aunt Cecily had warned would be my ruin. Of Richard Fairfax I tried not to think at all, for whenever I did, I experienced a sinking feeling in my stomach.

Unwilling to face Regina, who would probably want to talk of wedding arrangements, I asked Rosie to bring me a tray so that I could breakfast in my room. Afterward, lured by the sunshine outside, I decided to go for a walk on the cliff top. The sea breeze would soon chase away my depression. There I could think more clearly, without the deadening gloom of the Keep to oppress me.

Sea gulls wheeled and dipped about me as I stood on the cliff edge and looked down on the deserted beach. Their screaming and the crash of the waves on the rocks was a soothing accompaniment to thought. I had two choices, I argued with myself: I could stay here and become mistress of Mallory as Regina and Damian would have me do, or I could retract my promise, which would mean I must leave and return to London at once.

My heart sank at the prospect. Unpleasant as the thought of marriage to Damian might be, the alternative was no less pleasant. London held no attraction for me, but this place I had come to enjoy. I loved the tang of the pure air, the freedom of the vast moors, and even, oddly enough, the villagers down there below. Despite their surly silence there was something I could respect in their clannishness. In their unity lay their strength. In isolation lay vulnerability, as Regina and Damian clearly showed.

But as a Fairfax, you too would be isolated and weak, I told myself. True, but the fact was that I had given my word. It was too late now for debate. I must stay, and in staying I must marry Damian.

Thus resolved, I turned back towards the Keep. As I neared the gate in the thorn hedge I was moodily wondering how to explain to Richard. It would be a lame tale at best.

Suddenly I stopped. The gate was opening and someone was emerging from the Keep's grounds. I could have cried out for joy when I recognised the fair head that bent to duck under the archway, for it was Richard. And his smile of recognition was no less joyous than my own.

'Amity! I was looking for you!'

He seized my hands and stood looking down at me, his tanned face radiant for a moment. Then his smile receded and I felt my own soaring spirits droop as I remembered. I could not doubt now that I loved him, but I must say to him words I dreaded to speak.

'Have you just returned?' I asked timidly, anxious to delay the evil moment.

'Half an hour ago. I was looking for you. Rose told me you were out walking and I guessed where to find you. Come, let us walk along the cliff path a little way.'

There was a fluttering inside me as he took my elbow, but I fought hard to remain cool and think rationally. Perhaps it would be more seemly to keep silent about the subject of my forthcoming marriage, for it was really Regina's place to announce to her cousin the news of her brother's marriage. I felt guilty at finding a cowardly way out of my dilemma, but I knew Richard would have to discover sooner or later.

'Have you been well, Amity, while I was away?' His voice was gentle in its concern.

'Very well, I thank you. Did your business in London go well?' I felt we were speaking like strangers, not saying what we really wanted to say. Richard stopped abruptly and turned to face me.

'That is what I wanted to talk to you about, Amity. Let us sit on the grass a moment.'

I sat, and he seated himself beside me. For a moment he just stared out at the grey sea, and then he turned to me again.

'Amity, you know that before I went away there was between us a certain warmth, a friendship that promised to bloom, was there not?'

I could not look into those earnest blue eyes, nor answer him. I looked down at my folded hands and stayed silent, trying to calm the thumping inside me. A bronzed hand reached out to rest on mine.

'Amity, I think that feeling was mutual. But I have to tell you now that whatever might have grown between us cannot be allowed to do so. Duty must come first.'

I looked up quickly. Had he heard something of what was planned? And was he absolving me? He lifted a finger to touch my chin.

'I think you know that I was feeling a very deep regard for you, Amity, but it must remain only that. You see I went to London to see about selling my land in America. Now it has been arranged. Very soon I shall have the money with which to restore Mallory to what it once was.'

I was bewildered, unable to follow the drift of his words. He moved away from me and stared moodily out to sea again.

'Now all is clear,' he murmured as if to himself. 'Regina wants to keep Mallory, but mine is the prior claim, and I have the wherewithal to maintain the estate. If Regina and I were to marry, then honour is satisfied on both sides and Mallory is safe.'

I stared at him, stupefied. 'You – marry Regina?' I gasped.

'If she will have me, and I doubt she will refuse.'

'Have you asked her?'

'Not yet. I wanted to explain to you first. I wanted you to know that it is duty which enforces me to take this step. I owed it to you, Amity, because of what there was between us.'

I turned away lest he should see my scarlet cheeks. 'There was nothing between us,' I protested hotly.

'Not spoken, I know but I feel there was a growing understanding nonetheless.'

'You are mistaken, sir.'

'Sir? You are angry with me, Amity, and rightly so. But you must see it is my duty. Where the heart conflicts with duty, the latter must win if we are to maintain our self-respect. You do agree with me, don't you?'

'You will marry a woman you do not love?'

'I respect Regina, and she will never know I do not love her.'

'Is that not dishonest?'

'It is honorable, under the circumstances. I cannot rob her of Mallory.'

Anger and disillusionment swept over me like the race of waters on the rocks below. I turned to glare at Richard.

'Then you must know that she has other plans.'

'Other plans? What plans?'

I had not meant to tell him, but frustration and fury won the day. I spat out the words with a feeling almost of triumph that I had defeated his plans.

'She wants me to marry Damian.'

'You – and he? Impossible! You have not agreed?'

'I have. And why not? Is it so impossible for a gentleman to marry a mere companion?'

'But marriage to Damian, of all people.' The surprise in his voice gave way to scorn. 'And you reproached me for marrying someone I did not love. Would you replace one loveless marriage with another? You cannot love Damian.'

'I have compassion for him. And I will marry him!'

Richard rose slowly to his feet. 'Very well. Then there is no more to be said.'

And without another word he strode quickly away, back towards the Keep, leaving me sitting there alone to weep bitter tears of vexation and misery.

CHAPTER FIFTEEN

'Sometimes we are devils to ourselves.'
—Shakespeare, *Troilus and Cressida*

I think I might have stayed on the cliffs for quite some time after Richard's abrupt departure, for I was far too angry and somehow humiliated by the encounter to want to return to the Keep. But, some moments later, when I irritably brushed away the tears that blurred my eyes, I quickly forgot my feelings when I caught sight of the man below.

It was the stranger I had seen previously on the beach, watching Damian, but this time it was the stranger who was being watched. He was aware of it too, for he was walking quickly along the scum-scarred water's edge from the direction of the village, and every now and again he glanced back over his shoulder.

A dozen or so of the village fishermen, easily recognisable by their woollen jerseys and sealskin caps, were walking along after him, slowly, but with quiet determination in their step. More fishermen, in a couple of their small fishing boats I had heard Regina call their cobles, were watching as they rowed close inshore. No one spoke, but I could feel the tension in the salty air. The stranger quickened his pace, and it was evident from his nervous backward glances that he too sensed the mounting atmosphere. He was afraid, I knew it, and I felt fear for him.

He hesitated as he neared the mouth of the cave. Ahead of him the beach ended suddenly where the headland jutted out to sea, culminating in that long line of rocks they called the brigg. Escape that way was impossible. He had either to enter the cave or try to scramble up the cliff if he hoped to elude his pursuers. I saw his head dart this way and that, searching for a way out of his dilemma, and all the while the fishermen came slowly on. They knew he could not escape. There was no hurry.

I lay almost prone on the cliff path, watching in fascination. The stranger must have discovered their illicit activities, or at least the villagers suspected he might have. But surely they would not harm him, just warn him, perhaps to restrain his curious mind. But I felt fearful for him as I watched him hover on the beach, irresolute, while the fishermen closed on him, still neither speaking nor touching him, but simply circling about him warily until he was completely surrounded by them. Then they stopped, ten or twelve yards from him, while the stranger twisted slowly about, staring at the inimical circle of faces.

Ben Jagger was one, I could distinguish him by his red hair glinting in the sunlight. The whole group now stood motionless like some theatrical tableau, each one frozen in his place. I had a sudden sensation of having witnessed this bizarre scene before, and then I remembered. The rooks' court, up on the fields when I had been with Richard. The silent court of judges who had raised no threatening hand, but had sentenced their victim to death from fear.

Fear for the stranger rose in me. He too was motionless, as though hypnotised by the hostile stares about him. Powerless to run to his aid, I thought of Richard. He would know what to do. I must fetch Richard.

I managed to back away and reach the gate in the thorn hedge, fortunate that I was so close to it that I could reach it unobserved. Running, half-stumbling, I reached the Keep and breathlessly climbed the steps to ring the bell. The door was opened almost at once by Ethel. The young housemaid smiled.

'Why, here's Miss Lucas, ma'am,' she said. Then I saw that Regina was standing in the vestibule, and beside her the Reverend Parmenter was adjusting his top hat.

'Ah, Miss Lucas, I was just about to leave without having the good fortune to see you, or so I believed,' the vicar said genially.

Regina advanced a step. I noted she looked rather pale but composed. 'The good reverend and I have been making arrangements for the ceremony, Amity,' she told me.

'The ceremony?'

'Your wedding, my dear. It is to be next Wednesday. You will have a few days to prepare,' explained the vicar. 'May I be allowed to felicitate you, Miss Lucas, on your good fortune and offer my sincere wishes for your future happiness. Mr. Fairfax is a lucky man indeed.'

I saw his white hand, withdrawn from his glove, rise to take my hand in greeting, but in the same instant I detected another movement. I glanced upward. Above on the minstrel's gallery I saw Richard Fairfax turn and walk away.

Regina was occupied in accompanying the vicar to the front door. Leaving her to her duties I hastened up the stairs. I had only one thought in mind – to tell Richard of my fears for the stranger on the beach, whether he wished to speak to me or not.

It was evident he did not want my company, for as I knocked on his door I heard his impatient voice.

'Who is it?'

'It is I, Amity. I must speak with you.'

'Go away. I have nothing to say to you.'

'Richard – please! It is urgent.'

After some seconds' delay, the door opened. Richard's expression was cold and unwelcoming. I made to pass him into the room, but he raised his arm to lean on the jamb, barring my way.

'Is someone ill? Is it Uncle Eustace?'

'No. But someone else has dire need of your help.'

Slowly, as if reluctantly, he lowered his arm and allowed me to pass. Having closed the door he turned and regarded me coolly.

'Be brief, madam. You compromise yourself in entering my room. It is unseemly for a lady affianced to another.'

I hated the coldness in his tone and could not resist snapping out my reply.

'Damian spent the whole of last night in my room, and no one thinks the worse of him.'

'He is your betrothed. No one will question.'

I longed to explain, but the stranger's need was urgent. In

a few words I told Richard of the scene I had witnessed on the beach. As I spoke, hurriedly, I saw his coldness melt into interest.

'A gentleman, you say?'

'Yes. Probably the stranger staying at the inn, the one of whom Mrs. Pickering spoke. Oh, Richard, if you had seen the menace I could feel, the fishermen surrounding him. It was exactly like the rooks' court we saw. I fear for the stranger's safety, Richard, whoever he is.'

For a few moments he stood silent, but I saw the swift change that came over his face. I could guess he was reminded of those other rooks, long ago in the Shenandoah Valley. Suddenly he sprang to life. He strode past me, picked up his cape from a chair, and turned to me.

'I shall go to investigate.'

'Let me come with you.' I was already crossing to the door when he stopped me.

'No. You stay here. I shall return immediately.'

He took up a lamp and matches from the night table and swept out. I hurried after him, wondering why he took the lamp in the full noonday light. He turned in the corridor and walked quickly up to the East Wing.

'Where are you going?'

'Down the underground passage to the cave. The cliff path down to the village and along the beach would take too long.'

From the studded door I watched him enter the Rose Room and close the door after him. Frustrated, I turned back. Now all I could do was wait until he returned.

As I went to my room I felt admiration for Richard, for the way he had so speedily forgotten his own troubles in order to go to help another in need, for his altruism and for his promptness of action. As I had discovered about him, he thought and acted quickly, but always with careful judgment. It was mortifying to think I had given up all chances of a husband such as he in favour of an irresolute, capricious man like Damian. I had rejected a man of strength only to have to spend my life propping up a weak, unstable man. I thrust the thought from my mind. This was what an impetuous nature could lead one into. I was a fool, and no mistake.

Half an hour lengthened into an hour and still Richard had

not returned. At last, growing impatient, I went to the Rose Room to await him. All was silent, no sound of anyone else in the east wing save myself. I sat on the pink brocade chair by the marble fireplace, my eyes on the panelling where I knew the secret opening to be, and my ears strained for the first sound of his coming.

It was a long wait. I had time to study in detail the pretty but dust-covered drapes on the four-poster bed and the silver-topped jars on the dressing table. I kept my eyes averted from the naughty portrait with the morbid urn beneath. So engrossed I became in contemplating what kind of man would want to keep and worship the ashes of a dead girl, that I was startled when the door suddenly opened. Regina swept in, her eyebrows rising at the sight of me.

'Ah! Have you also come to inspect your room?' she asked.

'My room?'

'Yours – your dressing room if you wish, after the wedding. I also came to see what must be done before the day. These – memories,' she said with a wide sweep of the arm, 'must be removed, of course. It would be unmannerly to remind you of a former occupant.'

'Perhaps Damian will not wish to remove them,' I ventured.

'Nonsense. It was I who had everything kept as it was, to remind him of his fall from grace and the reason for it. Now there is no longer need for him to be reminded, once you are his wife.'

I felt sickened. It was not Damian's love which had treasured these objects, but a sister's desire to taunt and keep him obedient to her wish. As well as anger I felt disillusionment that Regina was not the kindly creature I had once believed. Richard's interpretation of Rachel's diary had been correct after all. Regina had wanted to maintain her mastery over Damian.

'I'll have Mrs. Garner remove the trinkets and take down the drapes to wash them,' Regina was saying thoughtfully. 'As to the portrait and the urn, we must see.'

'I would prefer them to be taken away.'

'No doubt. But Damian may have need of them. We shall see.'

240

Before I could argue, I heard the sound I had been awaiting. There was a scuffling, dragging sound behind the panelling. I saw Regina's start of alarm, and then the panelling slide aside. I darted forward when I caught sight of Richard's grimy face and bedraggled hair, and the figure he supported in his arms.

Regina was the first to recover her voice. 'In heaven's name, Richard, what are you about? And who is this man?'

'No time for explanation now,' Richard gasped, droplets of water falling from his sodden cloak on to the parquet floor as he leaned wearily against the wall. 'Send for Cooper to help me carry this man to bed. He is half-dead and must be tended immediately.'

'I'll go,' Regina replied quickly. 'You stay and help undress him, Amity.'

She hastened away. As I bent to unfasten the stranger's soaking jacket I gave a fleeting thought to Regina's calm acceptance of the situation. She would act coolly and quickly now and save questions until later. Richard knelt to help me.

'What had they done to him, Richard?'

'Tied him to a stake in a rock pool in the cave. The tide was coming in. In another half hour he would have been drowned.'

The man rolled his head and groaned. As he moved I had a fleeting impression of having seen him before, long ago. His black hair clung wetly about a tolerably handsome young face, but I could not for the life of me remember where I had seen that face before.

Cooper lumbered in, and in answer to Richard's order he hoisted the limp figure, now divested of its sodden jacket and shirt, over his broad shoulders and bore him away. As Richard went to follow I laid a hand on his wet sleeve.

'Do not detain me now. I have a patient who is in need of help,' Richard said hoarsely. He strode out, leaving a trail of wet footmarks on the floor. I stood in the doorway and called out after him.

'I was only going to offer my help to nurse him,' I said lamely.

'No need. Regina will perform that task admirably.'

I turned back into the Rose Room, uncertain where to go or what to do since it was so clear I was not needed. From force of habit I tidied the room, closing the panel and picking up the stranger's discarded clothes to take down to the kitchen to be dried out. As I straightened I saw Rachel's portrait, and caught my breath.

That was why I had thought I recognised the stranger. He had the same proud face and darkly handsome looks. It was only a passing resemblance of course, but in the next second I recollected something else. The station. The stranger on the train who had caught my eye. It was the same man who now lay unconscious in Mallory Keep.

As I took the dripping clothes downstairs my thoughts were racing. If it was the same man, had he been on his way to the Keep? He had certainly been in the village for several days. And was the resemblance to the dead Rachel merely a coincidence, or had he some reason for his coming?

Regina was in the kitchen. 'Hot water bottles, Mrs. Garner, please, as many as you can find, and be sharp about it. And send Rose up with more coal. I must return to him at once.'

'Rose is upstairs seeing to Mr. Eustace, madam.'

'Then send for her. The fire must be built up.'

'I'll go fetch her,' I offered, glad to be able to help in some small way.

'Tell her to bring the coal to the room next to mine,' Regina replied as we both left the kitchen. At the top of the stairs we parted and I turned towards Uncle Eustace's room.

Rose was just coming out bearing a tray in her hands. 'The mistress bids you fetch coal to the room next to hers, quickly, Rose. There is a guest, very ill.'

''Appen he's not the only one,' Rose replied, jerking her head towards the old man's room. 'He's not eaten a thing again. Too tired, I reckon. Not even speaking now, he isn't. Ought to have a doctor, if tha ask me.'

'Give me the tray. You see to the coal.'

With a grunt Rose surrendered the tray to me and went away. I entered Uncle Eustace's room as quietly as I could in case the old man was sleeping, but as I put down the tray

242

beside the bed I saw his eyes following my movements. He lay very pale and still in the bed, only his bony hand moving restlessly on the counterpane.

'Sir, will you not eat?' I asked him brightly. 'Regina will be concerned for you if you do not.'

His head moved slowly sideways in a gesture of refusal, and the glittering eyes focussed on the painting still standing on the easel. The gnarled hand rose weakly to point at it, and my gaze followed. I recognised the canvas I had last seen him working on, and the drowning man. Uncle Eustace's rheumy blue eyes fastened on mine in question, and I understood. Once more the old man's powers of prevision had been uncannily accurate.

'We found him, sir. Rest easy, for Regina and Mr. Richard are caring for him now. He did not drown after all, thanks to your warning.'

I saw the look of relief that came over his misty eyes and then suddenly his thin hand grasped mine. It was unnaturally cold, but there was fierce determination in the old man's croak.

'Damian – you promised not to harm him. You will help him, won't you?'

I nodded. 'Do you not know Damian and I are to be married, sir? I shall always be there to help as best I can.'

A flicker of a smile touched his lips before he gasped a few more words. 'Then I am content. With you beside him, *she* will leave him be at last. She will have to let go. Now I can go in peace.'

His words, as tenuous as gossamer on the air, frightened me. I drew my hand away and rose quickly. I must fetch Richard. The old man was undeniably very ill.

It was Regina who answered my knock at the door. 'What is it Amity? Our patient is very sick.' She stood in the doorway so that I could not enter, but I could see Richard's tall frame bent over the supine figure in the canopied bed.

'It's Uncle Eustace, Regina. I fear he is very sick.'

Regina's startled look swept from me to Richard. He, hearing my words, left his patient and crossed to the door.

'Come with me, Amity. Regina, see to the man.'

I had to run to keep up with Richard's quick stride. He

reached Uncle Eustace before me, and as I entered I saw him on one knee, feeling the old man's pulse and lifting an eyelid to examine his eye. Uncle Eustace lay motionless, a half-smile on his lips.

Richard glanced up at me. 'It would be best to summon Regina and Damian. Would you see to the other patient please, Amity?'

Foreboding filled me as I carried out his request. Uncle Eustace must be dying. I was filled with sorrow and a kind of anger that he should be thus suddenly wrested from life. Regina heard my message in silence and went to find her brother. I sat by the unconscious stranger and waited.

There was no sound in the room but the ticking of the clock on the mantelshelf and the snuffling, rather laboured breathing of the dark-haired man lying as pale as the sheets which covered him. Not knowing what I was supposed to do for him, I sat still and quiet so as not to disturb him, and the clock ticked on. Half an hour or more must have elapsed and still I heard nothing. Since Regina left there had been no sound of movement anywhere in the house. She and Richard and Damian must still be at the old man's bedside.

It was an unpleasant, uncanny time of waiting. It was growing dusk, but I did not light the lamp. Two men lay near to death in this grim old house. It seemed almost as though the Keep was revelling in some macabre way in its moment of triumph. It was a house that gloried in death and tragedy, and I hated it. And my sorrow for Uncle Eustace grew the greater when I realised that I had committed myself to become mistress of the house I hated.

But it was not the Keep itself, but rather the stark, terrible memories it held that permeated it with fear, I argued. If only the spirits could be exorcised. Then the Keep could become happy with the new atmosphere that could be engendered there. Stones and mortar do not create unhappiness; only those who dwell there.

The man in the bed was growing restless, tossing his damp head and breathing in short, shallow gasps. I grew uneasy. Perhaps I had better call Richard. Even as I debated, I heard a sound at last in the still house. I strained my ears to listen. Somewhere in the distance a woman's voice was laughing, a soft, mocking laugh. I stiffened. I had heard that laugh in the night once before.

'Rachel.' It was not my voice, but that of the man in the bed. His eyes were still closed though he tossed feverishly. I was afraid. He too, though unconscious, had seemed to sense the presence of Rachel, and I feared that her vengeful spirit was very near, waiting to claim both he and Uncle Eustace as though to prove her power to Damian. I decided to go and fetch Richard after all, my patient needed help.

I darted along the darkened corridor quickly and tapped at Uncle Eustace's door. Regina opened it and swept me in in silence. Richard stood by the bed. He looked up as I approached.

'It is over, Amity. He is gone.'

He closed the old man's eyes while I watched in disbelief. So quickly? Could a life be snuffed out this swiftly and without warning? Tears pricked behind my eyelids.

'Damian was not here at the end. He could not be found,' Richard said quietly, and I could hear the compassion in his voice. He folded the gnarled old hands across Uncle Eustace's chest and drew the coverlet over his face, but not before I had seen the reddened marks on the back of one of the old man's hands. It was clawmarks, I was certain of it, as though a cat had scratched him, and very recently too. My horrified gaze rose to Richard's face, calm and thoughtful as he looked down at me.

'Do not be too distressed, my dear, though I confess the world is the poorer for his passing. He was a wise and gentle old fellow. Come.'

He drew me outside and closed the door. Only then did I recollect the other patient. I told Richard of his painful efforts to breathe.

'And is he feverish?'

I nodded. Richard turned quickly.

'I feared it. Pneumonia. We shall have a battle to save him. Come to the writing-room after dinner so we may talk.'

He was gone, and I had not been asked to follow. I returned to my own room and sat, miserably unhappy, until the dinner gong recalled me from my gloomy thoughts. It was humbling to realise that in my self-absorption, brooding over my own problems, I had been shamefully unaware of Uncle Eustace and his increasing quietness, until he grew too feeble to eat. Again I blamed the malevolent atmosphere of the Keep. We had all of us been too self-preoccupied to notice the poor old man's passing.

None of us were laudable characters, I thought, as I descended the stairs to the dining-room. Regina and Damian were as culpable as I. Only Richard could not be accused of selfishness, for he had been away until today. My dislike of my husband-to-be was intensified as I thought about it, and my future sister-in-law was less than the practical, amiable lady I had once believed. I would be overjoyed now to find some way of evading this impossible marriage, but I had only myself to blame.

Regina's non-appearance at dinner was not to be wondered at. No doubt she was grieving over her uncle's unexpected death, and Richard was presumably fully occupied by his patient. Ellen informed me that Mr. Damian was still out.

'Up on t'moor wi' his dog, no doubt,' she pronounced in her thin-lipped way. ''Appen he'll not be back afore t'morning.'

'And Miss Regina?'

'She's wi' Doctor Richard, nursing t'stranger.'

As Ellen spoke, I heard the front doorbell clang. The parlourmaid looked up with a frown. Callers were unusual at such a late hour.

'Oh, that'll be Reverend Parmenter. The mistress sent Cooper down to fetch him. Will that be all, miss?'

By the time I left the dining-room the Keep was again shrouded in silence. The vicar was no doubt upstairs consoling Regina and making arrangements for the funeral. A sudden thought arrested me on the staircase. My wedding day was only three days away, but surely now it would have to be postponed. The thought helped to lift a little of the gloom from my mind.

I sat by the fire in the writing room for an hour, awaiting Richard. It was late when I heard the sound of hooves on the gravel outside, indicating the vicar's departure, but still Richard did not come. At midnight I closed the book I had been vainly trying to read, and blew out the lamp. He would

246

not come now. The patient must still be critically ill. I hoped he would survive, if only to deny the menace of this house. Whoever he was, I hoped fiercely that he would live.

As it turned out, I had plenty of time to mull over my feelings of guilt at neglecting Uncle Eustace and my despair over becoming Damian's bride. For the next day I again found myself left to my own devices, since Richard and Regina were still closetted in the stranger's bedroom. I met Regina by chance in the corridor, but our meeting was brief.

'How does he fare, Regina?'

'Not well. His fever is high and he is delirious.'

'Will he recover, do you think?'

Her eyes were far away as she shrugged. 'Who can say? He recovers consciousness for a moment or two, but he does not know where he is.'

'Does he speak?' I wondered if he had pronounced Rachel's name again.

'Only muttered words that made no sense.'

'Then you do not know yet who he is?'

'No. But it's strange, I have a feeling we have met somewhere, though it must be long ago.'

Long ago, because for years she had not left the shelter of the Keep, she meant. I wondered if she had seen a resemblance to Rachel as I had, but the puzzled look in her dark eyes made it unlikely.

'I must go and make broth for him and try to coax him to sup a little,' Regina said as she passed by me to the staircase. 'Oh, by the way, your wedding. I fear we must delay it a week. My uncle's funeral will now take place on Wednesday.'

How coolly she announced the change. Wednesday was to have been a day of nuptial rejoicing, and now it was to be a day of burying the dead. Regina seemed too engrossed with tending the sick man to appreciate the enormity of the change.

I did not see Richard at all that day, nor the next. On the eve of Uncle Eustace's funeral I was sitting alone in the parlour after dinner, attempting to continue my embroidery, when Regina entered. She looked pale and drawn, the scar

247

standing out darkly against the pallor of her skin, but her eyes shone.

She sank wearily into the chair opposite me. 'Be a dear and ring the bell for tea, will you, Amity. I have been too busy to eat, but I'd love some tea.'

Ellen came quickly in answer to the bell. Regina was lying back in the chair, her eyes closed, so I gave Ellen orders to bring a tray of tea and sandwiches for her mistress. It was only after she had brought the tray and gone away that Regina sat up.

'There is no need for you to attend the service tomorrow, Amity,' she said quietly. I recognised it was a request, not an invitation to choose, so I sat silent, hands folded on my embroidery frame.

'Just family – Damian and Richard and myself, no other mourners. Uncle would have preferred it that way, for he hated fuss.'

That was true, though I regretted not being able to pay my last respects to the old gentleman. Without being aware of it I had become very fond of him, and I still felt pangs of remorse at the way I had neglected him. I looked at Regina, thoughtfully sipping her tea, and wondered if she too felt a sense of guilt.

I inquired about her patient and saw how the light leapt back into her eyes. 'He is poorly still,' she told me. 'A terrible cough and the utmost difficulty in breathing. But Richard says if we can reduce his fever in the next twenty-four hours, there is hope. It will reach a crisis before tomorrow night.'

She gazed into the fire, silent for a few moments. When she spoke again her hand was trembling so that the cup rattled in the saucer. 'I pray to God that he will live, Amity. For some strange reason it is crucial to me. He *must* live.'

When she turned her black eyes upon me, staring wide and unnaturally brilliant, I feared for a moment that she too was unbalanced, like her brother. They were the eyes of a maniac, possessed of one obsessing thought. Just then the door opened, and I knew before I turned who had entered. Regina never gave such a warm smile to Damian.

'Come and sit, Richard, you must be exhausted,' she said

in tones of concern. 'You must have a good sleep tonight. I shall sit up.'

Richard sat, his eyes dull with weariness. 'No, Regina, thanks all the same.'

'Have no fear, I shall wake you if his condition alters. But I insist you sleep.'

'You too must be drained. I cannot ask it of you.'

I intervened timidly. 'I should be glad to sit up with the gentleman if you would permit.'

'It is not necessary.' Regina rose quickly. 'I'll call you to take over at dawn, Richard. Sleep well until then.'

Richard smiled wryly across at me as Regina closed the door after her. 'My cousin is a singularly determined lady, Amity. She will surrender her charge to no one, it seems. I think even I would not be allowed near him if I were not a doctor.'

'It was you who rescued him,' I pointed out.

'Nevertheless, it would be no claim on him if Regina so decided. I think my fair cousin has a strong but frustrated maternal instinct. She revels in mothering a helpless creature.'

'So the stranger replaces Damian,' I remarked.

'For the moment. And one cannot be too harsh on her for mothering Damian. Heaven knows, he needs the strength of another.'

He leaned forward in his chair, his blue eyes probing mine. 'Very soon it will be your responsibility, Amity. Are you sure you are willing to shoulder it? Will you not reconsider before it is too late?'

'Is that why you wanted to see me, to dissuade me once again from this marriage?' I challenged.

He smiled. 'To try, though I know your misguided sense of loyalty. I am sorry I could not come to meet you, but my patient was extremely ill.'

'I understood, but your mission was in vain in any event. I shall still be married next week.' I averted my head, to avoid the directness of his penetrating eyes.

'You do not love him!' I felt his hands grip mine and I struggled to release them, but in vain.

'Let me go. You have no reason to interfere,' I cried out.

249

'I have good reasons.'

'Then name them.'

'Very well.' He released my hands and sat back. Only then did I find the courage to look at him, his fine features illuminated by the firelight. Oh how tired he looked! For the world I would not harass him further, but he was resolved to continue this interview.

'For the first reason, I must tell you that the man upstairs recovered consciousness briefly and was able to answer a few questions. I asked his name. He told me, Lawrence.'

I was puzzled. 'But what has Mr. Lawrence to do with me?'

Richard shook his head. 'Not Mr. Lawrence, but Lawrence Longden, Amity.'

'Longden? The name is familiar.'

'It was Rachel's surname. Lawrence is her brother.'

'He told you?'

'Yes.'

I sank back in my chair, bemused by this piece of information. And yet it seemed obvious, for had I not myself noted the man's resemblance to the dead Rachel? But why was he here at Mallory, and so long after his sister's death? Why let eight or nine years elapse and then come back into the lives of the Fairfaxes?

'I'm afraid I still don't understand, Richard. What has Lawrence Longden to do with me?'

Richard leaned further forward. 'This house has had its share of grief, Amity, but I fear it is not ended. I do not want you to be here when trouble strikes again. That is why I not want you to marry Damian.'

'Trouble? What trouble, Richard?'

He stared down at his hands for a moment. 'Lawrence was not conscious for long, and even then he was so confused that he answered my questions without being fully aware of what he was saying. I asked him one more question before he fell asleep again.'

'Yes?'

'I asked him what brought him to Mallory so long after Rachel's death.'

'And he told you?'

250

'One word. Vengeance.'

I gasped. For long seconds there was complete silence in the parlour, save for the crackle of settling coals in the fire. Then Richard spoke softly again.

'So you see why I want you to renounce this marriage and leave here, Amity. For the sake of your safety you must pack up and leave. You have no part in ancient quarrels here.'

'And Regina – have you told her of this?'

'Not yet.'

'But she's up there with him now! She is the one who is in danger, not I!'

Richard rose wearily. 'She is in no danger, don't fret. Mr. Longden is too weak to lift a cup to his lips, let alone raise his hand in anger. I would not expose my cousin to unnecessary danger. But now I shall go and rest a while. Good night, Amity, and think well on what I have said.'

He was opening the door to leave before I remembered there was something left unsaid. I sat up and called after him.

'Richard, you said there were two reasons why I should not marry. What was the second one?'

He paused, leaning against the doorframe. I was thinking how tall and broad and handsome he was. Then his words struck me like a thunderbolt.

'Because I love you, you little fool. Surely you knew that already.'

CHAPTER SIXTEEN

'Go poor devil, get thee gone, why should I hurt thee?'
—Sterne, *Tristram Shandy*

The day of Uncle Eustace's funeral was as grey and dismal as befitted such a mournful occasion. The wind blew gustily about the old house and the clouds hung heavy with unshed rain over the battlemented roof. Unable to sleep, I rose early. Along the corridor I met Regina as she was closing the stranger's door and returning to her own room.

She waited when she saw me coming, trying to stifle a yawn.

'Good morning, Amity. I am about to go and sleep. Richard is with him now. Would you be so kind as to keep an eye on him for an hour when Richard and I go to the church?'

'To be sure. At what time?'

'Midday. I shall sleep until then. By the way, I have put a parcel in the writing room for you. Some material, to make a gown if you wish. I never had occasion to make use of it, and I think it might make a pretty wedding gown.'

'You are very kind. Is he awake?'

'Mr. Lawrence? No, he sleeps soundly. If he survives today, he will recover.'

'I am glad, for you have worked hard. Go and sleep now, Regina.'

With a thin smile she left me. It was still only seven o'clock, not yet time for breakfast, so I made my way to the writing room. There, on the polished oak table, stood the package. I unwrapped it curiously. On top of layers of the most beautiful oyster grey satin lay a folded sheet of paper:

'For you, Amity, knowing that your deft fingers will work a miracle from it. And in the smaller package you will find a square of Brussels lace, a family heirloom. Wear it for your bridal veil and treasure it to hand on in future years to a Fairfax daughter. With love from Regina.'

How thoughtful! As I admired the creamy lace a glow of gratitude and affection for my future sister-in-law suffused me. Whatever her faults, Regina could be kindness personified when she chose. I fingered the satin lovingly, savouring its soft sensuousness. It would make a magnificent gown, even if I were to wear it for an unlooked-for wedding.

Richard's words sprang back into my mind just as they had done a thousand times during that sleepless night. 'I love you, you little fool!' Never had this marriage been so hateful to me as now, even though Richard's declaration of love had been spat out at me like some scornful message of hate.

He had not meant to say it, I felt sure. He had been trapped into admitting it, but even so, I felt elated. He loved me just as I loved him. The cruel thing was that it had come too late. If only he had said it before his trip to London, before I committed myself to Damian. . . .

I could almost hear Aunt Cecily's reprimanding voice. 'No use crying over spilled milk, my girl. Once you've made your bed you must lie on it.' She was right, of course. No point at all in daydreaming over what might have been. Finally I picked up the parcel of satin and returned with it to my own room. I might as well start cutting it out right now, concentration on the task leaving me no time to fret.

Rose came in after about an hour, whistling and obviously happy, despite the gloomy weather. She looked surprised to see me up and busy already.

'Wilt tha have breakfast on a tray here, miss, seeing as tha'art busy?' she asked.

'Yes please, Rosie. Is it raining yet?'

'Nay, though it's not far off. Ben says as t'weather'll worsen soon. He says it'll be right nasty for a day or two.'

'Is he usually right?' I asked. I did so hope the weather would become more what one expected for a June wedding day.

'Oh, aye. Fishermen allus know. They can tell by t'gulls flying inland, by where t'fish is lying and that. It'll blow a real gale soon.'

Sunnily she cleared the hearth and laid fresh wood and coals. 'You seem happy, Rosie,' I remarked. 'Have you and Ben named the day at last?' I couldn't help remembering how morose she had been when last we talked.

' 'Appen August, he says, if his plans go right,' Rosie answered. 'And I reckon they will. He's a masterful man is my Ben. If he wants owt, he gets it as a rule. I do like masterful men, don't tha too, miss?'

I pricked myself with a pin. I ignored her questions, trying not to think of Richard. 'What plans has Ben got, Rose? Another consignment of contraband, I wonder?'

She rose quickly from the hearth and turned to face me. Her cheeks burned redly. 'I don't rightly know, miss, and that's a fact, 'cos Ben can be very close when he wants, but I don't reckon as tha should joke about it. Just because tha helped us once and didn't give us away . . .'

'I'm sorry, Rose. You're quite right.'

She looked at me suspiciously. 'Tha's wi' us, aren't tha, not against us?'

'Not exactly, Rosie. I would not take part in smuggling myself, but on the other hand I do not see evasion of duty as a crime. What you do is your affair.'

She looked down at my pieces of material, some of which I was pinning together, and I saw the mischievous smile on her pretty face. 'I'm right glad, miss, else I'd have to tell thee.'

'Tell me what, Rose?'

'That's a nice bit of stuff tha has there. Where did tha come by it, may I ask?'

'This satin? It was a gift from Miss Regina. Why do you ask?'

'I thowt as much.' The smile rippled into a merry laugh. 'You have a length of stuff my Ben gave Miss Regina last year after we'd had a good haul from France. I reckoned as I recognised it. A right good piece of stuff it is and all. Tha'll look a fair treat in that.'

And still laughing she went out. Despite my earlier gloom I found myself laughing too. I found it ironically amusing to discover I was to be married in satin which had been sneaked under the very noses of the revenue men. How lucky I had not adopted a condemnatory attitude towards the villagers' activities!

Towards midday I lay aside my sewing and went along to Regina's room. She was just emerging, clad entirely in black, with a crepe-veiled black hat obscuring her face almost completely. Today she would not feel embarrassed about her scar, for it was invisible beneath the veil.

I thanked her for the gift of the satin and the lace veil. With a smile she pressed my hand and beckoned me to follow. She tapped at the door of the next room and entered.

Richard was sitting beside the bed. He, also in black, rose as we entered.

'He sleeps soundly, Regina. With luck all will be well.'

'Pray heaven you are right. Sit quietly, Amity, and do not disturb him. We shall not be long.'

After they had gone downstairs I went to stand by the window. The rain was still holding off, but the gusts of wind caught at the black plumes on the heads of the horses below. I could see them, pawing the gravel as if anxious to bear Uncle Eustace away on his last journey. I watched the hearse lumber away slowly down the drive, and the family carriage carrying Regina and Damian and Richard follow respectfully behind. With all my heart I wished Uncle Eustace well on his voyage into the unknown world beyond this life.

A shallow cough made me turn back to the bed. A pair of bright, dark eyes were surveying me suspiciously. Lawrence Longden was awake, and judging by his penetrating stare, no longer delirious. I crossed to the bedside.

'How do you feel, sir? Would you like something to eat or a cup of tea?'

He ignored my question, his dark eyes roving about the room. 'Where am I?' he asked weakly.

'Have no fear, sir, you are safe in Mallory Keep. You have been very ill for some days.'

'Mallory,' he repeated feebly. 'The village, the beach . . .'

'That is all over now. You are at the Keep and will stay until you are fully recovered. The family was very concerned for you.'

'The family?'

'Miss Regina and Mr. Damian.' I hesitated to say the surname, but the sick man supplied it instantly.

'Damian Fairfax. I am in his house?'

I nodded. 'His sister, Miss Regina, has been tending you day and night. You owe your life to her, and to her cousin, Dr. Richard Fairfax.'

He groaned and rolled his head aside. After a moment the black eyes turned to stare at me again.

'Are you also a Fairfax, then?'

Again I hesitated. Not yet, I should have answered to be truthful, but instead I shook my head. 'My name is Amity Lucas, companion to Miss Regina.'

'And you say the family took me in not knowing who I am? They took in a complete stranger?'

'Yes. But we know now that you are Mr. Lawrence Longden.'

The suspicion leapt into his eyes again. 'How did you learn? Who told you?'

'You spoke your name yourself, sir, in your delirium. Dr. Richard saved you from the cave, and it was to him that you spoke your name.'

I could see by his eyes that he was wondering how much else he had revealed. Having matters on a clear footing has always seemed to me to be the easiest and most honest way to live, and so, deliberately, I went on.

'You told us also that you are Rachel's brother.' That he also spoke of vengeance, I could not bring myself to add. Perhaps that had only been a notion caused by the fever, so there was no reason to put the idea back in his mind again.

With a groan he rolled his head away from me again. Fearing to overtire him with prolonged conversation, I decided to let him sleep. I sat by him until his regular breathing assured me that he was once again asleep.

The room was growing darker as the skies lowered outside. I went to the window and gazed out, my spirits as heavy and gloom-laden as the leaden sky. I pressed my forehead against the cool window pane, thankful that at least Regina's patient was going to live. After a time I saw the carriage approaching slowly up the drive, and as it came, the first heavy drops of rain began to patter against the window.

I went to meet Regina in the vestibule. She took off her veiled hat and shook off the droplets of rain. Richard followed her in.

'How is he, Amity?'

'He was awake and speaking rationally, but now he is sleeping again.'

Richard darted upstairs without a word. Regina took my hand. 'It would seem all is well then. God be thanked.' She released me and went to the stairs. 'I shall take off my coat and then go to him.'

'Lunch is almost ready.'

'Later. I must see him first.'

At the top of the stairs she met Richard. I could hear their low exchange of words.

'Amity is right. The crisis is indeed over, Regina. He will live.'

'A few weeks of rest is all he needs now. I shall see he gets it. He shall be my special charge.'

The rain was battering in an unceasing sheet against the dining room windows during lunch. Richard and I sat opposite each other and neither of us spoke a word. I could not tell whether he was too angry with me to speak, or too engrossed in his own thoughts, but in any event I had no wish to talk. Uncle Eustace's death, the threat of Lawrence's revenge on the family, and my impending marriage combined to envelop me in gloom. I felt trapped and helpless. I peeped furtively at the bent fair head opposite and wished with all my heart that I could run to him and weep out my frustrations in the comfort of his arms, but it could never be. In my self-pity I was forgetting that he too probably felt just as cheated, obliged to leave Mallory soon on my account, deprived of his birthright.

Oh, how selfish I was! But try as I might, I could see no way to be fair to him without reneging on my promise to Regina and Damian – and to Uncle Eustace. One could not betray the dead. That was unthinkable.

Miserable, I picked at my dinner and found myself unable to eat the stewed prunes and custard. It was almost with relief that I heard Richard murmur, 'Excuse me,' rising and leav-

257

ing without anothe word. I yearned for his company, and yet could not bear him close to me.

It was the next day that Mrs. Garner intercepted me as I came downstairs. In her arms she was carrying a pile of neatly folded clothes.

'Here's the gentleman's clothes, miss, all clean and dried now. I thought as maybe he'd want them soon, now he's better.'

'I'll take them, Mrs. Garner, though I doubt he will need them for a few days yet. What is that little book?'

'Poetry. I found it in one of his pockets, all soggy it was, but I've dried it out as best I can.'

I took the clothes and the slim volume and went upstairs again. What a strange title the book had – *The Rubaiyat of Omar Khayyam*. I laid the piles of clothes on the little table outside Lawrence Longden's door so as not to knock and disturb him, but kept the book in my hand. I wandered on towards the writing room. There I could sit and read it in peace.

It was strange, haunting verse, and though I had paid little regard to poetry lessons in my school days, I found myself enjoying this unusual verse. The poet seemed saddened by the transcience of youth and love. One verse in particular caught my attention.

'Ah, love, could thou and I with Fate conspire
To grasp this sorry scheme of things entire,
Would not we shatter it to bits – and then
Remould it nearer to the heart's desire.'

Ah yes, I thought wistfully, if only one could remould one's life to be what one wanted it to be. If only I could change events so that I could be married to Richard instead of to Damian, to love and honour him as a wife should, instead of fearing and abhorring her husband. If only . . .

The door opened suddenly and Richard strode in. Startled by his unexpected appearance and ashamed at being caught out thinking forbidden thoughts about him, I coloured and fumbled with the book. Richard coughed and murmured an apology.

258

'I came for my bag. Have to go and fetch more ingredients to mix my patient an expectorant,' he said by way of explanation. 'Sorry if I startled you.'

I was too confused to answer. He picked up a large black bag from the floor by the table and came back, hesitating behind my chair. 'What were you reading?'

'Poetry.'

'May I see?'

I surrendered the little book and he glanced at the title. 'Ah, Fitzgerald. Do you like it?'

I was surprised he could name the translator, for I had not thought of Richard as a poetry reader. 'As much as I have read, I like it well enough. Have you read it?'

'When I was in London, before I came here. Strange how the words linger in the memory.'

'Can you remember it?'

I still had my back towards him, unable to turn and face him. As he began quoting, I could feel his breath on my hair.

'Ah, Moon of my Delight, who knowst no wane,
The Moon of Heaven is rising once again.
How oft hereafter, rising, shall she look
Through this same garden after me – in vain.'

Shivers ran down my spine at his words. Like me, he had found a significant verse to express his feelings, but while I was struggling to find some reply I heard the door close. He had gone, leaving the words of love and despair hovering tenuously on the darkening air.

Fighting back the tears that burned my eyelids, I snatched up the book, and when I was sure Richard was well out of sight, returned to Lawrence's room. I laid the book on top of the pile of clothes and went back to my own room. I passed the day miserably, trying to find pleasure in exerting my skill as a needlewoman on my wedding gown, but I could find none.

I saw little of Regina and Richard in the next day or so, and nothing at all of my bridegroom-to-be. Mrs. Garner told me that Regina stayed constantly with Mr. Lawrence, who was now sitting up and taking nourishment.

'She talks to him and reads to him, but he seems to have

259

little inclination to talk,' the housekeeper commented. She was arranging roses in a large pewter bowl in the parlour, and their heady scent filled the room with sweetness.

'No doubt he is still weak,' I replied. 'It is kind of Miss Regina to devote so much of her time to him.'

Mrs. Garner grunted and then licked her finger as if a thorn were the reason. 'Mr. Eustace didn't warrant all that fuss,' she remarked dryly.

It was two days before my wedding and the rain still fell unendingly. The wind was growing more savage and blustery; I could hear the branches of the tree outside angrily slapping against my window. My gown was almost finished and my fingers were sore from stitching. I tried it on before the mirror in my bedroom and begrudgingly had to admit that I had done a rather fine job. It fitted beautifully, clasping my waist with the closeness of a lover's embrace and flowing gracefully behind me. The silvery grey hue certainly enhanced my fair colouring. On a whim I took out the square of Brussels lace and draped it over my head. The effect was very becoming. I stared at my reflection, trying to visualise the tall bridegroom at my side. Try as I might, the phantom groom I saw was tanned and fair, not the scowling darkness of Damian Fairfax. I was about to wrench off the lace when my door opened.

'Oh, how lovely you look!' It was Regina, standing entranced, her hands clasped in pleasure. 'Turn around, let me look at you.'

'The hem needs turning up yet,' I replied, taking off the veil.

'Let me pin it for you.'

Regina took my pin box from the table and swept down in a graceful movement to kneel at my feet. I watched her curiously. There was about her a glow, an added grace I had not seen before. Her eyes sparkled, giving her face a vitality which made her almost beautiful. But for the disfiguring weal across her cheek she would be radiantly beautiful. She looked far more the eager bride than I did, I thought, catching sight of my doleful expression in the mirror.

For some minutes Regina concentrated on her task, until footsteps outside in the corridor made her look up.

'Damian,' she said. 'He has been asleep all day.' Putting aside the pin box she rose and ran to the door, flinging it wide just as her brother passed. 'Oh Damian, Lawrence is so much better that Richard says he may get up tomorrow.'

He stared blankly at her. 'Lawrence?' He murmured. He wore the dazed expression of one not yet fully awake.

'Lawrence Longden. You know, the man Richard saved from drowning.'

'*Longden?*'

Damian's voice was a croak, his eyes now wide with an expression of fear or disbelief, it was hard to tell which.

Regina clicked her tongue. 'Yes, dear. You forget, I told you about it. He is Rachel's brother, but do not dwell on that. You would remember better if you stayed home and slept at night instead of wandering about on the moor and having to sleep by day. I hope your bride will try to improve your habits.' She smiled at me, but I could feel only a prick of annoyance. Damian's reaction was more vociferous.

'No!' he bellowed, and then his gaze travelled past his sister and came to rest on me. Immediately he darted past her into my room and across to me. Gripping me by the shoulders he went on shouting. 'Do you see how they taunt me? Always they come, the living and the dead, to taunt me for my terrible sin! Will they never leave me in peace?'

'Hush, Damian, please!' I begged him, frightened by his fierce grip and the terrifying look in his black eyes.

'Please, for God's sake, Amity, make them go away and leave me in peace,' he implored, the roar dwindling to a whimper. Helplessly I looked to Regina, mutely begging her to intervene.

'There, there, Damian, what a lot of fuss about nothing,' she said comfortingly. 'Mr. Lawrence is a charming gentleman and has not the remotest intention of taunting you. It all happened a long time ago and everyone has forgotten.'

'I have not forgotten, nor ever shall,' he rasped, turning the glare on her. 'Have you forgotten Rachel's dying words – that she would always haunt me and hold me in her power? She does, she will! And she foretold that I would always be accursed.'

'You know that is not true,' Regina said levelly, 'or you

would not have the fortune to find so lovely a bride. Look at her, Damian. Is she not beautiful?'

He did not turn his eyes to me, but glowered instead at Regina. 'It *was* true. Was our child not born dead? That was a sign of God's displeasure at my treachery. I *am* acccursed, and shall be forever.'

It was as though they had both forgotten my presence, the way they talked across me. Regina moved forward, close to her brother.

'Listen to me, Damian. I had not meant to tell you, but must do so now to disprove your words. The child was born alive. I had Ramsden take him away up to Keep Farm through the underground passage. No one but I ever knew, for I delivered the child alone. Then I told you and Rachel that he was dead. I felt she would have less power over you if there was no child. So you are wrong. God was not angry with you. He knows human frailty.'

'My son – alive?' Damian murmúred. He was swaying slightly, like a man weakened by sickness. 'At Keep Farm?'

Regina nodded. The vitality I had seen in her face was gone now, sadness in its place. 'He was the boy you knew as Eric.'

For a second Damian stood immobile, then he flung up his hands in despair. 'The boy died of measles! And you tell me I am not cursed? *You* are wrong, Regina, not I. Nothing I touch will prosper, everything will rot and putrefy!'

'Not with Amity beside you. Look at her, so young and pure and innocent. She will lead you to the path of grace and redemption. Look at her.'

His smouldering gaze came slowly round to rest on me, but the haunted look did not leave his eyes. He came close, laid his great hands gently on my shoulders, and looked down at me.

'You are right. She is young and fair and her heart is pure. She gives me ease and rest which no one else can do . . .'

'You see, all will be well.'

'But does she realise what she must sacrifice for me? She will be but a shadow to replace my lost love, a substitute for a dream.'

'You did not love Rachel, you know it.'

'But she possesses me still! I cannot rid my mind of her! Do

262

you realise that when I lie with my bride, it will be Rachel I am embracing again? Forever I shall be committing again that sin which robbed me of my soul!'

I broke loose from him, fighting back the anger and humiliation which scorched in my veins. 'Go away, go away!' I gasped, sickened by what I had heard, and feeling like some eavesdropper who has heard ill of himself. Regina took my arm.

'Do not concern yourself, Amity, he will get over this mood. I shall talk to him privately,' she said soothingly, then taking her brother's arm she led him from my room. I sat on the bed, dazed and nauseated. I could not go on with this impossible marriage.

During that night the weather grew as tumultuous as the thoughts that raged through my brain. The wind lashed round the old Keep, buffeting and howling like enraged demons from hell. Ben Jagger had been uncannily accurate in his prediction of a week's bad weather leading to storm. By morning I had decided to tell Regina that I could not go on with the wedding. I had debated whether to talk it over with Richard first, but decided against it. I did not wish it to be thought that I was angling for his proposal first. Though I loved the man dearly, I had my pride.

Rose did not arrive at the usual hour with my tea and hot water. After a little while I dressed and went down to the kitchen myself. As I pushed the door open I saw Ben Jagger in sodden oilskins leaning on the kitchen table. Rosie was bent over the range, ladling hot water into a jug. Either they did not hear me or they took me for another of the servants, for Ben went on speaking.

'Tonight then, lass. Tha knows thy part?'

'Aye, Ben. I'll see to it. Have no fear.'

Ben caught sight of me and pulled off his cap. 'Morning, Miss Lucas, he said, rather over-loudly, I thought. 'Foul weather for thy wedding, I fear.'

Rose straightened and turned. 'Oh, I were just coming up to thee, miss. Sorry I've kept thee waiting.'

'I'll be off, then,' said Ben, pulling his cap on again.

'Surely there's no fishing in this weather, Mr. Jagger?' I questioned.

'Nay but there's a lot to be done about t'place. Lash barn roofs down, mend t'hen runs afore t'birds all escape,' he replied. 'Well, Rosie, tha'll go see as Widow Thackeray is all right for me, wilt tha? Think on, now, t'old lady has no one to see to her.'

'I've told thee I will, and I will,' Rose replied. 'Now be off, Ben Jagger. I've a lot to see to this morning.'

Jagger nodded a farewell to me and went out, the blast of wind through the open door catching the towels on the ceiling airer and scattering them about the flagstone floor and draping them across the milk and bread on the table. Rose gathered them up and folded them neatly.

'Will Miss Regina be down for breakfast today, Rose?' I asked her as she piled the towels on the dresser.

'Aye, she says so.'

Good. I would have the opportunity then to tell her of my decision, I thought. But I was deceived. She did not enter the dining room alone, but with Lawrence Longden holding her arm.

'There now, you've done it, Lawrence,' she said, smiling proudly. 'Have you met Miss Lucas?'

He nodded and said good morning. I could see he was rather weak after the effort of descending the stairs, but his manner was decidedly more affable and less suspicious than when I had last seen him. Regina's charm had evidently worked on him. And it was still working, for I could see the way he listened intently while she chatted over breakfast, and the look in his eyes was thoughtful and appraising.

He put down his porridge spoon after a while and leaned towards her. 'Regina, I must tell you something.'

'There is no need yet, Lawrence. Eat and grow strong. Later there will be plenty of time to talk.' I noted the tenderness in her tone when she spoke his name. Richard had been right once again. She was transferring her maternal solicitude from Damian to this stranger.

'But I must. I feel a hypocrite to be in your house if I do not speak,' Lawrence said urgently. Yet again I had the feeling of being invisible, that people were talking across me without being aware of me. I felt very uncomfortable.

'Really, Lawrence . . .'

'No, listen. When I came to Mallory I did not entertain the same feelings towards you that I do now. Things have changed dramatically.'

'But of course. You did not know us then.'

'You misunderstand. I mean I came here full of spite and hatred. I meant to do you harm. Now that I know you and respect you, my high regard and gratitude have changed matters completely. I was wrong to bear you such malice. I know my sister's wilfulness and should never have believed you and your brother solely to blame for what happened. Now I only have cause for gratitude to you.'

'There is no need for gratitude. I am happy to see you well and know my efforts were successful.'

'Eternal gratitude, for you saved my life, as Miss Lucas so rightly reminded me. I owe you my life, Regina.'

She blushed becomingly as Ellen entered with a dish of kippers. When she had gone, Regina spoke again quietly. 'We all of us repent our wrong attitudes when we come to realise our errors. I too repent of how I have made my brother suffer over the past. It was cruel of me to prolong his grief, but I shall try to make amends.'

I stared at her disbelievingly. Did she truly believe she could eradicate Damian's grief with a few words? Did she not realise that her years of domination over him, convincing him that his sinfulness had robbed him of all right to peace, even after death, could never be washed away? The poor man was doomed to suffer agonies of torment until his death because of what she had done refusing to let him marry Rachel and hiding his child away. Such was her power over her weak brother. I stared at her, recognising fully now her strength and determination and how it had crippled her brother's mind. I wondered who was really the devil that tortured Damian Fairfax – Rachel or Regina.

After breakfast Regina bore her guest away again to the writing room, to talk and play chess. I could see that with her complete absorption in Lawrence it was going to be difficult for me to talk to her. But it was the eve of the wedding. It had to be done today, or it would be too late.

But some kind of perversity made me keep stitching away at the hem of my wedding gown. It was almost as though I knew I could not avoid it, that I was predestined to marry Damian Fairfax tomorrow, however I might struggle, and anger and frustration chafed me.

Nearing lunch time I went downstairs. Richard was in the vestibule supervising Cooper who was manhandling a large valise across the floor towards the front door.

'Leave it there, Cooper, thank you,' Richard said, and as Cooper went off through the baize door towards the kitchens Richard turned and saw me. I came down the last few steps.

'What are you doing, Richard? Why is your valise here?'

'I am leaving after lunch.' His voice was as cold and brittle as the light in his blue eyes.

'Today? But you cannot!' Panic seized me at the thought of his leaving so abruptly, and with this chasm of coldness between us.

'You do not expect me to stay and have to watch you wed my cousin, surely?' he drawled in that delectable accent I had come to love so well. 'No, Miss Lucas, I wish you well of my eccentric cousin, but I fear you make a terrible mistake which you will always regret. I do not wish to be here to see your disillusionment.'

I must tell him now about my change of heart, but there was little privacy in the vestibule. Already he was turning away from me. Impulsively I took his elbow.

'Richard, please don't go. Come into the dining room, for I have something to tell you.'

He hesitated, and as he looked down at me I saw the hardness in his eyes gradually melt. But before we took the first step towards the dining room the bell at the front door began clanging wildly. Richard looked up, and in three strides he crossed the hall and wrenched open the front door.

A blast of wind drove in before it a sodden figure in a shawl. Richard slammed the door and took her arm. As the shawl fell back on her shoulders I recognised the plump face of Mrs. Pickering, rain running down her cheeks and her grey hair clinging round her head.

'Mrs. Pickering! What is wrong?' Richard cried. The woman swayed, gasping for breath. He led her to the hall seat and lowered her bulky frame into it. 'Amity, fetch brandy from the dining room,' he said to me.

266

There was a decanter on the sideboard. Hastily I poured a large glassful and hurried back. Richard took the glass and held it to Mrs. Pickering's lips.

'Now take your time. Sip this and get your breath back first,' he ordered her gently. Her eyes spoke her gratitude as she sipped, and a pool of water gradually spread about her feet.

'I struggled up t'cliff path to get thee,' she panted at last.

'The cliff path, in this gale? Then there *is* something wrong for you to risk your life so. Rest easy a moment, and then tell me.'

She took a few more sips and then leaned back. At last she could breathe easily enough to speak. 'It's our Sam, doctor. He's hurt. Tha mun help him.'

'I will. Now tell me what happened.'

'T'cottage at t'end of t'street – it were washed away in t'storm. Sam were trying to help t'family out. He did, afore t'waves carried t'last of t'cottage away, but a beam fell on him.'

'Is he still trapped?'

'Nay. The men got him out, but his leg's broken. T'bone is sticking out, doctor. He's in mortal bad pain.'

'I'll go at once.' Richard strode across to the baize door and flung it open. 'Cooper, Cooper!'

A woman's voice called back a message I could not hear. Richard shouted again. 'Then go tell him to saddle a horse for me – instantly – and send Rose up here.'

He turned to me. 'I'll fetch my bag. See Mrs. Pickering into Rose's charge. Get her clothes dried and give her a hot meal. I'll return as soon as I can.'

He bounded up the stairs three at a time and in seconds raced down again, cloaked and carrying his bag. He hurried past me, out of the front door, just as Rose emerged from the kitchens. She took her mother away downstairs, and I noted how little surprised she seemed to see her mother here, nor did she question why. A life of hardship led one to accept every contingency with equanimity, it seemed.

Young Ethel came downstairs carrying a pewter bowl of fallen roses. She smiled as she passed me. 'A pity them roses is all dropped,' she remarked. 'There's no more to be picked.

T'storm's beaten them all down. Pity. There's none for thy wedding tomorrow, miss. A wedding should never be without flowers.'

'No matter, Ethel,' I replied. 'By the way, I shall not take lunch. Please tell Mrs. Garner.'

She smiled again and went on downstairs to the kitchen. They were probably all busy down there, the housekeeper and the servants, preparing the wedding breakfast for tomorrow. Cold ham and salad with pickles, perhaps, and fruit and wine. Although they were busy on my account, I felt very lonely as I made my way back into the dining room so I could hear when Richard returned. There is nothing lonelier than to feel one is in the midst of activity and yet not part of it. The servants had their duties, Richard was exercising his skill on yet another patient, and Regina and Lawrence were growing more intimate in the privacy of the writing room. As to Damian's whereabouts I had no idea.

The afternoon passed and still the wind lashed and raged as I sat alone in the gloom of the dining room. My bridegroom, I thought morosely, would undoubtedly interpret this fiendish weather as a further sign of God's displeasure at his wedding. I felt miserable and lonely and for the first time I realised how much I missed old Uncle Eustace.

The gloom of the dining room, although it was only late afternoon, seemed to develop in intensity, bringing with it a chill, a feeling of imminent menace. I shivered. Time was passing by swiftly while I watched for Richard. I must act soon, but still I hesitated to interrupt Regina's tête-a-tête. I decided to go to my room and write her a letter of explanation. Then I would pack my bag and prepare to leave Mallory Keep.

Several times I dipped my pen in the inkstand and wrote a few lines, and every time it came out wrong and I tore up the paper and began again. But whatever I wrote I felt deceitful, to betray my benefactress in this cold way, at a distance, as though I could not bring myself to face her and admit my defeat. It would not do. I must see her and tell her in person.

It took only a few minutes to gather together my few belongings and pack them in my bag, for I did not pack the gowns Regina had given me, nor the silver-grey wedding gown that hung on the wardrobe door. That done, I glanced at the clock. It was nearing time for dinner. I would tell Regina over the dinner table of my decision, whether Lawrence Longden was there or not, and then shamelessly ask her for the last quarter's salary and the loan of the carriage in the morning to take me to the station.

Uncle Leonard and Aunt Cecily would be startled at my unexpected return, and I wondered what kind of explanation I could give them. I would have to look for another position very soon, and that would not be easy since Regina was unlikely to give me a reference in the circumstances. But these were small problems and ones to face another day, so I put them from my mind. When the dinner gong sounded I went downstairs. Now I must tell Regina.

She was already steated at the table, Lawrence next to her, when I entered. They were both laughing quietly, amused by some private joke. As I seated myself opposite Regina, she moved the candlestick in front of her, and I knew it was because Ellen had inadvertently placed it to the wrong side of her mistress's place, where it illuminated her scar. But as she moved it, talking still to Lawrence, I saw his hand move to cover hers on the candlestick base.

'Leave it, Regina. I can see you better as it is.'

He withdrew his hand, but hers still lay on the candlestick as she hesitated. Lawrence's voice was gentle.

'Why do you wish to move it? Is it because of your scar?' Regina hung her head. 'Then leave it where it is, I pray you, for I admire the woman I know as she is. I see no blight, for there is none. I want to see your face, to remember the angel of mercy who hovered always before me when I lay at death's door. Please do not move the candles.'

Slowly Regina's hand drew back and she raised her face to Lawrence. Never have I seen a woman look more radiant. Suddenly I realised – she was falling in love with Lawrence Longden and, unless I was much mistaken, he also with her.

'Regina,' I blurted out in desperation. 'I must tell you. I shall not marry Damian. I shall go home to London tomorrow.'

CHAPTER SEVENTEEN

'A poor devil has ended his cares.'
—Robert Browning, *Master Hughes of Saxe-Gotha*

It was starkly said, blunt and clumsy, but I was beginning to fear I should never have said it at all. Two bewildered faces stared at me, uncomprehending at first, startled at being thus rudely wrenched out of the rapport which bound them. For them I had not existed until this moment.

'Nonsense, my dear,' Regina said warmly, when at length she had taken in my words. 'It is common for brides to experience wedding-eve nerves. But it will pass.'

'No, it's not,' I said, rising to my feet to prove the seriousness of my intent. 'I have no intention of marrying your brother, tomorrow or ever, I am leaving Mallory Keep. I am sorry if it causes you disappointment, Regina, for you have been kindness itself to me, but my mind is made up, and there's an end to it.'

Ellen came in with the soup. I sat down again while she poured it, and after she had gone Regina leaned forward, her dark eyes searching mine.

'Amity, may I not now appeal to your kindness? Damian needs you. Could you not, out of the friendship we bear each other, find it in your heart. . . .'

'No, no, Regina! Please don't ask it of me!'

The door opened and Damian entered. As he came to the table, neither looking at nor speaking to any of us, Regina welcomed him.

'I'm so glad you've returned to join us at dinner, Damian. Where have you been all afternoon?'

'In the crypt, praying. But it is no use. I must go up to the Abbey tonight and offer Mass there.'

He was pulling out his chair to sit, when his dark eyes alighted on Lawrence. He stood, transfixed, staring, and then let out a howl of anguish, pointing a finger at Lawrence.

'See, even now Rachel's eyes come to taunt me! What hellhound are you that comes to torment me thus?' He wheeled about, clutching his head and moaning, and stumbled to the door. All three of us watched him go in stunned silence.

'Poor Father Damian,' murmured Lawrence. 'How he has changed. I remember him still as he was, a gentle giant of a priest with comfort and compassion for everyone. He was well-loved in our village.'

'He is sick, I fear,' Regina said in a muffled tone, and I sensed the guilt and remorse in her voice. Rachel alone was not to blame for the man's degeneration, but his well-meaning sister too, and at last she was beginning to realise it.

Unable to eat more, feeling agitated as I did, I begged to be excused. I do not think Regina and Lawrence were even aware of my leaving, so engrossed were they in each other. I had some hazy notion of repeating my intention to leave to Damian, if I could find him, so that Regina could not ignore it.

But in the hallway I met Richard, still cloaked, emerging from the servants' quarters. With delight I went to meet him, to tell him of my decision, but before I could speak he stopped me.

'Where's Rose? Have you seen her?' he demanded curtly.

'Not for hours. But Richard . . .'

'I must find her. It's important. Perhaps she's upstairs.'

He swept past me and up the staircase. I hurried after him, trying to keep up with him.

'Is Sam all right? Does Rose need to go back down to the village to him?'

'I've set his leg, but it's a bad break. I shall have to stay on for a few days to watch that infection does not set in.'

Reaching the gallery he flung open the door of the writing-room. It was empty. He turned to go to the parlour. 'Where can she be? I must find her.'

'What is it, Richard? Can I help?'

He looked down at me coldly. 'I doubt it. I overheard

something at the Pickerings' cottage which led me to believe something is afoot. Rose can tell me, even if I have to browbeat her into it.'

The parlour was empty too. I stood in Richard's way so he could not brush past me again.

'Tell me. Perhaps I can help. I *want* to help.'

He was looking down at me with a patient, patronising look which incensed me, but I was determined. With a sigh he explained.

'I was in the bedroom at the cottage, setting Sam's leg. Mrs. Pickering went out into the living-room when someone came in. I heard a voice – Jagger's I think – saying something about getting another sentry to replace Sam, and Rosie would see to her part, but time was short. Then there was a sudden silence. I imagine Mrs. Pickering signalled to him that there was a stranger in the bedroom who could overhear. Then the door slammed. When I came out, he had gone.'

'Did you ask Mrs. Pickering about it?'

'Of course, but she acted stupid, pretending not to know what I was talking about. But there's something odd happening, I can feel it. Can't you feel the tension in the air? And then, as I rode away past the church several men were going in the gate. One of them muttered about a choir practice. But something is up, I know. Maybe that big job Jagger spoke of weeks ago.'

'Jagger, yes, I remember now,' I murmured as recollection returned. 'He was in the kitchen this morning with Rose. I heard him speak of tonight.'

'Can you remember anything else he may have said?'

I racked my brain in an effort to recall. 'Nothing significant, I think. Oh yes, he reminded Rose to go up to an old lady's cottage, to make sure she was all right in the storm. That's all.'

Richard looked at me sharply. 'Which cottage? Where is it?'

'Up on Carnelian Point. The widow lives alone, he said.'

'What was her name? Was it Widow Thackeray?'

'Yes, that's it. Why?'

'Because Widow Thackeray is down in the village now. Sam Pickering fetched her down yesterday.' As he spoke,

Richard turned the knob of the parlour door and crossed the darkened room to the window. 'Now why should Jagger send Rose up on the Point to an empty cottage, I wonder?'

I stood behind him, looking out of the window up at the Point. As we watched, a dull red glow sprang into life and I heard Richard's quick intake of breath.

'A lantern at the window, behind a red curtain! A signal, if I am not mistaken, but for what? Surely they cannot attempt to land contraband safely on a night like this?'

All was blackness outside, save for the glow from the cottage window high on the cliff edge of Carnelian Point. The wind was still lashing fiercely around the Keep, at times a howling roar and then dropping to a whine for a few seconds before waxing again into a deafening crescendo. Suddenly Richard cocked his fair head to one side.

'Listen!'

I listened, but could hear nothing but the wind.

'Listen,' Richard urged. 'Surely you can hear it.' He opened the window, and for a moment I was deafened by the wind. Then I caught the faintest sound above the noise. I strained my ears, waiting for the wind to abate.

Yes! There it was, the distant sound of a bell. I looked up at Richard. 'I hear it – a bell. It must be the church bell, for you said the men were at choir practice.'

He shook his head slowly as he closed the window. 'That is no church bell. I recognise it, Amity. It is a ship's bell. There is a ship out there at sea and it has lost its bearings in the storm. Now I begin to see. It makes sense at last.'

'What does? I don't follow you.'

'The signal – it is to the ship. And that terrible line of rocks runs out to sea from the point. The light is to lure the ship on to the rocks!'

A wrecking! I could scarcely believe it. Already Richard was striding to the door. I hurried after him. 'What will you do?'

'Stop it, if I can. Put out the light if the ship has not already foundered. Think of it, all those poor devils on those needle-like rocks on a night like this. I must stop it!'

He ran down the stairs, calling for Cooper. Mercifully the rain had stopped at last, although the howling wind evidently

273

had no intention of abating. I stood on the minstrel's gallery and watched Richard go before I remembered what I had intended to tell him.

Tomorrow might be too late. I might have left Mallory Keep forever without seeing Richard again. I rushed back into the writing-room and opened the window, leaning out to watch for Richard. He must ride this way to reach cliff path.

I could just discern his fair head in the darkness as he cantered across the grounds towards the hedge of blackthorn. 'Richard!' I called out as loudly as I could, 'Richard! I am *not* going to marry Damian!'

The wind whipped up his answering cry, scattering the words like crumbs along the cliff to the dispassionate gulls, but I did not catch them. I did not even know if he had heard me.

Closing the window, I knelt on the windowseat to watch. Long minutes passed, and still the red light glowed steadily on the Point. Now and again when the wind dropped I could catch the faint sound of the ship's bell, and prayed that Richard would be in time to prevent the tragedy that seemed imminent. Richard was right; there was a feeling of presentiment in the air. The gaunt old house seemed wrapped in foreboding, as though awaiting a crisis.

As I sat watching the Point, I thought again about the men at the church. Of course! It came to me now; they were making for the underground entrance by the Devil's Arrow. From there they could reach the cave unseen and wait and watch for their victims to fall prey to the terrible rocks of the brigg. I rebelled inwardly at the thought of the fisherfolks' callous cruelty. After all, they were not usually cruel people, as I knew, but easily led by a man with the powerful personality of a Ben Jagger. To bring them to heel, they had need of a stronger master than Damian at Mallory Keep.

At last I saw the red light vanish and breathed a sigh of relief. Richard had succeeded. Now he had only to avoid the vengeful anger of the fishermen. For the first time I realised he might be in danger, for the Mallory folk were not easily thwarted, and especially by a stranger. I had visions of Jagger, with his fiery red hair and scowling countenance, barring Richard's way and bringing him down off his horse. Up

274

there on the cliffs, and with a gale still howling. . . . I remembered the story of how a horse had once before returned to the Keep, riderless, and Thomas Fairfax's body found next morning at the foot of the cliffs, and alarm filled me.

Dear God! Let nothing happen to him, I prayed inwardly. Let him return safely, and I can leave Mallory Keep in the morning content that he was unharmed. It would break my heart to leave him, but at least I would be happier knowing that he was safe. If only there was something I could do to help him. I felt so useless sitting idle while he risked his life.

A wild notion seized me. I thought of saddling up Twilight and galloping up to the Point after him. But even as I left the writing-room, heading for the stairs, a sound that distracted me caught my ears. It was a laugh, a woman's laugh, and it came through the open door leading to the east wing. Curiosity made me pause. It was not the first time I had heard that laugh late at night in that eerie wing of the house.

I turned back to the studded door. Along the dusty passageway I could see light falling aslant the corridor coming from the Rose Room. I crept nearer and listened.

'Really, Damian, you're surely not going out in weather like this?' It was Regina's voice, amused and bantering. 'You'd be far wiser to stay in your bed on such a night, and do remember you are to be married in the morning.'

'All the more reason why I must go! Do you not see, I must pray for blessing so that my marriage will not be accursed. I am doomed to eternal punishment, but she must not share my sorrow. I must pray for her and the children we may have. Let me go, Regina!'

Again that laugh, musical and yet taunting. 'And catch your death before you are wed? Nonsense!'

'I shall go through the passage up to the farm. It is not far from there to the Abbey. Let me pass, Regina.'

I stepped boldly up to the door. I wanted to tell Damian that prayer for me was unnecessary. Let him pray for another bride if he would, but I would not be she. I stood in the doorway. Regina, standing by the bed, did not seem to see me. Damian stood with his back to me, and I saw with surprise that he wore the black habit of a priest, with a rosary suspended from his rope girdle.

'Then while you are gone I shall remove Rachel's portrait,' Regina said smoothly. 'It is not fitting for it to hang in Amity's room.'

'Do not touch it!' Damian's voice was a roar of anger. 'I forbid you to touch it!'

'And the urn. I think we should permit Lawrence to carry Rachel's remains home to her family, where they may lie with her own folk.'

'No!' the roar was an enraged bellow now.

'Be reasonable, Damian. You have worshipped long enough at the shrine of Rachel's memory, and it was fitting that you should. But now, with a new bride, a new life, it is time to forget and begin again.'

'Forget? How can I ever forget? *You* have forgotten, the night Rachel died, the curse she laid upon me, the threat . . .'

'The delirium of a woman dying of childbed fever, my dear, no more.'

'No, no!' Damian turned his terrible black stare on his sister. 'And it was you who reminded me all these years of her curse, telling me that she was vain and perfidious like all women! You it was who told me she was right and I should never be free of her, for she would be a constant reminder of my weakness and my sinfulness! Why do you change now?'

'Because the time has come. We must move on, Damian, we cannot remain forever as we were.'

I stood speechless, hypnotised by the high tension which charged the atmosphere. Regina moved forward to touch her brother's sleeve. 'I admit I was wrong, Damian, to keep you suffering so long. But now I see a chance of happiness for you, for redemption. Take it, brother. Do as I advise.'

'Never! I have always listened to you, and you have mastered me, dominated my every thought and deed for these past eight years. Now leave me alone. I must find my own salvation.'

'And so you shall, with Amity to help. Now let me remove the portrait and the urn so as not to offend her.'

'Get back!' Damian spat out the words with venom. 'I see you now for what you are, Regina! Rachel was no fool – she

276

saw through you and your manipulating ways! She hated you, and you still bear the mark of Cain she branded on you!'

I saw Regina's fingers fly up to her scarred cheek and heard the gasp of disbelief.

'The mark of Cain?' she repeated in a whisper.

'Who slew his brother just as you have destroyed me!' Damian cried. As he turned I caught sight of his face for the first time, and his look terrified me, distorted as it was by hatred and fear. I saw him reach for the oil lamp that glowed on the little table below Rachel's portrait, and as he snatched it up, his sleeve caught the silver urn. The urn tottered, rolled and fell, spilling the contents on the parquet floor. Damian gazed down at the scattered ashes in horror, then raised the oil lamp high in the air, his eyes glittering with hate.

Regina recoiled, her arm raised to protect herself. Realising his intention, I made to leap forward to stop him.

'Damian, no, for God's sake!'

But as I moved, something small and firm pressed itself against my shins, making me stumble as I clutched at Damian's arm. I saw the lamp swing forward in a great arc, and I grabbed desperately. The lamp sailed across the room, missing Regina and falling on the bed. Instantly a sheet of flame leapt up to envelop the hangings, and in seconds the whole bed was a roaring wall of fire.

Regina moaned and sank to the floor in a faint. Damian stood transfixed, his black eyes maniacally reflecting the flames from the bed. I seized his arm.

'Damian, quickly! Carry Regina out before the fire spreads!'

But he did not move. Flames were licking at the curtains of the window now and a dense cloud of smoke was beginning to fill the little room. Greedily the fire devoured the dusty curtains.

'Damian! For pity's sake, help me with Regina!'

I struggled to lift her but she was too heavy. Slowly Damian came out of his trance and began to laugh, loudly and coarsely, throwing back his great shaggy head and bellowing with the most devilish sound I have ever heard. I left Regina and seized his arm.

'Pull yourself together! Lift her out before the flames reach her! Stop laughing, Damian. Lift her!'

He wrenched his arm from my grip, glaring at me as if I were some loathsome beast, and ran from the room. Helplessly I followed him to the door, crying after him to come back, but he ran on towards the spiral staircase down to the crypt. He was still uttering that inhuman laugh.

And then I saw it. At the head of the spiral staircase the black cat sat waiting, its green eyes glowing malevolently in the darkness. Slowly it uncurled itself and stood up, its head held majestically high, and as Damian turned at the top of the steps it stepped gracefully between his legs. He could not have seen it. With a cry of alarm he stumbled and fell headlong down the stone flight of steps.

The roar behind me made me rush back. I could hardly see Regina in the blanket of dense smoke. Coughing and choking I groped for her body on the floor. The fire was within inches of her feet. Unable to lift her, I seized her under the armpits and began dragging her, inch by inch, towards the door. I heard the windowpanes crack in the intense heat, and then as they shattered and fell the wind broke in through the opening, grabbing up the tongues of flame and spreading them along the panelled walls.

Perspiration poured from me as I struggled. Hazily I realised that the gritty substance over which I was dragging Regina's weighty body was the ashes of Rachel's body, but this was no time for philosophical reflection. In the doorway I paused to gasp for breath.

I looked up. Rachel's portrait stared down impassively at my efforts, but even as I looked, her expression changed. The haughty smile on the full lips curved slowly and triumphantly into a sneer. Was fear driving me mad?

A sheet of flame had engulfed the panelling now, and I realised as I stared at the proud, cruel face, distorted into a devilish caricature, that the oils were melting and running. I seized Regina and began heaving again until I had her safely outside in the corridor.

Which way to go? One way led to the chapel and the crypt, and no exit lay that way. In any case, a glance showed me that thick streamers of smoke were already issuing from under

Damian's door; the fire must have broken through the connecting door. There was no alternative. I must head for the studded door and the main wing of the Keep, even though six rooms lay between it and me.

Smoke was beginning to fill the corridor now. Try as I might, I had to let go of Regina's inert figure every few inches in order to gasp for air. I was beginning to feel very weak and faint. Pray heaven my strength would last out, for there was no time to run for help. The fire had found a ready accomplice in the wind, for together they raged on inexorably. Great sheets of flame now leapt from the door of the Rose Room and were beginning their havoc in the dusty, panelled corridor. I slapped Regina's face.

'Regina! For heaven's sake, Regina!'

But she did not waken. It was more than a fainting fit now, I realised. She was overcome by the smoke, and unless I got her out into the air quickly . . .

But I too was succumbing. Waves of giddiness swept over me as I struggled. The fire was gaining on me and I could feel its hot breath as the wall of flame advanced. Gathering the last of my strength I dragged Regina to within yards of the studded door, and then let go of her.

I stumbled to the door, wrenching at the knob. It did not give. I struggled to turn it, desperate to get help before unconsciousness claimed me. But still it would not yield. My last despairing thought was the realisation that either it had jammed or someone had closed and locked the door, and then I sank to the floor. And as I lay there, before darkness closed in on me, shutting out the red glow, I could swear that something small arched its furry back against my cheek. . . .

Eternity passed. When I opened my eyes it was in a strange, low-raftered room, and I was lying between crisply starched sheets in a strange bed. Rose's plump, pretty face hovered over me.

'Oh, tha'rt awake at last, Miss Lucas. Dost know it's close on midday?'

I struggled to sit up. 'Where am I, Rosie? Where is Miss Regina?'

'Have no fear, tha'rt both safe here at t'inn. Dr. Richard

got thee out o't'Keep. Everyone's safe now, 'cepting Mr. Damian. Dr. Richard is still up there looking for him.'

Richard was safe then, I realised with relief, and Regina too. But how on earth had he found us and saved us? Rose answered my unspoken question.

'Dr. Richard came up to t'Point and took me down to t'beach. He spoke to t'men, and while he were talking we saw t'great tower of fire up on t'cliff. We knew it were t'Keep. Dr. Richard marched the men up t'cliffs to come and put t'fire out. It weren't easy wi' that wind howling, but they did it. Only t'old east wing were burnt. Dr. Richard forced a door open and found thee and Miss Regina and carried thee out. He's a brave man is Dr. Richard, and no mistake.'

Indeed he was, and my love for him spilled over. I made to get out of bed, but Rose tried to stop me.

'Nay, stay, miss! T'doctor said as tha were to rest!'

'I am rested, Rose. I must go up to the Keep. Be a good girl and fetch my clothes for me.'

Reluctantly she took from the wardrobe the gown I wore last night, now scarcely recognisable as pale blue, for it was encrusted with dirt and soot. Rose watched me as I pulled it on.

'There's nowt left of t'east wing, tha'll see. Only a great heap of black stones. If Mr. Damian were in there, there's no hope for him. Only chance is that he were out on t'moor all night like he often is. But I doubt it. That ugly great dog of his is prowling round t'ruins up there, sniffing in t'smoke. 'Appen he's looking for his master.'

'And Dr. Richard is still there you say? Well, tell Miss Regina I am well and have gone out for a lungful of good, clean air.' I could not bring myself to face Regina yet and have to tell her I had seen her brother fall to his death. Later, perhaps.

As I hastened up the village street, the wind had dropped to a light breeze, and the air was bright with that promise of light before the sun breaks out from behind cloud. At the lych-gate outside the church, the Reverend Parmenter was standing looking up towards the Keep.

'Have you been up there?' I asked him.

He nodded. 'A sad business. That old wing built from the

280

abbey stones is gutted completely. You are a very lucky young lady, Miss Lucas.'

As he spoke I heard the clock strike noon. The thought crossed my mind that, had fate not taken a hand, I might have been becoming Damian's wife at this very moment. The vicar spoke again.

'I fear Mr. Damian was not so fortunate. It appears he must have perished in the fire.'

'I fear so. I saw him fall down the stairs to the crypt,' I replied quietly.

'The crypt? Then he is entombed there for ever, along with his ancestors, for the ruins of the wing prevent any chance of access. Poor man, for he was unhappy while he lived. God grant he may have found peace now.'

'Amen,' I concurred.

'Indeed, as the old ballad says:

'To Purgatory fire thou comest at last
And Christ receive thy soul.'

May the fire have purged him of all his cares, in truth. But good comes even out of evil. My belief is that the holocaust will mark the beginning of a new life for Mallory and all its folk.'

'I hope you may be right,' I murmured.

'To be sure. Dr. Richard found the opportunity to take the villagers to task for their sinful ways and command them to stop. He must have gained their respect, for they followed him readily enough to fight the fire. They're a proud race, these Mallory folk, and they won't submit easily, but they recognise and respect a man of strength. Last night's achievement augurs well for the new master of Mallory.'

Jagger was striding down the cliff path towards us, filthy and soot-begrimed. I left the vicar abruptly and hastened to meet him.

'Is Dr. Richard still up at the Keep?'

He pulled off his sealskin cap. 'Aye, miss. But he's given up hope of finding Mr. Fairfax. He said to tell thee as he'd be coming to thee soon.'

Joyfully I hurried past him, up the cliff path. Against the skyline I could see wisps of grey smoke spiralling upwards.

281

As I clambered up the narrow path, the breeze blew my hair over my face. I had been in too much of a hurry to coil and arrange it, and now strands of it blew in my mouth and I tasted salt on my lips.

I was nearing the crest of the hill, expecting to glimpse the first sight of the Keep, when instead I saw him. He was walking steadily down towards me, his head bent in thought. I felt a pang of compassion, seeing his fair hair greyed with ash and smoke, his face masked by soot and the streaks of perspiration. And I trembled. I was almost afraid to go and meet him.

I stood still. For a moment he walked on with his head down. And then he raised it and caught sight of me.

'Amity!'

White teeth gleamed through the grime in a broad smile and he flung his arms wide. My fears vanished. As I ran forward into his welcoming embrace there was an explosion of scattering sea gulls about our feet, and I was reminded of the first time I had climbed this path to meet my destiny at Mallory Keep.